27/3/25

£3

The
Complete
Dr. Thorndyke

Volume IX:

The Stoneware Monkey
Mr. Polton Explains
The Jacob Street Mystery

The Complete Dr. Thorndyke

Volume IX:

The Stoneware Monkey
Mr. Polton Explains
The Jacob Street Mystery

by

R. Austin Freeman

Edited by
David Marcum

ISBN Hardback 978-1-78705-689-3
ISBN Paperback 978-1-78705-690-9
AUK ePub ISBN 978-1-78705-691-6
AUK PDF ISBN 978-1-78705-692-3

These works are in the Public Domain in Great Britain
Portrait of Dr. Thorndyke by H.M. Brock (1908)

Published in the UK by
MX Publishing
335 Princess Park Manor, Royal Drive,
London, N11 3GX
www.mxpublishing.co.uk

David Marcum can be reached at:
thepapersofsherlockholmes@gmail.com

Cover design by Brian Belanger
www.belangerbooks.com and *www.redbubble.com/people/zhahadun*

CONTENTS

Introductions

Adventures

The Stoneware Monkey

Book One – *Narrated by James Oldfield, M.D.*

Book II – *Narrated by Christopher Jervis, M.D.*

(Continued on the next page . . . .)

Mr. Polton Explains

The Jacob Street Mystery

(Continued on the next page . . . .)

Part II – *The Unknown Factor*

The
Complete
Dr. Thorndyke

Volume IX:

The Stoneware Monkey
Mr. Polton Exlains
The Jacob Street Mystery

Dr. John Thorndyke

5A King's Bench Walk
in the late 1890's when
Thorndyke would have moved in

5A King's Bench Walk
Photographed by the Editor
during his
Sherlock Holmes Pilgrimage No. 3
(September 8th, 2016)

Meet Dr. Thorndyke
by R. Austin Freeman

My subject is Dr. John Thorndyke, the hero or central character of most of my detective stories. So I'll give you a short account of his real origin – of the way in which he did in fact come into existence.

To discover the origin of John Thorndyke I have to reach back into the past for at least fifty years, to the time when I was a medical student preparing for my final examination. For reasons which I need not go into I gave rather special attention to the legal aspects of medicine and the medical aspects of law. And as I read my text-books, and especially the illustrative cases, I was profoundly impressed by their dramatic quality. Medical jurisprudence deals with the human body in its relation to all kinds of legal problems. Thus its subject matter includes all sorts of crime against the person and all sorts of violent death and bodily injury: Hanging, drowning, poisons and their effects, problems of suicide and homicide, of personal identity and survivorship, and a host of other problems of the highest dramatic possibilities, though not always quite presentable for the purposes of fiction. And the reported cases which were given in illustration were often crime stories of the most thrilling interest. Cases of disputed identity such as the Tichbourne Case, famous poisoning cases such as the Rugeley Case and that of Madeline Smith, cases of mysterious disappearance or the detection of long-forgotten crimes such as that of Eugene Aram. All these, described and analysed with strict scientific accuracy, formed the matter of Medical Jurisprudence which thrilled me as I read and made an indelible impression.

But it produced no immediate results. I had to pass my examinations and get my diploma, and then look out for the means of earning my living. So all this curious lore was put away for the time being in the pigeon-holes of my mind – which Dr. Freud would call the *Unconscious* – not forgotten, but ready to come to the surface when the need for it should arise. And there it reposed for some twenty years, until failing health compelled me to abandon medical practice and take to literature as a profession.

It was then that my old studies recurred to my mind. A fellow doctor, Conan Doyle, had made a brilliant and well-deserved success by the creation of the immortal Sherlock Holmes. Considering that achievement, I asked myself whether it might not be possible to devise a

1

detective story of a slightly different kind – one based on the science of Medical Jurisprudence, in which, by the sacrifice of a certain amount of dramatic effect, one could keep entirely within the facts of real life, with nothing fictitious excepting the persons and the events. I came to the conclusion that it was, and began to turn the idea over in my mind.

But I think that the influence which finally determined the character of my detective stories, and incidentally the character of John Thorndyke, operated when I was working at the Westminster Ophthalmic Hospital. There I used to take the patients into the dark room, examine their eyes with the ophthalmoscope, estimate the errors of refraction, and construct an experimental pair of spectacles to correct those errors. When a perfect correction had been arrived at, the formula for it was embodied in a prescription which was sent to the optician who made the permanent spectacles.

Now when I was writing those prescriptions it was borne in on me that in many cases, especially the more complex, the formula for the spectacles, and consequently the spectacles themselves, furnished an infallible record of personal identity. If, for instance, such a pair of spectacles should have been found in a railway carriage, and the maker of those spectacles could be found, there would be practically conclusive evidence that a particular person had travelled by that train. About that time I drafted out a story based on a pair of spectacles, which was published some years later under the title of *The Mystery of 31 New Inn*, and the construction of that story determined, as I have said, not only the general character of my future work but of the hero around whom the plots were to be woven. But that story remained for some years in cold storage. My first published detective novel was *The Red Thumb-mark*, and in that book we may consider that John Thorndyke was born. And in passing on to describe him I may as well explain how and why he came to be the kind of person that he is.

I may begin by saying that he was not modelled after any real person. He was deliberately created to play a certain part, and the idea that was in my mind was that he should be such a person as would be likely and suitable to occupy such a position in real life. As he was to be a medico-legal expert, he had to be a doctor and a fully trained lawyer. On the physical side I endowed him with every kind of natural advantage. He is exceptionally tall, strong, and athletic because those qualities are useful in his vocation. For the same reason he has acute eyesight and hearing and considerable general manual skill, as every doctor ought to have. In appearance he is handsome and of an imposing presence, with a symmetrical face of the classical type and a Grecian nose. And here I may remark that his distinguished appearance is not merely a concession to my personal taste but is also a protest against the monsters of ugliness whom some detective writers have evolved.

These are quite opposed to natural truth. In real life a first-class man of any kind usually tends to be a good-looking man.

Mentally, Thorndyke is quite normal. He has no gifts of intuition or other supernormal mental qualities. He is just a highly intellectual man of great and varied knowledge with exceptionally acute reasoning powers and endowed with that invaluable asset, a scientific imagination (by a scientific imagination I mean that special faculty which marks the born investigator, the capacity to perceive the essential nature of a problem before the detailed evidence comes into sight). But he arrives at his conclusions by ordinary reasoning, which the reader can follow when he has been supplied with the facts, though the intricacy of the train of reasoning may at times call for an exposition at the end of the investigation.

Thorndyke has no eccentricities or oddities which might detract from the dignity of an eminent professional man, unless one excepts an unnatural liking for Trichinopoly cheroots. In manner he is quiet, reserved and self-contained, and rather markedly secretive, but of a kindly nature, though not sentimental, and addicted to occasional touches of dry humour. That is how Thorndyke appears to me.

As to his age. When he made his first bow to the reading public from the doorway of Number 4 King's Bench Walk he was between thirty-five and forty. As that was thirty years ago, he should now be over sixty-five. But he isn't. If I have to let him *grow old along with me*" I need not saddle him with the infirmities of age, and I can (in his case) put the brake on the passing years. Probably he is not more than fifty after all!

Now a few words as to how Thorndyke goes to work. His methods are rather different from those of the detectives of the Sherlock Holmes school. They are more technical and more specialized. He is an investigator of crime but he is not a detective. The technique of Scotland Yard would be neither suitable nor possible to him. He is a medico-legal expert, and his methods are those of medico-legal science. In the investigation of a crime there are two entirely different methods of approach. One consists in the careful and laborious examination of a vast mass of small and commonplace detail: Inquiring into the movements of suspected and other persons, interrogating witnesses and checking their statements particularly as to times and places, tracing missing persons, and so forth – the aim being to accumulate a great body of circumstantial evidence which will ultimately disclose the solution of the problem. It is an admirable method, as the success of our police proves, and it is used with brilliant effect by at least one of our contemporary detective writers. But it is essentially a police method.

The other method consists in the search for some fact of high evidential value which can be demonstrated by physical methods and which constitutes conclusive proof of some important point. This method also is used by the police in suitable cases. Finger-prints are examples of this kind of evidence, and another instance is furnished by the Gutteridge murder. Here the microscopical examination of a cartridge-case proved conclusively that the murder had been committed with a particular revolver, a fact which incriminated the owner of that revolver and led to his conviction.

This is Thorndyke's procedure. It consists in the interrogation of things rather than persons, of the ascertainment of physical facts which can be made visible to eyes other than his own. And the facts which he seeks tend to be those which are apparent only to the trained eye of the medical practitioner.

I feel that I ought to say a few words about Thorndyke's two satellites, Jervis and Polton. As to the former, he is just the traditional narrator proper to this type of story. Some of my readers have complained that Dr. Jervis is rather slow in the uptake. But that is precisely his function. He is the expert misunderstander. His job is to observe and record all the facts, and to fail completely to perceive their significance. Thereby he gives the reader all the necessary information, and he affords Thorndyke the opportunity to expound its bearing on the case.

Polton is in a slightly different category. Although he is not drawn from any real person, he is associated in my mind with two actual individuals. One is a Mr. Pollard, who was the laboratory assistant in the hospital museum when I was a student, and who gave me many a valuable tip in matters of technique, and who, I hope, is still to the good. The other was a watch- and clock-maker of the name of Parsons – familiarly known as Uncle Parsons – who had premises in a basement near the Royal Exchange, and who was a man of boundless ingenuity and technical resource. Both of these I regard as collateral relatives, so to speak, of Nathaniel Polton. But his personality is not like either. His crinkly countenance is strictly his own copyright.

To return to Thorndyke, his rather technical methods have, for the purposes of fiction, advantages and disadvantages. The advantage is that his facts are demonstrably true, and often they are intrinsically interesting. The disadvantage is that they are frequently not matters of common knowledge, so that the reader may fail to recognize them or grasp their significance until they are explained. But this is the case with all classes of fiction. There is no type of character or story that can be made sympathetic and acceptable to every kind of reader. The personal equation affects the reading as well as the writing of a story.

R. Austin Freeman
(1862-1943)

5A King's Bench Walk
in the early 1900's when
Thorndyke was in practice

Dr. Thorndyke: In the Footsteps
of Sherlock Holmes
by David Marcum

When Sherlock Holmes began his practice as a "Consulting Detective", his ideas of scientific criminal investigations caused the London police to look upon him as a mere "theorist". He was perceived as an amateur to be tolerated, often with amusement – until, that is, his assistance was required. Then they were more than willing to come knocking upon his door, asking for whatever help that they could receive. And usually this help took the form of brilliant solutions to bizarre and otherwise insoluble problems.

Holmes espoused methods and ideas that were considered ludicrous in the late 1800's. For instance, his frustration knew no bounds when a crime scene was disturbed. Holmes realized that so much could be determined from the physical evidence – footprints, fibers, and spatters. The police were happy to trod into and disturb the evidence as if they were herds of field beasts, with the equivalent level of intelligence.

However, Holmes's methods, and the science behind catching criminals, eventually won out and became so important that it's hard to now imagine the world without them. Many of the exact same techniques and methods that he advocated are now standard practice. From being an amateur with unusual ideas, Holmes is now recognized around the world as The Great Detective. In 2002, Holmes received a posthumous Honorary Fellowship from the British Royal Society of Chemistry, based on the fact that he was beyond his time in using chemistry and chemical sciences as a means of solving crimes.

And before that, in 1985, Scotland Yard introduced *HOLMES* (*Home Office Large Major Enquiry System*), an elaborate computer system designed to process the masses of information collected and evaluated during a criminal investigation, in order to ensure that no vital clues are overlooked. This system, providing total compatibility and consistency between all the police forces of England, Scotland, Wales, and Northern Ireland, as well as the Royal Military Police, has since been upgraded by the improved *HOLMES 2* – and like the first version, there is absolutely no doubt as to who is being honored and memorialized for his work in dragging criminology out of the dark ages.

Many famous Great Detectives followed in Holmes's footsteps – Nero Wolfe and Ellery Queen, Hercule Poirot and Solar Pons – each with their own methods and techniques, but before they began their careers, and while Holmes was still in practice in Baker Street, another London consultant – Dr. John Thorndyke – opened his doors, using the scientific methods developed and perfected by Holmes and taking them to a whole new level of brilliance.

Meet Dr. Thorndyke

Dr. John Evelyn Thorndyke was born on July 4th, 1870. We don't know about where he was raised, or if he has any family. At no point will we be introduced to a more brilliant brother who sometimes *is* the British Government. He was educated at the medical school of St. Margaret's Hospital in London, and while there, he met fellow student Christopher Jervis. They became friends but, after completing school in 1895, they lost touch with one another. Over the next six years, Thorndyke remained at St. Margaret's, taking on various jobs, hanging "about the chemical and physical laboratories, the museum and *post mortem* room," and learning what he could. He obtained his M.D. and his Doctor of Sciences, and then was called to the bar in 1896.

He'd prepared himself with the hope of obtaining a position as a coroner, but he learned of the unexpected retirement of one of St. Margaret's lecturers in medical jurisprudence. He applied for the position and, rather to his own surprise, it was awarded to him. (He would continue to maintain his association with the hospital, going on to become the Medical Registrar, Pathologist, Curator of the Museum, and then Professor of Medical Jurisprudence, all while maintaining his own private consulting practice.

It was when Thorndyke was named lecturer that he obtained his chambers at 5A King's Bench Walk, in the Inner Temple, that amazing and historic area between Fleet Street and the River. Founded over eight-hundred years ago by the Knights Templar, it is one of the four Inns of Court, (along with the Middle Temple, Lincoln's Inn, and Gray's Inn.) The buildings along King's Bench Walk, and particularly No.'s 4, 5, and 6, have a great deal of historical significance – and not just because Dr. John Thorndyke practiced at 5A for a number of years.

Thorndyke was quite fortunate to obtain a suite of rooms on multiple floors at this location, which leads to speculation about his influence and resources – a question which has no answer. In any case, it was there that he opened his practice and began to wait for clients and cases. He also made the acquaintance of elderly Nathaniel Polton, that man-of-all-work with the crinkly smile who ran the household, as well as Thorndyke's upstairs laboratory.

Like Sherlock Holmes during those early years in the 1870's when he had rooms in Montague Street next to the British Museum and spent his vast amounts of free time learning his craft, Thorndyke also found a way to make the empty hours more useful. He had the unique idea of imagining increasingly complex crimes – often a murder or series of them, for instance – and then, when he had planned every single aspect of the crime, he would turn around and work out the solution from the other side. While doing this, he made extensive notes of each of these theoretical exercises, and retained them for their later usefulness when encountering real-life crimes.

His first legal case was *Regina v Gummer* in 1897. Sadly, no further information about this affair is ever revealed to us, but we may be certain that Thorndyke used his considerable skills to bring it to a satisfactory conclusion, adding to his reputation as he did so.

In the meantime, Jervis had a more unfortunate story. As his time at school ended, his funds ran out rather unexpectedly, and after paying his various fees, he was left with earning his living as a medical assistant, or sometimes serving as a *locum tenens*, moving from one low-paying and temporary job to another, with no prospects of improvement.

Jervis is unemployed on the morning of March 22nd, 1901 when he encounters Thorndyke a few doors up from 5A King's Bench Walk. The two friends are happy to see one another, and before long, Jervis is involved in an investigation that will change his life in several ways, as recounted in *The Red Thumb Mark*.

But it should not be assumed that every Thorndyke adventure is narrated by Jervis in a typical Watsonian manner. In fact, the very next book, *The Eye of Osiris*, is instead told from the perspective of one of Thorndyke's students, Dr. Paul Berkeley. It is one of several that provide a look at Thorndyke – and Jervis – from a different perspective. But Jervis returns as narrator in the third novel, *The Mystery of 31 New Inn*, and we see Thorndyke through his eyes for a good many of both the novels and short stories.

Here a word might be mentioned about the Chronology of the Thorndyke stories. For some this is an irrelevant factor, but for others – like me – understanding the correct chronological placement of the stories is very important. Like the volumes that make up the Sherlock Holmes Canon, the Thorndyke stories aren't published in chronological order – a case set in 1907 (such as "Percival Bland's Proxy") might be collected before one that occurs in 1908, ("The Missing Mortgagee"), or it might not. For instance, *The Red Thumb Mark* (1907) is set in March and April 1901. (This chronological placement, by the way, is

9

determined by noticing that a specific date is given three times in the book – in the British fashion of day before month – *9.3.01* – or *March 9th, 1901*. The dates for the events of the rest of the book can be carefully worked out from this fixed point.)

The next book, *The Eye of Osiris* (1911) is primarily set in the summer of 1904 (with Chapter 1, something of a prologue, taking place in late 1902.) Then, the next book to follow, *The Mystery of 31 New Inn* (1912), jumps back to the spring of 1902, about a year after the events of *The Red Thumb Mark*, and before *The Eye of Osiris*. And one of the short stories, "The Man With the Nailed Shoes" occurs in September and October 1901, between the first two books. Clearly, there is a great deal of material for the chronologicist in the Thorndyke Chronicles.

As Jervis becomes a part of Thorndyke's world, following their reacquaintance in March 1901, he meets others in Thorndyke's circle, including policemen such as Superintendent Miller and Inspector Badger, lawyers like Robert Anstey, Marchmont, and Brodribb, and other physicians like Dr. Paul Berkeley and Dr. Humphrey Jardine. He also has more opportunity to learn from his friend as he begins his own studies in order to become a similar specialist in the medico-legal practice – although he'll never be another Thorndyke.

Through Jervis's eyes – as well as others along the way – we build up our knowledge of Dr. Thorndyke. In appearance, he is tall and athletic, just under six feet in height, slender, and weighing around one-hundred-and-eighty pounds. He is exceptionally handsome – and has been called the handsomest detective in literature. He has no vices, except – perhaps – that he enjoys a Trichinopoly cigar upon occasion when he is feeling especially triumphant – although there is one time when the criminal's knowledge of this fact leads to a clever attempt at Thorndyke's murder . . . .

There are several instances where Thorndyke displays a marked resemblance to Sherlock Holmes – and not just in his scientific approach to crime. The two men sometimes say similar things – such as when Holmes says "*It is quite a pretty little problem,*" (in "A Scandal in Bohemia") or ". . . *there are some pretty little problems among them*" (in "The Musgrave Ritual"). Thorndyke mimics this in *Felo de Se?* ("*There, Jervis,*" said he, "*is quite a pretty little problem for you to excogitate*") or "*Ah, there is a very pretty little problem for you to consider*" (in *The Eye of Osiris*).

And who can forget the many instances when Holmes refers to *data*:

- *"It is a capital mistake to theorize before one has data. Insensibly one begins to twist facts to suit theories, instead of theories to suit facts."* – "A Scandal in Bohemia"
- *"I had,"* said he, *"come to an entirely erroneous conclusion which shows, my dear Watson, how dangerous it always is to reason from insufficient data."* – "The Speckled Band"
- *"No data yet,"* he answered. *"It is a capital mistake to theorize before you have all the evidence. It biases the judgment."* – *A Study in Scarlet*
- *"The temptation to form premature theories upon insufficient data is the bane of our profession."* – *The Valley of Fear*
- *"Still, it is an error to argue in front of your data."* – "Wisteria Lodge"

Thorndyke's version? *". . . believe me, it is a capital error to decide beforehand what data are to be sought for."* – from *The Mystery of 31 New Inn*. There are others.

Then there is Holmes's quote from "The Man With the Twisted Lip":

"You have a grand gift of silence, Watson," said he. *"It makes you quite invaluable as a companion."*

Here's the Thorndyke equivalent:

"It has just been borne in upon me, Jervis," said he, *"that you are the most companionable fellow in the world. You have the heaven-sent gift of silence."*

And then there is the time, in "The Anthropologist at Large", that a client – expecting a Holmes-like performance as based on "The Blue Carbuncle" – presents Thorndyke with an object for examination:

"I understand," said he, *"that by examining a hat it is possible to deduce from it, not only the bodily characteristics of the wearer, but also his mental and moral qualities, his state of health, his pecuniary position, his past history, and even his domestic relations and the peculiarities of his place of abode. Am I right in this supposition?"*

The ghost of a smile flitted across Thorndyke's face as he laid the hat upon the remains of the newspaper. "We must

11

not expect too much," he observed. "Hats, as you know, have a way of changing owners . . . ."

Another area of intersection between Holmes and Thorndyke is the assembly of information. Recall Holmes's *"ponderous commonplace books in which he placed his cuttings"* as mentioned in "The Engineer's Thumb". We find, also in "The Anthropologist at Large", that Thorndyke does the same thing:

> [H]is method of dealing with [the morning newspaper] was characteristic. The paper was laid on the table after breakfast, together with a blue pencil and a pair of office shears. A preliminary glance through the sheets enabled him to mark with the pencil those paragraphs that were to be read, and these were presently cut out and looked through, after which they were either thrown away or set aside to be pasted in an indexed book.

No doubt and examination of Thorndyke's lodgings at 5A King's Bench Walk would reveal – in addition to a series of indexed commonplace books filled with clippings – a number of other items and aspects that would remind one of 221b Baker Street.

Like many locations where the detective's residence is almost a character in and of itself – Sherlock Holmes's London address at 221 Baker Street, and the New York homes of Ellery Queen on West 87th Street and Nero Wolfe's Brownstone on West 35th Street – Thorndyke's rooms at 5A King's Bench Walk are a living and vibrant place – from the entry way, where a heavy door known as "The Oak" leads visitors into a most comfortable wood-paneled sitting room, located on the (British) first floor, one flight up from the ground floor. On the next floor up, Polton has his laboratory and workshop, containing everything that is needed (or what might be manufactured) in order to solve the case.

On the next floor, underneath the attic, are bedrooms belonging to Thorndyke, Jervis, and Polton. Even after Jervis has married – and now you know that he does get married! – he continues to reside a good deal of the time in King's Bench Walk. As he explains in *When Rogues Fall Out* (1932, with the U.S. title of *Dr. Thorndyke's Discovery*):

> Here, perhaps, since my records of Thorndyke's practice have contained so little reference to my own personal affairs, I should say a few words concerning my domestic habits. As the circumstances of our practice often made it

12

desirable for me to stay late at our chambers, I had retained there the bedroom that I had occupied before my marriage; and, as these circumstances could not always be foreseen, I had arranged with my wife the simple rule that the house closed at eleven o'clock. If I was unable to get home by that time, it was to be understood that I was staying at the Temple. It may sound like a rather undomestic arrangement, but it worked quite smoothly, and it was not without its advantages. For the brief absence gave to my homecomings a certain festive quality, and helped to keep alive the romantic element in my married life. It is possible for the most devoted husbands and wives to see too much of one another.

Thorndyke's Other Appearances

Through the years, Thorndyke's reputation continues to grow, as presented through a number of adventures. Surprisingly, in light of the tens of thousands of Post-Canonical Sherlock Holmes that have come to light over the years, as discovered by latter-day Literary Agents taking over Watson's first Literary Agent, Sir Arthur Conan Doyle, stopped literary-agenting, there have been almost no additional Thorndyke cases brought to the public's attention. The few exceptions to this statement are *Goodbye, Dr. Thorndyke* (1972) by Norman Donaldson, and *Dr. Thorndyke's Dilemma* (1974) by John H. Dirckx. Both narratives deal with Thorndyke and Jervis in their latter years, and each is written by an expert in the field of Thorndyke scholarship.

Donaldson also wrote what might be the final scholarly word on the subject, *In Search of Dr. Thorndyke* (1971). In fact, he had intended his pastiche, *Goodbye, Dr. Thorndyke*, to be published as the conclusion to this book, but it ended up appearing separately.

To my knowledge, "The Great Fathomer", as Thorndyke is sometimes known, has rarely appeared in other locations. He is mentioned in the Solar Pons tale "The Adventure of the Proper Comma" by August Derleth, which finds Dr. Parker returning "from Thorndyke & Polton with an analysis of the capsules Mrs. Buxton had carried with her . . . ."

In my own book of authorized Solar Pons stories, *The Papers of Solar Pons* (2017), Thorndyke makes two appearances. "The Adventure of the Additional Heirs" has Pons and Parker visiting King's Bench Walk:

> *At 5A, we learned that our friend Thorndyke, the*
> *medical juris-practitioner, was out on some investigation or*
> *other, but Pons handed the papers,* sans *photograph, into the*
> *care of Polton, his crinkly-faced laboratory technician, with*
> *a detailed explanation of what he wished to learn. The man*
> *nodded and smiled, and without any extraneous chit-chat,*
> *shut the door, freeing us to return to Fleet Street. We paused*
> *at the edge of the walk to look at the photograph, still in*
> *Pons's hand.*

Later Thorndyke sends Pons a detailed report that helps toward the solution of the problem. And in "The Affair of the Distasteful Society", set in July 1921, Pons and Parker attend the first meeting of a group gathered to honor Sherlock Holmes, where the following conversation occurs:

> *"I see that you invited Thorndyke, and that little*
> *Belgian over on Farraway Street," said Rath.*
> *"And Sexton Blake as well," replied Sir Amory.*
> *"Sexton Blake is a fictional character, Sir Amory," said*
> *Pons with a smile.*

In my story, "The Adventure of the Two Sisters", included in *The New Adventures of Solar Pons*, Dr. Parker writes:

> *Pons was not the only detective who offered his services*
> *to the London populace, although he might have been the*
> *most well-known. We were friends with several others,*
> *including the former Belgian policeman who lived in*
> *Farraway Street, and another rather mysterious fellow in*
> *nearby Bottle Street. And of course, Pons went way back*
> *with Thorndyke, whose chambers were across town. It*
> *wasn't unusual for Pons and the others to regularly confer*
> *on investigations, or simply to sit down and share a few*
> *drinks and professional anecdotes.*

Thorndyke doesn't just appear in some of my Solar Pons adventures. He's also been referenced off-stage in a couple of Sherlock Holmes adventures that I've pulled from Watson's Tin Dispatch Box – and it's more than likely that others will follow. In "The "London Wheel", contained in *The MX Book of New Sherlock Holmes Stories* –

Part IV: 2016 Annual (2016), Holmes, looking through some documents, states:

> *"I believe," said Holmes, "that I have enough amateur legal training that I can get a sense of the implications of the clauses in question in both of these documents." He pulled the folded pages from his pocket. "I thought about sending a message to my* protégé *Thorndyke in King's Bench Walk for his opinion, as he could have been here very quickly, should he be at home at all and not out on his own business. However, I don't believe that will be necessary.*

Perhaps it is a point of interest that Thorndyke is referred to Holmes's protégé. Possibly more information will be forthcoming, such as that which is hinted in my story, "The Coombs Contrivance" (in *The Irregular Adventures of Sherlock Holmes!*). Set in 1889, when Thorndyke was nineteen years old, Holmes and Watson are discussing a precocious Baker Street Irregular:

> *[Holmes] pinched the bridge of his nose. "Do you trust Levi's judgment, Watson?"*
> *I considered. "For an eight-year-old, he's remarkably perceptive – as much as any of the other Irregulars who have assisted you. The Wiggins family, or the Peakes, or Thorndyke, before he went away to university."*

So was Thorndyke, perhaps, a gifted Irregular who learned from The Master, and then went on to create his own successful practice, taking what he learned to a next very successful level? Possibly. In my story "The Inner Temple Intruder", to be found in *Sherlock Holmes and the Great Detectives*, such an origin story is posited. As Robert Downey, Jr. succinctly stated when playing Holmes in 2009's *Sherlock Holmes*: "Food for thought!"

Thorndyke is also mentioned in Bob Byrne's Holmes story, "The Adventure of the Parson's Son" (*The MX Book of New Sherlock Holmes Stories – Part III: 1896-1929*), wherein Holmes, examining a piece of evidence, cries:

> *"Ha! I believe we have discredited the coat entirely. Though I wish I could get Thorndyke to examine it. Would that we were back in London."*

And it isn't just Thorndyke who has appeared elsewhere. His lawyer friend Marchmont has assisted Holmes and Watson in a small way a couple of my own: "The Coombs Contrivance" and the forthcoming adventure *Sherlock Holmes and The Eye of Heka.*

Although I have encouraged these Thorndyke cameos in my own stories or in Holmes and Pons books that I edit, his appearances elsewhere are much more fleeting. In the 2015 BBC radio series *The Rivals*, Inspector Lestrade, Holmes's most frequent associate at Scotland Yard, is placed into the events of the Thorndyke short story "The Moabite Cipher". And Thorndyke has only had a handful of other media appearances. In 1964, the BBC produced seven episodes (now lost) of *Thorndyke*, starring Peter Copley. The episodes were:

- "The Case of Oscar Brodski'
- "The Old Lag"
- "A Case of Premeditation"
- "The Mysterious Visitor"
- "The Case of Phyllis Annesley" – Adapted from "Phyllis Annesley's Peril"
- "Percival Bland's Brother" – Adapted from "Percival Bland's Proxy"
- "The Puzzle Lock"

From 1971 to 1973, Thames TV aired *The Rivals of Sherlock Holmes*, and two stories were adapted: "A Message from the Deep Sea" starring John Neville (who had also played Holmes in 1965's *A Study in Terror*), and "The Moabite Cipher" starring Barrie Ingram. Except for a 1963 BBC Radio adaption of *Mr. Pottermack's Oversight*, and a few on-air readings by a single performer, there have been no other Thorndyke adaptations – which is a terrible shame, as the stories certainly lend themselves to visual and audible interpretations. Perhaps a new generation will discover Thorndyke, Jervis, and the rest, and they will find popularity once again, as they did more than a century ago.

Copley, Neville, and Ingram as Thorndyke

16

A Few (Hundred) Words About R. Austin Freeman
Thorndyke's Chronicler

Richard Austin Freeman was born on April 11, 1862 in the Soho district of London. He was the son of a skilled tailor and the youngest of five children. As he grew, it was expected that he would become a tailor as well, but instead he had an interest in natural history and medicine, and so he obtained employment in a pharmacist's shop. While there, he qualified as an apothecary and could have gone on to manage the shop, but instead he began to study medicine at Middlesex Hospital.

Austin Freeman qualified as a physician in 1887, and in that same year he married. Faced with the twin facts of his new marital responsibilities and his very limited resources as a young doctor, he made the unusual decision to join the Colonial Service, spending the next seven years in Africa as an Assistant Colonial Surgeon. This continued until the early 1890's, when he contracted Blackwater Fever, an illness that eventually forced him to leave the service and return permanently to England.

For several years, he served as a *locum tenens* for various physicians, a bleak time in his life as he moved from job to job, his income low, and his health never quite recovered. (These experiences were reflected in the narratives of Doctors Jervis and Berkeley.) However, he supplemented his meager income and exercised his creativity during these years by beginning to write. His early publications included *Travels and Live in Ashanti and Jaman* (1898), recounting some of his African sojourns.

In 1900, Freeman obtained work as an assistant to Dr. John James Pitcairn (1860-1936) at Holloway Prison. Although he wasn't there for very long, the association between the two men was enough to turn Freeman's attention toward writing mysteries. Over the next few years, they co-wrote several under the pseudonym *Clifford Ashdown*, including *The Adventures of Romney Pringle* (1902), *The Further Adventures of Romney Pringle* (1903), *From a Surgeon's Diary* (1904-1905), and *The Queen's Treasure* (written around 1905-1906, and published posthumously in 1975.) The specifics of the two men's writing arrangement are unknown to the present day, although much research was carried out by Freeman scholar Percival Mason ("P.M.") Stone, who was actually able to confirm Pitcairn's involvement and influence. Following this association, which apparently helped to train Freeman to be a better writer and to focus on a recurring character, his luck changed, and he was able, within just a few years, to abandon the practice of

17

medicine, which had never been successful, and become a professional author.

In approximately 1904, Freeman began developing a mystery novella based on a short job that he had held at the Western Ophthalmic Hospital. This effort, "31 New Inn", was published in 1905, and it is the true first Dr. Thorndyke story. In it, we meet narrator Dr. Christopher Jervis, working as a *locum tenens*, moving from practice to practice in the same bleak existence that Freeman had experienced. Jervis becomes involved with a patient that may or may not be in danger. Unsure what to do, he recalls his former classmate, the brilliant Dr. John Thorndyke.

Curiously, this novella, (included in Volume II of this newly reissued collection *The Complete Dr. Thorndyke*), has numerous references to the events of the first Thorndyke novel, *The Red Thumb Mark*, which would not be published until 1907. Much of Freeman's life is obscure and unknown, including his writing processes and milestones, but clearly, with so much already clearly defined in this novella about Thorndyke and Jervis, he had firmly established not only fixed aspects of their histories, but the plot of *The Red Thumb Mark* as well, several years before the book's publication. One wonders why he chose to first publish "31 New Inn", since it occurs chronologically a whole year *after* the events of *The Red Thumb Mark*.

Interestingly – at least to a chronologicist such as myself – the original novella of "31 New Inn" is specifically set in April 1900, as indicated internally. However, when it was later revised to become the third Thorndyke novel, *The Mystery of 31 New Inn*, (1912, and included in Volume I of *The Complete Dr. Thorndyke*), the narrative's date is changed to 1902 – which fits, since the events definitely occur after *The Red Thumb Mark*, which takes place in March and April 1901.

Like Rex Stout's Nero Wolfe, who seemed to have sprung fully formed from his creator's brow, Thorndyke and his world are well-defined and immediately real. Although certain characters are added to the circle through the years, the basic layout – with Thorndyke, Jervis, and Polton (the man-of-all-work crinkly-smiled assistant) are always at 5A, ready to spring into action when Jervis – or one of the other varied narrators who show up throughout the series – arrive with a curious problem.

Freeman had found his voice with the Thorndyke books and short stories, and he was able to make use of his lifelong interest in medicine and natural science – often conducting extensive experiments to work out exactly how the solutions in his stories could be discovered. And in Thorndyke's early days, Freeman was able to turn the literary form inside out with the creation of the "Inverted Mystery Story", wherein the criminal is known from the beginning – the motive is explained, the planning and execution of the crime are observed, and the miscreant is left to believe that all is well and that he'll never be caught. And then, in the second part of the story, Thorndyke enters to inexorably follow the trail that is completely invisible to everyone else, scraping away, layer by layer and point by point, until the truth is inevitably revealed.

As Freeman explained:

> *Some years ago I devised, as an experiment, an inverted detective story in two parts. The first part was a minute and detailed description of a crime, setting forth the antecedents, motives, and all attendant circumstances. The reader had seen the crime committed, knew all about the criminal, and was in possession of all the facts. It would have seemed that there was nothing left to tell. But I calculated that the reader would be so occupied with the crime that he would overlook the evidence. And so it turned out. The second part, which described the investigation of the crime, had to most readers the effect of new matter.*

This format went on to be used by a great many authors through the years. For example several of the Lord Peter Wimsey narratives come close to being this type of story, and television's *Columbo* used this type of story-telling as its basis.

While these volumes are an attempt to reintroduce the modern reader to Thorndyke, and are a celebration of him and his world, it must be discussed at some point that Freeman held views that are unacceptable. Unlike Sir Arthur Conan Doyle, who spent his last decades championing spiritualism but never allowed it to creep into the Sherlock Holmes stories, Freeman sometimes did let his own prejudices make their way into the Thorndyke tales. In his book *Social Decay and Regeneration* (1921), he expressed his rather nationalistic view that England had become an "homogenized, restless, unionized working class". Worse, he inexcusably and detestably supported the eugenics movement, arguing that people with "undesirable" traits should not be allowed to reproduce by means such as "segregation, marriage restriction, and sterilization". He referred to immigrants as "Sub-Man", and argued that society needed to be protected from "degenerates of the destructive type."

Some have attempted to excuse his beliefs as being a product of his times. For instance, it has been written that he had a distrust of Jews because of the competition that his father, a tailor, had faced when Freeman was a boy. Later, he served in the Colonial Service in Africa during some of the worst years in terms of treatment of natives by the British, and as an older man, he existed in the Great Britain between the two wars when great upheavals disrupted much of what he had known and expected.

Sadly, there are occasional racial stereotypes and references in the Thorndyke books. As I explain in the *Editor's Caveat*, some of these stereotypes had to be unfortunately maintained within the story in order to accurately reflect the plot and the characters of those times. However, there are some words or phrases that were used in the original stories – vile racial epithets that have no business being repeated or perpetuated anywhere – that I have cheerfully and happily removed. (There weren't many of them, but any are too many.)

These books are intended to bring Dr. Thorndyke and his adventures to a new generation – and not to be an untouchable and sacred literary artifact, with every nasty stain preserved and archived for the historical record. As I warn in the *Caveat*, if readers find that they want to experience the original versions as they were first written, with those hateful words included, then they would be advised to go and seek out the original books, because you won't find that filth here. These versions celebrate Dr. Thorndyke and Dr. Jervis – who do not use the awful stereotyped language, I'm glad to say! – and as such, I felt no need whatsoever to include and perpetuate the objectionable and offensive material

From Thorndyke's creation until 1914, Freeman wrote four novels and two volumes of short stories. Then, with the commencement of the First World War, he entered military service. In February 1915, at the age of fifty-two, he joined the Royal Army Medical Corps. Due to his health, which had never entirely recovered from his time in Africa, he spent the duration of the war involved with various aspects of the ambulance corps, having been promoted very early to the rank of Captain. He wrote nothing about Thorndyke during this period, but he did publish one book concerning the adventures of a scoundrel, *The Exploits of Danby Croker* (1916).

Following the war, he resumed his previous life, writing approximately one Thorndyke novel per year, as well as three more volumes of Thorndyke short stories and a number of other unrelated items, until his death on September 28th, 1943 – likely related to Parkinson's Disease, which had plagued him in later years.

Upon learning the news, *Chicago Tribune* columnist Vincent Starrett wrote:

> *When all the bright young things have performed their appointed task of flatting the complexes of neurotic semi-literates, and have gone their way to oblivion, the best of the Thorndyke stories will live on – minor classics on the shelf that holds the good books the world.*

Raymond Chandler wrote in his famous essay, which initially appeared in a couple of magazines and then was published in the book of the same name, *The Simple Art of Murder* (1950):

> *This man Austin Freeman is a wonderful performer. He has no equal in his genre, and he is also a much better writer than you might think, if you were superficially inclined, because in spite of the immense leisure of his writing, he accomplishes an even suspense which is quite unexpected .. . There is even a gaslight charm about his Victorian love affairs, and those wonderful walks across London.*

In the introduction to *Great Stories of Detection, Mystery, and Horror* (1928), Dorothy L. Sayers, Chronicler of Lord Peter Wimsey, stated:

> *Thorndyke will cheerfully show you all the facts. You will be none the wiser . . . .*

Discovering Dr. Thorndyke

I first encountered Dr. Thorndyke in a rather backwards way – in passing only – and it took several decades to correct that mistake. In approximately 1980, my dad gave me Otto Penzler's *The Private Lives of Private Eyes, Spies, Crime Fighters, and Other Good Guys* (1977). This wonderful oversized book has biographies of twenty-five well-known heroes, along with lists of the original books featuring each one.

My dad bought it for me because it had a chapter about Sherlock Holmes. There were a few others in there that I recognized or had already read about– Ellery Queen and Perry Mason – and soon I would become fanatical about a few more – Nero Wolfe and Hercule Poirot. Over the next few years I would also find the chapters on James Bond and Lew Archer indispensable, and later than that I would come to appreciate the entries about Philip Marlowe, Sam Spade, Miss Marple, Philo Vance, and Lord Peter Wimsey. But there were a few that, to this day, I've never bothered to read – such as Modesty Blaise or Mr. Moto – and a few others that I skimmed but otherwise ignored. And one of these was the biography of Dr. Thorndyke.

That fact was easily understandable, as throughout the entire time that I was growing up in eastern Tennessee – and in the years since as well – I've never come across a Thorndyke book for sale here in the wild, either in a new bookstore or in a used one. If I'd found one, I might have bought and read it, liked it, and then sought out others. Instead, I was bound to discover Thorndyke by way of Sherlock Holmes.

I've been collecting traditional Sherlock Holmes pastiches since the same time that I discovered the Sherlockian Canon, when I was ten years old in 1975. Since that time, I've collected, read, and chronologicized literally thousands of them. It never gets old, and I'm constantly looking for more – and that means checking Amazon to see what new releases are on the horizon.

In 2012, someone – and I've never determined who – began releasing a variety of Holmes stories for Kindle under the author name *Dr. John H. Watson.* This wasn't too unusual – there have been a number of pastiches that officially list Watson as the author, rather than putting the editor of Watson's papers first. Of course, after determining that these latest entries weren't going to be available as real books, I bought the e-versions, and then printed them on real paper. (I cannot stand e-books – ephemeral electronic blips that you lease instead of buy. I'll only buy those titles if they aren't going to be released as legitimate books – and in this case, it's a good thing that I did, as each of these Kindle stories that I found and paid for were soon withdrawn.)

As I read these latest "Holmes" stories, I noticed that each had a definite style that captured the writing from the late 1800's or early 1900's. (No matter how modern pasticheurs try to achieve that, they never quite pull it off.) But in one of the first two or three titles that I read, I caught a couple of mistakes. In one story, Holmes and Watson leave 221 Baker Street and are immediately in the area around The Temple and Fleet Street, rather than in Marylebone, where Baker Street is properly located. On another occasion, the story's policeman – who had been identified up to that point as Inspector Lestrade – was inexplicably named *Superintendent Miller* – but only in one instance. And in another place in one of the stories, Holmes's address was stated to be *5A King's Bench Walk.*

It was then that some vague memory triggered in my head, and I realized why these stories had captured the style of the late Victorian and early Edwardian eras: *It was because they had actually been written then*. I recalled – from reading Otto Penzler's book of biographies so long ago - that 5A King's Bench Walk belonged to Dr. Thorndyke, and not Sherlock Holmes. Someone was taking the original Thorndyke stories, which I had never before read, and simply changing names: Dr. Thorndyke, Dr. Jervis, and Superintendent Miller became Sherlock Holmes, Dr. Watson, and Inspector Lestrade, respectively.

Between 2012 and 2014, the anonymous author continued to load new Kindle editions on Amazon of Thorndyke-converted to-Holmes stories, and I continued to buy them. As soon as I had one, I would read it, and then try to figure out the original Thorndyke story from which it was taken. When I'd done so, I'd post a review, identifying what this editor was doing, from where he or she was taking the story, and urging that person, whoever it was, give credit to R. Austin Freeman instead of listing the author as Dr. John H. Watson.

Soon after each of my reviews would appear, the story would be withdrawn. I don't know if it was because the editor had made enough money from the initial sales, or if my reviews alerted him or her that they're game had been uncovered. In any case, I still have the printed copies of each of these converted stories – possibly the only copies that are still in existence.

For the record, over that two year period, this editor produced sixteen converted tales – four of the original Thorndyke novels, and twelve short stories. One of the original short stories, "The Mandarin's Pearl", was converted twice, with slight variations – initially published as "The Dragon Pearl", withdrawn, and later revised and reloaded as "The Oriental Pearl":

- "The Bloodied Thumbprint" – Originally the first Thorndyke novel, *The Red Thumb Mark*;
- "The Eye of Ra" – Originally the second Thorndyke novel, *The Eye of Osiris*;
- "The Cat's Eye Mystery" – Originally the sixth Thorndyke novel, *The Cat's Eye*;
- "The Julius Dalton Mystery" – Originally the ninth Thorndyke novel, *The D'Arblay Mystery*;
- "The Green Jacket Mystery" – Originally "The Green Check Jacket";
- "Mr. Crofton's Disappearance" – Originally "The Mysterious Visitor";
- "The Coded Lock" – Originally "The Puzzle Lock";

- "The Duplicated Letter" – Originally "The Stalking Horse";
- "The Bullion Robbery" – Originally "The Stolen Ingots";
- "The Talking Corpse" – Originally "The Contents of a Mare's Nest";
- "The Blue Diamond Mystery" – Originally "The Fisher of Men";
- "The Dragon Pearl" – Originally "The Mandarin's Pearl". (This story was also reworked and published again as a Holmes story under the title "The Oriental Pearl");
- "The Ingenious Murder" – Originally "The Aluminium Dagger";
- "The Bloodhound Superstition" – Originally "The Singing Bone"; *and*
- "The Magic Box" – Originally "The Magic Casket".

For quite a while, I was happy to have these as Holmes stories, and I even considered converting the rest of the Thorndyke adventures into additions to the extended Holmes Canon as well. (For at that time I cared nothing for Dr. Thorndyke.) It was partly with these converted stories in mind that I was motivated to go ahead and publish *Sherlock Holmes in Montague Street* (2014, 2016), which did the same thing to the Martin Hewitt stories, making them early adventures of Holmes before he met Watson and moved to Baker Street. I had long before decided to my own satisfaction that Martin Hewitt *was* a young Sherlock Holmes, with his identity changed through the preparations of a different literary agent than Sir Arthur Conan Doyle.

The taking of old public-domain stories featuring other detectives as the main protagonists and switching them so that Holmes is the main character has also been done by Alan Lance Andersen for his collection *The Affairs of Sherlock Holmes* (2015, 2016), wherein various non-series Sax Rohmer stories from nearly a hundred years ago were reworked as Holmes tales. Other non-Holmes authors have sometimes done the same thing. Raymond Chandler revised some of his early short stories so that the original characters' names were changed to Philip Marlowe. Ross MacDonald – (Kenneth Millar) also rewrote his old stories as well, making them into Lew Archer cases instead. More recently, the British

ITV series *Marple* has taken non-Miss Marple Agatha Christie stories and converted them into episodes featuring that character.

So I had no problems with this type of change – and still don't. In fact, in my foreword to *Sherlock Holmes of Montague Street*, I wrote that I would rather have these converted Thorndyke stories as Holmes adventures, because I would rather read about Holmes than Thorndyke. But gradually my mind began to change, and I became more curious about Thorndyke, as presented in the proper fashion.

In 2013, I was able to go to London, as well as other places in England and Scotland, on the first (of three so far) Holmes Pilgrimages. For the most part, if a location wasn't related to Holmes, I didn't visit it. There were a few exceptions – I did intentionally visit Solar Pons's house at 7B Praed Street, Hercule Poirot's two residences, James Bond's flat in Chelsea – but everything else was pretty much pure Holmes.

One day, during my Holmesian rambles, I was making my way east down Fleet Street, and I visited both of the possible locations of "Pope's Court" (as featured in "The Red-Headed League"), Poppin's Court and Mitre Court. (The latter is also one of the locations where Denis Nayland Smith and Dr. Petrie had quarters in some of the Fu Manchu books.) I decided that Mitre Court was certainly the original of "Pope's Court", and I passed through it to find myself unexpectedly in The Temple.

That's the amazing thing about a Holmes Pilgrimage to London – one travels to a site and finds two more very close by. I had planned to visit The Temple, but hadn't realized that I was so close. And now here I was – and more interesting was the fact that I was walking along King's Bench Walk, which runs downhill from the Miter Court passage. I recalled that Thorndyke had lived at 5A, so I made my way there – but without too much awe on that day, because I hadn't actually read any Thorndyke adventures yet – just some converted Holmes stories.

After I returned home, the thought of that side-trip to Thorndyke's front door stuck in my mind, and I sought out and read the first novel in the series, *The Red Thumb Mark*. I was so impressed that I kept going, and discovered a wonderful series of books and stories – fascinating characters and mysteries, and very evocative descriptions of both the London and the countryside of those times.

When I returned on my second Holmes Pilgrimage in 2015, I took the second Thorndyke book with me, reading it while there – while also reading Holmes stories too, of course! This one, *The Eye of Osiris*, has a great deal of London atmosphere, and I spent part of one late afternoon tracking down locations in this book – or what's now left of them – in the area around Fetter Lane to the north of Thorndyke's home in The Temple. It was truly unforgettable.

And of course I made an intentional stop at King's Bench Walk on that 2015 trip, and again on Holmes Pilgrimage No. 3 in 2016. By that point I was a Thorndyke fan, and I took the trouble to write to the current occupiers of 5A before I traveled to see if I could step inside and perhaps spend a moment in Thorndyke's old quarters. Sadly, they did not respond – either because it was simply beneath them to do so, or possibly because they get too many people like me who want to make a literary pilgrimage to what is a functioning and thriving business location.

While making photographs at Thorndyke's old doorway, I had several chances to go inside when someone else would enter or leave – My ever-present deerstalker and I could have simply been bold enough to slip in and then talk my way onward. It worked at other places on my Holmes Pilgrimages – the laboratory at Barts where Holmes and Watson met, for instance, and the site of the (former?) Diogenes Club at No. 78 Pall Mall, where they acted just oddly enough to make me think that the club is still there. But for some reason, barging into Thorndyke's old chambers without proper permission didn't feel quite right. But if or when I make Holmes Pilgrimage No. 4, I'll definitely make an even greater effort to see the doctor's former rooms.

The Editor and his Deerstalker at 5A King's Bench Walk
September 2016

With many thanks . . . .

These last few years have been an amazing ride, and I've been able to play in the Sherlockian sandbox more than I'd ever imagined. (And subsequently, the Solar Pons sandbox, and now Thorndyke, too! Along the way, I've been able to meet some incredible people, both in person and in the modern electronic way, and also I've been able to read several hundred new Holmes adventures, as well as to be able to share them with others.

Still, what is most important is my amazingly wonderful wife (of over thirty years!) Rebecca, and our truly awesome son and my friend, Dan. I love you both, and you are everything to me! I am the luckiest guy in the world.

I have all the gratitude in the world for everyone that I've encountered along the way – It's an undeniable fact that Sherlock Holmes authors are the *best* people! I'd like to thank those who offer support, encouragement, and friendship, sometimes patiently waiting on me to reply as my time is directed in many other directions. Many many thanks to (in alphabetical order): Brian Belanger, Derrick Belanger, Bob Byrne, Roger Johnson, Mark Mower, Denis Smith, Tom Turley, Dan Victor, and Marcia Wilson.

In particular, I'd also like to especially thank Steve Emecz, who is always supportive of every idea that I pitch. It's been my particular good fortune that he crossed my path – it changed my life in a way that would have never happened otherwise, and I'm grateful for every opportunity!

I hope that these books will provide pleasure to those discovering Dr. Thorndyke for the first time, and to others who have known him for a long time. As always, I approach these matters from a Sherlockian perspective, so of course these stories, to me, are a peripheral extension of Holmes's world, and as such they are just more tiny threads woven into the ongoing Great Holmes Tapestry. However, they are wonderful on their own, and however one reads them, I wish great joy upon the journey.

David Marcum
(Revised October 2020)

Questions, comments, and story submissions
may be addressed to David Marcum at
thepapersofsherlockholmes@gmail.com

5A King's Bench Walk
in the late 1890's when
Thorndyke was in residence

Editor's *Caveat*

These stories have been prepared using modern text-converting software, and as such, occasional deviations in punctuation have occurred. Those who absolutely must have the original version, down to each jot and dash, should understand that this version was created in order to present Dr. Thorndyke's adventures to a modern audience, and not to preserve an absolute pristine model for the historical archives.

Similarly, these stories were written in a time when racial prejudice and stereotypes were much more common than today. While some of these stereotypes must be unfortunately maintained within the story in order to accurately reflect the plot and the characters of those times, there are some words that were used in the original stories – vile racial epithets that have no business being repeated or perpetuated anywhere – that I have cheerfully removed. (There weren't many of them, but *any* are *too many*.)

If readers find that they want to experience the original versions as they were first written, with those hateful and ignorant words included, then they would be advised to seek out the original books. These versions celebrate Dr. Thorndyke and Dr. Jervis – who do *not* use the awful stereotyped language, I'm glad to say! – and as such, I felt no need whatsoever to include objectionable and offensive material simply for the sake of honoring or archiving the historical record.

David Marcum
Editor

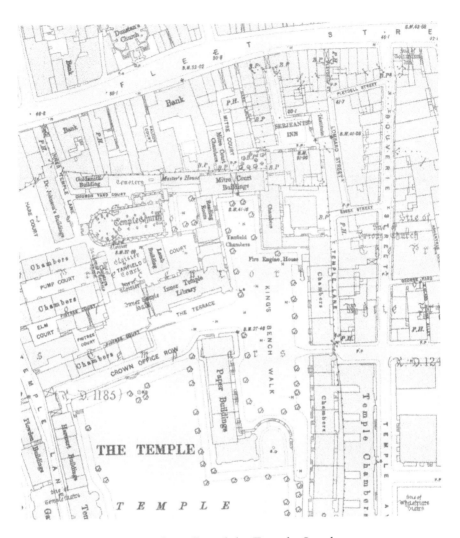

King's Bench Walk and the Temple, London
around 1900

1938 Hodder & Stoughton, London Cover

The Stoneware Monkey – As Sculpted by the Author

Book One
Narrated by
James Oldfield, M.D.

Chapter I
Hue-and-Cry

The profession of medicine has a good many drawbacks in the way of interrupted meals, disturbed nights, and long and strenuous working hours. But it has its compensations, for a doctor's life is seldom a dull life. Compared, for instance, with that of a civil servant or a bank official, it abounds in variety of experience and surroundings, to say nothing of the intrinsic interest of the work in its professional aspects. And then it may happen at any moment that the medical practitioner's duties may lead him into the very heart of a drama or a tragedy or bring him into intimate contact with crime.

Not that the incident which I am about to describe was, in the first place, directly connected with my professional duties. The initial experience might have befallen anyone. But it was my medical status that enlarged and completed that experience.

It was about nine o'clock on a warm September night that I was cycling at an easy pace along a by-road towards the town, or village, of Newingstead, in which I was temporarily domiciled as the *locum tenens* of a certain Dr. Wilson. I had been out on an emergency call to a small village about three miles distant and had taken my bicycle instead of the car for the sake of the exercise, and having ridden out at the speed that the occasion seemed to demand, was now making a leisurely return, enjoying the peaceful quiet of the by-way and even finding the darkness restful with a good headlight to show the way and a rear light to secure me from collisions from behind.

At a turn of the lane, a few twinkling lights seen dimly through spaces in the hedgerow told me that I was nearing my destination. A little reluctant to exchange the quiet of the countryside for the light and bustle of the town, I dismounted and, leaning my bicycle against a gate, brought out my pipe and was just dipping into my pocket for my tobacco pouch when I heard what sounded to me like the call of a police whistle.

I let go the pouch and put away my pipe as I strained my ears to listen. The sound had come from no great distance but I had not been able exactly to locate it. The cart track from the gate, I knew, skirted a small wood, from which a footpath joined it, and the sound had seemed to come from that direction. But the wood was invisible in the darkness, though I could judge its position by a group of ricks, the nearest of which loomed vaguely out of the murk.

I had switched off the lamps of my machine and was just considering the expediency of walking up the cart track to explore when the unmistakable shriek of a police whistle rang out, considerably nearer than the last and much shorter, and was succeeded by the sound of voices – apparently angry voices – accompanied by obscure noises as of bodies bursting through the undergrowth of the wood, from the direction of which the sounds now clearly proceeded. On this I climbed over the gate and started up the cart track at a quick pace, treading as silently as I could and keeping a bright lookout. The track led through the groups of ricks, the great shapes of which loomed up one after another, looking strangely gigantic in the obscurity, and near the last of them I passed a farm wagon and was disposed to examine it with my flashlight, but then judged it to be more prudent not to show a light. So I pushed on with the flashlight in my hand, peering intently into the darkness and listening for any further sounds.

But there were none. The silence of the countryside – now no longer restful, but awesome and sinister – was deepened rather than broken by the faint sounds that belonged to it, the half-audible "skreek" of a bat, the faint murmur of leaves and, far away, the fantastic cry of an owl.

Presently I was able to make out the wood as a vague shape of deeper darkness, and then I came on the little footpath that meandered away towards it. Deciding that this was the right direction, I turned on to it and followed it – not without difficulty, for it was but a narrow track through the grass – until I found myself entering the black shadows of the wood. Here I paused for a moment to listen while I peered into the impenetrable darkness ahead. But no sounds came to my ear save the hushed whisper of the trees. Whatever movement there had been was now stilled, and as I resumed my advance toward the wood I began to ask myself uneasily what this strange and sudden stillness might portend. But I had not gone more than a score of paces and was just entering the wood when the question was answered. Quite suddenly, almost at my feet, I saw the prostrate figure of a man.

Instantly I switched on my flashlight and as its beam fell on him it told the substance of the tragic story in a single flash. He was the constable whose whistle I had heard – it was still hanging loose at the end of its chain. He was bareheaded and at the first glance I thought he was dead, but when I knelt down by his side I saw that he was still breathing, and I now noticed a small trickle of blood issuing from an invisible wound above his ear. Very carefully I sought the wound by a light touch of my finger and immediately became aware of a soft area of the scalp, which further cautious and delicate palpation showed to be a depression of the skull.

I felt his pulse – a typical brain-compression pulse – and examined his eyes, but there was no doubt as to his condition. The dent in the skull was compressing his brain and probably the compression was being increased from moment to moment by internal bleeding. The question was, what was to be done? I could do nothing for him here, but yet I could hardly leave him to go in search of help. It was a horrible dilemma, whatever could be done for him would need to be done quickly, and the sands of his life were running out while I knelt helplessly at his side.

Suddenly I bethought me of his whistle. The sound of it had brought me to the spot and it must surely bring others. Picking it up, I put it to my lips and blew a loud and prolonged blast and, after a few moments' pause, another and yet another. The harsh, strident screech, breaking in on the deathly stillness of the wood and setting the sleeping birds astir, seemed to strike my overstrung nerves a palpable blow. It was positive pain to me to raise that hideous din, but there was nothing else to do. I must keep it up until it should be heard and should attract someone to this remote and solitary place.

It took effect sooner than I had expected, for I was in the act of raising the whistle once more to my lips when I heard sounds from within the wood as of someone trampling through the undergrowth. I threw the beam of my flashlight in that direction but took the precaution to stand up until I should have seen who and what the newcomer might be. Almost immediately there appeared a light from the wood which flashed out and then disappeared as if a lantern were being carried among tree trunks. Then it became continuous and was evidently turned full on me as the newcomer ran out of the wood and advanced towards me. For a few moments I was quite dazzled by the glare of his light, but as he came nearer, mine lighted him up and I then saw that he was a police constable. Apparently he had just observed the figure lying at my feet, for he suddenly quickened his pace and arrived so much out of breath that, for a moment or two, he was unable to speak, but stood with the light of his lantern cast on his unconscious comrade, breathing hard and staring down at him with amazement and horror.

"God save us!" he muttered at length. "What the devil has been happening? Who blew that whistle?"

41

"I did," I replied, upon which he nodded, and then, once more throwing his light on me, and casting a searching glance at me, demanded, "And who are you, and how do you come to be here?"

I explained the position very briefly and added that it was urgently necessary that the injured man should be got to the hospital as quickly as possible.

"He isn't dead, then?" said he. "And you say you are a doctor? Can't you do anything for him?"

"Not here," I answered. "He has got a deep depressed fracture of the skull. If anything can be done, it will have to be done at the hospital, and he will have to be moved very gently. We shall want an ambulance. Could you go and fetch one? My bicycle is down by the gate."

He considered for a few moments. Apparently he was in somewhat of a dilemma, for he replied, "I oughtn't to go away from here with that devil probably lurking in the wood. And you oughtn't to leave this poor chap. But there was another man coming along close behind me. He should be here any minute if he hasn't lost his way. Perhaps I'd better go back a bit and look for him."

He threw the beam from his lantern into the opening of the wood and was just starting to retrace his steps when there sounded faintly from that direction the voice of someone apparently hailing us.

"Is that you, Mr. Kempster?" the constable roared.

Apparently it was, though I could not make out the words of the reply, for a minute or so later a man emerged from the wood and approached us at a quick walk. But Mr. Kempster, like the constable, was a good deal the worse for his exertions and, for a time, was able only to stand panting, with his hand to his side, while he gazed in consternation at the prostrate form on the ground.

"Can you ride a bicycle, Mr. Kempster?" the constable asked.

Mr. Kempster managed to gasp out that he could, though he wasn't much of a rider.

"Well," said the constable, "we want an ambulance to take this poor fellow to the hospital. Could you take the doctor's bicycle and run along to the police station and just tell them what has happened?"

"Where is the bicycle?" asked Kempster.

"It is leaning against the gate at the bottom of the cart track," I replied, adding, "You can have my flashlight to find your way and I will see you down the path to the place where it joins the track."

He agreed, not unwillingly, I thought, having no great liking for the neighbourhood, so I handed him my flashlight and conducted him along the path to its junction with the cart track, when I returned to the place where the constable was kneeling by his comrade, examining him by the light of his lantern.

"I can't make this out," said he as I came up. "He wasn't taken unawares. There seems to have been a considerable scrap. His truncheon's gone. The fellow must have managed to snatch it out of his hand, but I can't imagine how that can have happened. It would take a pretty hefty customer to get a constable's truncheon out of his fist, especially as that's just what he'd be on his guard against."

"He seems to have been a powerful ruffian," said I, "judging by the character of the injury. He must have struck a tremendous blow. The skull is stove in like an egg-shell."

"Blighter!" muttered the constable. Then, after a pause, he asked, "Do you think he is going to die, Doctor?"

"I am afraid his chances are not very good," I replied, "and the longer we have to wait for that ambulance, the worse they will be."

"Well," he rejoined, "if Mr. Kempster hustles along, we shan't have very long to wait. They won't waste any time at the station."

He stood up and swept the beam of his lantern around, first towards the wood and then in the direction of the ricks. Suddenly he uttered an indignant snort and exclaimed, angrily, "Well, I'm damned! Here's Mr. Kempster coming back." He kept the light of his lantern on the approaching figure, and as it came within range he roared out, "What's the matter, sir? We thought you'd be half-way there."

Mr. Kempster hurried up, breathing hard and looking decidedly resentful of the constable's tone.

"There is no bicycle there," he said, sulkily. "Somebody must have made off with it. I searched all about there but there was not a sign of it."

The constable cursed as a well-trained constable ought not to curse.

"But that's put the lid on it," he concluded. "This murderous devil must have seen you come up, Doctor, and as soon as you were out of sight, he must have just got on your machine and cleared out. I suppose you had a headlight."

"I had both head and rear light," I replied, "but I switched them both off before I started up the cart track. But, of course, if he was anywhere near – hiding behind one of those ricks, for instance – he would have seen my lights when I came up to the gate."

"Yes," the constable agreed, gloomily, "it was a bit of luck for him. And now he's got clean away – got away for good and all unless he has left some sort of traces."

Mr. Kempster uttered a groan. "If he has slipped through your fingers," he exclaimed, indignantly, "there's about ten-thousand pounds' worth of my property gone with him. Do you realize that?"

"I do, now you've told me," replied the constable, adding unsympathetically, "and it's bad luck for you, but still, you know, you are better off than my poor mate here who was trying to get it back for you. But we mustn't stop here talking. If the man has gone, there is no use in my staying here. I'll just run back the way I came and report at the station. You may as well wait here with the doctor until I come back with the ambulance."

But Mr Kempster had had enough of the adventure.

"There is no use in my waiting here," said he, handing me my flashlight. "I'll walk back through the wood with you and then get along home and see exactly what that scoundrel has taken."

The constable made no secret of his disapproval of this course, but he did not actually put it into words. With a brief farewell to me, he turned the light of his lantern on the entrance to the wood and set off at a pace that kept his companion at a brisk trot. And as the light faded among the trees and the sound of their footsteps died away in the distance, I found myself once more alone with my patient, encompassed by the darkness and wrapped in a silence which was broken only by an occasional soft moan from the unconscious man.

It seemed to me that hours elapsed after the departure of the constable, hours of weary expectation and anxiety. I possessed myself of my patient's lantern and by its light examined him from time to time. Naturally, there was no improvement, indeed, each time that I felt his pulse it was with a faint surprise to find it still beating. I knew that, actually, his condition must be getting worse with every minute that passed, and it became more and more doubtful whether he would reach the hospital alive.

Then my thoughts strayed towards my bicycle and the unknown robber. We had taken it for granted that the latter had escaped on the machine, and in all probability he had. Yet it was possible that the cycle might have been stolen by some tramp or casual wayfarer and that the robber might be still lurking in the neighbourhood. However, that possibility did not disturb me, since he could have no object in attacking me. I was more concerned about the loss of my bicycle.

From the robber, my reflections drifted to the robbed. Who and what was Mr. Kempster? And what sort of property was it that the thief had made off with? There are not many things worth ten-thousand pounds which can be carried away in the pocket. Probably the booty consisted of something in the nature of jewelry. But I was not much interested. The value of property, and especially of such trivial property as jewelry, counts for little compared with that of a human life. My momentarily wandering attention quickly came back to the man lying motionless at my feet, whose life hung so unsteadily in the balance.

At last my seemingly interminable vigil came to an end. From the road below came the distinctive clang of an ambulance bell, and lights winked over the unseen hedgerow. Then the glare from a pair of powerful headlamps came across the field, throwing up the ricks in sharp silhouette, and telling me that the ambulance was passing in through the gate. I watched the lights growing brighter from moment to moment, saw them vanish behind the ricks, and presently emerge as the vehicle advanced up the cart track and at length turned on to the footpath.

It drew up eventually within a few paces of the spot where the injured man was lying, and immediately there descended from it a number of men, including a police inspector and the constable who had gone with Kempster. The former greeted me civilly and, looking down on his subordinate with deep concern, asked me a few questions while a couple of uniformed men brought out a stretcher and set it down by the patient. I helped them to lift him on to the stretcher and to convey the latter to its place in the ambulance. Then I got in, myself and, while the vehicle was being turned round, the inspector came to take a last look at the patient.

"I am not coming back with you. Doctor," said he. "I have got a squad of men with some powerful lights to search the wood."

"But," said I, "the man has almost certainly gone off on my bicycle."

"I know," said he. "But we are not looking for him. It's this poor fellow's truncheon that I want. If the thief managed to snatch it away from him, there are pretty certain to be finger-prints on it. At any rate, I hope so, for it's our only chance of identifying the man."

With this, as the ambulance was now ready to start, he turned away, and as we moved off towards the cart track, I saw him, with the constable and three plain-clothes men, advancing towards the wood which, by the combined effects of all their lights, was illuminated almost to the brightness of daylight.

Once out on the road, the smoothly-running ambulance made short work of the distance to the hospital. But yet the journey had not been short enough. For when the stretcher had been borne into the casualty room and placed on the table, the first anxious glance showed that the feebly-flickering light had gone out. In vain the visiting surgeon – who had been summoned by telephone – felt the pulse and listened to the heart. Poor Constable Murray – such, I learned, was his name – had taken his last turn of duty.

"A bad business," said the surgeon, putting away his stethoscope and passing his fingers lightly over the depression in the dead man's skull. "But I doubt whether we could have done much for him even if he had come in alive. It was a devil of a blow. The man was a fool to hit so hard, for now he'll have to face a charge of wilful murder – that is, if they catch him. I hope they will."

"I hope so, too," said I, "but I doubt whether they will. He seems to have found my bicycle and gone off on it, and I gather that nobody saw him near enough to recognize him."

"Hmm," grunted the surgeon, "that's unfortunate, and bad luck for you, too, though I expect you will get your cycle back. Meanwhile, can I give you a lift in my car?"

I accepted the offer gladly and, after a last look at the dead constable, we went out together to return to our respective homes.

Chapter II
The Inquiry

It was on the fourth day after my adventure that I received the summons to attend the inquest – which had been kept back to enable the police to collect such evidence as was available – and in due course presented myself at the little Town Hall in which the inquiry was to be held. The preliminaries had already been disposed of when I arrived, but I was in time to hear the coroner's opening address to the jury. It was quite short, and amounted to little more than the announcement of his intention to take the evidence in its chronological order, a very sensible proceeding, as it seemed to me, whereby the history of the tragedy would evolve naturally from the depositions of the witnesses. Of these, the first was Mr. Arthur Kempster, who, by the coroner's direction, began with a narrative of the events known to him.

"I am a diamond merchant, having business premises in Hatton Garden and a private residence at The Hawthorns, Newingstead. On Friday, the 16th of September, I returned from a trip to Holland and came direct from Harwich to The Hawthorns. At Amsterdam I purchased a parcel of diamonds and I had them in a paper packet in my inside waistcoat pocket when I arrived home, which I did just about dinner time. After dinner, I went to my study to examine the diamonds and to check their weight on the special scales which I keep for that purpose. When I had finished weighing them and had looked them over, one by one, I put away the scales and looked about for the lens which I use to examine stones as to their cutting. But I couldn't find the lens. Then I had a faint recollection of having used it in the dining room, which adjoins the study, and I went to that room to see if I might have left it there. And I had. I found it after a very short search and went back with it to the study. But when I went to the table on which I had put the diamonds, to my amazement I found that they had vanished. As nobody could possibly have come into the study by the door, I looked at the window, and then I saw that it was open, whereas it had been shut when I went to the dining room.

"I immediately rushed out through the dining room to the front door, and as I came out of it I saw a man walking quickly down the drive. He was nearly at the end of it when I ran out and, as soon as he heard me, he darted round the corner and disappeared. I ran down the drive as fast as I could go and, when I came out into the road, I could see him some distance ahead, running furiously in the direction of the country. I followed him as fast as I could, but I could see that he was gaining on me. Then, as I came to a side turning – Bascombe Avenue – I saw a policeman approaching along it and quite near. So I hailed him and gave the alarm, and when he ran up, I told him, very briefly, what had happened and, as the thief was still in sight, he ran off in pursuit. I followed as well as I could, but I was already out of breath and couldn't nearly keep up with him. But I saw the thief make off along the country road and get over a gate nearly opposite Clay Wood, and the policeman, who seemed to be gaining on the fugitive, also got over the gate, and I lost sight of them both.

"It seemed to me that it was useless to try to follow them, so I turned back towards the town to see if I could get any further assistance. Then, on the main road, I met Police Constable Webb and told him what had happened, and we started off together to the place where the thief had disappeared. We got over the gate, crossed a field, and entered the wood. But there we rather lost ourselves as we had missed the path. We heard a police whistle sounding from the wood while we were crossing the field, and we heard another shorter one just after we had entered. But we couldn't make out clearly the direction the sounds had come from, and we still couldn't find the path.

"Then, after a considerable time, we heard three long blasts of a whistle and at the same moment we saw a glimmer of light, so we ran towards the light – at least the constable did, for I was too blown to run any farther – and at last I found the path and came out of the wood and saw Dr. Oldfield standing by the deceased, who was lying on the ground. Constable Webb suggested that I should take Dr. Oldfield's bicycle and ride to the police station and the doctor gave me his flashlight to light me down the cart track to the gate where he had left the bicycle. But when I got to the gate, there was no sign of any bicycle, so I returned and reported to the constable, who then decided to go, himself, to the station, and we went back together through the wood. When we got back to the field he ran on ahead and I went back to my house."

"When you went to the dining room," said the coroner, "how long were you absent from the study?"

"About two minutes, I should say. Certainly not more than three."

"You say that the study window was closed when you went out of the room. Was it fastened?"

"No. It was open at the top. I opened it when I came in after dinner as it was a warm night and the room seemed rather close."

"Was the blind down?"

"There is no blind, only a pair of heavy curtains. They were drawn when I came into the room, but I had to pull them apart to open the window and I may not have drawn them close afterwards, in fact, I don't think I did."

"Do you think that anyone passing outside could have seen into the room?"

"Yes. The study is on the ground floor – perhaps a couple of feet above the level of the ground – and the windowsill would be about the height of a man's shoulder, so that a man standing outside could easily look into the room."

"Does the window face the drive?"

"No. It looks on the alley that leads to the back premises."

"You, apparently, did not hear the sound of the window sash being raised?"

"No, but I shouldn't, in the dining room. The sash slides up easily and I have all the sash pulleys of my windows kept oiled to prevent them from squeaking."

"Were the diamonds in an accessible position?"

"Yes, quite. They were lying, all together, on a square of black velvet on the table."

"Were they of any considerable value?"

"They were, indeed. The whole parcel would be worth about ten-thousand pounds. There were fifteen of them, and they were all very exceptional stones."

"Would you be able to recognize them if they could be traced?"

"I could easily identify the complete parcel, and I think I could identify the individual stones. I weighed each one separately and the whole group together, and I made certain notes about them of which I have given a copy to the police."

"Was anything taken besides the diamonds?"

"Nothing, not even the paper. The thief must have just grabbed up the stones and put them loose in his pocket."

This completed Mr. Kempster's evidence. Some of the jury would have liked more detailed particulars of the diamonds, but the coroner reminded them gently that the inquiry was concerned, not with the robbery but with the death of Constable Alfred Murray. As there were no other questions, the depositions were read and signed, and the witness was released.

Following the chronological sequence, I succeeded Mr. Kempster and, like him, opened my evidence with a narrative statement. But I need not repeat this, or the examination that amplified it, as I have already told the story of my connection with the case. Nor need I record Constable

Webb's evidence, which was mainly a repetition of Kempster's. When the constable had retired, the name of Dr. James Tansley was called and the surgeon whom I had met at the hospital came forward.

"You have made an examination of the body of the deceased," said the coroner when the preliminary questions had been answered. "Will you tell us what conditions you found?"

"On external examination," the witness replied, "I found a deep depression in the skull two-and-a-quarter inches in diameter starting from a point an inch-and-a half above the left ear, and a contused wound an inch-and-three-quarters in length. The wound and the depressed fracture of the skull both appeared to have been produced by a heavy blow from some blunt instrument. There was no sign of more than one blow. On removing the cap of the skull I found that the inner table – that is, the hard inner layer of the skull – had been shattered and portions of it driven into the substance of the brain, causing severe lacerations. It had also injured one or two arteries and completely divided one, with the result that extensive bleeding had occurred between the skull and the brain, and this would have produced great pressure on the surface of the brain."

"What would you say was the cause of death?"

"The immediate cause of death was laceration and compression of the brain but, of course, the ultimate cause was the blow on the head which produced those injuries."

"It is a mere formality, I suppose, to ask whether the injury could have been self-inflicted?"

"Yes. It is quite impossible that the blow could have been struck by the deceased himself."

This was the substance of the doctor's evidence. When it was concluded and the witness had been released, the name of Inspector Charles Roberts was called, and that officer took his place by the table. Like the preceding witnesses, he began, at the coroner's invitation, with a general statement.

"On receiving Constable Webb's report, as the Chief Constable was absent, I ordered the sergeant to get out the ambulance and I collected a search party to go with it. When we arrived at the spot where the deceased was lying, I saw him transferred to the ambulance under the doctor's supervision, and when it had gone, I took my party into the wood. Each member of the party was provided with a powerful flashlight, so that we had a good light to work by.

"We saw no sign of anyone hiding in the wood, but near the path we found the deceased's helmet. It was uninjured and had probably been knocked off by a branch of a tree. We searched especially for the

50

deceased's truncheon and eventually found it quite near to the place where he had been lying. I picked it up by the wrist strap at the end of the handle and carried it in that way until we reached the station, when I examined it carefully and could see that there were several finger-prints on it. I did not attempt to develop the prints, but hung up the truncheon by its strap in a cupboard, which I locked. On the following morning I delivered the key of the cupboard to the Chief Constable when I made my report."

"Did you find any traces of the fugitive?"

"No. We went down to the gate and found marks there on the earth where the bicycle had stood, and we could see where it had been wheeled off on to the road, but we were unable to make out any visible tracks on the road itself."

"Has the bicycle been traced since then?"

"Yes. Two days after the robbery it was found hidden in a cart shed near the London Road, about three miles from Clay Wood, towards London. I went over it carefully with developing powder to see if there were any finger-prints on it but, although there were plenty of finger-marks, they were only smears and quite unidentifiable."

This was the sum of the inspector's evidence, and as there were no questions, the officer was released and was succeeded by Chief Constable Herbert Parker, who took up and continued the inspector's account of the dead constable's truncheon.

"The key of the cupboard at the police station was delivered to me by Inspector Roberts as he has deposed. I unlocked the cupboard and took out the truncheon, which I examined in a good light with the aid of a magnifying lens. I could see that there were, on the barrel of the truncheon, several finger-prints, and by their position and grouping, I judged that they had been made by the thief when he snatched the truncheon out of the deceased's hand. They were quite distinct on the polished surface, but not sufficiently so to photograph without development, and I did not attempt to develop them because I thought that, having regard to their importance, it would be better to hand the truncheon intact to the experts at Scotland Yard. Accordingly, I packed the truncheon in such a way that the marked surfaces should be protected from any contact and took it up to the finger-print department at Scotland Yard, where I delivered it to the Chief Inspector, who examined it and developed the fingerprints with a suitable powder.

"It was then seen that there were four decipherable prints, evidently those of a left hand. One was a thumb-print and was perfectly clear, and the others, of the first three fingers, though less perfect, were quite recognizable. As soon as they had been developed, they were photographed, and when the photographs were ready, they were handed to the expert searchers who took them to the place where the collections are kept and went through the files with them. The result of the search was to make it certain that no such finger-prints were in any of the files, neither in those of the main collection, nor in those containing single finger-prints."

"And what does that amount to?"

"It amounts to this: That, since these finger-prints are not in the principal files – those containing the complete sets taken by prison officers – it is certain that this man has never been convicted, and since they are not in the single finger-print files, there is no evidence that he has ever been connected with any crime. In short – so far as the finger-prints are concerned – this man is not known to the police."

"That is very unfortunate," said the coroner. "It would seem as if there were practically no chance of ever bringing the crime home to him.

"There is little," he began, "that I need say to you, members of the jury. You have heard the evidence, and the evidence tells the whole sad story. I do not suppose that you will have any doubt that the gallant officer whose tragic and untimely death is the subject of this inquiry, was killed by the runaway thief. But I have to point out to you that if that is your decision, you are legally bound to find a verdict of wilful murder against that unknown man. The law is quite clear on the subject. If any person, while engaged in committing a felony, and in furtherance of such felony, kills, or directly causes the death of any other person, he is guilty of wilful murder, whether he did or did not intend to kill that person.

"Now, there is no evidence that this fugitive desired or intended to kill the constable. But he dealt him a blow which might have killed him and which, in fact, did kill him, and the fugitive was at the time engaged in committing a felony. Therefore, he is guilty of wilful murder. That is all, I think, that I need say."

The jury had apparently already made up their minds on the subject, for after but the briefest whispered consultation with them, the foreman announced that they had agreed on their verdict.

"We find," he continued as the coroner took up his pen, "that the deceased was murdered in Clay Wood by the unknown man who entered Mr. Kempster's house to commit a robbery."

The coroner nodded. "Yes," he said, "I am in entire agreement with you and I shall record a verdict of wilful murder against that unknown man, and I am sure you will concur with me in expressing our deepest sympathy with the family of this gallant officer whose life was sacrificed in the performance of a dangerous duty."

Thus, gloomily enough, ended the adventure that had brought me for the first time into intimate contact with serious crime. At least, it appeared to me that the adventure was at an end and that I had heard the last of the tragedy and of the sinister, shadowy figure that must have passed so near to me on the margin of the wood. It was a natural belief, since I had played but a super's part in the drama and seemed to be concerned with it no more, and since my connection with Newingstead and its inhabitants would cease when my principal, Dr. Wilson, should return from his holiday.

But it was, nevertheless, a mistaken belief, as will appear at a later stage of this narrative.

Chapter III
Peter Gannet

A problem that has occasionally exercised my mind is that of the deterioration of London streets. Why do they always deteriorate and never improve? The change seems to be governed by some mysterious law. Constantly we meet with streets, once fashionable but now squalid, whose spacious houses have fallen from the estate of mansions, tenanted by the rich and great, to that of mere tenements giving shelter to all grades of the poverty-stricken, from the shabby genteel to the definitely submerged, streets where the vanished coaches have given place to the coster's barrow and the van of the yelling coal vendor. But never, in my experience, does one encounter a street that has undergone a change in the reverse direction, that has evolved from obscurity to fashion, from the shabby to the modish.

The reflection is suggested to me by the neighbourhood in which I had recently taken up my abode, on the expiration of my engagement at Newingstead. Not that Osnaburgh Street, Marylebone, could fairly be described as squalid. On the contrary, it is a highly respectable street. Nevertheless, its tall, flat-faced houses with their spacious rooms and dignified doorways are evidently survivors from a more opulent past, and the whole neighbourhood shows traces of the curious subsidence that I have referred to.

The occasion of my coming to Osnaburgh Street was the purchase by me of a "death vacancy", very properly so described, for there was no doubt of the decease of my predecessor, and the fact of the vacancy became clearly established as I sat, day after day, the undisturbed and solitary occupant of the consulting room, incredulously turning over the pages of the old ledgers and wondering whether the names inscribed therein might perchance appertain to mythical persons, or whether those patients could, with one accord, have followed the late incumbent to his destination in Heaven or Gehenna.

Yet there were occasional calls or messages, at first from casual strangers or newcomers to the district, but presently, by introduction and recommendation, the vacancy grew into a visible "nucleus", which, expanding by slow degrees, seemed to promise an actual practice in the not too far distant future. The hours of solitary meditation in the consulting room began more frequently to be shortened by welcome interruptions, and my brisk, business-like walks through the streets to have some purpose other than mere geographical exploration.

Principally my little practice grew, as I have said, by recommendation. My patients seemed to like me and mentioned the fact to their friends, and thus it was that I made the acquaintance of Peter Gannet. I remember the occasion very clearly, though it seemed so insignificant at the time. It was a gloomy December morning, some three months after my departure from Newingstead, when I set forth on my "round" (of one patient), taking a short cut to Jacob Street, Hampstead Road, through the by-streets behind Cumberland Market and contrasting the drab little thoroughfares with the pleasant lanes around Newingstead. Jacob Street was another instance of the "law of decay" which I have mentioned. Now at the undeniably shabby genteel stage, it had formerly been the chosen resort of famous and distinguished artists. But its glory was not utterly departed for, as several of the houses had commodious studios attached to them, the population still included a leavening of artists, though of a more humble and unpretentious type. Mr. Jenkins, the husband of my patient, was a monumental mason, and from the bedroom window I could see him in the small yard below, chipping away at a rather florid marble headstone.

The introduction came when I had finished my leisurely visit and was about to depart.

"Before you go, Doctor," said Mrs. Jenkins, "I must give you a message from my neighbour, Mrs. Gannet. She sent her maid in this morning to say that her husband is not very well and that she would be glad if you would just drop in and have a look at him. She knows that you are attending me and they've got no doctor of their own. It's next door but one, Number 12."

I thanked her for the introduction and, having wished her good morning, let myself out of the house and proceeded to Number 12, approaching it slowly to take a preliminary glance at the premises. The result of the inspection was satisfactory as an index to the quality of my new patient, for the house was in better repair than most of its neighbours and the bright brass knocker and door-knob and the whitened door-step suggested a household rather above the general Jacob Street level. At the side of the house was a wide, two-leaved gate with a wicket, at which I glanced inquisitively. It seemed to be the entrance to a yard or factory, adapted to the passage of trucks or vans, but it clearly belonged to the house, for a bell-pull on the jamb of the gate had underneath it a small brass plate bearing the inscription, "*P. Gannet*".

In response to my knock, the door was opened by a lanky girl of about eighteen with long legs, a short skirt, and something on her head which resembled a pudding cloth. When I had revealed my identity, she conducted me along a tiled hall to a door, which she opened, and having announced me by name, washed her hands of me and retired down the kitchen stairs.

The occupant of the room, a woman, of about thirty-five, rose as I entered and laid down some needlework on a side table.

"Am I addressing Mrs. Gannet?" I asked.

"Yes," she replied. "I am Mrs. Gannet. I suppose Mrs. Jenkins gave you my message?"

"Yes. She tells me – which I am sorry to hear – that your husband is not very well."

"He is not at all well," said she, "though I don't think it is anything that matters very much, you know."

"I expect it matters to him," I suggested.

"I suppose it does," she agreed. "At any rate, he seems rather sorry for himself. He is sitting up in his bedroom at present. Shall I show you the way? I think he is rather anxious to see you."

I held the door open for her and, when she passed through, I followed her up the stairs, rapidly sorting out my first impressions. Mrs. Gannet was a rather tall, slender woman with light brown hair and slightly chilly blue eyes. She was decidedly good-looking, but yet I did not find her prepossessing. Comely as her face undoubtedly was, it was not – at least to me – a pleasant face. There was a tinge of petulance in its expression, a faint suggestion of unamiability. And I did not like the tone in which she had referred to her husband.

Her introduction of me was as laconic as that of her maid. She opened the bedroom door and standing at the threshold, announced, "Here's the doctor." Then, as I entered, she shut me in and departed.

"Well, Doctor," said the patient, "I'm glad to see you. Pull up a chair to the fire and take off your overcoat."

I drew a chair up to the fire gladly enough, but I did not adopt the other suggestion, for already I had learned by experience that the doctor who takes off his overcoat is lost. Forthwith he becomes a visitor and his difficulties in making his escape are multiplied indefinitely.

"So you are not feeling very well?" said I, by way of opening the proceedings.

"I'm feeling devilish ill," he replied. "I don't suppose it's anything serious, but it's deuced unpleasant. Little Mary in trouble, you know."

I didn't know, not having heard the expression before, and I looked at him inquiringly, and probably rather vacantly.

"Little Mary," he repeated. "Tummy. Bellyache, to put it bluntly."

"Ha!" said I, with sudden comprehension. "You are suffering from abdominal pain. Is it bad?"

"Is it ever good?" he demanded, with a sour grin.

"It certainly is never pleasant," I admitted. "But is the pain severe?"

"Sometimes," he replied. "It seems to come and go – Whoo!"

A change of facial expression indicated that, just now, it had come. Accordingly, I suspended the conversation until conditions should be more favourable and, meanwhile, inspected my patient with sympathetic interest. He was not as good-looking as his wife, and his appearance was not improved by a rather deep scar which cut across his right eyebrow, but he made a better impression than she, a strongly-built man, though not large, so far as I could judge, seeing him sitting huddled in his easy chair, of a medium complexion and decidedly lean. He wore his hair rather long and had a well-shaped moustache and a Vandyke beard. Indeed, his appearance in general was distinctly Vandykish, with his brown velveteen jacket, his open, deep-pointed collar, and the loose bow with drooping ends which served as a necktie. I also noted that his eyes looked red and irritable like those of a long-sighted person who is in need of spectacles.

"Phoo!" he exclaimed after a spell of silence. "That was a bit of a twister, but it's better now. Going to have a lucid interval, I suppose."

Thereupon I resumed the conversation, which, however, I need not report in detail. I had plenty of time and could afford to encourage him to enlarge on his symptoms, the possible causes of his illness, and his usual habits and mode of life. And as he talked, I looked about me, bearing in mind the advice of my teacher, Dr. Thorndyke, to observe and take note of a patient's surroundings as a possible guide to his personality. In particular I inspected the mantelpiece which confronted me and considered the objects on it in their possible bearings on my patient's habits and life history.

They were rather curious objects – examples of pottery of a singularly uncouth and barbaric type which I set down as the gleanings gathered in the course of travel in distant lands among primitive and aboriginal peoples. There were several bowls and jars – massive, rude and unshapely – of a coarse material like primitive stoneware, and presiding over the whole collection, a crudely modeled effigy of similar material, apparently the artless representation of some forest deity, or, perhaps a portrait of an aboriginal man. The childish crudity of execution carried my thoughts to Darkest Africa or the Ethnographical galleries of the British Museum, or to those sham primitive sculptures which have recently appeared on some of the public buildings in London. I looked again at Mr. Gannet and wondered whether his present trouble might be the aftermath of some tropical illness contracted in the forests or jungles where he had collected these strange and not very attractive curios.

Fortunately, however, I did not put my thoughts into words, but in pursuance of another of Dr. Thorndyke's precepts to "Let the patient do most of the talking", listened attentively while Mr. Gannet poured out the tale of his troubles. For, presently, he remarked, after a pause, "And it isn't only the discomfort. It's such a confounded hindrance. I want to get on with my work."

"By the way, what its your work?" I asked.

"I am a potter," he replied.

"A potter!" I repeated. "I didn't know that there were any pottery works in London – except, of course, Doultons."

"I am not attached to any pottery works," said he. "I am an artist potter, an individual worker. The pieces that I make are what is usually called studio pottery. Those are some of my works on the mantelpiece."

In the vulgar phrase, you could have knocked me down with a feather. For the moment I was bereft of speech and could only sit like a fool, gazing round-eyed and agape at these amazing products of the potter's art, while Gannet observed me gravely and, I thought, with slight disfavour.

"Possibly," he remarked, "you find them a little over-simplified."

It was not the expression that I should have used, but I grasped at it eagerly.

"I think I had that feeling at the first glance," I replied, "that and the – er – the impression that perhaps – ha – in the matter of precision and – er – symmetry – that is, to an entirely inexpert eye – er – "

"Exactly!" he interrupted. "Precision and symmetry are what the inexpert eye looks for. But they are not what the artist seeks. Mechanical accuracy he can leave to the ungifted toiler who tends a machine."

"I suppose that is so," I agreed. "And the – " I was about to say "image" but hastily corrected the word to "statuette" " – that is your work, too?"

"The figurine," he corrected. "Yes, that is my work. I was rather pleased with it when I had it finished. And apparently I was justified, for it was extremely well received. The art critics were quite enthusiastic, and I sold two replicas of it for fifty guineas each."

"That was very satisfactory," said I. "It is a good thing to have material reward as well as glory. Did you give it any descriptive title?"

"No," he replied. "I am not like those anecdote painters who must have a title for their pictures. I just called it 'Figurine of a Monkey'."

"Of a – oh, yes. Of a monkey. Exactly!"

I stood up, the better to examine it and then discovered that its posterior aspect bore something like a coil of garden hose, evidently representing a tail. So it obviously was a monkey and not a woodland god. The tail established the diagnosis, even as, in those sculptures that I have mentioned, the absence of a tail demonstrates their human character.

"And I suppose," said I, "you always sign your works?"

"Certainly," he replied. "Each piece bears my signature and a serial number and, of course, the number of copies of a single piece is rigidly limited. You will see the signature on the base."

With infinite care and tenderness, I lifted the precious figurine and inverted it to examine the base, which I found to be covered with a thick layer of opaque white glaze, rather out of character with the rough grey body but excellent for displaying the signature. The latter was in thin blue lines as if executed with a pen and consisted of something resembling a bird, supported by the letters, "*P.G.*" and underneath, "*Op. 571 A*".

"The goose is, I suppose," said I, "your sign manual or personal mark – it is a goose, isn't it?"

"No," he replied, a little testily. "It's a gannet."

"Of course it is," I agreed, hastily. "How dull of me not to recognize your rebus, though a gannet is not unlike a goose."

He admitted this, and watched me narrowly as I replaced the masterpiece on the little square of cloth which protected it from contact with the marble shelf. Then it occurred to me that perhaps I had stayed long enough, and as I buttoned my overcoat, I reverted to professional matters with a few parting remarks.

"Well, Mr. Gannet, you needn't be uneasy about yourself. I shall send you some medicine which I think will soon put you right. But if you have much pain, you had better try some hot fomentations or a hot water bottle – a rubber one, of course, and you would probably be more comfortable lying down."

"It's more comfortable sitting by the fire," he objected, and as it appeared that he was the best judge of his own comfort, I said no more, but having shaken hands, took my departure.

As I was descending the stairs, I met a man coming up, a big man who wore a monocle and was carrying a glass jug. He stopped for a moment when he came abreast, and explained, "I am just taking the invalid some barley water. I suppose that is all right? He asked for it."

"Certainly," I replied. "A most suitable drink for a sick person."

"I'll tell him so," said he, and with this we went our respective ways.

59

When I reached the hall, I found the dining room door open, and as Mrs. Gannet was visible within, I entered to make my report and give a few directions, to which she listened attentively, though with no great appearance of concern. But she promised to see that the patient should take his medicine regularly, and to keep him supplied with hot water bottles. "Though," she added, "I don't expect that he will use them. He is not a very tractable invalid."

"Well, Mrs. Gannet," said I, pulling on my gloves, "we must be patient. Pain is apt to make people irritable. I shall hope to find him better tomorrow. Good morning!"

At intervals during the day, my thoughts reverted to my new patient, but not, I fear, in the way that they should have done. For it was not his abdomen – which was my proper concern – that occupied my attention but his queer pottery and above all, the unspeakable monkey. My reflections oscillated between frank incredulity and an admission of the possibility that these pseudo-barbaric works might possess some subtle quality that I had failed to detect. Yet I was not without some qualifications for forming a judgment, for mine was a distinctly artistic family, Both my parents could draw, and my maternal uncle was a figure painter of some position who, in addition to his pictures, executed small, unpretentious sculptures in terra-cotta and bronze, and I had managed, when I was a student, to spare an evening a week to attend a life class. So I, at least, could draw, and knew what the human figure was like, and when I compared my uncle's graceful, delicately-finished little statuettes with Gannet's uncouth effigy, it seemed beyond belief that this latter could have any artistic quality whatever.

Yet it doesn't do to be too cocksure. It is always possible that one may be mistaken. But yet, again, it doesn't do to be too humble and credulous, for the simple, credulous man is the natural prey of the quack and the impostor. And the quack and the impostor flourish in our midst. The post-war Twentieth Century seems to be the golden age of "bunk".

So my reflections went around and around and brought me to no positive conclusion, and meanwhile, poor Peter Gannet's abdomen received less attention than it deserved. I assumed that a dose or two of bismuth and soda, with that fine old medicament, once so overrated and now rather under-valued – Compound Tincture of Cardamoms – would relieve the colicky pains and set the patient on the road to recovery, and having dispatched the mixture, I dismissed the medical aspects of the case from my mind.

But the infallible mixture failed to produce the expected effect, for when I called on the following morning, the patient's condition was unchanged. Which was disappointing (especially to him) but not disturbing. There was no suspicion of anything serious, no fever and no physical signs suggestive of appendicitis or any other grave condition. I was not anxious about him, nor was he anxious about himself, though slightly outspoken on the subject of the infallible mixture, which I promised to replace by something more effectual, repeating my recommendations as to hot water bottles or fomentations.

The new treatment, however, proved no better than the old. At my third visit I found my patient in bed, still complaining of pain and in a state of deep depression. But even now, though the man looked definitely ill, neither exhaustive questioning nor physical examination threw any light either on the cause or the exact nature of his condition. Obviously, he was suffering from severe gastro-intestinal catarrh. But why he was suffering from it, and why no treatment gave him any relief, were mysteries on which I pondered anxiously as I walked home from Jacob Street, greatly out of conceit with myself and inclined to commiserate the man who had the misfortune to be my patient.

Chapter IV
Dr. Thorndyke
Takes a Hand

It was on the sixth day of my attendance on Mr. Gannet that my vague but increasing anxiety suddenly became acute. As I sat down by the bedside and looked at the drawn, haggard, red-eyed face that confronted me over the bedclothes, I was seized by something approaching panic. And not without reason. For the man was obviously ill – very ill – and was getting worse from day to day, and I had to admit – and did admit to myself – that I was completely in the dark as to what was really the matter with him. My diagnosis of gastro-enteritis was, in effect, no diagnosis at all. It was little more than a statement of the symptoms, and the utter failure of the ordinary empirical treatment convinced me that there was some essential element in the case which had completely eluded me.

It was highly disturbing. A young, newly established practitioner cannot afford to make a hash of a case at the very outset of his career, as I clearly realized, though to do myself justice, I must say that this was not the consideration that was uppermost in my mind. What really troubled me was the feeling that I had failed in my duty towards my patient and in ordinary professional competence. My heart was wrung by the obvious suffering of the quiet, uncomplaining man who looked to me so pathetically for help and relief – and looked in vain. And then there was the further, profoundly disquieting consideration that the man was now very seriously ill and that if he did not improve, his condition would presently become actually dangerous.

"Well, Mr. Gannet," I said, "we don't seem to be making much progress. I am afraid you will have to remain in bed for the present."

"There's no question about that, Doctor," said he, "because I can't get out, at least I can't stand properly if I do. My legs seem to have gone on strike and there is something queer about my feet, sort of pins and needles, and a dead kind of feeling, as if they had got a coat of varnish over them."

"But," I exclaimed, concealing as well as I could my consternation at this fresh complication, "you haven't mentioned this to me before."

"I hadn't noticed until yesterday," he replied, "though I have been having cramps in my calves for some days. But the fact is that the pain in my gizzard occupies my attention pretty completely. It may have been coming on before I noticed it. What do you suppose it is?"

To this question I gave no direct answer, for I was not supposing at all. To me the new symptoms conveyed nothing more than fresh and convincing evidence that I was completely out of my depth. Nevertheless, I made a careful examination which established the fact that there was an appreciable loss of sensibility in the feet and some abnormal conditions of the nerves of the legs. Why there should be I had not the foggiest idea, nor did I make any great effort to unravel the mystery, for these new developments brought to a definite decision a half-formed intention that I had been harbouring for the last day or two.

I would seek the advice of some more experienced practitioner. That was necessary as a matter of common honesty, to say nothing of humanity. But I had hesitated to suggest a second opinion since that would not only have involved the frank admission that I was graveled – an impolitic proceeding in the case of a young doctor – but it would have put the expense of the consultant's fee on the patient, whereas I felt that, since the need for the consultation arose from my own incompetence, the expense should fall upon me.

"What do you think, Doctor, of my going into a nursing home?" he asked, as I resumed my seat by the bed.

I rather caught at the suggestion, for it seemed to make my plan easier to carry out.

"There is something to be said for a nursing home," I replied. "You would be able to have more constant and skilled attention."

"That is what I was thinking," said he, "and I shouldn't be such a damned nuisance to my wife."

"Yes," I agreed, "there's something in that. I will think about your idea and make a few inquiries, and I will look in again later in the day and let you know the result."

With this I rose and, having shaken his hand, took my departure, closing the door audibly and descending the stairs with a slightly heavy tread to give notice of my approach to the hall. When I arrived there, however, I found no sign of Mrs. Gannet and the dining room door was shut, and glancing towards the hat-rack on which my hat was awaiting me, I noted another hat upon an adjoining peg and surmised that it possibly accounted for the lady's non-appearance. I had seen that hat before. It was a somewhat dandified velour hat which I recognized as appertaining to a certain Mr. Boles – the man whom I had met on the stairs at my first visit and had seen once or twice since – a big, swaggering, rather good-looking young man with a noisy, bullying manner and a tendency to undue familiarity. I had disliked him at sight. I resented his familiarity, I suspected his monocle of a merely ornamental function, and I viewed with faint disapproval his relations with Mrs. Gannet – though, to be sure, they were some sort of cousins, as I had understood from Gannet, and he obviously knew all about their friendship.

So it was no affair of mine. But still, the presence of that hat gave me pause. It is awkward to break in on a *tete-a-tete*. However, my difficulty was solved by Boles himself, who opened the dining room door a short distance, thrust out his head, and surveyed me through his monocle – or perhaps with the less-obstructed eye.

"Thought I heard you sneaking down, Doc," said he. "How's the sufferer? Aren't you coming in to give us the news?"

I should have liked to pull his nose. But a doctor must learn early to control his temper – especially in the case of a man of Boles's size. As he held the door open, I walked in and made my bow to Mrs. Gannet, who returned my greeting without putting down her needlework. Then I delivered my report, briefly and rather vaguely, and opened the subject of the nursing home. Instantly, Boles began to raise objections.

"Why on earth should he go to a nursing home?" he demanded. "He is comfortable enough here. And think of the expense."

"It was his own suggestion," said I, "and I don't think it a bad one."

"No," said Mrs. Gannet. "Not at all. He would get better attention there than I can give him."

There followed something like a wrangle between the two, to which I listened impassively, inwardly assessing their respective motives. Obviously the lady favoured the prospect of getting the invalid off her hands, while as to Boles, his opposition was due to mere contrariety, to an instinctive impulse to object to anything that I might propose.

Of course, the lady had her way – and I had intended to have mine in any case. So, when the argument had petered out, I took my leave with a promise to return some time later to report progress.

As I turned away from the house, I rapidly considered the position. I had no further visits to make, so for the present, my time was my own, and as my immediate purpose was to seek the counsel of some more experienced colleague, and as my hospital was the most likely place in which to obtain such counsel, I steered a course for the nearest bus route by which I could travel to its neighbourhood. There, having boarded the appropriate omnibus, I was presently delivered at the end of the quiet street in which St. Margaret's Hospital is situated.

It seemed but a few months since I had reluctantly shaken from my feet the dust of that admirable institution and its pleasant, friendly medical school, and now, as I turned into the familiar street, I looked about me with a certain wistfulness as I recalled the years of interesting study and companionship that I had spent here as I slowly evolved from a raw freshman to a fully qualified practitioner. And as, approaching the hospital, I observed a tall figure emerge from the gate and advance towards me, the sight brought back to me one of the most engrossing aspects of my life as a student. For the tall man was Dr. John Thorndyke, a lecturer on Medical Jurisprudence, perhaps the most brilliant and the most popular member of the teaching staff.

As we approached, Dr. Thorndyke greeted me with a genial smile and held out his hand.

"I think," said he, "this is the first time we have met since you fluttered out of the nest."

"We used to call it the incubator," I remarked.

"I think 'nest' sounds more dignified," he rejoined. "There is something rather embryonic about an incubator. And how do you like general practice?"

"Oh, well enough," I replied. "Of course, it isn't as thrilling as hospital practice – though mine happens, at the moment, to be a bit more full of thrills than I care for."

"That sounds as if you were having some unpleasant experiences."

"I am," said I. "The fact is that I am up a tree. That is why I am here. I am going to the hospital to see if one of the older hands can give me some sort of tip."

"Very wise of you, Oldfield," Thorndyke commented. "'Would it seem impertinent if I were to ask what sort of tree it is that you are marooned in?"

"Not at all, sir," I replied, warmly. "It is very kind of you to ask. My difficulty is that I have got a rather serious case, and I am fairly graveled in the matter of diagnosis. It seems to be a pretty acute case of gastro-enteritis, but why the fellow should have got it and why none of my treatment should make any impression on it, I can't imagine at all."

Dr. Thorndyke's kindly interest in an old pupil seemed to sharpen into one more definitely professional.

"The term 'gastro-enteritis'," said he, "covers a good many different conditions. Perhaps a detailed description of the symptoms would be a better basis for discussion."

Thus encouraged, I plunged eagerly into a minute description of poor Gannet's symptoms – the abdominal pain, the obstinate and distressing nausea and physical and mental depression – with some account of my futile efforts to relieve them, to all of which Dr. Thorndyke listened with profound attention. When I had finished, he reflected for a few moments and then asked, "And that is all, is it?

65

Nothing but the abdominal trouble? No neuritic symptoms, for instance?"

"Yes, by Jove, there are!" I exclaimed. "I forgot to mention them. He has severe cramps in his calves, and there is quite distinct numbness of the feet with loss of power in the legs – in fact, he is hardly able to stand, at least so he tells me."

Dr. Thorndyke nodded, and after a short pause, asked, "And as to the eyes – anything unusual about them?"

"Well," I replied, "they are rather red and watery, but he put that down to reading in a bad light, and then he seems to have a slight cold in his head."

"You haven't said anything about the secretions," Dr. Thorndyke remarked. "I suppose you made all the routine tests?"

"Oh yes," I replied, "most carefully. But there was nothing in the least abnormal – no albumen, no sugar, nothing out of the ordinary."

"I take it," said Thorndyke, "that it did not occur to you to try Marsh's Test?"

"Marsh's Test!" I repeated, gazing at him in dismay. "Good Lord, no! The idea never entered my thick head. And you think it may actually be a case of arsenic poisoning?"

"It is certainly a possibility," he replied. "The complex of symptoms that you have described is entirely consistent with arsenic poisoning, and it doesn't appear to me to be consistent with anything else."

I was thunderstruck. But yet no sooner was the suggestion made than its obviousness seemed to stare me in the face.

"Of course!" I exclaimed. "It is almost a typical case. And to think that I never spotted it, after attending all your lectures, too! I am a fool. I am not fit to hold a diploma."

"Nonsense, Oldfield," said Thorndyke, "you are not exceptional. The general practitioner nearly always misses a case of poisoning. Quite naturally. His daily experience is concerned with disease, and as the effects of a poison simulate disease, he is almost inevitably misled. He has, by habit, acquired an unconscious bias towards what we may call 'normal' illness, whereas an outsider, like myself, coming to the case with an open mind, or even a bias towards the abnormal, is on the lookout for suspicious symptoms. But we mustn't rush to conclusions. The first thing is to establish the presence or absence of arsenic. That would be a good deal easier if we had him in hospital, but I suppose there would be some difficulty – "

"There would be no difficulty at all, sir," said I. "He has asked me to arrange for him to go to a nursing home."

"Has he?" said Thorndyke. "That almost seems a little significant – I mean that there is a slight suggestion of some suspicions on his own part. But what would you like to do? Will you make the test yourself, and carry on, or would you like me to come along with you and have a look at the patient?"

"It would be an enormous relief to me if you would see him, sir," I replied, "and it is awfully good of you to – "

"Not at all," said Thorndyke. "The question has to be settled, and settled without delay. In a poisoning case, the time factor may be vital. And if we should bring in a true bill, he should be got out of that house at once. But you understand, Oldfield, that I come as your friend. My visit has no financial implications."

I was disposed to protest, but he refused to discuss the matter, pointing out that no second opinion had been asked for by the patient. "But," he added, "we may want some reagents. I had better run back to the hospital and get my research case, which I had left to be called for, and see that it contains all that we are likely to need."

He turned and retraced his steps to the hospital where he entered the gateway, leaving me to saunter up and down the forecourt. In a few minutes he came out, carrying what looked like a small suitcase covered with green Willesden canvas, as there happened to to be a disengaged taxi at the main entrance, where it had just set down a passenger, Thorndyke chartered it forthwith. When I had given the driver the necessary directions, I followed my senior into the interior of the vehicle and slammed the door.

During the journey Dr. Thorndyke put a few discreet questions respecting the Gannet household, to which I returned correspondingly discreet answers. Indeed, I knew very little about the three persons – or four, including Boles – of whom it consisted and I did not think it proper to eke out my slender knowledge with surmises. Accordingly I kept strictly to the facts actually known to me, leaving him to make his own inferences.

"Do you know who prepares Gannet's food?" he asked.

"To the best of my belief," I replied, "Mrs. Gannet does all the cooking. The maid is only a girl. But I am pretty sure that Mrs. Gannet prepares the invalid's food – in fact, she told me that she did. There isn't much of it, as you may imagine."

"What is Gannet's business or profession?"

"I understand that he is a potter – an artist potter. He seems to specialize in some sort of stoneware. There are one or two pieces of his in the bedroom."

"And where does he work?"

"He has a studio at the back of the house, quite a big place, I believe, though I haven't seen it. But it seems to be bigger than he needs, as he lets Boles occupy part of it. I don't quite know what Boles does, but I fancy it is something in the goldsmithing and enamelling line."

Here, as the taxi turned from Euston Road into Hampstead Road, Thorndyke glanced out of the window and asked, "Did I hear you mention Jacob Street to the driver?"

"Yes, that is where Gannet lives. Rather a seedy-looking street. You don't know it, I suppose?"

"It happens that I do," he replied. "There are several studios in it, relics of the days when it was a more fashionable neighbourhood. I knew the occupant of one of the studios. But here we are, I think, at our destination."

As the taxi drew up at the house, we got out and he paid the cabman while I knocked at the door and rang the bell. Almost immediately the door was opened by Mrs. Gannet herself, who looked at me with some surprise and with still more at my companion. I hastened to anticipate questions by a tactful explanation.

"I've had a bit of luck, Mrs. Gannet. I met Dr. Thorndyke, one of my teachers at the hospital, and when I mentioned to him that I had a case which was not progressing very satisfactorily, he very kindly offered to come and see the patient and give me the benefit of his great experience."

"I hope we shall all benefit from Dr. Thorndyke's kindness," said Mrs. Gannet, with a smile and a bow to Thorndyke, "and most of all my poor husband. He has been a model of patience, but it has been a weary and painful business for him. You know the way up to his room."

While we were speaking, the dining room door opened softly and Boles's head appeared in the space, adorned with the inevitable eye-glass through which he inspected Thorndyke critically and was not, himself, entirely unobserved by the latter. But the mutual inspection was brief, for I immediately led the way up the stairs and was closely followed by my senior.

As we entered the sickroom after a perfunctory knock at the door, the patient raised himself in bed and looked at us in evident surprise. But he asked no question, merely turning to me interrogatively, whereupon I proceeded at once concisely to explain the situation. "It is very good of Dr. Thorndyke," said Gannet, "and I am most grateful and pleased to see him, for I don't seem to be making much progress. In fact, I seem to be getting worse."

"You certainly don't look very flourishing," said Thorndyke, "and I see that you haven't taken your arrowroot, or whatever it is."

68

"No," said Gannet, "I tried to take some, but I couldn't keep it down. Even the barley water doesn't seem to agree with me, though I am parched with thirst. Mr. Boles gave me a glassful when he brought it up with the arrowroot but I've been uncomfortable ever since. Yet you'd think that there couldn't be much harm in barley water."

While the patient was speaking, Thorndyke looked at him thoughtfully as if appraising his general appearance, particularly observing the drawn, anxious face and the red and watery eyes. Then he deposited his research case on the table and, remarking that the latter was rather in the way, carried it, with my assistance, away from the bedside over to the window, and in place of it drew up a couple of chairs. Having fetched a writing pad from the research case, he sat down and, without preamble, began a detailed interrogation with reference to the symptoms and course of the illness, writing down the answers in shorthand and noting all the dates. The examination elicited the statement that there had been fluctuations in the severity of the condition, a slight improvement being followed by a sudden relapse. It also transpired that the relapses, on each occasion, had occurred shortly after taking food or a considerable drink. "It seems," Gannet concluded, dismally, "as if starvation was the only possible way of avoiding pain."

I had heard all this before, but it was only now, when the significant facts were assembled by Thorndyke's skilful interrogation, that I could realize their unmistakable meaning. Thus set out they furnished a typical picture of arsenic poisoning. And so with the brief but thorough physical examination. The objective signs might have been taken from a text-book case.

"Well, Doctor," said Gannet, as Thorndyke stood up and looked down at him gravely, "what do you think of me?"

"I think," replied Thorndyke, "that you are very seriously ill and that you require the kind of treatment and attention that you cannot possibly get here. You ought to be in a hospital or a nursing home, and you ought to be removed there without delay."

"I rather suspected that myself," said Gannet. "In fact, the doctor was considering some such arrangement. I'm quite willing."

"Then," said Thorndyke, "if you agree, I can give you a private ward or a cubicle at St. Margaret's Hospital, and as the matter is urgent, I propose that we take you there at once. Could you bear the journey in a cab?"

"Oh, yes," replied Gannet, with something almost like eagerness, "if there is a chance of some relief at the end of it."

"I think we shall soon be able to make you more comfortable," said Thorndyke. "But you had better just look him over, Oldfield, to make sure that he is fit to travel."

As I got out my stethoscope to listen to the patient's heart, Thorndyke walked over to the table, apparently to put away his writing pad – but that was not his only purpose – for as I stooped over the patient with the stethoscope at my ears, I could see him (though the patient could not) carefully transferring some arrowroot from the bowl to a wide-mouthed jar. When he had filled it and put in the rubber stopper, he filled another jar from the jug of barley water and then quietly closed the research case.

Now I understood why he had moved the table away from the bed to a position in which it was out of the range of the patient's vision. Of course, the specimens of food and drink could not have been taken in Gannet's presence without an explanation, which we were not in the position to give, for although neither of us had much doubt on the subject. Still, the actual presence of arsenic had yet to be proved.

"Well, Oldfield," said Thorndyke, "do you think he is strong enough to make the journey?"

"Quite," I replied, "if he can put up with the discomfort of traveling in a taxi."

As to this, Gannet was quite confident, being evidently keen on the change of residence.

"Then," said Thorndyke, "perhaps you will run down and explain matters to Mrs. Gannet, and it would be just as well to send out for a cab at once. I suppose Madame is not likely to raise objections?"

"No," I replied. "She has already agreed to his going to a nursing home and, if she finds our methods rather abrupt, I must make her understand that the case is urgent."

The interview, however, went quite smoothly so far as the lady was concerned, though Boles was disposed to be obstructive.

"Do you mean that you are going to cart him off to the hospital now?" he demanded.

"That is what Dr. Thorndyke proposes," I replied.

"But why?" he protested. "You say that there is no question of an operation. Then why is he being bustled off in this way?"

"I think," said I, "if you will excuse me, I had better see about that cab," and I made a move towards the hall, whereupon Mrs. Gannet intervened, a little impatiently.

"Now don't waste time, Fred. Run along and get a taxi while I go up with the doctor and make Peter ready for the journey."

On this, Boles rather sulkily swaggered out into the hall and, without a word, snatched down the velour hat, jammed it on his head, and departed on his quest, slamming the street door after him. As the door closed, Mrs. Gannet turned towards the staircase and began to ascend and I followed, passing her on the landing to open the bedroom door.

When we entered the room, we found Thorndyke standing opposite the mantelpiece, apparently inspecting the stoneware image, but he turned and, bowing to the lady, suavely apologized for our rather hurried proceedings.

"There is no need to send any clothes with him," said he, "as he will have to remain in bed for the present. A warm dressing-gown and one or two blankets or rugs will do for the journey."

"Yes," she replied. "Rugs, I think, will be more presentable than blankets." Then turning to her husband, she asked, "Is there anything that you will want to take with you, Peter?"

"Nothing but my attaché case," he replied. "That contains all that I am likely to want, excepting the book that I am reading. You might put that in, too. It is on the small table."

When this had been done, Mrs. Gannet proceeded to make the few preparations that were necessary while Thorndyke resumed his study of the pottery on the mantelpiece. The patient was assisted to rise and sit on the edge of the bed while he was inducted into a thick dressing gown, warm woollen socks, and a pair of bedroom slippers.

"I think we are all ready, now," said Mrs. Gannet. Then, as there seemed to be a pause in the proceedings, she took the opportunity to address a question to Thorndyke.

"Have you come to any conclusion," she asked, "as to what it is exactly that my husband is suffering from?"

"I think," Thorndyke replied, "that we shall be able to be more definite when we have had him under observation for a day or two."

The lady looked a little unsatisfied with this answer – which certainly was rather evasive – as, indeed, the patient also seemed to note. But here the conversation was interrupted, providentially, by the arrival of Boles to announce that the cab was waiting.

"And now, old chap," said he, "the question is, how are we going to get you down to it?"

That problem, however, presented no difficulty, for when the patient had been wrapped in the rugs, Thorndyke and I carried him, by the approved ambulance method, down the stairs and deposited him in the taxi, while Boles and Mrs. Gannet brought up the rear of the procession, the latter carrying the invaluable attaché case. A more formidable problem was that of finding room in the taxi for two additional large men, but we managed to squeeze in and, amidst valedictory hand wavings from the two figures on the doorstep, the cab started on its journey.

It seemed that Thorndyke must have given some instructions at the hospital, for our arrival appeared to be not unexpected. A wheeled chair was quickly procured and in this the patient was trundled, under Thorndyke's direction, through a maze of corridors to the little private ward on the ground floor which had been allotted to him. Here we found a nurse putting the finishing touches to its appointments, and presently the sister from the adjacent ward came to superintend the establishment of the new patient. We stayed only long enough to see Gannet comfortably settled in bed, and then took leave of him and, in the corridor outside we parted after a few words of explanation.

"I am just going across to the chemical laboratories," said Thorndyke, "to hand Professor Woodfield a couple of samples for analysis. I shall manage to see Gannet tomorrow morning, and I suppose you will look in on him from time to time."

"Yes," I replied. "If I may, I will call and see him tomorrow."

"But of course you may," said he. "He is still your patient. If there is anything to report – from Woodfield, I mean – I will leave a note for you with Sister. And now I must be off."

We shook hands and went our respective ways, and as I looked back at the tall figure striding away down the corridor, research case in hand, I speculated on the report that Professor Woodfield would furnish on a sample of arrowroot and another of barley water.

Chapter V
A True Bill

Impelled by my anxiety to clear up the obscurities of the Gannet case, I dispatched the only important visit on my list as early on the following morning as I decently could and then hurried off to the hospital in the hope that I might be in time to catch Thorndyke before he left. It turned out that I had timed my visit fortunately, for as I passed in at the main entrance, I saw his name on the attendance board and learned from the hall porter that he had gone across to the school. Thither, accordingly, I directed my steps, but as I was crossing the garden, I met him coming from the direction of the laboratories and turned to walk back with him.

"Any news yet?" I asked.

"Yes," he replied. "I have just seen Woodfield and had his report. Of the two samples of food that I gave him for analysis, one – some of the arrowroot that you saw – contained no arsenic. The other – a specimen of the barley water – contained three-quarters of a grain of arsenic in the five fluid ounces of my sample. So, assuming that the jug held twenty fluid ounces, it would have contained about three grains of arsenic – that is, of arsenious acid."

"My word!" I exclaimed. "Why, that is a fatal dose, isn't it?"

"It is a possibly fatal dose," he replied. "A two grain dose has been known to cause death, but the effects of arsenic are very erratic. Still, we may fairly well say that if he had drunk the whole jugful, the chances are that it would have killed him."

I shuddered to think of the narrow escape that he – and I – had had. Only just in time had we – or rather Thorndyke – got him away from that house.

"Well," I said, "the detection of arsenic in the barley water settles any doubts that we might have had. It establishes the fact of arsenic poisoning."

"Not quite," Thorndyke dissented. "But we have established the fact by clinical tests. Woodfield and the House Physician have ascertained the presence of arsenic in the patient's body. The quantity was quite small, smaller than I should have expected, judging by the symptoms. But arsenic is eliminated pretty quickly, so we may infer that some days have elapsed since the last considerable dose was taken."

"Yes," said I, "and you were just in time to save him from the next considerable dose, which would probably have been the last. By the way, what are our responsibilities in this affair? I mean, ought we to communicate with the police?"

"No," he replied, very decidedly. "We have neither the duty nor the right to meddle in a case such as this, where the patient is a responsible adult in full control of his actions and his surroundings. Our duty is to inform him of the facts which are known to us and to leave him to take such measures as he may think fit."

That, in effect, is what we did when we had made the ordinary inquiries as to the patient's condition – which, by the way, was markedly improved.

"Yes," Gannet said, cheerfully, "I am worlds better, and it isn't from the effects of the medicine, because I haven't had any. I seem to be recovering of my own accord. Queer, isn't it? Or perhaps it isn't. Have you two gentlemen come to any conclusion as to what is really the matter with me?"

"Yes," Thorndyke replied in a matter-of-fact tone. "We have ascertained that your illness was due to arsenic poisoning."

Gannet sat up in bed and stared from one to the other of us with dropped jaw and an expression of the utmost astonishment and horror.

"Arsenic poisoning!" he repeated, incredulously. "I can't believe it. Are you sure that there isn't some mistake? It seems impossible."

"It usually does," Thorndyke replied, drily. "But there is no mistake. It is just a matter of chemical analysis, which can be sworn to and proved, if necessary, in a court of law. Arsenic has been recovered from your own body and also from a sample of barley water that I brought away for analysis."

"Oh!" said Gannet, "so it was in the barley water. I suppose you didn't examine the arrowroot?"

"I brought away a sample of it," replied Thorndyke, "and it was examined, but there was no arsenic in it."

"Ha!" said Gannet. "So it was the barley water. I thought there was something wrong with that stuff. But arsenic! This is a regular facer! What do you think I ought to do about it, Doctor?"

"It is difficult for us to advise you, Mr. Gannet," Thorndyke replied. "We know no more than that you have been taking poisonous doses of arsenic. As to the circumstances in which you came to take that poison, you know more than we do. If any person knowingly administered that poison to you, he – or she – committed a very serious crime, and if you know who that person is, it would be proper for you to inform the police."

"But I don't," said Gannet. "There are only three persons who could have given me the arsenic, and I can't suspect any one of them. There is

74

the servant maid. She wouldn't have given it to me. If she had wanted to poison anybody, it would have been her mistress. They don't get on very well, whereas the girl and I are on quite amiable terms. Then there is my wife. Well, of course, she is outside the picture altogether. And then there is Mr. Boles. He often brought up my food and drink, so he had the opportunity, but I couldn't entertain the idea of his having tried to poison me. I would as soon suspect the doctor – who had a better opportunity than any of them." He paused to grin at me, and then summed up the position. "So, you see, there is nobody whom I could suspect, and perhaps there isn't any poisoner at all. Isn't it possible that the stuff might have got into my food by accident?"

"I wouldn't say that it is actually impossible," Thorndyke replied, "but the improbability is so great that it is hardly worth considering."

"Well," said Gannet, "I don't feel like confiding in the police and possibly stirring up trouble for an innocent party."

"In that," said Thorndyke, "I think you are right. If you know of no reason for suspecting anybody, you have nothing to tell the police. But I must impress on you, Mr. Gannet, the realities of your position. It is practically certain that some person has tried to poison you, and you will have to be very thoroughly on your guard against any further attempts."

"But what can I do?" Gannet protested. "You agree that it is of no use to go to the police and raise a scandal. But what else is there?"

"The first precaution that you should take," replied Thorndyke, "would be to tell your wife all that you know, and advise her to pass on the information to Mr. Boles – unless you prefer to tell him, yourself – and to anyone else whom she thinks fit to inform. The fact that the poisoning has been detected will be a strong deterrent against any further attempts, and Mrs. Gannet will be on the alert to see that there are no opportunities. Then you will be wise to take no food or drink in your own house which is not shared by someone else and, perhaps, as an extra precaution, it might be as well to exchange your present maid for another."

"Yes," Gannet agreed, with a grin, "there will be no difficulty about that when my wife hears about the arsenic. She'll send the girl packing at an hour's notice."

"Then," said Thorndyke, "I think we have said all that there is to say. I am glad to see you looking so much better, and if you continue to improve at the same rate, we shall be able to send you out in a few days to get back to your pottery."

With this, he took leave of the patient, and I went out with him in case he should have anything further to say to me, but it was not until we had passed out at the main entrance and the porter had duly noted his departure, that he broke the silence. Then, as we crossed the court-yard, he asked, "What did you make of Gannet's statement as to the possible suspects?"

"Not very much," I replied, "but I rather had the feeling that he was holding something back."

"He didn't hold it back very far," Thorndyke commented, with a smile. "I gathered that he viewed Mr. Boles with profound suspicion and that he was not unwilling that we should share that suspicion. By the way, are you keeping notes of this case?"

I had to admit that I had nothing beyond the entries in the Day Book.

"That won't do," said he. "You may not have heard the last of this case. If there should, in the future, be any further developments, you ought not to be dependent on your memory alone. I advise you to write out now, while the facts are fresh, a detailed account of the case, with all the dates and full particulars of the persons who were in any way connected with the affair. I will send you a certified copy of Woodfield's analysis, and I should be interested to see your memoranda of the case to compare with my own notes."

"I don't suppose you will learn much from mine," said I.

"They will be bad notes if I don't," said he. "But the point is that if anything should hereafter happen to Gannet – anything, I mean, involving an inquest or a criminal charge – you and I would be called, or would volunteer, as witnesses, and our evidence ought to agree. Hence the desirability of comparing notes now when we can discuss any disagreements."

Our conversation had brought us to the crossroads, and here, as our ways led in opposite directions, we halted for a few final words and then parted, Thorndyke pursuing his journey on foot and I waiting at the bus stop for my omnibus.

During Gannet's stay in the hospital, I paid him one or two visits, noting his steady improvement and copying into my notebook the entries on his case sheet. But his recovery was quite uneventful, and after a few days, I struck him off my visiting list, deciding to await his return home to wind up the case.

But in the interval I became aware that he had, at least in one particular, acted on Thorndyke's advice. The fact was conveyed to me by Mrs. Gannet, who appeared one evening, in a very disturbed state, in my consulting room. I guessed at once what her mission was, but there was not much need for guessing as she came to the point at once.

"I have been to see Peter this afternoon," said she, "and he has given me a most terrible shock. He told me – quite seriously – that his illness was really not an illness at all, but that his condition was due to poison. He says that somebody had been putting arsenic into his food, and he quotes you and Dr. Thorndyke as his authorities for this statement. Is he off his head or did you really tell him this story?"

"It is perfectly true, Mrs. Gannet," I replied.

"But it can't be," she protested. "It is perfectly monstrous. There is nobody who could have had either the means or the motive. I prepared all his food with my own hands and I took it up to him myself. The maid never came near it – though I have sent her away all the same – and even if she had had the opportunity, she had no reason for trying to poison Peter. She was really quite a decent girl and she and he were on perfectly good terms. But the whole thing is impossible – fantastic. Dr. Thorndyke must have made some extraordinary mistake."

"I assure you, Mrs. Gannet," said I, "that no mistake has been made. It is just a matter of chemical analysis. Arsenic is nasty stuff, but it has one virtue: It can be identified easily and with certainty. When Dr. Thorndyke saw your husband, he at once suspected arsenic poisoning, so he took away with him two samples of the food – one of arrowroot and one of barley water – for analysis.

"They were examined by an eminent analyst and he found in the barley water quite a considerable quantity of arsenic – the whole jugful would have contained enough to cause death. You see, there is no doubt. There was the arsenic in the barley water. It was extracted and weighed, and the exact amount is known, and the arsenic itself has been kept and can be produced in evidence if necessary."

Mrs. Gannet was deeply impressed – indeed, for the moment, she appeared quite overwhelmed, for she stood speechless, gazing at me in the utmost consternation. At length she asked, almost in a whisper, "And the arrowroot? I took that up to him, myself."

"There was no arsenic in the arrowroot," I replied, and it seemed to me that she was a little relieved by my answer, though she still looked scared and bewildered. I could judge what was passing in her mind, for I realized that she remembered – as I did – who had carried the barley water up to the sickroom. But whatever she thought, she said nothing, and the interview presently came to an end after a few questions as to her husband's prospects of complete recovery and an urgent request that I should come and see him when he returned from the hospital.

That visit, however, proved unnecessary, for the first intimation that I received of Gannet's discharge from the hospital was furnished by his bodily presence in my wailing room. I had opened the communicating door in response to the *"ting"* of the bell (*"Please Ring and Enter"*) and Behold! There he was with velveteen jacket and Vandyke beard, all complete. I looked at him with the momentary surprise that doctors and nurses often experience on seeing a patient for the first time in his ordinary habiliments and surroundings, contrasting this big, upstanding, energetic-looking man with the miserable, shrunken wretch who used to peer at me so pitifully from under the bedclothes.

"Come to report, sir," said he, with a mock naval salute, "and to let you see what a fine job you and your colleagues have made of me."

I shook hands with him and ushered him through into the consulting room, still pleasantly surprised at the completeness of his recovery.

"You didn't expect to see me looking so well," said he.

"No," I admitted. "I was afraid you would feel the effects for some time."

"So was I," said he, "and in a sense I do. I am still aware that I have got a stomach, but apart from that dyspeptic feeling, I am as well as I ever was. I am eternally grateful to you and Dr. Thorndyke. You caught me on the hop – just in time. Another few days and I suspect it would have been a case of *hic jacet*. But what a rum affair it was. I can make nothing of it. Can you? Apparently, it couldn't have been an accident."

"No," I replied. "If the whole household had been poisoned, we might have suspected an accident, but the continued poisoning of one person could hardly have been accidental. We are forced to the conclusion that the poison was administered knowingly and intentionally by some person."

"I suppose we are," he agreed, "But what person? It's a regular corker. There are only three, and two of them are impossible. As to Boles, it is a fact that he brought up that jug of barley water and he poured out half-a-tumblerful and gave it me to drink. And he has brought me up barley water on several other occasions. But I really can't suspect Boles. It seems ridiculous."

"It is not for me to suggest any suspicions," said I. "But the facts that you mention are rather striking. Are there any other facts? What about your relations with Boles? There is nothing, I suppose, to suggest a motive?"

"Not a motive for poisoning me," he replied. "It is a fact that Boles and I are not as good friends as we used to be. We don't hit it off very well nowadays, though we remain, in a sort of way, partners. But I suspect that Boles would have cut it and gone off some time ago if it had not been for my wife. She and he have always been the best of friends – they are distant cousins of some kind – and I think they are quite attached to each other. So Boles goes on working in my studio for the sake of keeping in touch with her. At least, that is how I size things up."

78

It seemed to me that this was rather like an affirmative answer to my question, and perhaps it appeared so to him. But it was a somewhat delicate matter and neither of us pursued it any farther. Instead, I changed the subject and asked, "What do you propose to do about it?"

"I don't propose to do anything," he replied. "What could I do? Of course, I shall keep my weather eyelid lifting, but I don't suppose anything further will happen now that you and Dr. Thorndyke have let the cat so thoroughly out of the bag. I shall just go on working in my studio in the same old way, and I shall make no difference whatever in my relations with Boles. No reason why I should, as I really don't suspect him."

"Your studio is somewhere at the back of the house, isn't it?" I asked.

"At the side," he replied, "across the yard. Come along one day and see it," he added, cordially, "and I will unfold the whole art and mystery of making pottery. Come whenever you like and as soon as you can. I think you will find the show interesting."

As he issued this invitation (which I accepted gladly) he rose and picked up his hat, and we walked out together to the street door and said farewell on the door-step.

Chapter VI
Shadows in the Studio

Peter Gannett's invitation to me to visit his studio and see him at work was to develop consequences that I could not then have foreseen, nor shall I hint at them now, since it is the purpose of this narrative to trace the course of events in the order in which they occurred. I merely mention the consequences to excuse the apparent triviality of this part of my story.

At my first visit I was admitted by Mrs. Gannet, to whom I explained that this was a friendly call and not a professional visit. Nevertheless, I loitered awhile to hear her account of her husband and to give a few words of advice. Then she conducted me along the hall to a side door which opened on a paved yard, in which the only salient object was a large galvanized dust-bin. Crossing this yard, we came to a door which was furnished with a large, grotesque, bronze knocker and bore in dingy white lettering the word "*Studio*".

Mrs. Gannet executed a characteristic rat-tat on the knocker and, without waiting for an answer, opened the door and invited me to enter. I did, and found myself in a dark space, the front of which was formed by a heavy black curtain. As Mrs. Gannet had shut the door behind me, I was plunged in complete obscurity, but groping at the curtain, I presently drew its end aside and then stepped out into the light of the studio.

"Excuse my not getting up," said Gannet, who was seated at a large bench, "and also not shaking hands. Reasons obvious," and in explanation he held up a hand that was plastered with moist clay. "I am glad to see you, Doctor," he continued, adding. "Get that stool from Boles's bench and set it alongside mine."

I fetched the stool and placed it beside his at the bench, and having seated myself, proceeded to make my observations. And very interesting observations they were, for everything that met my eye – the place itself and everything in it – was an occasion of surprise. The whole establishment was on an unexpected scale. The studio, a great barn of a place, evidently, by its immense north window, designed and built as such, would have accommodated a sculptor specializing in colossal statues. The kiln looked big enough for a small factory, and the various accessories – a smaller kiln, a muffle furnace, a couple of grinding mills, a large iron mortar with a heavy pestle, and some other appliances – seemed out of proportion to what I supposed to be the actual output.

But the most surprising object was the artist, himself, considered in connection with his present occupation. Dressed correctly for the part in an elegant gown or smock of blue linen, and wearing a black velvet skull cap, "The Master" was, as I have said, seated at the bench, working at the beginnings of a rather large bowl. I watched him for a while in silent astonishment, for the method of work used by this "Master Craftsman" was that which I had been accustomed to associate with the Kindergarten. It was true that the latter had simply adopted, as suitable for children, the methods of ancient and primitive people, but these seemed hardly appropriate to a professional potter. However, such as the method was, he seemed to be quite at home with it and to work neatly and skilfully, and I was interested to note how little he appeared to be incommoded by a stiff joint in the middle finger of the right hand. Perhaps I might as well briefly describe the process.

On the large bench before him was a stout, square board, like a cook's pastry board, and on this was a plaster "bat", or slab, the upper surface of which had a dome-like projection (now hidden) to impart the necessary hollow to the bottom of the bowl. This latter (I am now speaking from subsequent experience) was made by coiling a roll, or cord, of clay into a circular disc, somewhat like a Catharine-wheel, and then rubbing the coils together with the finger to produce a flat plate. When the bottom was finished and cut true, the sides of the bowl were built up in the same way. At the side of the pastry board was an earthenware pan in which was a quantity of the clay cord, looking rather like a coil of gas tubing, and from this the artist picked out a length, laid it on top of the completed part of the side and, having carried it round the circumference, pinched it off and then pressed it down lightly, and rubbed and stroked it with his finger and a wooden modelling tool until it was completely united to the part below.

"Why do you pinch it off?" I inquired. "Why not coil it up continuously?"

"Because," he explained, "if you built a bowl by just coiling the clay cord round and round without a break, it would be higher one side than the other. So I pinch it off when I have completed a circle, and you notice that I begin the next tier in a different place, so that the joins don't come over each other. If they did, there would be a mark right up the side of the bowl."

"Yes," I agreed, "I see that, though it hadn't occurred to me. But do you always work in this way?"

"With the clay coils?" said he. "No. This is the quick method and the least trouble. But for more important pieces, to which I seek to impart the more personal and emotional qualities and at the same time to express the highest degree of plasticity, I dispense with the coil and work, as a sculptor does, with simple pellets of clay."

"But," said I, "what about the wheel? I see you have one, and it looks quite a high-class machine. Don't you throw any of your work on it?"

He looked at me solemnly, almost reproachfully, as he replied, "Never. The machine I leave to the machinist, to the mass-producer and the factory. I don't work for Woolworth's or the crockery shops. I am not concerned with speed of production or quantity of output or mechanical regularity of form. Those things appertain to trade. I, in my humble way, am an artist, and though my work is but simple pottery, I strive to infuse into it qualities that are spiritual, to make it express my own soul and personality. The clay is to me, as it was to other and greater masters of the medium – such as Della Robbia and Donatello – the instrument of emotional utterance."

To this I had nothing to say. It would not have been polite to give expression to my views, which were that his claims seemed to be extravagantly disproportionate to his achievements. But I was profoundly puzzled, and became more so as I watched him, for it appeared to me that what he was doing was not beyond my own powers, at least with a little practice, and I found myself half-unconsciously balancing the three obvious possibilities but unable to reach a conclusion.

Could it be that Gannet was a mere impostor, a pretender to artistic gifts that were purely fictitious? Or was he, like those mentally unbalanced "modernists" who honestly believe their crude and childish daubings to be great masterpieces, simply suffering from a delusion? Or was it possible that his uncouth, barbaric bowls and jars did really possess some subtle aesthetic qualities that I had failed to perceive merely from a lack of the necessary special sensibility? Modesty compelled me to admit the latter possibility. There are plenty of people to whom the beauties of nature or art convey nothing, and it might be that I was one of them.

My speculations were presently cut short by a thundering flourish on the knocker, at which Gannet started with a muttered curse. Then the door burst open and Mr. Frederick Boles swaggered into the studio, humming a tune.

"I wish you wouldn't make that damned row when you come in, Boles," Gannet exclaimed, irritably.

He cast an angry glance at his partner, or tenant, to which the latter responded with a provocative grin.

"Sorry, dear boy," said he. "I'm always forgetting the delicate state of your nerves. And here's the doctor. How de do, Doc? Hope you find your patient pretty well. Hmm? None the worse for all that arsenic that they tell me you put into his medicine? Ha ha!"

He bestowed on me an impudent stare through his eyeglass, removed the latter to execute a solemn wink, and then replaced it, after which, as I received his attentions quite impassively (though I should have liked to kick him), he turned away and swaggered across to the part of the studio which appeared to be his own domain, followed by a glance of deep dislike from Gannet which fairly expressed my own sentiments.

Mr. Boles was not a prepossessing person. Nevertheless, I watched his proceedings with some interest, being a little curious as to the kind of industry that he carried on, and presently, smothering my distaste – for I was determined not to quarrel with him – I strolled across to observe him at close quarters. He was seated on a rough, box-like stool, similar to the one which I had borrowed, at an ordinary jeweler's bench fitted with a gas blowpipe and a tin tray in place of the usual sheep-skin. At the moment he was engaged in cutting with an engraving tool a number of shallow pits in a flattened gold object which might have been a sketchy model of a *plaice* or *turbot*. I watched him for some time, a little mystified as to the result aimed at, for the little pits seemed, themselves, to have no determinate shape nor could I make out any plan in their arrangement. At length I ventured on a cautious inquiry.

"Those little hollows, I suppose, form the pattern on this – er – *object*?"

"Don't call it an object. Doc," he protested. "It's a pendant, or it will be when it is finished, and those hollows will form the pattern – or more properly, the surface enrichment – when they are filled with enamel."

"Oh, they are to be filled with enamel," said I, "and the spots of enamel will make the pattern. But I don't quite see what the pattern represents."

"Represents!" he repeated, indignantly, fixing his monocle (which he did not use while working) to emphasize the reproachful stare that he turned on me. "It doesn't represent anything. I'm not a photographer. The enamel spots will just form a symphony of harmonious, gem-like colour with a golden accompaniment. You don't want representation on a jewel. That can be left to the poster artist. What I aim at is harmony – rhythm – the concords of abstract colour. Do you follow me?"

"I think I do," said I. It was an outrageous untruth, for his explanation sounded like mere meaningless jargon. "But," I added, "probably I shall understand better when I have seen the finished work."

"I can show you a finished piece of the same kind now," said he, and laying down his work and the scorer, he went to the small cupboard in which he kept his materials and produced from it a small brooch which he placed in my hand and requested me to consider as "a study in polychromatic harmony".

It was certainly a cheerful and pleasant-looking object but strangely devoid of workmanship (though I noticed, on turning it over, that the pin and catch seemed to be quite competently finished), a simple elliptical tablet of gold covered with irregular-shaped spots of many-coloured enamel distributed over the surface in apparently accidental groups. The effect was as if drops of wax from a number of coloured candles had fallen on it.

"You see," said Boles, "how each of these spots of colour harmonizes and contrasts with all the others and reinforces them?"

"Yes, I see that," I replied, "but I don't see why you should not have grouped the spots into some sort of pattern."

Boles shook his head. "No," said he, "that would never do. The intrusion of form would have destroyed the natural rhythm of contrasting colour. The two things must be kept separate. Gannet is concerned with abstract form mainly uncomplicated with colour. My concern is with abstract colour liberated from form."

I made shift to appear as if this explanation conveyed some meaning to me and returned the brooch with a few appreciative comments. But I was completely fogged, so much so that I presently took the opportunity to steal away in order that I might turn matters over in my mind.

It was quite a curious problem. What was it that was really going on in that studio? There was a singular air of unreality about the industries that were carried on there. Gannet, with his archaic pottery, had been difficult enough to accept as a genuine artist, but Boles was even more incredible. And different as the two men were in all other respects, they were strangely alike in their special activities. Both talked what sounded like inflated, pretentious nonsense. Both assumed the airs of artists and *virtuosi*. And yet each of them appeared to be occupied with work which – to my eye – showed no sign of anything more than the simplest technical skill, and nothing that I could recognize as artistic ability.

Yet I had to admit that the deficiency might be in my own powers of perception. The curious phase of art known as "modernism" made me aware of widespread taste for pictures and sculpture of a pseudo-barbaric or primitive type, and the comments of the art critics on some of these works were not so very unlike the stuff that I had heard from Boles and Gannet. So perhaps these queer productions were actually what they professed to be and I was just a Philistine who couldn't recognize a work of art when I saw it.

But there was one practical question that rather puzzled me. What became of these wares? Admittedly, neither of these men worked for the retail shops. Then how did they dispose of their works, and who bought them? Both men were provided with means and appliances on a quite considerable scale and it was to be presumed that their output corresponded to the means of production, moreover, both were apparently obtaining a livelihood by their respective industries. Somewhere there must be a demand for primitive pottery and barbaric jewelry. But where was it? I decided – though it was none of my business – to make a few cautious inquiries.

Another matter, of more legitimate interest to me, was that of the relations of these two men. Ostensibly they were friends, comrades, fellow-workers, and in a sense, partners. But real friends they certainly were not. That had been frankly admitted by Gannet, and even if it had not been, his dislike of Boles was manifest and hardly dissembled. And, of course, it was natural enough if he suspected Boles of having tried to poison him, to say nothing of the rather doubtful relations of that gentleman with Mrs. Gannet. Indeed, I could not understand why, if he harboured this suspicion – of which Thorndyke seemed to entertain no doubt – he should have allowed the association to continue.

But if Gannet's sentiments towards Boles were unmistakable, the converse was by no means true. Boles's manners were not agreeable. They were coarse and vulgar – excepting when he was talking "high-brow" – and inclined to be rude. But though he was a bounder he was not consciously uncivil, and – so far as I could at present judge – he showed no signs of unfriendliness towards Gannet. The dislike appeared to be all on the one side.

Yet there must have been something more than met the eye. For if it was the fact – and I felt convinced that it was – that Boles had made a deliberate, cold-blooded attempt to poison Gannet, that attempt implied a motive which, to put it mildly, could not have been a benevolent one.

These various problems combined to make the studio a focus of profound interest to me, and as my practice at this period was productive principally of leisure, I spent a good deal of my time there – more, indeed, than I should have if Gannet had not made it so plain that my visits were acceptable. Sometimes I wondered whether it was my society that he enjoyed, or whether it might have been that my frequenting the studio gave him some sort of feeling of security. It might easily have been so, for, whenever I found him alone, I took the opportunity to satisfy myself that all was well with him. At any rate, he seemed always glad to see me, and for my part, I found the various activities of the two workers interesting to watch, quite independently of the curious problems arising out of their very odd relations.

By degrees my status changed from that of a mere spectator to something like that of a co-worker. There were many odd jobs to be done requiring no special skill and in these I was able to "lend a hand". For instance, there was the preparation of the "grog" – why so-called I never learned, for it was a most unconvivial material, being simply a powder made by pounding the fragments of spoiled or defective earthenware or broken saggars and used to temper the clay to prevent it from cracking in the fire. The broken pots or saggars were pounded in a great iron mortar until they were reduced to small fragments, when the latter were transferred to the grog mill and ground to powder. Then the powder was passed through a series of sieves, each marked with the number of meshes to the inch, and the different grades of powder – coarse, medium, and fine – stored in their appropriate bins.

Then there was the plaster work. Both men used plaster, and I was very glad to learn the technique of mixing, pouring, and trimming. Occasionally, Gannet would make a plaster mould of a successful bowl or jar (much to my surprise, for it seemed totally opposed to his professed principles) and "squeeze" one or two replicas, a process in which I assisted until I became quite proficient. I helped Boles to fire his queer-looking enamel plaques and to cast his uncouth gold ornaments and took over some of the pickling and polishing operations. And then, finally, there was the kiln, which interested me most of all. It was a coal-fired kiln and required a great deal of attention both before and during the firing. The preparation of the kiln Gannet attended to himself, but I stood by and watched his methods, observed the way in which he stacked the pieces, bedded in ground flint or bone-ash – he mostly used bone-ash – in the "saggars" (fire-clay cases or covers to protect the pieces from the flames) and at length closed the opening of the kiln with slabs of fire-clay.

But when the actual firing began, we were all kept busy. Even Boles left his work to help in feeding the fires, raking out the ashes and clearing the hearths, leaving Gannet free to control the draught and modify the fire to the required intensity. I was never able to observe the entire process from start to finish, for even at this time my practice called for some attention, but I was present on one occasion at the opening of the kiln – forty-eight hours after the lighting of the fires – and noted the care with which Gannet tested the temperature of the pieces before bringing them out into the cool air.

One day when I was watching him as he built up a wide-mouthed jar from a rough drawing – an extraordinarily rough drawing, very unskilfully executed, as I thought – which lay on the bench beside him, he made a new suggestion.

"Why shouldn't you try your hand at a bit of pottery, Doctor?" said he. "Just a simple piece. The actual building isn't difficult and you've seen how I do it. Get some of the stoneware body out of the bin and see what sort of job you can make of it."

I was not very enthusiastic about built pottery, for recently I had purchased a little treatise on the potter's art and had been particularly thrilled by the directions for "throwing" on the wheel. I mentioned the fact to Gannet, but he gave me no encouragement. For some reason he seemed to have an invincible prejudice against the potter's wheel.

"It's all right for commercial purposes," said he, "for speed and quantity. But there's no soul in the mechanical stuff. Building is the artist's method, the skilled hand translating thought directly into form."

I did not contest the matter. With a regretful glance at the wheel, standing idle in its corner, I fetched a supply of the mixed clay from the bin and proceeded to roll it into cords on the board that was kept for the purpose. But it occurred to me as an odd circumstance that, hating the wheel as he appeared to, he should have provided himself with one.

"I didn't buy the thing," he explained, when I propounded the question. "I took over this studio as a going concern from the executors of the previous tenant. He was a more or less commercial potter and his outfit suited his work. It doesn't suit mine. I don't want the wheel or that big mixing mill and I would sooner have had a smaller, gas-fired kiln. But the place was in going order and I got it dirt cheap with the outfit included, so I took it as it was and made the best of it."

My first attempt, a simple bowl, was no great success, being distinctly unsymmetrical and lopsided. But Gannet seemed to think quite well of it – apparently for these very qualities – and even offered to fire it. However, it did not satisfy me, and eventually I crumpled it up and returned it to the clay-bin, whence, after re-moistening, it emerged to be rolled out into fresh coils of cord. For I was now definitely embarked on the industry. The work had proved more interesting than I had expected, and as usually happens in the case of any art, the interest increased as the difficulties began to be understood and technical skill developed and grew.

"That's right, Doctor," said Gannet. "Keep it up and go on trying, and remember that the studio is yours whenever you like to use it, whether I am here or not." (As a matter of fact, he frequently was not, for both he and Boles took a good many days off, and rather oddly, I thought, their absences often coincided.) "And you needn't trouble to come in through the house. There is a spare key of the wicket which you may as well have. I'll give it to you now."

He took a couple of keys from his pocket and handed me one, whereby I became, in a sense, a joint tenant of the studio. It was an insignificant circumstance, and yet, as so often happens, it developed unforeseen consequences, one of which was a little adventure for the triviality of which I offer no apology since it, in its turn, had further consequences not entirely irrelevant to this history.

It happened that on the very first occasion on which I made use of the key, I found the studio vacant, and the condition of the benches suggested that both my fellow tenants were taking a day off. On the bench that I used was a half-finished pot, covered with damp cloths. I removed these and fetched a fresh supply of moist clay from the bin with the intention of going on with the work, when the wheel happened to catch my eye, instantly I was assailed by a great temptation. Here was an ideal opportunity to satisfy my ambition, to try my prentice hand with this delightful toy, which, to me, embodied the real romance of the potter's art.

I went over to the wheel and looked at it hungrily. I gave it a tentative spin and tried working the treadle, and finding it rather stiff, fetched Boles's oil-can, and applied a drop of oil to the pivots. Then I drew up a stool and took a few minutes' practice with the treadle until I was able to keep up a steady rotation. It seemed quite easy to me, as I was accustomed to riding a bicycle, and I was so far encouraged that I decided to try my skill as a thrower. Placing a basin of water beside the wheel, I brought the supply of clay from the bench and, working it into the form of a large dumpling, slapped it down on the damped hardwood disc, and having wetted my hands, started the rotation with a vigorous spin.

The start was not a perfect success, as I failed to centre the clay ball correctly and put on too much speed, with the result that the clay flew off and hit me in the stomach. However, I collected it from my lap, replaced it on the wheel-head, and made a fresh start with more care and caution. It was not so easy as it had appeared. Attending to the clay, I was apt to forget the treadle, and then the wheel stopped, and when I concentrated on the treadle, strange things happened to the clay. Still, by degrees, I got the "hang" of the process, recalling the instructions in my handbook and trying to practice the methods therein prescribed.

It was a fascinating game. There was something almost magical in the behaviour of the revolving clay. It seemed, almost of its own accord, to assume the most unexpected shapes. A light pressure of the wet hands and it rose into the form of a column, a cylinder or a cone. A gentle touch from above turned it miraculously into a ball, and a little pressure of the thumbs on the middle of the ball hollowed it out and transformed it into a bowl. It was wonderful and most delightful. And all the transformations had the charm of unexpectedness. The shapes that came were not designed by me, they simply came of themselves, and an inadvertent touch instantly changed them into something different and equally surprising.

For more than an hour I continued, with ecstatic pleasure and growing facility, to play this incomparable game. By that time, however, signs of bodily fatigue began to make themselves felt, for it was a pretty strenuous occupation, and it occurred to me that I had better get something done. I had just made a shallow bowl (or, rather, it had made itself), and as I took it gently between my hands, it rose, narrowed itself, and assumed the form of a squat jar with slightly in-turned mouth. I looked at it with pleased surprise. It was really quite an elegant shape and it seemed a pity to spoil it by any further manipulation. I decided to let well alone and treat it as a finished piece.

When I took my foot off the treadle and let the wheel run down, some new features came into view. The jar at rest was rather different from the jar spinning. Its surface was scored all over with spiral traces of "the potter's thumb", which stamped it glaringly as a thrown piece. This would not quite answer my purpose, which was to practice a playful fraud on Peter Gannet by foisting the jar on him as a built piece. The telltale spirals would have to be eliminated and other deceptive markings substituted.

Accordingly, I attacked it cautiously with a modelling tool and a piece of damp sponge, stroking it lightly in vertical lines and keeping an eye on one of Gannet's own jars, until all traces of the wheel had been obliterated and the jar might fairly have passed for a hand-built piece. Of course, a glance at the inside, which I did not dare to touch, would have discovered the fraud, but I took the chance that the interior would not be examined.

The next problem was the decoration. Gannet's usual method – following the tradition of primitive and barbaric ornament – was either to impress an encircling cord into the soft clay or to execute simple thumb-nail patterns. He did not actually use his thumb-nail for this purpose. A bone mustard-spoon produced the same effect and was more convenient. Accordingly I adopted the mustard-spoon, with which I carried a sort of rude *guilloche* round the jar, varied by symmetrically placed dents, made with the end of my clinical thermometer. Finally, becoming ambitious for something more distinctive, I produced my latch-key and, having made a few experiments on a piece of waste clay, found it quite admirable as a unit of pattern, especially if combined with the thermometer. A circle of key impressions radiating from a central thermometer dent produced a simple but interesting rosette which could be further developed by a circle of dents between the key-marks. It was really quite effective, and I was so pleased with it that I proceeded to enrich my masterpiece with four such rosettes, placing them as symmetrically as I could (not that the symmetry would matter to Gannet) on the bulging sides below the thumb-nail ornaments.

When I had finished the decoration and tidied it up with the modelling tool I stood back and looked at my work, not only with satisfaction but with some surprise. For, rough and crude as it was, it appeared to my possibly indulgent eye quite a pleasant little pot, and comparing it with the row of Gannet's works which were drying on the shelf, I asked myself once again what could be the alleged subtle qualities imparted by the hand of the master?

Having made a vacancy on the shelf by moving one of Gannet's pieces from the middle to the end, I embarked on the perilous task of detaching my jar from the wheel-head. The instrument that I employed was a thin wire with a wooden handle at each end, which we used for cutting slices of clay, a dangerous tool, for a false stroke would have cut the bottom off my jar. But Providence, which – sometimes – watches over the activities of the tyro, guided my hand, and at last the wire emerged safely, leaving the jar free of the surface to which it had been stuck. With infinite care and tenderness – for it was still quite soft – I lifted it with both hands and carried it across to the shelf, where I deposited it safely in the vacant space. Then I cleaned up the wheel, obliterating all traces of my unlawful proceedings, threw my half-finished built piece back into the clay-bin, and departed, chuckling over the surprise that awaited Gannet when he should come to inspect the pieces that were drying on the shelf.

As events turned out, my very mild joke fell quite flat, so far as I was concerned, for I missed the denouement. A sudden outbreak of measles at a local school kept me so busy that my visits to the studio had to be suspended for a time, and when at last I was able to make an afternoon call, the circumstances were such as to occupy my attention in a more serious and less agreeable manner. As this episode was later to develop a special significance, I shall venture to describe it in some detail.

On this occasion, I did not let myself in, as usual, by the wicket, for at the end of Jacob Street I overtook Mrs. Gannet and we walked together to the house, which I entered with her. It seemed that she had some question to ask her husband, and when I had opened the side door, she came out to walk with me across the yard to the studio. Suddenly, as we drew near to the latter, I became aware of a singular uproar within, a clattering and banging, as if the furniture were being thrust about and stools overturned, mingled with the sound of obviously angry voices. Mrs. Gannet stopped abruptly and clutched my arm.

"Oh, dear," she exclaimed, "there are those two men quarreling again. It is dreadful. I do wish Mr. Boles would move to another workshop. If they can't agree, why don't they separate?"

"They don't hit it off very well, then?" I suggested, listening attentively and conscious of a somewhat unfortunate expression – for they seemed to be hitting it off rather too well.

"No," she replied, "especially since – you know. Peter thinks Mr. Boles gave him the stuff, which is ridiculous, and Mr. Boles – I think I won't go in now," and with this she turned about and retreated to the house, leaving me standing near the studio door, doubtful whether I had better enter boldly or follow the lady's discreet example and leave the two men to settle their business.

It was very embarrassing. If I went in, I could not pretend to be unaware of the disturbance. On the other hand, I did not like to retreat when my intervention might be desirable. Thus I stood hesitating between considerations of delicacy and expediency until a furious shout in Boles's voice settled the question.

"You're asking for it, you know!" he roared, whereupon, flinging delicacy to the winds, I rapped on the door with my knuckles and entered. I had opened the door deliberately and rather noisily and I now stood for a few moments in the dark lobby behind the curtain while I closed it after me in the same deliberate manner to give time for any necessary adjustments. Sounds of quick movement from within suggested that these were being made, and when I drew aside the curtain and stepped in, the two men were on opposite sides of the studio. Gannet was in the act of buttoning a very crumpled collar and Boles was standing by his bench, on which lay a raising hammer that had a suspicious appearance of having been hastily put down there. Both men were obviously agitated. Boles, purple-faced, wild-eyed and furiously angry, Gannet, breathless, pale and venomous.

I greeted them in a matter-of-fact tone as if I had noticed nothing unusual, and went on to excuse and explain the suspension of my visits. But it was a poor pretense, for there were the overturned stools and there was Boles, scowling savagely and still trembling visibly, and there was that formidable-looking hammer the appearance of which suggested that I had entered only just in time.

Gannet was the first to recover himself, though even Boles managed to growl out a sulky greeting, and when I had picked up a fallen stool and seated myself on it, I made shift to keep up some sort of conversation and to try to bring matters back to a normal footing. I glanced at the shelf, but it was empty. Apparently the pieces that I had left drying on it had been fired and disposed of. What had happened to my jar, I could not guess and did not very much care. Obviously, the existing circumstances did not lend themselves to any playful interchanges between Gannet and me, nor did they seem to lend themselves to anything else, and I should have made an excuse to steal away but for my unwillingness to leave the two men together in their present moods.

I did not, however, stay very long – no longer, in fact, than seemed desirable. Presently, Boles, after some restless and apparently aimless rummaging in his cupboard, shut it, locked its door, and with a sulky farewell to me, took his departure, and as I had no wish to discuss the quarrel and Gannet seemed to be in a not very sociable mood, I took an early opportunity to bring my visit to an end.

It had been a highly disagreeable episode, and it had a permanent effect on me. Thenceforward, the studio ceased to attract me. Its pleasant, friendly atmosphere seemed to have evaporated. I continued to look in from time to time, but rather to keep an eye on Gannet, than to interest myself in the works of the two artists. Like Mrs. Gannet, I wondered why these two men, hating each other as they obviously did, should perversely continue their association. At any rate, the place was spoiled for me by the atmosphere of hatred and strife that seemed to pervade it, and even if the abundance of my leisure had continued – which it did not – I should still have been but an occasional visitor.

Chapter VII
Mrs. Gannet Brings
Strange Tidings

The wisdom of our ancestors has enriched us with the precept that the locking of the stable door fails in its purpose of security if it is postponed until after the horse has been stolen. Nevertheless (since it is so much easier to be wise after the event than before) this futile form of post-caution continues to be prevalent, of which truth my own proceedings furnished an illustrative instance. For having allowed my patient to be poisoned with arsenic under my very nose, and that, too, in the crudest and most blatant fashion, I now proceeded to devote my leisure to an intense study of Medical Jurisprudence and Toxicology.

Mine, however, was not a truly representative case. The actual horse had indeed been stolen, but still the stable contained a whole stud of potential horses. I might, and probably should, never encounter another case of poisoning in the practice of a life-time. On the other hand, I might meet with one tomorrow, or if not a poisoning case, perhaps some other form of crime which lay within the province of the medical jurist. There seemed to be plenty of them, judging by the lurid accounts of the authorities whose works I devoured, and I began almost to hope that my labours in their study would not be entirely wasted.

It was natural that my constant preoccupation with the detection and demonstration of crime should react more or less on my habitual state of mind. And it did. Gradually I acquired a definitely Scotland Yardish outlook and went about my practice – not neglectful, I trust, of the ordinary maladies of my patients – with the idea of criminal possibilities, if not consciously present, yet lurking on the very top surface of the subconscious. Little did my innocent patients or their equally innocent attendants suspect the toxicological balance in which symptoms and ministrations alike were being weighed, and little did the worthy Peter Gannet guess that, even while he was demonstrating the mysteries of stoneware, my perverted mind was canvassing the potentialities of the various glazes that he used for indirect and secret poisoning.

I mention these mental reactions to my late experience and my recent profound study of legal medicine in explanation of subsequent events. And I make no apology. The state of mind may seem odd, but yet it was very natural. I had been caught napping once and I didn't intend to be caught again, and that involved these elaborate precautions against possibilities whose probability was almost negligible.

It happened on a certain evening that in the intervals of my evening consultations, my thoughts turned to my friend, Peter Gannet. It was now some weeks since I had seen him, my practice having of late made a temporary spurt and left me little leisure. I had also been acting as *locum tenens* for the Police Surgeon, who was on leave. This further diminished my leisure and possibly accentuated the state of mind that I have described. Nevertheless, I was a little disposed to reproach myself for, solitary man as he was, he had made it clear that he was always pleased to see me. Indeed, it had seemed to me that I was the only friend that he had, for certainly Boles could not be regarded in that light, and if the quarrel between them had given me a distaste for the studio, that very occurrence did, in fact, emphasize those obligations of friendship which had led me at first visit to the studio.

I had then felt that it was my duty to keep an eye on him, since some person had certainly tried to poison him. That person had some reason for desiring his death and had no scruple about seeking to compass it, and as the motive, presumably, still existed, there was no denying that, calmly as he had taken the position, Peter Gannet stood definitely in peril of a further and more successful attempt – to say nothing of the chance of his being knocked on the head with a raising hammer in the course of one of his little disagreements with Boles. I ought not to have left him so long without at least a brief visit of inspection.

Thus reflecting, I decided to walk round to the studio as soon as the consultations were finished and satisfy myself that all was well, and as the time ran on and no further patients appeared, my eye turned impatiently to the clock, the hands of which were creeping towards eight, when I should be free to go. There were now only three minutes to run and the clock had just given the preliminary hiccup by which clocks announce their intention to strike, when I heard the door of the adjoining waiting room open and close, informing me that a last minute patient had arrived.

It was very provoking, but after all it was what I was there for. So dismissing Gannet from my mind, I rose, opened the communicating door, and looked into the waiting room.

The visitor was Mrs. Gannet, and at the first glance at her my heart sank. For her troubled, almost terrified, expression told me that something was seriously amiss, and my imagination began instantly to frame lurid surmises.

"What is the matter, Mrs. Gannet?" I asked, as I ushered her through into the consulting room. "You look very troubled."

94

"I am very troubled," she replied. "A most extraordinary and alarming thing has happened. My husband has disappeared."

"Disappeared!" I repeated in astonishment. "Since when?"

"That I can't tell you," she answered. "I have been away from home for about a fortnight, and when I came back I found the house empty. I didn't think much of it at the time, as I had said when I wrote to him that I was not certain as to what time I should get home, and I simply thought that he had gone out. But then I found my letter in the letter box, which seemed very strange, as it must have been lying there two days. So I went up and had another look at his bedroom, but everything was in order there. His bed had not been slept in – it was quite tidily made – and his toilet things and hairbrushes were in their usual place. Then I looked over his wardrobe, but none of his clothes seemed to be missing excepting the suit that he usually wears. And then I went down to the hall to see if he had taken his stick or his umbrella, but he hadn't taken either. They were both there, and what was more remarkable, both his hats were on their pegs."

"Do you mean to say," I exclaimed, "that there was no hat missing at all?"

"No. He has only two hats, and they were both there. So it seems as if he must have gone away without a hat."

"That is very extraordinary," said I. "But surely your maid knows how long he has been absent."

"There isn't any maid," she replied. "Our last girl, Mabel, was under notice and she left a week before I went away and, as there was no time to get a fresh maid, Peter and I agreed to put it off until I came back. He said that he could look after himself quite well and get his meals out if necessary. There are several good restaurants near.

"Well, I waited all yesterday in hopes of his return and I sat up until nearly one in the morning, but he never came home, and there has been no sign of him today."

"You looked in at the studio, I suppose?" said I.

"No, I didn't," she replied almost in a whisper. "That is why I have come to you. I couldn't summon up courage to go there."

"Why not?" I asked.

"I was afraid," she answered in the same low, agitated tone, "that there might be something – something there that – well, I don't quite know what I thought, but you know – "

"Yes, I understand," said I, rising – for the clock had struck and I was free. "But that studio ought to be entered at once. Your husband may have had some sudden attack or seizure and be lying there helpless."

I went out into the hall and wrote down on the slate the address where I was to be found if any emergency should arise. Then Mrs. Gannet and I set forth together, taking the short cuts through the back streets, with which I was now becoming quite familiar. We walked along at a quick pace, exchanging hardly a word, and as we went, I cogitated on the strange and disquieting news that she had brought. There was no denying that things had a decidedly sinister aspect. That Gannet should have gone away from home hatless and unprovided with any of his ordinary kit, and leaving no note or message, was inconceivable. Something must have happened to him. But what? My own expectation was that I should find his dead body in the studio, and that was evidently Mrs. Gannet's, too, as was suggested by her terror at the idea of seeking him there. But that terror seemed to me a little unnatural. Why was she so afraid to go into the studio, even with the expectation of finding her husband dead? Could it be that she had some knowledge or suspicion that she had not disclosed? It seemed not unlikely. Even if she had not been a party to the poisoning, she must have known, or at least strongly suspected, who the poisoner was, and it was most probable that she had been able to guess at the motive of the crime. But she would then realize, as I did, that the motive remained and might induce another crime.

When we reached the house, I tried the wicket in the studio gate, but it was locked, and the key which Gannet had given me was not in my pocket. Meanwhile, Mrs. Gannet had opened the street door with her latch-key and we entered the house together.

"Are you coming into the studio with me?" I asked as we went through the hall to the side door that opened on the yard.

"No," she replied. "I will come with you to the door and wait outside until you have seen whether he is there or not."

Accordingly, we walked together across the yard, and when we came to the studio door, I tried it. But it was locked, and an inspection by means of my flashlight showed that it had been locked from the inside and that the key was in the lock.

"Now," said I, "what are we to do? How are we going to get in?"

"There is a spare key," she replied. "Shall I go and get it?"

"But," I objected, "we couldn't get it into the lock. There is a key there already. And the wicket is locked, too. Have you got a spare key of that?"

She had, so we returned to the house, where she found the key and gave it to me. And as I took it from her trembling hand, I could see – though she made no comment – that the locked door with the key inside had given her a further shock. And certainly it was rather ominous. But if the wicket should prove also to be locked from the inside, all hope or doubt would be at an end. It was, therefore, with the most acute anxiety that I hurried out into the street, leaving her standing in the hall, and ran to the wicket. But to my relief, the key entered freely and turned in the lock and I opened the little gate and stepped through into the studio. Lighting myself across the floor with my flashlight I reached the switch and turned it on, flooding the place with light. A single glance around the studio showed that there was no one in it, alive or dead. Thereupon, I unlocked the yard door and threw it open, when I perceived Mrs. Gannet standing outside.

"Well, he isn't here," I reported, whereupon she came, almost on tiptoe, into the lobby and peered round the curtain.

"Oh dear!" she exclaimed, "what a relief! But still, where can he be? I can't help thinking that something must have happened to him."

As I could not pretend to disagree with her, I made no reply to this, but asked, "I suppose you have searched the house thoroughly?"

"I think so," she replied, "and I don't feel as if I could search any more. 'But if you would be so kind as to take a look round and make sure that I haven't overlooked anything – "

"Yes," said I, "I think that would be just as well. But what are you going to do tonight? You oughtn't to be in the house all alone."

"I couldn't be," she replied. "Last night was dreadful, but now my nerves are all on edge. I couldn't endure another night. I shall go to my friend, Miss Hughes – she lives in Mornington Crescent – and see if she will come and keep me company."

"It would be better if she would put you up for the night," said I.

"Yes, it would," she agreed. "Much better. I would rather not stay in this house tonight. As soon as you have made your inspection, I will run round and ask her."

"You needn't wait for me," said I. "Go round to her at once, as it is getting late. Give me the number of her house and I will call on my way home and tell you whether I have discovered any clue to the mystery."

She closed with this offer immediately, being, evidently, relieved to get away from the silent, desolate house. I walked back with her across the yard, and when I had escorted her to the street door and seen her start on her mission, I closed the door and went back into the house, not displeased to have the place to myself and the opportunity to pursue my investigations at my leisure and free from observation.

I made a very thorough examination, beginning with the attics at the very top of the house and working my way systematically downwards. On the upper floors there were several unoccupied rooms, some quite empty and others more or less filled with discarded furniture and miscellaneous lumber. All these I searched minutely, opening up every possible – and even impossible – hiding-place, and peering, with the aid of my pocket flashlight, into the dim and musty recesses of the shapeless closets in the corners of the roof or under the staircases. In the occupied bedrooms I knelt down to look under the beds, I opened the cupboards and wardrobes and prodded the clothes that hung from the pegs to make sure that they concealed no other hanging object. I even examined the chimneys with my lamp and explored their cavities with my walking-stick, gathering a little harvest of soot up my sleeves but achieving no other result and making no discoveries, excepting that, when I came to examine Gannet's bedroom, I noticed that the pots and pans and the effigy of the monkey had disappeared from the mantelpiece.

It was an eerie business and seemed to become more so (by a sort of autosuggestion) as I explored one room after another. By the time I had examined the great stone-paved kitchen and the rather malodorous scullery and searched the cavernous, slug-haunted cellars, even probing the mounds of coal with my stick, I had worked myself up into a state of the most horrid expectancy.

But still there was no sign of Peter Gannet. The natural conclusion seemed to be that he was not there. But this was a conclusion that my state of mind made me unable to accept. His wife's statement set forth that he had disappeared in his ordinary indoor apparel, in which it was hardly imaginable that he could have gone away from the house. But if he had not, then he must be somewhere on the premises. Thus I argued, with more conviction than logic, as I ascended the uncarpeted basement stairs, noting the surprisingly loud sound that my footsteps made as they broke in on the pervading silence.

As I passed into the hall, I paused at the hat-stand to verify Mrs. Gannet's statement. There were the two hats, sure enough, a shabby, broad-brimmed, soft felt which I knew well by sight, and a rather trim billycock which I had never seen him wear, but which bore his initials in the crown, as I ascertained by taking it down and inspecting it. And there was his stick, a rough oak crook, and his umbrella with a legible *P. G.* on the silver band. There was also another stick which I had never seen before and which struck me as being rather out of character with the Bohemian Gannet, a smart, polished cane with a gilt band and a gilt tip to the handle. I took it out of the stand, and as it seemed to me rather long, I lifted out the oak stick and compared the two, when I found that the cane was the longer by a full inch. There was nothing much in this, and as the band bore no initials, I was putting it back in the stand when my eye caught a minute monogram on the gilt tip. It was a confused device, as monograms usually are, but eventually I managed to resolve it into the two letters *F* and *B*.

Then it was pretty certain that the stick belonged to Frederick Boles, from which it followed that Boles had been to the house recently. But there was nothing abnormal in this, since he worked pretty regularly in the studio and usually approached it through the house. But why had he left his stick? And why had Mrs. Gannet made no mention of it – or, indeed, of Boles himself? For if he had been working here, he must have known when Gannet was last seen, for unless he had a latch-key, he must have been admitted by Gannet himself. Turning this over in my mind, I decided, before leaving the house, to take another look at the studio. It had certainly been empty when I had looked in previously, and there were no large cupboards or other possible hiding places. Still there was the chance that a more thorough examination might throw some light on Gannet's activities and on the question as to the time of his disappearance. Accordingly, I passed out by the side door, and crossing the yard, opened the studio door, switched on the lights, drew aside the curtain and stepped in.

Chapter VIII
Dr. Oldfield Makes
Surprising Discoveries

On entering the studio, I halted close by the curtain and stood awhile surveying the vast, desolate, forbidding interior with no definite idea in my mind. Obviously, there was no one there, dead or alive, nor any closed space large enough to form a hiding place. And yet as I stood there, the creepy feeling that had been growing on me as I had searched the house seemed to become even more intense. It may have been that the deathly silence and stillness of the place, which I had known only under the cheerful influence of work and companionship, cast a chill over me.

At any rate, there I stood, vaguely looking about me with a growing uncomfortable feeling that this great, bare room which had been the scene of Gannet's labours and the centre of his interests, had been in some way connected with his unaccountable disappearance.

Presently my vague, general survey gave place to a more detailed inspection. I began to observe the various objects in the studio and to note what they had to tell of Gannet's recent activities. There was the potter's wheel, carefully cleaned – though never used – according to his invariable orderly practice, and there was a row of "green" unfired jars drying on a shelf until they should be ready for the kiln. But when I looked at the kiln itself, I was struck by something quite unusual, having regard to Gannet's habitual tidiness. The fire-holes which led into the interior of the kiln were all choked with ash, and opposite to each was a large mound of the ash which had been raked out during the firing and left on the hearths. Now, this was singularly unlike Gannet's practice. Usually, as he raked out the ash, he shovelled it up into a bucket, and carried it out to the ash-bin in the yard, and as soon as the fires were out, he cleared each of the fireplaces of the remaining ash, leaving them clean and ready for the next firing.

Here, then, was something definitely abnormal. But there was a further discrepancy. The size of the mounds made it clear that there had been a rather prolonged firing and a "high fire". But where were the fired pieces? The shelves on which the pots were usually stored after firing were all empty and there was not a sign of any pottery other than the unfired jars. The unavoidable conclusion was that the "batch" must be still in the kiln. But if this were so, then Gannet's disappearance must have coincided with the end of the firing. But that seemed entirely to exclude the idea of a voluntary disappearance. It was inconceivable that he should have gone away leaving the fires still burning and the kiln unopened.

However, there was no need to speculate. The question could be settled at once by opening the kiln if it was sufficiently cool to handle. Accordingly, I walked over to it and cautiously touched the outside brick casing, which I found to be little more than lukewarm, and then I boldly unlatched and pulled open the big iron, fire-clay lined door, bringing into view the loose fire-bricks which actually closed the opening. As these, too, were only moderately warm, I proceeded to lift them out, one by one, which I was able to do the more easily since they had been only roughly fitted together.

It was not really necessary for me to take them all out, for, as soon as the upper tier was removed, I was able to throw the beam of my flashlight into the interior. And when I did so, I discovered, to my astonishment, that the kiln was empty.

The mystery, then, remained. Indeed, it grew more profound. For not only was the problem as to what had become of the fired pottery still unsolved, but there was the remarkable fact that the kiln must have been opened while it was still quite hot, a thing that Gannet would never have done, since a draught of cold air on the hot pottery would probably result in a disaster. And when I took away the rest of the fire-bricks and the interior of the kiln was fully exposed to view, another anomaly presented itself. The floor of the kiln, which during the firing would be covered with burnt flint or bone-ash, was perfectly clean. It had been carefully and thoroughly swept out, and this while the kiln was hot and while the fire-holes remained choked with ash.

As to the missing pottery, there was one possibility, though an unlikely one. It might have been treated with glaze and put into the glost oven. But it had not, for when I opened the oven and looked in, I found it empty and showing no sign of recent use.

It was all very strange, and the strangeness of it did nothing to allay my suspicion that the studio held the secret of Gannet's disappearance. I prowled round with uneasy inquisitiveness, scrutinizing all the various objects in search of some hint or leading fact. I examined the grog mill and noted that something white had been recently ground in it, and apparently ground dry, to judge by the coating of fine powder on the floor around it. I looked into the big iron mortar and noted that some white material had been pounded in it. I examined the rows of cupels on the shelves by Boles's little muffle, noted that they were badly made and of unusually coarse material, and wondered when Boles had made them.

I even looked into the muffle – finding nothing, of course – and observing that the floor of the studio seemed to have been washed recently, speculated on the possible reason for this very unusual proceeding.

But speculation got me no more forward. Obviously, there was something abnormal about the kiln. There had been a prolonged and intense fire, but of the fired ware there was not a trace. What conceivable explanation could there be of such an extraordinary conflict of facts? The possibility occurred to me that the whole batch might have been disposed of by a single transaction or sent to an exhibition. But a moment's reflection showed me that this would not do. There had not been time for the batch to be cooled, finished, glazed and refired, for the kiln was still quite warm inside.

The rough, box-like stool that Gannet had made to sit on at the bench was standing near the kiln. I slipped my hand through the lifting hole and drew the stool up to the open door in order more conveniently to examine the interior. But the examination yielded nothing. I threw the beam of light from my flashlight into every corner, but it simply confirmed my original observation. The kiln was empty, and no trace of its late contents remained beyond the few obscure white smears that the brush had left on the fire-clay floor.

I sat there for some minutes facing the open door and reflecting profoundly on this extraordinary problem. But I could make nothing of it, and at length, I started up to renew my explorations. For it had suddenly occurred to me that I had forgotten to examine the contents of the bins. But as I rose and turned round, I noticed a small white object on the floor which had evidently been covered by the stool before I had moved it. I stooped and picked it up, and at the first glance at it all my vague and formless suspicions seemed to run together into a horrible certainty.

The little object was the ungual phalanx, or terminal joint, of a finger – apparently a forefinger – burned to the snowy whiteness characteristic of incinerated bone. It was unmistakable. For if I lacked experience in some professional matters, at least my osteology was fresh, and as the instant recognition flashed on me, I stood as if rooted to the ground, staring at the little relic with a shuddering realization of all that it meant.

The mystery of the absent pottery was solved. There had never been any pottery. That long and fierce fire had burned to destroy the evidence of a hideous crime. And the other mysteries, too, were solved. Now I could guess what the white substance was that had been ground in the grog mill, how it came that the hastily-made cupels were of such

102

abnormally coarse material, and why it had been necessary to wash the studio floor. All the anomalies now fell into a horrid agreement and each served to confirm and explain the others.

I laid the little fragile bone tenderly on the stool and proceeded to re-examine the place by the light of this new and dreadful fact. First I went to the shelves by Boles's muffle and looked over the cupels, taking them in my hand the better to examine them. Their nature was now quite obvious. Instead of the finely powdered bone-ash of which they were ordinarily composed, they had been made by cramming fragments of crushed, incinerated bone into the cupel press, and the cohesion of these was so slight that one of the cupels fell to pieces in my hand.

Laying the loose fragments on the shelf, I turned away to examine the bins, of which there was a row standing against the wall. I began with the clay-bins, containing the material for the various "bodies" – stoneware, earthenware and porcelain. But when I lifted the lids, I saw that they contained clay and could contain nothing else. The grog-bins were nearly empty and showed nothing abnormal, and the same was true of the plaster-bin, though I took the precaution of dipping my hand deeply into the plaster to make sure that there was nothing underneath. When I came to the bone-ash-bin I naturally surveyed it more critically, for here, with the aid of the mill, the residue of a cremated body could have been concealed beyond the possibility of recognition.

I lifted off the lid and looked in, but at the first glance perceived nothing unusual. The bin was three parts full, and its contents appeared to be the ordinary finely powdered ash. But I was not prepared to accept the surface appearances. Rolling my sleeve up above the elbow, I thrust my hand deep down into the ash, testing its consistency by working it between my fingers and thumb. The result was what the cupels had led me to expect. About eight inches from the surface, the feel of the fine, smooth powder gave place to a sensation as if I were grasping a mixture of gravel and sand with occasional fragments of appreciable size. Some of these I brought up to the surface, dropping them into my other hand and dipping down for further specimens until I had collected a handful, when I carried them over the cupel shelves and, having deposited them on a vacant space, picked out one or two of the larger fragments and carried them across to the modelling stand to examine them by the light of the big studio lamp.

Of course, there could be no doubt as to their nature. Even to the naked eye, the characteristic structure of bone was obvious, and rendered more so by the burning away of the soft tissues. But I confirmed the diagnosis with the aid of my pocket lens, and then, having replaced the fragments on the shelf, I put the lid back on the bin and began seriously

103

to consider what I should do next. There was no need for further exploration. I had all the essential facts. I now knew what had happened to Peter Gannet, and any further elucidation lay outside my province and within that of those whose business it is to investigate crime.

Before leaving the studio, I looked about for some receptacle in which to pack the little finger bone, for I knew that it would crumble at a touch, and that, as it was the one piece of undeniable evidence, it must be preserved intact at all costs. Eventually I found a nearly empty match box and, having tipped out the remaining matches and torn a strip from my handkerchief, I rolled the little relic in this, packed it tenderly in the match box and bestowed the latter in my breast pocket. Then I took up my stick and prepared to depart, but just as I was starting towards the door, it occurred to me that I might as well take a few of the small fragments from the bin to examine more thoroughly at my leisure. Not that I had any doubts as to their nature, but the microscope would put the matter beyond dispute. Accordingly, I collected a handful from the shelf and, having wrapped them in the remainder of my handkerchief, put the little parcel in my pocket and then made my way to the door, switched off the lights, and went out, taking the door-key with me.

Coming out from the glare of the studio into the darkness, I had to light myself across the yard with my flashlight and, as I flashed it about, its beam fell on the big rubbish-bin which stood in a corner waiting for the dustman. For a moment, I was disposed to stop and explore it, but then I reflected that it was not my concern to seek further details, and as it was getting late and I still had to report to Mrs. Gannet, I went on into the house and, passing through the hall, let myself out into the street.

The distance from Jacob Street to Mornington Crescent is quite short, all too short for the amount of thinking that I had to do on the way thither – for it was only when I had shut the door and set forth on my errand that the awkwardness of the coming interview began to dawn on me. What was I to say to Mrs. Gannet? As I asked myself the question, I saw that it involved two others. The first was: How much did she know? Had she any suspicion that her husband had been made away with? I did not for a moment believe that she had been privy to the gruesome events that the studio had witnessed, but her agitation, her horror at the idea of spending the night in the house, and above all, her strange fear of entering the studio, justified the suspicion that, even if she knew nothing of what had happened, she had made some highly pertinent surmises.

Then, how much did I know? I had assumed quite confidently that a body had been cremated in the kiln and that the body was that of Peter Gannet. And I believed that I could name the other party to that grim transaction. But here I recalled Dr. Thorndyke's oft-repeated warnings to his students never to confuse inference or belief with knowledge and never to go beyond the definitely ascertained facts. But I had done this already, and now when I revised my convictions by the light of this excellent precept, I realized that the actual facts that I had ascertained (though they justified my inferences) were enough only to call for a thorough investigation.

Then should I tell Mrs. Gannet simply what I had observed and leave her to draw her own conclusions? Considered, subject to my strong distrust of the lady, this course did not commend itself. In fact, it was a very difficult question, and I had come to no decision when I found myself standing on Miss Hughes's door-step, and in response to my knock, the door was opened by Mrs. Gannet herself.

Still temporizing in my own mind, I began by expressing the hope that Miss Hughes was able to accommodate her.

"Yes," she replied, as she ushered me into the drawing room, "I am glad to say that she can give me the spare bedroom. She has been most kind and sympathetic. And how have you got on? You have been a tremendous time. I expected you at least half-an-hour ago."

"The search took quite a long time," I explained, "for I went through the whole house from the attics to the cellars and examined every nook and corner."

"And I suppose you found nothing, after all?"

"Not a trace in any part of the house."

"It was very good of you to take so much trouble," said she. "I don't know how to thank you, and you such a busy man, too. I suppose you didn't go into the studio again?"

"Yes," I replied. "I thought I would have another look at it, in rather more detail, and I did pick up some information there as to the approximate time when he disappeared, for I opened the big kiln and found it quite warm inside. I don't know how long it takes to cool. Do you?"

"Not very exactly," she answered, "but quite a long time, I believe, if it is kept shut up. At any rate, the fact that it was warm doesn't tell us much more than we know. It is all very mysterious, and I don't know what on earth to do next."

"What about Mr. Boles?" I suggested. "He must have been at the studio some time quite lately. Wouldn't it be as well to look him up and see if he can throw any light on the mystery?"

She shook her head, disconsolately. "I have," she said. "I went to his flat yesterday and again this morning, but I could get no answer to my knocking and ringing. And the caretaker man in the office says that he hasn't seen him for about a week, though he has been on the lookout for him on account of a parcel that the postman left. He has been up to the flat several times, but could get no answer. And there hasn't been any light in the windows at night, so he must be away from home."

"Did he know when you would be returning?"

"Yes," she replied. "And there is another strange thing. I wrote and told him what day I should be back and asked him to drop in and have tea with me. He not only never came, but he didn't even answer my letter."

I reflected on this new turn of events, which seemed less mysterious to me than it appeared to her. Then I cautiously approached the inevitable proposal.

"Well, Mrs. Gannet," said I, "it is, as you say, all very mysterious. But we can't just leave it at that. We have got to find out what has happened to your husband, and as we haven't the means of doing it ourselves, we must invoke the aid of those who have. We shall have to apply for help to the police."

As I made this proposal, I watched her attentively and was a little relieved to note that it appeared to cause her no alarm. But she was not enthusiastic.

"Do you think it is really necessary?" she asked. "If we call in the police, it will be in all the papers and there will be no end of fuss and scandal, and after all, he may come back tomorrow."

"I don't think there is any choice," I rejoined, firmly. "The police will have to be informed sooner or later, and they ought to be notified at once while the events are fresh and the traces more easy to follow. It would never do for us to seem to have tried to hush the affair up."

That last remark settled her. She agreed that perhaps the police had better be informed of the disappearance, and to my great satisfaction, she asked me to make the communication.

"I don't feel equal to it," said she, "and as you have acted as police surgeon and know the officers, it will be easier for you. Hadn't you better have the latch-key in case they want to look over the house?"

"But won't you want it yourself?" I asked.

"No," she replied. "Miss Hughes has invited me to stay with her for the present. Besides, I have a spare key and I brought it away with me, and of course, if Peter should come back, he has his own key."

With this she handed me the latch-key and when I had pocketed it I took my leave and set forth at a swinging pace for home, hoping that I should find no messages awaiting me and that a substantial meal would be ready for instant production. I was very well pleased with the way in which the interview had gone off and congratulated myself on having kept my own counsel. For now I need not appear in the investigation at all. The police would, of course, examine the studio, and the discoveries that they would make, on my prompting, could be credited to them.

When I let myself in, I cast an anxious glance at the message slate and breathed a benediction on the blank surface that it presented. And as a savoury aroma ascending from the basement told me that all was well there, too, I skipped off to the bathroom, there to wash and brush joyfully and reflect on the delight of being really hungry – under suitable conditions.

As I disposed of the excellent dinner – or supper – that my thoughtful housekeeper had provided, it was natural that I should ruminate on the astonishing events of the last few hours. And now that the excitement of the chase had passed off, I began to consider the significance of my discoveries. Those discoveries left me in no doubt (despite Thorndyke's caution) that my friend, Peter Gannet, had been made away with, and I owed it to our friendship, to say nothing of my duty as a good citizen, to do everything in my power to establish the identity of the murderer in order that he – or she – might be brought within the grasp of the law.

Now who could it be that had made away with my poor friend? I had not the faintest doubt as to, at least, the protagonist in that horrid drama. In the very moment of my realization that a crime had been committed, I had confidently identified the criminal. And my conviction remained unshaken. Nevertheless, I turned over the available evidence as it would have to be presented to a stranger and as I should have to present it to the police.

What could we say with certainty as to the personality of the murderer? In the first place, he was a person who had access to the studio. Then he knew how to prepare and fire the kiln. He understood the use and management of the grog mill and of the cupel press, and he knew which of the various bins was the bone-ash-bin. But, so far as I knew, there was only one person in the world to whom this description would apply – Frederick Boles.

Then, to approach the question from the other direction, were there any reasons for suspecting Boles? And the answer was that there were several reasons. Boles had certainly been at the house when Gannet was there alone, and had thus had the opportunity. He had now unaccountably disappeared, and his disappearance seemed to coincide with the date of the murder. He had already, to my certain knowledge, violently assaulted Gannet on at least one occasion. But far more to the point was the fact that he was under the deepest suspicion of having made a most determined attempt to kill Gannet by means of poison. Indeed, the word "suspicion" was an understatement. It was nearly a certainty. Even the cautious Thorndyke had made no secret of his views as to the identity of the poisoner. It was at this stage of my reflections that I had what, I think, Americans call a "hunch" – a brain wave, or inspiration. Boles had made at least one attempt to poison poor Gannet. We suspected more than one attempt, but of the one I had practically no doubt. Now one of the odd peculiarities of the criminal mind is its strong tendency to repetition. The coiner, on coming out of prison, promptly returns to the coining industry. The burglar, the forger, the pickpocket, all tend to repeat their successes, or even their failures. So, too, the poisoner, foiled at a first attempt, tries again, not only by the same methods, but nearly always makes use of the same poison.

Now Boles had been alone in the house with Gannet. He had thus had the opportunity, and it might be assumed that he had the means. Was it possible that he might have made yet another attempt and succeeded? It was true that the appearances rather suggested violence, and that this would be, from the murderer's point of view, preferable to the relatively slow method of poisoning. Nevertheless, a really massive dose of arsenic, if it could be administered, would be fairly rapid in its effects, and after all, in the assumed circumstances, the time factor would not be so very important.

But there was another consideration. Supposing Boles had managed to administer a big, lethal dose of arsenic – would any trace of the poison be detectible in the incinerated remains of the body? It seemed doubtful, though I had no experience by which to form an opinion. But it was certainly worthwhile to try, for if the result of the trial should be negative, no harm would have been done, whereas if the smallest trace of arsenic should be discoverable, demonstrable evidence of the highest importance would have been secured.

I have mentioned that, since the poisoning incident, I had taken various measures to provide against any similar case in the future, and among other precautions, I had furnished myself with a very complete apparatus for the detection of arsenic. It included the appliances for Marsh's Test – not the simple and artless affair that is used for demonstration in chemistry classes, but a really up-to-date apparatus, capable of the greatest delicacy and precision. And as a further precaution, I had made several trial analyses with it to make sure that, should the occasion arise, I could rely on my competence to use it.

And now the occasion had arisen. It was not a very promising one, as the probability of a positive result seemed rather remote. But I entered into the investigation with an enthusiasm that accelerated considerably my disposal of the rest of my dinner, and as soon as I had swallowed the last mouthful, I rose and proceeded forthwith to the dispensary which served also as a laboratory. Here I produced from my pocket the match box containing the finger bone and the parcel of crushed fragments from the bin. The match box I opened and tenderly transferred the little bone to a corked glass tube with a plug of cotton wool above and below it, and put the tube away in a locked drawer. Then I opened the parcel of fragments and embarked on the investigation.

I began by examining one or two of the fragments with a low power of the microscope and thereby confirming beyond all doubt my assumption that they were incinerated bone, and having disposed of this essential preliminary, I fell to work on the chemical part of the investigation. With the details of these operations – which, to tell the truth, I found rather tedious and troublesome – I need not burden the reader. Roughly, and in bare outline, the procedure was as follows: First, I divided the heap of fragments into two parts, reserving one part for further treatment if necessary. The other part I dissolved in strong hydrochloric acid and distilled the mixture into a receiver containing a small quantity of distilled water, a slow and tedious business which tried my patience severely, and which was, after all, only a preliminary to the actual analysis. But at last, the fluid in the retort dwindled to a little half-dry residue, whereupon I removed the lamp and transferred my attention to the Marsh's apparatus. With this I made the usual preliminary trial to test the purity of the reagents, and then set the lamp under the hard glass exit tube, watching it for several minutes after it had reached a bright red heat. As there was no sign of any darkening or deposit in the tube, I was satisfied that my chemicals were free from arsenic – as indeed I knew them to be from previous trials.

And now came the actual test. Detaching the receiver from the retort, I emptied its contents – the distilled fluid – into a well-washed measure glass and from this poured it slowly, almost drop by drop, into the thistle funnel of the flask in which the gas was generating. I had no expectation of any result – at least, so I persuaded myself. Nevertheless, as I poured in the "distillate", I watched the exit tube with almost tremulous eagerness. For it was my first real analysis, and after all the trouble that I had taken, a completely negative result would have seemed rather an anticlimax. Hence the yearning and half-expectant eye that turned ever towards the exit tube.

Nevertheless, the result, when it began to appear, fairly astonished me. It was beyond my wildest hopes. For even before I had finished pouring in the distillate, a dark ring appeared on the inside of the glass exit tube, just beyond the red hot portion, and grew from moment to moment in intensity and extent until a considerable area of the tube was covered with a typical "arsenic mirror." I sat down before the apparatus and watched it ecstatically, moved not only by the natural triumph of the tyro who has "brought it off" at the first trial, but by satisfaction at the thought that I had forged an instrument to put into the hands of avenging justice.

For now the cause of poor Gannet's death was established beyond cavil. My original surmise was proved to be correct. By some means, the murderer had contrived to administer a dose of arsenic so enormous as to produce an immediately fatal result. It must have been so. The quantity of the poison in the body must have been prodigious, for even after the considerable loss of arsenic in the kiln, there remained in the ashes a measurable amount, though how much I had not sufficient experience to judge.

I carried the analysis no farther. The customary procedure is to cut off the piece of tube containing the "mirror" of metallic arsenic and subject it to a further, confirmatory test. But this I considered unnecessary and, in fact, undesirable. Instead. I carefully detached the tube from the flask and, having wrapped it in several layers of paper, packed it in a cardboard postal tube and put it away with the finger bone in readiness for my interview with the police on the morrow.

Chapter IX
Inspector Blandy Investigates

On the following morning, as soon as I had disposed of the more urgent visits, I collected the proceeds of my investigations – the finger bone, the remainder of the bone fragments, and the glass tube with the arsenic mirror – and bustled off to the police station, all agog to spring my mine and set the machinery of the law in motion. My entry was acknowledged by the sergeant, who was perched at his desk, with an affable smile and the inquiry as to what he could do for me.

"I wanted rather particularly to see the Superintendent, if he could spare me a few minutes," I replied.

"I doubt whether he could," said the sergeant. "He's pretty busy just now. Couldn't I manage your business for you?"

"I think I had better see the Superintendent," I answered. "The matter is one of some urgency and I don't know how far it might be considered confidential. I think I ought to make my communication to him, in the first place."

"Sounds mighty mysterious," said the sergeant, regarding me critically. "However, we'll see what he says. Go in, Dawson, and tell the Superintendent that Dr. Oldfield wants to speak to him and that he won't say what his business is."

On this, the constable proceeded to the door of the inner office, on which he knocked and, having been bidden in a loud, impatient voice to "Come in," went in. After a brief delay, occupied probably by explanations, he reappeared, followed by the Superintendent, carrying in one hand a large note-book and in the other a pencil. His expression was not genial, but rather irritably interrogative, conveying the question, "Now, then. What about it?" And in effect, that was also conveyed by his rather short greeting.

"I should like to have a few words with you, Superintendent," I said, humbly.

"Well," he replied, "they will have to be very few. I am in the middle of a conference with an officer from Scotland Yard. What is the nature of your business?"

"I have come to inform you that I have reason to believe that a murder has been committed," I replied.

He brightened up considerably at this, but still he accepted the sensational statement with disappointing coolness.

"Do you mean that you think, or suspect, that a murder has been committed?" he asked in an obviously sceptical tone.

"It is more than that," I replied. "I am practically certain. I came to give you the facts that are known to me, and I have brought some things to show you which I think you will find pretty convincing."

He reflected for a moment, then, still a little irritably, he said, "Very well. You had better come in and let us hear what you have to tell us."

With this, he indicated the open door, and when I had passed through, he followed me and closed it after us.

As I entered the office, I was confronted by a gentleman who was seated at the table with a number of papers before him. A rather remarkable-looking gentleman, slightly bald, with a long, placid face and a still longer and acutely pointed nose, and an expression in which concentrated benevolence beamed on an undeserving world. I don't know what his appearance suggested, but it certainly did not suggest a detective inspector of the Criminal Investigation Department. Yet that was his actual status, as appeared when the Superintendent introduced him to me – by the name of Blandy – adding, "This is Dr. Oldfield, who has come to give us some information about a case of suspected murder."

"How good of him!" exclaimed Inspector Blandy, rising to execute a deferential bow and beaming a benediction on me as he pressed my hand with affectionate warmth. "I am proud, sir, to make your acquaintance. I am always proud to make the acquaintance of members of your learned and invaluable profession."

The Superintendent smiled sourly and offered me a chair.

"I suppose, Inspector," said he, "we had better adjourn our other business and take the doctor's information?"

"Surely, surely," replied Blandy. "A capital crime must needs take precedence. And as the doctor's time is even more valuable than ours, we can rely on him to economize both."

Accordingly, the Superintendent, with a distinct return to the "What about it?" expression, directed me shortly to proceed, which I did, and bearing in mind the inspector's polite hint, I plunged into the matter without preamble.

I need not record my statement in detail since it was but a repetition, suitably condensed, of the story that I have already told. I began with the disappearance of Peter Gannet, went on to my search of the house (to which the Superintendent listened with undissembled impatience) and then to my examination of the studio and my discoveries therein, producing the finger bone and the packet of fragments in corroboration. To the latter part of my statement both officers listened with evidently aroused interest, asking only such questions as were necessary to

112

elucidate the narrative – as, for instance, how I came to know so much about the kiln and Gannet's method of work.

At the conclusion of this part of my statement, I paused while the two officers pored over the little bone in its glass container and the open package of white, coral-like fragments. Then I prepared to play my trump card. Taking off the paper wrapping from the cardboard case, I drew out from the latter the glass tube and laid it on the table.

The Superintendent glared at it suspiciously while the inspector picked it up and regarded it with deep and benevolent interest.

"To my untutored eye," said he, "this dark ring seems to resemble an arsenic mirror."

"It is an arsenic mirror," said I.

"And what is its connection with these burnt remains?" the Superintendent demanded.

"That arsenic," I replied, impressively, "was extracted from a quantity of bone fragments similar to those that I have handed to you." And with this, I proceeded to give them an account of my investigations with the Marsh's apparatus, to which the Superintendent listened with open incredulity.

"But," he demanded, when I had finished, "what on earth led you to test these ashes for arsenic? What suggested to you that there might be arsenic in them?"

Of course, I had expected this question, but yet, curiously enough, I was hardly ready for it. The secret of the poisoning had been communicated to Gannet, but otherwise I had, on Thorndyke's advice, kept my own counsel. But now this was impossible. There was nothing for it but to give the officers a full account of the poisoning affair, including the fact that the discovery had been made and confirmed by Dr. Thorndyke.

At the mention of my teacher's name, both men pricked up their ears, and the Superintendent commented, "Then Dr. Thorndyke would be available as a witness."

"Yes," I replied, "I don't suppose he would have any objection to giving evidence on the natter."

"Objection be blowed!" snorted the Superintendent, "He wouldn't be asked. He could be subpoenaed as a common witness to the fact that this man, Gannet, was suffering from arsenic poisoning. However, before we begin to talk of evidence, we have got to be sure that there is something like a *prima facie* case. What do you think, Inspector?"

"I agree with you, Superintendent, as I always do," the inspector replied. "We had better begin by checking the doctor's observations on the state of affairs in Gannet's studio. If we find the conditions to be as

113

he has described them – which I have no doubt that we shall – and if we reach the same conclusions that he has reached, there will certainly be a case for investigation."

"Yes," the Superintendent agreed. "But our conclusions on the primary facts would have to be checked by suitable experts, and I suppose an independent analysis would be desirable. The doctor's evidence is good enough, but counsel likes to produce a specialist with a name and a reputation."

"Very true," said the inspector. "But the analysis can wait. It is quite possible that the arsenic issue may never be raised. If we find clear evidence that a human body has been burned to ashes in that kiln, we shall have the very strongest presumptive evidence that a murder has been committed. The method used doesn't really concern us, and an attempt to prove that the deceased was killed in some particular manner might only confuse and complicate the case."

"I was thinking," said the Superintendent, "of what the doctor has told us about the attempt to poison Gannet. The presence of arsenic in the bones might point to certain possible suspects, considered in connection with that previous attempt."

"Undoubtedly," agreed the inspector, "if we could prove who administered that arsenic. But we can't. And if Gannet is dead, I don't see how we are going to, he being the only really competent witness. No, Superintendent. My feeling is that we shall be wise to ignore the arsenic, or at any rate keep it up our sleeves for the present. But to come back to the immediate business, we want to see that studio, Doctor. How can it be managed without making a fuss?"

"Quite easily," I replied. "I have the keys, and I have Mrs. Gannet's permission to enter the house and to admit you, if you want to inspect the premises. I could hand you the keys if necessary, but I would much rather admit you myself."

"And very proper, too," said the inspector. "Besides, we should want you to accompany us, as you know all about the studio and we don't. Now when could you manage the personally conducted exploration? The sooner the better, you know, as the matter is rather urgent."

"Well," I replied, "I have got several visits to make, and it is about time that I started to make them. It won't do for me to neglect my practice."

"Of course it won't," the inspector agreed. "If duty calls you must away, and after all, a live patient is better than a dead potter. What time shall we say?"

"I think I shall be clear by four o'clock. Will that do?"

"It will do for me," replied the inspector, glancing inquiringly at his brother officer, and as the latter agreed, it was arranged that they should call at my house at four o'clock and that we should proceed together to the studio.

As I rose to depart, my precious mirror tube – despised by Blandy but dear to me – caught my eye, and I proceeded unostentatiously to resume possession of it, remarking that I would take care of it in case it should ever be wanted. As neither officer made any objection, I returned it to its case, and the packet of bone ash having served its purpose, I closed it and slipped it into my pocket with the tube.

On leaving the police station, I glanced rapidly through the entries in my visiting list and, having planned out a convenient route, started on my round, endeavouring – none too successfully – to banish from my mind all thoughts of the Gannet mystery that I might better concentrate my attention on the clinical problems that my patients presented. But if I suffered some distraction from my proper business, there was compensation in the matter of speed, for I dispatched my round of visits in record time, and even after a leisurely lunch, found myself with half-an-hour to spare before my visitors were due to arrive. This half-hour I spent with my hat on, pacing my consulting room in an agony of apprehension lest an inopportune professional call should hinder me from keeping my appointment. But fortunately no message came, and punctually at four o'clock Inspector Blandy was announced and conducted me to a large roomy car which was drawn up outside the house.

"The Superintendent couldn't come," Blandy explained, as he ushered me into the car. "But it doesn't matter. This is not a case for the local police. If there is anything in it, the C.I.D. will have to carry out the investigation."

"And what are you proposing to do now?" I asked.

"Just to check your report," he replied. "Personally, having seen you and noted your careful and exact methods, I accept it without any hesitation. But our people take nothing on hearsay if they can get observed facts, so I must be in a position to state those facts on my own knowledge and the evidence of my own eyesight – though as you and I know, my eyesight would have been of no use without yours."

I was beginning a modest disclaimer, suggesting that I was but an amateur investigator, but he would have none of it, exclaiming, "My dear Doctor, you undervalue yourself. The whole discovery is your own. Consider now what would have happened if I had looked into the studio as you did. What should I have seen? Nothing, my dear sir, nothing. My mere bodily senses would have perceived the visible objects but their significance would never have dawned on me. Whereas you, bringing an expert eye to bear on them, instantly detected the signs of some abnormal happenings. By the way, I am assuming that I am going to have the benefit of your co-operation and advice on this occasion."

I replied that I should be very pleased to stay for a time and help him (being, in fact, on the very tip-toe of curiosity as to his proceedings), on which he thanked me warmly, and was still thanking me when the car drew up opposite the Gannets' front door. We both alighted, Blandy lifting out a large, canvas covered suit-case, which he set down on the pavement while he stood taking a general view of the premises.

"Does that gate belong to Gannet's house?" he asked, indicating the wide, double-leaved studio door.

"Yes," I replied. "It opens directly into the studio. Would you like to go in that way? I have the key of the wicket."

"Not this time," said he. "We had better go in through the house so that I may see the lie of the premises."

Accordingly, I let him in by the front door and conducted him through the hall, where he looked about him inquisitively, giving special attention to the hat-rack and stand. Then I opened the side door and escorted him out into the yard, where again he inspected the premises and especially the walls and houses which enclosed the space. Presently he espied the rubbish-bin, and walking over to it, lifted its lid and looked thoughtfully into its interior.

"Is this domestic refuse?" he inquired, "or does it belong to the studio?"

"I think it is a general dump," I replied, "but I know that Gannet used it for ashes and anything that the dustmen would take away."

"Then," said he, "we had better take it in with us and look over the contents before the dustman has his innings."

As I had by this time got the studio door unlocked, we took the bin by its two handles and carried it in. Then, at the inspector's suggestion, I shut the door and locked it on the inside.

"Now, I suppose," said I, "you would like me to show you round the studio and explain the various appliances."

"Thank you, Doctor," he replied, "but I think we will postpone that, if it should be necessary after your singularly lucid description, and get on at once with the essential part of the inquiry."

"What is that?" I asked

"Our present purpose," he replied, beaming on me benevolently, "is to establish what the lawyers call the *corpus delicti:* To ascertain whether a crime has been committed, and if so, what sort of crime it is. We begin by finding out what those bone fragments really amount to. I have

116

brought a small sieve with me, but probably there is a better one here, preferably a fairly fine one."

"There is a set of sieves for sifting grog and other powders," said I. "The coarser ones are of wire gauze and the finer of bolting cloth, so you can take your choice. The number of meshes to the linear inch is marked on the rims."

I took him across to the place where the sieves were stacked and, when he had looked through the collection, he selected the finest of the wire sieves, which had twenty meshes to the inch. Then I found him a scoop, and when he had tipped the contents of one grog bin into another and placed the empty bin by the side of that containing the bone-ash, he spread out on the bench a sheet of white paper from his case, laid the sieve on the empty bin and fell to work.

For a time, the proceedings were quite uneventful, as the upper part of the bin was occupied by the finely-ground ash, and when a scoopful of this was thrown on to the sieve, it sank through at once. But presently, as the deeper layers were reached, larger fragments, recognizable as pieces of burnt bone, began to appear on the wire-gauze surface, and these, when he had tapped the sieve and shaken all the fine dust through, the inspector carefully tipped out on to the sheet of paper. Soon he had worked his way down completely past the deposit of fine powder, and now each scoopful consisted almost entirely of bone fragments, and as these lay on the gauze surface, Blandy bent over them, scrutinizing them with amiable intentness and shaking the sieve gently to spread them out more evenly.

"There can be no doubt," said he, as he ran his eye over a fresh scoopful thus spread out, "that these are fragments of bone, but it may be difficult to prove that they are human bones. I wish our unknown friend hadn't broken them up quite so small."

"You have the finger bone," I reminded him. "There's no doubt that that is human."

"Well," he agreed, "if you are prepared to swear positively that it is a human bone, that will establish a strong probability that the rest of the fragments are human. But we want proof if we can get it. In a capital case, the court isn't taking anything for granted."

Here he stooped closer over the sieve with his eyes riveted on one spot. Then very delicately with finger and thumb, he picked out a small object, and laying it on the palm of his other hand, held it out to me with a smile of concentrated benevolence. I took it from his palm, and placing it on my own, examined it closely, first with the naked eye and then with my pocket lens.

"And what is the diagnosis?" he asked, as I returned it to him.

117

"It is a portion of a porcelain tooth," I replied. "A front tooth, I should say, but it is such a small piece that it is impossible to be sure. But it is certainly part of a porcelain tooth."

"Ha!" said he, "there is the advantage of expert advice and cooperation. It is pronounced authoritatively to be certainly a porcelain tooth. But as the lower animals do not, to the best of my knowledge and belief, ever wear porcelain teeth, we have corroborative evidence that these remains are human. That is a great step forward. But how far does it carry us? Can you suggest any particular application of the fact?"

"I can," said I. "It is known to me that Peter Gannet had a nearly complete upper dental plate. I saw it in a bowl when he was ill."

"Excellent!" the inspector exclaimed. "Peter Gannet wore porcelain teeth, and here is part of a porcelain tooth. The evidence grows. But if he wore a dental plate, he must have had a dentist. I suppose you cannot give that dentist a name?"

"It happens that I can. He is a Mr. Hawley of Wigmore Street!"

"Really, now," exclaimed the inspector, "you are positively spoiling me. You leave me nothing to do. I have only to ask for information and it is instantly supplied."

He laid the fragment of tooth tenderly on the corner of the sheet of paper and made an entry in his note-book of the dentist's address. Then, having tipped the contents of the sieve on to the paper, he brought up another scoopful of bone fragments and shook it out on the gauze surface.

I need not follow the proceedings in detail. Gradually we worked our way through the entire contents of the bone-ash-bin, finishing up by holding the bin itself upside down over the sieve and shaking out the last grains. The net result was a considerable heap of bone fragments on the sheet of paper and no less than four other pieces of porcelain. As to the former, they were for the most part, mere crumbs of incinerated bone with just a sprinkling of lumps large enough to have some recognizable character. But the fragments of porcelain were more informative, for close examination and a few tentative trials at fitting them together left little doubt that they were all parts of the same tooth.

"But we won't leave it at that," said Blandy, as he dropped them one by one into a glass tube that he produced from his case. "We've got a man at Headquarters who is an expert at mending up broken articles. He'll be able to cement these pieces together so that the joins will hardly be visible. Then I'll take the tooth along to Mr. Hawley and see what he has to say to it."

He slipped the tube into his pocket and then, having produced from his case a large linen bag, shovelled the bone fragments into it, tied up its mouth and stowed it away in the case.

"This stuff," he remarked, "will have to be produced at the inquest, if we can identify it definitely enough to make an inquest possible. But I shall go over it again, a teaspoonful at a time, to make sure that we haven't missed anything, and then it will be passed to the Home Office experts. If they decide that the remains are certainly human remains, we shall notify the coroner."

While he was speaking his eyes turned from one object to another, taking in all the various fittings of the studio, and finally his glance lighted on Boles's cupboard and there remained fixed.

"Do you happen to know what is in that cupboard?" he asked.

"I know that it belongs to Mr. Boles," I replied, "and I think he uses it to keep his materials in."

"What are his materials?" the inspector asked.

"Principally gold and silver – especially gold. But he keeps some of his enamel material there and the copper plates for his plaques."

The inspector walked over to the cupboard and examined the keyhole narrowly.

"It isn't much of a lock," he remarked, "for a repository of precious metals. Looks like a common ward lock that almost any key would open. I think you said that Mr. Boles is not available at the moment?"

"I understand from Mrs. Gannet that he has disappeared from his flat and that no one knows where he is."

"Pity," said Blandy. "I hate the idea of opening that cupboard in his absence, but we ought to know what is in it. And, as I have a search warrant, it is my duty to search. Hmm! I happen to have one or two keys in my case. Perhaps one of them might fit this very simple lock."

He opened his case and produced from it a bunch of keys, and very odd-looking keys they were, so much so that I ventured to inquire, "Are those what are known as skeleton keys?"

He beamed on me with a slightly deprecating expression.

"The word 'skeleton'," said he, "as applied to keys, has disagreeable associations. I would rather call these 'simplified keys', just ordinary ward keys without wards. You will see how they act."

He illustrated their function by trying them one after another on the keyhole. At the third trial the key entered the hole, whereupon he gave it a turn and the door came open.

"There, you see," said he. "We break nothing, and when we go away we leave the cupboard locked as we found it."

The opened door revealed one or two shelves on which were glass pots of the powdered enamels, an agate mortar, and a few small tools. Below the shelves were several small but deep drawers. The inspector pulled out one of these and looked inquisitively into it as he weighed it critically in his hand.

"Queer-looking stuff, this, Doctor," said he, "and just feel the weight of it. All these lumps of gold in a practically unlocked cupboard. Are these the things that Mr. Boles makes?"

As he spoke he turned the drawer upside down on the paper that still covered the bench and pointed contemptuously to the heap of pendants, rings, and brooches that dropped out of it.

"Did you ever see such stuff?" he exclaimed. "Jewelry, indeed! Why, it might have been made by a plumber's apprentice. And look at the quantity of metal in it. Look at that ring. There's enough gold in it to make a bracelet. This stuff reminds me of the jewelry that the savages produce, only it isn't nearly so well made. I wonder who buys it. Do you happen to know?"

"I have heard," I replied, "that Mr. Boles exhibits it at some of the private galleries, and I suppose some of it gets sold. It must, you know, or he wouldn't go on making it."

Inspector Blandy regarded me with a rather curious, cryptic smile, but he made no rejoinder. He simply shot "the stuff" back into the drawer, replaced the latter, and drew out the next.

The contents of this seemed to interest him profoundly, for he looked into the drawer with an expression of amiable satisfaction and seemed to meditate on what he saw as if it conveyed some new idea to him. At length he tipped the contents out on to the paper and smilingly invited me to make any observations that occurred to me. I looked at the miscellaneous heap of rings, brooches, lockets, and other trinkets and noted that they seemed to resemble the ordinary jewelry that one sees in shop windows, excepting that the stones were missing.

"I don't think Mr. Boles made any of these," said I.

"I am quite sure he didn't," said Blandy, "but I think he took the stones out. But what do you make of this collection?"

"I should guess," I replied, "that it is old jewelry that he bought cheap to melt down for his own work."

"Yes," agreed Blandy, "he bought it to melt down and work up again. But he didn't buy it cheap if he bought from the trade. You can't buy gold cheap in the open market. Gold is gold, whether old or new. It has its standard price per ounce and you can't get it any cheaper, and you can always sell it at that price. I am speaking of the open market."

120

Once more he regarded me with that curious, inscrutable smile, and then, sweeping the jewelry back into its drawer, he passed on to the next.

This drawer contained raw material proper: Little ingots of gold, buttons from cupels or crucibles, and a few pieces of thin gold plate. It did not appear to me to present any features of interest, but evidently Blandy thought otherwise, for he peered into the drawer with a queer, benevolent smile for quite a considerable time. And he did not tip out its contents on to the bench. Instead, he took a pair of narrow-nosed pliers from one of the shelves and with these he delicately picked out the pieces of gold plate, and having examined them on both sides, laid them carefully on the paper.

"You seem to be greatly interested in those bits of plate," I remarked.

"I am," he replied. "There are two points of interest in them. First there is the fact that they are pieces of gold plate such as are supplied to the trade by bullion dealers. That goes to show that he bought some of his gold from the dealers in the regular way. He didn't get it all second hand. The other point is this."

He picked up one of the pieces of plate with the pliers and exhibited it to me, and I then observed that its polished surface was marked with the impression of a slightly greasy finger.

"You mean that finger-print?" I suggested.

"Thumb-print," he corrected, "apparently a left thumb, and on the other side, the print of a forefinger. Both beautifully clear and distinct, as they usually are on polished metal."

"Yes," said I, "they are clear enough. But what about it? They are Mr. Boles's finger-prints. But this is Mr. Boles's cupboard. We knew that he had used it and that he had frequented this studio. I don't see that the finger-prints tell you anything that you didn't know."

The inspector smiled at me, indulgently. "It is remarkable," said he, "how the scientific mind instantly seizes the essentials. But there is a little point that I think you have missed. We find that Mr. Boles is a purchaser of second-hand jewelry. Now, in the Finger-print Department we have records of quite a number of gentlemen who are purchasers of second-hand jewelry. Of course, it is quite incredible that Mr. Boles's finger-prints should be among them. But the scientific mind will realize that proof is better than belief. The finger-print experts will be able to supply the proof."

The hint thus delicately expressed conveyed a new idea to me and caused me to look with rather different eyes on the contents of the next, and last, drawer. These consisted of three small cardboard boxes, which, being opened, were found to contain unmounted stones. One was nearly half-filled with the less precious kinds – moonstones, turquoises, garnets, agates, carnelians and the like. The second held a smaller number of definitely precious stones such as rubies, sapphires, and emeralds, while the third contained only diamonds, mostly quite small. The inspector's comments expressed only the thought which had instantly occurred to me.

"These stones," said he, "must have been picked out of the secondhand stuff. I shouldn't think he ever buys any stones from the dealers, for only two of his pieces are set with gems, and those only with moonstone and carnelian. He doesn't seem to use stones often – too much trouble, easier to stick on a blob of enamel. So he must sell them. I wonder who buys them from him."

I could offer no suggestion on this point, and the inspector did not pursue the subject. Apparently the examination was finished, for he began to pack up the various objects that we had found in the drawers, bestowing especial care on the pieces of gold plate.

"As Mr. Boles seems to have disappeared," said he, "I shall take these goods into my custody. They are too valuable to leave in an unoccupied studio. And I must take temporary possession of these premises, as we may have to make some further investigations. We haven't examined the dust-bin yet, and it is too late to do it now. In fact, it is time to go. And what about the key, Doctor? I shall seal these doors before I leave – the wicket on the inside and the yard door on the outside – and the place will have to be watched. I should take it as a favour if you would let me have the key so that I need not trouble Mrs. Gannet. You won't be using it yourself."

As I saw that he meant to have it, and as it was of no further use to me, I handed it to him, together with the spare key of the wicket, on which he thanked me profusely and made ready to depart.

"Before we go," said he, "I will just make a note of Mrs. Gannet's present address in case we have to communicate with her, and you may as well give me Mr. Boles's, too. We shall have to get into touch with him, if possible."

I gave him both addresses, rather reluctantly as to the former, for I suspected that Mrs. Gannet was going to suffer some shocks. But there was no help for it. The police would have to communicate with her if only to acquaint her with the fact of her husband's death. But I was sorry for her, little as I liked her and little as I approved of her relations with Boles.

When the inspector had locked, bolted, and sealed the wicket, he took up his case and we went into the yard, where he locked the door with the key that I had left in it, pocketed the latter, and sealed the door.

Then we went out to the car and, when the driver had put away his book and his cigarette, we started homeward and arrived at my premises just in time for my evening consultations.

Chapter X
Inspector Blandy
is Inquisitive

My forebodings concerning Mrs. Gannet were speedily and abundantly justified. On the morning of the third day after the search of the studio, an urgent note from Miss Hughes, delivered by hand, informed me that her guest had sustained a severe shock and was in a state of complete nervous prostration. She had expressed a wish to see me and Miss Hughes hoped that I would call as soon as possible.

As the interview promised to be a somewhat lengthy one, I decided to dispose of the other patients on my modest visiting list and leave myself ample time for a leisurely talk, apart from the professional consultation. As a result, it was well past noon when I rang the bell at the house in Mornington Crescent. The door was opened by Miss Hughes herself, from whom I received forthwith the first instalment of the news.

"She is in an awful state, poor thing," said Miss Hughes. "Naturally, she was a good deal upset by her husband's extraordinary disappearance. But yesterday a gentleman called to see her – a police officer he turned out to be, though you'd never have suspected it to look at him. I don't know what he told her – it seems that she was sworn to secrecy – but he stayed a long time, and when he had gone and I went into the sitting room, I found her lying on the sofa in a state of collapse. But I mustn't keep you here talking. I made her stay in bed until you'd seen her, so I will take you up to her room."

Miss Hughes had not overstated the case. I should hardly have recognized the haggard, white-faced woman in the bed as the sprightly lady whom I had known. As I looked at her pallid, frightened face, turned so appealingly to me, all my distaste of her – it was hardly dislike – melted away in natural compassion for her obvious misery.

"Have you heard of the awful thing that has happened. Doctor?" she whispered when Miss Hughes had gone, discreetly shutting the door after her. "I mean what the police found in the studio."

"Yes, I know about that," I replied, not a little relieved to find that my name had not been mentioned in connection with the discovery. "I suppose that the officer who called on you was Inspector Blandy?"

"Yes, that was the name, and I must say that he was most polite and sympathetic. He broke the horrible news as gently as he could and told me how sorry he was to be the bearer of such bad tidings, and he did seem to be genuinely sorry for me. I only wished he would have left it at that. But he didn't. He stayed ever so long, telling me over and over again how sincerely he sympathized with me, and then asking questions – dozens of questions he asked until I got quite hysterical. I think he might have given me a day or two to recover a little before putting me through such a catechism."

"It does seem rather inconsiderate," said I, "but you must make allowances. The police have to act promptly and they naturally want to get at the facts as quickly as possible."

"Yes. That is the excuse he made for asking so many questions. But it was an awful ordeal. And although he was so polite and sympathetic, I couldn't help feeling that he suspected me of knowing more about the affair than I admitted. Of course he didn't say anything to that effect."

"I think that must have been your imagination," said I. "He couldn't have suspected you of any knowledge of the – er – the tragedy, seeing that you were away from home when it happened."

"Perhaps not," said she. "Still, he questioned me particularly about my movements while I was away and wanted all the dates – which, of course, I couldn't remember off-hand. And then he asked a lot of questions about Mr. Boles, particularly as to where he was on certain dates, and somehow he gave the impression that he knew a good deal about him."

"What sort of questions did he put about Mr. Boles?" I asked with some curiosity, recalling Blandy's cryptic reference to the finger-print files at Scotland Yard.

"It began with his asking me whether the two men, Peter and Fred, were usually on good terms. Well, as you know, Doctor, they were not. Then he asked me if they had always been on bad terms, and when I told him that they used to be quite good friends, he wanted to know exactly when the change in their relationship occurred and whether I could account for it in any way. I told him, quite truthfully, that I could not, and as to the time when they first fell out, I could only say that it was some time in the latter part of last year. Then he began to question me about Mr. Boles's movements – where he was on this and that date – and of course, I couldn't remember, if I had ever known. But his last question about dates I was able to answer. He asked me to try to remember where Mr. Boles was on the 19th of last September. I thought about it a little and then I remembered, because Peter had gone to spend a long week-end with him and I had taken the opportunity to make a visit to Eastbourne. As I was at Eastbourne on the 19th of September, I knew that Peter and Mr. Boles must have been at Newingstead on that date."

"Newingstead!" I exclaimed, and then stopped short.

"Yes," said she, looking at me in surprise. "Do you know the place?"

"I know it slightly," I replied, drawing in my horns rather suddenly as the finger-print files came once more into my mind. "I happen to know a doctor who is in practice there."

"Well, Mr. Blandy seemed to be very much interested in Mr. Boles's visit to Newingstead, and particularly with the fact that Peter was there with him on that day, and he pressed me to try to remember whether that date seemed to coincide with the change in their feelings to each other. It was an extraordinary question. I can't imagine what could have put the idea into his head. But when I came to think about it, I found that he was right, for I remember quite clearly that when I came back from Eastbourne I saw at once that there was something wrong. They weren't a bit the same. All the old friendliness seemed to have vanished and they were ready to quarrel on the slightest provocation. And they did quarrel dreadfully. I was terrified, for they were both strong men and both inclined to be violent."

"Did you ever get any inkling as to what it was that had set them against each other?"

"No. I suspected that something had happened when they were away together, but I could never find out what it was. I spoke to them both and asked them what was the matter, but I couldn't get anything out of either of them. They simply said that there was nothing the matter, that it was all my imagination. But I knew that it wasn't, and I was in a constant state of terror as to what might happen."

"So I suppose," said I, "that the – er – the murder has not come as a complete surprise?"

"Oh, don't call it a murder!" she protested. "It couldn't have been that. It must have been some sort of accident. When two strong and violent men start fighting, you never know how it will end. I am sure it must have been an accident – that is, supposing that it was Mr. Boles who killed Peter. We don't know that it was. It's only a guess."

I thought that it was pretty safe guess but I did not say so. My immediate concern was with the future, for Mrs. Gannet was my patient and I chose to regard her as my friend. She had been subjected to an intolerable strain, and I suspected that there was worse to come. The question was: What was to be done about it?

"Did the inspector suggest that he would require any further information from you?" I asked.

"Yes. He said that he would want me to come to his office at Scotland Yard one day pretty soon to make a statement and sign it. That will be an awful ordeal. It makes me sick with terror to think of it."

"I don't see why it should," said I. "You are not in any way responsible for what has happened."

"You know that I am not," said she, "but the police don't, and I am absolutely terrified of Mr. Blandy. He is a most extraordinary man. He is so polite and sympathetic, and yet so keen and searching, and he asks such unexpected questions and seems to have such uncanny knowledge of our affairs. And as I told you, I am sure he suspects that I had something to do with what has happened."

"I suppose he didn't seem to know anything about that mysterious affair of the arsenic poisoning?" I suggested.

"No," she replied, "but I am certain that he will worm it out of me when he has me in his office, and then he will think that it was I who put the poison into poor Peter's food."

At this point she broke down and burst into tears, sobbing hysterically and mingling incoherent apologies with her sobs. I tried to comfort her as well as I could, assuring her – with perfect sincerity – of my deep sympathy, for I realized that her fears were by no means unfounded. She probably had more secrets than I knew, and once within the dreaded office in the presence of a committee of detective officers, taking down in writing every word that she uttered, she might easily commit herself to some highly incriminating statements.

"It is a great comfort to me, Doctor," said she, struggling to control her emotion, "to be able to tell you all my troubles. You are the only friend that I have – the only friend, I mean, that I can look to for advice and help."

It wrung my heart to think of this poor, lonely woman in her trouble and bereavement, encompassed by perils at which I could only guess, facing those perils, friendless, alone and unprotected save by me – and who was I that I could give her any effective support? As I met the look of appeal that she cast on me, so pathetic and so confiding, it was borne in on me that she needed some more efficient adviser and that the need was urgent and ought to be met without delay.

"I am very willing," said I, "to help you, but I am not very competent. The advice that you want is legal, not medical. You ought to have a lawyer to protect your interests and to advise you."

"I suppose I ought," she agreed, "but I don't know any lawyers, and I trust in you because you know all about my affairs and because you have been such a kind friend. But I will do whatever you advise. Perhaps you know a lawyer whom you could recommend."

"The only lawyer whom I know is Dr. Thorndyke," I replied.

"Is he a lawyer?" she exclaimed in surprise. "I thought he was a doctor."

"He is both," I explained, "and what is more to the point, he is a criminal lawyer who knows all the ropes. He will understand your difficulties and also those of the police. Would you like me to see him and ask him to advise us?"

"I should be most grateful if you would," she replied, earnestly. "And you may take it that I agree to any arrangements that you may make with him. But," she added, "you will remember that my means are rather small."

I brushed this proviso aside in view of Thorndyke's known indifference to merely financial considerations and the fact that my own means admitted of my giving material assistance if necessary. So it was agreed that I should seek Thorndyke's advice forthwith and that whatever he might advise should be done.

"That will be a great relief," said she. "I shall have somebody to think for me, and that will leave me free to think about all that has to be done. There will be quite a lot of things to attend to. I can't stay here forever, though dear Miss Hughes protests that she loves having me. And then there are the things at the gallery. They will have to be removed when the exhibition closes. And there are some pieces on loan at another place – but there is no hurry about them."

"What exhibition are you referring to?" I asked.

"The show at the Lyntondale Gallery in Bond Street. It is a mixed exhibition and some of Peter's work is being shown and a few pieces of Mr. Boles's. Whatever is left unsold will have to be fetched away at once to make room for the next show."

"And the other exhibition?" I asked, partly from curiosity and partly to keep her attention diverted from her troubles.

"That is a sort of small museum and art gallery at Haxton. They show loan collections there for the purpose of educating the taste of the people, and Peter has lent them some of his pottery on two or three occasions. This time he sent only a small collection – half-a-dozen bowls and jars and the stoneware figure that used to be on his bedroom mantelpiece. I daresay you remember it."

"I remember it very well," said I. "It was a figure of a monkey."

"Yes, that was what he called it, though it didn't look to me very much like a monkey. But then I don't understand much about art. At any rate, he sent it, and as he set a good deal of value on it, I took it myself and delivered it to the director of the museum."

As we talked, principally on topics not directly connected with the tragedy, her agitation subsided by degrees until, by the time when my visit had to end, she had become quite calm and composed.

128

"Now don't forget," said I, as I shook her hand at parting, "that you have nothing further to fear from Inspector Blandy. You are going to have a legal adviser, and he won't let anybody put undue pressure on you."

Her gratitude was quite embarrassing, and as she showed signs of a slight recrudescence of emotion, I withdrew my hand (which she was pressing fervently) at the first opportunity and bustled out of the room.

On my way home, I considered my next move. Obviously, no time ought to be lost in making the necessary arrangements. But although I had the afternoon free, Thorndyke probably had not. He was a busy man and it would be futile for me to make a casual call on the chance of finding him at home and disengaged. Accordingly, as soon as I had let myself in and ascertained that there were no further engagements, I rang him up on the telephone to inquire when I could have a few words with him. In reply, a voice, apparently appertaining to a person named Polton, informed me that the doctor was out, that he would be in at three-thirty and that he had an engagement elsewhere at four-fifteen. Thereupon I made an appointment to call at three-thirty, and having given my name, rang off and proceeded without delay to dispatch my immediate business, including the dispensing of medicine, the writing up of the Day Book, and the wash and brush-up preliminary to lunch.

As I had no clear idea of the geography of the Temple, I took the precaution of arriving at the main gate well in advance of the appointed time, with the result that having easily located King's Bench Walk, I found myself opposite the handsome brick portico of Number 5A at the very moment when a particularly soft-toned bell ventured most politely to suggest that it was a quarter-past-three.

There was, therefore, no need to hurry. I whiled away a few minutes inspecting the portico and surveying the pleasant surroundings of the dignified old houses – doubtless still more pleasant before the fine, spacious square had become converted into a parking lot. Then I entered and took my leisurely way up the stairs to the first floor landing, where I found myself confronted by a grim-looking, iron bound door, above which was painted the name "Dr. Thorndyke." I was about to press the electric bell at the side of the door when I perceived, descending the stairs from an upper floor, a gentleman who appeared to belong to the premises, a small gentleman of a sedate and even clerical aspect, but very lively and alert.

"Have I the honour, sir, of addressing Dr. Oldfield?" he inquired, suavely.

I replied that I was, in fact, Dr. Oldfield. "But," I added, "I think I am a little before my time."

Thereupon, like Touchstone, he "drew a dial from his poke". and regarding it thoughtfully (but by no means "with a lacklustre eye"), announced that it was now twenty-four minutes and fifteen seconds past three. While he was making his inspection I looked at the watch, which was a rather large silver timepiece with an audible and very deliberate tick, and as he was putting it away, I ventured to remark that it did not appear to be quite an ordinary watch.

"It is not, sir," he replied, hauling it out again and gazing at it fondly. "It is an eight-day pocket chronometer – a most admirable timepiece, sir, with the full chronometer movement and even a helical balance spring."

Here he opened the case and then, in some miraculous way, turned the whole thing inside out, exhibiting the large, heavy balance and an unusual-looking balance spring which I accepted as helical.

"You can't easily see the spring detent," said he, "but you can hear it, and you will notice that it beats half-seconds."

He held the watch up towards my ear and I was able to distinguish the peculiar sound of the escapement. But at this moment he also assumed a listening attitude, but he was not listening to the watch, for after a few moments of concentrated attention, he remarked, as he closed and put away the chronometer.

"You are not much too early, sir. I think I hear The Doctor coming along Crown Office Row and Dr. Jervis with him."

I listened attentively and was just able to make out the faint sound of quick footsteps which seemed to be approaching, but I had not my small friend's diagnostic powers, which, however, were demonstrated when the footsteps passed in at the entry, ascended the stairs and materialized into bodily forms of Thorndyke and Jervis. Both men looked at me a little curiously, but any questions were forestalled by my new acquaintance.

"Dr. Oldfield, sir, made an appointment by telephone to see you at half-past three. I told him of your engagement at four-fifteen."

"Thank you, Polton," said Thorndyke. "So now, Oldfield, as you know the position, let us go in and make the best use of the available half-hour – that is, if this is anything more than a friendly call."

"It is considerably more," said I, as Mr. Polton opened the two doors and ushered us into a large room. "I have come on quite urgent business, but I think we can dispatch it easily in half-an-hour."

Here, Mr. Polton, after an interrogative glance at Thorndyke, took himself off, closing after him both the inner and outer doors.

"Now, Oldfield," said Jervis, setting out three chairs in a triangle, "sit down and let the engine run."

Thereupon we all took our seats facing one another and I proceeded, without preamble, to give a highly-condensed account of the events connected with Gannet's disappearance with a less-condensed statement of Mrs. Gannet's position in relation to them. To this account Thorndyke listened with close attention, but quite impassively and without question or comment. Not so Jervis. He did, indeed, abstain from interruptions, but he followed my recital with devouring interest, and I had hardly finished when he burst out, "But, my good Oldfield, this is a first-class murder mystery! It is a sin to boil it down into a mere abstract. I want details, and more details and, in short – or rather, in long – the whole story."

"I am with you, Jervis," said Thorndyke. "We must get Oldfield to tell us the story *in extenso*. But not now. We have an immediate and rather urgent problem to solve: How to protect Mrs. Gannet."

"Does she need protecting?" demanded Jervis. "The English police are not in the habit of employing 'third degree' methods."

"True," Thorndyke agreed. "The English police have usually the desire and the intention to deal fairly with persons who have to be interrogated. But an over-zealous officer may easily be tempted to press his examination – in the interests of justice, as he thinks – beyond the limits of what is strictly admissible. We must remember that, under our system of police procedure in the matter of interrogation, the various restrictions tend to weight the dice rather against the police and in favour of the accused person."

"But Mrs. Gannet is not an accused person," I protested.

"No," Thorndyke agreed. "But she may become one, particularly if she should make any indiscreet admissions. That is what we have to guard against. We don't know what the views of the police are, but one notes that our rather foxy friend, Blandy, was not disposed to be over-scrupulous. To announce to a woman that her husband has been murdered and his body burned to ashes, and then, while she is still dazed by the shock, to subject her to a searching interrogation, does not impress one as a highly considerate proceeding. I think her fear of Blandy is justified. No further interrogation ought to take place excepting in the presence of her legal adviser."

"She isn't legally bound to submit to any interrogation until she is summoned as a witness," Jervis suggested.

"In practice, she is," said Thorndyke. "It would be highly improper for her to withhold from the police any assistance that she could give them. And it would be extremely impolitic, as it would suggest that she had something serious to conceal. But it would be perfectly proper for her to insist that her legal adviser should accompany her and be present at the interrogation. And that is what will have to be done. She will have to be legally represented. But by whom? Can you make any suggestion, Jervis? It is a solicitor's job."

"What about the costs?" asked Jervis. "Is the lady pretty well off?"

"We can waive that question," said I. "The costs will be met. I will make myself responsible for that."

"I see," said Jervis. "Your sympathy takes a practical form. Well, if you are going to back the bill, we must see that it doesn't get too obese. A swagger solicitor wouldn't do. Besides, he would be too busy to attend in person. But we should want a good man. Preferably a young man with a rather small practice. Yes, I think I know the very man. What do you say, Thorndyke, to young Linnell? He was Marchmont's managing clerk, but he has gone into practice on his own account and he has distinct leanings towards criminal work."

"I remember him," said Thorndyke. "A very promising young man. Could you get into touch with him?"

"I will see him today before he leaves his office, and I think there is no doubt that he will undertake the case gladly. At any rate, Oldfield, you can take it that the matter is in our hands and that the lady will be fully protected, even if I have to accompany her to Scotland Yard myself. But you must play your hand, too. You are her doctor, and it is for you to see that she is not subjected to any strain that she is not fit to bear. A suitable medical certificate will put the stopper even on Blandy."

As Jervis ceased speaking, the soft-voiced bell of the unseen clock, having gently chimed the quarters, now struck (if one may use so violent an expression) the hour of four. I rose from my chair and, having thanked both my friends profusely for their help, held out my hand.

"One moment, Oldfield," said Thorndyke. "You have tantalized us with a bare *précis* of the astonishing story that you have to tell. But we want the unabridged edition. When are we to have it? We realize that you are rather tied to your practice. But perhaps we could look in on you when you have some time to spare, say, one evening after dinner. How would that do?"

"Why after dinner?" I demanded. "Why not come and dine with me and do the pow-wow after?"

"That would be very pleasant," said Thorndyke. "Don't you agree, Jervis?"

Jervis agreed emphatically, and as it appeared that both my friends were free that very evening, it was settled that we should meet again at Osnaburgh Street and discuss the Gannet case at length.

"And remember," said I, pausing in the doorway, "that consultation hours are usually more or less blank, so you can come as early as you like."

With this parting admonition, I shut the door after me and went on my way.

Chapter XI
Mr. Bunderby Expounds

As I emerged from the Temple gateway into Fleet Street I was confronted by a stationary omnibus, held up temporarily by a block in the traffic, and glancing at it casually, my eye caught, among the names on its rear board, those of Piccadilly and Bond Street. The latter instantly associated itself with the gallery of which Mrs. Gannet had spoken that morning, and the effect of the association was to cause me to jump on to the omnibus just as it started to move. I had nearly two hours to spare, and in that time could easily inspect the exhibition of Gannet's work.

I was really quite curious about this show, for Gannet's productions had always been somewhat of a mystery to me. They were so amazingly crude and so deficient, as I thought, in any kind of ceramic quality. And yet I felt there must be something more in them than I had been able to discover. There must be some deficiency in my own powers of perception and appreciation, for it was a fact that they had not only been publicly exhibited but actually sold, and sold at quite impressive prices, and one felt that the people who paid those prices must surely know what they were about. At any rate, I should now see the pottery in its appropriate setting and perhaps hear some comments from those who were better able than I to form a judgment.

I had no difficulty in finding the Lyntondale Gallery, for a flag bearing its name hung out boldly from a first floor window, and when I had paid my shilling entrance fee and a further shilling for a catalogue, I passed in through the turnstile and was straightway spirited aloft in an elevator.

On entering the principal room of the gallery, I was aware of a knot of people – about a dozen – gathered before a large glass case and appearing to surround a stout, truculent-looking gentleman with a fine, rich complexion and a mop of white hair which stood up like the crest of a cockatoo. But my attention was more particularly attracted by another gentleman, who stood apart from the knot of visitors and appeared to be either the proprietor of the gallery or an attendant. What drew my attention to him was an indefinite something in his appearance that seemed familiar. I felt that I had seen him somewhere before. But I could not place him, and while I was trying to remember where I might have seen him, he caught my eye and approached with a deferential smile.

"You have arrived quite opportunely, sir," said he. "Mr. Bunderby, the eminent art critic, is just about to give us a little talk on the subject of Peter Gannet's very remarkable pottery. It will be worth your while to hear it. Mr. Bunderby's talks are always most illuminating."

I thanked him warmly for the information, for an illuminating talk on this subject by a recognized authority was precisely what I wanted to hear, and as the cockatoo gentleman – whom I diagnosed as Mr. Bunderby – had just opened a show case and transferred one of the pieces to a small revolving stand, like a modeler's turntable, I joined the group that surrounded him and prepared to "lend him my ears".

The piece that he had placed on the stand was one of Gannet's roughest, an uncouth vessel, in appearance something between a bird's nest and a flowerpot. I noticed that the visitors stared at it in obvious bewilderment and Mr. Bunderby watched their expressions with a satisfied smile.

"Before speaking to you," said he, "of these remarkable works, I must say just a few words about their creator. Peter Gannet is a unique artist. Whereas the potters of the past have striven after more and yet more sophistication, Gannet has perceived the great truth that pottery should be simple and elemental, and with wonderful courage and insight, he has set himself to retrace the path along which mankind has strayed, back to that fountainhead of culture, the New Stone Age. He has cast aside the potter's wheel and all other mechanical aids, and relies solely on that incomparable instrument, the skilled hand of the artist.

"So in these works, you must not look for mechanical accuracy or surface finish. Gannet is, first and foremost, a great stylist, who subordinates everything to the passionate pursuit of essential form. So much for the man. And now we will turn to the pottery."

He paused a few moments and stood with half-closed eyes and his head on one side, contemplating the bowl on the stand. Then he resumed his discourse.

"I begin," said he, "by showing you this noble and impressive work because it is typical of the great artist by whose genius it was created. It presents in a nutshell – " (He might have said a coconut shell.) " – the aims, the ambitions and the inmost thoughts and emotions of its maker. Looking at it, we realize with respectful admiration the wonderful power of analysis, the sensibility – at once subtle and intense – that made its conception possible, and we can trace the deep thought, the profound research – the untiring search for the essentials of abstract form."

Here a lady, who spoke with a slight American intonation, ventured to remark that she didn't quite understand this piece. Mr. Bunderby fixed her with his truculent blue eye and replied, impressively, "You don't

135

understand it! But of course you don't. And you shouldn't try to. A great work of art is not to be *understood*. It is to be *felt*. Art is not concerned with intellectual expositions. Those it leaves to science. It is the medium of emotional transfer whereby the soul of the artist conveys to kindred spirits the reactions of his own sensibility to the problems of abstract form."

Here another Philistine intervened with the objection that he was not quite clear as to what was meant by "abstract form".

"No," said Mr. Bunderby, "I appreciate your difficulty. Mere verbal language is a clumsy medium for the expression of those elusive qualities that are to be felt rather than described. How shall I explain myself? Perhaps it is impossible. But I will try.

"The words 'abstract form', then, evoke in me the conception of that essential, pervading, geometric sub-structure which persists when all the trivial and superficial accidents of mere visual appearances have been eliminated. In short, it is the fundamental *rhythm* which is the basic aesthetic factor underlying all our abstract conceptions of spatial limitation. Do I make myself clear?"

"Oh, perfectly, thank you," the Philistine replied, hastily, and forthwith retired deep into his shell and was heard no more.

I need not follow Mr. Bunderby's discourse in detail. The portion that I have quoted is a representative sample of the whole. As I listened to the sounding phrases with their constantly recurring references to "rhythm" and "essential abstract form", I was conscious of growing disappointment. All this nebulous verbiage conveyed nothing to me. I seemed merely to be listening to Peter Gannet at second hand (though probably it was the other way about – that I had, in the studio talks, been listening to Bunderby at second hand). At any rate, it told me nothing about the pottery, and so far from resolving my doubts and misgivings, left me only still more puzzled and bewildered.

But enlightenment was to come. It came, in fact, when the whole collection seemed to have been reviewed. There was an impressive pause while Mr. Bunderby passed his fingers through his crest, making it stand up another two inches, and glared at the empty stand.

"And now," said he, "as a final *bonne bouche*, I am going to show you another facet of Peter Gannet's genius. May we have the decorated jar, Mr. Kempster?"

As the name was uttered, my obscure recognition of the proprietor was instantly clarified. But close as his resemblance was to the diamond merchant of Newingstead, he was obviously not the same man. Indeed he could not have been. Nevertheless, I observed him with interest as he advanced with slow steps, treading delicately and holding the precious jar in both hands, as if it had been the Holy Grail or a live bomb. At length he placed it, with infinite care and tenderness, on the stand, slowly withdrew his hands, and stepped back a couple of paces, still gazing at it reverentially.

"There," said Bunderby, "look at that!"

They looked at it and so did I – with bulging eyes and mouth agape. It was amazing – incredible. And yet it was impossible that I could be mistaken. Every detail of it was familiar, including the marks of my own latch-key and the little dents made by the clinical thermometer. Eagerly I awaited Bunderby's exposition, and when it came it surpassed even my expectations.

"I have reserved this, the gem of the collection, to the last because, though at first glance it is different from the others, it is typical. It affords the perfect and unmistakable expression of Peter Gannet's artistic personality. Even more than the other, it testifies to the rigorous, single-minded search for essential form and abstract rhythm. It is the fine flower of hand-built pottery. And mark you, not only does its hand-built character leap to the eye (the expert eye, of course), but it is obvious that by no method but that of direct modelling by hand could it have been created.

"Then consider the ornament. Note this charming guilloche, executed with the most masterly freedom with the thumb-nail – just the simple thumb-nail, a crude instrument, you may say, but no other could produce exactly this effect, as the ancient potters knew."

He ran his finger lovingly over the mustard-spoon impressions and continued, "Then look at these lovely rosettes. They tell us that when the artist created them he had in his mind the idea of 'what o'clocks' – the dandelion head. Profoundly stylized as the form is, generalized from the representational plane to that of ultimate abstraction, we can still trace the thought."

As he paused, one of the spectators remarked that the rosettes seemed to have been executed with the end of a key.

"They do," Bunderby agreed, "and it is quite possible that they were. And why not? The genius asks for no special apparatus. He uses the simple means that lie to his hand. But that hand is the hand of a master which transmutes to gold the very clay that feels its touch.

"So it has done in this little masterpiece. It has produced what we feel to be a complete epitome of abstract three-dimensional form. And then the rhythm! The rhythm!"

He paused, having apparently exhausted his vocabulary (if such a thing were possible). Then suddenly he looked at his watch and started.

137

"Dear me!" he exclaimed. "How the time flies! I must be running away. I have four more galleries to inspect. Let me thank you for the courteous interest with which you have listened to my simple comments and express the hope that some of you may be able to secure an example of the work of a great and illustrious artist. I had intended to say a few words about Mr. Boles's exquisite neo-primitive jewelry, but my glass has run out. I wish you all good afternoon."

He bowed to the assembly and to Mr. Kempster and bustled away, and I noticed that with his retirement all interest in the alleged masterpieces seemed to lapse. The visitors strayed away to other parts of the gallery and the majority soon strayed towards the door.

Meanwhile, Mr. Kempster took possession of the jar and carried it reverently back to its case. I followed him with my eyes and then with the rest of my person. For, like Mr. Tite Barnacle (or, rather, his visitor), I "wanted to know, you know". I had noticed a red wafer stuck to the jar, and this served as an introduction.

"So the masterpiece is sold," said I. "Fifteen guineas, according to the catalogue. It seems a long price for a small jar."

"It does," he admitted. "But it is a museum piece, hand-built and by an acknowledged master."

"It looks rather different from most of Gannet's work. I suppose there is no doubt that it is really from his hand?"

Mr. Kempster was shocked. "Good gracious, no!" he replied. "He drew up the catalogue himself. Besides – "

He picked up the jar quickly – No Holy Grail touch this time! – and turned it up to exhibit the bottom.

"You see," said he, "the piece is signed and numbered. There is no question as to its being Gannet's work."

If the inference was erroneous, the fact was correct. On the bottom of the jar was Gannet's distinctive mark, a sketchy gannet, the letters "P. G." with the number, *Op. 961*. That disposed of the possibility which had occurred to me that the jar might have been put among Gannet's own works by mistake, possibly by Mrs. Gannet. The fraud had evidently been deliberate.

As he replaced the jar on its shelf, I ventured to indulge my curiosity on another point.

"I heard Mr. Bunderby mention your name. Do you happen to be related to Mr. Kempster of Newingstead?"

"My brother," he replied. "You noticed the likeness, I suppose. Do you know him?"

"Very slightly. But I was down there at the time of the robbery, in fact. I had to give evidence at the inquest on the unfortunate policeman. It was I who found him by the wood."

"Ah, then you will be Dr. Oldfield. I read the report of the inquest and, of course, heard all about it from my brother. It was a disastrous affair. It appears that the diamonds were not covered by insurance, and I am afraid that it looks like a total loss. The diamonds are hardly likely to be recovered now. They are probably dispersed, and it would be difficult to identify them singly."

"I was sorry," said I, "to miss Mr. Bunderby's observations on Mr. Boles's jewelry. It seems to me to need some explaining."

"Yes," he admitted, "it isn't to everybody's taste. My brother, for instance, won't have it at any price, though he knows Mr. Boles and rather likes him. And speaking of Newingstead, it happens that Mr. Boles is a native of that place."

"Indeed. Then I suppose that is how your brother came to know him?"

"I can't say, but I rather think not. Probably he made the acquaintance through business channels. I know that he has had some dealings – quite small transactions – with Mr. Boles."

"But surely," I exclaimed, "Mr. Boles doesn't ever use diamonds in his neolithic jewelry?"

"Neo-primitive," he corrected with a smile. "No, I should think he was a vendor rather than a buyer, or he may have made exchanges. Like most jewelers, Mr. Boles picks up oddments of old or damaged jewelry, when he can get it cheap, to use as scrap. Any diamonds or faceted stones would be useless to him as he uses only simple stones, cabochon cut, and not many of those. But that is only a surmise based on remarks that Mr. Boles has let fall. I don't really know much about his affairs."

At this moment I happened to glance at a clock at the end of the gallery, and to my dismay saw that it stood at ten minutes to six. With a few words of apology and farewell, I rushed out of the gallery, clattered down the stairs and darted out into the street. Fortunately, an unoccupied taxi was drifting towards me and slowed down as I hailed it. In a moment I had given my address, scrambled in, and slammed the door, and was moving on at a pace that bid fair to get me home within a minute or two of six.

The short journey gave me little time for reflection. Yet in those few minutes I was able to consider the significance of my recent experiences sufficiently to be conscious of deep regret and disillusionment. Of the dead, one would wish not only to speak but to think nothing but good, and though Peter Gannet had been more an acquaintance than a friend, and one for whom I had entertained no special regard, I was troubled that I could no longer even pretend to think of him with respect. For the doubts that I had felt and tried to banish were doubts no longer. The bubble was pricked. Now I knew that his high pretensions were mere clap-trap, his "works of art" a rank imposture.

But even worse than this was the affair of "the decorated jar". To pass off as his own work a piece that had been made by another – though that other were but an incompetent beginner – was unspeakably shabby. To offer it for sale was sheer dishonesty. Not that I grudged the fifteen guineas, since they would benefit poor Mrs. Gannet, nor did I commiserate the "mug" who had paid that preposterous price. Probably, he deserved all he got – or lost. But it irked me to think that Gannet, whom I had assumed to be a gentleman, was no more than a common rogue.

As to Bunderby: Obviously, he was an arrant quack. An ignoramus, too, if he really believed my jar to have been hand-built, for a glance at its interior would have shown the most blatant traces of the wheel. But at this point my meditations were interrupted by the stopping of the taxi opposite my house. I hopped out, paid the driver, fished out my latch-key, and had it in the keyhole at the very moment when the first – and, as it turned out, also the last – of the evening's patients arrived on the door-step.

Chapter XII
A Symposium

To the ordinary housewife, the casual invitation to dinner of two large, able-bodied men would seem an incredible proceeding. But such is the way of bachelors – and perhaps it is not, after all, a bad way. Still, as I immured the newly-arrived patient in the waiting room, it did dawn on me that my housekeeper, Mrs. Gilbert, ought to be notified of the expected guests. Not that I had any anxiety, for Mrs. Gilbert appeared to credit me with the appetite of a Gargantua (and, in fact, I had a pretty good "twist"), and she seemed to live in a state of chronic anxiety lest I should develop symptoms of impending starvation.

Having discharged my bombshell down the kitchen stairs, I proceeded to deal with the patient – fortunately, a "chronic" who required little more than a "repeat" – and having safely launched him, bottle in hand, from the doorstep, repaired to the little glory-hole, known as "the study", to make provision for my visitors. Of their habits I knew nothing, but it seemed to me that a decanter of whisky, another of sherry, a siphon, and a box of cigars would meet all probable exigencies, and I had just finished these preparations when my guests arrived.

As they entered the study, Jervis looked at the table on which the decanters were displayed and grinned.

"It's all right, Thorndyke," said he. "Oldfield has got the restoratives ready. You won't want your smelling salts. But he is evidently going to make our flesh creep properly."

"Don't take any notice of him, Oldfield," said Thorndyke. "Jervis is a perennial juvenile. But he takes quite an intelligent interest in this case, and we are both all agog to hear your story. Where shall I put my note-book? I want to take rather full notes."

As he spoke, he produced a rather large block of ruled paper and fixed a wistful eye on the table, whereupon, having, after a brief discussion, agreed to take the restoratives as read, we transferred the whole collection – decanters, siphon, and cigar box – to the top of a cupboard, and Thorndyke laid his block on the vacant table and drew up a chair.

"Now, Oldfield," said Jervis, when we had all taken our seats and filled our pipes, "fire away. Art is long but life is short. Thorndyke is beginning to show signs of senile decay already, and I'm not as young as I was."

"The question is," said I, "where shall I begin?"

"The optimum place to begin," replied Jervis, "is at the beginning."

"Yes, I know. But the beginning of the case was the incident of the arsenic poisoning, and you know all about that."

"Jervis doesn't," said Thorndyke, "and I only came in at the end. Tell us the whole story. Don't be afraid of repetition and don't try to condense."

Thus directed, I began with my first introduction to the Gannet household and traced the history of my attendance up to the point at which Thorndyke came into the case, breaking off at the cessation of my visits to the hospital.

"I take it," said Jervis, "that full notes and particulars of the material facts are available if they should be wanted."

"Yes," Thorndyke replied, "I have my own notes and a copy of Woodfield's, and I think Oldfield has kept a record."

"I have," said I, "and I had intended to send you a copy. I must write one out and send it to you."

"Don't do that," said Jervis. "Lend it to me and I will have a typewritten copy made. But get on with the story. What was the next phase?"

"The next phase was the return home of Peter Gannet. He called on me to report and informed me that, substantially, he was quite fit."

"Was he, by Jove?" exclaimed Jervis. "He had made a pretty rapid recovery, considering the symptoms. And how did he seem to like the idea of coming home? Seem at all nervous?"

"Not at all. His view was that, as the attempt had been spotted and we should be on our guard, they wouldn't risk another. And apparently he was right – up to a certain point. I don't know what precautions he took – if he took any. But nothing further happened until – but we shall come to that presently. I will carry the narrative straight on."

This I did, making a brief and sketchy reference to my visits to the studio and the activities of Gannet and Boles. But at this point Jervis pulled me up.

"A little vague and general, this, Oldfield. Better follow the events more closely and in full detail."

"But," I protested, "all this has really nothing to do with the case."

"Don't you let Thorndyke hear you say that, my child. He doesn't admit that there is such a thing as an irrelevant fact, ascertainable in advance as such. Detail, my friend, detail, and again I say detail."

I did not take him quite literally, but I acted as if I did. Going back to the beginning of the studio episode, I recounted it with the minutest and most tedious circumstantiality, straining my memory in sheer malice to recall any trivial and unmeaning incident that I could recover, and winding up with a prolix and exact description of my prentice efforts with the potter's wheel and the creation of the immortal jar. I thought I had exhausted their powers of attention, but to my surprise Thorndyke asked, "And what did your masterpiece look like when you had finished it?"

"It was very thick and clumsy, but it was quite a pleasant shape. The wheel tends to produce pleasant shapes if you let it."

"Do you know what became of it?"

"Yes. Gannet fired it and passed it off as his own work. But I will tell you about that later. I only discovered the fraud this afternoon."

He nodded and made a note on a separate slip of paper and I then resumed my narrative, and as this was concerned with the discovery of the crime, I was genuinely careful not to omit any detail, no matter how unimportant it might appear to me. They both listened with concentrated attention, and Thorndyke apparently took my statement down verbatim in shorthand.

When I had finished with the gruesome discoveries in the studio, I paused and prepared to play my trump card, confident that, unlike Inspector Blandy, they would appreciate the brilliancy of my inspiration and its important bearing on the identity of the criminal. And I was not disappointed, at least as to the impression produced, for as I described how the "brain wave" had come to me, Thorndyke looked up from his note-book with an appearance of surprise and Jervis stared at me, open-mouthed.

"But, my dear Oldfield!" he exclaimed, "what in the name of Fortune gave you the idea of testing the ashes for arsenic?"

"Well, there had been one attempt," I replied, "and it was quite possible that there might have been another. That was what occurred to me."

"Yes, I understand," said he. "But surely you did not expect to get an arsenic reaction from incinerated bone?"

"I didn't, very much. It was just a chance shot, and I must admit that the result came quite as a surprise."

"The result!" he exclaimed. "What result?"

"I will show you," said I, and forthwith I produced from a locked drawer the precious glass tube with its unmistakable arsenic mirror.

Jervis took it from me and stared at it with a ludicrous expression of amazement, while Thorndyke regarded him with a quiet twinkle.

"But," the former exclaimed, when he had partially recovered from his astonishment, "the thing is impossible. I don't believe it!" Whereupon Thorndyke chuckled aloud.

"My learned friend," said he, "reminds me of that German professor who, meeting a man wheeling a tall cycle – a thing that he had never before seen the like of – demonstrated conclusively to the cyclist that it was impossible to ride the machine for the excellent reason that, if you didn't fall off to the right, you must inevitably fall off to the left."

"That's all very well," Jervis retorted, "but you don't mean to tell me that you accept this mirror at its face value?"

"It is certainly a little unexpected," Thorndyke replied, "but you will remember that Soderman and O'Connell state definitely that it has been possible to show the presence of arsenic in the ashes of cremated bodies."

"Yes. I remember noting their statement and finding myself unable to accept it. They cited no instances and they gave no particulars. A mere *ipse dixit* has no evidential weight. I am convinced that there is some fallacy in this case. What about your reagents, Oldfield? Is there a possibility that any of them might have been contaminated with arsenic?"

"No," I replied, "it is quite impossible. I tested them exhaustively. There was no sign of arsenic until I introduced the bone ash."

"By the way," Thorndyke asked, "did you use up all your material, or have you some left?"

"I used only half of it, so if you think it worthwhile to check the analysis, I can let you have the remainder."

"Excellent!" said Thorndyke. "A control experiment will settle the question whether the ashes do, or do not, contain arsenic. Meanwhile, since the mirror is an undeniable fact, we must provisionally adopt the affirmative view. I suppose you told the police about this?"

"Yes, I showed them the tube. Inspector Blandy spotted the arsenic mirror at a glance, but he took a most extraordinary attitude. He seemed to regard the arsenic as of no importance whatever – quite irrelevant, in fact. He would, apparently, like to suppress it altogether, which appears to me a monstrous absurdity."

"I think you are doing Blandy an injustice," said Thorndyke. "From a legal point of view, he is quite right. What the prosecution has to prove is, first, the fact that a murder has been committed, second, the identity of the person who has been murdered, and third, the identity of the person who committed the murder. Now the fact of murder is established by the condition of the remains and the circumstances in which they were found. The exact cause of death is, therefore, irrelevant. The arsenic has no bearing as proof of murder, because the murder is already proved. And it has no bearing on the other two questions."

"Surely," said I, "it indicates the identity of the murderer, in view of the previous attempt to poison Gannet."

144

"Not at all," he rejoined. "There was never any inquiry as to who administered that poison and there is no evidence. The court would not listen to mere surmises or suspicions. The poisoner is an unknown person, and at present the murderer is an unknown person. But you cannot establish the identity of an unknown quantity by proving that it is identical with another unknown quantity. No, Oldfield, Blandy is perfectly right. The arsenic would only be a nuisance and a complication to the prosecution. But it would be an absolute godsend to the defense."

"Why?" I demanded.

"Well," he replied, "you saw what Jervis's attitude was. That would be the attitude of the defense. The defending counsel would pass lightly over all the facts that had been proved and that he could not contest, and fasten on the one thing that could not be proved and that he could make a fair show of disproving. The element of doubt introduced by the arsenic might wreck the case for the prosecution and be the salvation of the accused. But we are wandering away from your story. Tell us what happened next."

I resumed my narrative, describing my visit to the police station and Blandy's investigations at the studio, dwelling expecially on the interest shown by the inspector in Boles's works and materials. They appeared to arouse a similar interest on the part of my listeners, for Jervis commented, "The plot seems to thicken. There is a distinct suggestion that the studio was the scene of activities other than pottery and the making of modernist jewelry. I wonder if those finger-prints will throw any light on the subject?"

"I rather suspect that they have," said I, "judging by the questions that Blandy put to Mrs. Gannet. He had got some information from somewhere."

"I don't want to interrupt the narrative," said Thorndyke, "but when we have finished with the studio, we might have Blandy's questions. They probably represent his views on the case and, as you say, they may enable us to judge whether he knows more about it than we do."

"There is only one more point about the studio," said I, "but it is a rather important one, as it seems to bear on the motive for the murder." And with this I gave a detailed account of the quarrel between Gannet and Boles, an incident that, in effect, brought my connection with the place and the men to an end.

"Yes," Thorndyke agreed, "that is important, for all the circumstances suggest that it was not a mere casual falling out but the manifestation of a deep-seated enmity."

"That was what I thought," said I, "and so, evidently, did Mrs. Gannet, and it was on this point that Blandy's questions were so particularly searching. First, he elicited the fact that the two men were formerly quite good friends and that the change had occurred quite recently. He inquired as to the cause of the change, but she was quite unable to account for it. Then he wanted to know when the change had occurred, but she was only able to say that it occurred sometime in the latter part of last year. The next questions related to Boles's movements about that time, and naturally, she couldn't tell him very much. And then he asked a most remarkable question, which was, could she remember where Boles was on the 19th of last September? And it happened that she could. For at that time Gannet had gone to spend a week-end with Boles and she had taken the opportunity to spend a week-end at Eastbourne. And as she remembered clearly that she was at Eastbourne on the 19th of September, it followed that on that date Boles and Gannet were staying together at a place called Newingstead."

At the mention of Newingstead, Thorndyke looked up quickly, but he made no remark, and I continued, "This information seemed greatly to interest Inspector Blandy, especially the fact that the two men were at Newingstead together on that date, and he pressed Mrs. Gannet to try to remember whether the sudden change from friendship to enmity seemed to coincide with that date. The question naturally astonished her, but on reflection, she was able to recall that she first noticed the change when she returned from Eastbourne."

"There is evidently something significant," said Jervis, "about that date and that place, but I can't imagine what it can be."

"I think," said I, "that I can enlighten you to some extent, for it happens that I also was at Newingstead on the 19th of last September."

"The deuce you were!" exclaimed Jervis. "Then it seems that you did not begin your story at the beginning, after all."

"I take it," said Thorndyke, "that you are the Dr. Oldfield who gave evidence at the inquest on Constable Murray?"

"That is so. But how do you come to know about that inquest? I suppose you read about it in the papers? But it is odd that you should happen to remember it."

"It isn't, really," said Thorndyke. "The fact is that Mr. Kempster – the man who was robbed, you remember – consulted me about the case. He wanted me to trace the thief, and if possible, to trace the diamonds, too. Of course, I told him that I had no means of doing anything of the kind. It was purely a police case. But he insisted on leaving the matter in my hands and he provided me with a verbatim report of the inquest from the local paper. Don't you remember the case, Jervis? I know you read the report."

"Yes," replied Jervis. "I begin to have a hazy recollection of the case. I remember now that a constable was murdered in a wood – killed with his own truncheon, wasn't he?"

"Yes," I replied, "and some very distinct finger-prints were found on the truncheon – finger-prints from a left hand, with a particularly clear thumb-print."

"Ha!" said Jervis. "Yes, of course, I remember, and I think I begin to 'rumble' Mr. Blandy, as Miller would say. Did you see those finger-prints on the gold plate?"

"I just had a look at them, though I was not particularly interested. But they were extremely clear – they would be, on polished gold plate. There was a thumb on one side and a forefinger on the reverse."

"Do you know whether they were left or right?"

"I couldn't tell, but Blandy said they were from a left hand."

"I expect he was right," said Jervis. "I am not fond of Blandy, but he certainly does know his job. It looks as if there were going to be some startling developments in this case. What do you think, Thorndyke?"

"It depends," replied Thorndyke, "on what Blandy found at the studio. If the finger-prints on the gold plate were the same as those found on the truncheon, they can be assumed to be those of the man who murdered the constable, and as Blandy will have assumed – quite properly – that they were the finger-prints of Boles, we can understand his desire to ascertain where Boles was on the day of the murder, and his intense interest in learning from Mrs. Gannet that Boles was actually at Newingstead on that very day. Further, I think we can understand his disinclination to have any dealings with the arsenic."

"I don't quite see why," said I.

"It is partly a matter of legal procedure," he explained. "Boles cannot be charged with any crime until he is caught. But if he is arrested, and his finger-prints are found to be the same as those on the truncheon, he will be charged with the murder of the constable. He may also be charged with the murder of Gannet. Thus when it comes to the trial, there will be two indictments. But, whereas – in the circumstances that we are assuming – the evidence against him in the matter of the murder at Newingstead appears to be conclusive and unanswerable, that relating to the murder of Gannet is much less convincing – in fact, there is hardly enough at present to support the charge.

"Hence it is practically certain that the first indictment would be the one to be proceeded with, and as this would almost certainly result in a conviction, the other would be of no interest. The police would not be willing to waste time and effort on preparing a difficult and inconclusive case which would never be brought to trial. That is how the matter presents itself to me."

"Yes," Jervis agreed, "that seems to be the position. But yet we can't dismiss the Gannet murder altogether. Boles is the principal suspect, but he hasn't the monopoly. He might have had an accomplice – an accessory, either before or after the fact. As I see the case, it seems to leave Mr. Boles fairly in the soup and Mrs. Gannet, so to speak, sitting on the edge of the tureen. But I may be wrong."

"I think you are," said I, with some warmth. "I don't believe that Mrs. Gannet has any guilty knowledge of the crime at all."

"I am inclined to agree with you, Oldfield," said Thorndyke. "But I think Jervis was referring to the views of the police, which may be different from ours."

At this moment the clock in the adjacent consulting room struck eight and, before its reverberations had died away, the welcome sound of the gong was heard summoning us to dinner. I conducted my guests to the dining room, and a quick glance at the table as I entered assured me that Mrs. Gilbert had been equal to the occasion. And that conviction deepened as the meal proceeded and evidently communicated itself to my guests, for Jervis remarked, after an appreciative sniff at his claret glass, "Oldfield seems to do himself pretty well for a struggling G.P."

"Yes," Thorndyke agreed. "I think we may congratulate him on his housekeeper."

"And his wine merchant," added Jervis. "I propose a vote of thanks to them both."

I bowed my acknowledgments and promised to convey the sentiments of the company to the proper quarters (which I did, subsequently, to our mutual satisfaction), and we then reverted to the activities proper to the occasion. Presently Jervis looked up at me as if a sudden thought had struck him.

"When you were describing Gannet's method of work, Oldfield, you didn't give us a very definite idea of the result. I gather that he posed as a special kind of artist potter. Did you consider that his productions justified that claim?"

"To tell the truth," I replied, "I didn't know what to think. To my eye his pottery looked like the sort of rough, crude stuff that is made by primitive people – but not so good – or the pottery that children turn out at the kindergartens. But you see I am not an expert. It seemed possible that it might have some subtle qualities which I was too ignorant to detect."

"A very natural state of mind for a modest man," said Thorndyke, "and a perfectly proper one, but a dangerous one, nevertheless. For it is

148

just that self-distrust, that modest assumption that 'there must be something in it, after all' that lets in the charlatan and the impostor. I saw some of Gannet's pottery in his bedroom, including that outrageous effigy, and I am afraid that I was less modest than you were, for I decided definitely that the man who made it was no potter."

"And you were absolutely right," said I. "The question has been settled conclusively, so far as I am concerned, this very day. I have just visited an exhibition of Gannet's works, and the bubble of his reputation was burst before my eyes. I will give you the particulars. It was quite a quaint experience."

With this I produced the catalogue from my pocket and having read to them Bunderby's introduction, I gave them a full description of the proceedings, including as much of Bunderby's discourse as I could remember, and finishing up with the amazing incident of the "decorated jar". They both listened with deep interest and with appreciative chuckles, and when I had concluded, Jervis remarked, "Well, the jar incident fairly puts the lid on it. Obviously, the whole of the pottery business was what the financiers call a 'ramp'. And I should say that Bunderby was in it up to the neck."

"That is not so certain," said Thorndyke. "He is either an ignoramus or a sheer impostor, and possibly both. It doesn't matter much, as he is apparently not our pigeon. But the affair of the jar – a mere beginner's experiment – is more interesting, for it concerns Gannet, who *is* our pigeon. As Jervis says, it explodes Gannet's pretensions as a skilled artist, and thus convicts him of deliberate imposture, but it also proves him guilty of an act, not only mean but quite definitely dishonest. For the jar might conceivably be sold."

"It *is* sold," said I, "for fifteen guineas."

"Which," Jervis pronounced, oracularly, "illustrates the proverbial lack of cohesion between a fool and his money. I wonder who the mug is."

"I didn't discover that – in fact, I didn't ask. But I picked up some other items of information. I had quite a long chat with Mr. Kempster, the proprietor of the gallery."

"Mr. Kempster?" Thorndyke repeated, with a note of interrogation.

"Yes, but not your Mr. Kempster. This man is the brother of your client and a good deal like him. That is how I came to speak to him."

"And what did you learn from Mr. Kempster?" Thorndyke asked.

"I learned, in the first place, that Boles is a Newingstead man, that he is acquainted with your Mr. Kempster, and that they have had certain business transactions."

"Of what kind?" asked Thorndyke.

149

"Either the sale or exchange of stones. It seems that Boles buys up oddments of old or damaged jewelry to melt down for his own work. If they contain any diamonds, he picks them out and passes them on to Kempster, either in exchange for the kind of stones that he uses, or else, I suppose, for cash. Apparently the transactions are on quite a small scale."

"Small or large," said Jervis, "it sounds a bit fishy. Wouldn't Blandy be interested?"

"I don't quite see why," said I. "Blandy is all out on the murder charge. It wouldn't help him if he could prove Boles to be a receiver, or even a thief."

"I think you are wrong there," said Thorndyke. "If you recall the circumstances of the diamond robbery, which led to the murder of the constable, you will see that what you have told us has a distinct bearing. It was assumed that the thief was a chance stranger who had strayed into the premises. But a man who was suspected of being either a receiver or a thief, who had had dealings with Kempster – possibly in that very house – and knew something of his habits, and who happened to be in Newingstead at the time of the robbery, would fit into the picture much better than a chance stranger. However, that case really turns on the finger-print. If the print on the truncheon is Boles's print, Boles will hang if he is caught, and if it is not, he is innocent both of the murder and of the robbery."

I did not pursue the topic any farther, and the conversation drifted into other channels. But suddenly it occurred to me that nothing had been said on the very subject that had occasioned the present meeting.

"By the way," said I, "you haven't told me what has been done about poor Mrs. Gannet. I hope you have been able to make some arrangements."

"We have," said Jervis. "You need have no further anxiety about her. I called on Linnell this afternoon and put the proposal to him, and he agreed, not only quite willingly but with enthusiasm, to undertake the case. He is keen on criminal practice, and for a solicitor he has an unusual knowledge of criminal law and procedure. So we can depend on him in both respects. He will see that Mrs. Gannet's rights and interests are properly safeguarded, and on the other hand, he won't obstruct and antagonize the police."

"I am relieved to hear that," said I, "for I was most distressed to think of the terrible position that this poor lady finds herself in. I feel the deepest sympathy for her."

"Very properly," said Thorndyke, "as her medical adviser, and I think I am disposed to agree with your view of the case. But we must be cautious. We must not take sides. In the words of a certain ecclesiastic,

'We must keep a warm heart and a cool head'. You will remember that when the arsenic poisoning occurred, both you and I, having regard to Mrs. Gannet's relations with Boles, felt that she was a possible suspect, either as an accessory or a principal. That view was perfectly correct, and I must remind you that nothing has changed since then. The general probabilities remain. I do not believe that she had any hand in this crime, but you and I may both be wrong. At any rate, the police will consider all the possibilities, and our business is to see that Mrs. Gannet gets absolutely fair treatment, and that we shall do."

"Thank you, sir," said I. "It is most kind of you to take so much interest, and so much trouble, in this case, seeing that you have no personal concern in it. Indeed, I don't quite know why you have interested yourselves in it in the way that you have done."

"That is easily explained," replied Thorndyke. "Jervis and I are medico-legal practitioners, and here is a most unusual crime of the greatest medico-legal interest. Such cases we naturally study for the sake of the knowledge and experience that may be gleaned from them. But there is another reason. It has repeatedly happened that when we have studied some unusual case from the outside for its mere professional interest, we have suddenly acquired a personal interest in it by being called on to act for one of the parties. Then we have had the great advantage of being able to take it up with full and considered knowledge of most of the facts."

"Then," I asked somewhat eagerly, "if you were asked to take up this case on behalf of Mrs. Gannet, would you be willing – assuming, of course, that the costs would be met?"

"The costs would not be an essential factor," he replied. "I think that if a charge should be brought against Mrs. Gannet, I would be willing to investigate the case – with an open mind and at her risk as to what I might discover – and if I were satisfied of her innocence, to undertake her defense."

"Only if you were satisfied of her innocence?"

"Yes. Reasonably satisfied when I had all the facts. Remember, Oldfield, that I am an investigator. I am not an advocate."

I found this slightly disappointing, but as no charge was probable, and as Thorndyke's view of the case was substantially similar to my own, I pursued the subject no farther. Shortly afterwards, we adjourned to the study and spent the remainder of the evening discussing Gannet's pottery and the various aspects of modernist art.

Chapter XIII
The Inquiry

The results of Mr. Linnell's activities on Mrs. Gannet's behalf were slightly disappointing, though she undoubtedly derived great encouragement from the feeling that his advice and support were always available. But Inspector Blandy was quietly but doggedly persistent in his search for information. Characteristically, he welcomed Linnell with almost affectionate warmth. It was such a relief to him to know that this poor lady now had a really competent and experienced legal adviser to watch over her interests. He had formerly been so distressed at her friendless and solitary condition. Now he was quite happy about her, though he deplored the necessity of troubling her occasionally with tiresome questions.

Nevertheless, he returned to the charge again and again in spite of Linnell's protests that all available information had been given. There were two points on which he yearned for more exact knowledge. The first related to the movements of Mr. Boles. The second to her own movements during the time that she had been absent from home. As to the first, the last time she had seen Boles was about a week before she went away, and she then understood that he was proposing to take a short holiday to Burnham-on-Crouch. Whether, in fact, he did go to Burnham she could not say. She had never seen or heard from him since that day. As to his usual places of resort, he had an aunt at Newingstead with whom he used to stay from time to time as a paying guest. She knew of no other place which he was in the habit of visiting, and she had no idea whatever as to where he might be now.

As to her own movements, she had been staying at Westcliff-on-Sea with an old servant who had a house there and let lodgings to visitors. While there, she had usually walked along the sea front to Southend in the mornings and returned to tea or dinner. Sometimes she spent the whole day at Southend and went to a theatre or other entertainment, coming back at night by train. Naturally she could not give exact dates or say positively where she was at a certain time on a given day, though she tried to remember. And when the questions were repeated on subsequent occasions, the answers that she gave inevitably tended to vary.

From these repeated questionings, it was evident to Linnell (from whom, as well as from Mrs. Gannet, I had these particulars) that, in the intervals, Blandy had checked all these statements by exhaustive

152

inquiries on the spot, and further, that he had been carefully studying the fast train service between Southend and London. Apparently he had discovered no discrepancy, but yet it seemed that he was not satisfied, that he still harboured a suspicion that Mrs. Gannet knew more about the affair than she had admitted and that she could, if she chose, give a useful hint as to where Boles was in hiding.

Such was the state of affairs when I received a summons to attend and give evidence at an inquest "on certain remains, believed to be human, found on the premises of No. 12 Jacob Street." The summons came rather as a surprise, and on receiving it I gave very careful consideration to the questions that I might be asked and the evidence that I should give. Should I, for instance, volunteer any statements as to the arsenic poisoning and my analysis of the bone-ash? As to the latter, I knew that Blandy would have liked me to suppress it, and my own enthusiasm on the subject had largely evaporated after witnessing Jervis's open incredulity. But I would be sworn to tell the whole truth, and as the analysis was a fact, it would have to be mentioned. However, as will be seen, the choice was not left to me: The far-sighted Blandy had anticipated my difficulty and provided the necessary counterblast.

On the morning of the inquest, I made a point of calling on Mrs. Gannet to satisfy myself that she was in a fit state to attend and to ascertain whether Linnell would be there to represent her. On both points I was reassured, for, though naturally a little nervous, she was quite composed and prepared to face courageously what must necessarily be a rather painful ordeal.

"I can never be grateful enough to you and Dr. Thorndyke," said she, "for sending Mr. Linnell to me. He is so kind and sympathetic and so wise. I should have been terrified of this inquest if I had had to go to it alone, but now that I know Mr. Linnell will be there to support me, I feel quite confident. For you know I really haven't anything that I need conceal."

"Of course you haven't," I replied, cheerfully, though without any profound conviction, "and there is nothing at all for you to worry about. You can trust Mr. Linnell to keep Inspector Blandy in order."

With this I took my departure, greatly relieved to find her in so satisfactory a state, and proceeded to dispatch my visits so as to leave the afternoon clear. For my evidence would probably occupy a considerable time and I wanted, if possible, to hear the whole of the inquiry, I managed this so successfully that I was able to present myself only a few minutes late and before the business had actually commenced.

Looking round the room as I entered, I was surprised to find but a mere handful of spectators, not more than a dozen, and these occupied two benches at the back, while the witnesses were accommodated on a row of chairs in front of them. Before seating myself on the vacant chair at the end, I glanced along the row, which included Blandy, Thorndyke, Jervis, Mrs. Gannet, Linnell, and one or two other persons who were unknown to me.

I had hardly taken my seat when the coroner opened the proceedings with a brief address to the jury.

"The general nature of this inquiry," said he, "has been made known to you in the course of your visit to the studio in Jacob Street. There are three questions to which we have to find answers. First, are these fragments of burnt bones the remains of a human being? Second, if they are, can we give a name and identity to that person? And third, how did that person come by his death? To these questions the obvious appearances and the known circumstances suggest certain answers, but we must disregard all preconceived opinions and consider the facts with an open mind. To do that, I think the best plan will be to trace, in the order of their occurrence, the events which seem to be connected with the subject of our inquiry. We will begin by taking the evidence of Dr. Oldfield."

Here I may say that I shall not follow the proceedings in detail since they dealt with matters with which the reader is already acquainted, and for such repetition as is unavoidable, I hereby offer a comprehensive apology.

When the preliminaries had been disposed of, the coroner opened his examination with the question, "When, and in what circumstances, did you first meet Peter Gannet?"

"On the 16th of December, 1930," I replied. "I was summoned to attend him professionally. He was then an entire stranger to me."

"What was the nature of his illness?"

"He was suffering from arsenic poisoning."

"Did you recognize the condition immediately?"

"No. The real nature of his illness was discovered by Dr. Thorndyke, whom I consulted."

Here, in answer to a number of questions, I described the circumstances of the illness up to the time when Peter Gannet called on me to report his recovery.

"Were you able to form any opinion as to whom administered the poison to Gannet?"

"No. I had no facts to go upon other than those that I have mentioned."

"You have referred to a Mr. Frederick Boles as being in attendance on Gannet. What was his position in the household?"

154

"He was a friend of the family and he worked with Gannet in the studio."

"What were his relations with Gannet? Were they genuinely friendly?"

"I thought so at the time, but afterwards I changed my opinion."

"What were the relations of Boles and Mrs. Gannet?"

"They were quite good friends."

"Should you say that their relations were merely friendly? Nothing more?"

"I never had any reason to suppose that they were anything more than friends. They seemed to be on the best of terms, but their mutual liking was known to Gannet and he used to refer to it without any sign of disapproval. He seemed to accept their friendship as quite natural and proper."

The questions now concerned themselves with what I may call the second stage, my relations with Gannet up to the time of the disappearance, including the quarrel in the studio which I had overheard. This evidently produced a deep impression and evoked a number of searching questions from the coroner and from one or two of the jury. Then came the disappearance itself, and as I told the story of my search of the house and my discoveries in the studio, the profound silence in the court and the intent looks of the jury testified to the eager interest of the listeners. When I had finished the account of my doings in the studio, the coroner (who I suspected had been primed by Blandy) asked, "What about the sample of bone-ash that you took away with you? Did you make any further examination of it?"

"Yes. I examined it under the microscope and confirmed my belief that it was incinerated bone, and I also made a chemical test to ascertain whether it contained any arsenic."

"Had you any expectation that it would contain arsenic?"

"I thought it just possible that it might contain traces of arsenic. It was the previous poisoning incident that suggested the examination."

"Did you, in fact, find any arsenic?"

"Yes. To my surprise, I discovered a considerable quantity. I don't know how much, as I did not attempt to estimate it, but I could see that there was a comparatively large amount."

"And what conclusion did you reach from this fact?"

"I concluded that the deceased, whoever he was, had died from the effects of a very large dose of arsenic."

"Is that still your opinion?"

"I am rather doubtful. There may have been some source of error which is not known to me, but the arsenic was certainly there. Really, its significance is a matter for an expert, which I am not."

This, substantially, brought my evidence to an end. I was followed by Sir Joseph Armadale, the eminent medico-legal authority, acting for the Home Office. As he took his place near the coroner, he produced and laid on the table a shallow, glass-topped box. In reply to the coroner's question, he deposed, "I have examined a quantity of fragments of incinerated bone submitted to me by the Commissioner of Police. Most of them were too small to have any recognizable character, but some were large enough to identify as parts of particular bones. These I found, in every case, to be human bones."

"Would you say that all these fragments are the remains of a human being?"

"That, of course, is an inference, but it is a reasonable inference. All I can say is that every fragment that I was able to recognize as part of a particular bone was part of a human bone. It is reasonable to infer that the unrecognisable fragments were also human. I have picked out all the fragments that were identifiable and put them in this box, which I submit for your inspection."

Here the box was passed round and examined by the jury, and while the inspection was proceeding, the coroner addressed the witness.

"You have heard Dr. Oldfield's evidence as to the arsenic that he found in the ashes. Have you any comments to make on his discovery?"

"Yes. The matter was mentioned to me by Inspector Blandy and I accordingly made an analysis to check Dr. Oldfield's findings. He is perfectly correct. The ashes contain a considerable quantity of arsenic. From two ounces of the ash I recovered nearly a tenth of a grain."

"And do you agree that the presence of that arsenic is evidence that the deceased died from arsenic poisoning?"

"No. I do not associate the arsenic with the body of the deceased at all. The quantity is impossibly large. As a matter of fact, I do not believe that, if the deceased had been poisoned even by a very large dose of arsenic, any trace of the poison would have been discoverable in the ashes. Arsenic is a volatile substance which changes into a vapour at a comparatively low temperature – about 300 degrees Fahrenheit. But these bones had been exposed for hours to a very high temperature – over 2000° Fahrenheit. I should say that the whole of the arsenic would have been driven off in vapour. At any rate, the quantity which was found in the ashes was quite impossible as a residue. The arsenic must have got into the ashes in some way after they had become ashes."

"Can you suggest any way in which it could have got into the ashes?"

"I can only make a guess. Inspector Blandy has informed me that he found a jar of arsenic in the studio among the materials for making glazes or enamels. So it appears that arsenic was one of the materials used, in which case it would have been possible for it to have got mixed with the ashes either in the grinding apparatus or in the bin. But that is only a speculative suggestion. There may be other possibilities."

"Yes," the coroner agreed. "But it doesn't matter much. The important point is that the arsenic was not derived from the body of the deceased, and you are clear on that?"

"Perfectly clear," replied Sir Joseph, and that completed his evidence.

The next witness was Mr. Albert Hawley, who described himself as a dental surgeon and deposed that he had attended Mr. Peter Gannet professionally and had made for him a partial upper denture which included the four incisors. The coroner then handed to him a small stoppered tube which I could see contained a tooth, remarking, "I think you have seen that before, but you had better examine it."

"Yes," the witness replied as he withdrew the stopper and shook the tooth out into the palm of his hand. "It was shown to me by Inspector Blandy. It is a porcelain tooth – a right upper lateral incisor – which has been broken into several fragments and very skilfully mended. It is of the type known as *Du Trey's*."

"Does it resemble any of the teeth in the denture which you made for Peter Gannet?"

"Yes. I used Du Trey's teeth in that denture, so this is exactly like the right upper lateral incisor in that denture."

"You can't say, I suppose, whether this tooth actually came from that denture?"

"No. The teeth are all alike when they come from the makers, and if I have to make any small alterations in adjusting the bite, no record is kept. But nothing seems to have been done to this tooth."

"If it were suggested to you that this tooth came from Gannet's denture, would you have any reason to doubt the correctness of that suggestion?"

"None whatever. It is exactly like a tooth in his denture and it may actually be that tooth. Only I cannot say positively that it is."

"Thank you," said the coroner. "That is all that we could expect of you, and I think we need not trouble you any further."

Mr. Hawley was succeeded by Inspector Blandy who gave his evidence with the ease and conciseness of the professional witness. His description of the researches in the studio and the discovery of the fragments of the tooth were listened to by the jury with the closest interest, though in the matter of sensation I had rather "stolen his thunder". But the turning out of Boles's cupboard was a new feature and several points of interest arose from it. The discovery, for instance, of a two-pound jar of arsenic, three-quarters full, was one of them.

"You had already learned of Dr. Oldfield's analysis?"

"Yes. He showed me the tube with the arsenic deposit in it, but I saw at once that there must be some mistake. It was too good to be true. There was too much arsenic for a cremated body."

"Did you gather what the arsenic was used for?"

"No. The cupboard contained a number of chemicals, apparently used for preparing enamels and fluxes, and I presumed that the arsenic was used for the same purpose."

The discovery of the finger-prints raised some other interesting questions, particularly as to their identity, concerning which the coroner asked, "Can you say whose finger-prints those were?"

"Not positively. But there were quite a lot of them on various objects, on bottles and jars, and some on tool-handles, and they were all from the same person, and as the cupboard was Boles's cupboard and the tools and bottles were his, it is fair to assume that the finger-prints were his."

"Yes," the coroner agreed, "that seems a reasonable assumption. But I don't see the importance of it, unless the finger-prints are known to the police. Is it expedient to ask whether they are?"

"I don't want to go into particulars," said Blandy, "but I may say that these finger-prints are known to the police and that their owner is wanted for a very serious crime against the person, a crime involving extreme violence. That is their only bearing on this case. If they are Boles's finger-prints, then Boles is known to be a violent criminal, and there seems to be evidence in this case that a violent crime has been committed."

"Have you had an opportunity of interviewing Mr. Boles?" the coroner asked.

The inspector smiled, grimly. "No," he replied. "Mr. Boles disappeared just about the time when the body was burned, and so far, he has managed to keep out of sight. Apparently he doesn't desire an interview."

That was the substance of the inspector's evidence and, as he was disposed to be evasive and reticent, the coroner discreetly refrained from pressing him. Accordingly, when the depositions had been read and signed, he was allowed to retire to his seat and the name of Letitia

Gannet was called. As she advanced to the table, where a chair was placed for her, I watched her with some uneasiness, for though I felt sure that she knew nothing that she had not already disclosed, the atmosphere of the court was not favourable. It was easy to see that the jury regarded her with some suspicion, and that Blandy's habitually benevolent expression but thinly disguised a watchful attention which was not entirely friendly.

As I had expected, the coroner began with an attempt to get more light on the incident of the arsenic poisoning, and Mrs. Gannet recounted the history of the affair in so far as it was known to her.

"Of what persons did your household consist at that time?" the coroner asked.

"Of my husband, myself, and one maid. Perhaps I should include Mr. Boles, as he worked in the studio with my husband and usually took his meals with us and was at the house a good deal."

"Who prepared your husband's food?"

"I did while he was ill. The maid did most of the other cooking."

"And the barley water? Who prepared that?"

"Usually I did, but sometimes Mr. Boles made it."

"And who took the food and drink to your husband's room?"

"I usually took it up to him myself, but sometimes I sent the maid up with it, and occasionally Mr. Boles took it up."

"Is the maid still with you?"

"No. As soon as I heard from my husband that there had been arsenic in his food, I sent the girl away with a month's wages in lieu of notice."

"Why did you do that? Did you suspect her of having put the arsenic in the food?"

"No, not in the least, but I thought it best to be on the safe side."

"Did you form any opinion as to who might have put it in?"

"No. There was nobody whom I could suspect. At first I thought that there must have been some mistake, but when Dr. Oldfield explained to me that no mistake was possible, I supposed that the arsenic must have got in by accident, and I think so still."

The next questions were concerned with the relations existing between Gannet and Boles and the time and circumstances of the break-up of their friendship.

"As to the cause of this sudden change from friendship to enmity – did you ever learn from either of the men what the trouble was?"

"Neither of them would admit that there was any trouble, though I saw that there must be. But I could never guess what it was."

159

"Did it ever occur to you that your husband might be jealous on account of your intimacy with Mr. Boles?"

"Never, and I am sure he was not. Mr. Boles and I were relatives – second cousins – and had known each other since we were children. We were always the best of friends, but there was never anything between us that could have occasioned jealousy on my husband's part, and he knew it. He never made the least objection to our friendship."

"You spoke of Mr. Boles as working with your husband in the studio. What, precisely, does that mean? Was Mr. Boles a potter?"

"No. He sometimes helped my husband, particularly in firing the kiln, but his own work, for the last year or two, was the making of certain kinds of jewellery and enamels."

"You say 'for the last year or two' – what was his previous occupation?"

"He was originally a dental mechanic, but when my husband took the studio, as it contained a jeweler's and enameler's plant, Mr. Boles came there and began to make jewellery."

Here I caught the eye of Inspector Blandy, and a certain fluttering of the eyelid recalled his observations on Mr. Boles's "neo-primitive" jewelry. But a dental mechanic is not quite the same as a plumber's apprentice.

The inquiry now proceeded to the circumstances of Peter Gannet's disappearance and the dates of the various events.

"Can you remember exactly when you last saw Mr. Boles?"

"I think it was on Tuesday, the 21st of April, about a week before I went away. He came to the studio and had lunch with us, and then he told us that he was going to spend a week or ten days at Burnham in Essex. I never saw or heard from him after that."

"You say that you went away. Can we have particulars as to when and where you went?"

"I left home on the 29th of April to stay for a fortnight at Westcliff-on-Sea with an old servant, Mrs. Hardy, who has a house there and lets rooms to visitors in the season. I returned home on Thursday, the 14th of May."

"Between those two dates, were you continuously at Westcliff, or did you go to any other places?"

To this she replied in the same terms that she had used in her answers to Blandy, which I have already recorded. Here again I suspected that the coroner had received some help from the inspector for he inquired minutely into the witness's doings from day to day while she was staying at Westcliff.

"In effect," said he, "you slept at Westcliff, but you frequently spent whole days elsewhere. During that fortnight, did you ever come to London?"

"No."

"If you had wished to spend a day in London, could you have done so without your landlady being aware of it?"

"I suppose so. There is a very good train service. But I never did."

"And what about Burnham? That is not so very far from Westcliff. Did you ever go there during your stay?"

"No. I never went farther than Southend."

"During that fortnight, did you ever write to your husband?"

"Yes, twice. The first letter was sent a day or two after my arrival at Westcliff and he replied to it a couple of days later. The second letter I wrote a few days before my return, telling him when he might expect me home. I received no answer to that, and when I got home I found it in the letter box."

"Can you give us the exact dates of those letters? You see that they are important as they give, approximately, the time of the disappearance. Can you remember the date of your husband's reply to your first letter? Or perhaps you have the letter itself."

"I have not. It was only a short note, and when I had read it I tore it up. My first letter was written and posted, I am nearly sure, on Monday, the 4th of May. I think his reply reached me by the first post on Friday, the 8th, so it would have been sent off on Thursday, the 7th. My second letter, I remember quite clearly, was written and posted on Sunday, the 10th of May, so it would have been delivered at our house early on Monday, the 11th."

"That is the one that you found in the letter box. Is it still in existence?"

"No. Unfortunately, I destroyed it. I took it from the letter box and opened it to make sure that it was my letter, and then, when I had glanced at it, I threw it on the fire that I had just lit. But I am quite sure about the date."

"It is a pity you destroyed the letter," said the coroner, "but no doubt your memory as to the date is reliable. Now we come to the incidents connected with the disappearance. Just give us an account of all that happened from the time when you arrived home."

In reply to this, Mrs. Gannet told the story of her alarming discovery in much the same words as she had used in telling it to me, but in greater detail, including her visit to me and our joint examination of the premises. Her statement was amplified by various questions from the coroner, but her answers to them conveyed nothing new to me with one or two exceptions. For instance, the coroner asked, "You looked at the hall stand and noticed that your husband's hats and stick were there. Did you notice another walking-stick?"

"I saw that there was another stick in the stand."

"Did you recognize it as belonging to any particular person?"

"No, I had never seen it before."

"Did you form any opinion as to whose stick it was?"

"I felt sure that it did not belong to my husband. It was not the kind of stick that he would have used, and as there was only one other person who was likely to be the owner – Mr. Boles – I assumed that it was his."

"Did you take it out and examine it?"

"No, I was not interested in it. I was trying to find out what had become of my husband."

"But you assumed that it was Mr. Boles's stick. Did it not occur to you as rather strange that he should have left his stick in your stand?"

"No. I suppose that he had gone out of the studio by the wicket and had forgotten about his stick. He was sometimes inclined to be forgetful. But I really did not think much about it."

"Was that stick in the stand when you went away from home?"

"No. I am sure it was not."

"You have mentioned that you called at Mr. Boles's flat. Why did you do that?"

"For two reasons. I had written to him telling him when I should be home and asking him to come and have tea with us. As he had not answered my letter and did not come to the house, I thought that something unusual must have happened. But especially I wanted to find out whether he knew anything about my husband."

"When you found that he was not at his flat, did you suppose that he was still at Burnham?"

"No, because I learned that he had returned about a week previously at night and had slept at the flat and had the next day gone away again."

"Did you know, or could you guess, where he had gone?"

"No, I had not the least idea."

"Have you any idea as to where he maybe at this moment?"

"Not the slightest."

"Do you know of any places to which he is in the habit of going?"

"The only place I know of is his aunt's house at Newingstead. But I understand from Inspector Blandy that inquiries have been made there and that his aunt has not seen or heard of him for some months. I know of no other place where he might be."

"When you were describing your search of the premises, you said that you did not look in the studio. Why did you not? Was it not the most likely place in which he might be?"

"Yes, it was. But I was afraid to go in. Since my husband and Mr. Boles had been on bad terms, they had quarrelled dreadfully. And they were both rather violent men. On one occasion – which Dr. Oldfield has mentioned – I heard them actually fighting in the studio, and I think it had happened on other occasions. So, when I could find no trace of my husband in the house, I began to fear that something might have happened in the studio. That was why I was afraid to go there."

"In short, you were afraid that you might find your husband's dead body in the studio. Isn't that what you mean?"

"Yes, I think that was in my mind. I suspected that something awful had happened."

"Was it only a suspicion? Or did you know that there had been some trouble?"

"I knew nothing whatever about any trouble. I did not even know whether the two men had met since I went away. And it was hardly a suspicion, only, remembering what had happened in the past, the possibility occurred to me."

When the coroner had written down this answer, he sat for a few moments looking reflectively at the witness. Apparently, he could think of nothing further to ask her, for, presently, turning to the jury, he said, "I think the witness has told us all that she knows about this affair, but possibly some members of the jury might wish to ask a further question."

There was a short pause, during which the members of the jury gazed solemnly at the witness. At length one enterprising juryman essayed a question.

"Could we ask Mrs. Gannet if she knows, or has any idea, who murdered her husband?"

"I don't believe," the coroner replied with a faint smile, "that we could ask that question, even if it were a proper one to put to a witness, because we have not yet decided that anyone murdered Peter Gannet, or even that he is dead. Those are precisely the questions that you will have to answer when you come to consider your verdict."

He paused and still regarded the jury inquiringly, but none of them made any sign, then, after waiting for yet a few more moments, he read the depositions, took the signature, released the witness, and pronounced the name of her successor, Dr. Thorndyke, who came forward and took the place which she vacated. Having been sworn, he deposed, in answer to the coroner's question, "I attended Peter Gannet in consultation with

Dr. Oldfield last January. I formed the opinion that he was suffering from arsenic poisoning."

"Had you any doubt on the subject?"

"No. His symptoms were the ordinary symptoms of poisoning by arsenic and, when I had him in the hospital under observation, it was demonstrated chemically that there was arsenic in his body. The chemical tests were made by Professor Woodfield and by me."

He then went on to confirm the account which I had given, including the analysis of the arrowroot and the barley water. When he had finished his statement, the coroner asked, tentatively, "I suppose you were not able to form an opinion as to how, or by whom, the poison was administered, or whether the poisoning might have been accidental?"

"No. I had no first-hand knowledge of the persons or the circumstances. As to accidental poisoning, I would not say that it was impossible, but I should consider it too improbable to be seriously entertained. The poisoning affected only one person in the house, and when the patient returned home after the discovery it did not recur. Those facts are entirely opposed to the idea of accidental poisoning."

"What do you say about the arsenic that Dr. Oldfield found in the ashes?"

"I agree with Sir Joseph Armadale that there must have been some contamination of the ashes. I do not associate the arsenic with the body of the person who was burned – assuming the ashes to be those of a burned human body."

"On that matter," said the coroner, "perhaps you will give us your opinion on the fragments which Sir Joseph Armadale has shown us."

He handed the box to Thorndyke, who took it and examined the contents with an appearance of the deepest interest, assisting his eyesight with his pocket lens. When he had – apparently – inspected each separate fragment, he handed the box back to the coroner, who asked, as he replaced it on the table.

"Well, what do say about those fragments?"

"I have no doubt," replied Thorndyke, "that they are all fragments of human bones."

"Would it be possible to identify the deceased from these fragments?"

"I should say that it would be quite impossible."

"Do you agree that the ashes as a whole may be assumed to be the remains of a burned human body?"

"That is an obviously reasonable assumption, though it is not susceptible of proof. It is the assumption that I should make in the absence of any reasons to the contrary."

That concluded Thorndyke's evidence, and when he retired, his place was taken by Professor Woodfield. But I need not record the Professor's evidence since it merely repeated and confirmed that of Thorndyke and Sir Joseph. With the reading and signing of his depositions the body of evidence was completed and when he had returned to his seat, the coroner proceeded to his summing up.

"In opening this inquiry," he began, "I said that there were three questions to which we had to find answers. First, are these ashes the remains of a human being? Second, if they are, can we identify that human being as any known person? And third, if we can so identify him, can we decide how he came by his death?

"Let us take these questions in their order. As to the first, it is definitely answered for us by the medical evidence. Sir Joseph Armadale and Dr. Thorndyke, both authorities of the highest eminence, have told us that all the fragments which are large enough to have any recognizable characters are undoubtedly portions of human bones, and they agree – as, indeed, common sense suggests – that the unrecognisable remainder of the ashes must also be presumed to be fragments of human bones. Thus our first question is answered in the affirmative. The bone ashes found in the studio are the remains of a human being.

"The next question presents much more difficulty. As you have heard from Dr. Thorndyke, the fragments are too small to furnish any clue to the identity of the deceased. Our efforts to discover who this person was must be guided by evidence of another kind. We have to consider the persons, the places, and the special circumstances known to us.

"As to the place, these remains were found in the studio occupied by Peter Gannet, and we learn that Peter Gannet has disappeared under most mysterious circumstances. I need not repeat the evidence in detail, but the fact that when he disappeared he was wearing only his indoor clothing seems to preclude the possibility of his having gone away from his home in any ordinary manner. Now the connection between a man who has mysteriously disappeared, and unrecognisable human remains found on his premises after his disappearance, appears strongly suggestive and invites the inquiry: What is the nature of the connection? To answer this, we must ask two further questions: When did the man disappear, and when did the remains make their appearance?

"Let us take the first question: We learn from Mrs. Gannet's evidence that she received a letter from her husband on the 8th of May. That letter, we may presume, was written on the 7th. Then she wrote and posted a letter to him on the 10th of May, and we may assume that it was delivered on the 11th. Most unfortunately, she destroyed that letter, so we

165

cannot be absolutely certain about the date on which it was delivered, but we can feel little doubt that it was delivered in the ordinary way on the 11th of May. If that is so, we can say with reasonable confidence that Peter Gannet was undoubtedly alive on the 7th of May, but inasmuch as Mrs. Gannet found her letter in the letter box, we must conclude that at the date of its delivery, Peter Gannet had already disappeared. That is to say that his disappearance occurred at some time between the 7th and the 11th of May.

"Now let us approach the problem from another direction. You have seen the kiln. It is a massive structure of brick and fire-clay with enormously thick walls. During the burning of the body, we know from the condition of the bones that its interior must have been kept for several hours at a temperature which has been stated in evidence as well over two-thousand degrees Fahrenheit – that is to say, at a bright red heat. When Dr. Oldfield examined it, the interior was just perceptibly warm. Now I don't know how long a great mass of brick and fire-clay such as this would take to cool down to that extent. Allowing for the fact that it had been opened to extract the ashes, as it had then been reclosed, its condition was undoubtedly favourable to slow cooling. We can confidently put down the time taken by the cooling which had occurred at several days, probably somewhere about a week. Now Dr. Oldfield's inspection was made on the evening of the 15th. A week before that was the 8th. But we have seen that the disappearance occurred between the 7th and the 11th of May, and the temperature of the kiln shows that the burning of the body must have occurred at some time before the 11th and almost certainly after the 7th. It thus appears that the disappearance of Peter Gannet and the destruction of the body both occurred between those two dates. The obvious suggestion is that the body which was burned was the body of Peter Gannet.

"Is there any evidence to support that conclusion? There is not very much. The most striking is the discovery among the ashes of a porcelain tooth. You have heard Mr. Hawley's evidence. He identifies that tooth as one of a very distinctive kind, and he tells us that it is identically and indistinguishably similar to a tooth on the denture which he supplied to Peter Gannet. He will not swear that it is the same tooth, only that it is the exact facsimile of that tooth. So you have to consider what are the probabilities that the body of some unknown person should have been burned in Peter Gannet's kiln and that that person should have worn a denture containing a right upper lateral incisor of the type known as Du Trey's, in all respects identical with that in Peter Gannet's denture, and how such probabilities compare with the alternative probability that the tooth came from Peter Gannet's own denture.

166

"There is one other item of evidence. It is circumstantial evidence and you must consider it for what it seems to be worth. You have heard from Dr. Oldfield and Dr. Thorndyke that some months ago Peter Gannet suffered from arsenic poisoning. Both witnesses agree that the suggestion of accidental poisoning cannot be entertained. It is therefore practically certain that some person or persons administered this poison to Gannet with the intention of causing his death. That intention was frustrated by the alertness of the doctors. The victim survived and recovered.

"But let us see how those facts bear on this inquiry. Some unknown person or persons desired the death of Peter Gannet and sought, by means of poison, to compass it. The attempted murder failed, but we have no reason to suppose that the motive ceased to exist. If it did not, then Peter Gannet went about in constant peril. There was some person who desired his death and who was prepared, given the opportunity, to take appropriate means to kill him.

"Apply these facts to the present case. We see that there was some person who wished Gannet to die and who was prepared to realize that wish by murdering him. We find in Gannet's studio the remains of a person who may be assumed to have been murdered. Gannet has unaccountably disappeared, and the date of his disappearance coincides with that of the appearance of these remains in his studio. Finally, among these remains, we find a tooth of a rather unusual kind which is in every respect identical with one known to have been worn by Peter Gannet. Those are the facts known to us, and I think you will agree with me that they yield only one conclusion: That the remains found in Peter Gannet's studio were the remains of Peter Gannet, himself.

"If you agree with that conclusion, we have answered two of the three questions to which we had to find answers. We now turn to the third: How, and by what means, did the deceased come by his death? It appears almost an idle question, for the body of the deceased was burned to ashes in a kiln. By no conceivable accident could this have happened, and the deceased could not have got into the kiln by himself. The body must have been put in by some other person and deliberately destroyed by fire. But such destruction of a body furnishes the strongest presumptive evidence that the person who destroyed the body had murdered the dead person. We can have no reasonable doubt that the deceased was murdered.

"That is as far as we are bound to go. It is not our function to fix the guilt of this crime on any particular person. Nevertheless, we are bound to take notice of any evidence that is before us which seems to point to a particular person as the probable perpetrator of the crime. And there is, in fact, a good deal of such evidence. I am not referring to the arsenic

167

poisoning. We must ignore that, since we have no certain knowledge as to who the poisoner was. But there are several important points of evidence bearing on the probable identity of the person who murdered Peter Gannet. Let us consider them.

"In the first place, there is the personality of the murderer. What do we know about him? Well, we know that he must have been a person who had access to the studio, and he must have had some acquaintance with its arrangements, knew where the various appliances were to be found, which of the bins was the bone-ash-bin, and so on. Then he must have known how to prepare and fire the kiln and where the fuel was kept, and he must have understood the use and management of the appliances that he employed – the grinding-mills and the cupel press, for instance.

"Do we know of any person to whom this description applies? Yes, we know of one such person, and only one – Frederick Boles. He had free access to the studio, for it was also his own workshop and he had the key. He was familiar with all its arrangements, and some of the appliances, such as the cupel press, were his own. He knew all about the kiln, for we have it in evidence that he was accustomed to helping Gannet light and stoke it when pottery was being fired. He agrees completely with the description, in these respects, which we know must have applied to the murderer and, I repeat, we know of no other person to whom it would apply.

"Thus there is a *prima facie* probability that the murderer was Frederick Boles. But that probability is conditioned by possibility. Could Boles have been present in the studio when the murder was committed? Our information is that he had been staying at Burnham. But he came home one night and passed that night at his flat and then went away again. What night was it that he spent at the flat? Now, Mrs. Gannet came home on the 14th of May, and she called at Boles's flat on the following day, the 15th. There she learned that he had come to the flat about a week previously, spent the night there and gone away the next day. Apparently, then, it would have been the night of the 8th that he spent at the flat, or it might have been the 7th or the 9th. But Gannet's death occurred between the 7th or the 11th. Consequently, Boles would appear to have been in London at the time when the murder was committed.

"But is there any evidence that he was actually on these premises at this time? There is. A walking-stick was found by Dr. Oldfield in the hall-stand on the night of the 15th. You have seen that stick and I pass it round again. On the silver mount of the handle you can see the initials '*F. B.*' – Boles's initials. Mrs. Gannet had no doubt that it belonged to Boles, and indeed there is no one else to whom it could belong. But she has told us that it was not in the hall-stand when she went away. Then it must have been deposited there since. But there is only one day on which it could have been deposited, the day after Boles's arrival at the flat. We thus have clear evidence that Boles was actually on the premises on the 8th, the 9th, or the 10th – that is to say, his presence on these premises seems to coincide in time with the murder of Peter Gannet, and we further note the significant fact that at the time when Boles came to the house, Gannet – if still alive – was there all alone.

"Thus the circumstantial evidence all points to Boles as the probable murderer and we know of no other person against whom any suspicion could rest. Add to this the further fact that the two men – Boles and the deceased – are known to have been on terms of bitter enmity and actually, on at least one occasion, to have engaged in violent conflict, and that evidence receives substantial confirmation.

"I think I need say no more than this. You have heard the evidence and I have offered you these suggestions as to its bearing. They are only suggestions. It is you who have to decide on your verdict, and I think you will have little difficulty in answering the three questions that I mentioned in opening this inquiry."

The coroner was right up to a certain point. The jury had apparently agreed on their verdict before he had finished speaking, but found some difficulty in putting it into words. Eventually, however, after one or two trials on paper, the foreman announced that he and his fellow jurors had reached a conclusion, which was that the ashes found in the studio were the remains of the body of Peter Gannet, and that the said Peter Gannet had been murdered by Frederick Boles at some time between the 7th and the 11th of May.

"Yes," said the coroner, "that is the only verdict possible on the evidence before us. I shall record a verdict of wilful murder against Frederick Boles." He paused, and glancing at Inspector Blandy, asked the latter, "Is there any object in my issuing a warrant?"

"No, sir," Blandy replied. "A warrant has already been issued for the arrest of Boles on another charge."

"Then," said the coroner, "that brings these proceedings to an end, and I can only hope that the perpetrator of this crime may shortly be arrested and brought to trial."

On this, the court rose. The reporters hurried away, intent on gorgeous publicity, the spectators drifted out into the street, and the four experts (including myself for this occasion only), after a brief chat with the coroner and the inspector, departed also and went their respective ways. And here it is proper for me to make my bow to the reader and retire from the post of narrator. Not that the story is ended, but that the pen now passes into another, and I hope more capable, hand. My function has been to trace the antecedents and describe the intimate circumstances of this extraordinary crime, and this I have done to the best of my humble ability. The rest of the story is concerned with the elucidation, and the centre of interest is now transferred from the rather drab neighbourhood of Cumberland Market to the historic precinct of the Inner Temple.

Book II
Narrated by
Christopher Jervis, M.D.

Chapter XIV
Dr. Jervis is Puzzled

The stage which the train of events herein recorded had reached when the office of narrator passed to me from the hands of my friend Oldfield, found me in a state of some mental confusion. It seemed that Thorndyke was contemplating some kind of investigation. But why? The Gannet case was no concern of ours. No client had engaged us to examine it, and a mere academic interest in it would not justify a great expenditure of valuable time and effort.

But further, what was there to investigate? In a medico-legal sense there appeared to be nothing. All the facts were known, and though they were lurid enough, they were of little scientific interest. Gannet's death presented no problem, since it was a bald and obvious case of murder, and if his mode of life seemed to be shrouded in mystery, that was not our affair – nor, indeed, that of anybody else, now that he was dead.

But it was precisely this apparently irrelevant matter that seemed to engage Thorndyke's attention. The ostensible business of the studio had, almost certainly, covered some other activities, doubtful if not actually unlawful, and Thorndyke seemed to be set on ascertaining what they were, whereas to me, that question appeared to be exclusively the concern of the police in their efforts to locate the elusive Boles.

I had the first inkling of Thorndyke's odd methods of approach to this problem on the day after our memorable dinner at Osnaburgh Street. On our way home, he had proposed that we should look in at the gallery where Gannet's pottery was on view, and I had agreed readily, being quite curious as to what these remarkable works were really like. So it happened naturally enough that when, on the following day, we entered the temple of the fine arts, my attention was at first entirely occupied with the exhibits.

I will not attempt to describe those astonishing works for I feel that my limited vocabulary would be unequal to the task. There are some things that must be seen to be believed, and Gannet's pottery was one of them. Outspoken as Oldfield had been in his description of them, I found myself totally unprepared for the outrageous reality. But I need not dwell on them. Merely remarking that they looked to me like the throw-outs from some very juvenile handiwork class, I will dismiss them – as I did, in fact – and proceed to the apparent purpose of our visit.

Perhaps the word "apparent" is inappropriate, for in truth, the purpose of our visit was not apparent to me at all. I can only record this incomprehensible course of events, leaving their inner meaning to emerge at a later stage of this history. By the time that I had recovered from the initial shock and convinced myself that I was not the subject of an optical illusion, Thorndyke had already introduced himself to the gallery proprietor, Mr. Kempster, and seemed to be discussing the exhibits in terms of the most extraordinary irrelevance.

"Having regard," he was saying, as I joined them, "to the density of the material and the thickness of the sides, I should think that these pieces must be rather inconveniently ponderous."

"They are heavy," Mr. Kempster admitted, "but you see they are collector's pieces. They are not intended for use. You wouldn't want, for instance, to hand this one across the dinner table."

He picked up a large and massive bowl and offered it to Thorndyke, who took it and weighed it in his two hands with an expression of ridiculous earnestness.

"Yes," he said, as he returned it to Mr. Kempster, "it is extremely ponderous for its size. What should you say it weighs? I should guess it at nearly eight pounds."

He looked solemnly at the obviously puzzled Kempster, who tried it again and agreed to Thorndyke's estimate. "But," he added, "there's no need to guess. If you are interested in the matter, we can try it. There is a pair of parcel scales in my office. Would you like to see what it really does weigh?"

"If you would be so kind," Thorndyke replied, whereupon Kempster picked up the bowl and we followed him in procession to the office, as if we were about to perform some sacrificial rite, where the uncouth pot was placed on the scale and found to be half an ounce short of eight pounds.

"Yes," said Thorndyke, "it is abnormally heavy even for its size. That weight suggests an unusually dense material."

He gazed reflectively at the bowl, and then, producing a spring tape from his pocket, proceeded carefully to measure the principal dimensions of the piece while Mr. Kempster looked on like a man in a dream. But not only did Thorndyke take the measurements. He made a note of them in his note-book together with one of the weight.

"You appear," said Mr. Kempster, as Thorndyke pocketed his note-book, "to be greatly interested in poor Mr. Gannet's work.'"

"I am," Thorndyke replied, "but not from the connoisseur's point of view. As I mentioned to you, I am trying, on Mrs. Gannet's behalf, to elucidate the very obscure circumstances of her husband's death."

"I shouldn't have supposed," said Kempster, "that the weight of his pottery would have had much bearing on that. But of course you know more about evidence than I do, and you know – which I don't – what obscurities you want to clear up."

"Thank you," said Thorndyke. "If you will adopt that principle, it will be extremely helpful."

Mr. Kempster bowed. "You may take it, Doctor," said he, "that, as a friend of poor Gannet's, though not a very intimate one, I shall be glad to be of assistance to you. Is there anything more that you want to know about this work?"

"There are several matters," Thorndyke replied. "In fact, I want to know all that I can about his pottery, including its disposal and its economic aspects. To begin with, was there much of it sold? Enough, I mean, to yield a living to the artist?"

"There was more sold than you might have expected, and the pieces realized good prices, ten to twenty guineas each. But I never supposed that Gannet made a living by his work. I assumed that he had some independent means."

"The next question," said Thorndyke, "is what became of the pieces that were sold? Did they go to museums or to private collectors?"

"Of the pieces sold from this gallery – and I think that this was his principal market – one or two were bought by provincial museums, but all the rest were taken by private collectors."

"And what sort of people were those collectors?"

"That," said Kempster, with a deprecating smile, "is a rather delicate question. The things were offered for sale in my gallery and the purchasers were, in a sense, my clients."

"Quite so," said Thorndyke. "It was not really a fair question, and not very necessary as I have seen the pottery. I suppose you don't keep any records of the sales or the buyers?"

"Certainly I do," replied Kempster. "I keep a Day Book and a ledger. The ledger contains a complete record of the sales of each of the exhibitors. Would you like to see Mr. Gannet's account?"

"I am ashamed to give you so much trouble," Thorndyke replied, "but if you would be so very kind – "

"It's no trouble at all," said Kempster, stepping across to a tall cupboard and throwing open the doors. From the row of books therein revealed, he took out a portly volume and laid it on the desk, turning over the leaves until he found the page that he was seeking.

"Here," he said, "is a record of all of Mr. Gannet's works that have been sold from this gallery. Perhaps you may get some information from it."

I glanced down the page while Thorndyke was examining it and was a little surprised at the completeness of the record. Under the general heading, "*Peter Gannet Esq.*" was a list of the articles sold, with a brief description of each, and in separate columns, the date, the price, and the name and address of each purchaser.

"I notice," said Thorndyke, "that Mr. Francis Broomhill of Stafford Square has made purchases on three occasions. Probably he is a collector of modernist work?"

"He is," replied Kempster, "and a special admirer of Mr. Gannet. You will observe that he bought one of the two copies of the figurine in stoneware of a monkey. The other copy, as you see, went to America."

"Did Mr. Gannet ever execute any other figurines?" Thorndyke asked.

"No," Kempster replied. "To my surprise, he never pursued that form of art, though it was a striking success. Mr. Bunderby, the eminent art critic, was enthusiastic about it, and as you see, the only copies offered realized fifty guineas each. But perhaps if he had lived he might have given his admirers some further examples."

"You speak of copies," said Thorndyke, "so I presume that they were admittedly replicas, probably squeezed in a mould or possibly slip-casts? It was not pretended that they were original modellings?"

"No, they couldn't have been. A small pottery figure must be made in a mould, either squeezed or cast, to get it hollow. Of course it would be modelled in the solid in the first place and the mould made from the solid model."

"There was a third specimen of this figurine," said Thorndyke, "I saw it in Gannet's bedroom. Would that also be a squeeze, or do you suppose it might be the original? It was certainly stoneware."

"Then it must have been squeezed from a mould," replied Kempster. "It couldn't have been fired solid, it would have cracked all to pieces. The only alternative would have been to excavate the solid original, which would have been extremely difficult and quite unnecessary, as he certainly had a mould."

"From your recollection of the figurines, should you say that they were as thick and ponderous as the bowls and jars?"

"I can't say, positively," replied Kempster, "but they could hardly have been. A figure is more likely to crack in the fire than an open bowl or jar, but the thinner it is, in reason, the safer it is from fire cracks. And it is just as easy to make a squeeze thin as thick."

This virtually brought our business with Mr. Kempster to an end. We walked out into the gallery with him when Thorndyke had copied out a few particulars from the ledger, but our conversation, apart from a brief discussion of Boles's jewellery exhibits, obviously had no connection with the purpose of our visit – whatever that might be. Eventually, having shaken his hand warmly and thanked him for his very courteous and helpful treatment of us, we took our departure, leaving him, I suspect, as much puzzled by our proceedings as I was myself.

"I suppose, Thorndyke," said I, as we walked away down Bond Street, "you realize that you have enveloped me in a fog of quite phenomenal density?"

"I can understand," he replied, "that you find my approach to the problem somewhat indirect."

"The problem!" I exclaimed. "What problem? I don't see that there is any problem. We know that Gannet was murdered and we can fairly assume that he was murdered by Boles. But whether he was or not is no concern of ours. That is Blandy's problem, and in any case, I can't imagine that the weight and density of Gannet's pottery has any bearing on it, unless you are suggesting that Boles biffed the deceased on the head with one of his own pots."

Thorndyke smiled indulgently as he replied, "No, Jervis. I am not considering Gannet's pots as possible lethal weapons, but the potter's art has its bearing on our problem, and even the question of weight may be not entirely irrelevant."

"'But what problem are you alluding to?" I persisted.

"The problem that is in my mind," he replied, "is suggested by the very remarkable story that Oldfield related to us last night. You listened to that story very attentively and no doubt you remember the substance of it. Now, recalling that story as a whole and considering it as an account of a series of related events, doesn't it seem to you to suggest some very curious and interesting questions?"

"The only question that it suggested to me was how the devil that arsenic got into the bone-ash. I could make nothing of that."

"Very well," he rejoined, "then try to make something of it. The arsenic was certainly there. We agree that it could not have come from the body. Then it must have got into the ash after the firing. But how? There is one problem. Take it as a starting point and consider what explanations are possible, and further, consider what would be the implications of each of your explanations."

"But," I exclaimed, "I can't think of any explanation. The thing is incomprehensible. Besides, what business is it of ours? We are not engaged in the case."

"Don't lose sight of Blandy," said he. "He hasn't shot his bolt yet. If he can lay hands on Boles, he will give us no trouble, but if he fails in that, he may think it worthwhile to give some attention to Mrs. Gannet. I don't know whether he suspects her of actual complicity in the murder, but it is obvious that he does suspect her of knowing and concealing the whereabouts of Boles. Consequently, if he can get no information from her by persuasion, he might consider the possibility of charging her as an accessory either before or after the fact."

"But," I objected, "the choice wouldn't lie with him. You are surely not suggesting that either the police or the Public Prosecutor would entertain the idea of bringing a charge for the purpose of extorting information – virtually as a measure of intimidation?"

"Certainly not," he replied, "unless Blandy could make out a *prima facie* case. But it is possible that he knows more than we do about the relations of Boles and Mrs. Gannet. At any rate, the position is that I have made a conditional promise to Oldfield that if any proceedings should be taken against her I will undertake the defense. It is not likely that any proceedings will be taken, but still it is necessary for me to know as much as I can learn about the circumstances connected with the murder. Hence these inquiries."

"Which seem to me to lead nowhere. However, as Kempster remarked, you know – which I do not – what obscurities you are trying to elucidate. Do you know whether there is going to be an inquest?"

"I understand," he replied, "that an inquest is to be held in the course of a few days and I expect to be summoned to give evidence concerning the arsenic poisoning. But I should attend in any case, and I recommend you to come with me. When we have heard what the various witnesses, including Blandy, have to tell, we shall have a fairly complete knowledge of the facts, and we may be able to judge whether the inspector is keeping anything up his sleeve."

As the reader will have learned from Oldfield's narrative – which this account overlaps by a few days – I adopted Thorndyke's advice and attended the inquest. But though I gained thereby a knowledge of all the facts of the case, I was no nearer to any understanding of the purpose that Thorndyke had in view in his study of Gannet's pottery, nor did I find myself entirely in sympathy with his interest in Mrs. Gannet. I realized that she was in a difficult and trying position, but I was less convinced

176

than he appeared to be of her complete innocence of any complicity in the murder or the very suspicious poisoning affair that had preceded it.

But his interest in her was quite remarkable. It went so far as actually to induce him to attend the funeral of her husband and even to persuade me to accept the invitation and accompany him – not that I needed much persuasion, for the unique opportunity of witnessing a funeral at which there was no coffin and no corpse – where "our dear departed brother" might almost have been produced in a paper bag – was not to be missed.

But it hardly came up to my expectations, for it appeared that the ashes had been deposited in the urn before the proceedings began, and the funeral service took its normal course, with the terra-cotta casket in place of the coffin. But I found a certain grim humour in the circumstance that the remains of Peter Gannet should be enshrined in a pottery vessel of obviously commercial origin which in all its properties – in its exact symmetry and mechanical regularity – was the perfect antithesis of his own masterpieces.

Chapter XV
A Modernist Collector

My experiences at Mr. Kempster's gallery were only a foretaste of what Thorndyke could do in the way of mystification, for I need not say that the most profound cogitation on Oldfield's story and on the facts which had transpired at the inquest had failed completely to enlighten me. I was still unable to perceive that there was any real problem to solve, or that, if there were, the physical properties of Gannet's pottery could possibly be a factor in its solution.

But obviously I was wrong. For Thorndyke was no wild goose hunter or discoverer of mare's nests. If he believed that there was a problem to investigate, I could safely assume that there was such a problem, and if he believed that Gannet's pottery held a clue to it, I could assume – and did assume – that he was right. Accordingly, I waited, patiently and hopefully, for some further developments which might dissipate the fog in which my mind was enshrouded.

The further developments were not long in appearing. On the third day after the funeral, Thorndyke announced to me that he had made, by letter, an appointment, which included me, with Mr. Francis Broomhill of Stafford Square, for a visit of inspection of his famous collection of works of modernist art. I gathered, subsequently, by the way in which we were received, that Thorndyke's letter must have been somewhat misleading, in tone if not in matter. But any little mental reservations as to our views on contemporary art were, I suppose, admissible in the circumstances.

Of course I accepted gleefully, for I was on the tiptoe of curiosity as to Thorndyke's object in making the appointment. Moreover, the collection included Gannet's one essay in the art of sculpture, which, if it matched his pottery, ought certainly to be worth seeing. Accordingly, we set forth together in the early afternoon and made our way to the exclusive and aristocratic region in which Mr. Broomhill had his abode.

The whole visit was a series of surprises. In the first place, the door was opened by a footman, a type of organism that I supposed to be virtually extinct. Then, no sooner had we entered the grand old Georgian house than we seemed to become enveloped in an atmosphere of unreality suggestive of Alice in Wonderland or of a nightmare visit to a lunatic asylum. The effect began in the entrance hall, which was hung with strange, polychromatic picture frames enclosing objects which obviously were not pictures but appeared to be panels or canvases on which some very extravagant painter had cleaned his palette. Standing about the spacious floor were pedestals supporting lumps of stone or metal, some – to my eye – completely shapeless, while others had faint hints of obscure anthropoidal character such as one might associate with the discarded failures from the workshop of some Easter Island sculptor. I glanced at them in bewilderment as the footman, having taken possession of our hats and sticks, solemnly conducted us along the great hall to a fine pedimented doorway, and opening a noble, many-panelled, mahogany door, ushered us into the presence.

Mr. Francis Broomhill impressed me favourably at the first glance, a tall, frail-looking man of about forty with a slight stoop and the forward poise of the head that one associates with near sight. He wore a pair of deep concave spectacles mounted in massive tortoise-shell frames. Looking at those spectacles with a professional eye, I decided that without them his eyesight would have been negligible. But though the pale blue eyes, seen through those powerful lenses, appeared ridiculously small, they were kindly eyes that conveyed a friendly greeting, and the quiet, pleasant voice confirmed the impression.

"It is exceedingly kind of you," said Thorndyke, when we had shaken hands, "to give us this opportunity of seeing your treasures."

"But not at all," was the reply. "It is I who am the beneficiary. The things are here to be looked at and it is a delight to me to show them to appreciative connoisseurs. I don't often get the chance, for even in this golden age of artistic progress, there still lingers a hankering for the merely representational and anecdotal aspects of art."

As he was speaking, I glanced round the room and especially at the pictures which covered the walls, and as I looked at them they seemed faintly to recall an experience of my early professional life when, for a few weeks, I had acted as *locum tenens* for the superintendent of a small lunatic asylum (or "mental hospital" as we say nowadays). The figures in them – when recognizable as such – all seemed to have a certain queer psychopathic quality as if they were looking out at me from a padded cell.

After a short conversation, during which I maintained a cautious reticence and Thorndyke was skilfully elusive, we proceeded on a tour of inspection round the room under the guidance of Mr. Broomhill, who enlightened us with comment and exposition, somewhat in the Bunderby manner. There was a quite considerable collection of pictures, all by modern artists – mostly foreign, I was glad to note – and all singularly alike. The same curious psychopathic quality pervaded them all, and the same odd absence of the traditional characteristics of pictures. The

179

drawing – when there was any – was childish, the painting was barbarously crude, and there was a total lack of any sort of mental content or subject matter.

"Now," said our host, halting before one of these masterpieces, "here is a work that I am rather fond of though it is a departure from the artist's usual manner. He is not often as realistic as this."

I glanced at the gold label beneath it and read, "*Nude. Israel Popoff*", and nude it certainly was – apparently representing a naked human being with limbs like very badly made sausages. I did not find it painfully realistic. But the next picture – by the same artist – fairly "got me guessing," for it appeared to consist of nothing more than a disorderly mass of streaks of paint of various rather violent colours. I waited for explanatory comments as Mr. Broomhill stood before it, regarding it fondly.

"This," said he, "I regard as a truly representative example of the Master, a perfect piece of abstract painting. Don't you agree with me?" he added, turning to me, beaming with enthusiasm.

The suddenness of the question disconcerted me. What the deuce did he mean by "abstract painting"? I hadn't the foggiest idea. You might as well – it seemed to me – talk about "abstract amputation at the hip-joint". But I had got to say something, and I did.

"Yes," I burbled incoherently, gazing at him in consternation. "Certainly – in fact, undoubtedly – a most remarkable and – er – " (I was going to say "cheerful" but mercifully saw the red light in time) "most interesting demonstration of colour contrast. But I am afraid I am not perfectly clear as to what the picture represents."

"Represents!" he repeated in a tone of pained surprise. "It doesn't represent anything. Why should it? It is a picture. But a picture is an independent entity. It doesn't need to imitate something else."

"No, of course not," I spluttered mendaciously. "But still, one has been accustomed to find in pictures representations of natural objects – "

"But why?" he interrupted. "If you want the natural objects, you can go and look at them, and if you want them represented, you can have them photographed. So why allow them to intrude into pictures?"

I looked despairingly at Thorndyke but got no help from that quarter. He was listening impassively, but from long experience of him, I knew that behind the stony calm of his exterior his inside was shaking with laughter. So I murmured a vague assent, adding that it was difficult to escape from the conventional ideas that one had held from early youth, and so we moved on to the next "abstraction". But warned by this terrific experience, I maintained thereafter a discreet silence tempered by

180

carefully prepared ambiguities, and thus managed to complete our tour of the room without further disaster.

"And now," said our host as we turned away from the last of the pictures, "you would like to see the sculptures and pottery. You mentioned in your letter that you were especially interested in poor Mr. Gannet's work. Well, you shall see it in appropriate surroundings, as he would have liked to see it."

He conducted us across the hall to another fine door which he threw open to admit us to the sculpture gallery. Looking around me as we entered, I was glad that I had seen the pictures first, for now I was prepared for the worst and could keep my emotions under control.

I shall not attempt to describe that chamber of horrors. My first impression was that of a sort of infernal Mrs. Jarley's, and the place was pervaded by the same madhouse atmosphere as I had noticed in the other room. But it was more unpleasant, for debased sculpture can be much more horrible than debased painting, and in the entire collection there was not a single work that could be called normal. The exhibits ranged from almost formless objects, having only that faint suggestion of a human head or figure that one sometimes notices in queer-shaped potatoes or flint nodules, to recognizable busts or torsos, but in these the faces were hideous and bestial and the limbs and trunks misshapen and characterized by a horrible obesity suggestive of dropsy or *myxoedema*. There was a little pottery, all crude and coarse, but Gannet's pieces were easily the worst.

"This, I think," said our host, "is what you specially wanted to see."

He indicated a grotesque statuette labelled "*Figurine of a Monkey: Peter Gannet*", and I looked at it curiously. If I had met it anywhere else it would have given me quite a severe shock, but here, in this collection of monstrosities, it looked almost like the work of a sane barbarian.

"There was some question," Mr. Broomhill continued, "that you wanted to settle, was there not?"

"Yes," Thorndyke replied. "In fact, there are two. The first is that of priority. Gannet executed three versions of this figurine. One has gone to America, one is on loan at a London Museum, and this is the third. The question is, which was made first?"

"There ought not to be any difficulty about that," said our host. "Gannet used to sign and number all his pieces and the serial number should give the order of priority at a glance."

He lifted the image carefully, and having inverted it and looked at its base, handed it to Thorndyke.

"You see," said he, "that the number is *571 B*. Then there must have been a *571 A* and a *571 C*. But clearly, this must have been the second

181

one made, and if you can examine the one at the museum, you can settle the order of the series. If that is *571 A*, then the American copy must be *571 C*, or vice versa. What is the other question?"

"That relates to the nature of the first one made. Is it the original model or is it a pressing from a mould? This one appears to be a squeeze. If you look inside, you can see traces of the thumb impressions, so it can't be a cast."

He returned it to Mr. Broomhill, who peered into the opening of the base and then, having verified Thorndyke's observation, passed it to me. I was not deeply interested, but I examined the base carefully and looked into the dark interior as well as I could. The flat surface of the base was smooth but unglazed and on it was inscribed in blue around the central opening "*Op. 571 B P. G.*" with a rudely drawn figure of a bird, which might have been a goose but which I knew was meant for a gannet, interposed between the number and the initials. Inside, on the uneven surface, I could make out a number of impressions of a thumb – apparently a right thumb. Having made these observations, I handed the effigy back to Mr. Broomhill, who replaced it on its stand, and resumed the conversation.

"I should imagine that all of the three versions were pressings, but that is only an opinion. What is your view?"

"There are three possibilities, and bearing in mind Gannet's personality, I don't know which of them is the most probable. The original figure was certainly modelled in the solid. Then *Opus 571 A* may either be that model, fired in the solid, or that model excavated and fired, or a squeeze from the mould."

"It would hardly have been possible to fire it in the solid," said Mr. Broomhill.

"That was Mr. Kempster's view, but I am not so sure. After all, some pottery articles are fired solid. Bricks, for instance."

"Yes, but a few fire cracks in a brick don't matter. I think he would have had to excavate it, at least. But why should he have taken that trouble when he had actually made a mould?"

"I can imagine no reason at all," replied Thorndyke, "unless he wished to keep the original. The one now at the museum was his own property and I don't think it had ever been offered for sale."

"If the question is of any importance," said our host – who was obviously of opinion that it was not – "it could perhaps be settled by inspection of the piece at the museum, which was probably the first one made. Don't you think so?"

"It might," Thorndyke replied, "or it might not. The most satisfactory way would be to compare the respective weights of the two pieces. An excavated figurine would be heavier than a pressing and, of course, a solid one would be much heavier."

"Yes," Mr. Broomhill agreed with a slightly puzzled air, "that is true. So I take it that you would like to know the exact weight of this piece. Well, there is no difficulty about that."

He walked over to the fireplace and pressed the bell-push at its side. In a few moments the door opened and the footman entered the room.

"Can you tell me, Hooper," Mr. Broomhill asked, "if there is a pair of scales that we could have to weigh this statuette?"

"Certainly, sir," was the reply. "There is a pair in Mr. Laws's pantry. Shall I bring them up, sir?"

"If you would. Hooper – with the weights, of course. And you might see that the pan is quite clean."

Apparently the pan was quite clean, for in a couple of minutes Hooper reappeared carrying a very spick-and-span pair of scales with a complete set of weights. When the scales had been placed on the table with the weights beside them, Mr. Broomhill took up the effigy with infinite care and lowered it gently on to the scale pan. Then, with the same care to avoid jars or shocks, he put on the weights, building up a little pile until the pan rose, when he made the final adjustment with a half-ounce weight.

"Three pounds, three-and-a-half ounces," said he. "Rather a lot for a small figure."

"Yes," Thorndyke agreed, "but Gannet used a dense material and was pretty liberal with it. I weighed some of his pottery at Kempster's gallery and found it surprisingly heavy."

He entered the weight of the effigy in his note-book and, when the masterpiece had been replaced on its stand and the scales borne away to their abiding place, we resumed our tour of the room. Presently Hooper returned, bearing a large silver tray loaded with the materials for afternoon tea, which he placed on a small circular table.

"You needn't wait, Hooper," said our host. "We will help ourselves when we are ready." As the footman retired, we turned to the last of the exhibits – a life-sized figure of a woman, naked, contorted, and obese, whose brutal face and bloated limbs seemed to shout for thyroid extract – and having expatiated on its noble rendering of abstract form and its freedom from the sickly prettiness of "mere imitative sculpture", our host dismissed the masterpieces and placed chairs for us by the table.

"Which museum is it," he asked, as we sipped the excellent China tea, "that is showing Mr. Gannet's work?"

"It is a small museum at Hoxton," Thorndyke replied, "known as 'The People's Museum of Modern Art'."

"Ah!" said Broomhill, "I know it. In fact, I occasionally lend some of my treasures for exhibition there. It is an excellent institution. It gives the poor people of that uncultured region an opportunity of becoming acquainted with the glories of modern art, the only chance they have."

"There is the Geffrye Museum close by," I reminded him.

"Yes," he agreed, "but that is concerned with the obsolete furniture and art of the bad old times. It contains nothing of this sort," he added, indicating his collection with a wave of the hand. Which was certainly true. Mercifully, it does not.

"And I hope," he continued, "that you will be able to settle your question when you examine the figurine there. It doesn't seem to me to matter very much, but you are a better judge of that than I am."

When we had taken leave of our kind and courteous host and set forth on our homeward way we walked for a time in silence, each occupied with his own thoughts. As to Thorndyke's ultimate purpose in this queer transaction, I could not make the vaguest guess, and I gave it no consideration. But the experience, itself, had been an odd one with a peculiar interest of its own. Presently I opened the subject with a question.

"Could you make anything of this stuff of Broomhill's or of his attitude to it?"

Thorndyke shook his head. "No," he replied. "It is a mystery to me. Evidently Broomhill gets a positive pleasure from these things, and that pleasure seem to be directly proportionate to their badness, to the absence in them of all the ordinary qualities – fine workmanship, truth to nature, intellectual interest, and beauty – which have hitherto been considered to be the essentials of works of art. It seems to be a cult, a fashion, associated with a certain state of mind, but what that state of mind is, I cannot imagine. Obviously it has no connection with what has always been known as *art*, unless it is a negative connection. You noticed that Broomhill was utterly contemptuous of the great work of the past, and that, I think, is the usual modernist attitude. But what can be the state of mind of a man who is completely insensitive to the works of the accomplished masters of the older schools, and full of enthusiasm for clumsy imitations of the works of savages or ungifted children, I cannot begin to understand."

"No," said I, "that is precisely my position." And with this the subject dropped.

Chapter XVI
At the Museum

"It is curious to reflect," Thorndyke remarked, as we took our way eastward along Old Street, "that this, which is commonly accounted one of the meanest and most squalid regions of the town, should be, in a sense, the last outpost of a disappearing culture."

"To what culture are your referring?" I asked.

"To that of the industrial arts," he replied, "of which we may say that it is substantially the foundation of all artistic culture. Nearly everywhere else those arts are dead or dying, killed by machinery and mass production, but here we find little groups of surviving craftsmen who still keep the lamp burning. To our right in Curtain Road and various small streets adjoining are skilled cabinet makers, making chairs and other furniture in the obsolete tradition of what Broomhill would call the 'bad old times' of Chippendale and his contemporaries. Nearby in Bunhill Row the last of the makers of fine picture frames have their workshops, and farther ahead in Bethnal Green and Spitalfields a remnant of the ancient colony of silk weavers is working with the hand-loom as was done in the eighteenth century."

"Yes," I agreed, "it seems rather an anomaly, and our present mission seems to rub in the discrepancy. I wonder what inspired the founders of The People's Museum of Modern Art to dump it down in this neighbourhood and almost in sight of the Geffrye Museum?"

Thorndyke chuckled softly. "The two museums," said he, "are queer neighbours, the one treasuring the best work of the past and the other advertising the worst work of the present. But perhaps we shan't find it as bad as we expect."

I don't know what Thorndyke expected, but it was bad enough for me. We located it without difficulty by means of a painted board inscribed with its name and description set over what looked like a reconstructed shop front, to which had been added a pair of massive folding doors. But those doors were closed and presumably locked, for a large card affixed to the panel with drawing pins bore the announcement, *"Closed Temporarily. Re-open 11:15".*

Thorndyke looked at his watch. "We have a quarter-of-an-hour to wait," said he, "but we need not wait here. We may as well take a stroll and inspect the neighbourhood. It is not beautiful, but it has a character of its own which is worth examining."

Accordingly, we set forth on a tour of exploration through the narrow streets where Thorndyke expounded the various objects of interest in illustration of his previous observations. In one street we found a row of cabinet makers' shops, through the windows of which we could see the half-finished carcases of wardrobes and sideboards and "period" chairs, seatless and unpolished, and I noticed that the names above the shops were mostly Jewish and many of them foreign. Then, towards Shoreditch, we observed a timber yard with a noble plank of Spanish mahogany at the entrance, and noted that the stock inside seemed to consist mainly of hardwoods suitable for making furniture. But there was no time to make a detailed examination for the clock of a neighbouring church now struck the quarter and sent us hurrying back to the temple of modernism, where we found that the card had vanished and the doors stood wide open, revealing a lobby and an inner door.

As we opened the latter and entered the gallery, we were met by an elderly, tired-looking man who regarded us expectantly.

"Are you Mr. Sancroft?" Thorndyke asked.

"Ah!" said our friend, "then I was right. You will be Dr. Thorndyke. I hope I haven't kept you waiting."

"Only a matter of minutes," Thorndyke replied, in his suavest manner, "and we spent those quite agreeably."

"I am so very sorry," said Sancroft, with evidently genuine concern, "but it was unavoidable. I had to go out, and as I am all alone here, I had to lock up the place while I was away. It is very awkward having no one to leave in charge."

"It must be," Thorndyke agreed, sympathetically. "Do you mean that you have no assistant of any kind, not even a doorkeeper?"

"No one at all," replied Sancroft. "You see, the society which runs this museum has no funds but the members' contributions. There's only just enough to keep the place going, without paying any salaries. I am a voluntary worker, but I have my living to earn. Mostly I can do my work in the curator's room – I am a law writer – but there are times when I have to go out on business, and then – well, you saw what happened this morning."

Thorndyke listened to this tale of woe, not only with patience but with a concern that rather surprised me.

"But," said he, "can't you get some of your friends to give you at least a little help? Even a few hours a day would solve your difficulties."

Mr. Sancroft shook his head wearily. "No," he replied. "It is a dull job, minding a small gallery, especially as so few visitors come to it, and I have found nobody who is willing to take it on. I suppose," he added, with a sad smile, "you don't happen to know of any enthusiast in modern

186

art who would make the sacrifice in the interests of popular enlightenment and culture?"

"At the moment," said Thorndyke, "I can think of nobody but Mr. Broomhill, and I don't suppose he could spare the time. Still, I will bear your difficulties in mind, and if I should think of any person who might be willing to help, I will try my powers of persuasion on him."

I must confess that this reply rather astonished me. Thorndyke was a kindly man, but he was a busy man and hardly in a position to enter into Mr. Sancroft's difficulties. And with him a promise was a promise, not a mere pleasant form of words, a fact which I think Sancroft hardly realized for his expression of thanks seemed to imply gratitude for a benevolent intention rather than any expectation of actual performance.

"It is very kind of you to wish to help me," said he. "And now, as to your own business. I understand that you want to make some sort of inspection of the works of Mr. Gannet. Does that involve taking them out of the case?"

"If that is permissible," Thorndyke replied. "I wanted, among other matters, to feel the weight of them."

"There is no objection to your taking them out," said Sancroft, "for a definite purpose. I will unlock the case and put the things in your custody for the time being. And then I will ask you to excuse me. I have a lease to engross, and I want to get on with it as quickly as I can."

With this he led us to the glass case in which Gannet's atrocities were exposed to view, and having unlocked it, made us a little bow and retired into his lair.

"That lease," Thorndyke remarked, "is a stroke of luck for us. Now we can discuss the matter freely."

He reached into the case and lifting out the effigy, began to examine it in the closest detail, especially as to the upturned base.

"The questions, as I understand them," said I, "are, first, priority, and second, method of work – whether it was fired solid, or excavated, or squeezed in a mould. The priority seems to be settled by the signature. This is *571 A*. Then it must have been the first piece made."

"Yes," Thorndyke agreed, "I think we may accept that. What do you say as to the method?"

"That, also, seems to be settled by the character of the base. It is a solid base without any opening, which appears to me to prove that the figure was fired solid."

"A reasonable inference," said Thorndyke, "from the particular fact. But if you look at the sides, you will notice on each a linear mark which suggests that a seam or join had been scraped off. You probably observed similar marks on Broomhill's copy, which were evidently the

187

remains of the seam from the mould. But the question of solidity will be best determined by the weight. Let us try that."

He produced from his pocket a portable spring balance and a piece of string. In the latter he made two "running bowlines," and, hitching them over the figure near its middle, hooked the "bight" of the string on to the balance. As he held up the latter, I read off from the index, "Three pounds, nine-and-a-half ounces. If I remember rightly, Broomhill's image weighed three pounds, three-and-a-half ounces, so this one is six ounces heavier. That seems to support the view that this figure was fired in the solid."

"I don't think it does, Jervis," said he. "Broomhill's copy was undoubtedly a pressing with a considerable cavity and not very thick walls. I should say that the solid figure would be at least twice the weight of the pressing."

A moment's reflection showed me that he was right. Six ounces obviously could not account for the difference between a hollow and a solid figure.

"Then," said I, "it must have been excavated. That would probably just account for the difference in weight."

"Yes," Thorndyke agreed, but a little doubtfully, "so far as the weight is concerned, that is quite sound. But there are these marks, which certainly look like the traces of a seam which has been scraped down. What do you say to them?"

"I should say that they are traces of the excavating process. It would be necessary to cut the figure in halves in order to hollow out the interior. I say that these marks are the traces of the join where the two halves were put together."

"The objection to that," said he, "is that the figure would not have been cut in halves. When a clay work, such as a terra-cotta bust, is hollowed out, the usual practice is to cut off the back in as thin a slice as possible, excavate the main mass of the bust, and when it is as hollow as is safe, to stick the back on with slip and work over the joins until they are invisible. And that is the obvious and reasonable way in which to do it. But these marks are in the middle, just where the seams would be in a pressing, and in the same position as those in Broomhill's copy. So that, in spite of the extra weight, I am disposed to think that this figure is really a pressing, like Broomhill's. And that is, on other grounds, the obvious probability. A mould was certainly made, and it must have been made from the solid figure. But it would have been much more troublesome to excavate the solid model than to make a squeeze from the mould."

As he spoke, he tapped the figure lightly with his knuckle as it hung from the balance, but the dull sound that he elicited gave no information either way, beyond proving – which we knew already from the weight – that the walls of the shell were thick and clumsy. Then he took off the string and, having offered the image to me for further examination (which I declined), he put it back in the case. Then we went into the curator's room to let Mr. Sancroft know that we had finished our inspection, and to thank him for having given us the facilities for making it.

"Well," said he, laying aside his pen, "I suppose that now you know all about Peter Gannet's works, which is more than I do. They are rather over the heads of most of our visitors, and mine, too."

"They are not very popular, then," Thorndyke ventured.

"I wouldn't say that," Sancroft replied with a faint smile. "The monkey figure seems to afford a good deal of amusement. But that is not quite what we are out for. Our society seeks to instruct and elevate, not to give a comic entertainment. I shan't be sorry when the owner of that figure fetches it away."

"The owner?" Thorndyke repeated. "You mean Mrs. Gannet?"

"No," replied Sancroft, "it doesn't belong to her. Gannet sold it, but as the purchaser was making a trip to America he got permission to lend it to us until such time as the owner should return and claim it. I am expecting him at any time now, and as I said, I shall be glad when he does come, for the thing is making the gallery a laughing-stock among the regular visitors. They are not advanced enough for the really extreme modernist sculpture."

"And suppose the owner never does turn up?" Thorndyke asked.

"Then I suppose we should hand it back to Mrs. Gannet. But I don't anticipate any difficulty of that sort. The purchaser – a Mr. Newman, I think – gave fifty pounds for it, so he is not likely to forget to call for it."

"No, indeed," Thorndyke agreed. "It is an enormous price. Did Gannet himself tell you what he sold it for?"

"Not Gannet. I never met him. It was Mrs. Gannet who told me when she brought it with the pottery."

"I suppose," said Thorndyke, "that the owner, when he comes to claim his property, will produce some evidence of his identity? You would hardly hand over a valuable piece such as this seems to be to anyone who might come and demand it, unless you happen to know him by sight?"

"I don't," replied Sancroft. "I've never seen the man. But the question of identity is provided for. Mrs. Gannet left a couple of letters with me from her husband which will make the transaction quite safe.

Would you like to see them? I know you are interested in Mrs. Gannet's affairs."

Without waiting for a reply, he unlocked and pulled out a drawer in the writing table, and having turned over a number of papers, took out two letters pinned together.

"Here they are," said he, handing them to Thorndyke, who spread them out so that we could both read them. The contents of the first one were as follows:

> *12 Jacob Street.*
> *April 13th, 1931*
>
> *Dear Mr. Sancroft,*
>
> *In addition to the collection of pottery, for exhibition on loan, I am sending you a stoneware figurine of a monkey. This is no longer my property as I have sold it to a Mr. James Newman, but as he is making a business trip to the United States, he has given me permission to deposit it on loan with you until he returns to England, this he expects to do in about three months' time. He will then call on you and present the letter of introduction of which I attach a copy, and you will then deliver the figurine to him and take a receipt from him which I will ask you kindly to send on to me.*
>
> *Yours sincerely,*
> *Peter Gannet*

The second letter was the copy referred to, and read thus:

> *Dear Mr. Sancroft,*
>
> *The bearer of this, Mr. James Newman, is the owner of the figurine of a monkey which I deposited on loan with you. Will you kindly deliver it to him, if he wants to have possession of it, or take his instructions as to its disposal? If he wishes to take it away with him, please secure a receipt for it before handing it over to him.*
>
> *Yours sincerely,*
> *Peter Gannet*

"You see," said Sancroft, as Thorndyke returned the letters, "he wrote on the 13ᵗʰ of April, so, as this is the 7ᵗʰ of July, he may turn up at any moment, as he will bring the letter of introduction with him, I shall be quite safe in delivering the figure to him, and the sooner the better. I am tired of seeing the people standing in front of that case and sniggering."

"You must be," said Thorndyke. "However, I hope Mr. Newman will come soon and relieve you of the occasion of sniggers. And I must thank you once more for the valuable help that you have given us, and you may take it that I shall not forget my promise to try to find you a deputy so that you can have a little more freedom."

With this, and a cordial handshake, we took our leave, once more I was surprised and even a little puzzled by Thorndyke's promise to seek a deputy for Mr. Sancroft. I could understand his sympathy with that overworked curator, but really, Mr. Sancroft's troubles were no affair of ours. Indeed, so abnormal did Thorndyke's attitude appear that I began to ask myself whether it was possible that some motive other than sympathy might lie behind it. No one, it is true, could be more ready than Thorndyke to do a little act of kindness if the chance came his way, but on the other hand, experience had taught me that no one's motives could be more difficult to assess than Thorndyke's. For there was always this difficulty – that one never knew what was at the back of his mind.

Chapter XVII
Mr. Snuper

When we arrived at our chambers we were met on the landing by Polton, who had apparently observed our approach from an upper window, and who communicated to us the fact that Mr. Linnell was waiting to see us.

"He has been here more than half-an-hour, so perhaps you will invite him to stay to lunch. I've laid a place for him, and lunch is ready now in the breakfast room."

"Thank you, Polton," said Thorndyke. "We will see what his arrangements are." And as Polton retired up the stairs, he opened the oak door with his latch-key and we entered the room. There we found Linnell pacing the floor with a distinctly unrestful air.

"I am afraid I have come at an inconvenient time, sir," he began, apologetically, but Thorndyke interrupted.

"Not at all. You have come in the very nick of time, for lunch is just ready, and as Polton has laid a place for you, he will insist on your joining us."

Linnell's rather careworn face brightened up at the invitation, which he accepted gratefully, and we adjourned forthwith to the small room on the laboratory floor which we had recently, for labour-saving reasons, adopted as the place in which meals were served. As we took our places at the table, Thorndyke cast a critical glance at our friend and remarked, "You are not looking happy, Linnell. Nothing amiss, I hope?"

"There is nothing actually amiss, sir," Linnell replied, "but I am not at all happy about the way things are going. It's that confounded fellow, Blandy. He won't let matters rest. He is still convinced that Mrs. Gannet knows, or could guess, where Boles is hiding, whereas, I am perfectly sure that she has no more idea where he is than I have. But he won't leave it at that. He thinks that he is being bamboozled and he is getting vicious – politely vicious, you know – and I am afraid he means mischief."

"What sort of mischief?" I asked.

"Well, he keeps letting out obscure hints of a prosecution."

"But," said I, "the decision for or against a prosecution doesn't rest with him. He is just a detective inspector."

"I know," said Linnell. "That's what he keeps rubbing in. For his part, he would be entirely opposed to subjecting this unfortunate lady to the peril and indignity of criminal proceedings – you know his oily way of speaking – but what can he do? He is only a police officer. It is his superiors and the Public Prosecutor who will decide. And then he goes on, in a highly confidential, friend-of-the-family sort of way, to point out the various unfortunate (and, as he thinks, misleading) little circumstances that might influence the judgment of persons unacquainted with the lady. And after all, he remarked to me in confidence, he found himself compelled to admit that if his superiors should decide (against his advice) to prosecute, they would be able, at least, to make out a *prima facie* case."

"I doubt whether they could," said I, "unless Blandy knows more than we know after attending the inquest."

"That is just the point," said Thorndyke. "Does he? Has he got anything up his sleeve? I don't think he can have, for if he had knowledge of any material facts, he would have to communicate them to his superiors. And as those superiors have not taken any action so far, we may assume that no such facts have been communicated. I suppose Blandy's agitations are connected with Boles?"

"Yes," Linnell replied. "He keeps explaining to me, and to Mrs. Gannet, how the whole trouble would disappear if only we could get into touch with Boles. I don't see how it would, but I do think that if Blandy could lay his hands on Boles, his interest in Mrs. Gannet would cease. All this fuss is to bring pressure on her to make some sort of statement."

"Yes," said Thorndyke, "that seems to be the position. It is not very creditable, and very unlike the ordinary practice of the police. But there is this to remember: Blandy's interest in Boles, and that of the police in general, is not connected with the murder in the studio, but with the murder of the constable at Newingstead. Blandy's idea is, I suspect – assuming that he seriously entertains a prosecution – that if Mrs. Gannet were brought to trial, she would have to be put into the witness box and then some useful information might be extracted from her in cross-examination. He is not likely to have made any such suggestions to his superiors, but seeing how anxious the police naturally are to find the murderer of the constable, they might be ready to give a sympathetic consideration to Blandy's view, if he could make out a really plausible case. And that is the question: What sort of case could he make out? Have you any ideas on that subject, Linnell? I take it that he would suggest charging Mrs. Gannet as an accessory after the fact."

"Yes, he has made that clear to both of us. If the Public Prosecutor decided to take action, the charge would be that she, knowing that a felony had been committed, subsequently sheltered or relieved the felon in such a way as to enable him to evade justice. Of course, it is the only charge that would be possible."

"So it would seem," said I. "But what facts has he got to support it? He can't prove that she knows where Boles is hiding."

"No," Linnell agreed, "at least, I suppose he can't. But there is that rather unfortunate circumstance that, when her husband was missing, she was – as she has admitted – afraid to enter the studio to see if he was there. Blandy fears that her behaviour might be interpreted as proving that she had some knowledge of what had happened."

"There isn't much in that," said I. "What are the other points?"

"Well, Blandy professes to think that the relations between Boles and Mrs. Gannet would tend to support the charge. No one suggests that their relations were in any way improper, but they were admittedly on affectionate terms."

"There is still less in that," said I. "The suggestion of a possible motive for doing a certain act is no evidence that the act was done. If Blandy has nothing better than what you have mentioned, he would never persuade a magistrate to commit her for trial. What do you say, Thorndyke?"

"It certainly looks as if Blandy held a remarkably weak hand," he replied. "Of course, we have to take all the facts together, but even so, assuming that he has nothing unknown to us in reserve, I don't see how he could make out a *prima facie* case."

"He has also," said Linnell, "dropped some obscure hints about that affair of the arsenic poisoning."

"That," said Thorndyke, "is pure bluff. He would not be allowed to mention it, and he knows he wouldn't. He said so explicitly, to Oldfield. It looks as if the threat of a prosecution were being made to exert pressure on Mrs. Gannet to make some revelation. Still, it is possible that he may manage to work up a case sufficiently plausible to induce the authorities to launch proceedings. Blandy is a remarkably ingenious and resourceful man, and none too scrupulous. He is a man whom one has to take seriously."

"And suppose he does manage to get a prosecution started," said Linnell, "what do you advise me to do?"

"Well, Linnell," Thorndyke replied, "you know the ordinary routine. We are agreed that the lady is innocent and you will act accordingly. As to bail, we will settle the details of that later, but we can manage any amount that may be required."

"Do you think that she might be admitted to bail?"

"But why not?" said Thorndyke. "She will be charged only as an accessory after the fact. That is not a very grave crime. The maximum

194

penalty is only two years' imprisonment, and in practice, the sentences are usually quite lenient. You will certainly ask for bail, and I don't see any grounds on which the police could oppose it.

"And now as to the general conduct of the case, I advise you very strongly to play for time. Delay the proceedings as much as you can. Find excuses to ask for remands, and in all possible ways keep the pot boiling as slowly as you can contrive. The longer the date of the final hearing can be postponed, the better will be the chance of finding a conclusive answer to the charge. I will tell you why, following Blandy's excellent example by taking you into my confidence.

"I have been examining this case in considerable detail, partly in Mrs. Gannet's interests and partly for other reasons, and I have a clear and consistent theory of the crime, both as to its motive and approximate procedure. But at present it is only a theory. I can prove nothing. The one crucial fact which will tell me whether my theory is right or wrong is still lacking. I cannot test the truth of it until certain things have happened. I hope that they may happen quite soon, but still, I have to wait on events. If those events turn out as I expect, I shall know that my construction of the crime has been correct, and then I shall be able to show that Mrs. Gannet could not possibly have been an accessory to it. But I can give no date because I cannot control the course of events."

Linnell was visibly impressed, and so was I – though less visibly. I was still in the same state of bewilderment as to Thorndyke's proceedings. I still failed to understand why he was busying himself in a case which did not seem to concern him – apart from his sympathy with Mrs. Gannet. Nor could I yet see that there was anything to discover beyond what we already knew.

Of course I had realized all along that I must have missed some essential point in the case, and now this was confirmed. Thorndyke had a consistent theory of the crime – which, indeed, might be right or wrong. But long experience with Thorndyke told me that it was pretty certainly right, though what sort of theory it might be I was totally unable to imagine. I could only, like Thorndyke, wait on events.

The rest of the conversation concerned itself with the question of bail. Oldfield we knew could be depended on for one surety, and by a little manoeuvring, it was arranged that Thorndyke should finance the other without appearing in the transaction. Eventually Linnell took his departure in greatly improved spirits, cheered by Thorndyke's encouragement and all the better for a good lunch and one or two glasses of sound claret.

Thorndyke's "confidence", if it mystified rather than enlightened me, had at least the good effect of arousing my interest in Mrs. Gannet and her affairs. From time to time during the next few days I turned them over in my mind, though with little result beyond the beneficial mental exercise. But in another direction I had better luck, for I did make an actual discovery. It came about in this way.

A few days after Linnell's visit, I had occasion to go to the London Hospital to confer with one of the surgeons concerning a patient in whom I was interested. When I had finished my business there and came out into the Whitechapel Road, the appearance of the neighbourhood recalled our expedition to the People's Museum, and I suddenly realized that I was within a few minutes' walk of that shrine of the fine arts. Now I had occasionally speculated on Thorndyke's object in making that visit of inspection and on his reasons for interesting himself in Sancroft's difficulties. Was it pure benevolence or was there something behind it? And there was the further question, had his benevolent intentions taken effect? The probability was that they had. He had given Sancroft a very definite promise, and it was quite unlike him to leave a promise unfulfilled.

These questions recurred to me as I turned westward along the Whitechapel Road, and I decided that at least some of them should be answered forthwith. I could now ascertain whether any deputy for Mr. Sancroft had been found, and if so, who that deputy might be. Accordingly, I turned up Commercial Street and presently struck the junction of Norton Folegate and Shoreditch and, traversing the length of the latter, came into Kingsland Road and so to the People's Museum.

One of my questions was answered as soon as I entered. There was no sign of Mr. Sancroft, but the priceless collection was being watched over by a gentleman of studious aspect who was seated in an armchair – a representative specimen of Curtain Road Chippendale – reading a book with the aid of a pair of horn-framed spectacles. So engrossed was he with his studies that he appeared to be unaware of my entrance, though, as I was the only visitor, I must have been a rather conspicuous object and worthy of some slight notice.

Taking advantage of his preoccupation, I observed him narrowly, and though I could not place him or give him a name, I had the distinct impression that I had seen him before. Continuing a strategic advance in his direction under cover of the glass cases, and still observing him as unobtrusively as I could, I had a growing sense of familiarity until, coming within a few yards of him, I suddenly realized who he was.

"Why," I exclaimed, "it is Mr. Snuper!"

He lowered his book and smiled, blandly. "Mr. Snuper it is," he admitted. "And why not? You seem surprised."

"So I am," I replied. "What on earth are you doing here?"

"To tell the truth," said he, "I am doing very little. You see me here, taking my ease and spending my very acceptable leisure profitably in reading books that I usually have not time to read."

I glanced at the book which he was holding and was not a little surprised to discover that it was Bell's *British Stalk-eyed Crustacea*. Observing my astonishment, he explained, apologetically, "I am a collector of British Crustacea in a small way – a very small way. The beginnings were made during a seaside holiday, and now I occasionally secure small additions from the fishmongers' shops."

"I shouldn't have thought," said I, "that the fishmongers' shops would have yielded many rare specimens."

"No," he agreed, "you wouldn't. But it is surprising how many curious and interesting forms of life you may discover among the heaps of shell-fish on a fishmonger's slab, especially the mussels and winkles. Only the day before yesterday, I obtained a nearly perfect specimen of *Stenorhynchus phalangium* from a winkle stall in the Mile End Road."

Now this was very interesting. I have often noticed how the discovery of some unlikely hobby throws most unexpected light on a man's character and personality. And so it was now. The enthusiastic pursuit of this comparatively erudite study presented a feature of Mr. Snuper's rather elusive personality that was quite new to me, and somewhat surprising. But I had not come here to study Mr. Snuper, and it suddenly occurred to me that that very discreet gentleman might be making this conversation expressly to divert my attention from other topics. Accordingly, I returned to my business with a direct question.

"But how do you come to be here?"

"It was Dr. Thorndyke's idea," he replied. "You see there was nothing doing in my line at the moment, and Mr. Sancroft was badly in need of someone who could look after the place while he went about his business, so the doctor suggested that I might as well spend my leisure here as at home, and do a kindness to Mr. Sancroft at the same time."

This answer left me nothing to say. The general question that I had asked was all that was admissible. I could not pursue the matter further, for that would have been a discourtesy to Thorndyke, to say nothing of the certainty that the discreet Snuper would keep his own counsel if there were any counsel to keep. So I brought the conversation gracefully to an end with a few irrelevant observations, and having wished my friend good day, went forth and set a course for Shoreditch Station.

But if it was not admissible for me to question Snuper, I was at liberty to turn the matter over in my mind. But that process had the effect rather of raising questions than of disposing of them. Snuper's account of his presence at the gallery was perfectly reasonable and plausible.

Thorndyke had no use for him at the moment and Sancroft had. That seemed quite simple. But was it the whole explanation? I had my doubts, and they were based principally on what I knew of Mr. Snuper.

Now Mr. Snuper was a very remarkable man. Originally he had been a private inquiry agent whom Thorndyke had employed occasionally to carry out certain observation duties which could not be discharged by either of us. But Snuper had proved so valuable – so dependable, so discreet, and so quick in the uptake – that Thorndyke had taken him on as a regular member of our staff. For apart from his other good qualities, he had a most extraordinary gift of inconspicuousness. Not only was he at all times exactly the kind of person whom you would pass in the street without a second glance, but in some mysterious way he was able to keep his visible personality in a state of constant change. Whenever you met him, you found him a little different from the man whom you had met before, with the natural result that you were constantly failing to recognize him. That was my experience, as it had been on this very occasion. I never discovered how he did it. He seemed to use no actual disguise (though I believe that he was a master of the art of make-up), but he appeared to be able, in some subtle way, to manage to look like a different person.

But whatever his methods may have been, the results made him invaluable to Thorndyke, for he could keep up a continuous observation on persons or places with practically no risk of being recognized.

Reflecting on these facts – on Mr. Snuper's remarkable personality, his peculiar gifts and the purposes to which they were commonly applied – I asked myself once more, could there be anything behind his presence at the People's Museum of Modern Art? And – so far as I was concerned – answer there was none. My discovery had simply landed me with one more problem to which I could find no solution.

Chapter XVIII
Mr. Newman

The premonitory rumblings which had so disturbed Linnell continued for some days, warning him to make all necessary preparations for the defense, and in spite of the scepticism which we all felt as to the practicability of a prosecution, the tension increased from day to day.

And then the bombshell exploded. The alarming fact was communicated to us in a hurried note from Linnell which informed us that a summons had been served on Mrs. Gannet that very morning, citing her to appear at the Police Court on the third day after that on which it was issued to answer to the charge of having, as an accessory after the fact of the murder of Peter Gannet, harboured, sheltered, or otherwise aided the accused person to evade justice.

Thorndyke appeared to be as surprised as I was, and a good deal more concerned. He read Linnell's note with a grave face and reflected on it with what seemed to me to be uncalled for anxiety.

"I can't imagine," said I, "what sort of evidence Blandy could produce. He can't know where Boles is, or he would have arrested him. And if he doesn't, he couldn't have discovered any evidence of any communications between Boles and Mrs. Gannet."

"No," Thorndyke agreed, "that seems quite clear. There can have been no intercepted letters from her, for the obvious reason that such letters would have had to be addressed in such a way as to reach him and thus reveal his whereabouts. And yet one feels that the police would not have taken action unless Blandy had produced enough facts to enable them to make out a *prima facie* case. Blandy might have been ready to gamble on his powers of persuasion, but the responsible authorities would not risk having the case dismissed by the magistrate. It is very mysterious. On my theory of the crime, it is practically certain that Mrs. Gannet could not have been an accessory either before or after the fact."

These observations gave me some clue to Thorndyke's anxiety, for they conveyed to me that Blandy's case, if he really had one, would not fit Thorndyke's theory. I put the suggestion to him in so many words, and he agreed frankly.

"The trouble is," said he, "that my scheme of the crime is purely hypothetical. It is based on a train of deductive reasoning from the facts which are known to us all. I am in possession of no knowledge other than that which is possessed equally by Blandy and by you. The reasoning by which I reached my conclusions seems to me perfectly sound. But I may have fallen into some fallacy, or it may be that there are some material facts which are not known to me, but which are known to Blandy. One of us is mistaken. Naturally, I hope that the mistake is Blandy's, but it may be mine. However, we shall see when the prosecution opens the case."

"I assume," said I, "that you will attend at the hearing."

"Undoubtedly," he replied. "We must be there to hear what Blandy has to say, if he gives evidence, and what sort of case the prosecution proposes to make out, and then we have to give Linnell any help that he may require. I suppose you will lend us the support of your presence?"

"Of course I shall come," I replied. "I am as curious as you are to hear what the prosecution has to say. I shall make a very special point of being there."

But that visit to the Police Court was never to take place, for on that very night the "events" on which Thorndyke had been waiting began to loom up on our horizon. They were ushered in by the appearance at our chambers of a young man of secretive bearing who, having been interviewed by Polton, had demanded personal audience of Thorndyke and had refused to indicate his name or business to any other person. Accordingly, he was introduced to us by Polton who, having conducted him into the presence, stood by and kept him under observation until he was satisfied that the visitor had no unlawful or improper designs. Then he retired and shut the door.

As the door closed, the stranger produced from an inner pocket a small packet wrapped in newspaper which he proceeded to open and, having extracted from it a letter in a sealed envelope, silently handed the letter to Thorndyke, who broke the seal and read through the evidently short note which it contained.

"If you will wait a few minutes," said he, placing a chair for the messenger, "I will give you a note to take with you. Are you going straight back?"

"Yes," was the reply. "He's waiting for me."

Thereupon Thorndyke sat down at the writing table and, having written a short letter, put it in an envelope, which he sealed with wax and handed to the messenger, together with a ten shilling note.

"That," said he, "is the fee for services rendered so far. There will be another at the end of the return journey. I have mentioned the matter in my letter."

The messenger received the note with an appreciative grin and a few words of thanks and, having disposed of it in some secret receptacle, wrapped the letter in the newspaper which had enclosed the other, stowed it away in an inner pocket, and took his departure.

"That," said Thorndyke, when he had gone, "was a communication from Snuper, who is deputizing for Sancroft at the People's Museum. He tells me that the owner of Gannet's masterpiece is going to call tomorrow morning and take possession of his property."

"Is that any concern of ours?" I asked.

"It is a concern of mine," he replied. "I am anxious not to lose sight of that monkey. There are several things about it which interest me, and if it is to be taken away from the museum, I want to learn, if I can, where it is going, in case I might wish at some future time to make a further examination of it. So I propose to go to the museum tomorrow morning and try to find out from Mr. Newman where he keeps his collection and how the monkey is to be disposed of. It is possible, for instance, that he may be a dealer, in which case there would be the danger of the monkey's disappearing to some unknown destination."

"I shouldn't think that he is a dealer," said I. "He would never get his money back. Probably he is a sort of Broomhill but, of course, he may live in the provinces or even abroad. At what time do you propose to turn up at the museum?"

"The place opens at nine o'clock in the morning, and Snuper expects Mr. Newman to arrive at about that time. I have told him that I shall be there at half-past eight."

Now on the face of it, the transaction did not promise any very thrilling experiences, but there was something a little anomalous about the whole affair. Thorndyke's interest in that outrageous monkey was quite incomprehensible to me, and I had the feeling that there was something more in this expedition than was conveyed in the mere statement of Thorndyke's intentions and objects. Accordingly, I threw out a tentative suggestion. "If I should propose to make one of the party, would my presence be helpful or otherwise?"

"My dear fellow," he replied, "your presence is always helpful. I had, in fact, intended to ask you to accompany me. Up to the present you have not seemed to appreciate the importance of the monkey in this remarkable case, but it is possible that you may gather some fresh ideas on the subject tomorrow morning. So come by all means. And now I must go and make the necessary preparations, and you had better do the same. We shall start from here not later than a quarter-to-eight."

With this he went up to the laboratory floor, whence, presently, I heard the distant tinkle of the telephone bell. Apparently he was making some kind of appointment, for shortly afterwards his footsteps were audible on the stairs descending to the entry, and I saw him no more until he came in to smoke a final pipe before going to bed.

On the following morning, Polton, having aroused me by precautionary and (as I thought, premature) thumpings on my door, served a ridiculously early breakfast and then took his stand on the door-step to keep a lookout for the taxi which had been chartered overnight. Evidently he had been duly impressed with the importance of the occasion, as apparently had the taxi man, for he arrived at half-past seven and his advent was triumphantly reported by Polton just as I was pouring out my second cup of tea. But after all there was not so very much time to spare, for in Fleet Street, Cornhill, and Bishopsgate, all the wheeled vehicles in London seemed to have been assembled to do us honour and retard our progress, it was a quarter-past-eight when we alighted opposite the Geffrye Museum and, having dismissed the taxi, began to walk at a leisurely pace northward along the Kingsland Road.

When we were a short distance from our destination, I observed a man walking towards us, and at a second glance, I actually recognized Mr. Snuper. As soon as he saw us, he turned about and walked back to the People's Museum, where he unlocked the door and entered. On our arrival we found the door ajar and Mr. Snuper lurking just inside, ready to close the door as soon as we had passed in.

"Well, Snuper," said Thorndyke, as we emerged from the lobby into the main room, "everything seems to have gone according to plan so far. You didn't give any particulars in your letter. How did you manage the adjournment?"

"It didn't require much management, sir," Snuper replied. "The affair came off by itself quite naturally. Mr. Sancroft didn't come to the museum yesterday. He had to go out of town on business and, of course, as I was here, there was no reason why he shouldn't go. So I was here all alone when Mr. Newman came just before closing time. He told me what he had come for and showed me the letter of introduction and the receipt which he had written out and signed. But I explained to him that I was not the curator and had no authority to allow any of the exhibits to be taken away from the museum. Besides, the case was locked and Mr. Sancroft had the key of the safe in which the other keys were kept, so I could not get the figure out even if I had been authorized to part with it.

"He was very disappointed and inclined to be huffy, but it couldn't be helped, and after all, he had only to wait a few hours. I told him that Mr. Sancroft would be here today and would arrive in time to open the museum as usual, so I expect Newman will turn up pretty punctually about nine o'clock. Possibly he will be waiting outside when Mr. Sancroft comes to let himself in."

This forecast, however, was falsified a few minutes later, for Mr. Sancroft arrived before his time and locked the door when he had

202

entered. Naturally, he knew nothing of what had been happening in his absence and was somewhat surprised to find Thorndyke and me in the museum. But whatever explanations were called for must have been given by Snuper, who followed Sancroft into the curator's room and shut the door behind him and, judging by the length of the interview, I assumed that Sancroft was being put in possession of such facts as it was necessary for him to know.

While this conference was proceeding, Thorndyke reconnoitered the galleries in what seemed to me a very odd way. He appeared to be searching for some place whence he could observe the entrance and the main gallery without being himself visible. Having tried one or two of the higher cases, and apparently finding them unsuitable, owing to his exceptional stature, he turned his attention to the small room which opened from the main gallery and was devoted entirely to water colours. The entrance of this room was exactly opposite the case which contained the "*Figurine of a Monkey*", and it also faced the main doorway. But it seemed to have a further attraction for Thorndyke for, on the wall nearly opposite to the entrance, hung a large water colour painting, the glass of which, taken at the proper angle, reflected the whole of the principal room, the main doorway, and the case in which the monkey was exhibited. I tried it when Thorndyke had finished his experiments, and found that, not only did it reflect a perfectly clear image, owing to the very dark colouring of the picture, but that the observer looking into it was quite invisible from the main gallery, or indeed, to anyone who did not actually enter the small room.

This was an interesting discovery, in its way. But the most interesting part of it was Thorndyke's motive in seeking this secret point of observation. Once more I decided that things were not quite what they had seemed. As I had understood the programme, Thorndyke was going to introduce himself to Mr. Newman and try to ascertain the destination and future whereabouts of the monkey. But with this purpose, Thorndyke's present proceedings seemed to have no connection.

However, there was not much time for speculation on my part, for at this point Mr. Snuper emerged from the curator's room and, walking up the gallery, unlocked the front door and threw it open and, as he returned, accompanied by a man who had slipped in as the door opened, I realized that the proceedings, whatever they might be, had begun.

"Keep out of sight for the present," Thorndyke directed me in a whisper and, forthwith, I flattened myself against the wall and fixed an eager gaze on the picture as well as I could without obstructing Thorndyke's view. In the reflection I could see Snuper and his companion advance until they were within a few yards of the place where we were lurking, and then I heard Snuper say, "If you will give me the letter and the receipt, I will take them in to Mr. Sancroft and get the key of the case, unless he wishes to hand the figure to you himself."

With this, he retired into the curator's room and shut the door, and as he disappeared, the stranger – presumably Mr. Newman – who, I could now see, carried a largish hand-bag, advanced to the case which contained the monkey and stood peering into it with his back to us, and so near that I could have put out my hand and touched him. As he stood thus, Thorndyke put his head round the jamb of the doorway to examine him by direct vision, and after a few moments' inspection, stepped out, moving quite silently on the solid parquet floor, and took up a position close behind him. Whereupon I, following his example, came out into the middle of the doorway and stood behind Thorndyke to see what was going to happen next.

For a few moments nothing happened, but just then I became aware of two men lurking in the lobby of the main entrance, half-hidden by the inner door and quite hidden from Newman by the case at which he was standing. Suddenly Newman seemed to become conscious of the presence of someone behind him, for he turned sharply and faced Thorndyke. Then I knew that something critical was going to happen, and I realized, too, that Thorndyke had got his "one crucial fact". For as the stranger's eyes met Thorndyke's, he gave one wild stare of horror and amazement and his face blanched to a deathly pallor. But he uttered no word, and after that one ghastly stare, turned about and appeared to resume his contemplation of the figurine.

Then three things happened in quick succession: First, Thorndyke took off his hat. Then the door of the curator's room opened and Snuper and Sancroft emerged, and then the two men whom I had noticed came out of the lobby and walked quickly up to the place where Newman and Thorndyke were standing. I looked at them curiously as they approached, and recognized them both. One was Detective Sergeant Wills of the C.I.D. The other was no less a person than Detective Inspector Blandy.

By this time Newman seemed, to some extent, to have recovered his self-possession, whereas Blandy, on the contrary, looked nervous and embarrassed. The former, ignoring the police officers, addressed himself to Sancroft, demanding the speedy conclusion of his business. But here Blandy intervened, with little confidence but more than his usual politeness.

"I must ask you to pardon me, sir," he began, "for interrupting your business, but there are one or two questions that I want you to be so kind as to answer."

Newman looked at him in evident alarm but replied gruffly, "I have no time to answer questions. Besides, you are a stranger to me, and I don't think I have any concern in your affairs."

"I am a police officer," Blandy explained, "and I – "

"Then I am sure I haven't," snapped Newman.

"I wanted to ask you a few questions in connection with a most unfortunate affair that happened at Newingstead last September," Blandy continued persuasively, but Newman cut him short with the brusque rejoinder, "Newingstead? I never heard of the place, and of course I know nothing about it."

Blandy looked at him with a baffled expression and then turned an appealing face to Thorndyke.

"Can you give us something definite, sir?" he asked.

"I thought I had," Thorndyke replied. "At any rate, I now accuse this man, Newman, as he calls himself, of having murdered Constable Murray at Newingstead on the 19th of last September. That justifies you in making the arrest, and then – well, you know what to do."

But still Blandy seemed undecided. The man's evident terror and the glare of venomous hatred that he cast on Thorndyke proved nothing. Accordingly the inspector, apparently puzzled and unconvinced, sought to temporize.

"If you would allow me, Mr. Newman," said he, "to take an impression of your left thumb, any mistake that may have been made could be set right in a moment. Now what do you say?"

"I say that I will see you damned first," Newman replied fiercely, edging away from the inspector and thereby impinging on the massive form of Sergeant Wills, which occupied the only avenue of escape.

"You've got a definite charge, you know, Inspector," Thorndyke reminded him in a warning tone, still narrowly watching the accused man, and something significant in the way the words were spoken helped Blandy to make up his mind.

"Well, then, Mr. Newman," said he, "if you won't give us any assistance, it's your own look-out. I arrest you on the charge of having murdered Police Constable Murray at Newingstead on the 19th of last September and I caution you that – "

The rest of the caution faded out, for Newman made a sudden movement and was in an instant clasped in the arms of Sergeant Wills, who had skilfully seized the prisoner's wrists from behind and held them immovably pressed against his chest. Almost at the same moment, Blandy sprang forward and grasped the prisoner's ears in order to secure his head and defeat his attempts to bite the sergeant's hands. But Newman was evidently a powerful ruffian, and his struggles were so violent that the two officers had the greatest difficulty in holding him, even when Snuper and I tried to control his arms. In the narrow interval between two glass cases, we all swayed to-and-fro, gyrating slowly and making uncomfortable contacts with sharp corners. Presently Blandy turned his streaming face towards Thorndyke and gasped. "Could you manage the print, Doctor? You can see I can't let go. The kit is in my right-hand coat pocket."

"I have brought the necessary things myself," said Thorndyke, producing from his pocket a small metal box. "It is understood," he added, as he opened the box, "that I am acting on your instructions."

Without waiting for a reply, he took out of the box a tiny roller which had been fixed by its handle in a clip, and having run it along the inside of the lid, which formed an inking-plate, he approached the squirming prisoner. Waiting his opportunity, he suddenly seized the left thumb and, holding it steady, ran the little roller over its bulb. Then he produced a small pad of smooth paper, and again watching for a moment when the thumb was fixed immovably, quickly pressed the pad on the inked surface. The resulting print was not a very perfect impression, but it showed the pattern clearly enough for practical purposes.

"Have you got the photograph with you?" he asked.

"Yes," replied Blandy, "but I can't – could you take hold of his head for a moment?"

Thorndyke laid the pad on the top of the nearest case and then, following Blandy's instructions, grasped the prisoner's head so as to relieve the inspector, Blandy then stepped back, and having taken up the pad, thrust his hand into his pocket and brought out a photograph mounted on a card. For a few moments he stood, eagerly glancing from the pad to the photograph and evidently comparing them point by point.

"Is it the right print?" Thorndyke asked.

Blandy did not answer immediately but continued his scrutiny with evidently growing excitement. At length he looked up, and forgetting his usual bland smile, replied, almost in a shout, "Yes, by God! It's the man himself!"

And then came the catastrophe.

Whether it was that the sergeant's attention was for the moment distracted by the absorbing interest of Blandy's proceedings, or that Newman had been watching his opportunity, I cannot say but, after a brief cessation of his struggles, as if he had become exhausted, he made a sudden violent effort and twisted himself out of his captors' grasp, darting instantly into the passage between two cases. Thither the sergeant followed, but the prisoner, with incredible quickness and dexterity, delivered a smashing blow on the chest which sent the officer staggering

206

backwards, the next moment, the prisoner was standing in the narrow space with an automatic pistol covering his pursuers.

I will do Blandy the justice (which I am glad to do, as I never liked the man) to say that he faced the deadly danger without a sign of fear or a moment's hesitation. How he escaped with his life I have never understood, for he dashed straight at the prisoner, looking into the very muzzle of the pistol. But by some miracle the bullet passed him by, and before another shot could be fired, he had grabbed the man's wrist and got some sort of control of the weapon. Then the sergeant and Snuper and I came to his assistance, and the old struggle began again, but with the material difference that each and all of us had to keep a wary eye on the barrel of the pistol.

Of the crowded and chaotic events of the next minute I have but the obscurest recollection. There comes back to me a vague idea of violent, strenuous effort, a succession of pistol shots with a sort of infernal obbligato accompaniment of shattering glass, the struggles of the sergeant to reach a back pocket without losing his hold on the prisoner, and the manoeuvres of Mr. Sancroft, at first ducking at every shot and finally retreating hurriedly – almost on all fours – into his sanctum. Nor when the end came, am I at all clear as to the exact manner of its happening. I know only that the firing ceased, and that almost as the last shot was fired, the writhing, struggling body became suddenly still and began limply to sag towards the floor, and that I then noticed in the man's right temple a small hole from which issued a little trickle of blood.

Blandy rose, and looking down gloomily at the prostrate body, cursed softly under his breath.

"What infernal luck!" he exclaimed. "I suppose he is dead?"

"I am afraid there is no doubt of that," I replied, as the last faint twitchings died away.

"Infernal luck," he repeated, "to have him slip through our fingers just as we had made sure of him."

"It was the making sure of him that did it," growled the sergeant. "I mean the finger-prints. We ought to have waited for them until we had got the darbies on."

"I know," said Blandy. "But you see I wasn't sure that we had got the right man. He didn't seem to me to answer to the description at all."

"The description of whom?" asked Thorndyke.

"Of Frederick Boles," replied Blandy. "This is Boles, isn't it?"

"No," replied Thorndyke. "This is Peter Gannet."

Blandy was thunderstruck. "But," he exclaimed, incredulously, "it can't be. We identified Gannet's remains quite conclusively."

"Yes," Thorndyke agreed, blandly, "that is what you were intended to do. The remains were actually those of Boles – with certain additions."

Blandy smiled sourly. "Well," said he, "this is a knockout. To think that we have been barking up the wrong tree all the time. But you might have given us the tip a bit sooner, Doctor."

"My dear Blandy," Thorndyke protested, "I told you all that I knew as soon as I knew it."

"You didn't tell us who this man Newman was."

"But, my dear Inspector," Thorndyke replied, "I didn't know myself. When I came here today, I suspected that Mr. Newman was Peter Gannet. But I didn't know until I had seen the man and recognized him and seen that he recognized me. I told you last night that it was merely a case of suspicion."

"Well, well," said Blandy, "it's no use crying over spilt milk. Is there a telephone in the office? If there is, you had better ring up the Police Station, Sergeant, and tell them to send an ambulance along as quickly as they can."

The tinkle of the telephone bell answered Blandy's question, and while the message was being sent and answered, Thorndyke and I proceeded to lay out the body, in view of the probability of premature *rigor mortis*. Then we adjourned to the curator's room, where Blandy showed a tendency to revert to the topic of the might-have-been. But our stay there was short, for the ambulance arrived in an almost incredibly short time, and when the body had been carried out by the stretcher bearers and the outer door shut, the inspector and the sergeant made ready to depart.

"There are some other particulars, Doctor," said Blandy, "that we shall want you to give us, if you will, but now I must get back to the Yard and report what has happened. They won't be over-pleased, but at least we have cleared up a rather mysterious case."

With this, he and the Sergeant went forth to their car, being let out by Mr. Sancroft who, having affixed a notice to the main door, shut it and locked it. Then he came back to the room and gazed round ruefully at the wreck of the People's Museum of Modern Art.

"The Lord knows," said he, "who is going to pay for all this damage. Seven glass cases smashed and the nose knocked off Israel Popoff's *Madonna*. It has been a shocking business, and there is that damned image – if you will excuse me – which has been the cause of all the trouble, still standing in one of the few undamaged cases. But I will soon have it out of there. Only the question is, what on earth is to be done with it? The beastly thing seems to be nobody's property now."

208

"It is the property of Mrs. Gannet," said Thorndyke. "I think it would be best if I were to take custody of it and hand it over to her. I will give you a receipt for it."

"You need not trouble about a receipt," said Sancroft, hauling out his keys and joyfully unlocking the case. "I accept you as Mrs. Gannet's representative and I am only too delighted to get the thing out of the museum. Shall I make it up into a parcel?"

"There is no need," replied Thorndyke, picking up Gannet's bag from the floor, on which it had been dropped when the struggle began. "This will hold it, and there is probably some packing inside."

He opened the bag, and finding it lined with a thick woollen scarf, took the figure from the open case, carefully deposited it in the folds of the scarf, and shut the bag.

That seemed to conclude our business, and after a few more words with the still agitated Sancroft and a brief farewell to Mr. Snuper, we accompanied the former to the door, whence we were let out into the street.

Chapter XIX
The Monkey Reveals
His Secret

By lovers of paradox we are assured that it is the unexpected that will always happens. But this is, to put it mildly, an exaggeration. Even the expected happens sometimes. It did, for instance, on the present occasion, for when we passed into the entry of our chambers on our return from the museum and began to ascend the stairs, I expected that Thorndyke would pass by the door of our sitting room and go straight up to the laboratory floor. And that is precisely what he did. He made directly for the larger workshop, and having greeted Polton as we entered, laid Gannet's bag on the bench.

"We need not disturb you, Polton," said he, noting that our assistant was busily polishing the pallets of a dead-beat escapement appertaining to a "regulator" that he was constructing. But Polton had already fixed an inquisitive eye on the bag and, coupling its presence with our mysterious expedition, had evidently sniffed something more exciting than clockwork.

"You are not disturbing me, sir," said he, laying the pallets on the table of the polishing lathe and bearing down with a purposeful air on the bag. "The clock is a spare time job. Can I give you any assistance?"

Thorndyke smiled appreciatively and, opening the bag, carefully took out the figure and stood it up on the bench.

"There, Polton," said he. "What do you think of that for a work of art?"

"My word!" exclaimed Polton, regarding the figure with profound disfavour, "but he is an ugly fellow. Now what part of the world might he have come from? South Sea Islands he looks like."

Thorndyke lifted the image and, turning it up to exhibit the base, handed it to Polton, who examined it with fresh astonishment.

"Why," he exclaimed, "it seems to have been made by a civilized man! It's English lettering, though I don't recognize the mark."

"It was made by an Englishman," said Thorndyke. "But do you find anything abnormal about it apart from its ugliness?"

Polton looked long and earnestly at the base, turned the figure over and examined every part of it, finally tapping it with his knuckles and listening attentively to the sound elicited.

"I don't think it is solid," said he, "though it is mighty thick."

"It is not solid," said Thorndyke, "We have ascertained that."

"Then," said Polton, "I don't understand it. The body looks like ordinary stoneware. But it can't be if it's hollow. There is no opening in it anywhere. But it couldn't have been fired without a vent-hole of some kind. It would have blown to pieces."

"Yes," Thorndyke agreed. "That is the problem. But have another look at the base. What do you say to that white glazed slip on which the signature is written?"

Polton inspected it afresh, and finally stuck a watchmaker's eyeglass in his eye to assist in the examination.

"I don't know what to make of it," said he. "It looks a little like a tin glaze, but I don't think it is. I don't see how it could be. What do you think it is, sir?"

"I suspect that it is some kind of hard white cement – possibly Keene's – covered with a clear varnish."

Polton looked up at him, and his expressive countenance broke out into a characteristic crinkly smile.

"I think you have hit it, sir," said he, "and I think I begin to ogle, as Mr. Miller would say. What are we going to do about it?"

"The obvious thing," said Thorndyke, "is to make what surgeons would call an exploratory puncture, drill a small hole in it and see what the base is really made of and what its thickness is."

"Would a drill go into stoneware?" I asked.

"No," replied Thorndyke, "not an ordinary drill. But I do not think that there is any stoneware in the middle of the base. You remember Broomhill's specimen? There was a good-sized elliptical opening in the base, and I imagine that this figure was originally the same, but that the opening has been filled up. What we have to ascertain is what it has been filled with and how far the filling goes into the cavity."

"We had better do it with a hand-drill," said Polton, "and steady the image on the bench, as it wouldn't be safe to fix it in the vise. Then it will be convenient if we want to enlarge the hole."

He wrapped the "image" in one or two thick dusters and laid it on the bench, when I took charge of it and held it as firmly as I could to resist the pressure of the drill. Then, having fitted an eighth-inch Morse into the stock, he began operations, cautiously, and with only a light pressure, but I noticed that at first the hard drill-point seemed to make very little impression.

"What do you suppose the filling consists of, sir?" Polton asked, as he withdrew the drill to examine the shallow pit its point had made, "and how far do you suppose it goes in?"

"My idea is," replied Thorndyke, "but it is only a guess – that there is a comparatively thin layer of Keene's cement and then a plug of plaster, perhaps three or four inches thick. Beyond that, I should expect to come to the cavity. I hope I am right, for if it should turn out to be Keene's cement all the way, we shall have some trouble in making a hole large enough for our purpose."

"What is our purpose?" I asked. "To see if there is anything in the cavity, I presume."

"Yes," Thorndyke replied, "though it is practically certain that there is. Otherwise, there would have been no object in stopping up the opening."

Here Polton returned to the charge, now sensibly increasing the pressure. Still, for a while, the drill seemed to make little progress. Then quite suddenly, as if some obstruction had been removed, it began to enter freely and had soon penetrated as far as the chuck would allow it to go.

"You said, three or four inches, I think, sir?" Polton remarked, as he withdrew the drill and examined the white powder in the grooves.

"Yes," Thorndyke replied, "but possibly more. A six-inch drill would be best, and you might use a stouter one – say a quarter-inch – to avoid the risk of its bending."

Polton made the necessary change and resumed operations with the larger drill, which soon enlarged the opening and then began quickly to penetrate the softer plaster. When it had entered about four inches, even this slight resistance seemed to cease, for it ran in suddenly right up to the chuck.

"Four inches it is, sir," said Polton, with a triumphant crinkle, as he withdrew the drill and inspected the grooves. "How big an opening will you want?"

"An inch might do," replied Thorndyke, "but an inch and a half would be better. I think that is possible without encroaching on the stoneware body. But you will see."

On this, Polton produced a set of reamers and a brace, and beginning with one which would just enter the hole, turned the brace cautiously while I continued to steady the figure. Meanwhile, Thorndyke, having cut off a piece of stout copper wire about eight inches long, fixed it in the vise and, with an adjustable die, cut a screw thread about an inch long on one end.

"We may as well see what the conditions are," said he, "before we go any further."

He took the wire out of the vise, and as Polton withdrew the third reamer – which had enlarged the hole to about half an inch – he passed the wire into the hole and began gently to probe the bottom of the cavity. Then he pressed it in somewhat more firmly and gave it one or two turns, slowly drawing it out while he continued to turn. When it finally emerged, its end held a small knob of cotton wool from which a little twisted strand of the same material extended into the invisible interior. I watched its emergence with profound interest and a certain amount of self-contempt, for obviously he had expected to find the interior filled with cotton wool as was demonstrated by the making of the cotton wool holder. And yet I, who knew as much of the essential facts as he did, had never guessed, and even now had only a vague suspicion of what its presence suggested.

As the operations with the reamers progressed, it became evident that the larger opening was possible, for the material cut through was still only cement and plaster. When the full inch and a half had been reached, Thorndyke fixed his wire in the chuck of the hand-drill, and passing the former into the wide hole, pressed the screw end into the mass of cotton wool, and began to turn the handle, slowly withdrawing it as he turned. When the end of the wire appeared at the opening, it bore a ball of cotton wool from which a thick strand, twisted by the rapid rotation of the wire into a firm cord, extended to the mass inside, and as Thorndyke slowly stepped back, still turning the handle, the cord grew longer and longer until at last its end slipped out of the opening, showing that the whole of the cotton wool had been extracted.

"Now," said Thorndyke, "let us see what all that cotton wool enclosed."

He laid aside the drill and, carefully lifting the figure, held it upright over the bench, when there dropped out a small, white paper packet tied up with thread. Having cut the thread, he laid the packet on the bench and opened it, while Polton and I craned forward inquisitively. I suppose we both knew approximately what to expect, and I was better able to guess than Polton, but the reality was quite beyond my expectations, and as for Polton, he was, for the moment, struck dumb. Only for the moment, however, for recovering himself, he exclaimed impressively, with his eyes fixed on the packet, "Never in all my life have I seen the like of this. Fifteen diamonds and every one of them a specimen stone. And look at the size of them! Why, that little lot must be worth a king's ransom!"

"I understand," said Thorndyke, "that they represent about ten-thousand pounds. That will be their market price, and you can add to that three human lives – not as their value, which it is not, but as their cost."

"I take it," said I, "that you are assuming these to be Kempster's diamonds?"

"It is hardly a case of assuming," he replied. "The facts seem to admit of no other interpretation. This was an experiment to test the correctness of my theory of the crime. I expected to find in this figure fifteen large diamonds. Well, we have opened the figure and here are the fifteen large diamonds. This figure belonged to Peter Gannet, and whatever was in it was put in by him, as is shown by the sealing on the base which bears his signature. But Peter Gannet has been proved to be the murderer of the constable, and that murderer was undoubtedly the man who stole Kempster's diamonds, and these diamonds correspond in number and appearance with the diamonds which were stolen. However, we won't leave it at a mere matter of appearance. Kempster gave me full particulars of the diamonds, including the weight of each stone, and of course the total weight of the whole parcel. We need hardly take the weight of each stone separately, but if we weigh the whole fifteen together and we find that the total weight agrees with that given by Kempster, even my learned and sceptical friend will admit that the identity is proved sufficiently for our present purposes."

I ventured mildly to repudiate the alleged scepticism but agreed that the verification was worthwhile, and when Thorndyke had carefully closed the packet, we all adjourned to the chemical laboratory, where Polton slid up the glass front of the balance and went through the formality of testing the truth of the latter with empty cans.

"What weight shall I put on, sir?" he asked.

"Mr. Kempster put the total weight at 380.4 grains. Let us try that."

Polton selected the appropriate weights, and when they had been checked by Thorndyke, they were placed in the pan and the necessary "rider" put on the beam to make up the fraction. Then Polton solemnly closed the glass front and slowly depressed the lever, and as the balance rose, the index deviated barely a hair's breadth from the zero mark.

"I think that is near enough," said Thorndyke, "to justify us in deciding that these are the diamonds that were stolen from Kempster."

"Yes," I agreed. "At any rate, it is conclusive enough for me. What do you propose to do with them? Shall you hand them to Kempster?"

"No," he replied. "I don't think that would be quite in order. Stolen property should be delivered to the police, even if its ownership is known. I shall hand these diamonds to the Commissioner of Police, explain the circumstances, and take his receipt for them. Then I shall notify Kempster and leave him to collect them. He will have no difficulty in recovering them as the police have a complete description of the stones. And that will finish the business, so far as I am concerned. I have more than fulfilled my obligations to Kempster and I have proved that Mrs. Gannet could not possibly have been an accessory to the murder of

214

her husband. Those were the ostensible objects of my investigation, apart from the intrinsic interest of the case, and now that they have both been achieved, it remains only to sing *Nunc Dimittis* and celebrate our success with a modest festivity of some kind."

"There is one other little matter that remains," said I. "Today's events have proved that your theory of the crime was correct, but they haven't shown how you arrived at that theory, and I have only the dimmest ideas on the subject. But perhaps the festivity will include a reasoned exposition of the evidence."

"I see nothing against that," he replied. "It would be quite interesting to me to retrace the course of the investigation, and if it would also interest you and Oldfield – who must certainly be one of the party – then we shall all be pleased."

He paused for a few moments, having, I think, detected a certain wistfulness in Polton's face, for he continued.

"A restaurant dinner would hardly meet the case, if a prolonged and necessarily confidential pow-wow is contemplated. What do you think, Polton?"

"I think, sir," Polton replied, promptly and with emphasis, "that you would be much more comfortable and more private in your own dining room, and you'd get a better dinner, too. If you will leave the arrangements to me, I will see that the entertainment does you credit."

I chuckled inwardly at Polton's eagerness. Not but that he would at any time have delighted in ministering, in our own chambers, to Thorndyke's comfort and that of his friends. But apart from these altruistic considerations, I felt sure that on this present occasion the "arrangements" would include some very effective ones for enabling him to enjoy the exposition.

"Very well, Polton," said Thorndyke. "I will leave the affair in your hands. You had better see Dr. Oldfield and find out what date will suit him, and then we will wind up the Gannet case with a flourish."

215

Chapter XX
Thorndyke Reviews
the Evidence

Our invitation to Oldfield came very opportunely, for he was just preparing for his holiday and had already got a *locum tenens* installed. So when, on the appointed evening, he turned up in buoyant spirits, it was as a free man, immune from the haunting fear of an urgent call.

Polton's artful arrangements for unostentatious eavesdropping had come to naught, for Thorndyke and I had insisted on his laying a place for himself at the table and joining us as the colleague that he had actually become in late years, rather than the servant that he still proclaimed himself to be. For the gradual change of status from servant to friend had occurred quite smoothly and naturally. Polton was a man in whom perfect manners were inborn, and as for his intellect – well, I would gladly have swapped my brain for his.

"This is very pleasant," said Oldfield, as he took his seat and cast an appreciative glance round the table, "and it is most kind of you, sir, to have invited me to the celebration, especially when you consider what a fool I have been and what a mess I made of my part of the business."

"You didn't make a mess of it at all," said Thorndyke.

"Well, sir," Oldfield chuckled, "I made every mistake that was humanly possible, and no man can do more than that."

"You are doing yourself a great injustice, Oldfield," Thorndyke protested. "Apparently you don't realize that you were the actual discoverer of the crime."

Oldfield laid down his knife and fork to gaze at Thorndyke.

"I, the discoverer!" he exclaimed, and then, "Oh, you mean that I discovered the ashes. But any other fool could have done that. There they were, plainly in sight, and it just happened that I was the first person to go into the studio."

"I am not so sure even of that," said Thorndyke. "There was some truth in what Blandy said to you. It was the expert eye which saw at once that something strange had happened. Most persons, going into the studio, would have failed to observe anything abnormal. But that is not what I am referring to. I mean that it was you who made the discovery that exposed the real nature of the crime and led to the identification of the criminal."

Oldfield shook his head, incredulously, and looked at Thorndyke as if demanding further enlightenment.

"What I mean," the latter explained, "is that here we had a crime, carefully and subtly planned and prepared in detail with admirable foresight and imagination. There was only a single mistake, and but for you, that mistake would have passed unnoticed and the scheme would have worked according to plan. It very nearly did, as you know."

Oldfield still looked puzzled, as well he might, for he knew, as I did, that all his conclusions had been wrong, and I was as far as he was from understanding what Thorndyke meant.

"Perhaps," Oldfield suggested, "you will explain in a little more detail what my discovery was?"

"Not now," replied Thorndyke. "Presently, we are going to have a reasoned analysis of the case. You will see plainly enough then."

"I suppose I shall," Oldfield agreed, doubtfully, "but I should have said that the entire discovery was your own, sir. I know that it came as a thunder-bolt to me, and so I expect it did to Blandy. And he must have been pretty sick at losing his prisoner, after all."

"Yes," said I, "he was. And it was unfortunate. Gannet ought to have been brought to trial and hanged."

"I am not sorry that he wasn't, all the same," said Oldfield. "It would have been horrible for poor Mrs. Gannet."

"Yes," Thorndyke agreed, "a trial and a hanging would have ruined her life. I am inclined to feel that the suicide, or accident, was all for the best, especially as there are signs that very warm and sympathetic relations are growing up between her and our good friend Linnell. One likes to feel that the future holds out to her the promise of some compensation for all the trials and troubles that she has had to endure."

"Still," I persisted, "the fellow was a villain and ought to have been hanged."

"He wasn't the worst kind of villain," said Thorndyke. "The murder of the constable was, if not properly accidental, at least rather in the nature of 'chance medley'. There could have been no intention to kill. And as to Boles, he probably offered considerable provocation."

From this point the conversation tended to peter out, the company's jaws being otherwise engaged. What there was ranged over a variety of topics – including Polton's magnum opus, the regulator, now in a fair way of being completed – and kept us entertained until the last of the dishes had been dealt with and removed and the port and the dessert had been set on the table. Then, when Oldfield and I had filled our pipes (Polton did not smoke but took an occasional, furtive pinch of snuff),

Thorndyke, in response to our insistent demands, put down his empty pipe and proceeded to the promised analysis.

"In order," he began, "to appreciate the subtlety and imagination with which this crime was planned, it is necessary to recall the whole sequence of events and to note how naturally and logically it evolved. It begins with a case of arsenic poisoning, a perfectly simple and ordinary case with all the familiar features. A man is poisoned by arsenic in his food. That food is prepared by his wife. The wife has a male friend to whom she is rather devoted, and she is not very devoted to her husband. Taken at its face value, there is no mystery at all. It appears to be just the old, old story.

"The poisoning is detected, the man recovers, and returns home to resume his ordinary habits. But any observer, noting the facts, must feel that this is not the end. There will surely be a sequel. A murder has been attempted and has failed, but the will to murder has been proved, and it presumably still exists, awaiting a fresh opportunity. Anyone knowing what has happened will naturally be on the lookout for some further attempt.

"Then, during his wife's absence at the seaside, the man disappears. She comes home and finds that he is missing. He has not gone away in any ordinary sense, for he has taken nothing with him, not even a hat. In her alarm she naturally seeks the advice of the doctor. But the doctor, recalling the poisoning incident, at once suspects a tragedy, and the more so since he knows of the violent enmity existing between the husband and the wife's friend. But he does not merely suspect a tragedy in the abstract. His suspicions take a definite shape. The idea of murder comes into his mind, and when it does it is associated naturally enough with the man who was suspected of having administered the poison. He is not, perhaps, fully conscious of his suspicions, but he is in such a state of mind that in the instant when the fact of the murder becomes evident, he confidently fills in the picture and identifies not only the victim but the murderer, too.

"Thus, you see how perfectly the stage had been set for the events that were to follow, how admirably the minds of all who knew the facts had been prepared to follow out a particular line of thought. There is the preliminary crime with Boles as the obvious suspect. There is the expectation that, since the motive remains, there will be a further attempt – by Boles. Then comes the expected sequel, and instantly, by the most natural and reasonable association, the *dramatis personae* of the first crime are transferred, in the same roles, to the second crime. It is all quite plain and consistent. Taking things at their face value, it seemed obvious that the murdered man must be Peter Gannet and his murderer, Frederick

218

Boles. I think that I should have been prepared to accept that view myself, if there had been nothing to suggest a different conclusion.

"But it was just at this point that Oldfield made his valuable contribution to the evidence. Providence inspired him to take a sample of the bone-ash and test it for arsenic, and to his surprise, and still more to mine, he proved that the ash did contain arsenic. Moreover, the metal was present, not as a mere trace but in measurable quantities. And there could be no doubt about it. Oldfield's analysis was carried out skilfully and with every precaution against error, and I repeated the experiment with the remainder of the sample and confirmed his results.

"Now here was a definite anomaly, a something which did not seem to fit in with the rest of the facts, and I am astonished that neither Blandy nor the other investigators appreciated its possible importance. To me an anomalous fact – a fact which appears unconnected, or even discordant with the body of known facts – is precisely the one on which attention should be focused. And that is what I did in this present case. The arsenic was undeniably present in the ashes, and its presence had to be accounted for.

"How did it come to be there? Admittedly, it was not in the body before the burning. Then it must have found its way into the ashes after their removal from the kiln. But how? To me there appeared to be only two possible explanations, and I considered each, comparing it with the other in terms of probability.

"First, there was the suggestion made at the inquest that the ashes might have become contaminated with arsenic in the course of grinding or transference to the bin. That, perhaps, sounded plausible if it was only a verbal formula for disposing of a curious but irrelevant fact. But when one tried to imagine how such contamination could have occurred, no reasonable explanation was forthcoming. What possible source of contamination was there? Arsenic is not one of the potter's ordinary materials. It would not have been present in the bin, nor in the iron mortar nor in the grinding mills. It was a foreign substance, so far as the pottery studio was concerned, and the only arsenic known to exist in the place was that which was contained in a stoppered jar in Boles's cupboard.

"Moreover, it had not the character of a mere chance contamination. Not only was it present in a measurable quantity, it appeared to be fairly evenly distributed throughout the ashes, as was proved by the fact that the Home Office chemist obtained results substantially similar to Oldfield's and mine. After a critical examination of this explanation, I felt that it explained nothing, that it did not agree with the facts, and was itself inexplicable.

219

"Then, if one could not accept the contamination theory, what was the alternative? The only other explanation that could be suggested was that the arsenic had been *intentionally mixed with the ashes*. At the first glance this did not look very probable. But if it was not the true explanation, it was at least intelligible. There was no impossibility, and in fact, the more I considered it, the less improbable did it appear.

"When this hypothesis was adopted provisionally, two further questions at once arose: If the arsenic was intentionally put into the ashes, who put it there, and for what purpose? Taking the latter question first, a reasonable answer immediately suggested itself. The most obvious purpose would be that of establishing a connection between the present crime and the previous arsenic poisoning, and when I asked myself what could be the object of trying to establish such a connection, again a perfectly reasonable answer was forthcoming. In the poisoning crime, the victim was Peter Gannet, and the would-be murderer was almost certainly Frederick Boles. Then the introduction of the arsenic as a common factor linking together the two crimes would have the purpose of suggesting a repetition of the characters of victim and murderer. That is to say, the ultimate object of putting the arsenic into the ashes would be to create the conviction that the ashes were the remains of Peter Gannet, that he had been murdered by means of arsenic, and that the murderer was Frederick Boles.

"But who would wish to create this conviction? Remember that our picture contains only three figures: Gannet, his wife, and Boles. If the arsenic had been planted, it must have been planted by one of those three. But by which of them? By Mrs. Gannet? Certainly not, seeing that she was under some suspicion of having been an accessory to the poisoning. And obviously Boles would not wish to create the belief that he was the murderer.

"Thus, of the three possible agents of this imposture, we had excluded two. There remained only Gannet. The suggestion was that he was dead and, therefore, could not have planted the arsenic. But could we accept that suggestion? The arsenic was (by the hypothesis) admittedly an imposture. But with the evidence of imposture, we could no longer take the appearances at their face value. The only direct evidence that the remains were those of Gannet was the tooth that was found in the ashes. It was, however, only a porcelain tooth and no more an integral part of Gannet's body than his shirt button or his collar stud. If the arsenic had been planted to produce a particular belief, it was conceivable that the tooth might have been planted for the very same purpose. It was in fact conceivable that the ashes were not those of Gannet and that consequently Gannet was not dead.

220

"But if Gannet had not been the victim of this murder, then he was almost certainly the murderer, and if Boles had not been the murderer, then he must almost certainly have been the victim. Both men had disappeared and the ashes were undoubtedly the remains of one of them. Suppose the remains to be those of Boles and the murderer to be Peter Gannet? How does that affect our question as to the planting of the arsenic?

"At a glance we can see that Gannet would have had the strongest reasons for creating the belief that the remains were those of his own body. So long as that belief prevailed, he was absolutely safe. The police would have written him off as dead and would be engaged in an endless and fruitless search for Boles. With only a trifling change in his appearance – such as the shaving off of his beard and moustache – he could go his way in perfect security. Nobody would be looking for him, nobody would even believe in his existence. He would have made the perfect escape.

"This result appeared to me very impressive. The presence of the arsenic was a fact. The hypothesis that it had been planted was the only intelligible explanation of that fact. The acceptance of that hypothesis was conditional on the discovery of some motive for planting it. Such a motive we had discovered, but the acceptance of that motive was conditional on the assumption that Peter Gannet was still alive.

"Was such an assumption unreasonable? Not at all. Gannet's death had rather been taken for granted. He had disappeared mysteriously, and certain unrecognisable human remains had been found on his premises. At once it had been assumed that the remains were his. The actual identification rested on a single porcelain tooth, but as that tooth was no part of his body and could, therefore, have been purposely planted in the ashes, the evidence that it afforded as to the identity of the remains was not conclusive. If any grounds existed for suspecting imposture, it had no evidential value at all. But apart from that tooth there was not, and never had been, any positive reasons for believing that those ashes were the remains of Peter Gannet.

"The completeness and consistency of the results thus arrived at, by reasoning from the hypothesis that the arsenic had been planted, impressed me profoundly. It really looked as if that hypothesis might be the true one, and I decided to pursue the argument and see whither it led, and especially to examine one or two other slight anomalies that I had noticed.

"I began with the crime itself. The picture presented (and accepted by the police) was this: Boles had murdered Gannet and cremated his body in the kiln, after dismembering it, if necessary, to get it into the cavity. He had then pounded the incinerated bones and deposited the fragments in the bone-ash bin. Then, after having done all this, he was suddenly overcome by panic and fled.

"But why had he fled? There was no reason whatever for him to flee. He was in no danger. He was alone in the studio and could lock himself in. There was no fear of interruption, since Mrs. Gannet was away at the seaside, and even if any chance visitor should have come, there was nothing visible to excite suspicion. He had done the difficult and dangerous part of the work and all that remained were the few finishing touches. If he had cleaned up the kiln and put it into its usual condition, the place would have looked quite normal, even to Oldfield, and as to the bone fragments, there was not only the grog-mill but also a powerful edge-runner mill in which they could have been ground to fine powder. If this powder had been put into the bone-ash-bin – the ordinary contents of which were powdered bone ash – every trace of the crime would have been destroyed. Then Boles could have gone about his work in the ordinary way or taken a holiday if he had pleased. There would have been nothing to suggest that any abnormal events had occurred in the studio or that Gannet was not still alive.

"Contrast this with the actual conditions that were found. The kiln had been left in a state that would instantly attract the attention of anyone who knew anything about the working of a pottery studio. The incinerated bones had been pounded into fragments, just too small to be recognizable as parts of any known person, but large enough to be recognized, not only as bones, but as human bones. After all the risk and labour of cremating the body and pounding the bones, there had still been left clear evidence that a man had been murdered.

"I think you will agree that the suggested behaviour of Boles is quite unaccountable, is entirely at variance with reasonable probabilities. On the other hand, if you consider critically the conditions that were found, they will convey to you, as they did to me, the impression of a carefully arranged tableau. Certain facts, such as the murder and the cremation, were to be made plain and obvious, and certain issues, such as the identities of victim and murderer, were to be confused. But furthermore, they conveyed to me a very interesting suggestion, which was that the tableau had been set for a particular spectator. Let us consider this suggestion.

"The crime was discovered by Oldfield, and it is possible that he was the only person who would have discovered it. His potter's eye, glancing at the kiln, noted its abnormal state and saw that something was wrong. Probably there was a good deal of truth, as well as politeness, in Blandy's remark that if he had come to the studio without his expert guide and adviser, though he would have seen the visible objects, he would have failed to interpret their meaning. But Oldfield had just the right knowledge. He knew all about the kiln, he knew the various bins and what was in them, and what the mills were for. So, too, with the little finger bone. Most persons would not have known what it was, but Oldfield, the anatomist, recognizes it at once as the ungual phalanx of a human index finger. He would seem to have been the pre-appointed discoverer.

"The suggestion is strengthened by what we know of the previous events, of Gannet's eagerness to cultivate the doctor's friendship, to induct him into all the mysteries of the studio and all the routine of the work that was carried on there. There is an appearance of Oldfield's being prepared to play the part of discoverer – a part that would naturally fall to him, since it was certain that when the blow fell, Mrs. Gannet would seek the help and advice of the doctor.

"The suggestion of preparation applies also to the arsenic in the ashes. If that arsenic was planted, the planting of it must have been a mere gamble, for it was most unlikely that anyone would think of testing the ashes for arsenic. But if there was any person in the world who would think of doing so, that person was most assuredly Oldfield. Any young doctor who has the misfortune to miss a case of arsenic poisoning is pretty certain thereafter to develop what the psychological jargonists would call 'an arsenic complex'. When any abnormal death occurs, he is sure to think first of arsenic.

"The whole group of appearances then suggested that Oldfield had been prepared to take a particular view and to form certain suspicions. But did not that suggestion carry us back still farther? What of the poisoning affair itself? If all the other appearances were false appearances, was it not possible that the poisoning was an imposture, too? When I came to consider that question, I recalled certain anomalies in the case which I had observed at the time. I did not attach great importance to them, since arsenic is a very erratic poison, but I noted them and I advised Oldfield to keep full notes of the case, and now that the question of imposture had arisen, it was necessary to reconsider them, and to review the whole case critically.

"We had to begin our review by reminding ourselves that practically the whole of our information was derived from the patient's statements. The phenomena were virtually all subjective. Excepting the redness of the eyes, which could easily have been produced artificially, there were no objective signs, for the appearance of the tongue was not characteristic. Of the subjective symptoms we were told, we did not observe them for ourselves. The abdominal pain was felt by the patient, not by us. So with the numbness, the loss of tactile sensibility, the tingling, the cramps, and the inability to stand, we learned of their existence from the patient and we could not check his statements. We accepted those statements as there appeared to be no reason for doubting them, but it was quite possible for them all to have been false. To an intelligent malingerer who had carefully studied the symptoms of arsenic poisoning, there would have been little difficulty in making up a quite convincing set of symptoms."

"But," Oldfield objected, "there really was arsenic in the body. You were not forgetting that?"

"Not at all," replied Thorndyke. "That was the first of the anomalies. You will remember my remarking to you that the quantity of arsenic obtained by analysis of the secretions was less than I expected. Woodfield and I were both surprised at the smallness of the amount – which was, in fact, not much greater than might have been found in a patient who was taking arsenic medicinally. But it was not an extreme discrepancy, since arsenic is rapidly eliminated, though the symptoms persist, and we explained it by assuming that no considerable dose had been taken quite recently. Nevertheless, it was rather remarkable, as the severity of the symptoms would have led us to expect a considerable quantity of the poison.

"The next anomaly was the rapidity and completeness of Gannet's recovery. Usually, in severe cases, recovery is slow and is followed by a somewhat long period of ill-health. But Gannet began to recover almost immediately, and when he left the hospital he seemed to be quite well.

"The third anomaly – not a very striking one, perhaps – was his state of mind on leaving hospital. He went back home quite happily and confidently, though his would-be murderer was still there, and he would not entertain any sort of inquiry or any measures to ascertain that murderer's identity. He seemed to assume that the affair was finished and that there was nothing more to fear.

"Now, looking at the case as a whole with the idea of a possible imposture in our minds, what did it suggest? Was there not the possibility that all the symptoms were simulated? That Gannet took just enough arsenic to supply the means of chemical demonstration (a fairly full daily dose of Fowler's Solution would do) and on the appropriate occasion, put a substantial quantity of arsenic into the barley water? In short, was it not possible that the poisoning affair was a deception from beginning to end?

"The answer to this question obviously was that it was quite possible, and the next question was as to its probability. But the answer to this also appeared to be affirmative, for on our hypothesis, the

224

appearances in the studio were false appearances, deliberately produced to create a certain erroneous belief. But those appearances were strongly supported by the previous poisoning crime and obviously connected with it. The reasonable conclusion seemed to be that the poisoning affair was a deception calculated to create this same erroneous belief (that an attempt had been made to murder Gannet) and to lead on naturally to the second crime.

"Now let us pause for a moment to see where we stand. Our hypothesis started with the assumption that the arsenic had been put into the ashes for a definite purpose. But we found that the only person who could have had a motive for planting it was Peter Gannet. Thus we had to conclude that Gannet was the murderer and Boles the victim. We have examined this conclusion, point by point, and we have found that it agrees with all the known facts and that it yields a complete, consistent, and reasonable scheme of the studio crime. Accordingly, we adopt that conclusion – provisionally, of course, for we are still in the region of hypothesis and have, as yet, actually proved nothing.

"But assuming that Gannet had committed this murder, it was evident that it must have been a very deliberate crime, long premeditated, carefully planned and carried out with extraordinary foresight and infinite patience. A crime of this kind implies a proportionate motive, a deep seated, permanent and intense motive. What could it have been? Was there anything known to us in Gannet's circumstances that might seem to account for his entertaining murder as a considered policy? Taking the usual motives for planned and premeditated murder, I asked myself whether any of them could apply to him. We may put them roughly into five categories: Jealousy, revenge, cupidity, escape, and fear. Was there any suggestion that Gannet might have been affected by any of them?

"As to jealousy, there was the undeniable fact that Mrs. Gannet's relations with Boles were unusual and perhaps indiscreet. But there was no evidence of any impropriety and no sign that the friendship was resented by Gannet. It did not appear to me that jealousy as a motive could be entertained.

"As to revenge, this is a common motive among Mediterranean peoples, but very rare in the case of Englishmen. Boles and Gannet disliked each other to the point of open enmity. An unpremeditated murder might easily have occurred, but there was nothing in their mere mutual dislike to suggest a motive for a deliberately planned murder. So, too, with the motive of cupidity, there was nothing to show that either stood to gain any material benefit by the death of the other. But when I came to consider the last two motives – escape and fear – I saw that there

225

was a positive suggestion which invited further examination, and the more it was examined, the more definite did it become."

"What, exactly, do you mean by 'escape'?" I asked.

"I mean," he replied, "the desire to escape from some intolerable position. A man, for instance, whose life is being made unbearable by the conduct of an impossible wife, may contemplate getting rid of her, especially if he sees the opportunity of making a happy and desirable marriage, or who is haunted by a blackmailer who will never leave him to live in peace. In either case, murder offers the only means of escape, and the motive to adopt that means will tend to develop gradually. From a mere desirable possibility, it will grow into a definite intention, and then there will be careful consideration of practicable and safe methods of procedure. Now in the present case, as I have said, it appeared to me that such a motive might have existed, and when I considered the circumstances, that impression became strongly confirmed. The possible motive came into view in connection with certain facts which were disclosed by Inspector Blandy's activities, and which were communicated to me by Oldfield when he consulted me about Mrs. Gannet's difficulties.

"It appeared that Blandy, having finished with the bone fragments, proceeded to turn out Boles's cupboard. There he found fairly conclusive evidence that Boles was a common receiver, which was not our concern. But he also found a piece of gold plate on which were some very distinct finger-prints. They were the prints from a left hand, and there was a particularly fine and clear impression of a left thumb. Of this plate Blandy took possession with the expressed intention of taking it to the Finger-print Department at Scotland Yard to see if Boles happened to be a known criminal. Presumably, he did so, and we may judge of the result by what followed. Two days later he called on Mrs. Gannet and subjected her to a searching interrogation, asking a number of leading questions, among which were two of very remarkable significance. He wanted to know where Boles was on the 19th of last September, and when it was that his friendship with Gannet suddenly turned to enmity. Both these questions she was able to answer, and the questions and the answers were highly illuminating.

"First, as to the questions. The 19th of September was the date of the Newingstead murder, and the murdered constable's truncheon bore a very distinct print of a left thumb – evidently that of the murderer. At a glance, it appeared to me obvious that the thumb-print on the gold plate had been found to correspond with the thumb print on the truncheon and that Boles had been identified thereby as the murderer of the constable. That was the only possible explanation of Blandy's question. And this

226

assumption was confirmed by the answer, by which it transpired that Boles was at Newingstead on that fatal day and that, incidentally, Gannet was with him, the two men, apparently, staying at the house of Boles's aunt.

"Blandy's other question and Mrs. Gannet's answer were also profoundly significant, for she recalled, clearly, that the sudden change in the relations of the two men was first observed by her when she met them after their return from Newingstead. They went there friends, they came back enemies. She knew of no reason for the change, but those were the facts.

"Here we may pause to fill in, as I did, the picture thus presented to us in outline. There are two men (whom we may conveniently call A and B) staying together at a house in Newingstead. On the 19th of September, one of them, A, goes forth alone. Between eight and nine in the evening he commits the robbery. At about nine o'clock he kills the constable. Then he finds Oldfield's bicycle and on it he pedals away some four miles along the London Road. Having thus got away from the scene of the crime, he dismounts and seeks a place in which to hide the bicycle. He finds a cart shed, and having concealed the bicycle in it, sets out to return to Newingstead. Obviously, he would not go back by the same route, with the chance of encountering the police, for he probably suspects that he has killed a man, and at any rate, he has the stolen diamonds on his person. He must necessarily make a detour so as to approach Newingstead from a different direction, and his progress would not be rapid, as he would probably try to avoid being seen. The cart shed was over four miles from Newingstead along the main road, and his detour would have added considerably to that distance. By the time that he arrived at his lodgings it would be getting late, at least eleven o'clock and probably later. Quite a late hour by village standards.

"The time of his arrival home would probably be noted by B. But there is something else he would note. A had been engaged in a violent encounter with the constable and could hardly fail to bear some traces of it on his person. The constable was by no means passive. He had drawn his truncheon and was using it when it was snatched away from him. We may safely assume that A's appearance, when he sneaked home and let himself into the house, must have been somewhat unusual.

"By the next morning the hue-and-cry was out. All the village knew of the robbery and the murder, and it would be inevitable that B should connect the crime with A's late homecoming and disordered condition. Not only did the times agree, but the man robbed, Arthur Kempster, was known to them both, and known personally at least by one of them. Then came the inquest with full details of the crime and the vitally important

227

fact that a clear finger-print, left by the murderer, was in the possession of the police. Both the men must have known what was proved at the inquest for a very full report of it was published in the local paper, as I know from having read a copy that Kempster gave me. Both men knew of the existence of the thumb-print, and one knew, and the other was convinced, that it was A's thumb-print.

"From these facts it was easy to infer what must have followed. For it appears that it was just at this time that the sudden change from mutual friendship to mutual enmity occurred. What did that change (considered in connection with the aforesaid facts) imply? To me it suggested the beginning of a course of blackmail. B was convinced that A was the robber and he demanded a share of the proceeds as the price of his silence. But A could not admit the robbery without also admitting the murder. Consequently, he denied all knowledge of either.

"Then began the familiar train of events that is characteristic of blackmail, that so commonly leads to its natural end in either suicide or murder. B felt sure that A had in his possession loot to the value of ten-thousand pounds and he demanded, with menaces, his share of that loot, demands that A met with stubborn denials. And so it went on with recurring threats and recriminations and violent quarrels.

"But it could not go on forever. To A the conditions were becoming intolerable. A constant menace hung over him. He lived in the shadow of the gallows. A word from B could put the rope round his neck, a mere denunciation without need of proof. For there was the deadly thumb-print, and they both knew it. To A a simple accusation showed the way directly to the execution shed.

"Was there no escape? Obviously, mere payment was of no use. It never is of use in the case of blackmail. For the blackmailer may sell his silence but he retains his knowledge. If A had surrendered the whole of the loot to B, he would still not have been safe. Still B would have held him in the hollow of his hand, ready to blackmail again when the occasion should arise. Clearly, there was no escape that way. As long as B remained alive, the life of A hung upon a thread.

"From this conclusion the corollary was obvious. If B's existence was incompatible with the safe and peaceful existence of A, then B must be eliminated. It was the only way of escape. And having come to this decision, A could give his attention, quietly and without hurry, to the question of ways and means, to the devising of a plan whereby B could be eliminated without leaving a trace, or at any rate, a trace that would lead in the direction of A. And thus came into being the elaborate, ingeniously devised scheme which I had been examining and which looked, at that time, so much like a successful one.

228

"The next problem was to give a name to each of the two men. *A* and *B* represented *Boles* and *Gannet*, but which was which? Was Boles, for instance, *A* the murderer, or *B* the blackmailer? By Blandy, Boles was confidently identified as the Newingstead murderer. But then Blandy accepted all the appearances at their face value. In his view Gannet was not in the picture. He was not a person – he was a mere basketful of ashes. The thumb-print had been found in Boles's cupboard on Boles's own material. Therefore it was Boles's thumb-print.

"But was this conclusion in accordance with ordinary probabilities? From Blandy's point of view it may have been, but from mine it certainly was not. So great was the improbability that it presented that, even if I had known nothing of the other facts, I should have approached it with profound scepticism. Consider the position: Here is a man whose thumb-print is filed at Scotland Yard. That print is capable of hanging him, and he knows it. Then is it conceivable that, if he were not an abject fool – which Boles was not – he would be dabbing that print on surfaces that anyone might see? Would he not studiously avoid making that print on anything? Would he not, when working alone, wear a glove on his left hand? And if by chance he should mark some object with that print, would he not be careful to wipe it off? Above all, if he were absconding as he was assumed to have absconded, would he leave a perfect specimen of that incriminating print in the very place which the police would be quite certain to search for the express purpose of discovering finger-prints? The thing was incredible. The very blatancy of it was enough to raise a suspicion of imposture.

"That, as I have said, is taking the thumb-print apart from any other facts or deductions. But now let us consider it in connection with what we have deduced. If we suggest that the thumb-print was Gannet's and that he had planted it where it was certain to be found by the police, at once we exchange a wild improbability for a very striking probability. For thus he would have contrived to kill an additional, very important, bird with the same stone. He has got rid of Boles, the blackmailer. But now he has also got rid of the Newingstead murderer. He has attached the incriminating thumb-print to the person of Boles, and as Boles has ceased to exist, the fraud can never be discovered. He has made himself absolutely safe, for the police have an exact description of Boles – who was at least three inches taller than Gannet and had brown eyes. So that even if, by some infinitely remote chance, Gannet should leave his thumb-print on some object and it should be found by the police, still he would be in no danger. They would assume as a certainty that it had been made by a tall, brown-eyed man, and they would search for that man – and never find him.

"Here, then, is a fresh agreement, and you notice that our deductions are mounting up, and that they conform to the great rule of circumstantial evidence: That all the facts shall point to the same conclusion. Our hypothesis is very largely confirmed, and we are justified in believing it to be the true one. That, at least, was my feeling at this stage. But still there remained another matter that had to be considered – an important matter, too, since it might admit of an actual experimental test. Accordingly I gave it my attention.

"I had concluded (provisionally) that Gannet was the Newingstead murderer. If he were, he had in his possession fifteen large diamonds of the aggregate value of about ten-thousand pounds. How would he have disposed of those diamonds? He could not carry them on his person, for apart from their great value, they were highly incriminating. Merely putting them under lock and key would hardly be sufficient, for Boles was still frequenting the house and he probably knew all about the methods of opening drawers and cupboards. Something more secure would be needed, something in the nature of an actual hiding place. But he was planning to dispose of Boles and then to disappear, and naturally, when the time should come for him to disappear, he would want to take the diamonds with him. But still he might be unwilling to have them on his person. How was this difficulty to be met?

"Here, once more, enlightenment came from the invaluable Oldfield. In the course of his search of the deserted house he observed that the pottery which had been on the mantelpiece of Gannet's bedroom had disappeared. Now this was a rather remarkable circumstance. The disappearance of the pottery seemed to coincide with the disappearance of Gannet, and one naturally asked oneself whether there could be any connection between the two events, and if so, what the nature of that connection might be. The pottery consisted, as I remembered, of a number of bowls and jars and a particularly hideous stoneware figure. The pots seemed to be of no special interest. But the figure invited inquiry. A pottery figure is necessarily made hollow, for lightness and to allow of even shrinkage during the firing, and the cavity inside would furnish a possible hiding place, though not, perhaps, a very good one, if the figure were of the ordinary type.

"But this figure was not of the ordinary type. I ascertained the fact from Oldfield, who had examined it and who gave me an exact description of it. And a most astonishing description it was, for it seemed to involve a physical impossibility. The figure, he informed me, had a flat base covered with some sort of white enamel on which was the artist's signature. There was no opening in it, nor was there any opening either at the back or the top. That was according to his recollection, and he could hardly have been mistaken, for he had examined the figure all over and he was certain that there was no hole in it anywhere.

"Now, here was a most significant fact. What could be the explanation? There were only two possibilities, and one of them could be confidently rejected. Either the figure was solid or an opening in it had been filled up. But it could not be solid, for there must be some cavity in a pottery figure to allow for shrinkage without cracking. But if it was hollow, there must have been some opening in it originally. For a hollow figure in which there was no opening would be blown to pieces by the expansion of the imprisoned air during the firing. The only possible conclusion was that an opening originally existing had been filled up, and this conclusion was supported by the condition of the base. It is there that the opening is usually placed, as it is hidden when the figure is standing, and there it had apparently been in this case, for the white, glazed enamel looked all wrong, seeing that the figure itself was salt-glazed, and in any case, it was certainly an addition. Moreover, as it must have been added after the firing, it could hardly have been a ceramic enamel but was more probably some kind of hydraulic cement such as Keene's. But whatever the material may have been, the essential fact was that the opening had been filled up and concealed, and the open cavity converted into a sealed cavity.

"Here, then, was an absolutely perfect hiding place, which had the additional virtue of being portable. But if it contained the diamonds, as I had no doubt that it did, it was necessary to find out without delay what had become of it. For wherever the diamonds were, sooner or later Gannet would be found there. In short, it seemed that the stoneware monkey might supply the crucial fact which would tell us whether our hypothesis was true or false.

"There was no difficulty in tracing the monkey, for Oldfield had learned that it had been sent, with the other pottery, to a loan exhibition at a museum in Hoxton. But before going there to examine it and check Oldfield's description, I had to acquire a few preliminary data. From Mr. Kempster of the Bond Street gallery I obtained the name and address of the owner of a replica of the figure, and as the question of weight might arise, I took the opportunity to weigh and measure one of Gannet's bowls.

"The owner of the replica, a Mr. Broomhill, gave us every facility for examining it, even to weighing it. We found that it was hollow, and judging by the weight, that it had a considerable interior cavity. There was an oval opening in the base of about an inch-and-a-half in the longer diameter, through which we could see the marks of a thumb, showing that the figure was a squeeze from a mould, and it was a little significant that all the impressions appeared to be those of a right thumb.

"Armed with these data, we went to the museum, where we were able to examine, handle and weigh Gannet's figure. It corresponded completely with Oldfield's description, for there was no opening in any part of it. The appearance of the base suggested that the original opening had been filled with Keene's cement and glazed with cellulose varnish. That the figure was hollow was proved by its weight, but this was about six ounces greater than that of Broomhill's replica, a difference that would represent, roughly, the weight of the diamonds, the packing and the cement stopping. Thus the observed facts were in complete agreement with the hypothesis that the diamonds had been concealed in the figure, and you will notice that they were inexplicable on any other supposition.

"We now went into the office and made a few inquiries, and the answers to these – quite freely and frankly given by the curator, Mr. Sancroft – disclosed a most remarkable and significant group of facts. It appeared that the figure had been sold a short time before it had been sent to the museum. The purchaser, Mr. James Newman, had then gone abroad but expected to return in about three months, when he proposed to call at the museum and claim his property. The arrangements to enable him to do so were very simple but very interesting. As Mr. Newman was not known personally to Mr. Sancroft (who also, by the way, had never met Peter Gannet), he would produce a letter of introduction and a written order to Mr. Sancroft to deliver the figurine to Newman, who would then give a receipt for it.

"These arrangements presented a rather striking peculiarity. They involved the very minimum of contacts. There was no correspondence by which an address would have had to be disclosed. Mr. Newman, a stranger to Sancroft, would appear in person, would present his order, receive his figurine and then disappear, leaving no clue as to whence he had come or whither he had gone. The appearances were entirely consistent with the possibility that Mr. Newman and Peter Gannet were one and the same person. And this I felt convinced was the fact.

"But if Newman was Gannet, what might we predict as to his personal appearance? He would almost certainly be clean shaven and there might be a certain amount of disguise. But the possibilities of disguise off the stage are very limited, and the essential personal characteristics remain. Stature cannot be appreciably disguised, and eye colour not at all. Gannet's height was about five-feet-eight and his eyes were of a pale grey. He had a scar across his left eyebrow and the middle finger of his right hand had an ankylosed joint. Neither the scar nor the

232

stiff joint could be disguised, and it would be difficult to keep them out of sight.

"We learned from Sancroft that the three months had expired and that Mr. Newman might be expected at any moment. Evidently, then, whatever was to be done must be done at once. But what was to be done? The final test was the identity of Newman, and that test could be applied only by me. I had to contrive, if possible, to be present when Newman arrived, for no subsequent shadowing of him was practicable. Until he was identified as Gannet he could not be stopped or prevented from leaving the country.

"At first it looked almost like an impossible problem, but certain peculiar circumstances made it comparatively easy. I was able to install my man, Snuper, at the museum to hold the fort in my absence. I gave him the description of Gannet and certain instructions which I need not repeat in detail as it never became necessary to act on them. By good luck it happened that Newman arrived in the evening when Snuper was in charge alone. He had no authority to deliver up the figure so he made an appointment for the following morning. Then he sent me a message stating what had happened and that Mr. Newman seemed to answer my description, whereupon I got into communication with Blandy and advised him to come to the museum on the chance that Newman might be the man whom he wanted for the Newingstead affair.

"You know the rest. Jervis and I were at the museum when Newman arrived and Blandy was lurking in the entry. But, even then, the case was still only a train of hypothetical reasoning. Nothing had really been proved. Even when I stood behind Newman waiting for him to discover my presence, it was still possible that he might turn and reveal himself as a perfectly innocent stranger. Only at the very last moment, when he turned to face me and I recognized him as Gannet and saw that he recognized me, did I know that there had been no flaw in my reasoning. It was a dramatic moment, and a more unpleasant one I hope never to experience."

"It was rather horrible," I agreed. "The expression on the poor devil's face when he saw you haunts me to this day. I was almost sorry for him."

"Yes," said Thorndyke, "it was a disagreeable duty. The pursuit had been full of interest, but the capture I would gladly have left to the police, if that had been possible. But it was not. Our mutual recognition was the crucial fact.

"And now, after all this logic chopping, perhaps a glass of wine would not come amiss. Let us pledge our colleague, Oldfield, who set

233

our feet on the right track. And I may remark, Polton, that one fluid drachm is not a glass of wine within the meaning of the act."

The abstemious Polton crinkled guiltily and poured another thirty minims into the bottom of his glass. Then we solemnly pledged our friend, who received the tribute with a rather sheepish smile.

"It is very good of you, sir," said he, "to give me so much undeserved credit, and most kind of you all to drink my health. I realize my limitations, but it is a satisfaction to me to know that, if my wits are none of the most brilliant, I have at least been the occasion of wit in others."

There is little more to tell. The repentant Blandy, by way of making amends to his late victim (and possibly of casting a discreet veil over his own mistakes), so arranged matters with the coroner that the inquest on "a man who called himself James Newman" was conducted with the utmost tact and the minimum of publicity, whereby the future of Mrs. Gannet was left unclouded and the susceptibilities of our friend Linnell unoffended.

As to the monkey, it experienced various vicissitudes before it finally came to rest in appropriate surroundings. First, by Mrs. Gannet, it was presented to Thorndyke "as a memorial". But we agreed that it was too ugly even for a memorial, and I secretly took possession of it and conveyed it to Oldfield, who accepted it gleefully with a cryptic grin which I did not, at the time, understand. But I understood it later when he informed me – with a grin which was not at all cryptic – that he had presented it to Mr. Bunderby.

The End

MR. POLTON EXPLAINS
R. AUSTIN FREEMAN

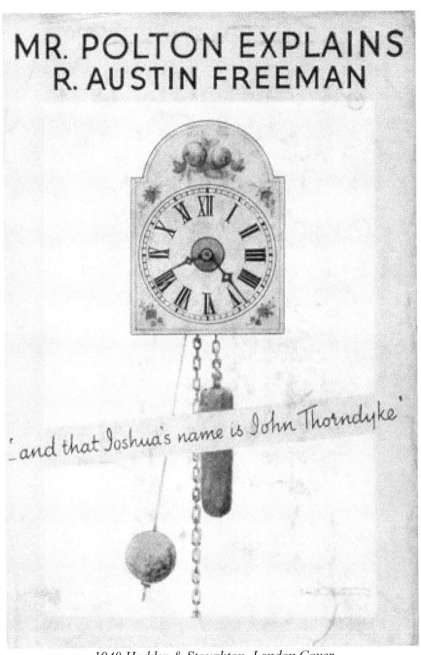

'...and that Joshua's name is John Thorndyke'

1940 Hodder & Stoughton, London Cover

237

Introductory Observations
by Mr. Polton

Friends of Dr. Thorndyke who happen to have heard of me as his servant and technical assistant may be rather surprised to see me making my appearance in the character of an author. I am rather surprised, myself, and I don't mind admitting that of all the tools that I have ever used, the one that is in my hand at the present moment is the least familiar and the most unmanageable. But mere lack of skill shall not discourage me. The infallible method, as I have found by experience, of learning how to do anything is to do it, and keep on doing it until it becomes easy. Use is second nature, as a copy-book once informed me.

But I feel that some explanation is necessary. The writing of this record is not my own idea. I am acting on instructions, and the way in which the matter arose was this. My master, The Doctor, was commissioned to investigate the case of Cecil Moxdale, Deceased, and a very queer case it was. So queer that, as The Doctor assures me, he would never have been able to come to a definite conclusion but for one little fact that I was able to supply. I think he exaggerates my importance and that he would have found it out for himself. Still, that one little fact did certainly throw a new light on the case, so, when the time came for the record of it to be written, both The Doctor himself and Dr. Jervis decided that I was the proper person to set forth the circumstances that made the final discovery possible.

That was all very well, but the question was: What were the circumstances and when did they begin? And I could find no answer, for as soon as I thought that I had found the beginning of the train of circumstances, I saw that it would never have happened if something had not happened before it. And so it went on. Every event in my life was the result of some other event and, tracing them back one after the other, I came to the conclusion that the beginning of the train of circumstances was also the beginning of me. For, obviously, if I had never been born, the experiences that I have to record could never have happened. I pointed this out to The Doctor, and he agreed that my being born was undoubtedly a contributory circumstance, and suggested that perhaps I had better begin with that. But, on reflection, I saw that this was impossible, for, although being born is undeniably a personal experience, it is, oddly enough, one which we have to take on hearsay and which it would therefore be improper to include in one's personal recollections.

Besides, although this history seems to be all about me, it is really an introduction to the case of Cecil Moxdale, Deceased, and my little contribution to the solving of that mystery was principally a matter of technical knowledge. There were some other matters, but my connection with the case arose out of my being a clock-maker. Accordingly, in these recollections, I shall sort out the incidents of my life, and keep, as far as possible, to those which present me in that character.

There is a surprising amount of wisdom to be gathered from copy-books. From one I learned that the boy is father to the man, and from another, to much the same effect, that the poet is born, not made. As there were twenty lines to the page, I had to repeat this twenty times, which was more than it merited. For the thing is obvious enough and, after all, there is nothing in it. Poets are not peculiar in this respect. The truth applies to all other kinds of persons, including fools and even clock-makers – that is, if they are real clock-makers and not just common men with no natural aptitude who have drifted into the trade by chance.

Now, I was born a clock-maker. It may sound odd, but such, I am convinced, is the fact. As far back as I can remember, clocks have always had an attraction for me quite different from that of any other kind of things. In later years my interests have widened, but I have still remained faithful to my old love. A clock (by which I mean a mechanical time-keeper of any kind) still seems to me the most wonderful and admirable of the works of man. Indeed, it seems something more – as if it were a living creature with a personality and a soul of its own, rather than a mere machine.

Thus I may say that by these beautiful creations my life has been shaped from the very beginning. Looking down the vista of years, I seem to see at the end of it the old Dutch clock that used to hang on the wall of our kitchen. That clock, and certain dealings with it on a particular and well-remembered day, which I shall mention presently, seem to mark the real starting-point of my journey through life. This may be a mere sentimental delusion, but it doesn't appear so to me. In memory, I can still see the pleasant painted face, changing in expression from hour to hour, and hear the measured tick that never changed at all, and to me, they are the face and the voice of an old and beloved friend.

Of my first meeting with that clock I have no recollection, for it was there when my Aunt Gollidge brought me to her home, a little orphan of three. But in that curious hazy beginning of memory when the events of our childhood come back to us in detached scenes like the pictures of a magic lantern, the old clock is the one distinct object, and as memories become more connected, I can see myself sitting in the little chair that Uncle Gollidge had made for me, looking up at the clock with an interest

240

and pleasure that were never exhausted. I suppose that to a child any inanimate thing which moves of its own accord is an object of wonder, especially if its movements appear to have a definite purpose.

But of explanations I have given enough and of apologies I shall give none, for if the story of my doings should appear to the reader as little worth as it does to me, he has but to pass over it and turn to the case to which it forms the introduction.

Part I – The Antecedents

Chapter I
The Young Horologist

"Drat that clock!" exclaimed my Aunt Judy. "Saturday night, too. Of course, it would choose Saturday night to stop."

She looked up malevolently at the stolid face and the motionless pendulum that hung straight down like a plumb-bob, and then, as she hopped up on a chair to lift the clock off its nail, she continued. "Get me the bellows, Nat."

I extricated myself with some difficulty from the little arm-chair. For dear Uncle Gollidge had overlooked the fact that boys grow and chairs do not, so that it was now a rather tight fit with a tendency to become, like a snail's shell, a permanent attachment. The separation accomplished, I took the bellows from the hook beside the fire-place and went to my aunt's assistance, she having, in her quick, brisk way, unhooked the pendulum and opened the little side doors of the case. Then I held the clock steady on the table while she plied the bellows with the energy of a village blacksmith, blowing out a most encouraging cloud of dust through the farther door-opening.

"We will see what that will do," said she, slapping the little doors to, fastening the catches, and hooking on the pendulum. Once more she sprang up on the chair, replaced the clock on its nail, gave the pendulum a persuasive pat, and descended.

"What is the time by your watch, Dad?" she asked. Old Mr. Gollidge paused in the story that he was telling and looked at her with mild reproach. A great story-teller was old Mr. Gollidge (he had been a ship's carpenter), but Aunt Judy had a way of treating his interminable yarns as mere negligible sounds like the ticking of a clock or the dripping of a leaky tap, and she now repeated her question, whereupon the old gentleman, having contributed to a large spittoon at his side, stuck his pipe in his mouth and hauled a bloated silver watch from the depths of his pocket as if he were hoisting out cargo from the lower hold.

"Watch seems to say," he announced, after looking at it with slight surprise, "as it's a quarter-past-six."

"Six!" shrieked Aunt Judy. "Why, I heard the church clock strike seven a full half-hour ago."

"Then," said the old gentleman, "'twould seem to be about three bells, say half-past seven. Watch must have stopped."

He confirmed the diagnosis by applying it to his ear, and then, having fished up from another pocket an old-fashioned bronze, crank-shaped key, opened the front glass of the watch, which had the winding-hole in the dial like a clock, inserted the key and proceeded to wind as if he were playing a little barrel-organ.

"Half-past seven, you say," said he, transferring the key to the centre square preparatory to setting the hands.

Aunt Judy looked up at the clock, which was still sluggishly wagging its pendulum but uttering no tick, and shook her head impatiently.

"It's no use guessing," said she. "We shall want to know the time in the morning. If you put on your slipper, Nat, you can run round and have a look at Mr. Abraham's clock. It isn't far to go."

The necessity for putting on my slipper arose from a blister on my heel which had kept me a bootless prisoner in the house. I began cautiously to insinuate my foot into the slipper and had nearly completed the operation when Aunt Judy suddenly interposed.

"Listen," said she, and as we all froze into immobility, the silence was broken by the church clock striking eight. Then old Mr. Gollidge deliberately set the hands of his watch, put it to his ear to make sure that it was going, and lowered it into his pocket, and Aunt Judy, mounting the chair, set the clock to time, gave the pendulum a final pat, and hopped down.

"We'll give it another chance," she remarked, optimistically, but I knew that her optimism was unfounded when I listened for the tick and listened in vain and, sure enough, the oscillations of the pendulum slowly died away until it hung down as motionless as the weight.

In the ensuing silence, old Mr. Gollidge took up the thread of his narrative.

"And then the boy comes up from the cuddy and says he seemed to hear a lot of water washin' about down below. So the mate he tells me for to sound the well, which I did and, of course, I found there was a foot or two of water in it. There always was. Reg'ler old basket, that ship was. Always a-drainin' in, a-drainin' in, and the pumps a-goin' something crool."

"Ought to have had a windmill," said Uncle Gollidge, taking a very black clay pipe from his mouth and expectorating skilfully between the bars of the grate, "same as what the Dutchmen do in the Baltic timber trade."

244

The old gentleman shook his head. "Windmills is all right," said he, "if you've got a cargo of soft timber what'll float anyway. But they won't keep a leaky ship dry. Besides – "

"Now, Nat," said Aunt Judy, hooking a Dutch oven on the bar of the grate, "bring your chair over and keep an eye on the black pudding, and you, Sam, just mind where you're spitting."

Uncle Sam, who rather plumed himself on his marksmanship, replied with a scornful grunt. I rose to my feet (the chair rising with me) and took up my station opposite the Dutch oven, the back flap of which I lifted to make an interested inspection of the slices of black pudding (longitudinal sections, as The Doctor would say) which were already beginning to perspire greasily, in the heat. Meanwhile, Aunt Judy whisked about the kitchen (also the general sitting-room) busily making ready for the morrow, and old Mr. Gollidge droned on tirelessly like the brook that goes on for ever.

Of the morrow's doings I must say a few words, since they formed a milestone marking the first stage of my earthly pilgrimage. It had been arranged that the four of us should spend the Sunday with Aunt Judy's younger Sister, a Mrs. Budgen, who lived with her husband in the country out Finchley way. But my unfortunate blistered heel put me out of the party, much to my regret, for these excursions were the bright spots in my rather drab existence. Aunt Budgen was a kindly soul who gave us the warmest of welcomes, as did her husband, a rather taciturn dairy-farmer. Then there was the glorious drive out of London on the front seat of the Finchley omnibus with its smart, white-hatted driver and the third horse stepping out gaily in front with jingling harness and swaying swingle-bar.

But the greatest delight of these visits was the meeting with my sister, Maggie, who had been adopted by Aunt Budgen at the time when Aunt Judy had taken me. These were the only occasions on which we met, and it was a joy to us both to ramble in the meadows, to call on the cows in the shippon, or to sit together on the brink of the big pond and watch the incredible creatures that moved about in its depths.

However, there were to be compensations. Aunt Judy expounded them to me as I superintended the black pudding, turning the Dutch oven when necessary to brown the opposite sides.

"I'm leaving you three pork sausages – they're rather small ones, but you are rather a small boy – and there are some cold potatoes which you can cut into slices and fry with the sausages, and mind you don't set the chimney on fire. Then there is a baked raisin pudding – you can hot that up in the oven – and a whole jar of raspberry jam. You can take as much of that as you like, so long as you don't make yourself ill, and I've left the key in the book-cupboard, but you must wash your hands before you take any of the books out. I am sorry you can't come with us, and Maggie will be disappointed, too, but I think you'll be able to make yourself happy. I know you don't mind being alone a bit."

Aunt Judy was right. I was a rather solitary boy, a little given to day-dreaming and, consequently, partial to my own society. But she prophesied better than she knew. Not only was I able to make myself happy in my solitude, but that Sunday stands out as one of the red-letter days of my life.

To be sure, the day opened rather cheerlessly. As I stood on the doorstep with my single boot and bandaged foot, watching the departure, I was sensible of a pang of keen disappointment and of something approaching loneliness. I followed the receding figures wistfully with my eyes as they walked away down the street in their holiday attire, Aunt Judy gorgeous in her silk dress and gaily-flowered bonnet and the two men in stiff black broadcloth and tall hats, to which old Mr. Gollidge's fine, silver-topped malacca gave an added glory. At the corner Aunt Judy paused to wave her hand to me, then she followed the other two and was lost to view.

I turned back sadly into the house, which, when I had shut the door, seemed dark and gloomy, and made my way to the kitchen. In view of the early start to catch the omnibus, I had volunteered to wash up the breakfast things, and I now proceeded to get this job off my hands, but as I dabbled at the big bowl in the scullery sink, my thoughts still followed the holiday makers. I saw them mounting the omnibus (it started from St. Martin's Church), and visualized its pea-green body with the blessed word *"Finchley"* in big gold letters. I saw the driver gather up the reins and the conductor spring up to the monkey-board, and then away the omnibus rattled, and my thoughts went on ahead to the sweet countryside and to Maggie, waiting for me at the stile, and waiting in vain. That was the most grievous part of the affair, and it wrung my heart to think of it. Indeed, if it had not been beneath the dignity of a young man of nine to shed tears, I think I should have wept.

When I had finished with the crockery, put the plates in the rack, and hung the cups on their hooks, I tidied up the sink and then drifted through into the kitchen, where I looked about me vaguely, still feeling rather miserable and unsettled. From the kitchen I wandered into the parlour, or "best room", where I unlocked the book cupboard and ran my eye along the shelves. But their contents had no attractions for me. I didn't want books, I wanted to run in the fields with Maggie and look on all the things that were so novel and strange to a London boy. So I shut the cupboard and went back to the kitchen, where, once more, I looked

246

about me, wondering what I should do to pass the time. It was too early to think of frying the sausages and, besides, I was not hungry, having eaten a substantial breakfast.

It was at this moment that my wandering glance lighted on the clock. There it hung, stolid-faced, silent, and motionless. What, I wondered, could be the matter with it? Often enough before had it stopped, but Aunt Judy's treatment with the bellows had always set it ticking again. Now the bellows seemed to have lost their magic and the clock would have to have something different done to it.

But what? Could it be just a matter of old age? Clocks, I realized, grow old like men and, thinking of old Mr. Gollidge, I realized also that old age is not a condition that can be cured. But I was loth to accept this view and to believe that it had *"stopped short, never to go again"*, like Grandfather's Clock in the song.

I drew up a high-chair and, mounting it, looked up earnestly at the familiar face. It was a pleasant old clock, comely and even beautiful in its homely way, reflecting the simple, honest outlook of the Black Forest peasants who had made it, the wooden dial painted white with a circle of fine bold hour-figures ("chapters" they call them in the trade), a bunch of roses painted on the arch above the dial, and each of the four corner-spaces, or spandrels, decorated with a sprig of flowers, all done quite skilfully and with the unerring good taste of the primitive artist.

From inspection I proceeded to experiment. A gentle pat at the pendulum set it swinging, but brought no sound of life from within, but when I turned the minute-hand, as I had seen Aunt Judy do, while the pendulum still swung, a faint tick was audible, halting and intermittent, but still a tick. So the clock was not dead. Then I tried a gentle pull at the chain which bore the weight, whereupon the tick became quite loud and regular, and went on for some seconds after I ceased to pull, when it once more died away. But now I had a clue to the mystery. The weight was not heavy enough to keep the clock going, but since the weight had not changed, the trouble must be something inside the clock, obstructing its movements. It couldn't be dust because Aunt Judy had blown it out thoroughly. Then what could it be?

As I pondered this problem I was assailed by a great temptation. Often had I yearned to look into the clock and see what its mysterious "works" were really like, but beyond a furtive peep when the bellows were being plied, I had never had an opportunity. Now, here was a perfect opportunity. Aunt Judy, no doubt, would have disapproved, but she need never know and, in any case, the clock wouldn't go, so there could be no harm. Thus reasoning, I unhooked the weight from the chain and set it down on the chair, and then, not without difficulty, reached up, lifted the clock off its nail and, descending cautiously with my prize, laid it tenderly on the table.

I began by opening the little side doors and the lifting them bodily off the brass hooks that served as hinges. Now I could see how to take off the pendulum and, when I had done this, I carried the clock to the small table by the window, drew up a chair and, seating myself, proceeded to study the interior at my ease. Not that there was much to study in its simple, artless mechanism. Unlike most of these "Dutch" clocks, it had no alarum (or perhaps this had been removed), and the actual "train" consisted of no more than three wheels and two pinions. Nothing more perfect for the instruction of the beginner could be imagined. There were, it is true, some mysterious wheels just behind the dial in a compartment by themselves and evidently connected with the hands, but these I disregarded for the moment, concentrating my attention on what I recognized as the clock, proper.

It was here that my natural mechanical aptitude showed itself, for by the time that I had studied the train in all its parts, considering each wheel in connection with the pinion to which it was geared, I had begun to grasp the principle on which the whole thing worked. The next proceeding was to elucidate the matter by experiment. If you want to know what effects a wheel produces when it turns, the obvious thing is to turn the wheel and see what happens. This I proceeded to do, beginning with the top wheel, as the most accessible, and turning it very gently with my finger. The result was extremely interesting. Of course, the next wheel turned slowly in the opposite direction but, at the same time, the wire pendulum-crutch wagged rapidly to-and-fro.

This was quite a discovery. Now I understood what kept the pendulum swinging and what was cause of the tick but, more than this, I now had a clear idea as to the function of the pendulum as the regulator of the whole movement. As to the rest of the mechanism, there was little to discover. I had already noticed the ratchet and pawl connected with the pulley, and now, when I drew the chain through, the reason why it moved freely in the one direction and was held immovable in the other was perfectly obvious, and this made clear the action of the weight in driving the clock.

There remained the group of wheels in the narrow space behind the dial. From their position they were less easy to examine, but when I turned the minute-hand and set them in motion, their action was quite easy to follow. There were three wheels and one small pinion, and when I moved the hand round they all turned. But not in the same direction. One wheel and the pinion turned in the opposite direction to the hand, while the other two wheels, a large one and a much smaller one, turned with the hand, and as the large one moved very slowly, being driven by the little pinion, whereas the small one turned at the same speed as the hand, I concluded that the small wheel belonged to the minute-hand, while the large wheel turned the hour-hand. And at this I had to leave it, since the actual connections could not be ascertained without taking the clock to pieces.

But now that I had arrived at a general understanding of the clock, the original problem reappeared. Why wouldn't it go? I had ascertained that it was structurally complete and undamaged. But yet when it was started it refused to tick and the pendulum did nothing but wag passively and presently cease to do even that. When it had stopped on previous occasions, the bellows had set it going again. Evidently, then, the cause of the stoppage had been dust. Could it be that dust had at last accumulated beyond the powers of the bellows? The appearance of the inside of the clock (and my own fingers) lent support to this view. Wheels and case alike presented a dry griminess that seemed unfavourable to easy running. Perhaps the clock simply wanted cleaning.

Reflecting on this, and on the difficulty of getting at the wheels in the narrow space, it suddenly occurred to me that my tooth-brush would be the very thing for the purpose. Instantly, I hopped off to my little bedroom and was back in a few moments with this invaluable instrument in my hand. Pausing only to make up the fire, which was nearly out, I fell to work on the clock, scrubbing wheels and pinions and whatever the brush would reach, with visible benefit to everything, excepting the brush. When the worst of the grime had been removed, I blew out the dislodged dust with the bellows and began to consider how I should test the results of my efforts. There was no need to hang the clock on its nail (and, indeed, I was not disposed to part with it so soon), but it must be fixed up somehow so that the weight and the pendulum could hang free. Eventually, I solved the problem by drawing the small table towards the large one, leaving a space of about nine inches between them, and bridging the space with a couple of narrow strips of wood from a broken-up packing-case. On this bridge I seated the clock, with its chain and the re-hung pendulum hanging down between the strips. Then I hooked on the weight and set the pendulum swinging.

The result was disappointing, but yet my labour had not been all in vain. Start of itself the clock would not, but a slight pull at the chain elicited the longed-for tick, and thereafter for a full minute it continued and I could see the scape wheel turning. But there was no enthusiasm. The pendulum swung in a dead-alive fashion, its excursions growing visibly shorter, until, at length, the ticking stopped and the wheel ceased to turn.

It was very discouraging. As I watched the pendulum and saw its movements slowly die away, I was sensible of a pang of keen disappointment. But still I felt that I had begun to understand the trouble and perhaps I might, by taking thought, hit upon some further remedy. I got up from my chair and wandered restlessly round the room, earnestly cogitating the problem. Something in the clock was resisting the pull of the weight. Now, what could it be? Why had the wheels become more difficult to turn?

So delightfully absorbed was I in seeking the solution of this mystery that all else had faded out of my mind. Gone was all my depression and loneliness. The Finchley omnibus was forgotten, Aunt Budgen was as if she had never been, the green meadows and the pond, and even dear Maggie, had passed clean out of my consciousness. The clock filled the field of my mental vision and the only thing in the world that mattered was the question, What was hindering the movement of its wheels?

Suddenly, in my peregrinations I received an illuminating hint. Stowed away in the corner was Aunt Judy's sewing-machine. Now sewing-machines and clocks are not very much alike, but they both have wheels, and it was known to me that Aunt Judy had a little oil-can with which she used to anoint the machine. Why did she do that? Obviously, to make the wheels run more easily. But if the wheels of a sewing-machine needed oil, why should not those of a clock? The analogy seemed a reasonable one and, in any case, there could be no harm in trying. Cautiously, and not without some qualms of conscience, I lifted the cover of the machine and, having found the little, long-snouted oil-can, seized it and bore it away with felonious glee.

My proceedings with that oil-can will hardly bear telling, they would have brought tears to the eyes of a clock-maker. I treated my patient as if it had been an express locomotive with an unlimited thirst for oil. Impartially, I flooded every moving part, within and without – pallets, wheel-teeth, pivots, arbors, the chain-pulley, the "motion wheels" behind the dial, and the centres of the hands. I even oiled the pendulum rod as well as the crutch that held it. When I had finished, the whole interior of the clock seemed to have broken out into a greasy perspiration, and even the woodwork was dark and shiny. But my thoroughness had one advantage: If I oiled all the wrong places, I oiled the right ones as well.

At length, when there was not a dry spot left anywhere, I put down the oil-can, and "in trembling hope" proceeded to make a fresh trial, and even now, after all these years, I can hardly record the incident without emotion. A gentle push at the pendulum brought forth at once a clear and resonant tick and, looking in eagerly, I could see the scape wheel turning with an air of purpose and the centre wheel below it moving steadily in the opposite direction. And it was no flash in the pan this time. The swing of the pendulum, instead of dying away as before, grew in amplitude and liveliness to an extent almost beyond belief. It seemed that, under the magical influence of the oil-can, the old clock had renewed its youth.

To all of us, I suppose, there have come in the course of our lives certain moments of joy which stand out as unique experiences. They never come a second time, for though the circumstances may seem to recur, the original ecstasy cannot be recaptured. Such a moment was this. As I sat and gazed in rapture at the old clock, called back to vigorous life by my efforts, I enjoyed the rare experience of perfect happiness. Many a time since have I known a similar joy, the joy of complete achievement (and there is no pleasure like it), but this was the first of its kind and, in its perfection, could never be repeated.

Presently, there broke in upon my ecstasy the sound of the church clock, striking two. I could hardly believe it, so swiftly had the hours sped. And yet certain sensations of which I suddenly became conscious confirmed it. In short, I realized that I was ravenously hungry and that my dinner had yet to be cooked. I set the hands of the clock to the incredible time and rose to seek the frying-pan. But, hungry as I was, I could not tear myself away from my darling, and in the end I compromised by substituting the Dutch oven, which required less attention. Thus I alternated between cookery and horology, clapping the pudding in the large oven and then sitting down once more to watch the clock until an incendiary sausage, bursting into flame with mighty sputterings, recalled me suddenly to the culinary department.

My cookery was not equal to my horology, at least in its results, yet never have I so thoroughly enjoyed a meal. Black and brittle the sausages may have been and the potatoes sodden and greasy. It was no matter. Hunger and happiness imparted a savour beyond the powers of the most accomplished chef. With my eyes fixed adoringly on the clock (I had "laid my place" where I could conveniently watch the movement as I fed), I devoured the unprepossessing viands with a relish that a gourmet might have envied.

Of the way in which the rest of the day was spent my recollection is rather obscure. In the course of the afternoon I washed up the plates and cleaned the Dutch oven so that Aunt Judy should be free when she came home, but even as I worked at the scullery sink, I listened delightedly to the tick of the clock, wafted to my ear through the open doorway. Later, I made my tea and consumed it, to an obbligato accompaniment of

251

raspberry jam, seated beside the clock and, when I was satisfied unto repletion, I washed the tea-things (including the tea-pot) and set them out tidily in their places on the dresser. That occupied me until six o'clock, and left me with a full three hours to wait before Aunt Judy should return.

Incredibly long hours they were, in strange contrast to the swift-footed hours of the morning. With anxious eyes I watched the minute hand creeping sluggishly from mark to mark. I even counted the ticks (and found them ninety-six to the minute), and listened eagerly for the sound of the church clock, at once relieved and disappointed to find that it told the same tale. For now my mood had changed somewhat. The joy of achievement became mingled with impatience for its revelation. I was all agog to see Aunt Judy's astonishment when she found the clock going and to hear what she would say. And now, in my mind's eye, the progress of the Finchley omnibus began to present itself. I followed it from stage to stage, crawling ever nearer and nearer to St. Martin's Church. With conscious futility I went out, again and again, to look up the street along which the revellers would approach, only to turn back for another glance at the inexorable minute-hand.

At length, the sound of the church clock striking eight admonished me that it was time to return the clock to its place on the wall. It was an anxious business, for, even when I had unhooked the weight, it was difficult for me, standing insecurely on the chair, to reach up to the nail and find the hole in the back-plate through which it passed. But at last, after much fumbling, with up-stretched arm and my heart in my mouth, I felt the clock supported and, having started the pendulum, stepped down with a sigh of relief and hooked on the weight. Now, all that remained to do was to put away the oil-can, wash my tooth-brush at the scullery, and take it back to my bedroom, and when I had done this and lit the gas, I resumed my restless fittings between the kitchen and the street door.

Nine had struck when, at long last, from my post on the doorstep, I saw the home-comers turn the corner and advance up the lamp-lighted street. Instantly, I darted back into the house to make sure that the clock was still going, and then, returning, met them almost on the threshold. Aunt Judy greeted me with a kindly smile and evidently misinterpreted my eagerness for their return, for, as she stooped to kiss me, she exclaimed, "Poor old Nat! I'm afraid it has been a long, dull day for you, and we were all sorry that you couldn't come. However, there is something to make up for it. Uncle Alfred has sent you a shilling and Aunt Anne has sent you some pears, and Maggie has sent you a beautiful pocket-knife. She was dreadfully disappointed that she couldn't give it to you herself, because she has been saving up her pocket-money for weeks to buy it, and you will have to write her a nice letter to thank her."

Now this was all very gratifying, and when the big basket was placed on the kitchen table and the treasures unloaded from it, I received the gifts with proper acknowledgements. But they aroused no enthusiasm, not even the pocket-knife, for I was bursting with impatience for someone to notice the clock.

"You don't seem so particularly grateful and pleased." said Aunt Judy, looking at me critically, and then, as I fidgetted about restlessly, she exclaimed, "What's the matter with the boy? He's on wires!"

She gazed at me with surprise, and Uncle Sam and the old gentleman turned to look at me curiously. And then, in the momentary silence, Aunt Judy's quick ear caught the tick of the clock. She looked up at it and then exclaimed, "Why, the clock's going – going quite well, too. Did you start it, Nat? But, of course, you must have done. How did you get it to go?"

With my guilty consciousness of the tooth-brush and the borrowed oil-can, I was disposed to be evasive.

"Well, you see, Aunt Judy," I explained, "it was rather dirty inside, so I just gave it a bit of a clean and put a little oil on the wheels. That's all."

Aunt Judy smiled grimly, but asked no further questions.

"I suppose," said she, "I ought to scold you for meddling with the clock without permission, but as you've made it go, we'll say no more about it."

"No," agreed old Mr. Gollidge, "I don't see as how you could scold the boy for doing a useful bit of work. The job does him credit and shows that he's got some sense, and sense is what gets a man on in life."

With this satisfactory conclusion to the adventure, I was free to enter into the enjoyment of my newly-acquired wealth and, having sampled the edible portion of it and tested the knife on a stick of fire-wood, spent the short remainder of the evening in rapturous contemplation of my new treasures and the rejuvenated clock. I had never possessed a shilling before, and now, as I examined Uncle Alfred's gift and polished it with my handkerchief visions of its immense potentialities floated vaguely through my mind, and continued to haunt me, in company with the clock, even when I had blown out my candle and snuggled down into my narrow bed.

Chapter II
The Pickpocket's Leavings

It was shortly after my eleventh birthday that I conceived a really brilliant idea. It was generated by a card in the shop window of our medical attendant, Dr. Pope – (In those days, doctors practising in humble neighbourhoods used to keep what were euphemistically described as "Open Surgeries", but which were, in effect, druggists' shops.) – bearing the laconic announcement, *"Boy Wanted"*. I looked at the card and debated earnestly the exact connotation of the word *"Wanted"*. It was known to me that some of my schoolfellows contrived to pick up certain pecuniary trifles by delivering newspapers before school hours or doing small jobs in the evenings. Was it possible that the boy wanted by Dr. Pope might thus combine remunerative with scholastic industry? There would be no harm in enquiring.

I entered and, finding the Doctor secretly compounding medicine in a sort of hiding-place at the end of the counter, proceeded to state my case without preamble.

The Doctor put his head round the corner and surveyed me somewhat disparagingly.

"You're a very small boy," he remarked.

"Yes, sir," I admitted, "but I am very strong for my size."

He didn't appear much impressed by this, but proceeded to enquire, "Did Mrs. Gollidge tell you to apply?"

"No, sir," I replied, "it's my own idea. You see, sir, I've been rather an expense to Aunt Judy – Gollidge, I mean – and I thought that if I could earn a little money, it would be useful."

"A very proper idea, too," said the Doctor, apparently more impressed by my explanation than by my strength. "Very well. Come round this evening when you leave school. Come straight here, and you can have some tea, and then you can take a basket of medicine and see how you get on with it. I expect you will find it a bit heavy."

"It will get lighter as I go on, sir," said I, on which the Doctor smiled quite pleasantly and, having admonished me to be punctual, retired to his hiding-place, and I departed in triumph.

But the Doctor's prediction turned out to be only too correct, for when I lifted the deep basket, stacked with bottles of medicine, I was rather shocked by its weight and had to remind myself of my own prediction that the weight would be a diminishing quantity. That was an encouraging reflection. Moreover, there had been agreeable preliminaries in the form of a Gargantuan tea, including a boiled egg and marmalade, provided by Mrs. Stubbs, the Doctor's fat and jovial housekeeper. So I hooked the basket boldly on my arm – and presently shifted it to the other one – and set forth on my round, consulting the written list provided for me and judiciously selecting the nearest addresses to visit first and thereby lighten the basket for the more distant ones.

Still, there was no denying that it was heavy work for a small boy, and when I had made a second round with a fresh consignment, I felt that I had had enough for one day, and when I returned the empty basket, I was relieved to learn that there was nothing more to deliver.

"Well," said the Doctor as I handed in the basket, "how did you get on?"

"All right, thank you, sir," I replied, "but I think it would be easier if I put rather less in the basket and made more journeys."

The Doctor smiled approvingly. "Yes," he agreed, "that's quite a sensible idea. Give your legs a bit more to do and save your arms. Very well, you think you can do the job?"

"I am sure I can, sir, and I should like to."

"Good," said he. "The pay will be three-and-sixpence a week. That suit you?"

It seemed to me an enormous sum, and I agreed gleefully, which closed the transaction and sent me homewards rejoicing and almost oblivious of my fatigue.

A further reward awaited me when I arrived home. Aunt Judy, it is true, had professed disapproval of the arrangement as interfering with my "schooling", but the substantial hot supper seemed more truly to express her sentiments. It recognized my new status as a working man and my effort to pull my weight in the family boat.

The next day's work proved much less arduous, for I put my plan into operation by sorting out the bottles into groups belonging to particular localities, and thus contrived never to have the basket more than half full. This brought the work well within my powers, so that the end of the day found me no more than pleasantly tired, and the occupation was not without its interest, to say nothing of the dignity of my position as a wage-earner. But the full reward of my industry came when, returning home on Saturday night, I was able to set down my three shillings and sixpence on the kitchen table before Aunt Judy, who was laying the supper. The little heap of silver coins, a florin, a shilling, and a sixpence, made a quite impressive display of wealth. I looked at it with proud satisfaction – and also with a certain wistful curiosity as to whether any of that wealth might be coming my way. I had faint hopes of the odd sixpence, and watched a little anxiously as Aunt Judy spread out the heap with a considering air. Eventually, she picked up the florin and the sixpence and, pushing the shilling towards me, suddenly put her arm round my neck and kissed me.

"You're a good boy, Nat," said she, and as she released me and dropped the money in her pocket, I picked up my shilling and turned away to hide the tears that had started to my eyes. Aunt Judy was not a demonstrative woman but, like many undemonstrative persons, could put a great deal of meaning into a very few words. Half-a-dozen words and a kiss sweetened my labours for many a day thereafter.

My peregrinations with the basket had, among other effects, that of widening the range of my knowledge of the geography of London. In my early days that knowledge was limited to the few streets that I traversed on my way to and from school, to certain quiet back waters in which one could spin tops at one's convenience or play games without undue interruption, and certain other quiet streets in which one was likely to find the street entertainer – the acrobat, the juggler, the fire-eater, or best of all, the Punch-and-Judy show.

But now the range of my travels coincided with that of Dr. Pope's practice and led me far beyond the limits of the familiar neighbourhood, and quite pleasant these explorations were, for they brought me into new streets with new shops in them which provided new entertainment. I think shops were more interesting then than they are in these days of mass-production and uniformity, particularly in an old-fashioned neighbourhood where the crafts were still flourishing. A special favourite was Wardour Street, with its picture-frame makers, its antique shops filled with wonderful furniture and pictures and statuettes and gorgeous clocks.

But the shop that always brought me to a halt was that of M. Chanot, the violin-maker, which had, hanging on the door-jamb by way of a trade sign, a gigantic bow (or fiddlestick, as I should have described it). It was stupendous. As I gazed at it with the fascination that the juvenile mind discovers in things gigantic or diminutive, my imagination strove to picture the kind of fiddle that could be played with it and the kind of Titan who could have held the fiddle. And then, as a foil to its enormity, there hung in the window an infant violin, a "kit" such as dancing-masters were wont to carry in the skirt pockets of their ample frock-coats.

A few doors from M. Chanot's was the shop of a second-hand bookseller which was also one of the attractions of the street, for it was from the penny and two-penny boxes that my modest library was chiefly recruited. On the present occasion, having paid my respects to the

Lilliputian fiddle and the Brobdingnagian bow, I passed on to see what treasures the boxes had to offer. Naturally, I tried the penny box first as being more adapted to my financial resources. But there was nothing in it which specially attracted me, whereupon I turned my attention to the two-penny box.

Now, if I were disposed to moralize, I might take this opportunity to reflect on the momentous consequences which may emerge from the most insignificant antecedents. For my casual rooting about in the two-penny box started a train of events which profoundly influenced my life in two respects, and in one so vitally that, but for the two-penny box, this story could never have been written.

I had turned over nearly all the contents of the box when from the lowest stratum I dredged up a shabby little volume the spine of which bore in faded gold lettering the title, "*Clocks and Locks, Denison*". The words instantly rivetted my attention. Shifting the basket to free both my hands, I opened the book at random and was confronted by a beautiful drawing of the interior of a common house-clock, clearly displaying the whole mechanism. It was a wonderful drawing. With fascinated eyes I pored over it, comparing it rapidly with the well-remembered Dutch clock at home and noting new and unfamiliar features. Then I turned over the leaves and discovered other drawings of movements and escapements on which I gazed in rapture. I had never supposed that there was such a book in the world.

Suddenly I was assailed by a horrible doubt. Had I got two-pence? Here was the chance of a lifetime – should I have to let it slip? Putting the basket down on the ground, I searched feverishly through my pockets, but search as I might even in the most unlikely pockets, the product amounted to no more than a single penny. It was an awful predicament. I had set my heart on that book, and the loss of it was a misfortune that I shuddered to contemplate. Yet there was the grievous fact, the price of the book was two pence and I had only a penny.

Revolving this appalling situation, I thought of a possible way out of the difficulty. Leaving my basket on the pavement (a most reprehensible thing to do, but no one wants to steal medicine, and there were only three bottles left), I stepped into the shop with the book in my hand and deferentially approached the book-seller, a stuffy-looking elderly man.

"I want to buy this book, sir," I explained, timorously, "but it is two-pence, and I have only got a penny. Will you keep it for me if I leave the penny as a deposit? I hope you will, sir. I very much want to have the book."

257

He looked at me curiously and, taking the little volume from me, glanced at the title and then turned over the leaves.

"Clocks, hey," said he. "Know anything about clocks?

"Not much, sir," I replied, "but I should like to learn some more."

"Well," said he, "you'll know all about them when you have read that book, but it is stiffish reading for a boy."

He handed it back to me, and I laid my penny on it and put it down on the counter.

"I will try to call for it this evening, sir," said I, "and pay the other penny, and you'll take great care of it, sir, won't you?"

My earnestness seemed to amuse him, but his smile was a kindly and approving smile.

"You can take it away with you," said he, "and then you will make sure of it."

Tears of joy and gratitude rose to my eyes, so that I had nearly taken up the penny as well as the book. I thanked him shyly but warmly and, picking up the precious volume, went out with it in my hand. But even now I paused to take another look at my treasure before resuming charge of the neglected basket. At length I bestowed the book in my pocket and, returning to my proper business, took up the basket and was about to sort out the remaining three bottles when I made a most surprising discovery. At the bottom of the basket, beside the bottles, lay a leather wallet. I gazed at it in astonishment. Of course it was not mine, and I had not put it there, nor, I was certain, had it been there when I went into the shop. Someone must have put it in during my short absence. But why should anyone present me with a wallet? It could hardly have been dropped into the basket by accident, but yet – I picked it out and examined it curiously, noting that it had an elastic band to keep it closed but that nevertheless it was open. Then I ventured to inspect the inside but, beyond a few stamps and a quantity of papers, it seemed to contain nothing of interest to me. Besides, it was not mine. I was still puzzling over it when I became aware of a policeman approaching down the street in company with a short, wrathful looking elderly gentleman who appeared to be talking excitedly while the constable listened with an air of resignation. Just as they reached me, the gentleman caught sight of the wallet and immediately rushed at me and snatched it out of my hand.

"Here you are, Constable," he exclaimed, "here is the stolen property and here is the thief, taken red-handed."

"Red-handed be blowed," said the constable. "You said just now that you saw the man run away, and you've led me a dance a-chasing him. You had better see if there is anything missing."

But the wrathful gentleman had already seen that there was.

"Yes!" he roared, "there were three five-pound notes, and they're gone! Stolen! Fifteen pounds! But I'll have satisfaction. I give this young villain in charge. Perhaps he has the notes on him still. We'll have him searched at the station."

"Now, now," said the constable, soothingly, "don't get excited, sir. Softly, softly, you catch the monkey. You said that you saw the man run off."

"So I did but, of course, this young rascal is a confederate, and I give him in charge."

"Wait a minute, sir. Let's hear what he's got to say. Now, young shaver, tell us how you came by that pocket-book."

I described the circumstances, including my absence in the shop, and the constable, having listened patiently, went in and verified my statement by questioning the bookseller.

"There, sir, you see," said he when he came out, "it's quite simple. The pickpocket fished the notes out of your wallet and then, as he was making off, he looked for some place where he could drop the empty case out of sight, and there was this boy's basket with no one looking after it – just the very place he wanted. So he dropped it in as he passed. Wouldn't have done to drop it in the street where someone might have seen it and run after him to give it back."

The angry gentleman shook his head. "I can't accept that," said he. "It's only a guess, and an unlikely one at that."

"But," the constable protested, "it's what they always do – drop the empty purses or pocket-books in a doorway or a dark corner or post them in pillar-boxes – anywhere to get the incriminating stuff out of sight. It's common sense."

But the gentleman was obdurate. "No, no," he persisted, "that won't do. The common sense of it is that I found this boy with the stolen property in his possession, and I insist on giving him in charge."

The constable was in a dilemma, but he was a sensible man and he made the best of it. "Well, sir," he said, "if you insist, I suppose we must walk round to the station and report the affair. But I can tell you that the inspector won't take the charge."

"He'll have to," retorted the other, "when I have made my statement."

The constable looked at him sourly and then turned to me almost apologetically.

"Well, sonny," said he, "you'll have to come along to the station and see what the inspector has to say."

"Can't I deliver my medicines first?" I pleaded. "The people may be wanting them, and there are only three bottles."

The policeman grinned but evidently appreciated my point of view, for he replied, still half-apologetically, "You're quite right, my lad, but I don't suppose they'll be any the worse for a few minutes more without their physic, and the station is quite handy. Come, now, step out."

But even now the irate gentleman was not satisfied.

"Aren't you going to hold him so that he doesn't escape?" he demanded.

Then, for the first time, the patient constable showed signs of temper. "No, sir," he replied, brusquely, "I am not going to drag a respectable lad through the streets as if he had committed a crime when I know he hasn't."

That settled the matter, and we walked on with the manner of a family party. But it was an uncomfortable experience. To a boy of my age, a police station is a rather alarming sort of place, and the fact that I was going to be charged with a robbery was a little disturbing. However, the constable's attitude was reassuring and, as we traversed Great Marlborough Street and at last entered the grim doorway, I was only moderately nervous.

The proceedings were, as my constabulary friend had foreseen, quite brief. The policeman made his concise report to the inspector, I answered the few questions that the officer asked, and the gentleman made his statement, incriminating me.

"Where did the robbery take place?" the inspector asked.

"In Berwick Street," was the reply. "I was leaning over a stall when I felt myself touched, and then a man moved away quickly through the crowd, and then I missed my wallet and gave chase."

"You were leaning over a stall," the inspector repeated. "Now, how on earth did he get at your wallet?"

"It was in my coat-tail pocket," the gentleman explained.

"In your coat-tail pocket!" the inspector repeated, incredulously. "With fifteen pounds in it, and you leaning over a stall in a crowded street! Why, sir, it was a free gift to a pickpocket."

"I suppose I can carry my wallet where I please," the other snapped.

"Certainly you can – at your own risk. Well, I can't accept the charge against this boy. There is no evidence – in fact, there isn't even any suspicion. It would be only wasting the magistrate's time. But I will take the boy's name and address and make a few inquiries. And I will take yours too and let you know if anything transpires."

He took my name and address (and my accuser made a note of them), and that, so far as I was concerned, finished the business. I took up my basket and went forth a free boy in company with my friend the policeman. In Great Marlborough Street we parted, he to return to his beat, and I to the remainder of my round of deliveries.

So ended an incident that had, at one time, looked quite threatening. And yet it had not really ended. Perhaps no incident ever does truly end. For every antecedent begets consequences. Coming events cast their shadows before them, but those shadows usually remain invisible until the events which have cast them have, themselves, come into view. Indeed, it befalls thus almost from necessity, for how can a shadow be identified otherwise than by comparison with the substance?

But I shall not here anticipate the later passages of my story. The consequences will emerge in their proper place. I may, however, refer briefly to the more immediate reactions, though these also had their importance later. The little book which I had purchased (and paid for the same evening) was a treatise on clocks and locks by that incomparable master of horology and mechanism, Edmund Beckett Denison (later to be known as Lord Grimthorpe). It was an invaluable book, and it became my chiefest treasure. Carefully wrapped in a protective cover of brown paper, the precious volume was henceforth my constant companion. The abstruse mathematical sections I had regretfully to pass over, but the descriptive parts were read and re-read until I could have recited them from memory. Even the drawings of the Great Westminster Clock, which had at first appeared so bewildering, became intelligible by repeated study, and the intricacies of gravity escapements and maintaining powers grew simple by familiarity.

Thus did the revered E. B. Denison add a new delight to my life. Not only was every clock-maker's window a thing of beauty and a provider of quiet pleasure, but an object so lowly as the lock of the scullery door – detached by Uncle Sam and by me carefully dismembered – was made to furnish an entertainment compared with which even the Punch and Judy show paled into insignificance.

Chapter III
Out of the Nest

A certain philosopher, whose name I cannot recall, has, I understand, discovered that there are several different kinds of time. He is not referring to those which are known to astronomers, such as sidereal mean or apparent time, which differ only in terms of measurement, but to time as it affects the young, the middle-aged and the old.

The discovery is not a new one. Shakespeare has told us that "*Time travels in divers paces with divers persons*", and, for me, the poet's statement is more to the point (and perhaps more true) than the philosopher's. For I am thinking of one "*who Time ambles withal*", or even "*who he stands still withal*" – to wit, myself in the capacity of Dr. Pope's bottle-boy. That stage of my existence seemed, and still seems, looking back on it, to have lasted for half-a-lifetime, whereas it occupied, in actual fact, but a matter of months.

It came to an end when I was about thirteen, principally by my own act. I had begun to feel that I was making unfair inroads on the family resources, for, though the school that I attended was an inexpensive one, it was not one of the cheapest. Aunt Judy had insisted that I should have a decent education and not mix with boys below our own class, and accordingly she had sent me to the school conducted by the clergy man of our parish, the Reverend Stephen Page, which was attended by the sons of the local shop-keepers and better-class working men. But modest as the school fees were, their payment entailed some sacrifice, for, though we were not poor, still Uncle Sam's earnings as a journeyman cabinet-maker were only thirty shillings a week. Old Mr. Golligde, who did light jobs in a carpenter's shop, made a small contribution, and there was half-a-crown a week from my wages but, when all was said, it was a tight fit and must have taxed Aunt Judy's powers of management severely to maintain the standard of comfort in which we lived.

Moved by these considerations (and perhaps influenced by the monotonous alternation of school and bottle-basket), I ventured to put the case to Aunt Judy and was relieved to find that she took my suggestions seriously and was obviously pleased with me for making them.

"There is something in what you say, Nat," she admitted. "But remember that your schooling has got to last you for life. It's the

262

foundation that you've got to build on, and it would be bad economy to skimp that."

"Quite right," Uncle Sam chimed in. "You can't make a mahogany table out of deal. Save on the material at the start and you spoil the job."

"Still," I urged, "a penny saved is a penny earned," at which Aunt Judy laughed and gave me a playful pat on the head.

"You are a queer, old-fashioned boy, Nat," said she, "but perhaps you are none the worse for that. Well, I'll see Mr. Page and ask him what he thinks about it, and I shall do exactly what he advises. Will that satisfy you?"

I agreed readily enough, having the profoundest respect and admiration for my schoolmaster. For the Reverend Stephen Page, though he disdained not to teach the sons of working men, was a distinguished man in his way. He was a Master of Arts – though of what arts I never discovered – and a Senior Wrangler. That is what was stated on the School Prospectus, so it must have been true, but I could never understand it, for a less quarrelsome or contentious man you could not imagine. At any rate, he was a most unmistakable gentleman and, if he had taught us nothing else, his example of good manners, courtesy, and kindliness would have been a liberal education in itself.

I was present at the interview, and very satisfactory I found it. Aunt Judy stated the problem and Mr. Page listened sympathetically. Then he pronounced judgement in terms that rather surprised me as coming from a schoolmaster.

"Education and schooling, Mrs. Gollidge, are not quite the same thing. When a boy leaves school to learn a trade, he is not ending his education. Some might say that he is only beginning it. At any rate, the knowledge and skill by which he will earn his living and maintain his family when he has one, and be a useful member of society, is the really indispensable knowledge. Our young friend has a good groundwork of what simple folk call book-learning and, if he wants to increase it, there are books from which he can learn. Meanwhile, I don't think that he is too young to begin the serious business of life."

That question, then, was settled, and the next one was how the beginning was to be made. As a temporary measure, "while we were looking about", Uncle Sam managed to plant me on his employer, Mr. Beeby, as workshop boy at a salary of five shillings a week. So it came about that I made my final round with the bottles, handed in the basket for the last time, drew my wages and, on the following morning, set forth in company with Uncle Sam en route for Mr. Beeby's workshop in Broad Street. There was only one occupant when we arrived – a round-shouldered, beetle-browed, elderly man with rolled-up shirt-sleeves, a

263

linen apron, and a square brown-paper cap such as work men commonly wore in those days, who was operating with a very small saw on a piece of wood that was clamped in the bench-vice.

He looked up as we entered and remarked, "So this is the young shaver, is it? There ain't much of him. He'll have to stand on six penny's-worth of coppers if he is going to work at a bench. Never mind, youngster. You'll be a man before your mother," and with this he returned to his work with intense concentration – (I discovered, presently, that he was cutting the pins of a set of dovetails.) – and Uncle Sam, having provided me with a broom, set me to work at sweeping up the shavings, picking up the little pieces of waste wood and putting them into the large open box in which they were thriftily stored for use in odd jobs. Then he took off his coat, rolled up his sleeves, and put on his apron and paper cap, in which costume he seemed to me to be invested with a new dignity, and when he fell to work with a queer-looking, lean-bodied plane on the edge of a slab of mahogany, miraculously producing on it an elegant moulding, I felt that I had never properly appreciated him.

Presently the third member of the staff arrived, a young journeyman named Will Foster. He had evidently heard of me, for he saluted me with a friendly grin and a few words of welcome while he was unrobing and getting into working trim. Then he, too, set to work with an air of business on his particular job, the carcase of a small chest of drawers, and I noticed that each of the three men was engaged on his own piece of work, independently of the others. And this I learned later was Mr. Beeby's rule, so far as it was practicable. "If a man carries his own job right through," he once explained to me, "and does it well, he gets all the credit, and if he does it badly, he takes all the blame." It seemed a sensible rule. But that was an age of individualism.

I shall not follow in detail my experiences during the few months that I spent in Mr. Beeby's workshop. My service there was but an interlude between school and my real start in life. But it was a useful interlude, and I have never regretted it. As I was not an apprentice, I received no formal instruction. But little was needed when I had the opportunity of watching three highly expert craftsmen and following their methods from the preliminary sketch to the finished work, and I did, in fact, get a good many useful tips besides the necessary instruction in my actual duties.

As to these, they gradually extended as time went on from mere sweeping, cleaning and tidying to more technical activities but, from the first, the glue-pots were definitely assigned to me. Once for all, the whole art and mystery of the preparation and care of glue was imparted to me. Every night I emptied and cleaned the glue-pots and put the fresh glue in to soak, for Mr. Beeby would have nothing to do with stale glue, and every morning, as soon as I arrived, I set the pots of fresh glue on the workshop stove. Then, by degrees, I began to learn the use of tools, to saw along a pencil line, to handle a chisel and a jack-plane (with the aid of an improvised platform to bring my elbows to the bench level) and to use the marking gauge and the try-square, so that, presently, I became proficient enough to be given small, rough jobs of sawing and planing to save the time of the skilled workmen.

It was all very interesting – (What creative work is not?) – and I was happy enough in the workshop with its pleasant atmosphere of quiet, unhurried industry. I liked to watch these three skilful craftsmen doing difficult things with unconscious ease and a misleading appearance of leisureliness, and I learned that this apparently effortless precision was really the result of habitual concentration. The fact was expounded to me by Mr. Beeby on an appropriate occasion.

"You've given yourself the trouble, my lad, of doing that twice over. Now the way to work quickly is to work carefully. Attend to what you are doing and see that you make no mistakes." It was a valuable precept, which I have never forgotten and have always tried to put into practice. Indeed, I find myself, to this day, profiting from Mr. Beeby's practical wisdom.

But though I was interested and happy in my work, my heart was not in cabinet-making. Clocks and watches still held my affections and, on most evenings, the short interval between supper and bedtime was occupied in reading and re-reading the books on horology that I possessed. I now had a quite respectable little library, for my good friend, Mr. Strutt, the Wardour Street bookseller, was wont to put aside for me any works on the subject that came into his hands, and I suspect that, in the matter of price, he frequently tempered the wind to the shorn lamb.

Thus, though I went about my work contentedly, there lurked always at the back of my mind the hope that some day a chance might present itself for me to get a start on the career of a clock-maker. Apprenticeship was not to be thought of, for the family resources were not equal to a premium. But there might be other ways. Meanwhile, I tended the glue-pots and cherished my dream in secret, and in due course, by very indirect means, the dream became a reality.

The chance came, all unperceived at first, on a certain morning in the sixth month of my servitude, when a burly, elderly man came into the workshop carrying a brown-paper parcel. I recognized him instantly as Mr. Abraham, the clock-maker, whose shop in Foubert's Place had been

265

familiar to me since my earliest childhood, and I cast an inquisitive eye on the parcel as he unfastened it on the bench, watched impassively by Mr. Beeby. To my disappointment, the unwrapping disclosed only an empty clock-case, and a mighty shabby one at that. Still, even an empty case had a faint horological flavour.

"Well," said Mr. Beeby, turning it over disparagingly, "it's a bit of a wreck. Shockingly knocked about, and some fool has varnished it with a brush. But it has been a fine case in its time, and it can be again. What do you want us to do with it? Make it as good as new, I suppose."

"Better," replied Mr. Abraham with a persuasive smile.

"Now, you mustn't be unreasonable," said Beeby. "That case was made by a first-class tradesman and no one could make it any better. No hurry for it, I suppose? May as well let us take our time over it."

To this Mr. Abraham agreed, being a workman himself and, after some brief negotiations as to the cost of the repairs, he took his departure. When he had gone, Mr. Beeby picked up the "wreck" and, exhibiting it to Uncle Sam, remarked, "It wants a lot of doing to it, but it will pay for a bit of careful work. Care to take it on when you've finished that table?"

Uncle Sam took it on readily, having rather a liking for renovations of good old work, and when he had clamped up some glued joints on his table, fell to work forthwith on the case, dismembering it, as a preliminary measure, with a thoroughness that rather horrified me, until it seemed to be reduced to little more than a collection of fragments. But I realized the necessity for the dismemberment when I saw him making the repairs and restorations on the separated parts, unhampered by their connections with the others.

I followed his proceedings from day to day with deep interest as the work grew. First, when all the old varnish had been cleaned off, the cutting away of damaged parts. Then the artful insetting of new pieces and their treatment with stain until from staring patches, they became indistinguishable from the old. So it went on, the battered old parts growing newer and smarter every day with no visible trace of the repairs and, at last, when the fresh polish was hard, the separated parts were put together and the transformation was complete. The shabby old wreck had been changed into a brand-new case.

"Well, Sam," said Mr. Beeby, looking at it critically as its restorer stood it on the newly finished table, "you've made a job of that. It's good now for another hundred years. Ought to satisfy Abraham. Nat might as well run round presently and let him know that it's finished."

"Why shouldn't he take it with him?" Uncle Sam suggested.

Mr. Beeby considered the suggestion and eventually, having admonished me to carry the case carefully, adopted it. Accordingly, the case was wrapped in one or two clean dusters and tied up with string, leaving the gilt top handle exposed for convenience of carrying, and I went forth all agog to see how Mr. Abraham would be impressed by Uncle Sam's wizardry.

I found that gentleman seated at his counter writing on a card and, as the inscription was in large Roman capitals, my eye caught at a glance the words, *"Smart Youth Wanted"*. He rounded off the final *D* and then looked up at me and enquired, "You are Mr. Beeby's apprentice, aren't you? Is that the case?"

"This is the case, sir," I replied, "but I am not an apprentice. I am the workshop boy."

"Oh!" said he, "I thought you were an apprentice, as you were working at the bench. Well, let's see what sort of a job they've made of the case. Bring it in here."

He preceded me into a small room at the back of the shop which was evidently the place where he worked, and here, having cleared a space on a side bench, he took the case from me and untied the string. When the removal of the dusters revealed the case in all its magnificence, he regarded it with a chuckle of satisfaction.

"It looks a bit different from what it did when you saw it last, sir," I ventured to remark.

He seemed a little surprised, for he gave me a quick glance before replying.

"You're right, my boy. I wouldn't have believed it possible. But there, every man to his trade, and Mr. Beeby is a master of his."

"It was my uncle, Mr. Gollidge, that did the repairs, sir," I informed him, bearing in mind Mr. Beeby's rule that the doer of a good job should have the credit. Again Mr. Abraham looked at me, curiously, as he rejoined, "Then your uncle is a proper tradesman, and I take my hat off to him."

I thanked him for the compliment, the latter part of which was evidently symbolical, as he was bareheaded, and then asked, "Is that the clock that belongs to the case, sir?" and I pointed to a bracket clock with a handsome brass, silver-circled dial which stood on a shelf, supported by a movement-holder.

"You're quite right," he replied. "That's the clock, all clean and bright and ready for fixing. Would you like to see it in its case? Because, if so, you may as well help me to put it in."

I agreed, joyfully, and as he released the movement from the holder, I unlocked and opened the back door of the case and "stood by" for

267

further instructions, watching intently every stage of the procedure. There was not much for me to do beyond steadying the case and fetching the screws and the screwdriver, but I was learning how a bracket clock was fixed into its case, and when, at last, the job was finished and the fine old clock stood complete in all its beauty and dignity, I had the feeling of at least, having been a collaborator in the achievement.

It had been a great experience. But all the time, a strong undercurrent of thought had been running at the back of my mind. "*Smart Youth Wanted*". Was I a smart youth? Honest self-inspection compelled me to admit that I was not. But perhaps the smartness was only a rhetorical flourish, and in any case, it doesn't do to be too modest. Eventually I plucked up courage to ask, "Were you wanting a boy, sir?"

"Yes," he replied. "Do you know of one who wants a job?"

"I was wondering, sir, if I should be suitable."

"You!" he exclaimed. "But you've got a place. Aren't you satisfied with it?"

"Oh, yes, sir, I'm quite satisfied. Mr. Beeby is a very good master. But I've always wanted to get into the clock trade."

He looked down at me with a broad smile. "My good boy," said he, "cleaning a clockmaker's window and sweeping a clockmaker's floor won't get you very far in the clock trade."

It sounded discouraging, but I was not put off. Experience had taught me that there are boys and boys. As Dr. Pope's bottle boy I had learned nothing and gained nothing but the weekly wage. As Mr. Beeby's workshop boy I had learned the rudiments of cabinet-making and was learning more every day.

"It would be a start, sir, and I think I could make myself useful," I protested.

"I daresay you could," said he – (He had seen me working at the bench.) " – and I would be willing to have you. But what about Mr. Beeby? If you suit him, it wouldn't be right for me to take you away from him."

"Of course, I should have to stay with him until he had got another boy."

"And there is your uncle. Do you think he would let you make the change?"

"I don't think he would stand in my way, sir. But I'll ask him."

"Very well," said he. "You put it to him, and I'll have a few words with Mr. Beeby when I call to settle up."

"And you won't put that card in the window, sir," I urged.

He smiled at my eagerness but was not displeased. Indeed, it was evident to me that he was well impressed and very willing to have me.

268

"No," he agreed, "I'll put that aside for the present."

Much relieved, I thanked him and took my leave, and as I wended homeward to dinner I prepared myself a little nervously, for the coming conference.

But it went off more easily than I had expected. Uncle Sam, indeed, was strongly opposed to the change – ("Just as the boy had got his foot in and was beginning to learn the trade.") – and he was disposed to enlarge on the subject of rolling stones. But Aunt Judy was more understanding.

"I don't know, Sam," said she, "but what the boy's right. His heart is set on clocks, and he'll be happier working among things that he likes than going on with the cabinet-making. But I'm afraid Mr. Beeby won't be pleased."

That was what I was afraid of. But here again my fears proved to be unfounded. On the principle of grasping the nettle, I attacked him as soon as we returned to the workshop after dinner, and certainly, as he listened to my proposal with his great eyebrows lowered in a frown of surprise, he seemed rather alarming, and I began to "look out for squalls". But when I had finished my explanations, he addressed me so kindly and in such a fatherly manner that I was quite taken aback and almost regretful that I had thought of the change.

"Well, my son," said he, "I shall be sorry to lose you. If you had stayed with me I would have given you your indentures free, because you have got the makings of a good workman. But if the clock trade is your fancy and you have a chance to get into it, you are wise to take that chance. A tradesman's heart ought to be in his trade. You go to Mr. Abraham and I'll give you a good character. And you needn't wait for me. Take the job at once and get a start, but look us up now and again and tell us how you are getting on."

I wanted to thank Mr. Beeby, but was too overcome to say much. However, he understood. And now – such is human perversity – I suddenly discovered an unsuspected charm in the workshop and an unwillingness to tear myself away from it, and when "knocking-off time" came and I stowed my little collection of tools in the rush basket to carry away, my eyes filled and I said my last "Good night" in an absurd, tremulous squeak.

Nevertheless, I took Mr. Abraham's shop in my homeward route and found it still open, a fact which I noted with slight misgivings as suggestive of rather long hours. As I entered, my prospective employer rose from the little desk at the end of the counter and confronted me with a look of enquiry, whereupon I informed him briefly of the recent developments and explained that I was now a free boy.

269

"Very well," said he, "then I suppose you want the job. It's five shillings a week and your tea – unless," he added as an afterthought, "you'd rather run round and have it at home. Will that suit you? Because, if it will, you can come to-morrow morning at half-past eight and I will show you how to take down the shutters."

Thus, informally, were my feet set upon the road which I was to tread all the days of my life – a road which was to lead me, through many a stormy passage, to the promised land which is now my secure abiding place.

Chapter IV
The Innocent Accessory

The ancient custom of hanging out a distinctive shop sign still struggles for existence in old-fashioned neighbourhoods. In ours there were several examples. A ham-and-beef merchant proclaimed the nature of his wares by a golden ham dangled above his shop front, a gold-beater more appropriately exhibited a golden arm wielding a formidable mallet, barbers in different streets displayed the phlebotomist's pole with its spiral hint of blood and bandages, and Mr. Abraham announced the horologer's calling by a large clock projecting on a bracket above his shop.

They all had their uses, but it seemed to me that Mr. Abraham's was most to the point. For whereas the golden ham could do no more for you than make your mouth water, leaving you to seek satisfaction within, and the barber's offer to "let blood" was a pure fiction (at least, you hoped that it was), Mr. Abraham's sign did actually make you a free gift of the time of day. Moreover, for advertising purposes the clock was more efficient. Ham and gold leaf supply only occasional needs, but time is a commodity in constant demand. Its sign was a feature of the little street observed by all wayfarers, and thus conferred distinction on the small, antiquated shop that it surmounted.

At the door of that shop the tenant was often to be seen, looking up and down the street with placid interest and something of a proprietary air, and so I found him, refreshing himself with a pinch of snuff, when I arrived at twenty-six minutes past eight on the morning after my engagement. He received me with unexpected geniality and, putting away the tortoise shell snuff-box and glancing up approvingly at the clock, proceeded forthwith to introduce me to the art and mystery of taking down the shutters, including the secret disposal of the padlock. The rest of the daily procedure – the cleaning of the small-paned window, the sweeping of the floor, and such dusting as was necessary – he indicated in general terms and, having shown me where the brooms and other cleaning appliances were kept, retired to the little workshop which communicated with the retail part of the premises, seated himself at the bench, fixed his glass in his eye, and began some mysterious operations on a watch. I observed him furtively in the intervals of my work, and when I had finished, I entered the workshop for further instructions, but by that time the watch had dissolved into a little heap of wheels and plates which lay in a wooden bowl covered by a sort of glass dish-cover, and that was the last that I saw of it. For it appeared that, when not otherwise engaged, my duty was to sit on a stool behind the counter and "mind the shop".

In that occupation, varied by an occasional errand, I spent the first day, and mighty dull I found it after the life and activity of Mr. Beeby's establishment, and profoundly was I relieved when, at half-past eight, Mr. Abraham instructed me to put up the shutters under his supervision. As I took my way home, yawning as I went, I almost wished myself back at Beeby's.

But it was a false alarm. The intolerable dullness of that first day was never repeated. On the following morning I took the precaution to provide myself with a book, but it was not needed, for, while I was cleaning the window, Mr. Abraham went forth, and presently returned with an excessively dirty "grandfather" clock – without its case – which he carried into the workshop and at once began to "take down" (*i.e.*, to take to pieces). As I had finished my work, I made bold to follow him and hover around to watch the operation and, as he did not seem to take my presence amiss, but chatted in quite a friendly way as he worked, I ventured to ask one or two questions, and meanwhile kept on the alert for a chance to "get my foot in".

When he had finished the "taking down" and had put away the dismembered remains of the movement in a drawer, leaving the two plates and the dial on the bench, he proceeded to mix up a paste of rotten-stone and oil, and then, taking up one of the plates, began to scrub it vigorously with a sort of overgrown tooth brush dipped in the mixture. I watched him attentively for a minute or two, and then decided that my opportunity had come.

"Wouldn't it save you time, sir, if I were to clean the other plate?" I asked.

He stopped scrubbing and looked at me in surprise. "That's not a bad idea, Nat," he chuckled. "Why shouldn't you? Yes, get a brush from the drawer. Watch me and do exactly as I do."

Gleefully, I fetched the brush and set to work, following his methods closely and observing him from time to time as the work progressed. He gave an eye to me now and again, but let me carry out the job completely, even to the final polishing and the "pegging out" of the pivot-holes with the little pointed sticks known as peg-wood. When I had finished, he examined my work critically, testing one or two of the pivot-holes with a clean peg, and finally, as he laid down the plate, informed me that I had made quite a good job of it.

That night I went home in a very different frame of mind. No longer did I yearn for Beeby's. I realized that I had had my chance and taken it. I had got my foot in and was now free of the workshop. Other jobs would come my way and they would not all be mere plate-cleaning. I should see to that. And I did. Cautiously and by slow degrees I extended my offers of help from plates to wheels and pinions, to the bushing of worn pivot-holes and the polishing of pivots on the turns. And each time Mr. Abraham viewed me with fresh surprise, evidently puzzled by my apparent familiarity with the mechanism of clocks, and still more so by my ability to make keys and repair locks, an art of which he knew nothing at all.

Thus, the purpose that had been in my mind from the first was working out according to plan. My knowledge of the structure and mechanism of time-keepers was quite considerable. But it was only paper knowledge, book-learning. It had to be supplemented by that other kind of knowledge that can be acquired only by working at the bench, before I could hope to become a clock-maker. The ambition to acquire it had drawn me hither from Mr. Beeby's, and now the opportunity seemed to be before me.

In fact, my way was made unexpectedly easy, for Mr. Abraham's inclinations marched with mine. Excellent workman as he was, skilful, painstaking and scrupulously conscientious, he had no enthusiasm. As Mr. Beeby would have said, his heart was not in his trade. He did not enjoy his work, though he spared no pains in doing it well. But by nature and temperament he was a dealer, a merchant, rather than a craftsman, and it was his ability as a buyer that accounted for the bulk of his income. Hence he was by no means unwilling for me to take over the more laborious and less remunerative side of the business, in so far as I was able, for thereby he was left with more free time to devote to its more profitable aspects.

Exactly how he disposed of this free time I could never quite make out. I got the impression that he had some other interests which he was now free to pursue, having a deputy to carry on the mere retail part of the business and attend to simple repairs. But however that may have been, he began occasionally to absent himself from the shop, leaving me in charge, and as time went on and he found that I managed quite well without him, his absences grew more frequent and prolonged until they occurred almost daily, excepting when there were important repairs on hand. It seemed an anomalous arrangement, but there was really nothing against it. He had instructed me in the simple routine of the business, had explained the artless "secret price marks" on the stock, and ascertained (I think from Beeby) that I was honest and trustworthy, and if he was able

273

to employ his free time more profitably, there was nothing further to be said.

It was on the occasion of one of these absences that an incident occurred which, simple as it appeared to be at the time, was later to develop unexpected consequences. This was one of the days on which Mr. Abraham went down into the land of Clerkenwell to make purchases of material and stock. Experience had taught me that a visit to Clerkenwell meant a day off and, there being no repairs on hand, I made my arrangements to pass the long, solitary day as agreeably as possible. It happened that I had recently acquired an old lock of which the key was missing, and I decided to pass the time pleasantly in making a key to fit it. Accordingly, I selected from the stock of spare keys that I kept in my cupboard a lever key the pipe of which would fit the drill-pin of the lock, but of which the bit was too long to enter, and with this and a small vice and one or two tools, I went out into the shop and prepared to enjoy myself.

I had fixed the vice to the counter, taken off the front plate of the lock (it was a good but simple lock with three levers), clamped the key in the vice and was beginning to file off the excess length of the bit, preparatory to cutting the steps, when a man entered the shop and, sauntering up to the counter, fixed an astonished eye on the key.

"Guv'nor in?" he enquired.

I replied that he was not.

"Pity," he commented. "I've broke the glass of my watch. How long will he be?"

"I don't think he will be back until the evening. But I can fit you a new glass."

"Can you, though?" said he. "You seem to be a handy sort of bloke for your size. How old are you?"

"Getting on for fourteen," I replied, holding out my hand for the watch which he had produced from his pocket.

"Well, I'm blowed," said he. "Fancy a blooming kid of fourteen running a business like this."

I rather resented his description of me, but made no remark. Besides, it was probably meant as a compliment, though unfortunately expressed. I glanced at his watch and, opening the drawer in which watch-glasses were kept, selected one of the suitable size, tried it in the bezel after removing the broken pieces, and snapped it in.

"Well, I'm sure!" he exclaimed as I returned the watch to him. "Wonderful handy cove you are. How much?"

I suggested sixpence, whereupon he fished a handful of mixed coins out of his pocket and began to sort them out. Finally he laid a sixpence on the counter and once more fixed his eyes on the vice.

"What are you doing to that lock?" he asked.

"I am making a key to fit it," I replied.

"Are you, reely?" said he with an air of surprise. "Actooally making a key? Remarkable handy bloke you are. Perhaps you could do a little job for me. There is a box of mine what I can't get open. Something gone wrong with the lock. Key goes in all right but it won't turn. Do you think you could get it to open if I was to bring it along here?"

"I don't know until I have seen it," I replied. "But why not take it to a locksmith?"

"I don't want a big job made of it," said he. "It's only a matter of touching up the key, I expect. What time did you say the guv'nor would be back?"

"I don't expect him home until closing time. But he wouldn't have anything to do with a locksmith's job, in any case."

"No matter," said he. "You'll do for me. I'll just cut round home and fetch that box." And with this he bustled out of the shop and turned away towards Regent Street.

His home must have been farther off than he had seemed to suggest, for it was nearly two hours later when he reappeared, carrying a brown-paper parcel. I happened to see him turn into the street, for I had just received a shop dial from our neighbour, the grocer, and had accompanied him to the door, where he paused for a final message.

"Tell the governor that there isn't much the matter with it, only it stops now and again, which is a nuisance."

He nodded and turned away, and at that moment the other customer arrived with the unnecessary announcement that "here he was". He set the parcel on the counter and, having untied the string, opened the paper covering just enough to expose the keyhole, by which I was able to see that the box was covered with morocco leather and that the keyhole guard seemed to be of silver. Producing a key from his pocket, he inserted it and made a show of trying to turn it.

"You see?" said he. "It goes in all right, but it won't turn. Funny, isn't it? Never served me that way before."

I tried the key and then took it out and looked at it and, as a preliminary measure, probed the barrel with a piece of wire. Then, as the barrel was evidently clean, I tried the lock with the same piece of wire. It was a ward lock, and the key was a warded key, but the wards of the lock and those of the key were not the same. So the mystery was solved: It was the wrong key.

"Well, now," my friend exclaimed, "that's very singler. I could have swore it was the same key what I have always used, but I suppose you know. What's to be done? Do you think you can make that key fit?"

Now, here was a very interesting problem. I had learned from the incomparable Mr. Denison that the wards of a lock are merely obstructions to prevent it from being opened with the wrong key, and that, since the fore edge of the bit is the only acting part of such a key, a wrong key can be turned into a right one by simply cutting away the warded part and leaving the fore edge intact. I had never tried the experiment, but here was an opportunity to put the matter to a test.

"I'll try, if you like," I replied. "That is, if you don't mind my cutting the key about a little."

"Oh, the key is no good to me if it won't open the lock. I don't care what you do to it."

With this, I set to work gleefully, first making a further exploration of the lock with my wire and then carrying the key into the workshop, where there was a fixed vice. There I attacked it with a hack-saw and a file, and soon had the whole of the bit cut away excepting the top and fore edge. All agog to see how it worked, I went back to the shop with a small file in my hand in case any further touches should be necessary and, inserting the key, gave a gentle turn. It was at once evident that there was now no resistance from the wards, but it did not turn freely. So I withdrew it and filed away a fraction from the fore edge to reduce the friction. The result was a complete success, for when I re-inserted it and made another trial, it turned quite freely and I heard the lock click.

My customer was delighted (and so was I). He turned the key backwards and forwards several times and once opened the lid of the box, but only half-an-inch – just enough to make sure that it cleared the lock. Then he took out the key, put it in his pocket, and proceeded to replace the paper cover and tie the string.

"Well," said he, "you are a reg'lar master craftsman, you are. How much have I got to pay?"

I suggested that the job was worth a shilling, to which he agreed.

"But who gets that shilling?" he enquired.

"Mr. Abraham, of course," I replied. "It's his shop."

"So it is," said he, "but you have done the job, so here's a bob for yourself, and you've earned it."

He laid a couple of shillings on the counter, picked up his parcel and went out, whistling gleefully.

Now all this time, although my attention had been concentrated on the matter in hand, I had been aware of something rather odd that was happening outside the shop. My customer had certainly had no

276

companion when he arrived, for I had seen him enter the street alone. But yet he seemed to have some kind of follower, for hardly had he entered the shop when a man appeared, looking in at the window and seeming to keep a watch on what was going on within. At first he did not attract my attention – for a shop window is intended to be looked in at. But presently he moved off, and then returned for another look, and while I was working at the key in the workshop, I could see him on the opposite side of the street, pretending to look in the shop windows there, but evidently keeping our shop under observation.

I did not give him much attention while I was working at my job, but when my customer departed, I went out to the shop door and watched him as he retired clown the street. He was still alone. But now, the follower, who had been fidgeting up and down the pavement opposite, and looking in at shop windows, turned and walked away down the street, slowly and idly at first, but gradually increasing his pace as he went, until he turned the corner quite quickly.

It was very queer and, my curiosity being now fairly aroused, I darted out of the shop and ran down the street, where, when I came to the corner, I could see my customer striding quickly along King Street, while the follower was "legging it" after him as hard as he could go. What the end of it was I never saw, for the man with the parcel disappeared round the corner of Argyll Place before the follower could come up with him.

It was certainly a very odd affair. What could be the relations of these two men? The follower could not have been a secret watcher, for there he was, plainly in view of the other. I turned it over in my mind as I walked back to the shop, and as I entered the transaction in the day-book ("*Key repaired, 1/–*") and dropped the two shillings into the till, having some doubt as to my title to the "bob for myself". (But its presence was detected by Mr. Abraham when we compared the till with the day-book, and it was, after a brief discussion, restored to me.) Even when I was making a tentative exploration of the shop dial and restoring the vanished oil to its dry bearings and pallets, I still puzzled over this mystery until, at last, I had to dismiss it as insoluble.

But it was not insoluble, though the solution was not to appear for many weeks. Nor, when my customer disappeared round the corner, was he lost to me forever. In fact, he re-visited our premises less than a fortnight after our first meeting, shambling into the shop just before dinner-time and greeting me as before with the enquiry, "Guv'nor in?"

"No," I replied, "he has just been called out on business, but he will be back in a few minutes." (He had, in fact, walked round, according to his custom about this time, to inspect the window of the cook's shop in Carnaby Street.) "Is there anything that I can do?"

"Don't think so," said he. "Something has gone wrong with my watch. Won't go. I expect it is a job for the guv'nor."

He brought out from his pocket a large gold watch, which he passed across the counter to me. I noted that it was not the watch to which I had fitted the glass and that it had a small bruise on the edge. Then I stuck my eyeglass in my eye and, having opened first the case and then the dome, took a glance at the part of the movement that was visible. That glance showed me that the balance-staff pivot was broken, which accounted sufficiently for the watch's failure to go. But it showed me something else – something that thrilled me to the marrow. This was no ordinary watch. It was fitted with that curious contrivance that English watchmakers call a *"tourbillion"* – a circular revolving carriage on which the escapement is mounted, the purpose being the avoidance of position errors. Now, I had never seen a *tourbillion* before, though I had read of them as curiosities of advanced watch construction, and I was delighted with this experience, and the more so when I read on the movement the signature of the inventor of this mechanism, *Breguet á Paris*. So absorbed was I with this mechanical wonder that I forgot the existence of the customer until he, somewhat brusquely, drew my attention to it. I apologized and briefly stated what was the matter with the watch.

"That don't mean nothing to me," he complained. "I want to know if there's much wrong with it, and what it will cost to put it right."

I was trying to frame a discreet answer when the arrival of Mr. Abraham relieved me of the necessity. I handed him the watch and my eyeglass and stood by to hear his verdict.

"Fine watch," he commented. "French make. Seems to have been dropped. One pivot broken, probably some others. Can't tell until I have taken it down. I suppose you want it repaired."

"Not if it is going to be an expensive job," said the owner. "I don't want it for use. I got a silver one what does for me. I bought this one cheap, and I wish I hadn't now. Gave a cove a flyer for it."

"Then you got it very cheap," said Mr. Abraham.

"S'pose I did, but I'd like to get my money back all the same. That's all I ask. Care to give me a flyer for it?"

Mr. Abraham's eyes glistened. All his immemorial passion for a bargain shone in them. And well it might. Even I could tell that the price asked was but a fraction of the real value. It was a tremendous temptation for Mr. Abraham.

But, rather to my surprise, he resisted it. Wistfully, he looked at the watch, and especially at the hall-mark, or its French equivalent, for nearly a minute, then, with a visible pang of regret, he closed the case and pushed the watch across the counter.

"I don't deal in second-hand watches," said he.

"Gor!" exclaimed our customer. "It ain't second hand for you. Do the little repairs what are necessary, and it's a new watch. Don't be a mug, Mister. It's the chance of a lifetime."

But Mr. Abraham shook his head and gave the watch a further push.

"Look here!" the other exclaimed, excitedly. "The thing's no good to me. I'll take four-pound-ten. That's giving it away, that is. Gor! You ain't going to refuse that! Well, say four pound. Four blooming jimmies! Why, the case alone is worth more than double that."

Mr. Abraham broke out into a cold sweat. It was a frightful temptation, for what the man said was literally true. But even this Mr. Abraham resisted, and eventually the owner of this priceless timepiece, realizing that "the deal was off", sulkily put it in his pocket and slouched out without another word.

"Why didn't you buy it, sir?" I asked. "It was a beautiful watch."

"So it was," he agreed, "and a splendid case – twenty-two carat gold, but it was too cheap. I would have given him twice what he asked if I had known how he came by it."

"You don't think he stole it, sir, do you?" I asked.

"I suspect someone did," he replied, "but whether this gent was the thief or only the receiver is not my affair."

It wasn't mine either, but as I recalled my former transaction with this "gent" I was inclined to form a more definite opinion, and thereupon I decided to keep my own counsel as to the details of that former transaction. But circumstances compelled me to revise that decision when the matter was reopened by someone who took a less impersonal view than that of Mr. Abraham. That someone was a tall, military-looking man who strode into our shop one evening about six weeks after the watch incident. He made no secret of his business for, as he stepped up to the counter, he produced a card from his pocket and introduced himself with the statement, "You are Mr. David Abraham, I think. I am Detective Sergeant Pitts."

Mr. Abraham bowed graciously and, disregarding the card, replied that he was pleased to make the officer's acquaintance, whereupon the sergeant grinned and remarked, "You are more easily pleased than most of my clients."

Mr. Abraham smiled and regarded the officer with a wary eye. "What can I have the pleasure of doing for you?" he asked.

"That's what I want to find out," said the sergeant. "I have information that, on or about the thirteenth of May, you made a skeleton key for a man named Alfred Coomey, alias John Smith. Is that correct?"

"No," Abraham replied, in a startled voice, "certainly not. I never made a skeleton key in my life. Don't know how to, in fact."

The officer's manner became perceptibly more dry. "My information," said he, "is that on the date mentioned, the said Coomey, or Smith, brought a jewel case to this shop and that you made a skeleton key that opened it. You say that is not true."

"Wait a moment," said Abraham, turning to me with a look of relief. "Perhaps the sergeant is referring to the man you told me about who brought a box here to have a key fitted when I was out. It would be about that date."

The sergeant turned a suddenly interested eye on me and remarked, "So this young shaver is the operator, is he? You'd better tell me all about it, and first, what sort of box was it?"

"I couldn't see much of it, sir, because it was wrapped in brown paper, and he only opened it enough for me to get at the keyhole. But it was about fifteen inches long by about nine broad, and it was covered with green leather, and the keyhole plate seemed to be silver. That is all that I could see."

"And what about the key?"

"It was the wrong key, sir. It went in all right, but it wouldn't turn. So I cut away part of the bit so that it would go past the wards and then it turned and opened the lock."

The sergeant regarded me with a grim smile.

"You seem to be a rather downy young bird," said he. "So you made him a skeleton key, did you? Now, how did you come to know how to make a skeleton key?"

I explained that I had read certain books on locks and had taken a good deal of interest in the subject, a statement that Mr. Abraham was able to confirm.

"Well," said the sergeant, "it's a useful accomplishment, but a bit dangerous. Don't you be too handy with skeleton keys, or you may find yourself taking a different sort of interest in locks and keys."

But here Mr. Abraham interposed with a protest.

"There's nothing to make a fuss about, Sergeant. The man brought his box here to have a key fitted, and my lad fitted a key. There was nothing incorrect or unlawful in that."

"No, no," the sergeant admitted, "I don't say that there was. It happens that the box was not his but, of course, the boy didn't know that. I suppose you couldn't see what was in the box?"

"No, sir. He only opened it about half-an-inch, just to see that it would open."

280

The sergeant nodded. "And as to this man, Coomey – do you think you would recognize him if you saw him again?"

"Yes, sir, I am sure I should. But I don't know that I could recognize the other man."

"The other man!" exclaimed the sergeant. "What other man?"

"The man who was waiting outside." And here I described the curious proceedings of Mr. Coomey's satellite and so much of his appearance as I could remember.

"Ha!" said the sergeant. "That would be the footman who gave Coomey the jewel-case. Followed him here to make sure that he didn't nip off with it. Well, you'd know Coomey again, at any rate. What about you, Mr. Abraham?"

"I couldn't recognize him, of course. I never saw him."

"You saw him later, you know, sir, when he came in with the watch," I reminded him.

"But you never told me – " Abraham began, with a bewildered stare at me, but the sergeant broke in, brusquely. "What's this about a watch, Mr. Abraham? You didn't mention that. Better not hold anything back, you know."

"I am not holding anything back," Abraham protested. "I didn't know it was the same man." And here he proceeded to describe the affair in detail and quite correctly, while the sergeant took down the particulars in a large, funereal note-book.

"So you didn't feel inclined to invest," said he with a sly smile. "Must have wrung your heart to let a bargain like that slip."

"It did," Abraham admitted, "but, you see, I didn't know where he had got it."

"We can take it," said the sergeant, "that he got it out of that jewel-case. What sort of watch was it? Could you recognize it?"

"I am not sure that I could. It was an old watch. French make, gold case, engine-turned with a plain centre. No crest or initials."

"That's all you remember, is it? And what about you, young shaver? Would you know it again?"

"I think I should, sir. It was a peculiar watch, made by Breguet of Paris, and it had a *tourbillion*."

"Had a what?" exclaimed the sergeant. "Sounds like some sort of disease. What does he mean?" he added, gazing at Mr. Abraham.

The latter gave a slightly confused description of the mechanism, explaining that he had not noticed it, as he had been chiefly interested in the case, whereupon the sergeant grinned and remarked that the melting-pot value was what had also interested Mr. Coomey.

"Well," he concluded, shutting up his note-book, "that's all for the present. I expect we shall want you to identify Coomey, and the other man if you can, and when the case comes up for the adjourned hearing, you will both have to come and give evidence. But I will let you know about that later." With this and a nod to Mr. Abraham and a farewell grin at me, he took his departure.

Neither to my employer nor myself was the prospect of visiting the prison and the court at all alluring, especially as our simultaneous absence would entail shutting up the shop, and it was a relief to us both when the sergeant paid us a second, hurried visit to let us know that, as the accused men had decided to plead guilty, our testimony would not be required. So that disposed of the business so far as we were concerned.

Chapter V
Mr. Parrish

It has been remarked, rather obviously, that it is an ill wind that blows nobody good, and also that one man's meat is another man's poison. The application of these samples of proverbial wisdom to this history is in the respective effects of a severe attack of bronchitis upon Mr. Abraham and me. The bronchitis was his, with all its attendant disadvantages, an unmitigated evil, whereas to me it was the determining factor of a beneficial change.

While he was confined to his bed, under the care of the elderly Jewess who customarily "did for him", my daily procedure was, when I had shut up the shop, to carry the contents of the till with the day-book to his bedroom that he might compare them and check the day's takings, and it was on one of these occasions, when he was beginning to mend, that the change in my prospects came into view.

"I have been thinking about you, Nat," said he. "You're an industrious lad, and you've done your duty by me since I've been ill, and I think I ought to do something for you in return. Now, you're set on being a clock-maker, but you can't get into the trade without serving an apprenticeship in the regular way. Supposing I were willing to take you on as my apprentice. How would you like that?"

I jumped at the offer, but suggested that there might be difficulties about the premium.

"There wouldn't be any premium," said he. "I should give you your indentures free and pay the lawyer's charges. Think it over, Nat, and see what your uncle and aunt have to say about it."

It didn't require much thinking over on my part, nor, when I arrived home in triumph and announced my good fortune, was there any difference of opinion as to the practical issue, though the respective views were differently expressed. Uncle Sam thought it "rather handsome of the old chap" (Mr. Abraham was about fifty-five), but Aunt Judy was inclined to sniff.

"He hasn't done badly all these months," said she, "with a competent journeyman for five shillings a week, and he'd be pretty well up a tree if Nat left him to get another job. Oh, he knows which side his bread's buttered."

There may have been some truth in Aunt Judy's comment, but I thought there was more wisdom in old Mr. Gollidge's contribution to the debate.

"It may be a good bargain for Mr. Abraham," said he, "but that don't make it a worse bargain for Nat. It's best that both parties should be suited."

In effect, it was agreed that the offer should be accepted, and when I conveyed this decision to Mr. Abraham, the necessary arrangements were carried through forthwith. The indentures were drawn up, on Mr. Abraham's instructions, by his solicitor, a Mr. Cohen, who brought them to the shop by appointment, and when they had been submitted to and approved by Aunt Judy, they were duly signed by both parties on a small piece of board laid on the invalid's bed, and I was then and there formally bound apprentice for the term of seven years to "*the said David Abraham, hereinafter called the Master*", who, for his part, undertook to instruct me in the art and mystery of clock-making. I need not recite the terms of the indenture in detail, but I think Aunt Judy found them unexpectedly liberal. To my surprise, I was to be given board and lodging, I was to receive five shillings a week for the first year and my wages were to increase by half-a-crown annually, so that in my last year I should be receiving the full wage of a junior journeyman, or improver.

These were great advantages, for henceforth not only would Aunt Judy be relieved of the cost of maintaining me, but she would now have an additional room to dispose of profitably. But beyond these material benefits, there were others that I appreciated even more. Now, as an apprentice, I was entitled to instruction in that part of the "art and mystery" which was concerned with the purchase of stock and material. It is true that, at the time, I did not fully realize the glorious possibilities contained in this provision. Only when, a week or so later, Mr. Abraham (hereinafter called the Master) was sufficiently recovered to descend to the shop, did they begin to dawn on me.

"We seem to be getting short of material," said he after an exploratory browse round the workshop. "I am not well enough to go out yet, so you'll have to run down to Clerkenwell and get the stuff. We'd better draw up a list of what we want."

We made out the list together, and then "the Master" gave me the addresses of the various dealers with full directions as to the route, adding, as I prepared to set forth, "Don't be any longer than you can help, Nat. I'm still feeling a bit shaky."

The truth of the latter statement was so evident that I felt morally compelled to curtail my explorations to the utmost that was possible. But it was a severe trial. For as I hurried along Clerkenwell Road I found myself in a veritable Tom Tiddler's Ground. By sheer force of will, I had to drag myself past those amazing shop windows that displayed – better and more precious than gold and silver – all the wonders of the clock-maker's art. I hardly dared to look at them. But even the hasty glance that I stole as I hurried past gave me an indelible picture of those unbelievable treasures that I can recall to this day. I see them now, though the years have made familiar the subjects of that first, ecstatic, impression: The entrancing tools and gauges, bench-drills and wheel-cutters, the lovely little watchmaker's lathe, fairer to me than the Rose of Sharon or the Lily of the Valley, the polishing heads with their buffs and brushes, the assembled movements, and the noble regulator with its quicksilver pendulum, dealing with seconds as common clocks do with hours. I felt that I could have spent eternity in that blessed street.

However, my actual business, though it was but with dealers in "sundries", gave me the opportunity for more leisured observations. Besides Clerkenwell Road, it carried me to St. John's Gate and Clerkenwell Green, from which, at last, I tore myself away and set forth at top speed towards Holborn to catch the omnibus for Regent Circus (now, by the way, called Oxford Circus). But all the way, as my carriage rumbled sleepily westward, the vision of those Aladdin caves floated before my eyes and haunted me until I entered the little shop and dismissed my master to his easy-chair in the sitting-room. Then I unpacked my parcels, distributed their contents in the proper receptacles, put away the precious price-lists that I had collected for future study, and set about the ordinary business of the day.

I do not propose to follow in detail the course of my life as Mr. Abraham's apprentice. There would, indeed, be little enough to record, for the days and months slipped by unreckoned, spent with placid contentment in the work which was a pleasure to do and a satisfaction when done. But apart from the fact that there would be so little to tell, the mere circumstances of my life are not the actual subject of this history. Its purpose is, as I have explained, to trace the antecedents of certain events which occurred many years later when I was able to put my finger on the one crucial fact that was necessary to disclose the nature and authorship of a very singular crime. With the discovery of that crime, the foregoing chapters have had at least some connection, and in what follows I shall confine myself to incidents that were parts of the same train of causation.

Of these, the first was concerned with my Uncle Sam. By birth he was a Kentish man, and he had served his time in a small workshop at Maidstone, conducted by a certain James Wright. When his apprenticeship had come to an end, he had migrated to London, but he had always kept in touch with his old master and paid him occasional visits. Now, about the end of my third year, Mr. Wright, who was getting too old to carry on alone, had offered to take him into partnership, and the offer being obviously advantageous, Uncle Sam had accepted and forthwith made preparations for the move.

It was a severe blow to me, and I think also to Aunt Judy. For though I had taken up my abode with Mr. Abraham, hardly an evening had passed which did not see me seated in the familiar kitchen (but not in my original chair) facing the old Dutch clock and listening to old Mr. Gollidge's interminable yarns. That kitchen had still been my home as it had been since my infancy. I had still been a member, not only of the family, but of the household – absent, like Uncle Sam, only during working hours. But henceforth I should have no home – for Mr. Abraham's house was a mere lodging, no family circle and, worst of all, no Aunt Judy.

It was a dismal prospect. With a sinking heart I watched the preparations for the departure and counted the days as they slid past, all too quickly, and when the last of the sands had run out and I stood on the platform with my eyes fixed on the receding train, from a window of which Aunt Judy's arm protruded, waving her damp handkerchief, I felt as might have felt some marooned mariner following with despairing gaze the hull of his ship sinking below the horizon. As the train disappeared round a curve, I turned away and could have blubbered aloud, but I was now a young man of sixteen, and a railway station is not a suitable place for the display of the emotions.

But in the days that followed, my condition was very desolate and lonely, and yet, as I can now see, viewing events with a retrospective eye, this shattering misfortune was for my ultimate good. Indeed, it yielded certain immediate benefits. For, casting about for some way of disposing of the solitary evenings, I discovered an institution known as the Working Men's College, then occupying a noble old house in Great Ormond Street, whereby it came about that the homely kitchen was replaced by austere but pleasant class rooms, and the voice of old Mr. Gollidge recounting the mutiny on the *Mar' Jane* by those of friendly young graduates explaining the principles of algebra and geometry, of applied mechanics and machine-drawing.

The next incident, trivial as it will appear in the telling, had an even more profound effect in the shaping of my destiny. Indeed, but for that trifling occurrence, this history could never have been written. So I proceed without further apologies.

On a certain morning at the beginning of the fourth year of my apprenticeship, my master and I were in the shop together reviewing the stock when a rather irate-looking elderly gentleman entered and, fixing a truculent eye on Mr. Abraham, demanded, "Do you know anything about equatorial clocks?" Now, I suspect that Mr. Abraham had never heard of an equatorial clock, all his experience having been in the ordinary trade. But it would never do to say so. Accordingly he temporized.

"Well, sir, they don't, naturally, come my way very often. Were you wanting to purchase one?"

"No, I wasn't, but I've got one that needs some slight repair or adjustment. I am a maker of philosophical instruments and I have had an equatorial sent to me for overhaul. But the clock won't budge, won't start at all. Now, clocks are not philosophical instruments and I don't pretend to know anything about 'em. Can you come round and see what's the matter with the thing?"

This was, for me, a rather disturbing question, for our visitor was none other than the gentleman who had accused me of having stolen his pocket-book. I had recognized him at the first glance as he entered, and had retired discreetly into the background lest he should recognize me. But now I foresaw that I should be dragged forth into the light of day. And so it befell.

"I am afraid," Mr. Abraham said, apologetically, "that I can't leave my business just at the moment. But my assistant can come round with you and see what is wrong with your equa – with your clock."

Our customer looked at me, disparagingly, and my heart sank. But either I had changed more than I had supposed in the five years that had elapsed, or the gentleman's eyesight was not very acute (it turned out that he was distinctly near-sighted). At any rate, he showed no sign of recognition, but merely replied gruffly, "I don't want any boys monkeying about with that clock. Can't you come yourself?"

"I am afraid I really can't. But my assistant is a perfectly competent workman, and I take full responsibility for what he does."

The customer grunted and scowled at me.

"Very well," he said, with a very bad grace. "I hope he's better than he looks. Can you come with me now?"

I replied that I could and, having collected from the workshop the few tools that I was likely to want, I went forth with him, keeping slightly in the rear and as far as possible out of his field of view. But, to my relief, he took no notice of me, trudging on doggedly and looking straight before him.

We had not far to go, for, when we had passed halfway down a quiet street in the neighbourhood of Oxford Market, he halted at a door distinguished by a brass plate bearing the inscription: "*W. Parrish, Philosophical Instrument Maker*", and, inserting a latch-key, admitted himself and me. Still ignoring my existence, he walked down a long passage ending in what looked like a garden door but which, when he opened it, proved to be the entrance to a large workshop in which were a lathe and several fitted benches but, at the moment, no human occupants other than ourselves.

"There," said he, addressing me for the first time, but still not looking at me, "that's the clock. Just have a look at it, and mind you don't do any damage. I've got a letter to write, but I'll be back in a few minutes."

With this he took himself off, much to my satisfaction, and I proceeded forthwith to make a preliminary inspection. The "patient" was a rather large telescope mounted on a cast-iron equatorial stand. I had never seen an equatorial before except in the form of a book-illustration, but from this I was able easily to recognize the parts and also the clock, which was perched on the iron base with its winding-handle within reach of the observer. This handle I tried, but found it fully wound (it was a spring-driven clock, fitted with governor balls and a fly, or fan), and I then proceeded to take off the loose wooden case so as to expose the movement. A leisurely inspection of this disclosed nothing structurally amiss, but it had an appearance suggesting long disuse and was desperately in need of cleaning.

Suspecting that the trouble was simply dirt and dry pivots, I produced from my bag a little bottle of clock-oil and an oiler and delicately applied a small drop of the lubricant to the empty and dry oil-sinks and to every point that was exposed to friction. Then I gave the ball-governor a cautious turn or two, whereupon my diagnosis was immediately confirmed, for the governor, after a few sluggish revolutions as the oil worked into the bearings, started off in earnest, spinning cheerfully and in an obviously normal fashion.

This was highly satisfactory. But now my curiosity was aroused as to the exact effect of the clock on the telescope. The former was geared by means of a long spindle to the right ascension circle, and on this was a little microscope mounted opposite the index. To the eyepiece of this microscope I applied my eye, and was thrilled to observe the scale of the circle creeping almost imperceptibly past the vernier. It was a great experience. I had read of these things in the optical textbooks, but here was this delightful mechanism made real and active before my very eyes. I was positively entranced as I watched that slow, majestic motion, in fact I was so preoccupied that I was unaware of Mr. Parrish's re-entry until I heard his voice, when I sprang up with a guilty start.

"Well," he demanded, gruffly, "have you found out – Oh, but I see you have."

"Yes, sir," I said, eagerly, "it's running quite well now, and the right ascension circle is turning freely – though, of course, I haven't timed it."

"Ho, you haven't, hey?" said he. "Hmm. Seem to know all about it, young fellow. What was the matter with the clock?"

"It only wanted a little adjustment," I replied, evasively, for I didn't like to tell him that it was only a matter of oil. "But," I added, "it really ought to be taken to pieces and thoroughly cleaned."

"Ha!" said he, "I'll let the owner do that. If it goes, that is all that matters to me. You can tell your master to send me the bill."

He still spoke gruffly, but there was a subtle change in his manner. Evidently, my rapid performance had impressed him, and I thought it best to take the undeserved credit, though I was secretly astonished that he, a practical craftsman, had not been able to do the job himself.

But I had impressed him more than I realized at the time. In fact, he had formed a ridiculously excessive estimate of my abilities, as I discovered some weeks later when he brought a watch to our shop to be cleaned and regulated, and stipulated that I should do the work myself "and not let the old fellow meddle with it". I assured him that Mr. Abraham (who was fortunately absent) was a really skilful watchmaker, but he only grunted incredulously.

"I want the job done properly," he insisted, "and I want you to do it yourself."

Evidently Mr. Abraham's evasions in the matter of equatorial clocks had been noted and had made an unfavourable impression. It was unreasonable – but Mr. Parrish was an unreasonable man – and, like most unreasonable beliefs, it was unshakable. Nor did he make any secret of his opinion when, on subsequent occasions during the next few months, he brought in various little repairs and renovations and sometimes interviewed my principal. For Mr. Parrish had no false delicacy – nor very much of any other kind. But Mr. Abraham took no offence. He knew (as Aunt Judy had observed) which side his bread was buttered, and as he was coming more and more to rely on me, he was willing enough that my merits should be recognized.

So through those months, my relations with Mr. Parrish continued to grow closer and my future to shape itself invisibly. Little did I guess at the kind of grist that the Mills of God were grinding.

Chapter VI
Fickle Fortune

"*The best-laid plans of mice and men gang aft agley.*" The oft-quoted words were only too apposite in their application to the plans laid by poor Mr. Abraham for the future conduct of his own affairs and mine. Gradually, as the years had passed, it had become understood between us that, when the period of my apprenticeship should come to an end, I should become his partner and he should subside into the partial retirement suitable to his increasing age.

It was an excellent plan, advantageous to us both. To him it promised a secure and restful old age, to me an assured livelihood, and we both looked forward hope fully to the time, ever growing nearer, when it should come into effect.

But, alas! It was never to be. Towards the end of my fourth year, his old enemy, bronchitis, laid its hand on him and sent him, once more, to his bedroom. But this was not the customary sub-acute attack. From the first it was evident that it was something much more formidable. I could see that for myself, and the doctor's grave looks and evasive answers to my questions confirmed my fears. Nor was evasion possible for long. On the fifth day of the illness, the ominous word "pneumonia" was spoken, and Miriam Goldstein, Mr. Abraham's housekeeper, was directed to summon the patient's relatives.

But, promptly as they responded to the call, they were too late for anything more than whispered and tearful farewells. When they arrived, with Mr. Cohen the solicitor, and I conducted them up to the sick room, my poor master was already blue-faced and comatose, and it was but a few hours later, when they passed out through the shop with their handkerchiefs to their eyes, that Mr. Cohen halted to say to me in a husky under tone, "You can put up the shutters, Polton," and then hurried away with the others.

I shall not dwell on the miserable days that followed, when I sat alone in the darkened shop, vaguely meditating on this calamity, or creeping silently up the stairs to steal a glance at the shrouded figure on the bed. Of all the mourners, none was more sincere than I. Quiet and undemonstrative as our friendship had been, a genuine affection had grown up between my master and me. And not without reason. For Mr. Abraham was not only a kindly man, he was a good man, just and fair in all his dealings, scrupulously honest, truthful and punctual, and strict in

290

the discharge of his religious duties. I respected him deeply and he knew it, and he knew that in me he had a faithful friend and a dependable comrade. Our association had been of the happiest and we had looked forward to many years of pleasant and friendly collaboration. And now he was gone, and our plans had come to nought.

In those first days I gave little thought to my own concerns. It was my first experience of death, and my mind was principally occupied by the catastrophe itself, and by sorrow for the friend whom I had lost. But on the day after the funeral I was suddenly made aware of the full extent of the disaster as it affected me. The bearer – sympathetic enough – of the ill tidings was Mr. Cohen, who had called to give me my instructions.

"This is a bad look-out for you, Polton," said he. "Mr. Abraham ought to have made some provision on your behalf, and I think he meant to. But it was all so sudden. It doesn't do to put off making your will or drafting a new one."

"Then how do I stand, sir?" I asked.

"The position is that your apprenticeship is dissolved by your master's death, and I, as the executor, have to sell the business as a going concern, according to the provisions of the will, which was made before you were apprenticed. Of course, I shall keep you on, if you are willing, to run the business until it is sold. Perhaps the purchaser may agree to take over your indentures or employ you as assistant. Meanwhile, I will pay you a pound a week. Will that suit you?"

I agreed, gladly enough, and only hoped that the purchaser might not make too prompt an appearance. But in this I was disappointed, for, at the end of the third week, Mr. Cohen notified me that the business was sold, and on the following day brought the new tenant to the premises, a rather raffish middle-aged man who smelt strongly of beer and bore the name of Stokes.

"I have explained matters to Mr. Stokes," said Mr. Cohen, "and have asked him if he would care to take over your indentures, but I am sorry to say that he is not prepared to. However, I leave you to talk the matter over with him. Perhaps you can persuade him to change his mind. Meanwhile, here are your wages up to the end of the week, and I wish you good luck."

With this he departed, and I proceeded, forthwith, to try my powers of persuasion on Mr. Stokes. "It would pay you to take me on, sir," I urged. "You'd get a very cheap assistant. For though I am only an apprentice, I have a good knowledge of the trade. I could do all the repairs quite competently. I can take a watch down and clean it. In fact, Mr. Abraham used to give me all the watches to clean."

I thought that would impress him, but it didn't. It merely amused him.

"My good lad," he chuckled, "you are all behind the times. We don't take watches down, nowadays, to clean 'em. We just take off the dial, wind 'em up, wrap 'em in a rag soaked in benzine, and put 'em in a tin box and let 'em clean themselves."

I gazed at him in horror. "That doesn't seem a very good way, sir," I protested. "Mr. Abraham always took a watch down to clean it."

"Ha!" Mr. Stokes replied with a broad grin, "of course he would. That's how they used to do 'em at Ur of the Chaldees when he was serving his time. Hey? Haw haw! No, my lad. My wife and I can run this business. You'll have to look elsewhere for a billet."

"And about my bedroom, sir. Could you arrange to let me keep it for the present? I don't mean for nothing, of course."

"You can have it for half-a-crown a week until you have found another place. Will that do?"

I thanked him and accepted his offer, and that concluded our business, except that I spent an hour or two showing him where the various things were kept, and in stowing my tools and other possessions in my bedroom. Then I addressed myself to the problem of finding a new employer, and that very afternoon I betook myself to Clerkenwell and began a round of all the dealers and clock-makers to whom I was known.

It was the first of many a weary pilgrimage, and its experiences were to be repeated in them all. No one wanted a half-finished apprentice. My Clerkenwell friends were all master craftsmen and they employed only experienced journeymen, and the smaller tradesmen to whom the dealers referred me were mostly able to conduct their modest establishments without assistance. It was a miserable experience which, even now, I look back on with discomfort. Every morning I set out, with dwindling hope, to search unfamiliar streets for clockmakers' shops or to answer obviously inapplicable advertisements in the trade journals, and every evening I wended – not homewards, for I had no home – but to the hospitable common room of the Working Men's College, where, for a few pence, I could get a large cup of tea and a slab of buttered toast to supplement the scanty scraps of food that I had allowed myself during the day's wanderings. But presently even this was beyond my means, and I must needs, for economy, buy myself a half-quarter "household" loaf to devour in my cheerless bedroom to the accompaniment of a draught from the water-jug.

In truth, my condition was becoming desperate. My tiny savings – little more than a matter of shillings – were fast running out in spite of an economy in food which kept me barely above the starvation level. For I

292

had to reserve the rent for my bedroom, that I might not be shelterless as well as famished, so long as any fraction of my little hoard remained. But as I counted the pitiful collection of shillings and sixpences at the bottom of my money-box – soon they needed no counting – I saw that even this was coming to an end and that I was faced by sheer destitution. Now and again the idea of applying for help to Aunt Judy or to Mr. Beeby drifted through my mind, but either from pride or obstinacy or some more respectable motive, I always put it away from me. I suppose that, in the end, I should have had to pocket my pride, or whatever it was, and make the appeal, but it was ordained otherwise.

My capital had come down to four shillings and sixpence, which included the rent for my bedroom due in five days' time, when I took a last survey of my position. The end seemed to be fairly in sight. In five days I should be penniless and starving, without even a night's shelter. I had sought work in every likely and unlikely place and failed ever to come within sight of it. Was there anything more to be done? Any possibility of employment that I had overlooked? As I posed the question again and again, I could find no answer but a hopeless negative. And then, suddenly, I thought of Mr. Parrish. He at least knew that I was a workman. Was it possible that he might find me something to do?

It was but a forlorn hope, for he was not a clock-maker, and of his trade I knew nothing. Nevertheless, no sooner had the idea occurred to me than I proceeded to give effect to it. Having smartened myself up as well as I could, I set forth for Oxford Market as briskly as if I had a regular appointment and, having the good luck to find him at home, put my case to him as persuasively as I was able in a few words.

He listened to me with his usual frown of impatience and, when I had finished, replied in his customary gruff manner, "But my good lad, what do you expect of me? I am not a clock-maker and you are not an instrument-maker. You'd be no use to me."

My heart sank, but I made one last, despairing effort. "Couldn't you give me some odd jobs, sir, such as filing and polishing, to save the time of the skilled men? I shouldn't want much in the way of wages."

He began to repeat his refusal, more gruffly than before. And then, suddenly, he paused, and my heart thumped with almost agonized hope.

"I don't know," he said, slowly and with a considering air. "Perhaps I might be able to find you a job. I've just lost one of my two workmen and I'm rather short-handed at the moment. If you can use a file and know how to polish brass, I might give you some of the rough work to do. At any rate, I'll give you a trial and see what you can do. But I can't pay you a workman's wages. You'll have to be satisfied with fifteen shillings a week. Will that do for you?"

Would it do! It was beyond my wildest hopes. I could have fallen on his neck and kissed his boots (not simultaneously, though I was fairly supple in the joints in those days). Tremulously and gratefully, I accepted his terms, and would have said more, but he cut me short.

"Very well. You can begin work to-morrow morning at nine, and you'll get your wages when you knock off on Saturday. That's all. Off you go."

I wished him "good morning!" and off I went, in an ecstasy of joy and relief reflecting incredulously on my amazing good fortune. Fifteen shillings a week! I could hardly believe that my ears had not deceived me. It was a competence. It was positive affluence.

But it was prospective affluence. My actual possessions amounted to four shillings and sixpence, but it was all my own, for the half-crown that had been ear marked for rent was now available for food. Still, this was Monday morning and wages were payable on Saturday night, so I should have to manage on nine pence a day until then. Well, that was not so bad. In those days, you could get a lot of food for nine-pence if you weren't too particular and knew where to go. At the cook's shop in Carnaby Street where I used to buy Mr. Abraham's mid-day meal and my own, we often fed sumptuously on sixpence apiece, and now the recollection of those simple banquets sent me hurrying thither, spurred on by ravenous hunger and watering at the mouth as imagination pictured that glorious, steamy window.

As I turned into Great Marlborough Street, I encountered Mr. Cohen, just emerging from the Police Court, where he did some practice as advocate. He stopped to ask what I was doing and, when I had announced my joyful tidings, he went on to cross-examine me on my experiences of the last few weeks, listening attentively to my account of them and looking at me very earnestly.

"Well, Polton," he said, "you haven't been putting on a great deal of flesh. How much money have you got?"

I told him, and he rapidly calculated the possibilities of expenditure.

"Ninepence a day. You won't fatten a lot on that. Where did you get the money?"

"I used to put by a little every week when I was at work, sir," I explained, and I could see that my thrift commended itself to him.

"Wise lad," said he, in his dry, legal way. "The men who grow rich are the men who spend less than they earn. Come and have a bit of dinner with me. I'll pay," he added, as I hesitated.

I thanked him most sincerely, for I was famished, as I think he had guessed, and together we crossed the road to a restaurant kept by a Frenchman named Paragot. I had never been in it, but had sometimes

294

looked in with awe through the open doorway at the sybarites within, seated at tables enclosed in pews and consuming unimaginable delicacies. As we entered, Mr. Cohen paused for a few confidential words with the proprietor's sprightly and handsome daughter, the purport of which I guessed when the smiling damsel deposited our meal on the table and I contrasted Mr. Cohen's modest helping with the Gargantuan pile of roast beef, Yorkshire pudding, and baked potatoes which fairly bulged over the edge of my plate.

"Have a drop of porter," said Mr. Cohen. "Do you good once in a way," and, though I would sooner have had water, I thought it proper to accept. But if the taste of the beer was disagreeable, the pleasant pewter tankard in which it was served was a refreshment to the eye. And I think it really did me good. At any rate, when we emerged into Great Marlborough Street, I felt like a giant refreshed, which is something to say for a young man of four-feet-eleven.

As we stood for a moment outside the restaurant, Mr. Cohen put his hand in his pocket and produced a half-sovereign.

"I'm going to lend you ten shillings, Polton," said he. "Better take it. You may want it. You can pay me back a shilling a week. Pay at my office. If I am not there, give it to my clerk and make him give you a receipt. There you are. That's all right. Wish you luck in your new job. So long."

With a flourish of the hand, he bustled off in the direction of the Police Court, leaving me grasping the little gold coin and choking with gratitude to this – I was going to say "Good Samaritan", but I suppose that would be a rather left-handed compliment to an orthodox Jew with the royal name of Cohen.

I spent a joyous afternoon rambling about the town and looking in shop windows and, as the evening closed in, I repaired to a coffee-shop in Holborn and consumed a gigantic cup of tea and two thick slices of bread and butter ("pint of tea and two doorsteps", in the vernacular). Then I turned homeward, if I may use the expression in connection with a hired bedroom, resolving to get a long night's rest so as to be fresh for the beginning of my new labours in the morning.

Chapter VII
Introduces a Key
and a Calendar

When I entered the workshop which was to be the scene of my labours for the next few months, I found in it two other occupants: An elderly workman who was engaged at a lathe and a youth of about my own age who was filing up some brass object that was fixed in a vice. They both stopped work when I appeared, and looked at me with evident curiosity, and both greeted me in their respective ways, the workman with a dry "Good morning", and the other with a most peculiar grin.

"You're the new hand, I suppose," the former suggested, adding, "I don't know what sort of a hand you are. Can you file flat?"

I replied that I could, whereupon he produced a rough plate of brass and handed it to me.

"There," said he. "That casting has got to be filed smooth and true and then it's got to be polished. Let's see what you can do with it."

Evidently he had no extravagant expectations as to my skill, for he watched me critically as I put my tool-bag on the bench and selected a suitable file from my collection (but I could see that he viewed the bag with approval), and every few minutes he left his work to see how I was getting on. Apparently, the results of his observations were reassuring, for his visits gradually became less frequent, and finally he left me to finish the job alone.

During that first day I saw Mr. Parrish only once, for he did his own work in a small private workshop, which was always kept locked in his absence, as it contained a very precious dividing machine, with which he engraved the graduations on the scales of measuring instruments such as theodolites and sextants. This, with some delicate finishing and adjusting, was his province in the business, the larger, constructive work being done by his workmen. But on this occasion he came into the main workshop just before "knocking-off time" to hear the report on my abilities.

"Well, Kennet," he demanded in his gruff way, "How has your new hand got on? Any good?"

Mr. Kennet regarded me, appraisingly, and after a brief consideration, replied, "Yes, I think he'll do."

It was not extravagant praise, but Mr. Kennet was a man of few words. That laconic verdict established me as a permanent member of the staff.

In the days that followed, a quiet friendliness grew up between us. Not that Mr. Kennet was a specially prepossessing person. Outwardly a grey-haired, shrivelled, weasel-faced little man, dry and taciturn in manner and as emotionless as a potato, he had his kindly impulses, though they seldom came to the surface. But he was a first-class craftsman who knew his trade from *A* to *Z*, and measured the worth of other men in terms of their knowledge and skill. The liking that, from the first, he took to me, arose, I think, from his observation of my interest in my work and my capacity for taking pains. At any rate, in his undemonstrative way, he made me aware of his friendly sentiments, principally by letting me into the mysteries and secrets of the trade and giving me various useful tips from the storehouse of his experience.

My other companion in the workshop was the youth whom I have mentioned, who was usually addressed and referred to as Gus, which I took to represent Augustus. His surname was Haire, and I understood that he was some kind of relation of Mr. Parrish's, apparently a nephew, as he always spoke of Mr. Parrish as his uncle, though he addressed him as "Sir". His position in the workshop appeared to be that of a pupil, learning the business – as I gathered from him – with a view to partnership and succession. He lived on the premises, though he frequently went away for the week-ends to his home, which was at Malden in Essex.

The mutual liking of Mr. Kennet and myself found no counterpart in the case of Gus Haire. I took an instant distaste of him at our first meeting, which is rather remarkable, since I am not in the least addicted to taking sudden likes or dislikes. It may have been his teeth, but I hope not, for it would be unpardonable to allow a mere physical defect to influence one's judgment of a man's personal worth. But they were certainly rather unpleasant teeth and most peculiar. I have never seen anything like them, before or since. They were not decayed. Apparently, they were quite sound and strong, but they were covered with brown spots and mottlings which made them look like tortoise-shell. They were also rather large and prominent, which was unfortunate, as Gus was distinctly sensitive about them. Whence the remarkable grin which had so impressed me when we first met. It was habitual with him, and it startled me afresh every time. It began as a fine broad grin displaying the entire outfit of tortoise-shell. Then suddenly, he became conscious of his teeth, and in an instant the grin was gone. The effect was extraordinary, and not by any means agreeable.

297

Still, as I have said, I hope it was not the teeth that prejudiced me against him. There were other, and much better, reasons for my disliking him. But these developed later. My initial distaste of him may have been premonitory. In some unimaginable way, I seemed instinctively to have recognized an enemy.

As to his hardly-concealed dislike of me, I took it to be merely jealousy of Kennet's evident preference, for that thorough-going craftsman had no use for Gus. The lad was lazy, inattentive, and a superlatively bad workman, faults enough to damn him in Kennet's eyes. But there were other matters, which will transpire in their proper place.

In these early days, I was haunted by constant anxiety as to the security of my position. There was really not enough for me to do. Mr. Parrish was getting on in years and some of his methods were rather obsolete. Newer firms with more up-to-date plant were attracting orders that would formerly have come to him, so that his business was not what it had been. But even of the work that was being done I could, at first, take but a small share. Later, when I had learned more of the trade, Kennet was able to turn over to me a good deal of his own work, so that I became, in effect, something like a competent journeyman. But in the first few weeks I often found myself with nothing to do, and was terrified lest Mr. Parrish should think that I was not earning my wage.

It was a dreadful thought. The idea of being set adrift once more to tramp the streets, hungry and despairing, became a sort of permanent nightmare. I worked with intense care and effort to learn my new trade and felt myself making daily progress. But still, "Black Care rode behind the horseman". Something had to be done to fill up the hours of idleness and make me seem to be worth my pay. But what?

I began by taking down the workshop clock and cleaning it. Then I took off the lock of the workshop door, which had ceased to function, and made it as good as new, which seemed at the time to be a fortunate move, for, just as I was finishing it, Mr. Parrish came into the workshop and stopped to watch my proceedings.

"Ha!" said he, "so you are a locksmith, too. That's lucky, because I have got a job for you. The key of my writing-table has broken in the lock and I can't get the drawer open. Come and see what you can do with it."

I picked up my tool-bag and followed him to his workshop (which also served as an office), where he showed me the closed drawer with the stem of the broken key projecting about a quarter of an inch.

"There must be something wrong with the lock," said he, "for the key wouldn't turn, and when I gave it an extra twist it broke off. Flaw in the key, I expect."

I began by filing a small flat on the projecting stump, and then, producing a little hand-vice from my bag, applied it to the stump and screwed it up tight. With this I was able to turn the key a little backwards and forwards, but there was evidently something amiss with the lock, as it would turn no further. With my oiler, I insinuated a touch of oil on to the bit of the key and as much of the levers as I could reach and continued to turn the key to and fro, watched intently by Mr. Parrish and Gus (who had left his work to come and look on). At last, when I ventured to use a little more force, the resistance gave way and the key made a complete turn with an audible click of the lock.

As I withdrew the key, Mr. Parrish pulled out the drawer, which, as I saw, contained, among other things, a wooden bowl half-filled with a most untidy collection of mixed money: Shillings, half-crowns, coppers, and at least two half-sovereigns. I looked with surprise at the disorderly heap and thought how it would have shocked poor Mr. Abraham.

"Well," said Mr. Parrish, "what's to be done? Can you make a new key?"

"Yes, sir," I replied, "or I could braze the old one together."

"No," he replied, "I've had enough of that key. And what about the lock?"

"I shall have to take that off in any case, because the ironmonger won't sell me a key-blank unless I show the lock. But it will have to be repaired."

"Very well," he agreed. "Take it off and get the job done as quickly as you can. I don't want to leave my cash-drawer unlocked."

I had the lock off in a few moments and took it away, with the broken key, to the workshop, where I spent a pleasant half-hour taking it to pieces, cleaning it, and doing the trifling repairs that it needed, and all the time, Gus Haire watched me intently, following me about like a dog and plying me with questions. I had never known him to be so interested in anything. He even accompanied me to the ironmonger's and looked on with concentrated attention while I selected the blank. Apparently, locksmithing was more to his taste than the making of philosophical instruments.

But the real tit-bit of the entertainment for him was the making of the new key. His eyes fairly bulged as he followed the details of the operation. I had in my bag a tin box containing a good-sized lump of stiff moulding-wax, which latter I took out and, laying it on the bench, rolled it out flat with a file-handle. Then, on the flat surface, I made two impressions of the broken key, one of the profile of the bit and the other of the end, showing the hole in the "pipe" and, having got my pattern, I fell to work on the blank. First, I drilled out the bore of the pipe, then I filed up the blank roughly to the dimensions with the aid of callipers and, when I had brought it to the approximate size, I began carefully to shape the bit and cut out the "steps" for the levers, testing the result from time to time by fitting it into the impressions.

At length, when it appeared to fit both impressions perfectly, I tried it in the lock and found that it entered easily and turned freely to and fro, moving the bolt and levers without a trace of stiffness. Naturally, I was quite pleased at having got it right at the first trial. But my satisfaction was nothing compared with that of my watcher, who took the lock from me and turned the key to-and-fro with as much delight as if he had made it himself. Even Kennett, attracted by Gus's exclamations, left his work – (He was making a reflecting level – just a simple mirror with a hole through it, mounted in a suspension frame.) – to come and see what it was all about.

But Gus's curiosity seemed now to be satisfied, for, when I took the lock and the new key to Mr. Parrish's workroom, he did not accompany me. Apparently, he was not interested in the mere refixing of the lock, whereas Mr. Parrish watched that operation with evident relief, for when I had finished, he tried the key several times, first with the drawer open and then with it closed, finally locking the drawer and pocketing the key with a grunt of satisfaction.

"Where's the broken key?" he demanded as I prepared to depart. "I'd better have that."

I ran back to the workshop, where I found Gus back at his vice, industriously filing something, and Kennet still busy with his level. The latter looked round at me as I released the key from the hand-vice, and I explained that I had forgotten to give the broken key to Mr. Parrish. He nodded and still watched me as I retired with it in my hand to return it to its owner, and when I came back to the workshop he put down his level and strolled across to my bench, apparently to inspect the slab of wax. I also inspected it, and saw at once that it was smaller than when I had left it, and I had no doubt that the ingenious Gus had "pinched" a portion of it for the purpose of making some private experiments. But I made no remark and, having obliterated the key-impressions with my thumb, I peeled the wax off the bench, squeezed it up into a lump, and put it into my bag. Whereupon Kennet went back to his level without a word.

But my suspicions of Master Gus's depredations were confirmed a few days later when Kennet and I happening to be alone in the workshop, he came close to me and asked, in a low tone, "Did you miss any of that wax of yours the other day?"

"Yes, I did, and I'm afraid I suspected that Gus had helped himself to a bit."

"You were right," said Kennet. "He cut a piece off and pocketed it. But before he cut it off, he made two impressions of the key on it. I saw him. He thought I didn't, because my back was turned to him. But I was working on that level, and I was able to watch him in the mirror."

I didn't much like this, and said so.

"More don't I," said Kennet. "I haven't said anything about it, because it ain't my concern. But it may be yours. So you keep a look-out. And remember that I saw him do it."

With this and a significant nod he went back to the lathe and resumed his work.

The hardly-veiled hint that "it might be my concern" was not very comfortable to reflect on, but there was nothing to be done beyond keeping my tool-bag locked and the key in my pocket, which I was careful to do, and as the weeks passed, and nothing unusual happened, the affair gradually faded out of my mind.

Meanwhile, conditions were steadily improving. I had now learned to use the lathe and even to cut a quite respectable screw and, as my proficiency increased, and with it my value as a workman, I began to feel my position more secure. And even when there was nothing for me to do in the workshop, Mr. Parrish found me odd jobs about the house, repairing locks, cleaning his watch, and attending to the various clocks, so that I was still earning my modest wage. In this way I came by a piece of work which interested me immensely at the time, and which had such curious consequences later that I venture to describe it in some detail.

It was connected with a long-case, or "grandfather" clock, which stood in Mr. Parrish's workroom a few feet from his writing-table. I suspect that it had not been cleaned within the memory of man and, naturally, there came a time when dirt and dry pivots brought it to a standstill. Even then, a touch of oil would probably have kept it going for a month or two, but I made no such suggestion. I agreed emphatically with Mr. Parrish's pronouncement that the clock needed a thorough overhaul.

"And while you've got it to pieces," he continued, "perhaps you could manage to fit it with a calendar attachment. Do you think that would be possible?"

I pointed out that it had a date disc, but he dismissed that with contempt.

"Too small. Want a microscope to see it. No, no, I mean a proper calendar with the day of the week and the day of the month in good bold characters that I can read when I am sitting at the table. Can you do that?"

I suggested that the striking work would be rather in the way, but he interrupted, "Never mind the striking work. I never use it. I hate a jangling noise in my room. Take it off if it's in the way. But I should like a calendar if you could manage it."

Of course, there was no difficulty. A modification of the ordinary watch-calendar movement would have answered. But when I described it, he raised objections.

"How long does it take to change?" he asked.

"About half-an-hour, I should think. It changes during the night."

"That's no use," said he. "The date changes in an instant, on the stroke of midnight. A minute to twelve is, say, Monday, a minute after twelve is Tuesday. That ought to be possible. You make a clock strike at the right moment, why couldn't you do the same with a calendar? It must be possible."

It probably was, but no calendar movement known to me would do it. I should have to invent one on an entirely different principle if my powers were equal to the task. It was certainly a problem, but the very difficulty of it was an attraction, and in the end I promised to turn it over in my mind, and meanwhile I proceeded to take the clock out of its case and bear it away to the workshop. There, under the respectful observation of Gus and Mr. Kennet, I quickly took it down and fell to work on the cleaning operations, but the familiar routine hardly occupied my attention. As I worked, my thoughts were busy with the problem that I had to solve, and gradually my ideas began to take a definite shape. I saw, at once, that the mechanism required must be in the nature of an escapement, that is to say, that there must be a constant drive and a periodical release. I must not burden the reader with mechanical details, but it is necessary that I should give an outline of the arrangement at which I arrived after much thought and a few tentative pencil drawings.

Close to the top of the door of the case I cut two small windows, one to show the date numbers and the other the days of the week. Below these was a third window for the months, the names of which were painted in white on a band of black linen which travelled on a pair of small rollers. But these rollers were turned by hand and formed no part of the mechanism. There was no use in complicating the arrangements for the sake of a monthly change.

And now for the mechanism itself! The names of the days were painted in white on a black drum, or roller, three inches in diameter, and the date numbers were painted on an endless black ribbon which was carried by another drum of the same thickness but narrower. This drum had at each edge seven little pins, or pegs, and the ribbon had, along each edge, a series of small eyelet holes which fitted loosely on the pins, so that, as the drum turned, it carried the ribbon along for exactly the right distance. Both drums were fixed friction-tight on a long spindle, which also carried at its middle a star wheel with seven long, slender teeth, and at its end a ratchet pulley over which ran a cord carrying the small driving-weight. Thus the calendar movement had its own driving-power and made no demands on that of the clock.

So much for the calendar itself, and now for its connection with the clock. The mechanism "took off" from the hour-wheel which carries the hour-hand and makes a complete turn in twelve hours, and which, in this clock, had forty teeth. Below this, and gearing with it, I fixed another wheel, which had eighty teeth, and consequently turned once in twenty-four hours. I will call this the "day-wheel". On this wheel I fixed, friction-tight so that it could be moved round to adjust it, what clockmakers call a "snail", which is a flat disc cut to a spiral shape, so that it looks like the profile of a snail's shell. Connecting the snail with the calendar was a flat, thin steel bar (I actually made it from the blade of a hacksaw) which I will call the "pallet-bar". It moved on a pivot near its middle and had at its top end a small pin which rested against the edge of the snail and was pressed against it by a very weak spring. At its lower end it had an oblong opening with two small ledges, or pallets, for the teeth of the star-wheel to rest on. I hope I have made this fairly clear. And now let us see how it worked.

We will take the top end first. As the clock "went", it turned the snail round slowly (half-as-fast as the hour-hand), and as the snail turned, it gradually pushed the pin of the pallet-bar, which was resting against it, farther and farther from its centre, until the end of the spiral was reached. A little further turn and the pin dropped off the end of the spiral ("the step") down towards the centre. Then the pushing-away movement began again. Thus it will be seen that the rotation of the snail (once in twenty-four hours) caused the top end of the pallet-bar to move slowly outwards and then drop back with a jerk.

Now let us turn to the lower end of the pallet-bar. Here, as I have said, was an oblong opening, interrupted by two little projecting ledges, or pallets. Through this opening the star-wheel projected, one of its seven teeth resting (usually) on the upper pallet, and held there by the power of the little driving weight. As the snail turned and pushed the top end of the pallet-bar outwards, the lower end moved in the opposite direction, and the pallet slid along under the tooth of the wheel. When the tooth reached the end of the upper pallet, it dropped off on to the lower pallet and remained there for a few minutes. Then, when the pin dropped into the step of the snail, the lower pallet was suddenly withdrawn from under the tooth, which left the wheel free to turn until the next tooth was stopped by the upper pallet. Thus the wheel made the seventh of a revolution, but so, also, did the two drums which were on the same spindle, with the result that a new day and date number were brought to their respective windows, and the change occupied less than a second.

The above is only a rough sketch of the mechanism, omitting the minor mechanical details, and I hope it has not wearied the reader. To me, I need not say, the work was a labour of love which kept me supremely happy. But it also greatly added to my prestige in the workshop. Kennet was deeply impressed by it, and Gus followed the construction with the keenest interest and with a display of mechanical intelligence that rather surprised me. Even Mr. Parrish looked into the workshop from time to time and observed my progress with an approving grunt.

When the construction was finished, I brought the case into the workshop and there set the clock up – at first without the dial – to make the final adjustments. I set the snail to discharge at twelve noon, as midnight was not practicable, and the three of us used to gather round the clock as the appointed hour approached, for the gratification of seeing the day and date change in an instant at the little windows. When the adjustment was perfect, I stopped the clock at ten in the morning and we carried it in triumph to its usual abiding place, where, when I had tried the action to see that the tick was even, I once more stopped the pendulum and would have left it to the care of its owner. But Mr. Parrish insisted that I should come in in the evening and start it myself and further, that I should stay until midnight and see that the date did actually change at the correct moment. To which I agreed very readily, whereby I not only gained a supper that was a banquet compared with my customary diet and had the satisfaction of seeing the date change on the very stroke of midnight, but I received such commendations from my usually undemonstrative employer that I began seriously to consider the possibility of an increase in my wages in the not too distant future.

But, alas! The future had something very different in store for me.

Chapter VIII
Mr. Parrish Remembers

For a month or two after the agreeable episode just recounted, the stream of my life flowed on tranquilly and perhaps rather monotonously. But I was quite happy. My position in Mr. Parrish's establishment seemed fairly settled and I had the feeling that my employer set some value on me as a workman. Not, however, to the extent of increasing my salary, though of this I still cherished hopes. But I did not dare to raise the question, for at least I had an assured livelihood, if a rather meagre one, and so great was my horror of being thrown out of employment that I would have accepted the low wage indefinitely rather than risk my security. So I worked on contentedly, poor as a church mouse, but always hoping for better times.

But at last came the explosion which blew my security into atoms. It was a disastrous affair and foolish, too, and what made it worse was that it was my own hand that set the match to the gunpowder. Very vividly do I recall the circumstances, though at first they seemed trivial enough. A man from a tool-maker's had come into the workshop to inspect a new slide-rest that his firm had fitted to the lathe. When he had examined it and pronounced it satisfactory, he picked up the heavy bag that he had brought and was turning towards the door when Mr. Parrish said, "If you have got the account with you, I may as well settle up now."

The man produced the account from his pocket-book and handed it to Mr. Parrish, who glanced at it and then, diving into his coat-tail pocket, brought out a leather wallet (which I instantly recognized as an old acquaintance) and, extracting from it a five-pound note, handed the latter to the man in exchange for the receipt and a few shillings change. As our visitor put away the note, Mr. Parrish said to me, "Take Mr. Soames's bag, Polton, and carry it out to the cab."

I picked up the bag, which seemed to be filled with tool-makers' samples, and conveyed it out to the waiting "growler", where I stowed it on the front seat and, waiting with the door open, saw Mr. Soames safely into the vehicle and shut him in. Returning into the house, I encountered Mr. Parrish, who was standing at the front door, and then it was that some demon of mischief impelled me to an act of the most perfectly asinine folly.

"I see, sir," I said with a fatuous smirk, "that you still carry your wallet in your coat-tail pocket."

He halted suddenly and stared at me with a strange, startled expression that brought me to my senses with a jerk. But it was too late. I saw that the fat was in the fire, though I didn't guess how much fat there was or how big was the fire. After a prolonged stare, he commanded, gruffly, "Come into my room and tell me what you mean."

I followed him in, miserably, and when he had shut the door, I explained, "I was thinking, sir, of what the inspector at the police station said to you about carrying your wallet in your tail pocket. Don't you remember, sir?"

"Yes," he replied, glaring at me ferociously, "I remember. And I remember you, too, now that you have reminded me. I always thought that I had seen you before. So you are the young rascal who was found in possession of the stolen property."

"But I didn't steal it, sir," I pleaded.

"Ha!" said he. "So you said at the time. Very well. That will do for the present."

I sneaked out of the room very crest-fallen and apprehensive. "For the present!" What did he mean by that? Was there more trouble to come? I looked nervously in at the workshop, but as the other occupants had now gone to dinner, I took myself off and repaired to an a-la-mode beef shop in Oxford Market, where I fortified myself with a big basinful of the steaming compound and "topped up" with a halfpennyworth of apples from a stall in the market. Then I whiled away the remainder of the dinner hour rambling about the streets, trying to interest myself in shop windows, but unable to rid myself of the haunting dread of what loomed in the immediate future.

At length, as the last minutes of the dinner hour ran out, I crept back timorously, hoping to slink unnoticed along the passage to the workshop. But even as I entered, my forebodings were realized. For there was my employer, evidently waiting for me, and a glance at his face prepared me for instant dismissal. He motioned to me silently to follow him into his room, and I did so in the deepest dejection, but when I entered and found a third person in the room, my dejection gave place to something like terror. For that third person was Detective Sergeant Pitts.

He recognized me instantly, for he greeted me drily by name. Then, characteristically, he came straight to the point.

"Mr. Parrish alleges that you have opened his cash drawer with a false key and have, from time to time, taken certain monies from it. Now, before you say anything, I must caution you that anything you may say will be taken down in writing and may be used in evidence against you. So be very careful. Do you wish to say anything?"

"Certainly I do," I replied, my indignation almost overcoming my alarm. "I say that I have no false key, that I have never touched the drawer except in Mr. Parrish's presence, and that I have never taken any money whatsoever."

The sergeant made a note of my reply in a large black note-book and then asked, "Is it true that you made a key to fit this drawer?"

"Yes, for Mr. Parrish, and he has that key and the broken one from which it was copied. I made no other key."

"How did you make that key? By measurements only, or did you make a squeeze?"

"I made a squeeze from the broken key and, as soon as the job was finished, I destroyed it."

"That's what he says," exclaimed Mr. Parrish, "but it's a lie. He kept the squeeze and made another key from it."

The sergeant cast a slightly impatient glance at him and remarked, drily, "We are taking his statement," and continued. "Now, Polton, Mr. Parrish says that he marked some, or all, of the money in that drawer with a *P*. scratched just behind the head. If you have got any money about you, perhaps you would like to show it to us."

"Like, indeed!" exclaimed Mr. Parrish. "He'll have to be searched whether he likes it or not."

The sergeant looked at him angrily but, as I proceeded to turn out my pockets and lay the contents on the table, he made no remark until Mr. Parrish was about to pounce on the coins that I had laid down, when he said, brusquely, "Keep your hands off that money, Mr. Parrish. This is my affair."

Then he proceeded to examine the coins, one by one, laying them down again in two separate groups. Having finished, he looked at me steadily and said, "Here, Polton, are five coins: Three half-crowns and a shilling and a sixpence. All the half-crowns are marked with a *P*. The other coins are not marked. Can you explain how you came by those half-crowns?"

"Yes, sir. I received them from Mr. Parrish when he paid me my wages last Saturday. He gave me four half-crowns, two forms and a shilling, and he took the money from that drawer."

The sergeant looked at Mr. Parrish. "Is that correct?" he asked.

"I paid him his wages – fifteen shillings – but I don't admit that those are the coins I gave him."

"But," the sergeant persisted, "did you take the money from that drawer?"

"Of course I did," snapped Parrish. "It's my petty-cash drawer."

"And did you examine the coins to see whether they were marked?"

"I expect I did, but I really don't remember."

"He did not," said I. "He just counted out the money and handed it to me."

The sergeant gazed at my employer with an expression of bewilderment.

"Well, of all – " he began, and then stopped and began again. "But what on earth was the use of marking the money and then paying it out in the ordinary way?"

The question stumped Mr. Parrish for the moment. Then, having mumbled something about "a simple precaution", he returned to the subject of the squeeze and the key. But the sergeant cut him short.

"It's no use just making accusations without proof. You've got nothing to go on. The marked money is all bunkum, and as to the key, you are simply guessing. You've not made out any case at all."

"Oh, haven't I?" Parrish retorted. "What about that key and the lock that he repaired and the stolen money? I am going to prosecute him, and I call on you to arrest him now."

"I'm not going to arrest him," said the sergeant, "but if you still intend to prosecute, you'd better come along and settle the matter with the inspector at the station. You come, too, Polton, so that you can answer any questions."

Thus did history repeat itself. Once more, after five years, did I journey to the same forbidding destination in company with the same accuser and the guardian of the law. When we arrived at the police station and were about to enter, we nearly collided with a smartly dressed gentleman who was hurrying out, and whom I recognized as my late benefactor, Mr. Cohen. He recognized me at the same moment and stopped short with a look of surprise at the sergeant.

"Why, what's this, Polton?" he demanded. "What are you doing here?"

"He is accused by this gentleman," the sergeant explained, "of having stolen money from a drawer by means of a false key."

"Bah!" exclaimed Mr. Cohen. "Nonsense. He is a most respectable lad. I know him well and can vouch for his excellent character."

"You don't know him as well as I do," said Mr. Parrish, viciously.

Mr. Cohen turned on him a look of extreme disfavour and then addressed the sergeant.

"If there is going to be a prosecution, Sergeant, I shall undertake the defence. But I should like to have a few words with Polton and hear his account of the affair before the charge is made."

To this Mr. Parrish was disposed to object, muttering something about "collusion" but, as the inspector was engaged at the moment, the sergeant thrust my adviser and me into a small, empty room and shut the door. Then Mr. Cohen began to ply me with questions, and so skilfully were they framed that in a few minutes he had elicited, not only the immediate circumstances, but also the material antecedents, including the incident of the wax squeeze and Mr. Kennet's observations with the reflecting level. I had just finished my recital when the sergeant opened the door and invited us to step into the inspector's office.

Police officers appear to have astonishing memories. The inspector was the same one who had taken – or rather refused – the charge on my former visit, and I gathered that not only was his recognition of accused and accuser instantaneous, but that he even remembered the circumstances in detail. His mention of the fact did not appear to encourage Mr. Parrish, who began the statement of his case in a rather diffident tone, but he soon warmed up, and finished upon a note of fierce denunciation. He made no reference to the marked coins, but the sergeant supplied the deficiency with a description of the incident to which the inspector listened with an appreciative grin.

"It comes to this, then," that officer summed up. "You have missed certain money from your cash-drawer and you suspect Polton of having stolen it because he is able to make a key."

"And a very good reason, too," Mr. Parrish retorted, defiantly.

"You have no proof that he did actually make a key?"

"He must have done so, or he wouldn't have been able to steal the money."

The inspector exchanged glances of intelligence with the sergeant and then turned to my adviser.

"Now, Mr. Cohen, you say you are acting for the accused. You have heard what Mr. Parrish has said. Is there any answer to the charge?"

"There is a most complete and conclusive answer," Mr. Cohen replied. "In the first place I can prove that Polton destroyed the wax squeeze immediately when he had finished the key. Further, I can prove that, while Polton was absent, trying the key in the lock, some other person abstracted a piece of the wax and made an impression on it with the broken key. He thought he was unobserved, but he was mistaken. Someone saw him take the wax and make the squeeze. Now, the person who made that squeeze was a member of Mr. Parrish's household, and so would have had access to Mr. Parrish's office in his absence."

"He wouldn't," Mr. Parrish interposed. "I always lock my office when I go away from it."

"And when you are in it," the inspector asked, "where is the key?"

"In the door, of course," Mr. Parrish replied impatiently.

309

"On the outside, where anyone could take it out quietly, make a squeeze and put it back. And somebody must have made a false key if the money was really stolen. The drawer couldn't have been robbed when you were in the office."

"That is exactly what I am saying," Mr. Parrish protested. "This young rogue made two keys, one of the door and one of the cash-drawer."

The inspector took a deep breath and then looked at Mr. Cohen.

"You say, Mr. Cohen, that you can produce evidence. What sort of evidence?"

"Absolutely conclusive evidence, sir," Mr. Cohen replied. "The testimony of an eye-witness who saw Polton destroy his squeeze and saw the other person take a piece of the wax and make the impression. If this case goes into Court, I shall call that witness and he will disclose the identity of that person. And then I presume that the police would take action against that person."

"Certainly," replied the inspector. "If Mr. Parrish swears that money was stolen from that drawer and you prove that some person, living in the house, had made a squeeze of the drawer-key, we should, naturally, charge that person with having committed the robbery. Can you swear, Mr. Parrish, that the money was really stolen and give particulars of the amounts?"

"Well," replied Mr. Parrish, mightily flustered by these new developments, "to the best of my belief – but if there is going to be a lot of fuss and scandal, perhaps I had better let the matter drop and say no more about it."

"That won't do, Mr. Parrish," my champion said, sharply. "You have accused a most respectable young man of a serious crime, and you have actually planted marked money on him and pretended that he stole it. Now, you have got either to support that accusation – which you can't do, because it is false – or withdraw the charge unconditionally and acknowledge your mistake. If you do that, in writing, I am willing to let the matter drop, as you express it. Otherwise, I shall take such measures as may be necessary to establish my client's innocence."

The pretty obvious meaning of Mr. Cohen's threat was evidently understood, for my crestfallen accuser turned in dismay to the inspector with a mumbled request for advice, to which the officer replied, briskly, "Well. What's the difficulty? You've been guessing, and you've guessed wrong. Why not do the fair thing and admit your mistake like a man?"

In the end, Mr. Parrish surrendered, though with a very bad grace, and when Mr. Cohen had written out a short statement, he signed it, and Sergeant Pitts attested the signature and Mr. Cohen bestowed the document in his wallet, which brought the proceedings to an end. Mr. Parrish departed in dudgeon, and I – when I had expressed my profound gratitude to Mr. Cohen for his timely help – followed him, in considerably better spirits than when I had arrived.

But as soon as I was outside the police station, the realities of my position came back to me. The greater peril of the false charge and possible conviction and imprisonment I had escaped, but the other peril still hung over me. I had now to return to my place of employment, but I knew that there would be no more employment for me. Mr. Parrish was an unreasonable, obstinate man, and evidently vindictive. No generous regret for the false accusation could I expect, but rather an exacerbation of his anger against me. He would never forgive the humiliation that Mr. Cohen had inflicted on him.

My expectations were only too literally fulfilled. As I entered the house, I found him waiting for me in the hail with a handful of silver in his fist.

"Ha!" said he, "so you have had the impudence to come back. Well, I don't want you here. I've done with you. Here are your week's wages, and now you can take yourself off."

He handed me the money and pointed to the door, but I reminded him that my tools were in the workshop and requested permission to go and fetch them.

"Very well," said he, "you can take your tools, and I will come with you to see that you don't take anything else."

He escorted me to the workshop, where, as we entered, Kennet looked at us with undissembled curiosity, and Gus cast a furtive and rather nervous glance over his shoulder. Both had evidently gathered that there was trouble in the air.

"Now," said Mr. Parrish, "look sharp. Get your things together and clear out."

As the order was given, in a tone of furious anger, Gus bent down over his bench and Kennet turned to watch us with a scowl on his face that suggested an inclination to take a hand in the proceedings. But if he had had any such intention, he thought better of it, though he continued to look at me, gloomily, as I packed my bag, until Mr Parrish noticed him and demanded, angrily, "What are you staring at, Kennet? Mind your own business and get on with your work."

"Polton got the sack?" asked Kennet.

"Yes, he has," was the gruff reply.

"What for?" Kennet demanded with equal gruffness.

"That's no affair of yours," Parrish replied. "You attend to your own job."

"Well," said Kennet, "you are sending away a good workman, and I hope he'll get a better billet next time. So long, mate." And with this he turned back sulkily to his lathe, while I, having now finished packing my bag, said "Good-bye" to him and was forthwith shepherded out of the workshop.

As I took my way homeward – that is, towards Foubert's Place – I reflected on the disastrous change in my condition that a few foolish words had wrought, for I could not disguise from myself the fact that my position was even worse than it had been when poor Mr. Abraham's death had sent me adrift. Then, I had a reasonable explanation of my being out of work, Just now I should not dare to mention my last employer. I had been dismissed on suspicion of theft. It was a false suspicion and its falsity could be proved. But no stranger would go into that question. The practical effect was the same as if I had been guilty. I should have to evade any questions as to my last employment.

A review of my resources was not more encouraging. I had nine shillings left from my last wages and the fifteen shillings that Mr. Parrish had just paid me, added to which was a small store in my money-box that I had managed to put by from week to week. I knew the amount exactly and, casting up the entire sum of my wealth, found that the total was two pounds, three shillings and sixpence. On that I should have to subsist and pay my rent until I should obtain some fresh employment, and the ominous question as to how long it would last was one that I did not dare to consider.

When I had put away my tool-bag in the cupboard and bestowed the bulk of my money in the cash-box, I took a long drink from the water-jug to serve in lieu of tea and set forth towards Clerkenwell to use what was left of the day in taking up once more the too-familiar quest.

Chapter IX
Storm and Sunshine

Over the events of the succeeding weeks I shall pass as lightly as possible. There is no temptation to linger or dwell in detail on these dismal recollections, which could be no more agreeable to read than to relate. Nevertheless, it is necessary that I should give at least a summary account of them, since they were directly connected with the most important event of my life.

But it was a miserable time, repeating in an intensified form all the distressing features of that wretched interregnum that followed Mr. Abraham's death. For then I had at least begun my quest in hope, whereas now something like despair haunted me from the very beginning. I knew from the first how little chance I had of finding employment, especially since I could not venture to name my last employer, but that difficulty never arose, for no one ever entertained my application. The same old obstacle presented itself every time: I was not a qualified journeyman, but only a half-time apprentice.

Still I went on doggedly, day after day, trapesing the streets until I think I must have visited nearly every clockmaker in London and a number of optical-instrument makers as well, and as the days passed, I looked forward with ever-growing terror to the inevitable future towards which I was drifting. For my little store of money dwindled steadily. From the first I had cut my food down to an irreducible minimum.

Tea and butter I never tasted, but even a loaf of bread with an occasional portion of cheese, or a faggot or a polony, cost something, and there was the rent to pay at the end of every week. Each night, as I counted anxiously the shrinking remainder which stood between me and utter destitution, I saw the end drawing ever nearer and nearer.

Meanwhile, my distress of mind must have been aggravated by my bodily condition, for though the meagre scraps of food that I doled out to myself with miserly thrift were actually enough to support life, I was in a state of semi-starvation. The fact was obvious to me, not only from the slack way in which my clothes began to hang about me, but from the evident signs of bodily weakness. At first I had been able to tramp the streets for hours at a time without resting, but now I must needs seek, from time to time, some friendly doorstep or window-ledge to rest awhile before resuming my fruitless journeyings.

Occasionally, as I wandered through the streets, realizing the hopelessness of my quest, there passed through my mind vaguely the idea of seeking help from some of my friends – from Mr. Beeby or Mr. Cohen, or even Aunt Judy. But always I put it off as a desperate measure only to be considered when everything else had failed, and Aunt Judy I think I never considered at all. I had last written to her just after I had finished the calendar – a buoyant, hopeful letter, conveying to her the impression that a promising future was opening out to me, as I indeed believed. She would be quite happy about me, and I could not bear to think of the bitter disappointment and disillusionment that she would suffer if I were to disclose the dreadful reality. Besides, she and dear, honest Uncle Sam were but poor people, living decently, but with never a penny to spare. How could I burden them with my failure? It was not to be thought of.

But, in fact, as the time ran on, I seemed to become less capable of thought. My alarm at the approaching catastrophe gave place to a dull, fatalistic despair almost amounting to indifference. Even when I handed Mr. Stokes my last half-crown for rent – in advance – and knew that another week would see me without even a night's shelter, I seemed unable clearly to envisage the position. There still remained an uncounted handful of coppers. I was not yet penniless.

But there was something more in my condition than mere mental dulness. At intervals I became aware of it myself. Not only did my thoughts tend to ramble in a confused, dreamlike fashion, mingling objective realities with things imagined, I was conscious of bodily sensations that made me suspect the onset of definite illness – a constant, distressing headache, with attacks of shivering (though the weather was warm) and a feeling as if a stream of icy water were being sprayed on my back. And now the gnawing hunger from which I had suffered gave place to an intense repugnance to food. On principle, I invested the last but one of my pence in a polony. But I could not eat it, and when I had ineffectively nibbled at one end, I gave up the attempt and put it in my pocket for future use. But I had a craving for a drink of tea, and my last penny was spent at a coffee-shop, where I sat long and restfully in the old-fashioned "pew" with a big mug of the steaming liquor before me.

That is my last connected recollection of this day. Whither I went after leaving the coffee-shop I have no idea. Hour after hour I must have wandered aimlessly through the streets, for the night had fallen when I found myself sitting on the high step of a sheltered doorway with my aching head supported by my hands. A light rain was pattering down on the pavement, and no doubt it was to escape this that I had crept into the doorway. But I do not remember. Indeed, my mind must have been in a very confused state, for I seemed to wake up as from a dream or a spell of unconsciousness when a light shone on me and a voice addressed me.

"Now, young fellow, you can't sit there. You must move on."

I raised my head and received the full glare of the lantern in my face, which caused me instantly to close my eyes. There was a short pause, and then the voice resumed, persuasively, "Come, now, my lad, up you get."

With the aid of my hands on the step, I managed to rise a little way, but then sank down again with my back against the door. There was another pause, during which the policeman – now faintly visible – stooped over me for a closer inspection. Then a second voice interposed, "What's this? He can't be drunk, a kid like that."

"No, he isn't," the first officer replied. He grasped my wrist, gently, in a very large hand, and exclaimed, "God! The boy's red-hot. Just feel his wrist."

The other man did so and brought his lantern to bear on me. Then they both stood up and held a consultation of which I caught only a few stray phrases such as, "Yes, Margaret's is nearest," and, finally, "All right. Run along to the stand and fetch one. Four-wheeler, of course."

Here, one of the officers disappeared, and the other, leaning over me, asked in a kindly tone what my name was and where I lived. I managed to answer these questions, the replies to which the officer entered in a book, but the effort finished me, and I dropped forward again with my head in my hands. Presently a cab drew up opposite the doorway, and the two officers lifted me gently and helped me into it, when I saw by the light of its lamps that they were a sergeant and a constable. The latter got in with me and slammed the door with a bang that seemed like the blow of a hammer on my head, and the cab rattled away noisily, the jar of its iron tyres on the granite setts shaking me most abominably.

Of that journey I have but the haziest recollection. I know that I huddled in the corner with my teeth chattering, but I must have sunk into a sort of stupor, for I can recall nothing more than a muddled, dream-like, consciousness of lights and people, of being lifted about and generally discommoded, of having my clothes taken off and, finally, of being washed by a white-capped woman with a large sponge – a proceeding that made my teeth chatter worse than ever.

Thenceforward time ceased to exist for me. I must have lain in a dull, torpid condition with occasional intervals of more definite consciousness. I was dimly aware that I was lying in a bed in a large, light room in which there were other people, and which I recognized as a hospital ward. But mostly my mind was a blank, conscious only of

315

extreme bodily discomfort and a dull headache that never left me a moment of ease.

How long I continued in this state, indifferent to, and hardly conscious of my surroundings, but always restless, weary and suffering, I have no idea (excepting from what I was told afterwards). Days and nights passed uncounted and unperceived, and the memory of that period which remains is that of a vague, interminable dream.

The awakening came, I think, somewhat suddenly. At any rate, I remember a day when I, myself, was conscious of a change. The headache and the restlessness had gone, and with them the muddled, confused state of mind. I was now clearly aware of what was going on around me, though too listless to take particular notice, lying still with my eyes closed or half-closed, in a state of utter exhaustion, with a sensation of sinking through the bed. Vaguely, the idea that I was dying presented itself, but it merely floated through my mind without arousing any interest. The effort even of thinking was beyond my powers.

In the afternoon of this day the physician made his periodical visit. I was aware of droning voices and the tread of many feet as he and the little crowd of students moved on from bed to bed, now passing farther away and now coming nearer. Presently they reached my bed, and I opened my eyes sleepily to look at them. The physician was a short, pink-faced gentleman with upstanding silky white hair and bright blue eyes. At the moment he was examining the chart and case paper and discussing them with a tall, handsome young man whom I recognized as one of the regular disturbers of my peace. I took no note of what they were saying until he handed the chart-board to a white-capped lady (another of the disturbers) with the remark, "Well, Sister, the temperature is beginning to remit, but he doesn't seem to be getting any fatter."

"No, indeed," the sister replied. "He is an absolute skeleton, and he's most dreadfully weak. But he seems quite sensible to-day."

"Hmm. Yes," said the physician. Then, addressing the students, he continued. "A rather difficult question arises. We are in a dilemma. If we feed him too soon we may aggravate the disease and send his temperature up. If we don't feed him soon enough we may – well, we may feed him too late. And in this case there is the complication that the patient was apparently in a state of semi-starvation when he was taken ill, so he had no physiological capital to start with. Now, what are we to do? Shall we take the opinion of the learned house physician?" He smiled up at the tall young gentleman and continued. "You've had him under observation, Thorndyke. Tell us what you'd do."

"I should take what seems to be the lesser risk," the house physician replied, promptly, "and begin feeding him at once."

316

"There!" chuckled the physician. "The oracle has spoken, and I think we agree. We usually do agree with Mr. Thorndyke, and when we don't, we're usually wrong. Ha! ha! What? Very well, Thorndyke. He's your patient, so you can carry out your own prescription."

With this, the procession moved on to the next bed, and I closed my eyes and relapsed into my former state of dreamy half-consciousness. From this, however, I was presently aroused by a light touch on my shoulder and a feminine voice addressing me.

"Now, Number Six, wake up. I've brought you a little supper, and the doctor says you are to take the whole of it."

I opened my eyes and looked sleepily at the speaker, a pleasant-faced, middle-aged nurse who held in one hand a glass bowl, containing a substance that looked like pomade, and in the other a spoon, and with the latter she began to insinuate very small quantities of the pomade into my mouth, smilingly ignoring my feeble efforts to resist. For though the taste of the stuff was agreeable enough, I still had an intense repugnance to food and only wanted to be left alone. But she was very patient and very persistent, giving me little rests and then rousing me up and coaxing me to make another effort. And so, I suppose, the pomade was at last finished, but I don't know, for I must have fallen asleep and must have slept several hours, since it was night when I awoke and the ward was in semi-darkness. But the pomade had done its work. The dreadful sinking feeling had nearly gone and I felt sufficiently alive to look about me with a faintly-awakening interest, which I continued to do until the night sister espied me and presently bore down on me with a steaming bowl and a feeding cup.

"Well, Number Six," said she, "you've had quite a fine, long sleep, and now you are going to have some nice, hot broth, and perhaps, when you have taken it, you'll have another sleep." Which turned out to be the case, for though I recall emptying the feeding-cup, I remember nothing more until I awoke to find the sun light streaming into the ward and the nurse and Mr. Thorndyke standing beside my bed.

"This is better, Number Six," said the latter. "They tell me you have been sleeping like a dormouse. How do you feel this morning?"

I replied in a ridiculous whisper that I felt much better, at which he smiled, pleasantly, and remarked that it was the first time he had heard my voice. "If you can call it a voice," he added. Then he felt my pulse, took my temperature and, having made a few notes on the case-paper, departed with another smile and a friendly nod.

I need not follow my progress in detail. It was uninterrupted, though very slow. By the end of the following week my temperature had settled down and I was well on my way to recovery. But I was desperately weak and wasted to a degree of emaciation that I should have supposed to be impossible in a living man. However, this seemed to be a passing phase, for now, so far from feeling any repugnance to food, I hailed the appetizing little meals that were brought to me with voracious joy.

As my condition improved, Mr. Thorndyke's visits tended to grow longer. When the routine business had been dispatched, he would linger for a minute or two to exchange a few words with me (very few on my side and mostly playful or facetious on his) before passing on to the next bed, and whenever, during the day or night, he had occasion to pass through the ward, if I were awake, he would always greet me, at least, with a smile and a wave of the hand. Not that he specially singled me out for these attentions, for every patient was made to feel that the house physician was interested in him as a man and not merely as a "case".

Nevertheless, I think there was something about me that attracted his attention in a particular way, for on several occasions I noticed him looking me over in an appraising sort of fashion, and I thought that he seemed especially interested in my hands. And apparently I was right, as I learned one afternoon when, having finished his round, he came and sat down on the chair by my bedside to talk to me. Presently he picked up my right hand and, holding it out before him, remarked, "This is quite a lady-like hand, Polton." (He had dropped "Number Six".) "Very delicate and soft. And yet it is a good, serviceable hand, and I notice that you use it as if you were accustomed to do skilled work with it. Perhaps I am wrong, but I have been wondering what your occupation is. You are too small for any of the heavy trades."

"I am a clockmaker, sir," I replied, "but I have put in some time at cabinet-making and I have had a turn at making philosophical instruments, such as levels and theodolites. But clockmaking is my proper trade."

"Then," said he, "Providence must have foreseen that you were going to be a clockmaker and furnished you with exactly the right kind of hands. But you seem to have had a very varied experience, considering your age."

"I have, sir, though it wasn't all of my own choosing. I had to take the job that offered itself, and when no job offered, it was a case of wearing out shoe-leather."

"Ha!" said he. "And I take it that you had been wearing out a good deal of shoe-leather at the time when you were taken ill."

"Yes, sir. I had been having a very bad time."

I suppose I spoke somewhat dismally, for it had suddenly dawned on me that I should leave the hospital penniless and with worse prospects than ever. He looked at me thoughtfully and, after a short pause, asked, "Why were you not able to get work?"

I considered the question and found it difficult to answer, and yet I wanted to explain, for something told me that he would understand and sympathize with my difficulties, and we all like to pour our troubles into sympathetic ears.

"There were several reasons, sir, but the principal one was that I wasn't able to finish my apprenticeship. But it's rather a long story to tell to a busy gentleman."

"I'm not a busy gentleman for the moment," said he with a smile. "I've finished my work for the present, and I shall be a very interested gentleman if you care to tell me the story. But perhaps you would rather not recall those bad times."

"Oh, it isn't that, sir. I should like to tell you if it wouldn't weary you."

As he once more assured me of his interest in my adventures and misadventures, I began, shyly and awkwardly, to sketch out the history of my apprenticeship, with scrupulous care to keep it as short as possible. But there was no need. Not only did he listen with lively interest, but when I became unduly sketchy he interposed with questions to elicit fuller details, so that, becoming more at my ease, I told the little story of my life in a consecutive narrative, but still keeping to the more significant incidents. The last, disastrous, episode, however, I related at length – mentioning no names except that of Mr. Cohen – as it seemed necessary to be circumstantial in order to make my innocence perfectly clear, and I was glad that I did so, for my listener followed that tragedy of errors with the closest attention.

"Well, Polton," he said when I had brought the narrative up to date, "you have had only a short life, but it has been a pretty full one – a little too full, at times. If experience makes men wise, you should be bursting with wisdom. But I do hope you have taken in your full cargo of that kind of experience."

He looked at his watch and, as he rose, remarked that he must be getting back to duty, and having thanked me for "my most interesting story", walked quickly but silently out of the ward, leaving me with a curious sense of relief at having unburdened myself of my troubles to a confessor so kindly and sympathetic.

That, however, was not the last of our talks, for thenceforward he adopted the habit of making me little visits, sitting on the chair by my bedside and chatting to me quite familiarly without a trace of patronage. It was evident that my story had greatly interested him, for he occasionally put a question that showed a complete recollection of all that I had told him. But more commonly he drew me out on the subject of clocks and watches. He made me explain, with drawings, the construction and mode of working of a gravity escapement and the difference between a chronometer and a lever watch. Again, he was quite curious on the subject of locks and keys and of instruments such as theodolites, of which he had no experience, and though mechanism would seem to be rather outside the province of a doctor, I found him very quick in taking in mechanical ideas and quite keen on acquiring the little items of technical knowledge that I was able to impart.

But these talks, so delightful to me, came to a rather sudden end, at least for a time, for one afternoon, just as he was leaving me, he announced, "By the way, Polton, you will be handed over to a new house physician tomorrow. My term of office has come to an end." Then, observing that I looked rather crestfallen, he continued. "However, we shan't lose sight of each other. I am taking charge of the museum and laboratory for a week or two while the curator is away and, as the laboratory opens on the garden, where you will be taking the air when you can get about, I shall be able to keep an eye on you."

This was some consolation for my loss, and something to look forward to, and it begot in me a sudden eagerness to escape from bed and see what I could do in the way of walking. Apparently, I couldn't do much, for when the sister, in response to my entreaties, wrapped me in a dressing-gown and, with a nurse's aid, helped me to totter to the nearest armchair, I sat down with alacrity and, at the end of half-an-hour, was very glad to be conducted back to bed.

It was not a very encouraging start, but I soon improved on it. In a few days I was crawling about the ward unassisted, with frequent halts to rest in the armchair, and by degrees the rests grew shorter and less frequent, until I was able to pace up and down the ward quite briskly. And at last came the joyful day when the nurse produced my clothes (which appeared to have been cleaned since I last saw them) and help me to put them on and, it being a warm, sunny morning, the sister graciously acceded to my request that I might take a little turn in the garden.

That was a red-letter day for me. Even now I recall with pleasure the delightful feeling of novelty with which I took my journey downwards in the lift, swathed in a dressing-gown over my clothes and fortified by a light lunch (which I devoured, wolfishly), and the joy with which I greeted the sunlit trees and flower-beds as the nurse conducted me along a path and deposited me on a seat. But better still was the sight of a tall figure emerging from the hospital and advancing with long strides along the path. At the sight of him my heart leaped, and I watched him anxiously lest he should take another path and pass without seeing me.

My eagerness surprised me a little at the time, and now, looking back, I ask myself how it had come about that Mr. Thorndyke was to me so immeasurably different from all other men. Was it some prophetic sense which made me dimly aware of what was to be? Or could it be that I, an insignificant, ignorant lad, had somehow instinctively divined the intellectual and moral greatness of the man? I cannot tell. In a quiet, undemonstrative way he had been gracious, kindly and sympathetic, but beyond this there had seemed to be a sort of magnetism about him which attracted me, so that to the natural respect and admiration with which I regarded him was unaccountably added an actual personal devotion.

Long before he had drawn near, he saw me and came straight to my seat. "Congratulations, Polton," he said, cheerfully, as he sat down beside me. "This looks like the beginning of the end. But we mustn't be impatient, you know. We must take things easily and not try to force the pace."

He stayed with me about five minutes, chatting pleasantly, but principally in a medical strain, advising me and explaining the dangers and pitfalls of convalescence from a severe and exhausting illness. Then he left me, to go about his business in the laboratory, and I followed him with my eyes as he entered the doorway of a range of low buildings. But in a few moments he reappeared, carrying a walking-stick and, coming up to my seat, handed the stick to me.

"Here is a third leg for you, Polton," said he, "a very useful aid when the natural legs are weak and unsteady. You needn't return it. It is an ancient derelict that has been in the laboratory as long as I have known the place."

I thanked him and, as he returned to the laboratory, I rose and took a little walk to try the stick, and very helpful I found it, but even if I had not, I should still have prized the simple ash staff for the sake of the giver, as I have prized it ever since. For I have it to this day, and the silver band that I put on it bears the date on which it was given.

A few days later Mr. Thorndyke overtook me as I was hobbling along the path with the aid of my "third leg".

"Why, Polton," he exclaimed, "you are getting quite active and strong. I wonder if you would care to come and have a look at the laboratory."

I grasped eagerly at the offer, and we walked together to the building and entered the open doorway – left open, I presumed when I was inside, to let out some of the smell. The premises consisted of the laboratory proper, a large room with a single long bench, and a great number of shelves occupied by stoppered glass jars of all sizes, mostly filled with a clear liquid in which some very queer-looking objects were

321

suspended. (One, I was thrilled to observe, was a human hand.) On the lower shelves were ranged great covered earthenware pots which I suspected to be the source of the curious, spirituous odour. Beyond the laboratory was a work room furnished with a lathe, two benches, and several racks of tools.

When he had shown me round, Mr. Thorndyke seated me in a Windsor armchair close to the bench where he was working at the cutting, staining, and mounting of microscopical sections for use in the medical school. When I had been watching him for some time, he looked round at me with a smile.

"I suspect, Polton," said he, "that you are itching to try your hand at section-mounting. Now, aren't you?"

I had to confess that I was, whereupon he, most good-naturedly, provided me with a glass bowl of water and a pile of watch-glasses and bade me go ahead, which I did with the delight of a child with a new toy. Having cut the sections on the microtome and floated them off into the bowl, I carried out the other processes in as close imitation of his methods as I could, until I had a dozen slides finished.

"Well, Polton," said he, "there isn't much mystery about it, you see. But you are pretty quick at learning – quicker than some of the students whom I have to teach."

He examined my slides with the microscope and, to my joy, pronounced them good enough to go in with the rest, and he was just beginning to label them when I perceived, through the window, the nurse who had come to shepherd the patients into dinner. So, with infinite regret, I tore myself away, but not until I had been rejoiced by an invitation to come again on the morrow.

The days that followed were among the happiest of my life. Every morning – and, later, every afternoon as well – I presented myself at the laboratory and was greeted with a friendly welcome. I was allowed to look on at, and even to help in, all kinds of curious, novel and fascinating operations. I assisted in the making of a plaster cast of a ricketty boy's deformed legs, in the injecting with carmine gelatine of the blood-vessels of a kidney, and in the cutting and mounting of a section of a tooth. Every day I had a new experience and learned something fresh, and in addition was permitted and encouraged to execute repairs in the workroom on various invalid instruments and appliances. It was a delightful time. The days slipped past in a dream of tranquil happiness.

I have said "the days", but I should rather have said the hours that I spent in the laboratory. They were hours of happiness unalloyed. But with my return to the ward came a reaction. Then I had to face the realities of life, to realize that a dark cloud was rising, ever growing darker and more threatening. For I was now convalescent, and this was a hospital, not an almshouse. My illness was over and it was nearly time for me to go. At any moment now I might get my discharge, and then – but I did not dare to think of what lay before me when I should go forth from the hospital door into the inhospitable streets.

At last the blow fell. I saw it coming when, instead of sending me out to the garden, the sister bade me stay by my bed when the physician was due to make his visit. So there I stood, watching the procession of students moving slowly round the ward with the feelings of a condemned man awaiting the approach of the executioner. Finally, it halted opposite my bed. The physician looked at me critically, spoke a few kindly words of congratulation, listened to the sister's report and, taking the chart-board from her, wrote a few words on the case paper, returned the board to her and moved on to the next bed!

"When do I go out, Sister?" I asked, anxiously, as she replaced the board on its peg.

She evidently caught and understood the note of anxiety, for she replied very gently, with a quick glance at my downcast face, "The day after to-morrow," and turned away to rejoin the procession.

So the brief interlude of comfort and happiness was over and once more I must go forth to wander, a wretched Ishmaelite, through the cheerless wilderness. What I should do when I found myself cast out into the street, I had no idea. Nor did I try to form any coherent plan. The utter hopelessness of my condition induced a sort of mental paralysis, and I could only roam about the garden (whither I had strayed when sentence had been pronounced) in a state of vague, chaotic misery. Even the appetizing little supper was swallowed untasted and, for the first time since the dawn of my convalescence, my sleep was broken and troubled.

On the following morning I presented myself as usual at the laboratory. But its magic was gone. I pottered about in the workroom to finish a repairing job that I had on hand, but even that could not distract me from the thought that I was looking my last on this pleasant and friendly place. Presently, Mr. Thorndyke came in to look at the instrument that I was repairing – it was a rocking microtome – but soon transferred his attention from the instrument to me.

"What's the matter, Polton?" he asked. "You are looking mighty glum. Have you got your discharge?"

"Yes, sir," I replied. "I am going out to-morrow."

"Ha!" said he. "And from what you have told me, I take it that you have nowhere to go."

I admitted, gloomily, that this was the case.

"Very well," said he. "Now I have a little proposal that I want you to consider. Come and sit down in the laboratory and I'll tell you about it."

He sat me in a Windsor armchair and, seating himself on the bench stool, continued, "I am intending to set up in practice, not in an ordinary medical practice, but in that branch of medicine that is connected with the law and is concerned with expert medical and scientific evidence. For the purposes of my practice I shall have to have a laboratory, somewhat like this, with a workshop attached, and I shall want an assistant to help me with the experimental work. That assistant will have to be a skilled mechanic, capable of making any special piece of apparatus that may be required, and generally handy and adaptable. Now, from what you have told me and what I have seen for myself, I judge that you would suit me perfectly. You have a working knowledge of three crafts, and I have seen that you are skilful, painstaking, and quick to take an idea, so I should like to have you as my assistant. I can't offer much of a salary at first, as I shall be earning nothing, myself, for a time, but I could pay you a pound a week to begin with and, as I should provide you with food and a good, big bed and sitting room, you could rub along until something better turned up. What do you say?"

I didn't say anything. I was speechless with emotion, with the sudden revulsion from black despair to almost delirious joy. My eyes filled and a lump seemed to rise in my throat.

Mr. Thorndyke evidently saw how it was with me and, by way of easing the situation, he resumed. "There is one other point. Mine will be a bachelor establishment. I want no servants, so that, if you come to me, you would have to render a certain amount of personal and domestic services. You would keep the little household in order and occasionally prepare a meal. In fact, you would be in the position of my servant as well as laboratory assistant. Would you object to that?"

Would I object! I could have fallen down that instant and kissed his boots. What I did say was that I should be proud to be his servant and only sorry that I was not more worthy of that honourable post.

"Then," said he, "the bargain is struck, and each of us must do his best to make it a good bargain for the other."

He then proceeded to arrange the details of my assumption of office, which included the transfer of five shillings "to chink in my pocket and pay the cabman," and, when all was settled, I went forth, at his advice, to take a final turn in the garden, which I did with a springy step and at a pace that made the other patients stare.

As I entered the ward, the sister came up to me with a rather troubled face.

"When you go out to-morrow, Number Six, what are you going to do? Have you any home to go to?"

"Yes, Sister," I replied, triumphantly. "Mr. Thorndyke had just engaged me as his servant."

"Oh, I am so glad," she exclaimed. "I have been rather worried about you. But I am quite happy now, for I know that you will have the very best of masters."

She was a wise woman, was that sister.

I pass over the brief remainder of my stay in hospital. The hour of my discharge, once dreaded, but now hailed with joy, came in the middle of the forenoon and, as my worldly goods were all on my person, no preparations were necessary. I made the round of the ward to say farewell to my fellow-patients and, when the sister had given me a hearty handshake (I should have liked to kiss her), I was conducted by the nurse to the secretary's office and there formally discharged. Then, pocketing my discharge ticket, I made my way to the main entrance and presented myself at the porter's lodge.

"Ah!" said the porter when I had introduced myself, "so you are Mr. Thorndyke's young man. Well, I've got to put you into a hansom and see that you know where to go. Do you?"

"Yes," I answered, producing the card that my master had given me and reading from it. "The address is '*Dr. John Thorndyke, 5A King's Bench Walk, Inner Temple, London, E.G.*'"

"That's right," said he, "and remember that he's Doctor Thorndyke now. We call him Mister because that's the custom when a gentleman is on the junior staff, even if he is an M.D. Here's a hansom coming in, so we shan't have to fetch one."

The cab came up the courtyard and discharged its passenger at the entrance, when the porter hailed the driver and, having hustled me into the vehicle, sang out the address to which I was to be conveyed and waved his hand to me as we drove off and I returned his salutation by raising my hat.

I enjoyed the journey amazingly, surveying the busy streets over the low doors with a new pleasure and thinking how cheerful and friendly they looked. I had never been in a hansom before and I suppose I never shall again. For the hansom is gone, and we have lost the most luxurious and convenient passenger vehicle ever devised by the wit of man.

That cabman knew his business. Londoner as I was, the intricacies of his route bewildered me completely, and when he came to the surface, as it were, in Chancery Lane, which I recognized, he almost immediately finished me off by crossing Fleet Street and passing through a great gateway into a narrow lane bordered by ancient timber houses. Half-way

325

down this lane he turned into another, at the entrance to which I read the name, "Crown Office Row," and this ended in a great open square surrounded by tall houses. Here I was startled by a voice above my head demanding, "You said *Five A*, didn't you?"

I looked up, and was astonished to behold a face looking down on me through a square opening in the roof, but I promptly answered "Yes," whereupon the face vanished and I saw and heard a lid shut down, and a few moments later the cab drew up opposite the portico of a house on the eastern side of the square. I hopped out and, having verified the number, asked the cabman what there was to pay, to which he replied, concisely, "Two bob," and, leaning down, held out his hand. It seemed a lot of money but, of course, he knew what his fare was, so, having handed up the exact amount, I turned away and stepped into the entry, on the jamb of which was painted "*First Pair, Dr. John Thorndyke*".

The exact meaning of this inscription was not quite clear to me, but as the ground floor was assigned to another person, I decided to explore the staircase, and having ascended to the first-floor landing, was reassured by observing the name "*Dr. Thorndyke*" painted in white lettering over a doorway, the massive, iron-bound door of which was open, revealing an inner door garnished by a small and very tarnished brass knocker. On this I struck a single modest rap, when the door was opened by Dr. Thorndyke, himself.

"Come in, Polton!" said he, smiling on me very kindly and shaking my hand. "Come into your new home – which is my home, too, and I hope it will be a happy one for us both. But it will be what we make it. Perhaps, if your journey hasn't tired you, you would like me to show you over the premises."

I said that I was not tired at all, so he led me forth at once and we started to climb the stairs, of which there were four flights to the third-floor landing.

"I have brought you to the top floor," said The Doctor, "to introduce you to your own domain. The rest of the rooms you can explore at your leisure. This is your bedroom."

He threw open a door, and when I looked in I was struck dumb with astonishment and delight. It was beyond my wildest dreams – a fine, spacious room with two windows, furnished in a style of which I had no previous experience. A handsome carpet covered the floor, the bed surpassed even the hospital beds, there were a wardrobe, a chest of drawers, a set of bookshelves, a large table by one of the windows and a small one beside the bed, a fine easy chair and two other chairs. It was magnificent. I had thought that only noblemen lived in such rooms. And yet it was a very picture of homely comfort.

I was struggling to express my gratitude when The Doctor hustled me down to the second floor to inspect the future laboratory and workshop. At present they were just large, empty rooms, but the kitchen was fully furnished and in going order, with a gas-cooker and a dresser filled with china, and the empty larder was ready for use.

"Now," said The Doctor, "I must run off to the hospital in a few minutes, but there are one or two matters to settle. First, you will want some money to fit yourself out with clothes. I will advance you ten pounds for that purpose. Then, until we are settled down, you will have to get your meals at restaurants. I will give you a couple of pounds for those and any stores that you may lay in, and you will keep an account and let me know when you want any more money. And remember that you are a convalescent, and don't stint your diet. I think that is all for the present except the latch-keys, which I had better give you now."

He laid the money and the two keys on the table, and was just turning to go when it occurred to me to ask if I should get an evening meal prepared for him. He looked at me with a smile of surprise and replied, "You're a very enterprising convalescent, Polton, but you mustn't try to do too much at first. No, thank you. I shall dine in the board-room to-night and get home about half-past nine."

When he had gone, I went out and, having taken a substantial lunch at a restaurant near Temple Bar, proceeded to explore the neighbourhood with a view to household stores. Eventually I found in Fetter Lane enough suitable shops to enable me to get the kitchen and the larder provided for a start and, having made my purchases, hurried home to await the delivery of the goods. Then I spent a delightful afternoon and evening rambling about the house, planning the workshop, paying repeated visits to my incomparable room, and inaugurating the kitchen by preparing myself an enormous high tea, after which, becoming extremely sleepy, I went down and paced up and down the Walk to keep myself awake.

When The Doctor came home I would have expounded my plans for the arrangement of the workshop. But he cut me short with the admonition that convalescents should be early birds, and sent me off to bed, where I sank at once into a delicious slumber and slept until it was broad daylight and a soft-toned bell informed me that it was seven o'clock.

This day is the last that I shall record, for it saw the final stage of that wonderful transformation that changed the old Nathaniel Polton, the wretched, friendless outcast, into the pampered favourite of Fortune.

When I had given The Doctor his breakfast (which he praised, warmly, but begged me to remember in future that he was only one man) and seen him launched on his way to the hospital, I consumed what he had left on the dish – one fried egg and a gammon rasher – and, having tidied up The Doctor's bedroom and my own, went forth to wind up the affairs of Polton, the destitute, and inaugurate Polton, the opulent, to "ring out the old and ring in the new". First, I visited a "gentlemen's outfitters", where I purchased a ready-made suit of a sober and genteel character – (I heard the shopman whisper something about "medium boy's size".) – and other garments appropriate to it, including clerical grey socks, a pair of excellent shoes and a soft felt hat. The parcel being a large and heavy one I bought a strong rug-strap with which to carry it, and so was able, with an occasional rest, to convey it to Foubert's Place, where I proposed to settle any arrears of rent that Mr. Stokes might claim. However, he claimed none, having let my room when I failed to return. But he had stored my property in an attic, from which he very kindly assisted me to fetch it, so that I had, presently, the satisfaction of seeing all my worldly goods piled up on the counter – the tool-chest that I had made in Mr. Beeby's workshop, my whole collection of clockmaker's tools, and my beloved books, including Mr. Denison's invaluable monograph. When they were all assembled, I went out and chartered a four-wheeled cab, in which I stowed them all – chest, tools, books, and the enormous parcel from the out-fitters. Then I bade Mr. Stokes a fond farewell, gave the cabman the address (at which he seemed surprised, and I am afraid that I was a rather shabby little ragamuffin) shut myself in the cab and started for home.

Home! I had not known the word since Aunt Judy and Uncle Sam had flitted away out of my ken. But now, as the cab rattled over the stones until it made my teeth chatter, I had before me the vision of that noble room in the Temple which was my very own, to have and to hold in perpetuity, and the gracious friend and master whose presence would have turned a hovel into a mansion.

As soon as we arrived, I conveyed my goods – in relays – upstairs, and when I had paid off the cabman, I proceeded to dispose of them. The tools I deposited in the future workshop as the first instalment of its furnishing, the books and parcel I carried up to my own apartment. And there the final scene was enacted. When I had arranged my little library lovingly in the bookshelves, I opened the parcel and laid out its incredible contents on the bed. For a while I was so overcome by their magnificence that I could only gloat over them in ecstasy. I had never had such clothes before, and I felt almost shy at their splendour. However, they were mine, and I was going to wear them, and so reflecting, I proceeded boldly to divest myself of the threadbare, frayed and faded habiliments that had served me so long until I had stripped to the uttermost rag (and rag is the proper word). Then I inducted myself cautiously into the new garments, finishing up (in some discomfort) with a snowy and rather stiff collar, a silk neck-tie, and the sober but elegant black coat.

For quite a long time I stood before the mirror in the wardrobe door surveying, with something of amused surprise and a certain sense of unreality, the trimly-dressed gentleman who confronted me. At length, I turned away with a sigh of satisfaction and, having carefully put away the discarded clothing for use in the workshop, went down to await The Doctor's return.

And here I think I had better stop, leaving Dr. Jervis to relate the sequel. Gladly would I go on – having now got into my stride – to tell of my happy companionship with my beloved master, and how he and I fitted out the workshop, and then, working on our joiner' bench, gradually furnished the laboratory with benches and shelves. But I had better not. My tale is told, and now I must lay down my pen and hold my peace. Yet still I love to look back on that wonderful morning in the hospital laboratory when a few magical words banished in an instant the night of my adversity and ushered in the dawn.

But it was not only the dawn, it was the sunrise. And the sun has never set. A benevolent Joshua has ordained that I shall live the days of my life in perpetual sunshine, and that Joshua's name is John Thorndyke.

Part II – The Case of Moxdale, Deceased
Narrated by Christopher Jervis, M.D.

Chapter X
Fire

To an old Londoner, the aspect of the town in the small hours of the morning, in "the middle watch" as those dark hours are called in the language of the mariner, is not without its attractions. For however much he may love his fellow-creatures, it is restful, at least for a time, to take their society in infinitesimal doses, or even to dispense with it entirely, and to take one's way through the empty and silent streets free to pursue one's own thoughts undistracted by the din and hurly-burly that prevail in the daylight hours.

Thus I reflected as I turned out of Marylebone Station at about half-past two in the morning and, crossing the wide, deserted road, bore away south-east in the direction of the Temple. Through what side streets I passed I cannot remember, and in fact never knew, for, in the manner of the born-and-bred Londoner, I simply walked towards my destination without consciously considering my route. And as I walked in a silence on which my own footfalls made an almost startling impression, I looked about me with something like curiosity and listened for the occasional far-off sounds which told of some belated car or lorry wending its solitary way through some distant street.

I was approaching the neighbourhood of Soho and passing through a narrow street lined by old and rather squalid houses, all dark and silent, when my ear caught a sound which, though faint and far-away, instantly attracted my attention – the clang of a bell, not rung, but struck with a hammer and repeating the single note in a quick succession of strokes – the warning bell of a fire-engine. I listened with mild interest – it was too far off to concern me – and compared the sound with that of the fire-engines of my young days. It was more distinctive, but less exciting. The bell gave its message plainly enough, but it lacked that quality of urgency and speed that was conveyed by the rattle of iron tyres on the stones and the sound of galloping horses.

Ding, ding, ding, ding, ding – The sound was more distinct. Then the engine must be coming my way, and even as I noted the fact, the clang of another bell rang out from the opposite direction, and suddenly I became aware of a faintly pungent smell in the air. Then, as I turned a corner, I met a thin cloud of smoke that was drifting up the street and noticed a glow in the sky over the house-tops, and presently, reaching another corner, came into full view of the burning house, though it was still some distance away, near the farther end of the street.

I watched it with some surprise as I walked quickly towards it, for there seemed to be something unusual in its appearance. I had not seen many burning houses but none that I had seen had looked quite like this one. There was a furious intensity in the way that it flared up that impressed me as abnormal. From the chimneys, flames shot up like the jets from a gas-blowpipe, and the windows emitted tongues of fire that looked as if they were being blown out by bellows. And the progress of the fire was frightfully rapid, for even in the short time that it took me to walk the length of the street there was an evident change. Glowing spots began to appear in the roof flames poured out of the attic windows, and smoke and flame issued from the ground floor, which seemed to be some kind of shop.

No crowd had yet collected, but just a handful of chance wayfarers like myself and a few policemen, who stood a little distance away from the house, looking on the scene of destruction and listening anxiously to the sounds of the approaching engines, now quite near and coming from several different directions.

"It's a devil of a blaze," I remarked to one of the constables. "What is it? An oil-shop?"

"It's worse than that, sir," he replied. "It's a film dealer's. The whole place chock full of celluloid films. It's to be hoped that there isn't anybody in the house, but I'm rather afraid there is. The caretaker of the offices next door says that there is a gentleman who has rooms on the first floor. Poor look-out for him if he is in there now. He will be burned to a cinder by this time."

At this moment the first of the engines swung round the corner and swept up to the house with noiseless speed, discharging its brass-helmeted crew, who began immediately to prepare for action: Opening the water-plugs, rolling out lengths of hose, and starting the pumps. In a minute or two, four other engines arrived, accompanied by a motor fire-escape, but the latter, when its crew had glanced at the front of the house, was trundled some distance up the street out of the way of the engines. There was obviously no present use for it, nor did there seem to be much left for the engines to do, for, almost at the moment when the first jet of water was directed at the flaming window-space, the roof fell in with a crash and a roar, a volume of flame and sparks leaped up into the sky, and through the holes which had once been windows an uninterrupted sheet of fire could be seen from the top of the house to the bottom. Evidently, the roof in its fall had carried away what had been left of the floors, and the house was now no more than an empty shell with a mass of flaming debris at its base.

Whether the jets of water that were directed in through the window-holes had any effect, or whether the highly inflammable material had by this time all been burnt, I could not judge but, after the fall of the roof, the fire began almost suddenly to die down, and a good deal of the firemen's attention became occupied by the adjoining house, which had already suffered some injury from the fire and now seemed likely to suffer more from the water. But in this I was not greatly interested and, as the more spectacular phase of the disaster seemed to have come to an end, I extricated myself from the small crowd that had now collected and resumed my progress towards the Temple and the much-desired bed that awaited me there.

To a man who has turned in at past four o'clock in the morning, competition with the lark is not practicable. It was getting on for eleven when I emerged from my bedroom and descended the stairs towards the breakfast-room, becoming agreeably conscious of a subtle aroma which memory associated with bacon and coffee.

"I heard you getting up, sir," said Polton with a last, satisfied glance at the breakfast-table, "and I heard you come in last night, or rather this morning, so I have cooked an extra rasher. You did make a night of it, sir."

"Yes," I admitted, "it was rather a late business, and what made me still later was a house on fire somewhere near Soho which I stopped for a while to watch. A most tremendous blaze. A policeman told me that it was a celluloid film warehouse, so you can imagine how it flared up."

I produced this item of news designedly, knowing that it would be of interest, for Polton, the most gentle and humane of men, had an almost morbid love of the horrible and the tragic. As I spoke, his eyes glistened, and he commented with a sort of ghoulish relish, "Celluloid films! And a whole warehouse full of them, too! It must have been a fine sight. I've never seen a house on fire – not properly on fire, only just smoke and sparks. Was there a fire-escape?"

"Yes, but there was nothing for it to do. The house was like a furnace."

"But the people inside, sir. Did they manage to get out in time?"

"It's not certain that there was anybody in the house. I heard something about a gentleman who had rooms there, but there was no sign of him. It is not certain that he was there, but if he was, he is there still. We shall know when the firemen and salvage men are able to examine the ruins."

"Ha!" said Polton, "there won't be much of him left. Where did you say the place was, sir?"

"I can't tell you the name of the street, but it was just off Old Compton Street. You will probably see some notice of the fire in the morning paper."

Thereupon, Polton turned away as if to go in search of the paper, but at the door he paused and looked back at me.

"Speaking of burning houses, sir," said he, "Mr. Stalker called about half-an-hour ago. I told him how things were, so he said he would probably look in again in an hour's time. If he does, will you see him downstairs or shall I bring him up?"

"Oh, bring him up here. We don't make a stranger of Mr. Stalker."

"Yes, sir. Perhaps he has come to see you about this very fire."

"He could hardly have got any particulars yet," said I. "Besides, fire insurance is not in our line of business."

"No, sir," Polton admitted, "but it may be about the gentleman who had the rooms. A charred body might be in your line if they happen to know that there is one among the ruins."

I did not think it very likely, for there had hardly been time to ascertain whether the ruins did or did not contain any human remains. Nevertheless, Polton's guess turned out to be right, for when Stalker (having declined a cup of coffee and then explained, according to his invariable custom, that he happened to be passing this way and thought he might as well just look in) came to the point, it appeared that his visit was concerned with the fire in Soho.

"But, my dear Stalker," I protested, "we don't know anything about fires."

"I know," he replied with an affable smile. "The number of things that you and Thorndyke don't know anything about would fill an encyclopaedia. Still, there are some things that you do know. Perhaps you have forgotten that fire at Brattle's oil-shop, but I haven't. You spotted something that the fire experts had overlooked."

"Thorndyke did. I didn't until he pointed it out."

"I don't care which of you spotted it," said he. "I only know that, between you, you saved us two- or three thousand pounds."

I remembered the case quite well, and the recollection of it seemed to justify Stalker's attitude.

"What do you want us to do?" I asked.

"I want you just to keep an eye on the case. The question of fire-raising will be dealt with by the Brigade men and the Salvage Corps. They are experts and they have their own methods. You have different methods and you bring a different sort of expert eye to bear on the matter."

"I wonder," said I, "why you are so Nosey-Parkerish about this fire. There hasn't been time for you to get any particulars."

"Indeed!" said he. "We don't all stay in bed until eleven o'clock. While you were slumbering I was getting a report and making enquiries."

"Ha!" I retorted. "And while you were slumbering I was watching your precious house burning, and I must say that it did you credit."

Here, in response to his look of surprise, I gave him a brief account of my morning's adventure.

"Very well," said he when I had finished. "Then you know the facts and you can understand my position. Here is a house, full of inflammable material, which unaccountably bursts into flames at three o'clock in the morning. That house was either unoccupied or had a single occupant who was presumably in bed and asleep, as he apparently made no attempt to escape."

I offered a vague suggestion of some failure of the electric installation such as a short circuit or other accident, but he shook his head.

"I know that such things are actually possible," said he, "but it doesn't do to accept them too readily. A man who has been in this business as long as I have acquired a sort of intuitive perception of what is and what is not a normal case, and I have the feeling that there is something a little queer about this fire. I had the same feeling about that oil-shop case, which is why I asked Thorndyke to look into it. And then there are rumours of a man who was sleeping in the house. You heard those yourself. Now, if that man's body turns up in the debris, there is the possibility of a further claim, as there was in the oil-shop case."

"But, my dear Stalker!" I exclaimed, grinning in his face. "This is foresight with a vengeance. This fire may have been an incendiary fire. There may have been a man sleeping in the house and he may have got burned to death, and that man may have insured his life in your Society. How does that work out by the ordinary laws of chance? Pretty long odds, I think."

"Not so long as you fancy," he replied. "Persons who lose their lives in incendiary fires have a tendency to be insured. The connection between the fire and the death may not be a chance connection. Still, I will admit that, beyond a mere suspicion that there may be something

334

wrong about this fire, I have nothing to go on. I am asking you to watch the case '*ex abundantia cautelae*' as you lawyers say. And the watching must be done now while the evidence is available. It's no use waiting until the ruins have been cleared away and the body – if there is one – buried."

"No," I agreed, "Thorndyke will be with you in that. I will give him your instructions when I see him at lunch-time, and you can take it that he won't lose any time in collecting the facts. But you had better give us something in writing, as we shall have to get authority to inspect the ruins and to examine the body if there is one to examine."

"Yes," said Stalker, "I'll do that now. I have some of our letter-paper in my case."

He fished out a sheet and, having written a formal request to Thorndyke to make such investigations as might be necessary in the interests of the Griffin Assurance Company, handed it to me and took his departure. As his footsteps died away on the stairs, Polton emerged from the adjacent laboratory and came in to clear away the breakfast-things. As he put them together on the tray, he announced, "I've read the account of the fire, sir, in the paper, but there isn't much more than you told me. Only the address – Billington Street, Soho."

"And now," said I, "you would like to go and have a look at it, I suppose?"

"Well," he admitted, "it would be interesting after having heard about it from you. But you see, sir, there's lunch to be got ready. The Doctor had his breakfast a bit earlier than you did, and not quite so much of it."

"Never mind about lunch," said I. "William can see to that." (William, I may explain, was a youth who had lately been introduced to assist Polton and relieve him of his domestic duties, and a very capable under-study he had proved. Nevertheless, Polton clung tenaciously to what he considered his privilege of attending personally to "The Doctor's" wants, which, in effect, included mine.) "You see, Polton," I added by way of overcoming his scruples, "one of us ought to go, and I don't want to. But The Doctor will want to make an inspection at the earliest possible moment and he will want to know how soon that will be. At present, the ruins can't have cooled down enough for a detailed inspection to be possible, but you could find out from the man in charge how things are and when we could make our visit. We shall want to see the place before it has been considerably disturbed and, if there are any human remains, we shall want to know where the mortuary is."

On this Polton brightened up considerably. "Of course, sir," said he, "If could be of any use, I should like to go, and I think William will be able to manage, as it is only a cold lunch."

With this he retired, and a few minutes later I saw him from the window hurrying along Crown Office Row, carefully dressed and carrying a fine, silver-topped cane and looking more like a dignitary of the Church than a skilled artificer.

When Thorndyke came in, I gave him an account of Stalker's visit as well as of my own adventure.

"I don't quite see," I added, "what we can do for him or why he is in such a twitter about this fire."

"No," he replied. "But Stalker is enormously impressed by our one or two successes and is inclined to over-estimate our powers. Still, there seem to be some suspicious features in the case, and I notice, on the placards, a rumour that a man was burned to death in the fire. If that is so, the affair will need looking into more narrowly. But we shall hear more about that when Polton comes back."

We did. For when, just as we had finished lunch, our deputy returned, he was able to give us all the news up to the latest developments. He had been fortunate enough to meet Detective Sergeant Wills, who was watching the case for the police, and had learned from him that a body had been discovered among the debris, but that there was some mystery about its identity, as the tenant of the rooms was known to be away from home on a visit to Ireland. But it was not a mere matter of hearsay, for Polton had actually seen the body brought out on a stretcher and had followed it to the mortuary.

"You couldn't see what its condition was, I suppose?" said I.

"No, sir," he replied, regretfully. "Unfortunately, it was covered up with a waterproof sheet."

"And as to the state of the ruins – did you find out how soon an examination of them will be possible?"

"Yes, sir. I explained matters to the Fire Brigade officer and asked him when you would be able to make your inspection. Of course, everything is too hot to handle just now. They had the greatest difficulty in getting at the corpse, but the officer thought that by to-morrow morning they will be able to get to work, and he suggested that you might come along in the forenoon."

"Yes," said Thorndyke, "that will do. We needn't be there very early, as the heavier material – joists and beams and the debris of the roof – will have to be cleared away before we shall be able to see anything. We had better make our visit to the mortuary first. It is possible

336

that we may learn more from the body than from the ruins. At any rate, it is within our province, which the ruins are not."

"Judging from what I saw," said I, "there will be mighty little for anyone to learn from the ruins. When the roof fell, it seemed to go right through to the basement."

"Will you want anything got ready, sir?" Polton asked, a little anxiously.

Thorndyke apparently noted the wistful tone, for he replied, "I shall want you to come along with us, Polton, and you had better bring a small camera with the adjustable stand. We shall probably want photographs of the body, and it may be in an awkward position."

"Yes, sir," said Polton. "I will bring the extension as well, and I will put out the things that you are likely to want for your research-case."

With this, he retired in undissembled glee, leaving us to discuss our arrangements.

"You will want authorities to examine the body and the ruins," said I. "Shall I see to them? I have nothing special to do this afternoon."

"If you would, Jervis, it would be a great help," he replied. "I have some work which I should like to finish up, so as to leave to-morrow fairly free. We don't know how much time our examinations may take."

"No," said I, "especially as you seem to be taking the case quite seriously."

"But, my dear fellow," said he, "we must. There may be nothing in it at all but, in any case, we have got to satisfy Stalker and do our duty as medico-legal advisers to The Griffin."

With this he rose and went forth about his business, while I, having taken possession of Stalker's letter, set out in quest of the necessary authorities.

Chapter XI
The Ruins

In the medico-legal mind the idea of horror, I suppose, hardly has a place. It is not only that sensibilities tend to become dulled by repeated impacts, but that the emotions are, as it were, insulated by the concentration of attention on technical matters. Speaking, however, dispassionately, I must admit that the body which had been disinterred from the ruins of the burned house was about as horrible an object as I had ever seen. Even the coroner's officer, whose emotional epidermis might well have grown fairly tough, looked at that corpse with an undisguised shudder, while as to Polton, he was positively appalled. As he stood by the table and stared with bulging eyes at the dreadful thing, I surmised that he was enjoying the thrill of his life. He was in a very ecstasy of horror.

To both these observers, I think, Thorndyke's proceedings imparted an added touch of gruesomeness, for my colleague – as I have hinted – saw in that hideous object nothing but a technical problem, and he proceeded in the most impassive and matter-of-fact way to examine it feature by feature and note down his observations as if he were drawing up an inventory. I need not enter into details as to its appearance. It will easily be imagined that a body which had been exposed to such intense heat that not only was most of its flesh reduced to mere animal charcoal, but the very bones, in places, were incinerated to chalky whiteness, was not a pleasant object to look on. But I think that what most appalled both Polton and the officer was the strange posture that it had assumed – a posture suggesting some sort of struggle or as if the man had been writhing in agony or shrinking from a threatened attack. The body and limbs were contorted in the strangest manner, the arms crooked, the hands thrust forward, and the skeleton fingers bent like hooks.

"Good Lord, sir!" Polton whispered, "how the poor creature must have suffered! And it almost looks as if someone had been holding him down."

"It really does," the coroner's officer agreed, "as if somebody was attacking him and wouldn't let him escape."

"It does look rather horrid," I admitted, "but I don't think you need worry too much about the position of the limbs. This contortion is almost certainly due to shrinkage of the muscles after death as the heat dried them. What do you think, Thorndyke?"

"Yes," he agreed. "It is not possible to draw any conclusions from the posture of a body that has been burned to the extent that this has, and burned so unequally. You notice that, whereas the feet are practically incinerated, there are actually traces of the clothing on the chest, apparently a suit of pyjamas, to judge by what is left of the buttons."

At this moment the door of the mortuary opened to admit a newcomer, in whom we recognized a Dr. Robertson, the divisional surgeon and an old acquaintance of us both.

"I see," he remarked, as Thorndyke laid down his tape-measure to shake hands, "that you are making your examination with your usual thoroughness."

"Well," Thorndyke replied, "the relevant facts must be ascertained now or never. They may be of no importance, but one can't tell that in advance."

"Yes," said Robertson, "that is a sound principle. In this case, I don't much think they are. I mean data in proof of identity, which are what you seem to be collecting. The identity of this man seems to be established by the known circumstances, though not so very clearly, I must admit."

"That seems a little obscure," Thorndyke remarked. "Either the man's identity is known, or it isn't."

The divisional surgeon smiled. "You are a devil for accuracy, Thorndyke," said he, "but you are quite right. We aren't here to make guesses. But the facts as to the identity appear to be pretty simple. From the statement of Mr. Green, the lessee of the house, it seems that the first-floor rooms were let to a man named Gustavus Haire, who lived in them, and he was the only person resident in the house, so that, when the business premises closed down for the day and the employees went home, he had the place to himself."

"Then," said Thorndyke, "do we take it that this is the body of Mr. Gustavus Haire?"

"No," replied Robertson, "that is where the obscurity comes in. Mr. Haire has – fortunately for him – gone on a business visit to Dublin but, as Mr. Green informs us, during his absence he allowed a cousin of his, a Mr. Cecil Moxdale, to occupy the rooms, or at least to use them to sleep in to save the expense of an hotel. The difficulty is that Moxdale was not known personally to Mr. Green, or to anybody else, for that matter. At present, he is little more than a name. But, of course, Haire will be able to give all the necessary particulars when he comes back from Ireland."

"Yes," Thorndyke agreed, "but meanwhile there will be no harm in noting the facts relevant to the question of identity. The man may have made a will, or there may be other reasons for establishing proof of his identity independently of Haire's statements. I have made notes of the principal data, but I am not very happy about the measurements. The contorted state of the body makes them a little uncertain. I suggest that you and Jervis take a set of measurements each, independently, and that we compare them afterwards."

Robertson grinned at me, but he took the tape measure without demur and proceeded quite carefully to take the principal dimensions of the contorted body and the twisted limbs and, when he had finished, I repeated the measurements, noting them down in my pocket-book. Then we compared our respective findings – which were in substantial agreement – and Thorndyke copied them all down in his note-book.

"When you came in, Robertson," said he, "we were discussing the posture of the body, and we had concluded that the contortion was due to shrinkage and had no significance. Do you agree?"

"I think so. It is not an unusual condition, and I don't see what significance it could have. The cause of death is practically established by the circumstances. But it certainly is a queer posture. The head especially. The man looks as if he had been hanged."

"He does," Thorndyke agreed, "and I want you to take a careful look at the neck. I noticed Jervis looking at it with a good deal of interest. Has my learned friend formed any opinion?"

"The neck is certainly dislocated," I replied, "and the odontoid process is broken. I noted that, but I put it down to the effects of shrinkage of the neck muscles, and possibly to some disturbance when the body was moved."

Robertson stooped over the body and examined the exposed neck-bones narrowly, testing the head for mobility and finding it quite stiff and rigid.

"Well," said he, "the neck is undoubtedly broken, but I am inclined to agree with Jervis, excepting that, as the neck is perfectly rigid, I don't think that the dislocation could have been produced by the moving of the body. I should say that it is the result of shrinkage. In fact, I don't see how else it could have been caused, having regard to the circumstances in which the body was found."

Thorndyke looked dissatisfied. "It always seems to me," said he, "that when one is examining a particular fact, it is best to forget the circumstances, to consider the fact without prejudice and without connection with anything else, and then, as a separate proceeding, to relate it to the circumstances."

The divisional surgeon chuckled. "This," said he, "is what the Master instils into his pupils. And quite right, too. It is sound doctrine. But still, you know, we must be reasonable. When we find the body of a

340

man among the debris of a house which has been burned out, and the evidence shows that the man was the only occupant of that house, it seems a little pedantic to enquire elaborately whether he may not have died from the effects of manual strangulation or homicidal hanging."

"My point," Thorndyke rejoined, as a parting shot, "is that our function is to ascertain the objective facts, leaving their interpretation to the coroner and his jury. Looking at that odontoid process, I find that the appearance of the fragments where the break took place is more consistent with the fracture having occurred during life than after death and during the subsequent shrinkage. I admit that I do not see how the fracture can have happened in the known – or assumed – circumstances, and I further admit that the appearances are not at all decisive."

I took another careful look at the fractured bone and was disposed to agree with Thorndyke, but I had also to agree with Robertson when he closed the discussion with the remark, "Well, Thorndyke, you may be right, but in any case the point seems to be of only academic interest. The man was alone in the house, so he couldn't have died from homicide, and I have never heard of anyone committing suicide by dislocating his neck."

Nevertheless, he joined us in a very thorough examination of the body for any other traces of injury (of which I need hardly say there were none) and for any distinctive appearances which might help to determine the identity in case the question should arise. I noticed him closely examining the teeth, and as they had already attracted my attention, I asked, "What do you make of those teeth? Is that roughening and pitting of the enamel due to the heat, or to some peculiarity of the teeth themselves?"

"Just what I was wondering," he replied. "I think it must be the result of the fire, for I don't recognize it as a condition that I have ever seen on living teeth. What do you think, Thorndyke?"

"I am in the same position as yourself," was the reply. "I don't recognize the condition. It is not disease, for the teeth are quite sound and strong. On the other hand, I don't quite understand how that pitting could have been produced by the heat. So I have just noted the appearance in case it should have any significance later."

"Well," said Robertson, "if Thorndyke is reduced to an open verdict, I suppose we may follow suit," and with this we returned to the general examination. When we had finished, he helped us to lift the stretcher, on which the body had been left, from the table to the floor to enable Polton to expose the photographs that Thorndyke required as records and, when these had been taken, our business at the mortuary was finished.

341

"I suppose," said Robertson, "you are going to have a look at the ruins, now. It seems a trifle off the medico-legal track, but you may possibly pick up some information there. I take it that you are acting for the insurance company?"

"Yes," replied Thorndyke, "on instructions. As you say, it seems rather outside our province, as the company appears to be interested only in the house. But they asked me to watch the case, and I am doing so."

"You are indeed," Robertson exclaimed. "All that elaborate examination of the body seems to be completely irrelevant, if the question is only, How did the house catch fire? You carry thoroughness to the verge of fanaticism."

Thorndyke smiled. "Not fanaticism," said he, "merely experience, which bids us gather the rosebuds while we may. The question of to-day is not necessarily the question of tomorrow. At present we are concerned with the house, but there was a dead body in it. A month hence that body may be the problem, but by then it will be underground."

Robertson grinned at me. "'Twas ever thus," he chuckled. "You can't get a rise out of Thorndyke – for the reason, I suppose, that he is always right. Well, I wish you luck in your explorations and hope to meet you both at the inquest."

With this, he took his departure and, as Polton had now got his apparatus packed up, we followed him and made our way to what the papers described as "*The Scene of the Conflagration*".

It was a rather melancholy scene, with a tinge of squalor. The street was still wet and muddy, but a small crowd stood patiently, regardless of the puddles, staring up at the dismal shell with its scorched walls and gaping windows – the windows that I had seen belch forth flames but which now showed only the cold light of day. A rough hoarding had been put up to enclose the ground floor, and at the wicket of this a Salvage Corps officer stood on guard. To him Thorndyke addressed himself, producing his authority to inspect the ruins.

"Well, sir," said the officer, "you'll find it a rough job, with mighty little to see and plenty to fall over. And it isn't over-safe. There's some stuff overhead that may come down at any moment. Still, if you want to look the place over, I can show you the way down."

"Your people, I suppose," said Thorndyke, "have made a pretty thorough inspection. Has anything been discovered that throws any light on the cause or origin of the fire?"

The officer shook his head. "No, sir," he replied. "Not a trace. There wouldn't be. The house was burned right out from the ground upwards. It might have been lighted in a dozen places at once and there would be nothing to show it. There isn't even part of a floor left. Do you think it is worthwhile to take the risk of going down?"

"I think I should like to see what it looks like," said Thorndyke, adding, with a glance at me, "but there is no need for you and Polton to risk getting a brick or a chimney-pot on your heads."

Of course, I refused to be left out of the adventure, while, as to Polton, wild horses would not have held him back.

"Very well, gentlemen," said the officer, "you know your own business." And with this he opened the wicket and let us through to the brink of a yawning chasm which had once been the cellars. The remains of the charred beams had been mostly hauled up out of the way, but the floor of the cellars was still hidden by mountainous heaps of bricks, tiles, masses of charred wood, and all-pervading white ash, amidst which three men in leather, brass-bound helmets were working with forks and shovels and with their thickly-gloved hands, removing the larger debris such as bricks, tiles, and fragments of boards and joists, while a couple of large sieves stood ready for the more minute examination of the dust and small residue.

We made our way cautiously down the ladder, becoming aware of a very uncomfortable degree of warmth as we descended and noting the steam that still rose from the wet rubbish. One of the men stopped his work to look at us and offer a word of warning.

"You'd better be careful where you are treading," said he. "Some of this stuff is still red underneath, and your boots aren't as thick as mine. You'd do best to stay on the ladder. You can see all there is to see from there, which isn't much. And mind you don't touch the walls with your hands."

His advice seemed so reasonable that we adopted it, and seated ourselves on the rungs of the ladder and looked about the dismal cavern as well as we could through the clouds of dust and steam.

"I see," said Thorndyke, addressing the shadowy figure nearest to us, "that you have a couple of sieves. Does that mean that you are going to sift all the small stuff?

"Yes," was the reply. "We are going to do this job a bit more thoroughly than usual on account of the dead man who was found here. The police want to find out all they can about him, and I think the insurance people have been asking questions. You see, the dead man seems to have been a stranger, and he hasn't been properly identified yet. And I think that the tenant of the house isn't quite satisfied that everything was according to Cocker."

"And I suppose," said Thorndyke, "that whatever is found will be kept carefully and produced at the inquest?

"Yes. Everything that is recovered will be kept for the police to see. The larger stuff will be put into a box by itself, and the smaller things which may be important for purposes of identification are to be sifted out and put into a separate box so that they don't get mixed up with the other things and lost sight of. But our instructions are that nothing is to be thrown away until the police have seen it."

"Then," Thorndyke suggested, "I presume that some police officer is watching the case. Do you happen to know who he is?"

"We got our instructions from a detective sergeant – name of Wills, I think – but an inspector from Scotland Yard looked in for a few minutes this morning, a very pleasant-spoken gentleman he was. Looked more like a dissenting minister than a police officer."

"That sounds rather like Blandy," I remarked, and Thorndyke agreed that the description seemed to fit our old acquaintance. And so it turned out, for when, having finished our survey of the cellars, we retired up the ladder and came out of the wicket, we found Sergeant Wills and Inspector Blandy in conference with the officer who had admitted us. On observing us, Blandy removed his hat with a flourish and made demonstrations of joy.

"Well, now," he exclaimed, "this is very pleasant. Dr. Jervis, too, and Mr. Polton with photographic apparatus. Quite encouraging. No doubt there will be some crumbs of expert information which a simple police officer may pick up."

Thorndyke smiled a little wearily. Like me, he found Blandy's fulsome manner rather tiresome. But he replied amiably enough, "I am sure, Inspector, we shall try to be mutually helpful, as we always do. But at present I suspect that we are in much the same position – just observers waiting to see whether anything significant comes into sight."

"That is exactly my position," Blandy admitted. "Here is a rather queer-looking fire and a dead man in the ruins. Nothing definitely suspicious, but there are possibilities. There always are when you find a dead body in a burned house. You have had a look at the ruins, sir. Did you find anything suggestive in them?"

"Nothing whatever," Thorndyke replied, "nor do I think anyone else will. The most blatant evidences of fire-raising would have been obliterated by such total destruction. But my inspection was merely formal. I have no expert knowledge of fires but, as I am watching the case for the Griffin Company, I thought it best to view the ruins."

"Then," said Blandy with a slightly disappointed air, "you are interested only in the house, not in the body?"

"Officially that is so but, as the body is a factor in the case, I have made an examination of it with Dr. Robertson, and if you want copies of

344

the photographs that Polton has just taken at the mortuary, I will let you have them."

"But how good of you!" exclaimed Blandy. "Certainly, Doctor, I should like to have them. You see," he added, "the fact that this dead man was not the ordinary resident makes one want to know all about him and how he came to be sleeping in that house. I shall be most grateful for the photographs, and if there is anything that I can do – "

"There is," Thorndyke interrupted. "I learn that you are, very wisely, making a thorough examination of the debris and passing the ashes through a sieve."

"I am," said Blandy, "and what is more, the sergeant and I propose to superintend the sifting. Nothing from a pin upwards will be thrown away until it has been thoroughly examined. I suppose you would like to see the things that we recover."

"Yes," replied Thorndyke, "when you have finished with them, you might pass them on to me."

Blandy regarded Thorndyke with a benevolent and slightly foxy smile and, after a moment's pause, asked deferentially, "Was there anything in particular that you had in your mind, Doctor? I mean, any particular kind of article?"

"No," Thorndyke replied. "I am in the same position as you are. There are all sorts of possibilities in the case. The body tells us practically nothing, so we can only pick up any stray facts that may be available, as you appear to be doing."

This brought the interview to an end. Blandy and the sergeant disappeared through the wicket, and we went on our way homewards to see what luck Polton would have with his photographs.

Chapter XII
Light on the Mystery

For the reader of this narrative, the inquest on the body that had been recovered from the burnt house will serve, as it did to me, to present the known facts of the case in a coherent and related group – a condition which had been made possible by the stable and mummified state of the corpse. For, as the body was now virtually incorruptible, it had been practicable to postpone the inquiry until the circumstances had been investigated by the police and the principal facts ascertained, at least sufficiently for the purpose of an inquest.

When we arrived, the preliminaries had just been completed. The jury, having viewed the body, had taken their places and the coroner was about to open the proceedings. I need not report his brief address, which merely indicated the matters to be inquired into, but will proceed to the evidence. The first witness was Mr. Henry Budge, and he deposed as follows: "On the 19th of April, about a quarter-to-three in the morning, I started with my neighbour, James Place, to walk home from the house of a friend in Noel Street, where we had been spending the previous evening playing cards. My way home to Macclesfield Street lay through Billington Street, and Mr. Place walked that way with me. All the houses that we passed were in darkness with the exception of one in Billington Street in which we noticed a light showing through the Venetian blinds of two of the windows. Mr. Place pointed them out to me, remarking that we were not the only late birds. That would be about three o'clock."

"Was the light like ordinary lamp, or electric light? the coroner asked.

"No. It looked more like fire-light – rather red in colour and not very bright. Only just enough to make the windows visible."

"Will you look at this photograph of the house, in which the windows are marked with numbers, and tell us which were the ones that were lighted up?"

The witness looked at the photograph and replied that the lighted windows were those marked *8* and *9*, adding that the one marked *7* seemed to be quite dark.

"That," said the coroner, "is important as showing that the fire broke out in the bed-sitting room on the first floor. Number seven is the window of the store or workroom. Yes?"

"Well, we didn't take any particular notice. We just walked on until we came to Little Pulteney Street, where Place lives, and there we stopped at a corner talking about the evening's play. Presently, Place began to sniff, and then I noticed a smell as if there was a chimney on fire. We both crossed the road and looked up over the tops of the houses, and then we could see smoke drifting across and we could just make out the chimney that it seemed to be coming from. We watched it for a few minutes, and then we saw some sparks rising and what looked like a reddish glow on the smoke. That made us both think of the house with the lighted window, and we started to walk back to have another look. By the time we got into Billington Street we could see the chimney quite plain with lots of sparks flying out of it, so we hurried along until we came opposite the house, and then there was no mistake about it. All three windows on the first floor were brightly lighted up, and in one of them the Venetian blinds had caught, and now small flames began to show from the top of the chimney. We consulted as to what we should do, and decided that Place should run off and find a policeman while I tried to knock up the people of the house. So Place ran off, and I crossed the road to the front door of the house at the side of the shop."

"And did you make a considerable noise?"

"I am afraid I didn't. There was no proper knocker, only one of these new things fixed to the letter-box. I struck that as hard as I could and I pressed the electric bell, but I couldn't tell whether it sounded or not. So I kept on with the silly little knocker."

"Did you hear any sounds of any kind from within the house?"

"Not a sign, though I listened at the letter-box."

"How long were you there alone?"

"Three or four minutes, I should think. Perhaps a little more. Then Place came running back with a policeman, who told me to go on knocking and ringing while he and Place roused up the people in the houses next door. But by this time the house was fairly alight, flames coming out of all three first-floor windows and a light beginning to show in the windows of the floor above. And then it got too hot for me to stay at the door, and I had to back away across the street."

"Yes," said the coroner, glancing at the jury, "I think the witness has given us a very clear and vivid description of the way and the time at which the fire broke out. The rest of the story can be taken up by other witnesses when we have heard Mr. Place."

The evidence of James Place, given quite briefly, merely confirmed and repeated that of Mr. Budge, with the addition of his description of his meeting with the policeman. Then the latter, Edwin Pearson by name, was called and, having been sworn, deposed that on the 19th of April at about 3:14 a.m. he was accosted at the corner of Meard Street, Soho, by the last witness, who informed him that there was a house on fire in Billington Street. He immediately ran off with Place to the nearest fire alarm and sent off the warning. That was at 3:16 a.m. by his watch. Then he and the last witness hurried off to Billington Street, where they found the house alight as Mr. Budge had described it, and had endeavoured to rouse the inmates of the burning house and the two adjoining houses, and were still doing so when the first of the engines arrived. That would be about 3:24 a.m.

Here the narrative passed to the officer in charge of the engine which had been the first on the scene and, when he had been sworn, the coroner remarked, "You realize that this is an inquiry into the death of the man whose body was found in the burnt house. The information that we want is that which is relevant to that death. Otherwise, the burning of the house is not specially our concern."

"I understand that," replied the witness – whose name had been given as George Bell. "The principal fact bearing on the death of the deceased is the extraordinary rapidity with which the fire spread, which is accounted for by the highly inflammable nature of the material that the house contained. If the deceased was asleep when the fire broke out, he might have been suffocated by the fumes without waking up. A mass of burning cellulose would give off volumes of poisonous gas."

"You have made an examination of the ruins. Did you find any evidence as to how the fire started?"

"No. The ruins were carefully examined by me and by several other officers, but no clue to the origin of the fire could be discovered by any of us. There was nothing to go on. Apparently, the fire started in the first-floor rooms, and it would have been there that the clues would be found. But those rooms were completely destroyed. Even the floors had been carried away by the fall of the roof, so that there was nothing left to examine."

"Does it appear to you that there is anything abnormal about this fire?"

"No. All fires are, in a sense, abnormal. The only unusual feature in this case is the great quantity of inflammable material in the house. But the existence of that was known."

"You find nothing to suggest a suspicion of fire-raising? The time, for instance, at which it broke out?"

"As to the time, there is nothing remarkable or unusual in that. The beginning of a fire may be something which makes no show at first – a heap of soot behind a stove or a spark on some material which will smoulder but not burst into flame. It may go on smouldering for quite a

348

long time before it reaches some material that is really inflammable. A spark on brown paper, for instance, might smoulder slowly for an hour or more, then, if the glowing part spread and came into contact with a celluloid film, there would be a burst of flame and the fire would be started, and in such a house as this, the place might be well alight in a matter of minutes."

"Then you have no suspicion of incendiarism?"

"No, there is nothing positive to suggest it. Of course, it can't be excluded. There is simply no evidence either way."

"In what way might the fire have originated?"

The witness raised his eyebrows in mild protest, but he answered the rather comprehensive question without comment.

"There are a good many possibilities. It might have been started by the act of some person. That is possible in this case, as there was a person in the house, but there is no evidence that he started the fire. Then there is the electric wiring. Something might have occurred to occasion a short circuit – a mouse or a cockroach connecting two wires. It is extremely uncommon with modern wiring, and in this case, as the fuses were destroyed, we can't tell whether it happened or not. And then there is the possibility of spontaneous combustion. That does occur occasionally. A heap of engineer's cotton waste soaked with oil will sometimes start burning by itself. So will a big bin of sawdust or a large mass of saltpetre. But none of these things are known to have been in this house."

"As to human agency: Suppose this person had been smoking in bed?"

"Well, that is a dangerous habit but, after all, it would be only guess-work in this case. I have no evidence that the man was smoking in bed. If there is such evidence, then the fire might have been started in that way, though, even then, it would not be a certainty."

This concluded Mr. Bell's evidence and, when he had been allowed to retire, the coroner commented, "As you will have observed, members of the jury, the expert evidence is to the effect that the cause of the fire is unknown – that is to say that none of the recognized signs of fire-raising were found. But possibly we may get some light on the matter from consideration of the circumstances. Perhaps we had better hear what Mr. Green can tell us before we take the medical evidence."

Accordingly, Mr. Walter Green was called and, having been sworn, deposed, "I am the lessee of the premises in which the fire occurred, and I carried on in them the business of a dealer in films of all kinds: Kine films, X-ray films, and the ordinary films for use in cameras. I do not manufacture, but I am the agent for several manufacturers, and I also

349

deal to some extent in projectors and cameras, both kine and ordinary. I always kept a large stock of films. Some were kept in the ground-floor shop for immediate sale, and the reserve stock was stored in the rooms on the second and third floors."

"Were these films inflammable?"

"Nearly all of them were highly inflammable."

"Then this must have been a very dangerous house. Did you take any special precautions against fire?"

"Yes. The store-rooms were always kept locked, and the rule was that they were only to be entered by daylight and that no smoking was allowed in them. We were naturally very careful."

"And were the premises insured?"

"Yes, both the building and the contents were fully insured. Of course, the rate of insurance was high in view of the special risk."

"How many persons were ordinarily resident in the house?"

"Only one. Formerly the premises used to be left at night entirely unoccupied but, as there was more room than we needed, I decided to let the first floor. I would sooner have let it for use as offices, but my present tenant, Mr. Gustavus Haire, applied for it as a residential flat, and I let it to him, and he has resided in it for the last six months."

"Was he in residence at the time of the fire?"

"No. Fortunately for him, he was absent on a visit to Ireland at the time. The gentleman who met his death in the fire was a relative of Mr. Haire's to whom he had lent the flat while he was away."

"We will come to the question of the deceased presently, but first we might have a few particulars about Mr. Haire, as to his occupation, for instance."

"I really don't know very much about him. He seems to be connected with the film and camera trade, mostly, I think, as a traveller and agent for some of the wholesale firms. But he does some sort of dealing on his own account, and he seems to be something of a mechanic. He has done some repairs on projectors for me, and once he mended up a gramophone motor that I bought second hand. And he does a little manufacturing, if you can call it by that name – he makes certain kinds of cements and varnishes. I don't know exactly how much or what he does with them, but I presume that he sells them, as I can't think of any use that he could have for the quantities that he makes."

"Did he carry on this industry on your premises?"

"Yes, in the small room that adjoined the bedroom, which he also used as a workroom for his mechanical jobs. There was a cupboard in it in which he used to keep his stocks of varnish and the solvents for making them – mostly acetone and amyl acetate."

"Aren't those solvents rather inflammable?"

"They are very inflammable, and the varnish is still worse, as the basis is cellulose."

"You say that you don't know how much of this stuff he used to make in that room. Haven't you any idea?"

"I can't suggest a quantity, but I know that he must have made a good deal of it, because he used to buy some, at least, of his material from me. It consisted mostly of worn-out or damaged films, and I have sold him quite a lot from time to time. But I believe he had other sources of supply."

"And you say he used to store all this inflammable material – the celluloid, the solvents, and the varnish – in that small room?"

"Yes, but I think that when the little room got full up, he used to overflow into the bedroom – in fact, I know he did, for I saw a row of bottles of varnish on the bedroom mantelpiece, one of them a Winchester quart."

"Then you have been into Mr. Haire's rooms? Perhaps you could give us a general idea as to their arrangement and what was in them."

"I have only been in them once or twice, and I didn't take very much notice of them, as I just went in to talk over some matters which we had been discussing. There were two rooms: A small one – that would have the window marked 7 in the photograph. It was used as a workroom and partly as a store for the cements and varnishes. It contained a smallish deal table which had a vice fixed to it and served as a work bench. It was littered with tools and bits of scrap of various kinds and there was a gas-ring on a sheet of iron. Besides the table, there was a stool and a good-sized cupboard, rather shallow and fitted with five or six shelves which seemed to be filled principally with bottles.

"The other room was quite a fair size – about twenty feet long and twelve feet wide. It was used as a bed-sitting room and was quite comfortably furnished. The bed was at the end opposite window number 9, with the dressing-table and washstand near it. At the other end was a mahogany table, a small sideboard, a set of book-shelves, three single chairs, an easy chair by the fireplace, and a grandfather clock against the wall in the corner. There was some sort of carpet on the floor and a rug before the fireplace. That is all I remember about the furniture of the room, but what dwells in my memory is the appalling untidiness of the place. The floor was littered with newspapers and magazines, the mantelpiece and the sideboard were filled up with bottles and boxes and pipes and all sorts of rubbish, and there were brown-paper parcels all over the place – stacked along the walls and round the clock and even under the bed."

351

"Do you know what was in those parcels?"

"I don't know, but I strongly suspect that they contained his stock of films. I recognized one as a parcel that he had had from me."

The coroner looked at the witness with a frown of astonishment.

"It seems incredible," he exclaimed. "These rooms must have been even more dangerous than the rest of the house."

"Much more," the witness agreed, "for, in the business premises, the films were at least securely packed. We didn't keep them loose in paper parcels."

"No. It is perfectly astonishing. This man, Haire, might as well have been living and sleeping in a powder magazine. No wonder that the fire started in his flat. The necessary conditions seem to have been perfect for the start of a fire. But still we have no evidence as to what actually started it. I suppose, Mr. Green, you have no suggestion to offer on that question?

"Of course, I have no certain knowledge, though I have a very definite suspicion. But a suspicion is not evidence."

"No, but I suppose that you had something to go on. Let us hear what you suspect and why you suspect it."

"My opinion is based on a conversation that I had with Mr. Haire shortly before he went away. It occurred in a little restaurant in Wardour Street where we both used to go for lunch. He was telling me about his proposed visit to Dublin. He said he was not sure how long he might be away, but he thought it would be as well for him to leave me his address in case anyone should call on any matter that might seem urgent. So he wrote down the address of the firm on whom he would be calling and gave it to me, and I then said, jestingly, that, as there would be no one in the house while he was away, I hoped he would deposit his jewellery and plate and other valuable property in the bank before he left.

"He smiled and promised that he would, but then he remarked that, in fact, the house would probably not be empty, as he had agreed to let a cousin of his have the use of the rooms to sleep in while he was away. I was not very pleased to hear this, and I remarked that I should not much care to hand the keys of any rooms of mine to another person. He agreed with me, and admitted that he would rather have avoided the arrangement, 'But,' he said, 'what could I do? The man is my cousin and quite a decent fellow. He happens to be coming up to town just at the time when I shall be away, and it will be a great convenience to him to have a place where he can turn in and save the expense of an hotel. He may not use the rooms after all, but if he does, I don't expect that you will see much of him, as he will only be coming to the rooms to sleep. His days will be occupied in various business calls. I must admit,' he

352

added, 'that I wish him at Halifax, but he asked me to let him have the use of the rooms, and I didn't feel that I could refuse.'

"'Well,' I said, 'I should have refused. But he is your cousin, so I suppose you know all about him.'

"'Oh, yes,' he replied, 'he is quite a responsible sort of man, and I have cautioned him to be careful.'

"That struck me as a rather curious remark, so I said, 'How do you mean? What did you caution him about?' and he replied, 'Oh, I just cautioned him not to do himself too well in the matter of drinks in the evening, and I made him promise not to smoke in bed.'

"'Does he usually smoke in bed?' I asked, and he replied, 'I think he likes to take a book to bed with him and have a read and a smoke before going to sleep. But he has promised solemnly that he won't.'

"'Well,' I said, 'I hope he won't. It is a shockingly dangerous habit. He might easily drop off to sleep and let his cigarette fall on the bed-clothes.'

"'He doesn't smoke cigarettes in bed,' said Haire. 'He smokes a pipe. His favourite is a big French clay bowl in the form of a death's head with glass eyes and a cherry-wood stem. He loves that pipe. But you need not worry – he has sworn not to smoke in bed.'

"I was not very happy about the affair, but I didn't like to make a fuss. So I made no further objection."

"I think," said the coroner, "that you ought to have forbidden him to lend the rooms. However, you didn't. Did you learn what this man's name was?"

"Yes, I asked Mr. Haire, in case I should see the man and have occasion to speak to him. His name was Moxdale – Cecil Moxdale."

"Then we may take it that the body which is the subject of this inquiry is that of Cecil Moxdale. Did you ever see him?"

"I think I saw him once. That would be just before six in the evening of the 14th of April. I was standing inside the doorway of my premises when Mr. Haire passed with another man, whom I assumed to be Mr. Moxdale from his resemblance to Mr. Haire. The two men went to the street door which is the entrance to Mr. Haire's staircase and entered together."

"Could you give us any description of Moxdale?"

"He was a biggish man – about five-feet-nine or -ten – with dark hair and a rather full dark moustache. That is all I noticed. I only took a passing glance at him."

"From what you said just now," the coroner suggested, "I suppose we may assume that you connect the outbreak of the fire with this unfortunate man?"

353

"I do," the witness replied. "I have no doubt that he lit up his pipe, notwithstanding his promise, and set his bedclothes on fire. That would account for everything, if you remember that there were a number of parcels under the bed which were almost certainly filled with inflammable films."

"Yes," the coroner agreed. "Of course, it is only a surmise, but it is certainly a very probable one. And that, I suppose, Mr. Green, is all that you have to tell us."

"Yes, sir," was the reply, "that is about all I know of the case."

The coroner glanced at the jury and asked if there were any questions and, when the foreman replied that there were none, the witness was allowed to retire when the depositions had been read and signed.

There was a short pause, during which the coroner glanced at the depositions and, apparently, reflected on the last witness's evidence. "I think," he said at length, "that, before going further into the details of this deplorable affair, we had better hear what the doctors have to tell us. It may seem, having regard to the circumstances in which the deceased met his death and the condition of the body, that the taking of medical evidence is more or less of a formality but, still, it is necessary that we should have a definite statement as to the cause of death. We will begin with the evidence of the divisional surgeon, Dr. William Robertson."

As his name was mentioned, our colleague rose and stepped up to the table, where the coroner's officer placed a chair for him.

Chapter XIII
The Facts and the Verdict

"You have, I believe," said the coroner when the I preliminary questions had been answered, "made an examination of the body which is now lying in the mortuary?"

"Yes, I examined that body very thoroughly. It appears to be that of a strongly-built man about five-feet-ten inches in height. His age was rather difficult to judge, and I cannot say more than that he was apparently between forty and fifty, but even that is not a very reliable estimate. The body had been exposed to such intense heat that the soft tissues were completely carbonized and, in some parts, entirely burned away. Of the feet, for instance, there was nothing left but white incinerated bone."

"The jury, when viewing the body, were greatly impressed by the strange posture in which it lay. Do you attach any significance to that?"

"No. The distortion of the trunk and limbs was due to the shrinkage of the soft parts under the effects of intense heat. Such distortion is not unusual in bodies which have been burned."

"Can you make any statement as to the cause of death?"

"My examination disclosed nothing on which an opinion could be based. The condition of the body was such as to obliterate any signs that there might have been. I assume that the deceased died from the effects of the poisonous fumes given off by the burning celluloid – that he was, in fact, suffocated. But that is not properly a medical opinion. There is, however, one point which I ought to mention. The neck was dislocated and the little bone called the odontoid process was broken."

"You mean, in effect," said the coroner, "that the neck was broken. But surely a broken neck would seem to be a sufficient cause of death."

"It would be in ordinary circumstances, but in this case I think it is to be explained by the shrinkage. My view is that the contraction of the muscles and the soft structures generally displaced the bones and broke off the odontoid process."

"Can you say, positively, that the dislocation was produced in that way?"

"No. That is my opinion, but I may be wrong. Dr. Thorndyke, who examined the body at the same time as I did, took a different view."

"We shall hear Dr. Thorndyke's views presently. But doesn't it seem to you a rather important point?"

"No. There doesn't seem to me to be much in it. The man was alone in the house and must, in any case, have met his death by accident. In the circumstances, it doesn't seem to matter much what the exact, immediate cause of death may have been."

The coroner looked a little dissatisfied with this answer, but he made no comment, proceeding at once to the next point.

"You have given us a general description of the man. Did you discover anything that would assist in establishing his identity?"

"Nothing beyond the measurements and the fact that he had a fairly good set of natural teeth. The measurements and the general description would be useful for identification if there were any known person with whom they could be compared. They are not very specific characters, but if there is any missing person who might be the deceased, they might settle definitely whether this body could, or could not, be that of the missing person."

"Yes," said the coroner, "but that is of more interest to the police than to us. Is there anything further that you have to tell us?"

"No," replied the witness, "I think that is all that I have to say."

Thereupon, when the depositions had been read and signed the witness retired and his place was taken by Thorndyke.

"You examined this body at the same time as Dr. Robertson, I think?" the coroner suggested.

"Yes, we made the examination together, and we compared the results so far as the measurements were concerned."

"You were, of course, unable to make any suggestion as to the identity of the deceased?"

"Yes. Identity is a matter of comparison, and there was no known person with whom to compare the body. But I secured, and made notes of, all available data for identification if they should be needed at any future time."

"It was stated by the last witness that there was a dislocation of the neck with a fracture of the odontoid process. Will you explain that to the jury and give us your views as to its significance in this case?"

"The odontoid process is a small peg of bone which rises from the second vertebra, or neck-bone, and forms a pivot on which the head turns. When the neck is dislocated, the displacement usually occurs between the first and the second vertebra, and then, in most cases, the odontoid process is broken. In the case of the deceased, the first and second vertebrae were separated and the odontoid process was broken. That is to say that the deceased had a dislocated neck, or, as it is commonly expressed, a broken neck."

"In your opinion, was the neck broken before or after death?"

"I should say that it was broken before death – that, in fact, the dislocation of the neck was the immediate cause of death."

"Do you say positively that it was so?"

"No. I merely formed that opinion from consideration of the appearances of the structures. The broken surfaces of the odontoid process had been exposed to the fire for some appreciable time, which suggested that the fracture had occurred before the shrinkage. And then it appeared to me that the force required to break the process was greater than the shrinkage would account for. Still, it is only an opinion. Dr. Robertson attributed the fracture to the shrinkage, and he is as likely to be right as I am."

"Supposing death to have been caused by the dislocation: What significance would you attach to that circumstance?"

"None at all, if the facts are as stated. If the man was alone in the house when the fire broke out, the exact cause of death would be a matter of no importance."

"Can you suggest any way in which the neck might have been broken in the circumstances which are believed to have existed?"

"There are many possible ways. For instance, if the man was asleep and was suddenly aroused by the fire, he might have scrambled out of bed, entangled the bedclothes, and fallen on his head. Or again, he might have escaped from the bedroom and fallen down the stairs. The body was found in the cellar. There is no evidence as to where the man was when death took place."

"At any rate, you do not consider the broken neck in any way incompatible with accidental death?"

"Not in the least and, as I said before, Dr. Robertson's explanation may be the correct one, after all."

"Would you agree that, for the purposes of this inquiry, the question as to which of you is right is of no importance?"

"According to my present knowledge and belief, I should say that it is of no importance at all."

This was the sum of Thorndyke's evidence and, when he had signed the depositions and returned to his seat, the name of Inspector Blandy was called, whereupon that officer advanced to the table and greeted the coroner and the jury with his habitual benevolent smile. He polished off the preliminaries with the readiness born of long experience and then, having, by the coroner's invitation, seated himself, he awaited the interrogation.

"I believe, Inspector," the coroner began, "that the police are making certain investigations regarding the death of the man who is the subject of this inquiry. Having heard the evidence of the other witnesses, can you give us any additional facts?"

"Nothing very material," Blandy replied. "The inquiries which we are making are simply precautionary. A dead man has been found in the ruins of a burnt house, and we want to know who that man was and how he came to be in that house, since he was admittedly not the tenant of the premises. As far as our inquiries have gone, they have seemed to confirm the statement of Mr. Green that the man was the one referred to by Mr. Haire as Cecil Moxdale. But our inquiries are not yet complete."

"That," said the coroner, "is a general statement. Could you give us the actual facts on which your conclusions are based?"

"The only facts bearing on the identity of the deceased have been obtained by an examination of various things found among the ashes of the burned house. The search was made with the greatest care, particularly that for the smaller objects which might have a more personal character. When the larger objects had been removed, the fine ash was all passed through sieves so that nothing should be overlooked. But everything that was found has been preserved for further examination if it should be necessary."

"You must have got a rather miscellaneous collection," the coroner remarked. "Have you examined the whole lot?"

"No. We have concentrated on the small personal articles, and these seem to have yielded all the information that we are likely to get, and have practically settled the question of identity. We found, for instance, a pair of cuff-links of steel, chromium plated, on which the initials *C.M.* were engraved. We also found a clay pipe-bowl in the form of a death's head which had once had glass eyes and still had the remains of the glass fused in the eye-sockets. This had the initials *C.M.* scratched deeply on the under-surface of the bowl."

"That was a very significant discovery," the coroner remarked, "having regard to what Mr. Green told us. Yes?"

"There was also a stainless-steel plate which seemed to have belonged to an attaché case or a suit-case and which had the initials *C.M.* engraved on it, and a gold watch, of which the case was partly fused, but on which we could plainly make out the initials *G.H.*"

"*G.H.*," the coroner repeated. "That, then, would be Mr. Haire's watch. Isn't that rather odd?"

"I think not, sir," replied Blandy. "These were Mr. Haire's rooms, and they naturally contained articles belonging to him. Probably he locked up this valuable watch before going on his travels."

"Did you find any other things belonging to him?"

"Nothing at all significant. There was a vice and some tools and the remains of an eight-day clock which apparently belonged to him, and there were some other articles that might have been his, but they were mixed up with the remains of projectors and various things which had probably came from the shop or the stores above. But the small personal articles were the really important ones. I have brought those that I mentioned for your inspection."

Here he produced from his attaché case a small glass-topped box in which the links, the steel name-plate, the death's-head pipe-bowl, and the half-fused gold watch were displayed on a bed of cotton wool, and handed it to the coroner who, when he had inspected it, passed it to the foreman of the jury.

While the latter and his colleagues were poring over the box, the coroner opened a fresh line of inquiry.

"Have you tried to get into touch with Mr. Haire?" he asked.

"Yes," was the reply, "and I am still trying, unsuccessfully up to the present. The address that Mr. Haire gave to Mr. Green was that of Brady and Company, a firm of retail dealers in photographic materials and appliances. As soon as I got it from Mr. Green, I communicated with the Dublin police, giving them the principal facts and asking them to find Mr. Haire, if they could, and pass on to him the information about the fire and also to find out from him who the man was whose body had been found in the burnt house.

"The information that I have received from them is to the effect that they called on Bradys about mid-day on the 19th, but Mr. Haire had already left. They learned that he had made a business call on Bradys on the morning of the 16th, having arrived in Dublin the previous night. He called again on the 18th, and then said that he was going on to Cork, and possibly from there to Belfast. In the interval, it seemed that he had made several calls on firms engaged in the photographic trade, but Bradys had the impression that he had left Dublin on the evening of the 18th.

"That is all that I have been able to discover so far, but there should be no great difficulty in tracing Mr. Haire, and even if it should not be possible, he will probably be returning from Ireland quite soon, and then he will be able to give us all the particulars that we want about this man, Cecil Moxdale – if that is his name."

"Yes," said the coroner, "but it will be too late for this inquiry. However, there doesn't seem to be any great mystery about the affair. The man's name was given to us by Mr. Green, and the identity seems to be confirmed by the initials on the articles which were recovered from the ruins – particularly the pipe, which had been described to us by Mr. Green as belonging to Cecil Moxdale. We know practically nothing about the man, but still we know enough for the purpose of this inquiry. It might be expedient to adjourn the proceedings until fuller particulars are available, but I hardly think it is necessary. I suppose, Inspector, you have nothing further to tell us?"

"No, sir," replied Blandy. "I have told you all that I know about the affair."

"Then," said the coroner, "that completes the evidence, and I think, members of the jury, that there is enough to enable you to decide on your verdict."

He paused for a moment, and then proceeded to read the depositions and secure the signature and, when this had been done and Blandy had retired to his seat, he opened his brief summing up of the evidence.

"There is little that I need say to you, members of the jury," he began. "You have heard the evidence, all of which has been quite simple and all of which points plainly to the same conclusion. You have to answer four questions: Who was the deceased? And Where, When, and By what means did he come by his death?

"As to the first question: Who was he? The evidence that we have heard tells us no more than that his name was Cecil Moxdale and that he was a cousin of Mr. Gustavus Haire. That is not much but, still, it identifies him as a particular individual. As to the conclusiveness of the evidence on this point, that is for you to judge. To me, the identity seems to be quite clearly established.

"As to the time and place of his death, it is certain that it occurred in the early morning on the 19th of April in the house known as 34 Billington Street, Soho. But the question as to how he came by his death is not quite so clear. There is some conflict of opinion on the part of the two medical witnesses respecting the immediate cause of death. But that need not trouble us, for they are agreed that, whatever might have been the immediate cause of death, the ultimate cause – with which we are concerned – was some accident arising out of the fire. There appears to be no doubt that the deceased was alone in the house at the time when the fire broke out and, that being so, his death could only have been due to some misadventure for which no one other than himself could have been responsible.

"There is, indeed, some evidence that he may, himself, have been responsible both for the outbreak of the fire and for his own death. There is a suggestion that he may, in spite of his promise to Mr. Haire, have indulged in the dangerous practice of smoking in bed. But there is no positive evidence that he did, and we must not form our conclusions on guesses or inferences.

"That is all that I need say, and with that I shall leave you to consider your verdict."

There was, as the coroner had justly remarked, very little to consider. The facts seemed quite plain and the conclusion perfectly obvious. And that was evidently the view of the jury, for they gave the matter but a few minutes' consideration, and then returned the verdict to the effect that the deceased, Cecil Moxdale, had met his death by misadventure due to the burning of the house in which he was sleeping.

"Yes," the coroner agreed, "that is the obvious conclusion. I shall record a verdict of Death by Misadventure."

On this, the Court rose and, after a few words with the coroner and Robertson, Thorndyke and I, accompanied by Polton (who had been specially invited to attend), took our departure and shaped a course for King's Bench Walk.

Chapter XIV
A Visit from Inspector Blandy

With the close of the inquest, our connection with the case of the burnt house in Billington Street and Cecil Moxdale, Deceased, seemed to have come to an end. No points of doubt or interest had arisen, or seemed likely to arise hereafter. We appeared to have heard the last of the case and, when Thorndyke's notes and Polton's photographs had been filed, we wrote it off as finished with. At least, I did. But later events suggested that Thorndyke had kept it in mind as a case in which further developments were not entirely impossible.

My view of the case was apparently shared by Stalker, for when, being in the City on other business, we dropped in at his office, he expressed himself to that effect.

"An unsatisfactory affair from our point of view," he commented, "but there was nothing that we could really boggle at. Of course, when an entire insured stock is destroyed, you have to be wary. A trader who has a redundant or obsolete or damaged stock can make a big profit by burning the whole lot out and recovering the full value from the insurance society. But there doesn't seem to be anything of that kind. Green appears to be perfectly straight. He has given us every facility for checking the value of the stock, and we find it all correct."

"I suppose," said I, "you couldn't have raised the question of negligence in allowing a casual stranger to occupy a bedroom in his box of fireworks. He knew that Moxdale wasn't a very safe tenant."

"There is no evidence," Thorndyke reminded me, "that Moxdale set fire to the house. He probably did, but that is a mere guess on our part."

"Exactly," Stalker agreed, "and even if he did, he certainly did not do it consciously or intentionally. And, by the way, speaking of this man Moxdale: It happens, oddly enough, that his life was insured in this office. So he has let us in for two payments."

"Anything considerable?" Thorndyke asked.

"No. Only a thousand."

"Have you paid the claim?"

"Not yet. In fact, no claim has been made up to the present, and it isn't our business to hunt up the claimants. But we shall have to pay, for I suppose that even you could not make out a case of suicide."

"No," Thorndyke admitted, "I think we can exclude suicide. At any rate, there was nothing to suggest it. You accept the identity?"

"There doesn't seem to be much doubt," replied Stalker, "but the next of kin, or whoever makes the claim, will have to confirm the statements of Green and Haire. But I don't think there is anything in the question of identity. Do you?"

"So far as I know, the question was fairly well settled at the inquest, and I don't think it could be contested unless some positive evidence to the contrary should be produced. But we have to bear in mind that the identity was based on the statement of Walter Green and that his evidence was hearsay evidence."

"Yes," said Stalker, "I will bear that in mind when the claim is put in – if it ever is. If no claim is made, the question will not be of any interest to me."

So that was the position. Stalker was not interested and, consequently, we, as his agents, had no further interest in the case and, so far as I was concerned, it had passed into complete oblivion when my recollection of it was revived by Thorndyke. It was at breakfast time a week or two after our conversation with Stalker that my colleague, who was, according to his habit, glancing over the legal notices in *The Times*, looked up at me and remarked, "Here is a coincidence in a small way. I don't remember having ever met with the name of Moxdale until we attended the late inquest. It certainly is not a common name."

"No," I agreed, "I don't think I ever heard it excepting in connection with Cecil Moxdale, Deceased. But what is the coincidence?"

"Here is another Moxdale, also deceased," he replied, handing me the paper and indicating the paragraph. It was an ordinary solicitor's notice beginning, "*Re: Harold Moxdale deceased who died on the third of April, 1936*", and calling on creditors and others to make their claims by a certain specified date, of no interest to me apart from the mere coincidence of the name. Nor did Thorndyke make any further comment, though I observed that he cut out the notice and, having fixed it with a dab of paste to a sheet of paper, added it to the collection of notes forming the Moxdale dossier. Then, once more, the "case" seemed to have sunk into oblivion.

But a few days later it was revived by no less a person than Inspector Blandy, and the manner of its revival was characteristic of that extremely politic gentleman. It was about half-past-eight one evening when, after an early dinner, Thorndyke, Polton, and I were holding a sort of committee meeting to review and re-classify the great collection of microscope slides of hairs, fibres, and other "comparison specimens" which had accumulated in the course of years. We had just finished the first of the new cabinets and were labelling the drawers when an unfamiliar knock, of an almost apologetic softness, was executed on the small brass knocker of the inner door.

"Confound it!" I exclaimed, impatiently. "We ought to have shut the oak. Who the deuce can it be?"

The question was answered by Polton who, as he opened the door and peered out, stepped back and announced, "Inspector Blandy."

We both stood up, and Thorndyke, with his customary suavity, advanced to greet the visitor and offer him a chair.

"Pray, gentlemen," exclaimed Blandy, casting an inquisitive glance over the collection on the table, "do not let me disturb you – though, to be sure, I can see that I am disturbing you. But the disturbance need be only of the briefest. I have come – very improperly, without an appointment – merely to tender apologies and to make all too tardy amends. When I have done that, I can go, and leave you to pursue your investigations."

"They are not investigations," said Thorndyke. "We are just going over our stock of test specimens and re-arranging them. But what do you mean by apologies and reparations? We have no grievance against you."

"You are kind enough to say so," replied Blandy, "but I am, nevertheless, a defaulter. I made a promise and have not kept it. *Mea culpa.*" He tapped his chest lightly with his knuckles and continued. "When I had the pleasure of meeting you in the ruins of the burned house, I promised to let you have an opportunity of examining the various objects that were retrieved from the debris. This evening, it suddenly dawned on me that I never did so. I was horrified and, in my impulsive way, I hurried, without reflection, to seek your forgiveness and to make such amends as were possible."

"I don't think, Blandy," said Thorndyke, "that the trifling omission mattered. We seemed to have all the information that we wanted."

"So we did, but perhaps we were wrong. At any rate, I have now brought the things for you to see, if they are still of any interest. It is rather late, I must admit."

"Yes, by Jove!" I agreed. "It is the day after the fair. But what things have you brought, and where are they?"

"The exhibits which you saw at the inquest, I have here in my attaché case. If you would like me to leave them with you for examination at your leisure, I can do so, but we shall want them back. The other things are a box in my car and, as we have finished with them, you can dispose of them as you please when you have examined them, if you think the examination worthwhile."

"I take it," said Thorndyke, "that you have been through them pretty thoroughly. Did you find anything in any way significant?"

364

The inspector regarded Thorndyke with his queer, benevolent smile as he replied, "Not significant to me, but who knows what I may have overlooked? I could not bring to bear on them either your intellect, your encyclopaedic knowledge, or your unrivalled means of research." Here he waved his hand towards the table and seemed to bestow a silent benediction on the microscopes and the trays of slides. "Perhaps," he concluded, "these simple things might have for you some message which they have withheld from me."

As I listened to Blandy's discourse, I found myself speculating on the actual purpose of his visit. He could not have come to talk this balderdash or to deliver the box of trash that he had brought with him. What object, I wondered, lay behind his manoeuvres? Probably it would transpire presently but, meanwhile, I thought it as well to give him a lead.

"It is very good of you, Blandy," said I, "to have brought us these things to look at, but I don't quite see why you did it. Our interest in the affair ended with the inquest, and I take it that yours did too. Or didn't it?"

"It did not," he replied. "We were then making certain inquiries through the Irish police, and we have not yet obtained the information that we were seeking. The case is still incomplete."

"Do you mean," Thorndyke asked, "that Mr. Haire has not been able to tell you all that you wanted to know?"

"We have not been able to get into touch with Mr. Haire, which is a rather remarkable fact, and becomes still more remarkable as the time passes and we get no news of him."

"In effect, then," said Thorndyke, "Mr. Haire has disappeared. Have you taken any special measures to trace him?"

"We have taken such measures as were possible," replied Blandy. "But we are in a difficult position. We have no reliable description of the man and, if we had, we could hardly proceed as if we were trying to trace a 'wanted' man. It is curious that he should not have turned up in his usual places of resort, but there is nothing incriminating in the fact. We have no reason to suppose that he is keeping out of sight. There is nothing against him. No one could suspect him of having had any hand in starting the fire, as he was not there and another man was. But still, it is a little mysterious. It makes one wonder whether there could have been something that we overlooked."

"Yes," Thorndyke agreed, "there does certainly seem to be something a little queer about the affair. As I understand it, Haire went away with the stated intention of making a short visit to Dublin. He was known to have arrived there on a certain day and to have made two calls at a business house. He is said to have announced his intention to go on to Belfast, but it is not known whether he did, in fact, go there. Nothing at all is known as to his movements after he had left the dealer's premises. From that moment, no one, so far as we know, ever saw him again. Isn't that the position?"

"That is the position exactly, sir," replied Blandy, "and a very curious position it is if we remember that Haire was a man engaged in business in London and having a set of rooms there containing his household goods and personal effects."

"Before the fire," I remarked. "There wasn't much left of either after the flare up. He hadn't any home then to come back to."

"But, sir," Blandy objected, "what reason is there for supposing that he knew anything about the fire? He was somewhere in Ireland when it happened. But a fire in a London by-street isn't likely to be reported in the Irish papers."

"No," I admitted, "that is true, and it only makes the affair still more queer."

There was a short silence. Then Thorndyke raised a fresh question. "By the way, Inspector," said he, "there was a legal notice in *The Times* a few days ago referring to a certain Moxdale, Deceased. Did you happen to observe it?"

"Yes, my attention was called to it by one of my colleagues and, on the chance that there might be some connection with the other Moxdale, Deceased, I called on the solicitors to make a few enquiries. They are quite a respectable firm – Home, Croner, and Home of Lincoln's Inn – and they were as helpful as they could be, but they didn't know much about the parties. The testator, Harold Moxdale, was an old gentleman, practically a stranger to them, and the other parties were nothing more than names. However, I learned that the principal beneficiary was the testator's nephew, Cecil Moxdale, and that, if he had not had the misfortune to be burned, he would have inherited a sum of about four-thousand pounds."

"It is possible," I suggested, "that it may not be the same Cecil Moxdale. You say that they did not know anything about him. Did you try to fix the identity?"

"It wasn't necessary," replied Blandy, "for the next beneficiary was another nephew named Gustavus Haire, and as we knew that Haire and Moxdale were cousins, that settled the identity."

As Blandy gave this explanation, his habitual smile became tinged with a suggestion of foxiness, and I noticed that he was furtively watching Thorndyke to see how he took it. But there was no need, for my colleague made no secret of his interest.

366

"Did you learn whether these two bequests were in any way mutually dependent?" he asked.

Blandy beamed on him almost affectionately. It was evident that Thorndyke's reactions were those that had been desired.

"A very pertinent question, sir," he replied. "Yes, the two bequests were mutually contingent. The entire sum to be divided between the two nephews was about six-thousand pounds. Of this, four-thousand went to Cecil and two thousand to Gustavus. But it was provided that if either of them should pre-decease the testator, the whole amount should go the survivor."

"My word, Blandy!" I exclaimed. "This puts quite a new complexion on the affair. As Harold Moxdale died, if I remember rightly, on the 30th of April, and Cecil died on the 19th of the same month, it follows that the fire in Billington Street was worth four-thousand pounds to Mr. Gustavus Haire. A decidedly illuminating fact."

Blandy turned his benign smile on me. "Do you find it illuminating, sir?" said he. "If you do, I wish you would reflect a few stray beams on me."

Thorndyke chuckled, softly. "I am afraid, Jervis," said he, "that the inspector is right. This new fact is profoundly interesting – even rather startling. But it throws no light whatever on the problem."

"It establishes a motive," I retorted.

"But what is the use of that?" he demanded. "You, as a lawyer, know that proof of a motive to do some act is no evidence, by itself, that the person who had the motive did the act. Haire, as you imply, had a motive for making away with Moxdale. But before you could even suggest that he *did* actually make away with him, you would have to prove that he had the opportunity and the intention, and even that would carry you no farther than suspicion. To support a charge, there would have to be some positive evidence that the act was committed."

"Exactly, sir," said Blandy, "and the position is that we have not a particle of evidence that Haire had any intention of murdering his cousin, and there is clear evidence that he had no opportunity. When the fire broke out, he was in Ireland and had been there five days. That is, for practical purposes, an absolutely conclusive alibi."

"But," I persisted, "aren't there such things as time-fuses or other timing appliances?"

Blandy shook his head. "Not in a case like this," he replied. "Of course, we have considered that question, but there is nothing in it. In the case of a man who wants to set fire to a lock-up shop or empty premises, it is possible to use some such appliance – a time-fuse, or a candle set on some inflammable material, or an alarm clock – to give him time to show himself a few miles away and establish an alibi, and even then the firemen usually spot it. But here you have a flat, with somebody living in it, and the owner of that flat on the other side of the Irish Channel, where he had arrived five days before the fire broke out.

"No, sir, I don't think Mr. Haire is under any suspicion of having raised the fire. The thing is a physical impossibility. And I don't know of any other respect in which he is under suspicion. It is odd that we can't discover his whereabouts, but there is really nothing suspicious in it. There is no reason why he should let anyone know where he is."

I did not contest this, though my feeling was that Haire was purposely keeping out of sight, and I suspected that Blandy secretly took the same view. But the inspector was such an exceedingly downy bird that it was advisable not to say too much. However, I now understood – or thought I did – why he had made this pretext to call on us, he was at a dead end and hoped to interest Thorndyke in the case and thereby get a lead of some kind. And now, having sprung his mine, he reverted to the ostensible object of his visit.

"As to this salvage stuff," said he. "Would you like me to leave these small things for you to look over?"

I expected Thorndyke to decline the offer, for there was no mystery about the things, and they were no affair of ours in any case. But, to my surprise, he accepted and, having checked the list, signed the receipt which Blandy had written out.

"And as to the stuff in the box, perhaps Mr. Polton might show my man where to put it."

At this, Polton, who had been calmly examining and sorting the test-slides during the discussion (to which I have no doubt he had given close attention), rose and suggested that the box should be deposited in the laboratory in the first place, and when Thorndyke had agreed, he departed to superintend the removal.

"I am afraid," said Blandy, "that you will find nothing but rubbish in that box. That, at least, is what it appeared like to me. But, having studied some of your cases, I have been deeply impressed by your power of extracting information from the most unpromising material, and it is possible that these things may mean more to you than they do to me."

"It is not very likely," Thorndyke replied. "You appear to have extracted from them all the information that one could expect. They have conveyed to you the fact that Cecil Moxdale was apparently the occupant of the rooms at the time of the fire, and that is probably all that they had to tell."

368

"It is all they had to tell me," said Blandy, rising and picking up his attaché case, "and it is not all that I want to know. There is still the problem of how the fire started, and they throw no light on that at all."

"You have got the clay pipe," I suggested. "Doesn't that tell the story?"

He smiled at me with amiable reproach as he replied, "We don't want the material for plausible guesses. We want facts, or at least a leading hint of some kind, and I still have hopes that you may hit on something suggestive."

"You are more optimistic than I am," replied Thorndyke, "but I shall look over the material that you have brought and, if it should yield any facts that are not already known to you, I promise to let you have them without delay."

Blandy brightened up appreciably at this and, as he turned to depart, he expressed his gratitude in characteristic terms.

"That, sir, is most generous of you. It sends me on my way rejoicing in the consciousness that my puny intelligence is to be reinforced by your powerful intellect and your encyclopaedic knowledge. I thank you, gentlemen, for your kindly reception of an intruder and a disturber of your erudite activities, and I wish you a very good evening."

With this, the inspector took his departure, leaving us both a little overpowered by his magniloquence and me a little surprised by Thorndyke's promise which had evoked it.

Chapter XV
Polton on the Warpath

As the inspector's footsteps died away on the stairs, we looked at one another and smiled.

"That was a fine peroration, even for Blandy," I remarked. "But haven't you rather misled the poor man? He is evidently under the delusion that he has harnessed you firmly to his chariot."

"I only promised to look over his salvage, which I am quite ready to do for my own satisfaction."

"I don't quite see why. You are not likely to learn anything from it, and even if you were, this affair is not our concern."

"I don't know that we can say that," he replied. "But we needn't argue the point. I don't mind admitting that mere professional curiosity is a sufficient motive to induce me to keep an eye on the case."

"Well, that would be good news for Blandy, for it is obvious that he is completely stumped, and so am I, for that matter – assuming that there is anything abnormal about the case. I don't feel convinced that there is."

"Exactly," said Thorndyke. "That is Blandy's difficulty. It is a very odd and puzzling case. Taking the group of circumstances as a whole, it seems impossible to accept it as perfectly normal, but yet, when one examines the factors separately, there is not one of them at which one can cavil."

"I am not sure that I follow that," said I. "Why can we not accept the circumstances as normal? I should like to hear you state the case as it presents itself to you."

"Well," he replied, "let us first take the facts as a whole. Here is a house which, in some unknown way, catches fire in the small hours of the morning. In the debris of that house is found the body of a man who has apparently been burned to death."

"Yes," I agreed, with a grin, "the body certainly had that appearance."

"It transpires later," Thorndyke continued, disregarding my comment, "that the death of that man, A, benefits another man, B, to the extent of four-thousand pounds. But the premises in which the fire occurred belong to and are controlled by B, and they had been lent by B to A for his occupation while B should be absent in Ireland. The event by which the benefit accrues to B – the death of Harold Moxdale – has occurred quite a short time after the fire. Finally, the tenant, B, who had ostensibly gone away from his residence to make a short visit to Ireland, has never returned to that residence or made any communication to his landlord – has, in fact, disappeared."

"Blandy doesn't admit Haire has disappeared," I objected

"We mustn't take Blandy's statements too literally. In spite of his disclaimers, it is evident that he is hot on the trail of Mr. Gustavus Haire, and the fact is that, in the ordinary sense of the word, Haire has disappeared. He has absented himself from his ordinary places of resort, he has communicated with nobody, and he has left no traces by which the police could discover his whereabouts.

"But now take the facts separately. The origin of the fire is a mystery, but there is not a particle of evidence of incendiarism. The only person who could have been suspected had been overseas several days before the fire broke out."

"Do you consider that his absence at the time puts him quite outside the picture? I mean, don't you think that the fire could have been started by some sort of timing apparatus?"

"Theoretically, I have no doubt that it could. But it would have had to be a rather elaborate apparatus. The common alarm clock would not have served. But really the question seems to be of only academic interest for two reasons. First, the fire experts were on the look-out for some fire-raising appliance and found no trace of any. Second, the presence of Moxdale in the rooms seems to exclude the possibility of any such appliance having been used and, third, even the appliance that you are postulating would not have served its purpose with anything like calculable certainty."

"You mean that it might not have worked, after all?"

"No. What I mean is that it could not have been adjusted to the actual purpose, which would have been to cause the death of the man. It would have been useless to fire the house unless it were certain that the man would be in it at the time and that he would not be able to escape. But neither of these things could be foreseen with any degree of certainty. No, Jervis, I think that, on our present knowledge, we must agree with Blandy and the others that no suspicion of arson stands against Gustavus Haire."

"That is what he says, but it is obvious that he does suspect Haire."

"I was speaking in terms of evidence," Thorndyke rejoined. "Blandy admits that he has nothing against Haire and therefore cannot treat the disappearance as a flight. If he met Haire, he couldn't detain him or charge him with any unlawful act. But he feels – and I think quite rightly – that Haire's disappearance is a mystery that needs to be explained. Blandy, in fact, is impressed by the case as a whole, by the appearance of a connected series of events with the suggestion of a purpose behind it. He won't accept those events as normal events, brought about merely by chance, but he sees no way of challenging them so as to start an inquiry. That is why he came to us. He hopes that we may be able to give him some kind of leading fact."

"And so you are proposing to go over the box of rubbish that he has brought on the chance that you may find the leading fact among it?"

"I think we may as well look over it," he replied. "It is wildly improbable that it will yield any information, but you never know. We have, on more than one occasion, picked up a useful hint from a most unlikely source. Shall we go up and see what sort of rubbish the box contains?"

We ascended to the laboratory floor, where we found Polton looking with undissembled distaste at a large packing-case filled to the brim with miscellaneous oddments, mostly metallic, and all covered with a coating of white ash.

"Looks as if Mr. Blandy has turned out a dust bin," Polton commented, "and passed the contents on to us. A rare job it was getting it up the stairs. Shall I put the whole of the stuff out on the bench?"

"You may as well," replied Thorndyke, "though I think Blandy might have weeded some of it out. Door-handles and hinges are not likely to yield much information."

Accordingly, we all set to work transferring the salvage to the large bench, which Polton had tidily covered with newspaper, sorting it out to some extent as we did so, and making a preliminary inspection. But it was a hopeless-looking collection, for the little information that it conveyed we possessed already. We knew about the tools from the little workshop, the projectors, and the remains of gramophones and kinematograph cameras and, as to the buttons, studs, keys, pen-knives, and other small personal objects, they were quite characterless and could tell us nothing.

Nevertheless, Thorndyke glanced at each item as he picked it out of its dusty bed and laid it in its appointed place on the bench, and even Polton began presently to develop an interest in the proceedings. But it was evidently a merely professional interest, concerning itself exclusively with the detached fragments of the gramophone motors and other mechanical remains, and particularly with the battered carcase of the grandfather clock, and I strongly suspected that he was simply on the look-out for usable bits of scrap. Voicing my suspicion, I suggested, "This ought to be quite a little windfall for you, Polton. A lot of this clockwork seems to be quite sound – I mean as to the separate parts."

He laid down the clock (as tenderly as if it had been in going order) and regarded me with a cunning and crinkly smile.

"It's an ill wind, sir, that blows nobody good. My reserve stock of gear-wheels and barrels and other spare parts will be all the richer for Mr. Blandy's salvage. And you can't have too many spares – you never know when one of them may be the very one that you want. But might I suggest that, as this is a rather dirty job, you let me finish setting the things out and come and look over them at your leisure in the morning, when I have been through them with a dusting-brush."

As I found the business not only dirty but rather boresome – and in my private opinion perfectly futile – I caught at the suggestion readily, and Thorndyke and I then retired to the sitting-room to resume our operations on the test-slides, after cleansing our hands.

"We seem to have been ejected," I remarked as we sat down to the table. "Perhaps our presence hindered the collection of scrap."

Thorndyke smiled. "That is possible," said he. "But I thought that I detected an awakening interest in the inspection. At any rate, it will be as well to let him sort out the oddments before we go through them. He is a good observer, and he might notice things that we should overlook and draw our attention to them."

"You don't really expect to get any information out of that stuff, do you?" I asked.

"No," he replied. "The inspection is little more than a formality, principally to satisfy Blandy. Still, Jervis, we have our principles, and one of them – and a very important one – is to examine everything, no matter how insignificant. This won't be the first rubbish-heap that we have inspected, and it may be that we shall learn something from it, after all."

Thorndyke's suggestion of "an awakening interest" on Polton's part was curiously confirmed on the following day and thereafter. For, whereas I made my perfunctory inspection of the rubbish and forthwith – literally – washed my hands of it, and even Thorndyke looked it over with little enthusiasm, Polton seemed to give it a quite extraordinary amount of attention. By degrees, he got all the mechanical oddments sorted out into classified heaps, and once I found him with a small sieve, carefully sifting the ash and dirt from the bottom of the box. And his interest was not confined to the contents of that unclean receptacle, for, having been shown the gold watch which the inspector had left with us, he skilfully prised it open and examined its interior through his eyeglass with the most intense concentration.

Moreover, I began to notice something new and unusual in his manner and appearance – a suggestion of suppressed excitement and a

373

something secret and conspiratorial in his bearing. I mentioned the matter to Thorndyke but, needless to say, he had noticed it and was waiting calmly for the explanation to transpire. We both suspected that Polton had made some sort of discovery, and we both felt some surprise that he had not communicated it at once.

And then, at last, came the disclosure, and a most astonishing one it was. It occurred a few mornings after Blandy's visit, when Thorndyke and I, happening to go up together to the laboratory, found our friend at the bench, poring over one of the heaps of mechanical fragments with a pair of watchmaker's tweezers in his hand.

"Well, Polton," I remarked, "I should think that you have squeezed the inspector's treasures nearly dry."

He looked up at me with his queer, crinkly smile and replied, "I am rather afraid that I have, sir."

"And now, I suppose, you know all about it?"

"I wouldn't say that, sir, but I know a good deal more than when I started. But I don't know all that I want to know."

"Well," I said, "at any rate, you can tell us who set fire to that house."

"Yes, sir," he replied, "I think I can tell you that, without being too positive."

I stared at him in astonishment, and so did Thorndyke. For Polton was no jester and, in any case, was much too well-mannered to let off jokes at his principals.

"Then," said I, "tell us. Who do you say it was?"

"I say that it was Mr. Haire," he replied with quiet conviction.

"But, my dear Polton," I exclaimed. "Mr. Haire was in Dublin when the fire broke out, and had been there five days. You heard the inspector say that it was impossible to suspect him."

"It isn't impossible for me," said Polton. "He could have done it quite well if he had the necessary means. And I am pretty sure that he had the means."

"What means had he?" I demanded.

"Well, sir," he replied, "he had an eight-day long-case clock."

Of course, we knew that. The clock had been mentioned at the inquest. Nevertheless, Polton's simple statement impinged on me with a quite startling effect, as if some entirely new fact had emerged. Apparently it impressed Thorndyke in the same way, for he drew a stool up to the bench and sat down beside our mysterious little friend.

"Now, Polton," said he, "there is something more than that. Tell us all about it."

Polton crinkled nervously as he pondered the question.

"It is rather a long and complicated story," he said, at length. "But I had better begin with the essential facts. This clock of Mr. Haire's was not quite an ordinary clock. It had a calendar movement of a very unusual kind, quite different from the simple date disc which most of these old clocks have. I know all about that movement because it happens that I invented it and fitted it to a clock, and I am practically certain that this is the very clock.

"However, that doesn't matter for the moment, but I must tell you how I came to make it and how it worked. In those days, I was half-way through my time as apprentice, and I was doing some work for a gentleman who made philosophical instruments – his name was Parrish. Now, Mr. Parrish had a clock of this kind – what they call a 'grandfather' nowadays – and it had the usual disc date in the dial. But that was no use to him because he was rather near-sighted. What he wanted was a calendar that would show the day of the week as well as the date, and in good big characters that he could read when he was sitting at his writing-table, and he asked me if I could make one. Well, of course, there was no difficulty. The simple calendar work that is sometimes fitted to watches would have done perfectly. But he wouldn't have it because it works rather gradually. It takes a few minutes at least to make the change."

"But," said I, "surely that is of no consequence."

"Not the slightest, sir. The change occurs in the night when nobody can see it, and the correct date is shown in the morning. But Mr. Parrish was a rather precise, pernickety gentleman, and he insisted that the change ought to be made in an instant at the very moment of midnight, when the date does really change. So I had to set my wits to work to see what could be done, and at last I managed to design a movement that changed instantaneously.

"It was quite a simple affair. There was a long spindle, or arbor, on which were two drums, one having the days of the week in half-inch letters on it and the other carrying a ribbon with the thirty-one numbers painted the same size. I need not go into full details, but I must explain the action, because that is what matters in this case. There was a twenty-four hour wheel – we will call it the day-wheel – which took off from the hour-wheel, and this carried a snail which turned with it."

"You don't mean an actual snail, I presume," said I.

"No, sir. What clockmakers call a snail is a flat disc with the edge cut out to a spiral shape, the shape of one of those flat water-snails. Resting against the edge of the snail by means of a projecting pin was a light steel bar with two pallets on it, and there was a seven-toothed star-wheel with long, thin teeth, one of which was always resting on the

375

pallets. I may say that the whole movement excepting the day-wheel was driven by a separate little weight, so as to save the power of the clock.

"And now let me explain how it worked. The day-wheel, driven by the clock, made a complete turn in twenty-four hours, and it carried the snail round with it. But as the snail turned, its spiral edge gradually pushed the pallet-bar away. A tooth of the star-wheel was resting on the upper pallet, but when the snail had nearly completed its turn, it had pushed the bar so far away that the tooth slipped off the upper pallet on to the lower one – which was quite close underneath. Then the snail turned a little more and the pin came to the end of the spiral – what we call 'the step' – and slipped off, and the pallet-bar dropped back and let the tooth of the star-wheel slip off the lower pallet. Then the star-wheel began to turn until the next tooth was stopped by the upper pallet, and so it made a seventh of a turn and, as it carried the two drums round with it, each of those made the seventh of a turn and changed the date in less than a second. Is that clear, sir?"

"Quite clear," replied Thorndyke (speaking for himself), "so far as the mechanism goes, but not so clear as to your deductions from it. I can see that this quite innocent calendar movement could be easily converted into a fire-raising appliance. But you seem to suggest that it was actually so converted. Have you any evidence that it was?"

"I have, sir," replied Polton. "What I have described is the calendar work just as I made it. There is no doubt about that, because when I took off the copper dial, there was the day-wheel with the snail on it still in place. Perhaps you noticed it."

"I did, but I thought it was part of some kind of striking-work."

"No, sir. The striking-work had been removed to make room for the calendar-work. Well, there was the day-wheel and the snail, and I have found the pallet-bar and the star-wheel and some of the other parts, so it is certain that the calendar movement was there. But there was something else. Somebody had made an addition to it, for I found another snail and another pallet-bar almost exactly like those of the calendar. But there was this difference – the day-snail had marked on it twelve lines, each denoting two hours, but this second snail had seven lines marked on it, and those seven lines couldn't have meant anything but seven days."

"That is a reasonable assumption," said Thorndyke.

"I think, sir, that it is rather more than an assumption. If you remember that the star-wheel and the spindle that carried the two drums made one complete revolution in seven days, you will see that, if this snail had been fixed on to the spindle, it would also have made a revolution in seven days. But do you see what follows from that?"

"I don't," said I, "so you may as well explain."

"Well, the day-snail turned once a day and, at the end of its turn, it suddenly let the pin drop into the step, released the star-wheel and changed the date in an instant. But this second snail would take a week to turn and, at the end of the week, the pin would drop into the step, and in an instant something would happen. The question is, what was it that would have happened?"

"Yes," Thorndyke agreed, "that is the question, and first, can you think of any normal and innocent purpose that the snail might have served?"

"No, sir. I have considered that question, and I can't find any answer. It couldn't have been anything connected with the calendar, because the weeks aren't shown on a calendar. There's no need. When Sunday comes round, you know that it is a week since last Sunday, and no one wants to number the weeks."

"It is conceivable," I suggested, "that someone might have had some reason for keeping count of the weeks, though it does seem unlikely. But could this addition be connected with the phases of the moon? They are sometimes shown on clocks."

"They are, usually, on these old clocks," replied Polton, "but this movement would have been of no use for that purpose. The moon doesn't jump from one phase to the next. It moves gradually, and the moon-disc on a clock shows the changes from day to day. Besides, this snail would have been unnecessary. A moon-disc could have been taken directly off the spindle and moved forward one tooth at each change of date. No, sir, I can think of no use for that snail but to do some particular thing at a given time on a given day. And that is precisely what I think it was made for."

I could see that Thorndyke was deeply impressed by this statement, and so was I. But there were one or two difficulties, and I proceeded to point them out.

"You speak, Polton, of doing something at a given time on a given day. But your calendar gave no choice of time. It changed on the stroke of midnight. But this fire broke out at three o'clock in the morning."

"The calendar changed at midnight," replied Polton, "because it was set to that time. But it could have been set to any other time. The snail was not fixed immovably on the pivot. It was held fast by a set-screw, but if you loosened the screw, you could turn the snail and set it to discharge at any time you pleased."

"And what about the other snail?" Thorndyke asked.

"That was made in exactly the same way. It had a thick collet and a small set-screw. So you see, sir, the movement was easily controllable. Supposing you wanted it to discharge at three o'clock in the morning in five days' time, first you set the hands of the clock to three hours after midnight, then you set the day-snail so that the step was just opposite the pin, and you set the week-snail so that the pin was five marks from the step. Then both the snails would be in the correct position by the day-wheel, and at three in the morning on the fifth day both snails would discharge together and whatever you had arranged to happen at that time would happen to the moment. And you notice, sir, that until it did happen, there would be nothing unusual to be seen or heard. To a stranger in the room, there would appear to be nothing but an ordinary grandfather clock with a calendar – unless the little windows for the calendar had been stopped up, as I expect they had been."

Here Thorndyke anticipated a question that I had been about to put, for I had noticed that Polton had described the mechanism, but had not produced the parts for our inspection, excepting the carcase of the clock, which was on the bench.

"I understand that you have the two snails and pallet-bars?

"Yes, sir, and I can show them to you if you wish. But I have been making a model to show how the mechanism worked, and I thought it best for the purposes of evidence, to make it with the actual parts. It isn't quite finished yet, but if you would like to see it – "

"No," replied Thorndyke, instantly realizing, with his invariable tact and sympathy, that Polton wished to spring his creation on us complete, "we will wait until the model is finished. But to what extent does it consist of the actual parts?"

"As far as the calendar goes, sir, almost entirely. The day-wheel was on the clock-plate where you saw it. Then I found the snail and the spindle with the star-wheel still fixed to it. That is practically the whole of it excepting the wooden drums, which, of course, have gone.

"As to the week-mechanism, I have got the snail and the pallet-bar only. There may not have been much else, as the week-snail could have been set on the spindle and would then have turned with the star-wheel."

"There would have had to be a second star-wheel, I suppose," Thorndyke suggested.

"Not necessarily, sir. If it was required for only a single discharge, a pivoted lever, or something that would drop right out when the pallet released it, would do. I have found one or two wheels that might have been used, but they may have come from the gramophone motors or the projectors, so one can't be sure."

"Then," said I, "you can't say exactly what the week-mechanism was like, or that your model will be a perfect reproduction of it?

"No, sir," he replied, regretfully. "But I don't think that really matters. If I produce a model, made from the parts found in the ruins,

378

that would be capable of starting a fire, that will dispose of the question of possibility."

"Yes," said Thorndyke, "I think we must admit that. When will your model be ready for a demonstration?"

"I can promise to have it ready by to-morrow evening," was the reply.

"And would you be willing that Inspector Blandy should be present at the demonstration?"

The answer was most emphatically in the affirmative, and the gratified crinkle with which the permission was given suggested keen satisfaction at the chance of giving the inspector a shock.

So the matter was left, and Thorndyke and I retired, leaving our ingenious friend to a despairing search among the rubbish for yet further traces of the sinister mechanism.

Chapter XVI
Polton Astonishes the Inspector

Polton's revelation gave us both a good deal of material for thought and, naturally, thought generated discussion.

"How does Polton's discovery impress you?" I asked. "Is it a real one, do you think, or is it possible that he has only found a mare's nest?"

"We must wait until we have seen the model," Thorndyke replied. "But I attach great weight to his opinions for several reasons."

"As, for instance – ?"

"Well, first there is Polton himself. He is a profound mechanician, with the true mechanician's insight and imagination. He reads a certain function into the machine which he has mentally reconstructed, and he is probably right. Then there is the matter which we were discussing recently – the puzzling, contradictory nature of the case. We agreed that the whole group of events looks abnormal, that it suggests a connected group of events, intentionally brought about, with an unlawful purpose behind it, but there is not a particle of positive evidence connecting anyone with those events in the character of agent. The crux of the matter has been from the first the impossibility of connecting Haire with the outbreak of the fire. His alibi seemed to be unchallengeable, for not only was he far away, days before the fire broke out, and not only was there no trace of any fire-raising appliance, but the presence of the other man in the rooms seemed to exclude the possibility of any such appliance having been used.

"But if Polton's discovery turns out to be a real one, all these difficulties disappear. The impossible has become possible, and even probable. It has become possible for Haire to have raised the fire while he was hundreds of miles away, and the appliance used was so ordinary in appearance that it would have passed unnoticed by the man who was living in the rooms. If Polton is right, he has supplied the missing link which brings the whole case together."

"You speak of probability," I objected. "Aren't you putting it too high? At the most, Polton can prove that the mechanism could have been used for fire-raising, but what is the evidence that it was actually so used?"

"There is no direct evidence," Thorndyke admitted. "But consider all the circumstances. The fire, itself, looked like the work of an incendiary, and all the other facts supported that view. The fatal objection was the apparent physical impossibility of the fire having been purposely raised. But Polton's discovery – if we accept it provisionally – removes the impossibility. Here is a mechanism which could have been used to raise the fire, and for which no other use can be discovered. That, I say, establishes a probability that it was so used, and that probability would remain even if it could be proved that the mechanism had some legitimate function."

"Perhaps you are right," said I. "At any rate, I think Blandy will agree with you. Is he coming to the demonstration?"

"Yes. I notified him and invited him to come. I couldn't do less and, in fact, though I have no great love for the man, I respect his abilities. He will be here punctually at eight o'clock to-night."

In effect, the inspector was more than punctual, for he turned up, in a state of undisguised excitement, at half-past seven. I need not repeat his adulatory greeting of my colleague, nor the latter's disclaimer of any merit in the matter. But I noted that he appeared to be genuinely grateful for Thorndyke's help and much more frank and open in his manner than he had usually been.

As the demonstration had been arranged for eight, we occupied the interval by giving him a general outline of the mechanism while he fortified himself with a glass of sherry (which Thorndyke had, in some way, ascertained to be his particular weakness) and listened with intense attention. At eight o'clock, exactly, by Polton's newly-completed regulator, the creator of that incomparable time-keeper appeared and announced that the model was ready for inspection, and we all, thereupon, followed him up to the laboratory floor.

As we entered the big workroom, Blandy cast an inquisitive glance round at the appliances and apparatus that filled the shelves and occupied the benches. Then he espied the model and, approaching it, gazed at it with devouring attention.

It was certainly an impressive object, and at the first glance I found it a little confusing, and not exactly what I had expected, but as the demonstration proceeded, these difficulties disappeared.

"Before I start the movement," Polton began, "I had better explain one or two things. This is a demonstration model, and it differs in some respects from the actual mechanism. That mechanism was attached to an eight-day clock, and it moved once in twenty-four hours. This one moves once in an abbreviated day of thirty seconds."

"Good gracious!" exclaimed Blandy. "How marvellous are the powers of the horologist! But I am glad that it is only a temporary arrangement. At that rate, we should all be old men in about twenty minutes."

"Well, sir," said Polton, with an apologetic and crinkly smile, "you wouldn't want to stand here for five days to see it work. But the calendar movement is exactly the same as that in Mr. Haire's clock – in fact, it is made from the actual parts that I found in your box, excepting the two wooden drums and the ratchet pulley that carries the cord and weight. Those I had to supply, but the spindle that carries the drums, I found with the star-wheel on it.

"As we haven't got the clock, I have made a simple little clock to turn the snail, like those that are used to turn an equatorial telescope. You can ignore that. But the rest of the movement is driven by this little weight, just as the original was. Then, as to the addition that someone had made to the calendar, I have fixed the week-snail to the end of the spindle. I don't suppose that is how it was done, but that doesn't matter. This shows how the snail and pallet-bar worked, which is the important point."

"And what is that contraption in the bowl?" asked Blandy.

"That," Polton replied a little evasively, "you can disregard for the moment. It is a purely conjectural arrangement for starting the fire. I don't suggest that it is like the one that was used. It is merely to demonstrate the possibility."

"Exactly," said Blandy. "The possibility is the point that matters."

"Well," Polton continued, "that is all that I need explain. I have fitted the little clock with a dial and one hand so that you can follow the time and, of course, the day of the week and the day of the month are shown on the two drums. And now we can set it going. You see that the day-drum shows Sunday and the date-drum shows the first, and the hand on the dial shows just after three o'clock, so it has just turned three o'clock on Sunday morning. And, if you look at the week-snail, you will see that it is set to discharge on the fifth day – that is, at three o'clock on Friday morning. And now here goes."

He pulled up the little weight by its cord and released some sort of stop. Forthwith the little conical pendulum began to gyrate rapidly, and the single hand to travel round the dial, while Polton watched it ecstatically and chanted out the events as they occurred.

"Six a.m., nine a.m., twelve noon, three p.m., six p.m., nine p.m., midnight."

Here he paused with his eye on the dial, and we all watched expectantly as the hand moved swiftly towards the figure three. As it approached there was a soft click accompanied by a slight movement of the two drums. Then the hand reached the figure and there was another click and, immediately, the two drums turned, and Sunday, the first, became Monday, the second.

So the rather weird-looking machine went on. The little pendulum gyrated madly, the hand moved rapidly round the dial, and at each alternate three o'clock there came the soft click, and then the two drums moved together and showed a new day. Meanwhile, Polton continued to chant out his announcements – rather unnecessarily, as I thought, for the thing was obvious enough.

"Tuesday, the third, Wednesday, the fourth, Thursday, the fifth, six a.m., nine a.m., noon, three p.m., six p.m., nine p.m., midnight – now, look out for Friday morning."

I think we were all as excited as he was, and we gazed at the dial with the most intense expectancy as the hand approached the figure, and the first warning click sounded. Then the hand reached the hour mark and, immediately, there was a double click, followed by a faint whirring sound, and suddenly a cloud of white smoke shot up from the bowl and was instantly followed by a sheet of flame.

"My word!" exclaimed Blandy, "there's no nonsense about that. Would you mind showing us how that was done, Mr. Polton?"

"It was quite a simple and crude affair," Polton replied, apologetically, "but, you see, I am not a chemist."

"The simpler, the better," said Blandy, "for it was quite effectual. I wish you had shown it to us before you let it off."

"That's all right, sir," said Polton. "I've got another ready to show you, but I thought I would like you to see how it worked before I gave you the details."

"Quite right, too, Polton," said I. "The conjurer should always do the trick first, and not spoil the effect by giving the explanation in advance. But we want to see how it was done, now."

With a crinkly smile of satisfaction, Polton went to a cupboard, from which he brought out a second enamelled iron bowl and, with the greatest care, carried it across to the bench.

"It is quite a primitive arrangement, you see," said he. "I have just put a few celluloid films in the bowl, and on the top one I have put a ring of this powder, which is a mixture of loaf sugar and chlorate of potash, both finely powdered and thoroughly stirred together. In the middle of the ring is this little wide mouthed bottle, containing a small quantity of strong sulphuric acid. Now, as soon as any of the acid touches the mixture, it will burst into flame, so all that is necessary to start the fire is to capsize the bottle and spill the acid on the chlorate mixture.

"You see how I did that. When the escapement discharged, it released this small wheel, which was driven by a separate spring, and the wheel then began to spin and wind up this thin cord, the other end of which was attached to this spindle carrying this long wire lever. As soon

383

as the cord tightened up, it carried the lever across the bowl until it struck the little bottle and knocked it over. You notice that I stood the bottle inside an iron washer so that it couldn't slide, but must fall over when it was struck."

"A most remarkable monument of human ingenuity," commented Blandy, beaming benevolently on our gratified artificer. "I regard you, Mr. Polton, with respectful astonishment as a worker of mechanical miracles. Would it be possible to repeat the experiment for the benefit of the less gifted observer?"

Polton was only too delighted to repeat his triumph. Removing the first bowl, in which the fire had now died out, he replaced it with the second one and then proceeded to wind up the separate spring.

"There is no need to set it to the exact day," said he, "as it is only the ignition that you want to see. I will give you notice when it is ready to discharge, and you had better not stand too close to the bowl in case the acid should fly about. Now, there are two days to run, that is one minute."

We gathered round the bowl as near as was safe, and I noticed with interest the perfect simplicity of the arrangement and its infallible efficiency – so characteristic of Polton. In a couple of minutes the warning was given to "Look out!" and we all stepped back a pace. Then we heard the double click, and the cord – actually bookbinder's thread – which had fallen slack when the spring had been re-wound – began to tighten. As soon as it was at full tension the spindle of the long wire lever began to turn, carrying the latter at increasing speed towards the bowl. Passing the rim, it skimmed across until it met the bottle and, giving it a little tap, neatly capsized it. Instantly, a cloud of white smoke shot up, the powder disappeared and a tongue of flame arose from the heap of films at the bottom of the bowl.

Blandy watched them with a smile of concentrated benevolence until the flame had died out. Then he turned to Polton with a ceremonious bow.

"Sir," said he, "you are a benefactor to humanity, an unraveller of criminal mysteries. I am infinitely obliged to you. Now I know how the fire in Billington Street arose, and who is responsible for the lamented death of the unfortunate gentleman whose body we found."

Polton received these tributes with his characteristic smile, but entered a modest disclaimer. "I don't suggest, sir, that this is exactly the method that was used."

"No," said Blandy, "but that is of no consequence. You have demonstrated the possibility and the existence of the means. That is enough for our purposes. But as to the details, have you formed any

384

opinion on the methods by which the fire was communicated to the room from its starting-point?"

"Yes, sir," Polton replied, "I have considered the matter and thought out a possible plan, which I feel sure must be more or less right. From Mr. Green's evidence at the inquest, we learned that the whole room was littered with parcels filled with used films, and it appeared that these parcels were stacked all 'round the walls, and even piled round the clock and under the bed. It looked as if those parcels, stacked round and apparently in contact, formed a sort of train from the clock, 'round the room, to the heap under the bed.

"Now, I think that the means of communication was celluloid varnish. We know that there was a lot of it about the room, including a row of bottles on the mantelpiece. This varnish is extremely inflammable. If some of it got spilt on the floor, alight, it would run about, carrying the flame with it and lighting up the films as it went. I think that is the way the fire was led away from the clock. You probably know, sir, that the cases of these tall clocks are open at the bottom. The plinth doesn't make a watertight contact with the floor and, even if it did, it would be easy to raise it an eighth of an inch with little wedges. My idea is that the stuff for starting the fire was in the bottom of the clock-case. It must have been, for we know that the mechanism was inside the clock, and there couldn't have been anything showing outside. I think that the bottom of the clock was filled with loose films, but underneath them were two or three bottles of celluloid varnish, loosely corked, and on top, the arrangement that you have just seen, or some other.

"When the escapement tipped the bottle over – or started the fire in some other way – the films would be set alight, and the flames would either crack the varnish-bottles right away or heat the varnish and blow out the corks. In any case, there would be lighted varnish running about inside the clock, and it would soon run out under the plinth, stream over the floor of the room and set fire to the parcels of films, and when one parcel was set alight, the fire would spread from that to the next, and so all over the room. That is my idea as to the general arrangement. Of course, I may be quite wrong."

"I don't think you are, Polton," said Thorndyke, "at least in principle. But to come to details, wouldn't your suggested arrangement take up a good deal of space? Wouldn't it interfere with the pendulum and the weights?"

"I think there would be plenty of room, sir," replied Polton. "Take the pendulum first. Now, these tall-case clocks are usually about six feet high, sometimes a little more. The pendulum is about forty-five inches overall and suspended from near the top. That brings the rating-nut to about twenty-four inches above the floor level – a clear two feet to spare for the films and the apparatus. Then as to the weights, there was only one weight, as the striking-gear had been taken away. It is a rule that the weight ought not to touch the floor even when the clock is quite run down. But supposing it did, there would be about four feet from the bottom of the weight to the floor when the clock was fully wound – and we can assume that it was fully wound when the firing mechanism was started. As the fall per day would be not more than seven inches, the weight would be thirteen inches from the floor at the end of the fifth day, or at three a.m. on the fifth day, twenty inches.

"That leaves plenty of room in any case. But you have to remember that the weight, falling straight down, occupies a space of not more than four inches square. All round that space there would be the full two feet or even more at the sides, keeping clear of the pendulum. I don't think, sir, that the question of space raises any difficulty."

"I agree with you, Polton," said Thorndyke. "You have disposed of my objection completely. What do you say, Inspector?"

The inspector smiled benignly and shook his head. "What can I say?" he asked. "I am rendered almost speechless by the contemplation of such erudition, such insight, and such power of mental synthesis. I feel a mere dilettante."

Thorndyke smiled appreciatively. "We are all gratified," said he, "by your recognition of Mr. Polton's merits. But, compliments apart, how does his scheme strike you?"

"It strikes me," replied Blandy, subsiding into a normal manner (excepting his smile, which was of the kind that "won't come off"), "as supplying an explanation that is not only plausible but is probably the true explanation. Mr. Polton has shown that our belief that it was impossible for Mr. Haire to have raised the fire was a mistaken belief, that the raising of the fire was perfectly possible, that the means and appliances necessary for raising it were there, and that those means and appliances could have no other purpose. From which we are entitled to infer that those means were so used, and that the fire was actually raised, and was raised by Mr. Gustavus Haire."

"Yes," Thorndyke agreed, "I think that is the position, and with that we retire, temporarily, at any rate, and the initiative passes to you. Mr. Haire is a presumptive fire-raiser. But he is your Haire, and it is for you to catch him, if you can."

Chapter XVII
Further Surprises

The air of finality with which Thorndyke had, so to speak, handed the baby back to Inspector Blandy might have been deceptive, but I don't think it even deceived the inspector. Certainly it did not deceive me. Never had I known Thorndyke to resign from an unsolved problem, and I felt pretty certain that he was at least keeping this particular problem in view and, in his queer, secretive way, trying over the various possible solutions in his mind.

This being so, I made no pretence of having dismissed the case, but took every opportunity of discussing it, not only with Thorndyke but especially with Polton, who was the actual fountain of information. And there were, about this time, abundant opportunities for discussion, for we were still engaged, in our spare time, in the great work of re-arranging and weeding out our large collection of microscopical slides for which Polton had recently made a new set of cabinets. Naturally, that artist assisted us in sorting out the specimens, and it was in the intervals of these activities that I endeavoured to fill in the blanks of my knowledge of the case.

"I have been thinking," I remarked on one of these occasions, "of what you told us, Polton, about that clock of Mr. Haire's. You are of opinion that it is actually the clock to which you fitted the calendar for Mr. Parrish. I don't know that it is a point of any importance, but I should like to know what convinces you that this is the identical clock, and not one which might have been copied from yours, or invented independently."

"My principal reason for believing that it is the same clock is that it is made from the same kind of oddments of material that I used. For instance, I made the pallet-bar from an old hack-saw blade which I happened to have by me. It was not specially suitable, and an ordinary clock-maker would almost certainly have used a strip of brass. But the pallet-bar of this clock has been made from a hack-saw blade."

He paused and seemed to reflect for a while. Then he continued. "But there is another point, and the more I have thought about it the more it has impressed me. Mr. Parrish had a nephew who lived with him and worked as a pupil in the workshop, a lad of about my own age or a little younger. Now this lad's name was Haire, and he was always called Gus. I supposed at the time that Gus stood for Augustus, but when I heard at the inquest the name of Gustavus Haire, I wondered if it might happen to be the same person. You can't judge by a mere similarity of names, since there are so many people of the same name. But when I saw this clock, I thought at once of Gus Haire. For he was in the workshop when I made the calendar, and he watched me as I was working on it and got me to explain all about it, though the principle on which it worked was obvious enough to any mechanic."

"Should you describe Gus Haire as a mechanic?" I asked.

"Yes, of a sort," Polton replied. "He was a poor workman, but he was equal to a simple job like the making of this calendar, especially when he had been shown, and certainly to the addition that had been made to it."

"And what sort of fellow was he – morally, I mean?" Polton took time to consider this question. At length he replied, "It is not for me to judge any man's character, and I didn't know very much about him. But I do know this as a fact: That on a certain occasion when I was making a new key for Mr. Parrish's cash drawer to replace one which was broken, Gus pinched a piece of my moulding wax and took a squeeze of the broken key, and that, later, Mr. Parrish accused me of having opened that drawer with a false key and taken money from it. Now, I don't know that Gus made a false key and I don't know that any money was actually stolen, but when a man takes a squeeze of the key of another man's cash drawer, he lays himself open to a reasonable suspicion of an unlawful intention."

"Yes, indeed," said I. "A decidedly fishy proceeding, and from what you have just told us, it looks as if you were right – as if the clock were the original clock and Mr. Gustavus Haire the original Gus, though it is not quite clear how Mr. Parrish's clock came into his possession."

"I don't think, sir," said he, "that it is difficult to imagine. Mr. Parrish was his uncle and, as he was an old man even then, he must be dead long since. The clock must have gone to someone, and why not to his nephew?"

"Yes," I agreed, "that is reasonable enough. However, we don't know for certain and, after all, I don't see that the identity of either the clock or the man is of much importance. What do you think, Thorndyke?"

My colleague removed his eye from the microscope and, laying the slide in its tray, considered the question. At length he replied, "The importance of the point depends on how much Polton remembers. Blandy's difficulty at the moment is that he has no description of Gustavus Haire sufficiently definite for purposes of identification. Now, can we supply that deficiency? What do you say, Polton? Do you think

388

that if you were to meet Gus Haire after all these years you would recognize him?"

"I think I should, sir," was the reply. And then he added as an afterthought, "I certainly should if he hadn't lost his teeth."

"His teeth!" I exclaimed. "Was there anything very distinctive about his teeth?"

"Distinctive isn't the word, sir," he replied. "They were most extraordinary teeth. I have never seen anything like them. They looked as if they were made of tortoiseshell."

"You don't mean that they were decayed?"

"Lord, no, sir. They were sound enough, good strong teeth and rather large. But they were such a queer colour. All mottled over with brown spots. And those spots wouldn't come off. He tried all sorts of things to get rid of them – Armenian bole, charcoal, even jeweller's red stuff – but it was no use. Nothing would shift those spots."

"Well," I said, "if those teeth are still extant, they would be a godsend to Blandy, for a written description would enable a stranger to identify the man."

"I doubt if it would, sir," Polton remarked with a significant smile. "Gus was extremely sensitive about those teeth, and showed them as little as possible when he talked or smiled. In those days he couldn't produce much in the way of a moustache, but I expect he does now, and I'll warrant he doesn't crop it too close."

"That is so," Thorndyke confirmed. "The only description of Haire that the police have, as I understand, is that given by Mr. Green and that of the man who interviewed Haire in Dublin. Green's description is very vague and sketchy, while the Dublin man hardly remembered him at all except by name, and that only because he had kept the card which Haire had presented. But both of these men mentioned that Haire wore a full, drooping moustache."

"Still," I persisted, "the teeth are a very distinctive feature, and it would seem only fair to Blandy to give him the information."

"Perhaps it might be as well," Thorndyke agreed. Then, returning to the subject of Polton's old acquaintance, he asked, "You say that Gus lived with his uncle. Why was that? Was he an orphan?"

"Oh, no, sir. Only his people lived in the country, not very far away, for he used to go down and stay with them occasionally at week-ends. It was somewhere in Essex. I have forgotten the name of the place, but it was a small town near the river."

"It wouldn't be Maldon?" Thorndyke suggested.

"That's the place, sir. Yes, I remember now." He stopped suddenly and, gazing at his principal with an expression of astonishment, exclaimed, "Now, I wonder, sir, how you knew that he lived at Maldon."

Thorndyke chuckled. "But, my dear Polton, I didn't know. I was only making a suggestion. Maldon happens to agree with your description."

Polton shook his head and crinkled sceptically. "It isn't the only waterside town in Essex," he remarked, and added, "No, sir. It's my belief that you knew that he lived at Maldon, though how you knew I can't imagine."

I was disposed to agree with Polton. There was something a little suspicious in the way in which Thorndyke had dropped pat on the right place. But further questions on my part elicited nothing but an exasperating grin and the advice to me to turn the problem over in my mind and consider any peculiarities that distinguished Maldon from other Essex towns, advice that I acted upon at intervals during the next few days with disappointingly negative results.

Nevertheless, Polton's conviction turned out to be justified. I realized it when, one morning about a week later, I found Polton laying the breakfast-table and placing the "catch" from the letter-box beside our respective plates. As I entered the room, he looked at me with a most portentous crinkle and pointed mysteriously to a small package which he had just deposited by my colleague's plate. I stooped over it to examine the typewritten address, but at first failed to discover anything significant about it, then, suddenly, my eye caught the postmark, and I understood. That package had been posted at Maldon.

"The Doctor is a most tantalizing person, sir," Polton exclaimed. "I don't mind admitting that I am bursting with curiosity as to what is in that package. But I suppose we shall find out presently."

Once more he was right. In fact, the revelation came that very evening. We were working our way through the great collection of test specimens, examining and discussing each slide, when Thorndyke looked up from the microscope and electrified Polton and me by saying, "By the way, I have got a specimen of another kind that I should like to take your opinion on. I'll show it to you."

He rose and stepped across the room to a cabinet, from which he took a small cardboard box of the kind that dentists use for the packing of dental plates. Opening this, he took from it the wax model of an upper denture, complete with teeth, and laid it on the table.

There was a moment's silence as we both gazed at it in astonishment and Thorndyke regarded us with a quizzical smile. Then

Polton, whose eyes seemed ready to drop out, exclaimed, "God bless my soul! Why, they are Mr. Haire's teeth!"

Thorndyke nodded. "Good!" said he. "You recognize these teeth as being similar to those of Gus Haire?

"They aren't similar," said Polton, "they are identically the same. Of course, I know that they can't actually be his teeth, but they are absolutely the same in appearance – the same white, chalky patches, the same brown stains, and the same little blackish-brown specks. I recognized them in a moment, and I have never seen anything like them before or since. Now, I wonder how you got hold of them."

"Yes," said I, "that is what I have been wondering. Perhaps the time has come for the explanation of the mystery."

"There is not much mystery," he replied. "These teeth are examples of the rare and curious condition known as 'mottled teeth', of which perhaps the most striking feature is the very local distribution. It is known in many different places, and has been studied very thoroughly in the United States, but wherever it is met with it is confined to a quite small area, though within that area it affects a very large proportion of the inhabitants, so large that it is almost universal. Now, in this country, the most typically endemic area is Maldon and, naturally, when Polton described Gus Haire's teeth and told us that Gus was a native of Essex, I thought at once of Maldon."

"I wonder, sir," said Polton, "what there is about Maldon that affects people's teeth in this way. Has it been explained?"

"Yes," Thorndyke replied. "It has been found that wherever mottled teeth occur, the water from springs and wells contains an abnormal amount of fluorine, and the quantity of the fluorine seems to be directly related to the intensity of the mottling. Mr. Ainsworth, whose admirable paper in the *British Dental Journal* is the source of my information on the subject, collected samples of water from various localities in Essex and analysis of these confirmed the findings of the other investigators. That from Maldon contained the very large amount of five parts per million."

"And how did you get this specimen?" I asked.

"I got into touch with a dental surgeon who practises in Maldon and explained what I wanted. He was most kind and helpful and, as he has taken an interest in mottled teeth and carefully preserved all his extractions, he was able to supply me not only with this model to produce in court if necessary, but with a few spare teeth for experiments such as section-cutting."

"You seem to have taken a lot of trouble," I remarked, "but I don't quite see why."

"It was just a matter of verification," he replied. "Polton's description was clear enough for us as we know Polton, but for the purposes of evidence, the actual identification on comparison is infinitely preferable. Now we may say definitely that Gus Haire's teeth were true mottled teeth, and if Gus Haire and Gustavus Haire are one and the same person, as they appear to be, then we can say that Mr. Haire has mottled teeth."

"But," I objected, "does it matter to us what his teeth are like?"

"Ah!" said he. "That remains to be seen. But if it should turn out that it does matter, we have the fact."

"And are we going to pass the fact on to Blandy? It seems to be more his concern than ours."

"I think," he replied, "that, as a matter of principle, we ought to, though I agree with Polton that the information will not be of much value to him. Perhaps we might invite him to drop in and see the specimen and take Polton's depositions. Will you communicate with him?"

I undertook to convey the invitation, and when the specimen had been put away in the cabinet, we dismissed the subject of mottled teeth and returned to our task of revision.

But that invitation was never sent, for, on the following morning, the inspector forestalled it by ringing us up on the telephone to ask for an interview, he having, as he informed us, some new and important facts which he would like to discuss with us. Accordingly, with Thorndyke's concurrence, I made an appointment for that evening, which happened to be free of other engagements.

It was natural that I should speculate with some interest on the nature of the new facts that Blandy had acquired. I even attempted to discuss the matter with Thorndyke, but he, I need not say, elected to postpone discussion until we had heard the facts. Polton, on the other hand, was in a twitter of curiosity, and I could see that he had made up his mind by hook or by crook to be present at the interview, to which end, as the hour of the appointment drew near, he first placed an easy-chair for the inspector, flanked by a small table furnished with a decanter of sherry and a box of cigarettes, and then covered the main table with a portentous array of microscopes, slide-trays, and cabinets. Having made these arrangements, he seated himself opposite a microscope and looked at his watch, and I noticed thereafter that the watch got a good deal more attention than the microscope.

At length, punctually to the minute, the inspector's modest rat-tat sounded on the knocker, and Polton, as if actuated by a hidden spring, shot up from his chair like a Jack-in-the-box and tripped across to the door. Throwing it open, with a flourish, he announced "Inspector

Blandy", whereupon Thorndyke and I rose to receive our guest and, having installed him in his chair, filled his glass, and opened the cigarette-box, while Polton stole back to his seat and glued his eye to the microscope.

My first glance at the inspector as he entered assured me that he expected to spring a surprise on us. But I didn't intend to let him have it all his own way. As he sipped his sherry and selected a cigarette from the box, I anticipated his offensive and took the initiative. "Well, Blandy, I suppose we may assume that you have caught your Haire?"

"I deprecate the word 'caught' as applied to Mr. Haire," he answered, beaming on me, "but, in fact, we have not yet had the pleasure of meeting him. It is difficult to trace a man of whom one has no definite description."

"Ah!" said I, "that is where we are going to help you. We can produce the magic touchstone which would identify the man instantly."

Here I took the denture-box from the table, where it had been placed in readiness and, having taken out the model, handed it to him. He regarded it for a while with an indulgent smile and then looked enquiringly at me.

"This is a very singular thing, Dr. Jervis," said he. "Apparently a dentist's casting-model. But the teeth look like natural teeth."

"They look to me like deuced unnatural teeth," said I, "but, such as they are, they happen to be an exact facsimile of Mr. Haire's teeth."

Blandy was visibly impressed, and he examined the model with a new interest.

"I am absolutely astounded," said he, "not so much at the strange appearance of the teeth, though they are odd enough, as by your apparently unbounded resources. May I ask how you made this extraordinary discovery?"

Thorndyke gave him a brief account of the investigation which Polton confirmed and amplified, to which he listened with respectful attention.

"Well," he commented, "it is a remarkable discovery, and would be a valuable one if the identity had to be proved. In the existing circumstances it is not of much value, for Mr. Haire is known to wear a moustache, and we may take it that his facial expression is not at all like that of the Cheshire Cat. And you can't stop a stranger in the street and ask him to show you his teeth."

He handed the model back to me and, having refreshed himself with a sip of wine, opened the subject of his visit.

"Speaking of identity, I have learned some new facts concerning the body which was found in Mr. Haire's house. I got my information from a rather unexpected source. Now, I wonder whether you can guess the name of my informant."

Naturally, I could not and, as Thorndyke refused to hazard a guess, the inspector disclosed his secret with the air of a conjuror producing a goldfish from a hat box. "My informant," said he, "is Mr. Cecil Moxdale."

"What!" I exclaimed. "The dead man!"

"The dead man," he repeated, "thereby refuting the common belief that dead men tell no tales."

"This is most extraordinary," said I, "though, as a matter of fact, the body was never really identified. But why did Moxdale not come forward sooner?"

"It seems," replied Blandy, "that he was travelling in the South of France at the time of the fire and, naturally, heard nothing about it. He has only just returned and, in fact, would not have come back so soon but for the circumstance that he happened to see a copy of *The Times* in which the legal notice appeared in connection with his uncle's death."

"Then I take it," said Thorndyke, "that he made his first appearance at the solicitor's office."

"Exactly," replied Blandy, "and there he learned about his supposed death, and the solicitors communicated with me. I had left them my address and asked them to advise me in the case of any new developments."

There was a short pause, during which we all considered this "new development". Then Thorndyke commented, "The reappearance of Moxdale furnishes conclusive negative evidence as to the identity of the body. Could he give any positive evidence?"

"Nothing that you could call evidence," replied Blandy. "Of course, he knows nothing. But he has done a bit of guessing, and there may be something in what he says."

"As to the identity of the body?" Thorndyke asked.

"Yes. He thinks it possible that the dead man may have been a man named O'Grady. The relations between Haire and O'Grady seem to have been rather peculiar – intimate but not friendly. In fact, Haire appears to have had an intense dislike for the other man, but yet they seem to have associated pretty constantly, and Moxdale has a strong impression that O'Grady used to 'touch' Haire for a loan now and again, if they were really loans. Moxdale suspects that they were not, in short, to put it bluntly he suspects that Haire was being blackmailed by O'Grady."

"No details, I suppose?"

"No. It is only a suspicion. Moxdale doesn't know anything and he doesn't want to say too much, naturally, as Haire is his cousin."

"But how does this bear on the identity of the body?"

"Doesn't it seem to you to have a bearing? The blackmailing, I mean, if it can be established. Blackmailers have a way of dying rather suddenly."

"But," I objected, "it hasn't been established. It is only a suspicion, and a rather vague one at that."

"True," he admitted, "and very justly observed. Yet we may bear the suspicion in mind, especially as we have a fact which, taken in connection with that suspicion, has a very direct bearing on the identity of the body. Moxdale tells me that O'Grady had an appointment with Haire at his, Haire's, rooms in the forenoon of the fourteenth of April, the very day on which Haire must have started for Dublin. He knows this for a fact, as he heard O'Grady make the appointment. Now, that appointment, at that place and on that date, strikes me as rather significant."

"Apparently, Moxdale finds it significant, too," said I. "The suggestion seems to be that Haire murdered O'Grady and went away, leaving his corpse in the rooms."

"Moxdale didn't put it that way," said Blandy.

"He suggested that O'Grady might have had the use of the rooms while Haire was away. But that is mere speculation, and he probably doesn't believe it himself. Your suggestion is the one that naturally occurs to us, and if it is correct, we can understand why Haire is keeping out of sight. Don't you think so?"

The question was addressed to Thorndyke with a persuasive smile. But my colleague did not seem to be impressed.

"The figure of O'Grady," he said, "seems to be rather shadowy and elusive – as, in fact, does the whole story. But perhaps Moxdale gave you a more circumstantial account of the affair."

"No, he did not," replied Blandy. "But my talk with him was rather hurried and incomplete. I dropped in on him without an appointment and found him just starting out to keep an engagement, so I only had a few minutes with him. But he voluntarily suggested a further meeting to go into matters in more detail, and I then ventured to ask if he would object to your being present at the interview, as you represent the insurance people, and he had no objection at all.

"Now, how would you like me to bring him along here so that you could hear his account in detail and put such questions as you might think necessary to elucidate it? I should be glad if you would let me, as you know so much about the case. What do you say?"

Thorndyke was evidently pleased at the proposal and made no secret of the fact, for he replied, "It is very good of you, Blandy, to make this suggestion. I shall be delighted to meet Mr. Moxdale and see if we can clear up the mystery of that body. Does your invitation include Jervis?"

"Of course it does," Blandy replied, heartily, "as he is a party to the inquiry, and Mr. Polton, too, for that matter, seeing that he discovered the crucial fact. But, you understand that Moxdale knows nothing about that."

"No," said Thorndyke, "but if it should seem expedient for the purposes of the examination to let him know that the fire was raised by Haire, do you agree to my telling him?"

The inspector looked a little dubious. "We don't want to make any unnecessary confidences," said he. "But, still, I think I had better leave it to your discretion to tell him anything that may help the inquiry."

Thorndyke thanked him for the concession and, when one of two dates had been agreed on for the interview, the inspector took his leave, wreathed in smiles and evidently well satisfied with the evening's work.

Chapter XVIII
Thorndyke Administers a Shock

"I wonder, sir," said Polton, as the hour approached for the arrival of our two visitors, "how we had better arrange the room. Don't want it to look too much like a committee meeting. But there's rather a lot of us for a confidential talk."

"It isn't so particularly confidential," I replied. "If there are any secrets to be revealed, they are not Moxdale's. He didn't pose as a dead man. The deception was Haire's."

"That's true, sir," Polton rejoined with evident relief. "Still, I think I won't make myself too conspicuous, as he may regard me as an outsider."

The plan that he adopted seemed to me to have exactly the opposite effect to that intended, for, having arranged four chairs around the fireplace with a couple of small tables for wine and cigars, he placed a microscope and some trays of slides on the large table, drew up a chair and prepared to look preoccupied.

At eight o'clock precisely our visitors arrived and, as I admitted them, I glanced with natural curiosity at "the deceased", and was impressed rather favourably by his appearance. He was a good-looking man, about five-feet-nine or -ten in height, broad-shouldered, well set-up, and apparently strong and athletic, with a pleasant, intelligent face, neither dark nor fair, a closely-cropped dark moustache, and clear grey eyes. He greeted me with a friendly smile, but I could see that, in spite of Polton's artful plans, he was a little taken aback by the size of the party, and especially by the apparition of Polton, himself, seated necromantically behind his microscope.

But Thorndyke soon put him at his ease and, when the introductions had been effected (including "Mr. Polton, our technical adviser"), we took our seats and opened the proceedings with informal and slightly frivolous conversation.

"We should seem to be quite old acquaintances, Mr. Moxdale," said Thorndyke, "seeing that I have had the honour of testifying to a coroner's jury as to the cause of your death. But that sort of acquaintanceship is rather one-sided."

"Yes," Moxdale agreed, "it is a queer position. I come back to England to find myself the late Mr. Moxdale and have to introduce myself as a resurrected corpse. It is really quite embarrassing."

"It must be," Thorndyke agreed, "and not to you alone for, since you have resigned from the role of the deceased, you have put on us the responsibility of finding a name for your understudy. But the inspector tells us that you can give us some help in our search."

"Well," said Moxdale, "it is only a guess, and I may be all abroad. But there was someone in that house when it was burned and, as I was not that someone, I naturally ask myself who he could have been. I happen to know of one person who might have been there, and I don't know of any other. That's the position. Perhaps there isn't much in it, after all."

"A vulgar saying," Blandy remarked, "has it that half-a-loaf is better than no bread. A possible person is at least something to start on. But we should like to know as much as we can about that person. What can you tell us?"

"Ah!" said Moxdale, "there is the difficulty. I really know nothing about Mr. O'Grady. He is little more than a name to me, and only a surname at that. I can't even tell you his Christian name."

"That makes things a bit difficult," said Blandy, "seeing that we have got to trace him and find out whether he is still in existence. But at any rate, you have seen him and can tell us what he was like."

"Yes, I have seen him – once, as I told you – and my recollection of him is that he was a strongly-built man about five-feet-nine or -ten inches high, medium complexion, grey eyes, dark hair, and moustache and no beard. When I saw him, he was wearing a black jacket, striped trousers, grey overcoat, and a light-brown soft felt hat."

"That is quite a useful description," said Blandy, "for excluding the wrong man, but not so useful for identifying the right one. It would apply to a good many other men, and the clothes were not a permanent feature. You told me about your meeting with him. Perhaps you wouldn't mind repeating the account for Dr. Thorndyke's benefit."

"It was a chance meeting," said Moxdale. "I happened to be in the neighbourhood of Soho one day about lunch-time and it occurred to me to drop in at a restaurant that Haire had introduced me to, Moroni's in Wardour Street. I walked down to the further end of the room and was just looking for a vacant table when I caught sight of Haire, himself, apparently lunching with a man who was a stranger to me. As Haire had seen me, I went up to him and shook hands, and then, as I didn't know his friend, was going off to another table when he said, 'Don't go away, Cecil. Come and take a chair at this table and let me introduce you to my friend, O'Grady. You've heard me speak of him and he has heard me speak of you.'"

398

"Accordingly, as O'Grady stood up and offered his hand, I shook it and sat down at the table and ordered my lunch, and in the interval before it arrived we chatted about nothing in particular, especially O'Grady, who was very fluent and had a rather pleasant taking manner. By the time my food was brought, they had finished their lunch and, having got their bills from the waiter, settled up with him. Then O'Grady said, 'Don't let me break up this merry party, but Time and Tide, you know – I must be running away. I am glad to have had the pleasure of meeting you, Moxdale, and turning a mere name into a person.'

"With this he got up and put on his overcoat and hat – I noticed the hat particularly because it was rather a queer colour – and when he had shaken hands with me, he said to Haire, just as he was turning to go, 'Don't forget our little business on Thursday. I shall call for you at eleven o'clock to the tick, and I shall bring the stuff with me. Better make a note of the time. So long.' and with a smile and a wave of the hand to me, he bustled away.

"When he had gone, I remarked to Haire that O'Grady seemed to be rather a pleasant, taking sort of fellow. He smiled grimly and replied, 'Yes, he is a plausible rascal, but if you should happen to meet him again, I advise you to keep your pockets buttoned. He is remarkably plausible.'

"I tried to get him to amplify this statement, but he didn't seem disposed to pursue the subject, and presently he looked at his watch and then he, too, took his departure. That is the whole story, and there isn't much in it excepting the date of the appointment. The Thursday referred to would be the fourteenth of April, and that, I understand, is the day on which Haire started for Dublin."

"You say, you understand," said Thorndyke. "Have you not seen the account of the inquest?"

"No. But Mr. Home, my solicitor, has given me a summary of it with all the material facts, including my own untimely decease. But I needn't have said I understand, because I happen to know."

"That Mr. Haire did start on that day?" Thorndyke queried.

"Yes. I actually saw him start."

"That is interesting," said Blandy. "Could you give us the particulars?"

"With pleasure," replied Moxdale "It happened that on that day – or rather that night – I was starting for the South of France. I had left my luggage in the cloak-room at Victoria earlier in the day, as I had some calls to make, and when I had done all my business, I strolled to Wardour Street and dropped in at Moroni's for a late dinner or supper. And there I found Haire, who had just come in on the same errand. He was taking the night train for Holyhead, and as I was travelling by the night train to Folkestone, we both had plenty of time. So we made our dinner last out and we dawdled over our coffee until it was past ten o'clock. Then Haire, who had a heavy suit-case with him, said he thought he would take a taxi across to Euston so, when we had paid our bills, we went out together to look for a cab. We found one disengaged in Shaftesbury Avenue and, when Haire had put his suit-case inside, he called out 'Euston' to the driver, got in, said 'Good-night' to me, and off he went."

"Did he say whether O'Grady had kept his appointment?" Thorndyke asked.

"He just mentioned that he had called. Nothing more, and of course I asked no questions."

"You seemed to think," said Thorndyke, "that the body that was found after the fire might be that of O'Grady. What made you think that?"

"Well, really," Moxdale replied, "I hardly know. It was just an idea, suggested, I suppose, by the fact that O'Grady went to the rooms and I didn't know of anybody else. I thought it possible that Haire might have let him use the rooms while he was away, as O'Grady lives out of town – somewhere Enfield way."

The inspector looked dissatisfied. "Seems rather vague," he remarked. "You were telling me something about a suspicion of blackmailing. Could you give us some particulars on that subject?"

"My dear Inspector," exclaimed Moxdale, "I haven't any particulars. It was just a suspicion, which I probably ought not to have mentioned, as I had nothing definite to go upon."

"Still," Blandy persisted, "you must have had some reasons. Is Haire a man who could be blackmailed?"

"That I can't say. He isn't a pattern of all the virtues, but I know of nothing that a blackmailer could fix on. And he is my cousin, you know. I think what raised the suspicion was the peculiar relations between the two men. They were a great deal together, but they were not really friends. Haire seemed to me to dislike O'Grady intensely, and I gathered from chance remarks that he let drop that O'Grady had got a good deal of money out of him from time to time. In what way I never knew. It may have been in the form of loans, but if not, it would rather look like blackmail."

There was a short silence. Then Blandy, dropping his oily manner for once, said, rather brusquely, "Now, Mr. Moxdale, you have suggested that the burned body might have been that of O'Grady. You have told us that O'Grady was in those rooms on the fourteenth of April, and you have suggested that O'Grady was blackmailing Haire. Now I put it to

400

you that what you really suspect is that, on that day, Haire made away with O'Grady and concealed his body in the rooms."

Moxdale shook his head. "I never suspected anything of the kind. Besides, the thing wasn't practicable. Is it likely that he would have gone off to Ireland leaving the body in his rooms?"

"You are not forgetting the fire," Blandy reminded him.

"I don't see that the fire has anything to do with it. Haire couldn't foresee that someone would set his rooms on fire at that particularly opportune moment."

"But that is precisely what he did foresee," said Thorndyke. "That fire was not an accident. It was carefully prepared and started by a timing mechanism on a pre-arranged date. That mechanism was discovered and reconstructed by our colleague, Mr. Polton."

The statement was, no doubt, a startling one, but its effect on Moxdale was beyond what I should have expected. He could not have looked more horrified if he had been accused of setting the mechanism himself.

"So you see," Thorndyke continued, "that Haire is definitely implicated and, in fact, the police are prepared to arrest him on charges connected with both the fire and the body."

"Yes," said the inspector, "but the trouble is that we have no photograph or any sufficient description by which to identify him."

"Speaking of identification," said Thorndyke, "we learn that his teeth are rather peculiar in appearance. Can you tell us anything about them?"

Moxdale looked distinctly uncomfortable at this question, though I could not imagine why. However, he answered, somewhat hesitatingly, "Yes, they are rather queer-looking teeth, as if they were stained by tobacco. But it isn't tobacco-staining, because I remember that they were just the same when he was a boy."

Having given this answer, he looked from Blandy to Thorndyke and, as neither asked any further question, he remarked, cheerfully, "Well, I think you have squeezed me pretty dry, unless there is something else that you would like me to tell you."

There was a brief silence. Then Thorndyke said in a very quiet, matter-of-fact tone, "There is one other question, Mr. Moxdale. I have my own opinion on the subject, but I should like to hear your statement. The question is: What made you go to Dublin after you had killed Mr. Haire?"

A deathly silence followed the question. Moxdale was thunderstruck. But so were we all. Blandy sat with dropped jaw, staring at Thorndyke, and Polton's eyes seemed ready to start from their sockets.

At length, Moxdale, pale as a corpse, exclaimed in a husky voice, "I don't understand you, sir. I have told you that I saw Mr. Haire start in a taxi for Euston."

"Yes," Thorndyke replied. "But at the moment when you saw Mr. Haire get into the cab, his dead body was lying in his rooms."

Moxdale remained silent for some moments. He seemed completely overwhelmed and, watching him, I saw that abject terror was written in every line of his face. But he made one more effort. "I assure you, sir," he said, almost in a whisper, "that you have made some extraordinary mistake. The thing is monstrous. You are actually accusing me of having murdered my cousin!"

"Not at all," replied Thorndyke. "I said nothing about murder. I referred simply to the physical fact that you killed him. I did not suggest that you killed him feloniously. I am not accusing you of a crime. I merely affirm an act."

Moxdale looked puzzled and yet somewhat reassured by Thorndyke's answer. But he was still evasive.

"It seems," said he, "that it is useless for me to repeat my denial."

"It is," Thorndyke agreed. "What I suggest is that you give us a plain and truthful account of the whole affair."

Moxdale looked dubiously at the inspector and said in a half-interrogative tone, "If I am going to be charged with having compassed the death of my cousin, it seems to me that the less I say, the better."

The inspector, thus appealed to, suddenly recovered his self-possession, even to the resumption of his smile, and I could not but admire the quickness with which he had grasped the position. "As a police officer," he said, "I am not permitted to advise you. I can only say that if you choose to make a statement you can do so, but I have to caution you that any statement that you may make will be taken down in writing and may be used in evidence against you. That doesn't sound very encouraging, but I may remind you that you are, at present, not charged with any offence, and that a statement made voluntarily in advance is more effective than the same statement made in answer to a charge."

"And I," said Thorndyke, "not being a police officer, may go farther and suggest that a statement may possibly obviate the necessity for any charge at all. Now, come, Mr. Moxdale," he continued, persuasively, taking from his pocket a foolscap envelope, "I will make you a proposal. In this envelope is a signed statement by me setting forth briefly my reconstruction, from evidence in my possession, of the circumstances of Mr. Haire's death. I shall hand this envelope to the inspector. Then I suggest that you give us a straight-forward account of those circumstances. When he has heard your account, the inspector will open the envelope and read my statement. If our two statements agree, we may take it that they are both true. If they disagree, we shall have to examine the discrepancies. What do you say? I advise you, strongly, to give us a perfectly frank statement."

The persuasive and even friendly tone in which Thorndyke spoke evidently made a considerable impression on Moxdale, for he listened attentively with a thoughtful eye on the speaker, and when Thorndyke had finished he reflected awhile, still keeping his eyes fixed on my colleague's face. At length, having made up his mind, he said, with something like an air of relief, "Very well, sir, I will take your advice. I will give you a full and true account of all that happened on that dreadful day, suppressing nothing."

He paused for a few moments to collect his thoughts and then continued, "I think I should begin by telling you that my cousin stood to gain four-thousand pounds by my death if I should die before my uncle, Harold Moxdale."

"We knew that," said Blandy.

"Ah! Well, then, there is another matter. I don't like to speak ill of the dead, but the truth is that Haire was an unscrupulous rascal – a downright bad man."

"We knew that, too," said Blandy, "when we learned that he had set fire to the house."

"Then I need not dwell on it, but I may add that he had a deep grudge against me for being the more favoured beneficiary of my uncle's will. In fact, his jealousy had induced a really virulent hatred of me which was apt to break out at times, though we usually preserved outwardly decent relations.

"And now to come to the actual incident. I am the part-proprietor of a sort of international trade directory, and I do a good deal of the canvassing for advertisements, particularly in France. I live out at Surbiton and only go to the office occasionally. Now, a few days before the disaster – the eleventh of April, I think it was – I had a letter from Haire telling me that he was making a business trip to Dublin to try to arrange some agencies and suggesting that he should do some business for me at the same time. I wasn't very keen, as I knew that I was not likely to see any of the money that he might collect. However, I agreed, and eventually arranged to meet him on the fourteenth, on which day I proposed to start by a night train for the South of France. He suggested that he should call for me at my office at half-past four, that we should have some tea and then go to his rooms to talk things over.

"In due course, he turned up at the office, I finished my business, took my bag, and went with him to some tea-rooms, where we had a leisurely tea, and we then went on to his rooms, which we reached about ten minutes to six. As we passed the entrance of the business premises, I saw a man standing just inside, and he saw us, too, for he called out 'Good evening' to Haire, who returned his greeting, addressing him as Mr. Green, and it struck me that Mr. Green looked rather hard at me, as if he thought he recognized me. Then Haire opened the street door with his latch-key and conducted me up the stairs to the first floor, where he opened the door of his rooms with another latch-key, which looked like a Yale.

"Now, all the time that I had been with Haire, and especially at the tea-rooms, I had been aware of something rather queer in his manner, a suggestion of suppressed excitement, and he seemed nervous and jumpy. But when we got inside his rooms and he had shut the door, it grew much more marked, so much so that I watched him rather closely, noticing that he appeared restless and flustered, that there was a wild look in his eyes and that his hands were trembling quite violently.

"I didn't like the look of him at all, and I don't mind admitting that I began to get the wind up, for I couldn't forget that four-thousand pounds, and I knew that poor old Uncle Harold was in a bad way and might die at any moment. But he was not dead yet. There was still time for me to die before him. So I kept an eye on Haire and held myself in readiness in case he really meant mischief.

"But he nearly had me, after all. He had given me a list of the Dublin firms to look at and, while I was reading it, he got behind me to look over my shoulder. Suddenly, he made a quick move and I felt him slip a noose of soft cord over my head. I was only just in time to thrust my right hand up inside the noose when he pulled it tight. But, of course, he couldn't strangle me while my hand was there and, seeing that, he made violent efforts to drag it away while I struggled for my life to keep hold of the noose.

"It was a horrible business. Haire was like a mad man. He tugged and wrenched at the cord, he clawed at me with his free hand, he kicked me and drove his knee into my back while I hung on for dear life to the noose. By degrees I worked round until I faced him, and tried to grab his arm with my left hand while he tugged with all his might at the cord. Then we began to gyrate round the room in a kind of hideous waltz, each pounding at the other with his free hand.

"At last, in the course of our gyrations, we collided with a chair, and he fell backwards on the seat with me on top of him, his head overhanging the seat and my left hand at his throat. When we fell, the

404

whole of my weight must have been on that left hand, for it slid under his chin and thrust it violently upwards. And as his chin went up, I felt and heard a faint click, his head fell loosely to one side and, in a moment, his grasp on the cord relaxed. For an instant or two his arms and legs moved with a sort of twitching motion. Then he lay quite still.

"Cautiously, I picked myself up and looked down at him. He was sprawling limply across the chair, and a glance at his face told me that he was dead. Evidently, the sudden drive of my left hand had broken his neck.

"Shaken as I was, I drew a deep breath of relief. It had been a near thing. An instant's hesitation with my right hand and I should now have been lying with blackening face and starting eyes and the fatal noose secured tightly around my neck. It was a horrible thought. Only by a hair's-breadth had I escaped. Still, I had escaped, and now I was free of that peril forever.

"But my relief was short-lived. Suddenly, I realized that, if I had escaped one danger, I was faced by another. Haire was dead, but it was my hand that had brought about his death. Who was to know that I had not murdered him? Very soon, relief gave way to alarm, alarm to panic. What was I to for my own safety? My first impulse was to rush out and seek a policeman, and that is what I ought to have done. But I dared not. As I took off the noose and held it in my hand, it seemed to whisper a terrible warning of what might yet befall me.

"Suppose I were just to steal away and say nothing to anyone of what had happened. Haire lived alone. No one ever came to his rooms. It might be months before the body should be discovered. Why not go away and know nothing about it? But, no, that wouldn't do. Mr. Green had seen me enter the rooms and perhaps he knew who I was. When the body was found, he would remember that I had been with Haire the last time he was seen alive.

"I sat down with my back to the corpse and thought hard, trying to decide what I should do. But for a while I could think of no reasonable plan. The figure of Mr. Green seemed to block every way of escape. Suddenly, my wandering gaze lighted on the list of Dublin firms lying where I had dropped it. I looked at it idly for a few moments, then, in a flash, I saw a way of escape.

"Haire had intended – so he had told me – to start for Ireland that very night. Well, he should start – by proxy. The people whom he was going to call on were strangers, for he had never been in Dublin before. I would make those calls for him, announcing myself by his name and presenting his card. Thus Haire would make an appearance in Dublin, and that appearance could be cited as evidence that he was alive on that day. Then, when at some later date, his body should be found, it would be beyond question that he must have died at some time after his return from Ireland. My connection with his death would have disappeared and I could snap my fingers at Mr. Green.

"As soon as the scheme was clear in my mind I set to work to execute it, and as I worked, I thought out the details. First I stripped the corpse and dressed it in the pyjamas from the bed. Then, having thrown the bed-clothes into disorder, I placed the body half in the bed, half outside, with the head bent sideways and resting on the floor. The obvious suggestion would be that he had fallen out of bed and broken his neck – a mere accident implicating nobody.

"When I had folded his clothes and put them away tidily on a chair, I looked at my watch. It was barely twenty past six. The whole of this horrid drama had been played out in less than half-an-hour. I sat down to rest awhile – for it had been a strenuous affair while it lasted – and looked about the room to see that I was leaving no traces, but there were none, excepting my bag, and that I should take away with me. The Venetian blinds were lowered – I had noticed that when we came in – and I decided to leave them so, as that was probably how Haire was accustomed to leave them when he went away. So I sat and thought out the rest of my plan. The place was strangely quiet, for by now Mr. Green and his people had apparently shut up their premises and gone away, and there was not a sound in the room save the solemn tick of the big clock in the corner.

"Presently I rose and began, at my leisure, to complete my preparations. There was no need for hurry. It was now only half-past-six by the big clock, and I knew that the Holyhead Express did not leave Euston until eight forty-five. I looked over an open bureau and took from it a few of Haire's business cards and a little sheaf of his bill-heads. When I had stowed these in my bag, I had finished, and as all was still quiet, I picked up the bag, turned away with a last, shuddering glance at the grotesque figure that sprawled over the side of the bed, let myself out as silently as I could, and stole softly down the stairs.

"I need not follow the rest of my proceedings in detail. I caught my train and duly arrived in Dublin about seven o'clock the next morning. I went to a small private hotel – Connolly's – where I wrote in the visitors' book, 'G. Haire, Billington Street, London', and when I had washed and shaved and had breakfast, I went out and made the first of my calls, Brady and Company, where I stayed quite a long time gossiping with the manager. We didn't complete any definite transaction, but I left one of Haire's cards with some particulars written on the back. I made two more calls on that day, the 15th and, during the next three days I visited several other firms, always leaving one of Haire's cards. I stayed in Dublin until the 18th, which I thought was long enough to give the proper impression of a business tour and, in the evening of that day, just before closing time, I made a second call at Brady's, to impress myself on the manager's memory. Then, having already settled up at the hotel, I went straight to the station and caught the 7:50 train which runs in connection with the Holyhead express. I arrived at Euston in the early morning, about 5:55, and took a taxi straight across to Victoria, where, after a wash and a leisurely breakfast, I caught the nine o'clock Continental train, embarking at Folkestone about eleven.

"After that I followed my usual route and went about my ordinary business, canvassing the Bordeaux district for renewals. But I didn't complete the tour, for it happened that in an hotel at Bordeaux I came across a rather out-of-date copy of *The Times* and, glancing through the legal notices, I was startled to see that of Home, Cronin, and Home, announcing the death of my uncle. As this was some weeks old, I thought I had better pack up and start for home at once to get into touch with the solicitors.

"But I had to go warily, for I didn't know what might have happened while I had been abroad. Had Haire's body been discovered? And, if so, what had been done about it? These were questions that would have to be answered before I could safely present myself at Home's office. I thought about it during the journey and decided that the first thing to do was to go and have a look at the house and see whether the Venetian blinds were still down, and if they were not, to try to pick up some information in the neighbourhood. So when I got to Victoria I put my bag in the cloak room and took a bus to Piccadilly Circus, from whence I made my way to Billington Street. I walked cautiously down the street, keeping a sharp look-out in case Mr. Green should be at his door, and avoiding the appearance of looking for the house. But my precautions were unnecessary, for, when I came to the place, behold! There was no house there! Only some blackened walls, on which the housebreakers were operating with picks.

"As I was standing gazing at the ruins, an idler approached me.

"'Proper old blaze, that was, Mister. Flared up like a tar barrel, it did.'

"'Ah!' said I, 'then you actually saw the fire?'

"'Well, no,' said he, 'I didn't see it, myself, but I heard all about it. I was on the coroner's jury.'

"'The coroner's jury!' I exclaimed. 'Then there were some lives lost?'

407

"'Only one,' he replied, 'and the queer thing was that he wasn't the proper tenant, but just a stranger what had had the rooms lent to him for a few days. He was identified by a clay pipe what had his initials, *C.M.*, scratched on it.'

"'*C.M.*!' I gasped. 'What did those letters stand for?'

"'Cecil Moxdale was the poor chap's name, and it seemed that he had been smoking that pipe in bed and set the bed-clothes alight. Probably a bit squiffy, too.'

"Now, here was a pretty state of affairs. Mysterious, too. For the clay pipe wasn't mine. I never smoke a pipe. But obviously, my calculations had been completely upset, and I was in a pretty tight place, for my trip to Dublin had only introduced a fresh complication. I should have to announce myself as alive, and then the fat would be in the fire. For if the body wasn't mine, whose was it? If the dead man was Haire, then who was the man in Dublin? And if the man in Dublin was Haire, then who the deuce was the dead man? It was a regular facer.

"Of course, I could have maintained that I knew nothing about the affair. But that wouldn't do, for there was that infernal Mr. Green. No, I should have to make up some story that would fit the facts and, turning it over in my mind, I decided to invent an imaginary person and let the police find him if they could. He must be virtually a stranger to me, and he must be sufficiently like me to pass as the man whom Green saw going into the rooms with Haire. So I invented Mr. O'Grady and told a pretty vague story about him – but I needn't say any more. You know the rest. And now, Inspector, what about that statement that you have?"

Blandy smiled benignly and, opening the envelope, drew from it a single sheet of paper, and when he had quickly glanced at its contents, he positively beamed. "Dr. Thorndyke's statement," said he, "is, in effect, a very brief summary of your own."

"Well, let's have it," said Moxdale.

"You shall," said Blandy, and he proceeded, with unctuous relish, to read the document.

> *Summary of the circumstances attending the death of Gustavus Haire as suggested by evidence in my possession.*
>
> *Haire had planned to murder Cecil Moxdale, presumably, to secure the reversion of a bequest of four-thousand pounds, and then, by means of a certain mechanism, to start a fire in the rooms while he was absent in Dublin. He prepared the rooms by filling them with inflammable material and planted certain marked, uninflammable objects to enable Moxdale's body to be*

identified. On the 14th of April, he set the mechanism to discharge in the early morning of the 19th. At about six p.m. on the 14th he brought Moxdale to the rooms and attempted to murder him. But the attempt failed, and in the struggle which ensued, Haire's neck became dislocated. Then Moxdale, knowing that he had been seen to enter the premises with Haire, and fearing that he would be accused of murder, decided to go to Dublin and personate Haire to make it appear that Haire was then alive. He started for Dublin in the evening of the 14th and remained there until the evening of the 18th, when he apparently returned to England.

"That is all that is material," Blandy concluded, "and, as your statement is in complete agreement with Dr. Thorndyke's – which I have no doubt is supported by conclusive evidence – I, personally, accept it as true."

Moxdale drew a deep breath. "That is a blessed relief," he exclaimed. "And now what is to be done? Are you going to arrest me?"

"No," replied Blandy, "certainly not. But I think you had better walk back with me to headquarters and let us hear what the senior officers propose. May I take your summary with me, Doctor?"

"By all means," Thorndyke replied, "and make it clear that I am ready to produce the necessary evidence."

"I had taken that for granted, Doctor," said Blandy as he put the envelope in his pocket. Then he rose to depart, and Moxdale stood up.

"I am thankful, sir," said he, "that I took your advice, and eternally grateful to you for having dissipated this nightmare. Now, I can look to the future with some sort of confidence."

"Yes," Thorndyke agreed, "I don't think that you need feel any great alarm, and I wish you an easy passage through any little difficulties that may arise."

With this, Moxdale shook our hands all round and, when the inspector had done likewise, the two men moved towards the door, escorted by Polton.

Chapter XIX
The Evidence Reviewed

"**B**rilliant finish to a most remarkable case," I commented as our visitors' footsteps died away upon the stairs, "and a most magnificent piece of bluff on the part of my revered senior."

Thorndyke smiled and Polton looked shocked.

"I shall not contest your description, Jervis," said the former, "but, in fact, the conclusion was practically a certainty."

"Probability," I corrected.

"In practice," said he, "we have to treat the highest degrees of probability as certainties, and if you consider the evidence in this case as a whole, I think you will agree that only one possible conclusion emerged. The element of bluff was almost negligible."

"Probably you are right," I admitted. "You usually are, and you certainly were in this case. But the evidence was so complex and conflicting that I find it difficult to reconstitute it as a whole. It would interest me very much to hear you sort it out into a tidily arranged argument."

"It would interest me, too," said he, "to retrace our investigation and observe the curious way in which the different items of evidence came to light. Let us do so, taking the events in the order of their occurrence and noting the tendency of the evidence to close in on the final conclusion.

"This was a very singular case. The evidence did not transpire gradually but emerged in a number of successive and perfectly distinct stages, each stage being marked by the appearance of a new fact which reacted immediately on our previous conclusions. There were seven stages, each of which we will examine separately, noting how the argument stood at the end of it.

"The first is the inquest, including the *post mortem*. Perhaps we had better deal with the body first. There were only two points of interest, the neck and the teeth. The dislocation of the neck appeared to me to have occurred before death and I took it to be, most probably, the immediate cause of death. As to the teeth, there was nothing very striking in their appearance, just a little pitting of the enamel. But from the arrangement of the little pits in irregular transverse lines, corresponding roughly to the lines of growth, I did not believe them to have been due to the heat but to have existed during life. I thought it possible that the deceased might have had mottled teeth which had been bleached out in the fire but, as I

410

had never seen a case of mottled teeth, I could not form a definite opinion. I just noted the facts and satisfied myself that the pitting showed clearly in Polton's photograph of the dead man's face.

"And now let us consider the body of evidence which was before us when the inquest was finished and the inferences that it suggested. To me – and also to Blandy – the appearances as a whole conveyed the idea of deliberate arson, of a fire which had been arranged and started for a definite purpose. And since the death of Cecil Moxdale seemed to be part of the plan – if there was a plan – it was reasonable to suspect that this was the purpose for which the fire was raised.

"What especially led me to suspect arson was the appearance of preparation. The room, itself crammed with highly inflammable material, seemed to have been expressly prepared for a fire. But most suspicious to me was the information given by Haire to Green. It seemed designed to create in Green's mind (as it actually did) the fear that a fire might occur. But more than this, it prepared him, if a fire should occur, to decide at once upon the way in which it had been caused. Nor was that all. Haire's statement even suggested to Green the possibility of a fatal accident, and in the event of such a fatality occurring, it provided Green in advance with the data for identifying any body that should be found.

"Then there were the objects found in the ruins which confirmed Green's identification. They were marked objects composed of highly refractory material."

"They would have to be," I objected, "if they were found. All the combustible objects would have been destroyed."

"True," he admitted. "But still it was a striking coincidence that these imperishable objects should happen to bear the initials of a man whose corpse was unrecognizable. The clay pipe was especially significant, seeing that people do not usually incise their initials on their pipe-bowls. But a clay pipe is, as nearly as possible, indestructible by heat. No more perfect means of identification, in the case of a fire, could be devised than a marked clay pipe. To me, these most opportune relics offered a distinct suggestion of having been planted for the very purpose which they served.

"But there is one observation to make before finishing with the positive aspects of the case. It was assumed that the man who was in the house when the fire broke out was a live man, and it was agreed that that live man was Cecil Moxdale. Now, I did not accept, unreservedly, either of these assumptions. To me, the appearances suggested that the man was already dead when the fire started. As to the identity, the probability seemed to be that the man was Moxdale, but I did not regard the fact as

411

having been established conclusively. I kept in my mind the possibility of either a mistake or deliberate deception.

"And now, what conclusions emerged from these considerations? To me – and to Blandy – they suggested a crime. My provisional hypothesis was that Haire had made away with Moxdale and raised the fire to cover the murder, that the crime had been carefully planned and prepared, and that, for some reason, Haire was especially anxious that the body should be identified as that of Cecil Moxdale. That, as I said, was the positive aspect of the case. Now let us look at the negative.

"There were two facts that conflicted with my hypothesis. The first was that when the fire broke out, Haire was in Dublin and had been there for five days. That seemed to be an unanswerable alibi. There was no trace of any sort of fire-raising apparatus known to the experts or the police, indeed, no apparatus was known which would have been capable of raising a fire after an interval of five days. The large and complicated appliances used for the automatic lighting of street lamps do not come into the problem – they would not have been available to Haire and, in fact, no trace of anything of the kind was found. Apparently, it was a physical impossibility that the fire could have been started by Haire.

"The second objection to my hypothesis was in the nature of the injury. A dislocation of the neck is, in my experience, invariably an accidental injury. I have never heard of a homicidal case. Have you?"

"No," I answered, "and, in fact, if you wanted to dislocate a man's neck, I don't quite know how you would go about it."

"Exactly," he agreed. "It is too difficult and uncertain a method for a murderer to use. So that, in this case, if the broken neck was the cause of death, the man would appear to have died from the effects of an accident.

"Thus, the position at the end of the first stage was that, although the case as a whole looked profoundly suspicious, there was not a particle of positive evidence of either arson or murder.

"The second stage was introduced by the disappearance of Haire. This was most mysterious. Why did Haire not return at the expected time? There was no reason why he should not, even if my hypothesis were true. For if he had raised a fire to cover a murder, his plan had succeeded to perfection. The fire had been accepted as an accident, the body had been identified, and the man's death had been attributed to misadventure. And not only was there no reason why Haire should not have come home, there was a very good reason why he should. For his absence tended to start inquiries, and inquiries were precisely what he would have wished to avoid. I could think of no explanation of his disappearance. There was a suggestion that something had gone wrong, but there was no suggestion whatever as to what it was. Nevertheless, the

412

fact of the disappearance tended to make the already suspicious group of events look even more suspicious.

"The third stage was reached when we learned that Moxdale senior was dead and heard of the provisions of his will. Then it appeared that Haire stood to benefit to the extent of four-thousand pounds by the death of Cecil Moxdale. This, of course, did not, by itself, establish a probability that Haire had murdered Moxdale, but if that probability had already been suggested by other facts, this new fact increased it by supplying a reasonable and adequate motive. At this stage, then, I definitely suspected Haire of having murdered Moxdale, though still not without some misgivings. For the apparently insuperable difficulty remained. It seemed to be a physical impossibility that Haire could have started the fire.

"Then came Polton's astonishing discovery, and immediately the position was radically altered. Now, it was shown, not only that it was possible for Haire to have started the fire, but that it was nearly certain that he had done so. But this new fact reacted on all the others, giving them an immensely increased evidential value. I had now very little doubt that Haire had murdered Moxdale.

"But the mystery of Haire's disappearance remained. For he was all unaware of Polton's discovery. To him, it should have seemed that all had gone according to plan and that it was perfectly safe for him to come back. Then why was he keeping out of sight? Why did he not return, now that his uncle was dead and the stake for which he had played was within his grasp? I turned this problem over and over in my mind. What was keeping him away? Something had gone wrong. Something of which we had no knowledge. What could it be?

"Once more, that dislocated neck presented itself for consideration. It had always seemed to me an anomaly, out of character with the known circumstances. How came Moxdale to have a broken neck? All the evidence pointed to a murder, long premeditated, carefully planned, and elaborately prepared. And yet the murdered man seemed to have died from an accidental injury.

"Here another point recurred to me. The body had been identified as that of Cecil Moxdale. But on what evidence? Simply on the hearsay evidence of Green and the marked objects found in the ruins. Of actual identification there had been none. The body probably was Moxdale's. The known facts suggested that it was – but there was no direct proof. Suppose, after all, that it were not. Then whose body could it be? Evidently, it must be Haire's, for our picture contained only these two figures. But this assumption involved an apparent impossibility, for, at the time of the fire, Haire was in Dublin. But the impossibility

413

disappeared when we realized that again there had been no real identification. The men whom Haire called upon in Dublin were strangers. They knew him as Haire simply because he said that he was Haire and presented Haire's card. He might, quite easily, have been some other man, personating Haire. And if he were, that other person must have been Moxdale.

"It seemed a far-fetched suggestion, but yet it fitted the facts surprisingly well. It agreed, for instance, with the dislocated neck, for if Haire had been killed, he had almost certainly been killed accidentally. And it explained the disappearance of the Dublin 'Haire', for Moxdale's object in personating Haire would have been to prove that Haire had been alive after the 14th of April, when the two men had been seen to enter Haire's premises together, and for this purpose it would be necessary only for him to 'enter an appearance' at Dublin. When he had done that, he would naturally return from Ireland to his ordinary places of resort.

"Thus the fourth stage of the investigation left us with the virtual certainty that Haire had raised the fire, the probability that he had murdered Moxdale, but the possibility that the murder had failed and that Haire had been killed accidentally in the struggle. There were two alternatives, and we had no means of deciding which of them was the true one.

"Then, once more, Polton came to our help with a decisive fact. Haire had mottled teeth and was a native of Maldon. Instantly, as he spoke, I recalled the teeth of the burned corpse and my surmise that they might have been mottled teeth. At once, I got into communication with a dental practitioner at Maldon who, though I was a stranger to him, gave me every possible assistance, including a wax denture of mottled teeth and some spare teeth for experimental purposes. Those teeth I examined minutely, comparing them with those of the body as shown in Polton's enlarged photograph of the face and, disregarding the brown stains, which the fire had bleached out, the resemblance was perfect. I did, as a matter of extra precaution, incinerate two of the spare teeth in a crucible. But it was not necessary. The first comparison was quite convincing. There was no doubt that the burnt body was that of a man who had mottled teeth and very little doubt that it was Haire's body."

"But," I objected, "Moxdale might have had mottled teeth. He was Haire's cousin."

"Yes," Thorndyke agreed, "there was that element of uncertainty. But there was not much in it. The mere relationship was not significant, as mottled teeth are not transmitted by heredity but are purely environmental phenomena. But, of course, Moxdale might also have

414

been born and grown up at Maldon. Still, we had the definite fact that Haire was known to have had mottled teeth and that the dead man had had teeth of the same, very rare, kind. So this stage left us with the strong probability that the body was Haire's, but the possibility that it might be that of Moxdale.

"But at the next stage this question was settled by the reappearance of Moxdale in the flesh. That established the identity of the body as a definite fact. But it also established the identity of the personator. For if the dead man was Haire, the live man at Dublin must have been Moxdale. There appeared to be no alternative possibility.

"Nevertheless, Moxdale essayed to present us with one in the form of a moderately plausible story. I don't know whether Blandy believed this story. He professed to, but then Blandy is – Blandy. He was certainly puzzled by it, as we can judge by his anxiety to bring Moxdale here that we might question him, and we have to remember that he did not know what we knew as to the identity of the body. For my part, I never entertained that story for a moment. It sounded like fiction pure and simple, and a striking feature of it was that no part of it admitted of verification. The mysterious O'Grady was a mere shadow, of whom nothing was known and nothing could be discovered, and the alleged blackmailing was not supported by a single tangible fact. Moreover, O'Grady, the blackmailer, did not fit the facts. The murder which had been so elaborately prepared was, specifically, the murder of Cecil Moxdale. Not only was it Moxdale whose identification was prepared for – the motive for the murder was connected with Moxdale.

"However, it doesn't do to be too dogmatic. One had to accept the infinitely remote possibility that the story might be true, at least in parts. Accordingly I grasped at Blandy's suggestion that he should bring Moxdale here and give us the opportunity to put the story to the test of comparison with the known facts.

"We need not consider that interview in detail. It was an ingenious story that Moxdale told, and he told it extremely well. But still, as he went on, its fictional character became more and more pronounced and its details more and more elusive. You probably noticed that when I asked for a description of O'Grady, he gave an excellent one – which was an exact description of himself. It had to be, for O'Grady must needs correspond to Green's description of the man whom he saw with Haire, and that description applied perfectly to Moxdale.

"I followed the narrative with the closest attention, waiting for some definite discrepancy on which one could fasten. And at last it came. Moxdale, unaware of what we knew, made the inevitable false step. In his anxiety to prove that Haire was alive and had gone to Dublin, he gave a circumstantial account of his having seen Haire into the taxi en route for Euston at past ten o'clock at night. Now, we knew that Haire had never gone to Dublin. Moreover we knew that, by ten o'clock, Haire had been dead some hours, and we knew, also, that, by that time, the personator must have been well on his way to Holyhead, since he appeared in Dublin early the next morning.

"Here, then, was a definitely false statement. It disposed at once of any possibility that the story might be true, and its effect was to make it certain that the Dublin personator was Moxdale, himself. I was now in a position to tax Moxdale with having killed Haire and carried out the personation, and I did so with studied abruptness in order to force him to make a statement. You see there was not very much bluff about it, after all."

"No," I admitted. "It was not really bluff. I withdraw the expression. I had not realized how complete the evidence was. But your question had a grand dramatic effect."

"That, however, was not its object," said Thorndyke. "I was anxious, for Moxdale's own sake, that he should make a true and straightforward statement. For if he had stuck to his fictitious story, he would certainly have been charged with having murdered Haire and, as Blandy very justly observed, a story told by an accused man from the witness-box is much less convincing than the same story told voluntarily before any charge has been made. Fortunately, Moxdale, being a sensible fellow, realized this and took my advice."

"What do you suppose the police will do about it?" I asked.

"I don't see why they should do anything," he replied. "No crime has been committed. A charge of manslaughter could not be sustained, since Moxdale's action was purely defensive and the death was the result of an accident."

"And what about the question of concealment of death?"

"There doesn't seem to be much in that. Moxdale did not conceal the body, he merely tried to dissociate himself from it. He did not, it is true, report the death as he ought to have done. That was rather irregular and so was the personation. But I think that the police will take the view that, in the absence of any criminal intention, there is no need, on grounds of public policy, for them to take any action."

Thorndyke's forecast proved to be correct. The Assistant Commissioner asked us for a complete statement of the evidence, and when this had been supplied (including a demonstration by Polton), he decided that no proceedings were called for. It was, however, necessary to amend the finding of the coroner's jury, not only for the purposes of registration, but for that of obtaining probate of Harold Moxdale's will.

416

Accordingly, Thorndyke issued a certificate of the death of Gustavus Haire, and thereby put the finishing touch to one of the most curious cases that had passed through our hands.

The End

418

The

JACOB STREET

MYSTERY

R.AUSTIN
FREEMAN

A 'Dr.Thorndyke' novel

U.S. Title: *The Unconscious Witness*
1942 Hodder & Stoughton, London Cover

Part I – A Plot in the Making

Chapter I
The Eavesdropper

On a pleasant, sunny afternoon near the end of May, when the late spring was just merging into early summer, Mr. Thomas Pedley ("Tom Pedley" to his friends, or more usually plain "Tom") was seated on a substantial sketching stool before a light bamboo easel on which was fixed an upright canvas measuring eighteen-inches-by-twelve. To an expert eye, his appearance, his simple, workmanlike outfit, the leisurely ease with which he handled his brush, and the picture which was growing into shape on the canvas, would all have suggested a competent and experienced landscape painter.

And such, in fact, was Tom Pedley. From his early boyhood, some forty-odd years ago, drawing and painting had been his one absorbing passion, coupled with that love of the countryside that marks the born landscape artist. To him that countryside, largely unspoiled in his early days, was an inexhaustible source of delight and a subject of endless study and meditation. In his daily rambles through meadow or woodland, by farmyards or quiet hamlets, every journey was a voyage of exploration yielding fresh discoveries, new truths of characteristic form, and subtle, unexpected colour to be added to his growing store of knowledge of those less obvious aspects of nature which it is the landscape painter's mission to reveal. And as the years passed and the countryside faded away under the withering touch of mechanical transport, that knowledge grew more and more precious. Now, the dwindling remnants had to be sought and found with considered judgment and their scanty material eked out with detail brought forth from the stores of the remembered past.

The picture which was shaping itself on the canvas was an example of this application of knowledge gained by experience. On the wall of a gallery it would have suggested to the spectator an open glade in some vast woodland. In fact, the place was no more than a scrubby little copse, the last surviving oasis in the squalid desert of a "developing" neighbourhood. From his "pitch", ensconced in a clump of bushes, Tom could hear, faint and far away, the strident hoots of motor cars, the rumble of omnibuses, and the clatter of lorries, and but a hundred yards

421

distant was the path by which he had come, a rutted track that led from a half-built street at one end to a dismantled farmyard at the other.

Nevertheless, apart from the traffic noises, the place was strangely peaceful and quiet, its silence accentuated by the natural sounds that pervaded it. Somewhere in the foliage hard by, a thrush sang joyously, and on a branch just overhead a chaffinch repeated again and again his pleasant little monotonous song. And the solitude was as perfect as the quiet. The rough path seemed to be untrodden by the foot of man for, during the two hours that Tom had been at work, not a soul had passed along it.

At length, as he paused to fill his pipe and take a thoughtful survey of his picture, the sound of voices was followed by the appearance of two men walking slowly along the path, conversing earnestly though in low tones. Tom could not hear what they were saying, though the impression conveyed to him was that their manner was rather the reverse of amicable. But in fact he gave them little attention beyond noting the effect of the dark, sharply defined shapes against the in definite background, and even this interested him but little as his subject required no figures, and certainly not one in a bowler hat. So he continued filling his pipe and appraising his afternoon's work as they walked by without noticing him – actually, he was almost invisible from the path – and as they passed out of sight he produced his matchbox and was about to strike a light when a third figure, that of a woman, made its appearance, moving in the same direction as the others.

This time Tom's attention was definitely aroused, and he sat motionless with the unlighted match in his hand, peering out through the chinks in the bushes which concealed him. The woman's behaviour was very peculiar. She was advancing rather more quickly than the two men, but with a silent, stealthy tread, and from her movements she seemed to be listening and trying to keep the men in sight while keeping out of sight, herself.

Tom watched her disapprovingly. He disliked "snoopers" of all sorts, but especially those who were eavesdroppers as well. However, this was none of his business and, when she had passed out of his field of vision, he lit his pipe, took up his brush, and straightway forgot all about her.

But he had not finished with her after all. He had been painting but a few minutes when she reappeared, and now her behaviour was still more odd. She was returning at a quicker pace but with the same stealthy movements, listening and looking back over her shoulder with something like an air of alarm. Suddenly, when she was nearly opposite Tom's

422

pitch, she slipped into an opening in the bushes and disappeared from his sight.

This was really rather queer. Once more he transferred his brush to the palette hand and, as he listened intently, felt in his pocket for the matchbox for, of course, his pipe had gone out, as a painter's pipe continually does. Very soon his ear caught the sound of footsteps – light, quick footsteps – approaching from the direction of the farmyard. Then a man came into view, walking quickly but with a soft and almost stealthy tread and looking about him watchfully as he went.

Tom, sitting stock-still in his leafy ambush, followed the retreating figure with an inquisitive eye, recognizing him as the shorter of the two men who had passed down the path and wondering what had become of the other. Then the man disappeared in the direction of the street, and still Tom sat like a graven image, waiting to see if there were any further developments.

He had not long to wait. Hardly had the sound of the man's footsteps died away when the woman stole forth from her hiding-place and stood for a few seconds listening intently and peering up the path in the direction in which the man had gone. Then she began slowly and warily to follow, and presently she, too, passed out of sight among the trees.

Tom thoughtfully lit his pipe and reflected. It was a queer affair. What was it all about? The woman was obviously spying on the men, apparently listening to their talk, and mighty anxious to keep out of sight. That was all there was to it so far as he was concerned, and as he was not really concerned in it at all, he decided that it was a "dam' rum go" and dismissed it from his mind.

But the dismissal was not quite effective. The incident had broken the continuity of his ideas and he found it difficult to start afresh. For a few minutes he struggled to pick up the threads, adding a touch here and there, then, once more, he leaned back and surveyed his work, finally getting up from his stool and stepping back a pace or two to see it better as a whole. Now, one of the most important things that experience teaches a painter is when to leave off, and Tom, having considered his picture critically, decided that the time had come. He had painted steadily for a full two hours, and he was a rapid worker in spite of his leisurely manner, rapid because he knew what he wanted to do, made few mistakes, and painted very directly with a rigid economy of work.

Having decided that his picture was finished, excepting perhaps for a little work in the studio to "pull it together," he proceeded forthwith to pack up, closing the folding palette and stowing it in the light wooden colour box, strapping the painting in the canvas carrier, and rolling the used brushes in the painting rag. When he had put these things tidily in his satchel, he folded up the easel and stool, fixed them in the carrying-strap, slung the satchel on his shoulder and, having taken a last look at his subject, pushed his way through the undergrowth towards the path.

Arriving at the rutted track, he stood for a few seconds looking up and down it as he refilled his pipe. He was not an inquisitive man, but he felt a mild curiosity as to what had become of the man who had passed and had not returned. His previous explorations had given him the impression that the path, or cart track, came to a dead end where the wood petered out and the new devastations began. Apparently, he had been wrong, there must be some continuation of the track, perhaps holding out possibilities for the landscape painter.

Having lit his pipe, he strolled along the path for some three-hundred yards until he emerged from the shade of the wood into open daylight. And then both his questions were disposed of. The track, or at least the cart-ruts, was visible, passing through the remains of a gateway and meandering through the devastated farmyard towards an area in which stacks of bricks and dumps of various building material foreshadowed a new eruption of houses similar to those that were to be seen beyond. Hard by, on his right hand, was an old, rat-eaten hayrick and, a few yards farther away, a ruinous cart-shed of which the thatched roof had rotted away, exposing the decayed rafters. At these melancholy relics of the vanished farm Tom glanced regretfully, then he turned back and retraced his steps along the path.

He had trudged some two-hundred yards when there was borne to his ear the sound of horse's hoofs and the rumble of wheels, evidently approaching from the direction of the street, and as he came nearly opposite his "pitch", a two-wheeled cart appeared round a curve. He stopped to watch it and to note the interesting effect of the rustic-looking vehicle on the winding track, standing out sharply in dark silhouette against its background of sun-lighted foliage. As it drew near, he backed into the wood to make way for it and exchanged greetings with the man who was leading the horse, and when it had passed, he turned to look at it and make a mental note of its changed appearance in the altered conditions of light, until it disappeared round a bend of the track, whereupon he resumed his advance towards the town, stepping out briskly and becoming aware of an increasing interest in the meal which was awaiting him at the end of his journey. At the top of the path where it opened on the half-built street, he paused for a few moments to look disparagingly on the unlovely scene, which but a year ago had still been country. Then, having exchanged a few words with an elderly bricklayer

424

who appeared to be standing guard over a stack of bricks, he strode away towards the main road to take up his position at the bus stop.

Here he had a considerable time to wait, and he spent it pacing up and down, looking expectantly at each turn in the direction whence the omnibus would come. From a young policeman who presently strolled past, he obtained a rather vague statement as to the time when it was due, with the discouraging addition that the last one had passed about five minutes ago. So Thomas resumed his sentry-go and meanwhile turned over in his mind once again that very queer episode in the wood, and he was still cogitating on it when the omnibus appeared and put a welcome end to his vigil.

It was not a long journey, in terms of modern transport, and the rather squalid domain of the speculative builder soon gave place to the established town. Tom's natural stopping-place would have been the Hampstead Road, but he elected to alight at Marylebone Church and approach his destination by way of Osnaburgh Street and Cumberland Market, whereby he presently emerged into a quiet, shabby street of tall, shabby, but commodious old houses, and so to a green-painted wooden gate bearing the number *38A* and flanked by a small brass plate on the jamb inscribed "*T. Pedley*" and surmounted by a big brass bell-pull.

As Thomas inserted his latch-key and opened the gate, he disclosed a feature common to many of the adjacent houses: A narrow passage opening into a paved yard, for Jacob Street was largely a street of studios. Once it had been a fashionable street, the abode of famous painters and sculptors. Now, the famous artists had gone, but the studios remained, some tenanted by artists of humbler status, but most of them converted into workshops. In either case, Jacob Street was a highly eligible place for persons of small means who wanted roomy premises for, as studios are in little demand nowadays and are useless for residential purposes, the rents were surprisingly low, though the accommodation was, of its special kind, admirable.

The studio into which Tom admitted himself after crossing the yard was better adapted for residence than some of the others, being more moderate in height, and he had further adapted it by erecting a light wooden partition in one corner, enclosing a large cubicle which served him as a bedroom. With this and a tall folding screen to enclose the fireplace in winter, or to conceal the sink and the gas cooking-stove when he had visitors, Tom had converted the great bare studio into a convenient and fairly comfortable flat.

Having cleaned his palette, washed his brushes, and washed himself in a big bowl in the sink, he opened a hay-box (disguised by an upholstered top to look like, and serve as, an ottoman) and took out a couple of casseroles which he set on the neatly laid dinner table, opened a bottle of beer and decanted the contents into a fine white stoneware jug, drew up a chair, sat down with a sigh of contentment, and lifted off the lids of the casseroles, one of which proved to contain potatoes (cooked in their jackets) and the other a nondescript kind of stew based on a dismembered fowl.

The table and its appointments offered a summary of Tom Pedley's character and personality. His simple philosophy of life was fairly expressed in his own statement that "a man's wealth can be estimated in terms of what he can do without." Now, the things that Tom could do without were the luxuries and extras that consume money. For entertainments other than museums and public galleries he had no use. He had hardly ever ridden in a taxi, he never smoked cigars, and his single bottle of whisky had lain unopened for a couple of years. He lived plainly, spent little, wasted nothing, and took care of what he had.

By thus thriftily ordering his life, he was able to indulge himself in the things that mattered to him. The beer-jug was a museum piece, as was also the fine ale-glass with its charming engraved design of hops and barley. The little French cheese reposed in a covered dish of Moorcroft ware, the pile of apples in a handsome bowl of beaten bronze, and a finely carved wooden trencher supported the brown loaf. Every object on the table, even including the casseroles, was pleasant and comely to look at, though not necessarily costly, and had been the subject of carefully considered choice. For Tom was an artist to his finger-tips. To him art was no Sunday religion. He loved to have beautiful things around him, not merely to look at but to live with, and he could afford to indulge his fancy, since he did his own domestic work and knew that his treasures were safe from the devastating duster of servant maid or charwoman.

So Tom sat in the fine "Chippendale Windsor" chair at the picturesque gate-leg table and consumed his dinner with placid enjoyment, keeping himself entertained, as is the way of solitary men, with a train of reflections. Principally, his thoughts tended to concern themselves with the curious episode in the wood, which seemed to haunt him to a quite unreasonable extent, for it had been but a trivial affair, and he was not deeply interested in it. Nevertheless, his memory persisted in recalling the incident and filling in details of which he had been unaware at the time, until he was able to visualize a curiously complete picture of the scene and the action. Then his lively imagination took charge and wove a little story around those three figures, and this interested him so much that it presently occurred to him that here was the making of quite a good subject picture of a simple kind, and he decided to try an experimental sketch and see what he could make of it.

426

When he had finished his dinner, he proceeded to wash up, still turning the project over in his mind. The washing up was not a protracted business, for he had learned to economize in the use of plates and dishes. There was, in fact, only one plate and a knife and fork and, when these had been dealt with and tidily stowed away, together with the casseroles, in a great French armoire, he was ready to begin. Taking his fresh painting from the canvas-carrier, he set it on an easel and, selecting a smaller spare canvas, put that on another easel alongside, set his palette, and fell to work, first roughing in some of the background from his painting and then proceeding to the disposition of the figures.

The subject of the projected picture was to be "*The Eavesdropper*", and this seemed to require that the woman should be the principal figure, placed as near as possible in the foreground and painted in some detail on a sufficient scale. Accordingly, he began with her, first blocking in a flat grey silhouette to get the form and the pose and then proceeding to colour and detail. And as he worked he was surprised to find how much he remembered and how little he had to invent. The gleam of sunlight which had fallen on the woman as she retired, lighting up her hair like burnished gold and picking out bright spots on her clothing, came back to him vividly, and when he had put in a few lively touches of positive colour to render the effect, there seemed little more to do. Roughly as the figure was indicated, it recalled the appearance of the woman exactly as he had seen her.

The same was true of the male figures, though as they were more distant they could be painted more simply. In their definitely urban dress they were not very pictorial but, as this was only a preliminary sketch, Tom decided to keep to the actual facts. And here again he was surprised to note how much he had seen in those casual glances without conscious observation. In fact, when he had put in the two figures from memory not only had he rendered admirably the argumentative pose and action but he had put in more distinctive detail than the distance of the figures required.

For over an hour he worked away with great enjoyment until the little sketch was completed so far as it need be. Then he "knocked off", cleaned his palette, washed his brushes and, after a glance at the old "hood" clock on the wall, proceeded to smarten himself up with a view to an informal call on his bachelor friend, Dr. Oldfield, who lived hard by in Osnaburgh Street, with whom it was his custom to spend an occasional evening in pleasant, companionable gossip and perhaps a game of chess. But they were not often reduced to that resource, for the doctor was something of an artist, and they had plenty of material for interesting and sympathetic conversation.

When he had refilled his tobacco pouch from a tin and brushed his hat, Tom stood awhile before the easel considering critically the newly finished sketch. It had been interesting enough in the doing but, now that it was done, he found it a little disappointing. As a subject picture, it was somewhat indefinite and lacking in matter. In short, it was hardly a subject picture at all, but rather a landscape with figures. However, it could be reconsidered and perhaps elaborated if that should seem worthwhile and, having reached this conclusion, Tom took his gloves and stick and set forth en route for Osnaburgh Street.

Chapter II
Mr. Blandy

One afternoon about a week after his expedition to the wood, Tom Pedley was engaged in his studio in tidying up the painting that he had done on that occasion. At the moment he was working with a sharp scraper, cutting off objectionable lumps of paint and generally levelling down the surface preparatory to some further touches to "pull the painting together". He had just stepped back to take a look at the picture as a whole when the jangling of the studio bell in the yard outside announced a visitor, whereupon he went out and, traversing the yard and the passage, threw open the large outer gate, disclosing a small person carrying a leather bag.

"Why, it's Mr. Polton," he exclaimed in a tone of relief.

"Yes, sir," said the small gentleman, greeting him with a pleasant and curiously crinkly smile. "I thought I might take the liberty of calling — "

"Now, don't talk nonsense," Tom interrupted. "You know quite well that I am always delighted to see you. Come along in."

"It is very good of you, sir, to say that," said Polton, as Tom shut the gate and led the way down the passage, "but I hope I am not disturbing you. I see," he added with a glance at the scraper, "that you are at work."

"Only doing a scrape down," said Tom, "and you wouldn't disturb me if I wanted to go on. But it's close on tea-time. I should have been knocking off in any case."

As he spoke, he glanced up at the old clock, and Polton, following his glance, drew out a large watch and remarked that the clock was about ten seconds fast, "Which," he added, "is not bad going for a timepiece that is nearly three-hundred years old."

As Tom proceeded to fill the kettle and put a match to the gas-ring, Polton placed his bag on the table and, opening it, brought forth a green baize bundle tied up with tape. Unfastening this, he produced a brilliantly burnished tankard which, after a gentle rub with his handkerchief, he held out for Tom's inspection.

"This, sir," said he, "is what brought me here. You said some time ago that you were on the look-out for a pewter tankard, and you made a drawing, if you remember, sir, to show me the shape that you wanted. Now I happened to see this one on a junk-stall in Shoreditch, so I ventured to get it for you."

"But how good of you to think of me!" exclaimed Tom. "And what a perfectly magnificent specimen! And a junk-stall, too, of all unlikely places. By the way, what am I in your debt for it?"

"I got it for a shilling," Polton replied.

Tom looked at him in amazement. "A shilling!" he repeated incredulously. "You don't really mean a shilling. Why, it's quite a valuable piece."

"Well, you see, sir," Polton explained in an apologetic tone, "it had had some bad usage. It was very dirty and it had been all battered out of shape, so it really was not worth more than a shilling. I didn't take advantage of the man. But pewter is a kindly material if you know how to deal with it. I just took out the bruises, put it back into shape, and cleaned up the surface. That was all. I am glad you like it, sir."

"I am perfectly delighted with it," said Tom. He paused, and for one instant – but only one – he thought of offering a consideration for the time and labour that had wrought the transformation. Then he continued, "Here is the shilling, Polton. But it isn't payment. I take the tankard as a gift. You have turned a bit of worthless junk into a museum piece which will be an abiding joy to me, and I am more grateful than I can tell you."

Polton crinkled shyly and, by way of closing the subject, wandered round to the easel to inspect the painting. For some seconds he stood, regarding the picture with a sort of pleased surprise. At length he remarked, "A wonderful art, sir, is that of the painter. To me it looks almost like a kind of magic. Here is a beautiful woodland glade that you have made to appear so real that I seem to feel as if I could walk into it. You must have gone a long way from the bricks and mortar to find a scene like that."

Tom laughed. "A very natural delusion, Polton but, as a matter of fact, I was almost in sight of the bricks and mortar when I was painting. That bit of woodland is just the last remnant of the country in the midst of a new housing estate. It is within a bus ride of this place, and not a long ride at that."

"Indeed, sir," exclaimed Polton. "Now whereabouts would that be?"

"It is out Hendon way. A place called Linton Green, and the wood is still known by its old name, Gravel-pit Wood."

As Tom spoke the name, Polton started and gazed at the picture with a most singular expression.

"Gravel-pit Wood. Linton Green," he repeated in a strange hushed voice. "The very wood in which that poor gentleman was murdered!"

"Oh!" said Tom in a tone of mild interest. "I never heard of that. How long ago was it?"

"The murder was committed last Tuesday."

430

"Last Tuesday!" Tom repeated incredulously. "Why, that is the day on which I painted the picture. Do you know what time it happened?"

"It would have been somewhere about four o'clock in the afternoon."

"Then," Tom exclaimed, "I must have actually been in the wood at the very time when the murder was being committed!"

"Yes, sir," Polton agreed. "I rather thought you must when you mentioned the wood, because the police have issued a description of a man who was seen there about that time, and it seems to be a description of you."

The two men looked at each other in silence for some moments, then Tom commented with a grim smile. "Well, this is a pretty kettle of fish. Do you happen to remember any of the details? I hardly ever see a newspaper, so this is the first that I have heard of the affair."

"I remember all about it," replied Polton, "but I needn't trust to my memory, as I have cut out all the reports of the case and I have got the cuttings in my pocket. You see, sir," he added deprecatingly, "I am rather interested in murders. Perhaps it is because I have the honour of serving a very eminent criminal lawyer. At any rate, I always cut out the reports and paste them into a book for reference."

With this explanation, he produced from his pocket a large wallet from which he extracted a sheaf of newspaper cuttings. Sorting them out rapidly, he selected one, which he handed to Tom.

"That, sir," said he, "is one the which will serve your purpose best. It is from a weekly paper and it gives a summary of the case with all that is known at present. Perhaps you would like to glance through it while I get the tea ready. I know where you keep all the things."

Tom thanked him and sat down to study the cutting while Polton, having examined the kettle, opened the big armoire and began noiselessly to set out the tea-things on the table. The report was headed "*Mysterious Crime in a Wood*", and ran as follows:

> *In the new and rising suburb of Linton Green, near Hendon, there still exists a small patch of woodland, now little more than a dozen acres in extent, known as Gravel-pit Wood. Here, about five o'clock in the afternoon of last Tuesday, a most shocking discovery was made by a labourer who was engaged on the new buildings. This man, Albert Whiffin by name, was sent by the foreman with a message to the clerk of the works whose temporary office was in the half-built street on the other side of the wood. He approached along the cart-track which crosses the wood and*

had nearly reached the entrance when his attention was attracted by a white object among the grass at the corner of a disused cart-shed, and he went off the path to see what it was. Drawing near, he saw that it was the ivory handle of an umbrella and naturally advanced to pick it up, but as he reached the corner of the shed and was just stooping to pick up the umbrella, he was horrified to perceive the body of a man lying among the nettles and rubbish in one of the stalls of the shed. A single glance convinced him that the man was dead, and he made no further examination, but hurried away with the umbrella in his hand, ran across the wood, and reported his discovery to the clerk of the works. The latter sent off a messenger on a bicycle to the police station, and within a few minutes a sergeant and an inspector arrived and were conducted by Whiffin to the shed where the body was lying. It was seen to be that of a well-dressed man about sixty years of age, and the identity was at once established by visiting cards in the pocket, confirmed by the initials engraved on the silver band of the umbrella. These showed the deceased to be Mr. Charles Montagu, of The Birches, Hall Road, Linton Green.

But how had he met with his death? The circumstances plainly pointed to murder, and this was confirmed by evident signs of a struggle in the nettles and the long grass. But, strangely enough, there were no wounds or other injuries. The clothing was somewhat disordered, the collar was crumpled, and there appeared to be slight bruises on the neck, but nothing that would serve to account for death. When, however, the divisional surgeon arrived and made his examination, he decided, provisionally, that death was due to poisoning either by prussic acid or some cyanide. Thereupon a search was made for some container, which resulted in the discovery among the nettles of a small bottle bearing traces of a liquid which had the smell of bitter almonds.

As to the time at which death occurred, as the surgeon made his examination at 5:35 p.m. and he decided that the deceased had been dead not more than two hours, it would seem that it must have taken place about four o'clock. The time is important in connection with the only clue to the mystery. About half-past-four, a carter taking a load of bricks along the track through the wood met a man coming from the direction of the cart-shed. This man was seen also by a bricklayer's labourer, emerging from the wood into the half-built street, and he was seen again by a young constable, who noticed him particularly and has given a description of him which agrees exactly with that of the other two witnesses, and which has been circulated by the police, with a request to the man to communicate with them.

The description is as follows: Height about five-feet-ten, strongly built, age from forty-five to fifty, grey eyes, brown hair and short brown moustache, dressed in a buff tweed knickerbocker suit with buff stockings and brown shoes, buff soft felt hat with rather broad brim, brown canvas satchel over left shoulder, folding stool and some kind of stand or easel strapped together and carried by a handle in the left hand, and a couple of wooden frames, apparently picture canvases, in a holder carried in the right hand.

The constable, who encountered the man at the bus stop in the Linton Green Road, waiting for the east-bound omnibus, reports that he seemed to be rather anxious to get on, as he inquired when the next omnibus was due and was apparently annoyed to learn that the last one had only just passed. He spoke in a deep, strong voice with the accent of an educated man. The conductor of the omnibus also noticed the man and remembered that he alighted at Marylebone Church, but did not see which way he went after alighting.

At the inquest, which was held on Friday, little further light was thrown on the mystery. The medical evidence proved that the deceased died from poisoning by a strong solution of potassium cyanide, either taken by himself or forcibly administered by some other person. There were slight bruises on the neck but nothing to indicate extreme violence and, in a medical sense, there was nothing to show that the poison was not taken by the deceased himself. The police evidence, however, was more definite. The poison bottle bore a number of finger-prints, but although these were very imperfect, the experts were able to say, positively, that they were not those of the deceased or of any person known to the police. This fact, as the coroner pointed out in his summing-up, taken with the signs of a struggle, made it nearly certain that the poison was forcibly administered to the deceased by some other person. The coroner also commented on the significance of the deceased 's profession.

433

Mr. Montagu was a financier – in effect, a moneylender – and a moneylender is apt to have enemies with strong reasons for compassing his death. In the present case, no such person was at present known. As to the mysterious artist, his identity had not yet been ascertained as he had not been traced and had not come forward, and nothing was known of his connection, if any, with the tragedy.

At the conclusion of the summing-up, the jury promptly returned a verdict of Wilful Murder by Some Person or Persons Unknown, and that is how the matter stands. Perhaps, when the police are able to get in touch with the elusive artist, some fresh facts may come to light."

As Tom finished his reading, he handed the cutting back to Polton, who returned it carefully to his wallet and, having put the teapot on the table, silently awaited comments.

"Well," said Tom, "as I remarked before, it's a pretty kettle of fish. I am the mysterious and elusive artist and a possible for the title of murderer. However, the elusiveness can be mended. I had better pop along to the police station to-morrow morning and let them know who I am."

"Yes, sir," Polton agreed earnestly. "That is very necessary. But why wait till to-morrow? Why not go round this evening? The police may succeed at any moment in tracing you, and it would be so much better if you were to go to them of your own accord than to leave them to find you. Don't forget that they have reasonable grounds for suspicion. This murder has been the talk of the town for nearly a week. The papers have been full of it, including the excellent description of you. Probably you are the only person in London who has not heard of it."

Tom laughed, grimly. "By Jove, Polton!" said he. "You are talking like a prosecuting counsel. But you are quite right. I am a suspected person, and it won't do for me to look as if I were in hiding. I will amble round to the police station this very evening."

But Tom's wise decision came too late. Less than half-an-hour later, when they had finished tea, and Polton, having insisted on washing up, was in the act of stowing the tea-things in the great armoire, the jingling of the studio bell was heard from without and Tom went forth to answer the summons. When he opened the gate he discovered on the threshold a tall, clerical-looking man, who saluted him with a deferential bow and a suave smile.

"Have I the pleasure," the stranger inquired, "of addressing Mr. Thomas Pedley?"

434

"You have," Tom replied with a faint grin. "At any rate, I am Thomas Pedley."

"So I had supposed," the other rejoined, glancing at the brass plate, "and I am delighted to make your acquaintance, as I believe that you may be able to help me in certain investigations in which I am engaged. Perhaps I should explain that I am a police officer, and if you would like to see my authority – "

"No, thanks," replied Tom. "I think I know what your business is and, in fact, I was going to call at the police station this very evening. However, this will be better. Come along in."

He preceded the officer across the yard and ushered him into the studio, where Polton was discovered standing on a stool setting the clock to time by his watch.

"Well, I'm sure!" the officer exclaimed. "Here is a delightful surprise. My old and esteemed friend, Mr. Polton! And what a singular coincidence. Have you known Mr. Pedley long?"

"A good time," replied Polton. "We first met in an antique shop in Soho. Parrott's. You remember Parrott – his name was really Pettigrew, and he was the villain who murdered Mr. Penrose."

"I remember the case," said the officer, "though I was not concerned in it. But there is another coincidence, for, by a strange chance, it is a murder case that is the occasion of my visit here."

Tom did not quite perceive the coincidence but he made no remark, waiting for the officer to open the proceedings. Meanwhile Polton tentatively approached his hat, with the suggestion that "perhaps they would rather discuss their business alone."

"You needn't go on my account," said the officer. "There are no secrets." And as Tom expressed himself to the same effect, Polton gladly relinquished the hat and sat down with undisguised satisfaction to listen.

"Now, Mr. Pedley," the officer began, "I am going to ask you a few questions, and it is my duty to explain that you are not bound to answer any if the answer would tend – in the silly official phrase – to *incriminate* you."

"I'll bear that in mind," said Tom, with a broad grin.

"Yes," said the officer, with a responsive smile. "Ridiculous expression, but we must observe the formalities. Well, as a start, can you remember where you were and what you were doing on Tuesday, the eighteenth of May?"

"Last Tuesday. Yes. In the afternoon I was in Gravel-pit Wood, Linton Green. I got there about two o'clock and I came away about half-past-four, or perhaps a little earlier. In the interval, I was painting a picture of the wood, which I will show you if you care to see it."

435

"Thank you," said the officer. "I should like very much to see it, presently. But meanwhile another question arises. It appears from what you tell me that you must actually have been in the wood while the murder was being committed, and yet, although there was an urgent broadcast appeal for information and similar appeals in the Press, you never came forward or made any sign whatever, not even though those appeals were coupled with a description of yourself, and so, in effect, addressed to you personally. Now, why did you not communicate with the police?"

"The explanation is perfectly simple," replied Tom. "Until a couple of hours ago, when Mr. Polton told me about it, I had no knowledge that any murder had been committed."

The officer received this statement with a bland and benevolent smile.

"A perfectly simple explanation," he agreed, "and yet, if I were disposed to cavil – which I am not – I might think of the broadcast and the daily papers with their staring headlines and wonder – but, as I say, I am not."

"I dare say," said Tom, "that it sounds odd. But I have no wireless and I hardly ever see a paper. At any rate, it is the fact that I had never heard of the crime until Mr. Polton mentioned it and showed me an account of it which he had cut out of a newspaper."

Here Polton interposed with a deferential crinkle. "If it would not seem like a liberty, sir, I should like to say that Mr. Pedley showed me the picture and told me where and when he had painted it, and he seemed very much shocked and surprised when I informed him about the murder."

The officer regarded the speaker with a smile of concentrated benevolence.

"Thank you, Mr. Polton," said he. "Your very helpful statement disposes of the difficulty completely. Now, perhaps, I may have the privilege of seeing the picture."

Tom rose and, fetching a rough studio frame from a stack by the wall, slipped the canvas into it and replaced it on the easel.

"There it is," said he, "not quite finished but perhaps all the better for that as a representation."

"Yes," the officer agreed, "as my interest in it is merely topographical, though I can see that it is a very lovely work of art." He stood before the easel beaming on the picture as if pronouncing a benediction on it, but nevertheless scrutinizing it minutely. Presently he produced from a roomy inner pocket a small portfolio from which he took a section of the six-inch Ordnance Map pasted on thin card. "Here,

436

Mr. Pedley," said he, "is a large-scale map of the wood. Do you think you could show me the position of the spot which this picture represents?"

Tom took the map from him and studied it for a few moments while he felt in his pocket for a pencil.

"I think," said be, indicating a spot with the pencil point, "that this will be the place. I am judging by the curve of the footpath, as the individual trees are not shown. Shall I make a mark?"

"If you please," the officer replied, and when Tom had marked a minute cross and handed the card back to its owner, the latter produced a boxwood scale and a pair of pocket dividers, with which he took off the distance from the cross to the nearest point on the path and measured it on the scale.

"A hundred-and-seven yards, I make it," said he. "What do you say to that?"

"Yes," Tom answered, "that seems about right."

"Very well. You were about a hundred yards from the path. From where you were, could you see any person that might pass along that path?"

"I could, and I did. Not very clearly, because I was sitting on a low stool and I could only see out through the chinks in the foliage. But while I was working there, I saw three persons pass down the path, and two of them came back."

"And do you suppose that those persons saw you?"

"I am pretty certain that they didn't. They couldn't, you know. Sitting low among the bushes, as I was, I must have been quite invisible from the path."

"Yes," the officer agreed, "but you could see them. Now, what can you tell me about them?"

"All I can tell you is that they behaved in a rather queer way. At least, one of them did." And here Tom proceeded to give a minute and circumstantial account of what he had seen.

"But my dear Mr. Pedley!" the officer exclaimed, beaming delightedly on the narrator. "This is most important and illuminating. The woman is a new feature of the case. By the way, did anyone else pass?"

"No. These were the only people that I saw until just as I was coming away, when I met a man bringing a cart full of bricks through the wood."

"Then there can be no doubt as to who those people were. One was Mr. Montagu, the other was the murderer, and the woman must have been connected with one or both of the men. What time was it when they passed down?"

"About four o'clock or perhaps a few minutes earlier. It would be about ten minutes or a quarter-of-an-hour later when the man came back."

"Yes," said the officer, "that seems to agree with the evidence. And now we come to the most important point of all: Can you give us any description of them, and do you think you would recognize them if you saw them again?"

"As to recognizing them, I am very doubtful. Certainly I couldn't swear to any of them. And I don't think I could give much of a description. They were a good distance away and I saw them only through the chinks between the branches, and wasn't taking very much notice. However, I will see what I can remember."

With this he embarked on a description of the three persons, rather vague and general, though helped out by questions from the officer, who jotted down the answers in his notebook.

"Yes," the latter remarked as Tom concluded, "not so bad. But yet, Mr. Pedley, I feel that you must have seen more than that. You are not an ordinary observer. You are a painter. Now, a painter's eye is a noticing eye and a remembering eye. Supposing you were to try to paint the scene from memory – "

"By Jove!" Tom interrupted, "I'm glad you said that, for it happens that that is just what I did do, and on the very day, while my memory was fresh. I thought the incident might make the subject for a picture, 'The Eavesdropper', and that evening I roughed out a trial sketch. I will show it to you."

From a collection of unfinished works on a shelf he produced the sketch and set it on the easel beside the larger picture, from which the background had been copied.

"Ha!" said the officer. "Now you see that I was right. The brush is mightier than the word. This tells us a lot more than your description. It shows us what the people really looked like. This figure is evidently Mr. Montagu, hat and coat quite correct, and you have even shown the ivory handle of the umbrella. And the other two are not mere figures – they look like particular persons."

"Yes," agreed Polton, who had been gazing at the sketch with delighted interest, "Mr. Blandy is quite right. But it is really very wonderful. Those two men have their backs to us, and the woman's face has practically no features, and yet I feel that they are real persons and that I should know them again if I were to meet them. Can you explain it, Mr. Pedley?"

"Well," Tom replied, "I can only say that this is an impression of the scene at a particular moment, and that is how these people looked at that moment. You identify a person not only by his face, but by his size, shape, proportions, and characteristic posture and movements. You can often recognize a man by his walk long before you can distinguish his features."

"Exactly," said Blandy, "and that is why our recognizing officers like to watch the remand prisoners in the exercise yard. They can often spot a disguised man by his general make-up and the way he walks or stands, and I am inclined to think that this sketch might be useful to a specialist of that kind. Would it be possible to borrow it and have a photograph made to accompany your description?"

Before Tom could reply, Polton broke in eagerly.

"Why not let me do the photograph for you, Inspector? I could bring my camera here so that you wouldn't have to borrow the sketch. I should like to do it, if you'd let me."

Inspector Blandy beamed on him with ineffable amiability.

"How very good of you, Mr. Polton," said he. "Always so helpful. But it would be a good photograph, and you would have a copy to add to your little collection. I am inclined to accept gratefully if Mr. Pedley will grant us permission."

Mr. Pedley granted his permission without demur, whereupon the inspector, having arranged a date of delivery with Polton, prepared to take his leave.

"By the way," said he, picking up his hat and putting it down again, "there are two little points that we may as well clear up. First, as to the stature of the unknown man and the woman. The man looks distinctly shorter than Mr. Montagu, who was about five-feet-ten. What do you say?"

"Yes," replied Tom. "I should put him at about five-feet-seven. The woman looked taller, but then women do. I should say that she was about the same height."

The inspector made a note of the answer and then said, "When you met the carter, you seemed to be coming from the bottom of the wood."

"I was. As one of the men had not come back, it seemed that the path, which I had supposed ended at the bottom of the wood, must continue beyond, so I went down to see if it did. When I saw that it crossed the farmyard I came back and started homeward."

"Then you must have passed the cart-shed. Isn't it rather remarkable that you should not have noticed the body, or, at any rate, the umbrella?"

"Not at all. There is an old hayrick between the path and the cart-shed. I never saw more than a corner of the shed, and it was the wrong corner. Whiffin, you remember, was coming from the farmyard."

"Yes," said the inspector. "I had forgotten the rick, but I suspect the lady found it useful for stalking purposes. Well," he added, once more taking up his hat, "I think that is all, excepting that it remains for me to offer my most humble and hearty thanks for your invaluable help. It has been a great privilege for me to listen to your very illuminating observations and to be made the beneficiary of your remarkable technical knowledge and skill."

With this final flourish he made his way to the door escorted by Tom, who conducted him to the gate and launched him into the outer world.

"Rather an oily customer, that, for a police officer," Tom remarked when he returned to the studio, to find Polton still gloating over the sketch. "Don't you think so?"

Polton crinkled knowingly, as he replied, "Mr. Blandy is an exceedingly polite gentleman. But he is a very able detective officer, as sharp as a needle and as slippery as an eel. You've got to be very careful with Mr. Blandy. I hope, sir, that you didn't mind my offering to do the photograph. You see, sir, I thought it best that a valuable thing like that should not go out of your possession."

"That was very good of you, Polton. But bless you, it isn't a valuable thing. It is practically a throw-out."

"Oh, don't say that, sir. I have been admiring it and thinking what a charming little picture it is and how wonderfully full of interest. When will it be convenient for me to come and take the photograph?"

"You needn't trouble to bring the camera here. Take the canvas with you and do the job in your own place and, as it seems to have taken your fancy, you had better keep it and let me have a photograph, in case I should decide to paint the subject. The photograph will do just as well for me."

Polton was disposed to protest, but Tom stolidly wrapped the canvas in paper and handed it to him, and a few minutes later he departed, crinkling with pleasure and gratitude, with the little parcel under his arm.

Chapter III
Mrs. Schuiller

In all the busy town that seethed around him, there can have been but few persons whose lives were as untroubled as was that of Thomas Pedley. He had, in fact, not a care in the world. His work yielded a modest income which was more than enough to supply his modest needs, and the doing of that work was a pleasure that time could not stale. He never tired of painting. If he had come into a fortune, he would still have gone on painting for the mere joy of the occupation, and might then have missed the added satisfaction of living by his industry. At any rate, he craved no fortune and envied no one, except, perhaps, those artists whose work he considered better than his own.

Thus, through the uneventful years, Tom pursued "the noiseless tenor of his way" in quiet happiness and perfect contentment, up to the period at which this history now arrives, when we have to record the appearance of a cloud upon his usually serene horizon. It was only a small cloud, but its little shadow was enough to cause a sensible disturbance of his habitually placid state of mind.

The trouble was not connected with the Gravel-pit Wood incident. That had never occasioned him any anxiety, even though he had been aware – with a slightly amused interest – that the police had by no means forgotten his existence. But as the weeks had passed and the "Unsolved Mystery" had gradually faded from the pages of the daily papers, so had it faded from his own memory and ceased to be of any concern to him.

The cloud was, in fact, a feminine cloud. His troubles, like those of Milton Perkins, were connected with the female of his species. For Tom, as the reader has probably inferred, was a bachelor, and it was his considered intention to remain a bachelor. Wherefore, though he liked women well enough, he avoided all feminine intimacies and kept a wary eye on any unattached spinsters who came his way – and as for widows, he viewed them with positive alarm.

Now it happened that, on a certain afternoon, Tom was working with great enjoyment at a subject picture which his dealer had commissioned when the jangling of the studio bell announced a visitor. With a snort of annoyance, he laid down his palette and brushes and went forth to confront the disturber of his peace, when he discovered on the threshold a rather tall woman, dressed – and painted – in the height of fashion, who turned at the sound of the opening gate, and greeted him with a smile that made his flesh creep.

"You are Mr. Pedley, I think," said she.

Tom was of the same opinion, and said so.

"I hope you won't consider me troublesome," she said in a wheedling tone, "but I should be so grateful if you would lend me a sheet of Whatman. I have a piece of work to do, and I want to start on it at once, but I have run out of paper."

Now, if the smile had made Tom's flesh creep, the request positively made it crawl. For he knew – and so must she if she were a painter – that there was an excellent artists' colourman's shop within five minutes' walk of the place where they were standing – from whence, indeed, Tom got most of his supplies. It looked suspiciously like a pretext for making his acquaintance.

"Perhaps I should explain," she continued, "that I am your next-door neighbour – Mrs. Schiller."

Tom bowed. He had observed the recent appearance of a brass plate bearing this name, and was now slightly reassured. At least, she was a married woman – unless she was a widow! In any case, he couldn't keep her waiting on the doorstep.

"I'll let you have a sheet with pleasure," said he. "Won't you come in?"

She complied with alacrity and, as he conducted her along the passage, he asked, "What sort of surface would you like? I generally use *140, Net*."

"That will do perfectly, if you can spare me a sheet. I will let you have it back – at least, not the same sheet, you know, but an equivalent."

"You needn't," said Tom, with a view to heading her off from another visit. "I have a good stock. Just laid in a fresh quire, and I don't use a lot as I work mostly in oil. This is my show."

He indicated the open door and, as she stepped into the studio, his visitor looked around with a little squeak of surprise.

"But how enormous!" she exclaimed. "And how magnificent! I do envy you. My studio isn't really a studio at all. It is just my sitting room, though it is quite a good room, with a nice big window. You must let me show it to you, sometime."

Tom groaned inwardly. A very pushing young person, this. He began to suspect that she must be a widow, and decided that he must "mind his eye".

"Well," he replied, "you don't really need a place of this size to paint in, though, of course, it's a convenience to have plenty of elbow room."

442

He went to a set of wide shelves and, drawing out the imperial size portfolio in which he kept his stock of paper, opened it on the table, and selected a sheet, which he rolled slightly and secured with a turn of string.

Meanwhile, his visitor had taken her stand before the easel and was inspecting the nearly finished picture, a simple, open-air subject such as Tom liked to paint, showing a group of gipsies on a heathy common, tending their fire, with a couple of vans in the background.

"But how wonderful!" she exclaimed. "And how curious and interesting."

Tom paused in the act of tying the knot and looked round suspiciously.

"Why curious?" he asked.

"I mean," she explained, "the extraordinary representationalism. It might almost be a photograph. Do you always paint like this?"

Now Tom held privately the opinion that the comparison of a finished, realistic painting to a photograph was the hallmark of the perfect ignoramus. But he did not say so. He merely answered the question.

"I try to get as near as I can to the appearances of nature but, of course, the best of us fall a long way short."

"Exactly," said she. "Imitative painting must be very difficult, and after all, you can't compete with the photographer. That is the advantage of abstract art. You are not trying to imitate anything in particular. You just let your personality express itself in terms of abstract form and colour. Have you ever experimented in the new progressive art?"

"No," replied Tom. "This is the way I paint, and it seems to me to be the right way, and I suppose my dealers and private clients take the same view, as they are willing to buy my pictures at a fair price. At any rate, such as it is, I had better get on with it."

By way of enforcing this blunt refusal of the attempted discussion, he held out the roll of paper and glanced wistfully at his palette.

"Yes," she agreed, taking the paper from him with an engaging smile, "I mustn't waste your time now, though I should like to talk this question over with you some day. But now I will take myself off, and thank you so much for the loan of the paper. I promise faithfully to repay it."

Once more Tom assured her that no repayment was necessary, though he now realized, hopelessly, that the promise would certainly be kept. Nevertheless, as he bade her *adieu* on the doorstep and watched her trip round to her own door, he resolved afresh to "mind his eye" and ward off any attempt to establish more definitely intimate relations, an admirable resolution but one which, to a scrupulously polite gentleman such as Tom Pedley, presented certain difficulties in practice, as he was very soon to discover. For, of course, the loan of the paper was repaid promptly – on the following day, in fact, and Tom's efforts, as he received the rolled sheet, to "close the incident" failed ignominiously. He did not on this occasion invite his fair visitor to come in. But though he conducted the transaction on the doorstep, the closure of the incident was but the prelude to the opening of another.

"I won't detain you now," said she with a smile that displayed between her scarlet lips a fine set of teeth, "but I do want you to see my studio, and especially I want you to tell me what you think of my work. A few words of criticism from an experienced artist like you would be so helpful. Now, you will come, won't you? Any time that suits you. This afternoon if you like, say about four o'clock. How would that do?"

Of course, it wouldn't do at all if there were any possibility of escape. But there was not. Tom looked at her helplessly, mumbling polite acknowledgments and thinking hard. But what could he say? Obviously he could not refuse, and this being clear to him, he decided to get the visit over at once and take precautions against its repetition.

"Very well," said she, "then we will say four o'clock, and if you are very good and don't slate my pictures too much, I will give you a nice cup of tea."

With a friendly nod and a further display of teeth, she tripped away briskly in the direction of Hampstead Road, and Tom, muttering objurgations, retired to bestow the sheet of paper in the portfolio.

It need hardly be said that the afternoon's visit did nothing towards "closing the incident". As she opened the street door in response to his ring at the bell, removing a cigarette to execute a smile of welcome, his hostess received him as though he had been "the companion of her childhood and the playmate of her youth". She shook his hand with affectionate warmth and, still holding it, led him into a large front room where a brand new easel, flanked by a small table, stood close to the window. Tom cast a comprehensive glance around and rapidly assessed the occupant in professional terms. Apart from the easel and the colour-box, brushes and water pot on the table, it was just a typical woman's sitting room, in which the tea-table with its furnishings seemed more at home than the easel.

"This is my humble workshop," said his hostess, "a poor affair compared with your noble studio, but still – "

"It would probably have been good enough for Turner or DeWint," said Tom. "It's the painter that matters, not the studio. Shall we have a look at some of your work?"

444

"Yes, let's," she replied brightly, leading him towards the easel. "This is my latest. I am not quite satisfied with it but I don't think I will carry it any further for fear of spoiling it. What do you think?"

Tom stared at the object on the easel and gibbered inarticulately. A half-sheet of Whatman had been pinned untidily on a board and covered with curved streaks of bright colour – evidently laid, very wet, on damped paper, producing an effect like that of an artist's colourman's sheet of samples.

"Well," he stammered, recovering himself slightly, "I don't see what more you could do to it. Perhaps the – er – the subject is – er – just a little obscure. Not perfectly obvious, you know. Possibly – er – "

"Oh, there isn't any subject," she explained, "not in an imitative sense, that is. It is just an essay in abstract colour. I propose to call it '*A Symphony in Green and Blue*'. Do you think it sounds pretentious to call it a symphony?"

"I wouldn't say pretentious," he replied, "but I don't much like calling things by wrong names. It isn't a symphony, you know. A symphony is a combination of sounds, whereas this work is a – is a – well, it's a painting."

Mrs. Schiller laughed softly. "You were going to say 'it's a picture', and then you thought better of it. Now didn't you?"

"Well," Tom admitted with an apologetic grin, "it isn't quite what I should call a picture, but then I really don't know anything about this new form of art. I suppose it is an abstract picture."

"That is just what it is, an entirely non-representational abstraction of colour. Rather an extreme example, perhaps, so we will change it for something more representational."

She fished out a portfolio from under a settee and took from it a small mounted drawing which she stood up on the easel.

"The first one," she explained, "is a study of abstract colour. Now this one is an essay in abstract form. But it has a subject. I have called it '*Adam and Eve*'. How do you like it?"

Tom considered this new masterpiece with knitted brows and a feeling of growing bewilderment. It represented two human figures such as might have been drawn by an average child of nine or ten with no natural aptitude for art, in a heavy, clumsy pencil outline filled in with daubs of colour, As the serious production of a sane adult, the thing was incredible.

"They are a good deal alike," Tom remarked, by way of saying something.

"Yes," she agreed, "but of course they would be, as they haven't any clothes, poor things. The bigger one would naturally be Adam, though it really doesn't matter. The title is only a convention. The picture is really a study in essential form."

"I see," said Tom, though he didn't, but he continued to gaze at the work with bulging eyeballs while the lady looked over his shoulder with a curious cryptic smile – which vanished instantly when he turned towards her. After a prolonged inspection with no further comment, he cast a furtive glance at the portfolio, whereupon his hostess removed the figure subject and replaced it by another painting, apparently representing a human head and shoulders and, in character, very much like those "portraits" with which untalented schoolchildren adorn blank spaces in their copybooks. Such, in fact, Tom at first assumed it to be, but the artist hastily corrected him.

"Oh, no," said she. "It is not imitative. I have called it '*Madonna*', but it is just a study in simplification based on the architectural structure of the human head, with all the irrelevant details eliminated."

"Yes," Tom commented, "I noticed that there had been a good deal of elimination. Those brown patches, I suppose, represent the hair?"

"They don't represent it," she replied. "They merely acknowledge and connote its existence. Perhaps, in a non-representational work, they are really superfluous, but they are useful in elucidating the pattern."

This explanation left Tom speechless as did the other selections from the portfolio. They were all much of the same kind, either meaningless streaks of colour or childish drawings of men and animals. Some of them he judged to be landscapes from the appearance in them of green, mop-like shapes, which might have "connoted" trees, and in one the simplified landscape was inhabited by abstract animals suggesting the cruder productions of a toy-shop.

"Well," said Mrs. Schiller as she returned the last of them to the portfolio, "that is my repertoire, and now that you have seen them all, I want you to tell me frankly what you think of them. You need not mind being outspoken. Candid criticism is what I want from you."

"But my dear Mrs. Schiller," Tom exclaimed despairingly, "I am quite incompetent to criticize your work. I know nothing whatever about this modernist art excepting that it is a totally different thing from the art which I have always known and practised. And we can't discuss it because we are not speaking the same language. When I paint a picture I aim at beauty and interest, and since there is nothing so beautiful as nature, I keep as close to natural appearances as I can. And as a picture is a work of imagination and not a mere representation like an illustration in a scientific textbook, I try to arrange my objects in a pleasing composition and to make them convey some interesting ideas. But,

446

apparently, modernist art avoids truth to nature and any kind of intellectual or emotional interest. I don't understand it at all."

"But," she objected, "don't you find beauty in abstract form?"

"I have always supposed," he replied, "that abstract form appertains to mathematics, whereas painting and sculpture are concerned with visible and tangible things. But really, Mrs. Schiller, it's of no use for me to argue the question. We are talking and thinking on different planes."

"I suppose we really are," she agreed, "but it's rather disappointing. I had hoped to profit by your experience, but I see now that it has no bearing on modern art. But never mind, we will drown our disagreements in the teapot. Will you take this chair while I boil the kettle, or would you prefer a softer one?"

"I like a hard chair," replied Tom.

"So do I. Odd, isn't it, that women seem to want a chair stuffed like a feather bed and piled up with cushions? I could never understand why, seeing that they are lighter than men, as a rule, and better covered."

"Perhaps," Tom suggested, as he subsided on to the wooden-seated chair, "it is because they wear less clothes and want the cushions for warmth."

"Well, at any rate," said she, as she put a match to the gas-ring on the hearth which supported a handsome copper kettle, "we are on the same plane in the matter of chairs, so we have one agreement to start with."

She drew up a light mahogany armchair and, seating herself, gave her attention to the kettle, and while it was heating she continued the discussion with a whimsical mock-seriousness that Tom found quite pleasant. In fact, there was no denying that Mrs. Schiller's personality was distinctly attractive if one could forget the atrocities of her painting, and Tom, who liked women well enough so long as they did not want him to marry them, realized with some surprise that he was finding the little informal function quite agreeable (though he was still resolved that this visit should "close the incident"). The excellent China tea was brewed to perfection, the table appointments, including the kettle, were pleasant to look on, and his hostess's bright flippancies kept him mildly amused.

Presently the conversation reverted to the subject of painting, and Tom ventured to seek some solution of the mystery that had perplexed him.

"Have you always painted in the modernist manner?" he asked.

"Always!" she repeated with a smile. "I haven't always painted at all. It is a completely new venture on my part, and it came about quite by chance – a very odd chance it seems when I look back on it. A girl friend

447

of mine asked me to go with her to a show at a gallery in Leicester Square, an exhibition of works of modern masters. I didn't want to go, because I had never felt the least interest in pictures and didn't know anything about them, but she insisted that I must go because everybody was talking about these pictures, and the art critics declared they were the latest discoveries in art.

"So I went and, to my surprise, I was tremendously impressed and interested. The pictures were so different from anything that I had ever seen before, so quaint and curious. They looked as if they might have been done by children. I was really charmed with them, so much so that I decided to try if I could do anything like them. And I found that I could. Isn't it strange? I had never drawn or painted before, and yet I found it quite easy to do. Don't you think it is very remarkable?"

"Very remarkable," Tom agreed quite sincerely, though not quite in the sense that she meant. For him the mystery was now completely solved, though there were other matters concerning which he was curious.

"Do you send into the exhibitions?" he asked. "It is rather necessary if you expect to make a living by your work."

"I haven't actually exhibited," she replied, "but I am getting a collection together in readiness, and I go to see the modernist shows to see what sort of prices works of my kind fetch, or, at least, are offered at. They seem to me rather high, but I notice that very few of the pictures are sold."

"Yes," said Tom, "there are not many picture-buyers nowadays, and the few picture-lovers who do buy mostly prefer work of the traditional kind. But your best plan would be to try some of the dealers who specialize in modernist works. They would know what your pictures are worth in their market, and they might be able to give you some useful advice. They might even buy some of your works – at their own price, of course."

"That's an excellent idea," said she. "I will certainly try it. Perhaps you could give me the names of one or two dealers. Would you?"

Tom shook his head. "My dealers would be no good for you. They are old-fashioned fellows who deal in old-fashioned work. No modernist stuff for them. They'd be afraid of frightening away their regular customers."

"That doesn't sound very encouraging," she remarked with a wry smile.

"I suppose it doesn't," Tom admitted, and in the pause that followed it was suddenly borne in on him that these comradely confidences were not very favourable to the "closure of the incident". And then, in the vulgar but convenient phrase, he "put the lid on it".

"You appear," said he, "to work exclusively in water colour. Do you find that more suitable than oil?"

"The truth is," she replied, "that I have never tried oil painting because I don't quite know how to go about it, I mean as to mixing the paint and putting it on with those queer-looking stiff-haired brushes. But I should like to paint in oil, or at least give the medium a trial." She paused for a few moments. Then in an insinuating tone she continued, "I wonder whether my kind and helpful neighbour would come to my assistance."

Tom looked at her apprehensively. "I suppose I'm the neighbour," said he, "but I don't quite see what you want me to do."

"It is only a modest request," she urged, "but I should be so grateful if, sometime when you are at work, you would let me come and look on."

"But to what purpose?" he demanded. "My painting and your painting are not the same kind of thing at all."

"I know," she agreed. "But, after all, modernist painters use the same materials and implements as artists of the more old-fashioned type. Now, you know all about the methods of oil painting and, if I could watch you when you are working, I should see how you do it, and then I should be able, with a little practice, to do it myself. Won't you let me come once or twice? I promise not to waste your time or interrupt you by talking."

Tom looked at the smiling, wheedlesome face and realized that he was cornered. It would be churlish to refuse, and indeed, utterly unlike him to withhold any help from a fellow artist, no matter how bad. But still it was necessary for him to "mind his eye". It would never do to give this enterprising young woman the run of his studio.

"When I am at work," he said at length, "I like to be alone and concentrate on what I am doing, but I shall be very pleased to give you a demonstration of the technique of oil painting. What I would suggest is that you bring in one of your pictures, and that I make a copy of it in oil, while you look on. Then you can ask as many questions as you please and I will give you any tips as to the management of the medium that seem necessary. How will that do?"

"But it is the very thing that I would have asked for if I had dared. I am delighted, and more grateful than I can tell you. Perhaps you will let me know when I may come for the demonstration."

"I will," he replied. "It won't be for a day or two, but when I have finished the picture that I have in hand, I will drop a note into your letter-

449

box giving one or two alternative dates. And I hope," he continued as he rose to depart, "that you will like the medium and do great things in it."

As he re-entered his studio and occupied himself in cleaning his palette and brushes and doing a few odd jobs, he cogitated profoundly on the events of the afternoon. One thing was plain to him: The "closure of the incident" was "off". The good lady had fairly taken possession of him. Already she had established herself definitely as an acquaintance, and he saw clearly that the next interview would put her on the footing of a friend. It was an unfortunate affair, but he must make the best of it and continue to "mind his eye" – if the word "continue" was strictly applicable.

As to the woman herself, he was completely puzzled. He could make nothing of her. Was she simply an impostor or did she suffer from some extraordinary delusion? The plain and obvious facts were that she could not draw at all, that her watercolour painting was that of an untalented child, and that she seemed to have no artistic ideas or the capacity to invent a subject. But was it possible that she had some kind of artistic gifts which he was unable to gauge? The supposition seemed to be negatived by her own admission that she had never felt any interest in pictures, for the outstanding characteristic of real talent is the early age at which it shows itself. Pope "lisped in numbers, for the numbers came". Mozart and Handel were accomplished musicians, and even composers, when they were small children. John Millais was a masterly draughtsman at the age of five. Bonington died in the twenties with a European reputation, and so with Fred Walker, Chantrey, and a host of others. No, a person who reaches middle age without showing any sign of artistic aptitude is certainly not a born artist.

The only possible conclusion seemed to be that Mrs. Schiller was either a rank impostor or the subject of some strange delusion, and at that he had to leave it. After all, it was not his affair. His concern was to see that he was not involved in any entanglements, and the lady's masterful ways promised to give him full occupation in that respect without troubling about her artistic gifts.

Chapter IV
Mr. Vanderpuye

There are persons, unfortunately too common, who seem to be incapable of doing anything well. Impatience to get the job finished and inability to concentrate on the doing beget slipshod work and faulty results. Conversely, there are some more happily constituted who cannot bring themselves to do anything badly. Of this type Tom Pedley was a representative specimen. To the simplest task he gave his whole attention and would not leave it until it was done to a finish, even though the task was no more than the washing of a teacup or the polishing of a spoon. Hence the demonstration of oil technique, though he secretly regarded it as a waste of time, was carried out with as much thoroughness as if Mrs. Schiller had been a pupil of the highest promise.

"I have brought two of my pictures," the lady explained when she made her appearance on the appointed day, "the '*Symphony in Green and Blue*' the '*Adam and Eve*' subject. Which do you think will be the more suitable?"

"May as well do them both," replied Tom, "as one has some sort of shape in it and the other hasn't. We'll begin with the '*Symphony*'. You seem to have used mighty big brushes and kept the paper uncommonly wet."

"Oh, I didn't use any brushes at all. I just soaked the paper in water, mixed up some emerald oxide and French ultramarine in separate saucers and poured it on in long streaks. When I tilted the board, of course, the streaks ran together and produced those subtle gradations of colour that I have tried to express by the word *Symphony*."

"I see," said Tom with an appreciative grin. "Deuced good method. Labour-saving, too. Well, you can't do that sort of thing in oil. Got to do the blending with the brush unless you work with the knife. I'll show you."

He set up the "*Symphony*" on the easel with a fourteen-by-twelve canvas by its side. Then, on a clean palette, he squeezed out three blobs of colour: Emerald Oxide, French Ultramarine, and Flake White, and, taking up the palette knife, mixed one or two tints to match those of the "*Symphony*".

"We'll follow your methods as far as we can in oil," said he. "We begin with streaks of the deepest colour, add lighter tints at the edges, and then paint them into one another to produce the subtle gradations. Like this."

He fell to work with a couple of large brushes, keeping an attentive eye on the "*Symphony*" and giving from time to time a few words of explanation as to the management of the brush and the mixing of the tints. At the end of a quarter-of-an-hour's work he had produced a copy of the "*Symphony*" which might have been a facsimile but for the difference in the medium. His pupil watched him and listened to his explanations without saying a word until he had finished. Then, as he stepped back and laid down his palette, she exclaimed, "How extraordinary! You've made a perfect copy, and so quickly, too. It is really wonderful, and it looks so easy."

"Easy!" Tom repeated. "Of course it's easy. Any – er – anyone – " (He had nearly said "any fool".) " – can put streaks of colour on a canvas and paint their edges into one another. But, of course," he added hurriedly, "you've got to invent the streaks. Now we'll have a go at '*Adam and Eve*'."

This, however, presented more difficulty. Try as he would, he could not quite attain the childish effect of the original. His figures persisted in looking slightly human and even in differentiating themselves into a recognizable man and woman.

"There," he said as he stepped back and regarded his performance with a grim smile, "I think that will do, though it isn't a fair copy. I seem to have missed some of the 'essential form', but that doesn't matter. You see the method. And now, as a wind up, I'll just show you how to work with the knife. That may suit you better than the brush."

He placed on the easel a slab of millboard and, taking a couple of small, thin-bladed, trowel-shaped knives, rapidly executed another rendering of the "Symphony," while his pupil watched with delighted surprise. Finally, he showed her how to clean the palette and wash the brushes, admonishing her that a tidy worker takes care of his tools and doesn't waste his materials.

"And now," he concluded, "you know all about it. Facility will come with practice, and the ideas you have already, so all you've got to do is to provide yourself with the materials and fire away."

"I will certainly do that," said she, "but I can't tell you how grateful I am." She came close up to him, looking earnestly in his face and laying her hands on his arms (and for one awful moment he thought she was going to kiss him) and exclaimed, "It was so kind of you to take all this trouble for a mere stranger. I think you are a perfect dear. But we aren't really strangers, are we?"

"Well," Tom admitted cautiously, "I've certainly seen you before."

"Now, don't be an old bear," she protested smilingly. "Seen me before, indeed! But never mind. You haven't done with me yet. I want you to come with me to the artists' colourman and show me what I must get for a start. You will do that for me, won't you? Say yes, like a duck."

"Can't very well do that," objected Tom, "as I've never heard a duck say yes, but I'll come to the shop with you and see that you don't waste your money on foolishness. Might as well nip along now and get it done with. Shop's close by. Only take us a few minutes. What do you say?"

She said "Yes" with a sly and very understanding smile, and Tom realized too late that his studied gruffness, so far from fending her off, had only put her on a more intimate footing. So they went forth together, and when Tom had superintended her purchases and seen her provided with the bare necessaries for a beginning, he took up the bulky parcel and escorted her home, and as he handed her the parcel and said "Good-bye" on her doorstep, the effusiveness of her gratitude made him thankful that the farewells were exchanged in a public thoroughfare.

He turned away with a troubled face and a sinking heart. No self-delusion was now possible. He had failed utterly to "mind his eye" and had been definitely adopted, willy-nilly, by this remarkable young woman as her special friend and comrade. And there seemed to be no escape. A coarser and less genial man would have administered an effective rebuff, but Tom was a kindly soul, courteous and considerate by nature and habit and with all the old bachelor's deference to women. Unwillingly, he had to accept the conviction that this unwanted friendship was an established fact to which, henceforth, his old simple, self-contained way of life should be subject.

And so it proved. His new friend was not actually intrusive. She recognized that he was a solitary man who liked to work alone. But somehow it happened that hardly a day passed in which she did not make some kind of appearance. Of course, he had to go in to see her experiments in the new medium (at which he gazed stolidly, his capacity for astonishment having been exhausted) and give her further purely technical advice. Then she would drop in at the studio now and again to ask a question, to offer some little service or to bring some small gift, and the number of chance meetings in the neighbouring streets was such as to confound all the known laws of probability. Thus, insensibly, the intimacy grew and with it the space which she occupied in his life.

Tom observed the process with anxious foreboding and cursed the ill luck that had brought her into his orbit. But presently he began to realize that things were not so bad as he had feared. In the first place, she was not a widow. There was a husband in the background – apparently a

453

German background, a dim figure, but still an undeniable bar to matrimony. So the principal danger was excluded. Then certain other reassuring facts became evident. At first her astonishing familiarity had horrified him, and the endearing phrases and epithets she used had seemed positively alarming, but he soon grew accustomed to being addressed as "Tom" or even "Tommy", and as to the endearments, they appeared to be no more than a playful habit. He realized this as he noted the essential correctness of her conduct when they were together. Never was there the slightest tendency to sentimentality or philandering.

She might call him "my dear" or "duck" or even "Tommy, darling", but the mere words seemed harmless enough – though foolish – in view of her perfectly matter-of-fact behaviour, and Tom, now reassured and satisfied that no real entanglement threatened, made shift to put up with what he regarded as a "damn silly and rather objectionable habit".

As to the woman herself, her personality was not unpleasing. Sprightly, humorous, and amusing, she might have been a quite acceptable companion if he had wanted one – which he emphatically did not – and if she had shown any glimmer of sensibility to art as he understood it. But, though she soon dropped the art-journalist's jargon and tried to interest herself in his work, she really knew nothing and cared nothing about normal art, and lacking that interest, they had nothing in common.

Her appearance, on the other hand, rather interested him and, in his capacity as an occasional portrait painter, he gave it some attention. He would have described her as a luridly picturesque woman: Blonde, showy, and made up in the height of an ugly fashion, with vermilion lips, rouged and powdered cheeks, pencilled eyebrows, and a remarkable mass of fuzzy hair, which had apparently once been bobbed and was now in process of being unbobbed. That hair interested him especially. He had never seen anything quite like it. In colour it was a very light brown, approaching flaxen, but there was something unusual in its texture, something that gave it a peculiar shimmering character when it caught the light and seemed to make the colour variable. Considering the problem of rendering it in a portrait, Tom studied its changing lights and compared it with the greenish-hazel eyes and as much of the complexion as he could make out, finally reaching the conclusion that it was some sort of fake, but what sort of fake he could not imagine.

For the rest, she was a rather tall woman, perhaps five-feet-seven without her high heels, fairly good-looking, with rather small features but a prominent chin and a strong lower jaw. Her most attractive aspect was undoubtedly the profile, and Tom, studying this with a professional eye, decided that it would make quite a good medallion. He even made one or two trial sketches from memory in his notebook with a half-formed intention of offering to paint a medallion portrait, but he abandoned that idea as he realized that the necessary sittings would tend further to cement a friendship that was already too close.

By which it will be seen that Tom was still, so to speak, fighting a rearguard action, still seeking to limit this unsought intimacy. Although he now knew that she could have no matrimonial designs on him, and he no longer feared any attempt to establish a questionable relationship, he disliked the association. He had never wanted a female friend and he resented the way in which this woman had attached herself to him. An eminently self-contained and rather solitary man, his principal wish was to be left alone to live his own life and, as time went on, he found it more and more irksome to have that life pervaded by another personality, and not even a sympathetic one at that. But he saw no prospect of escape, short of a definite snub, of which he was incapable, and in the end he gave up the struggle and, with a sigh of regret for the peace and freedom that were gone, resigned himself to making the best of the new conditions.

But the hour of his deliverance was at hand, little as he could have foreseen it, and little as he suspected the benign character of the agent when he arrived bearing, all unknown, the order of release. And as the darkest hour is that before the dawn, so the beginning of his emancipation occurred at a moment when he felt that the nuisance of this forced intimacy was becoming intolerable.

It was about four o'clock in the afternoon and the lady had just dropped in at the studio with an invitation to tea, which he had firmly declined.

"Oh, rubbish," she protested. "You are always too busy to come and have tea with me – at least you say you are, and I don't believe you. It's just an excuse. Is it my tea or my society you that don't like?"

"My dear Mrs. Schiller – " Tom began, but she cut him short.

"Oh, not Mrs. Schiller! Haven't I told you again and again not to call me by that horrible name? Call me Lotta. I'm sure it's a very nice name."

"It's a most admirable name. Well – er – Lotta – "

"Well, my dear, if you won't come to have tea with me, I shall stay here and make yours for you and help you to drink it, and then I'll take myself off and leave my darling old bear to the peaceful enjoyment of his den. You'll let me stay, Tom, dear, won't you?"

It was at this moment that the studio bell, jangling imperatively out in the yard, broke into the discussion.

"Shall I run out and see who it is?" asked Lotta.

"No. I'd better go. May be able to settle the business on the doorstep."

He strode out along the passage, hoping that it might be so. But when he opened the door and discovered on the threshold his old friend, Mr. Polton, accompanied by a stranger, he knew that no evasion was possible. He would have to invite them in.

"Good afternoon, sir," said Polton, greeting him with a cheerful and crinkly smile. "I have taken the liberty of bringing you a client who would like you to paint his portrait. Am I right in using the word 'client'?"

"Well, we usually call them sitters, though that does sound a little suggestive of poultry. But it doesn't matter. Won't you come in?"

They came in, and as they walked slowly along the passage, Polton completed the introductions. The prospective sitter, a light-coloured, good-looking African gentleman, was a Mr. William Vanderpuye, a native of Elmina on the Gold Coast, who was at present attending a course of lectures on Medical Jurisprudence at St. Margaret's Hospital.

"He is also doing some practical work in our laboratory," Polton explained further, "as Dr. Thorndyke's pupil. That is how I came to have the pleasure of making his acquaintance."

At this point they reached the studio door, which Tom threw open, inviting them to enter. Accordingly they entered, and then, becoming aware of the other occupant of the studio, they both stopped short and, for a moment, three inquisitive pairs of eyes made a rapid mutual inspection. Sweating with embarrassment and cursing under his breath, Tom haste to introduce his three guests, and then, by way of giving the lady an opportunity to retire, explained, "Mr. Vanderpuye is going to do me the honour of sitting to me for his portrait."

"Oh, how interesting!" she exclaimed. "But now I expect you will want to arrange about the sittings, so I suppose I had better run away and leave you to your consultation."

As she spoke, she directed a subtly appealing glance at Mr. Vanderpuye, who replied instantly and with emphasis, "Not at all, Mrs. Schiller. You mustn't let me drive you away. We are not going to talk secrets, but just to arrange about the portrait. Besides," he added, a little ambiguously, "it seems that you paint yourself, so you may be able to advise us."

"That is very gracious of you," said she, "and if you would really like me to stay, I should be delighted to hear all about the portrait, and I will make you a nice cup of tea as a thank offering for the invitation."

She began, forthwith, to set out the tea-things while Polton filled the kettle and put it on the gas-ring, and Tom looked on with mixed feelings

456

which changed from moment to moment. He could easily have dispensed with Lotta's company, but as he noted the way in which his new patron's eyes followed her movements, he began to suspect that it might be all for the best. Apparently, he was Lotta's only male friend. It would be a great relief to him if she should get another.

With this idea in his mind, he observed the trend of events while tea was being consumed (as also did Mr. Polton, to whom the lady was a startling mystery) and found it encouraging. Of a set purpose, as it seemed, Lotta kept the ball of conversation rolling almost entirely between herself and Mr. Vanderpuye, addressing him in a tone of deference which he evidently found flattering. Indeed, the African gentleman was obviously much impressed by the fair Lotta, and openly admiring, which was not unnatural, for she was a good-looking woman (if one did not object to the "abstract colour"), who could make herself extremely agreeable when she tried. And she was obviously trying now.

"I am inclined to envy Mr. Pedley his opportunity," said she. "You are such an admirable subject for a portrait."

"Do you really think so?" he exclaimed, delighted. "I was rather afraid that the complexion – and the hair, you know – "

"Oh, but that is what I meant by the opportunity. Your warm olive complexion creates all sorts of possibilities in the way of colour harmonies, so unlike the pale, relatively colourless European face. Perhaps," she continued reflectively, "that may account for the fact that the African peoples seem to be born colourists. Don't you think so?"

"It may be so," Vanderpuye agreed. "They certainly like colour, and plenty of it. My steward, at home, used to wear a scarlet flannel suit and green carpet slippers."

"But what a lovely combination!" exclaimed Lotta. "Such a subtle and delicate contrast! Don't you agree with me?"

Mr. Vanderpuye was prepared to agree to anything, and did so with a genial smile, thereby revealing such a set of teeth as seldom gladdens the eye of the modern European.

"But, of course," he added, "I don't know much about the matter except that I like bright colours myself, whereas you are an artist and have, no doubt, studied the subject profoundly."

"I have," she admitted. "Colour is the engrossing interest of my life. So much do I love it that I am often impelled to paint pictures consisting entirely of colour without any other motive. Symphonies and concertos in colour, you know."

"They must be very beautiful, I am sure," said Vanderpuye, "though I don't quite understand how you can make a picture of colour alone. Perhaps, some day, I may have the privilege of seeing your works."

"Would you like to? If you would, I should be only too proud and delighted to show them to you. I live next door to Mr. Pedley, so you could easily drop in sometime after one of your sittings."

"It would be better to make an appointment," suggested Vanderpuye. "What time would you like me to attend for the sitting, Mr. Pedley?"

"I should prefer the morning light," replied Tom, "say from nine to twelve. How would that suit you, Mr. Vanderpuye?"

"Admirably," was the reply. "And as to the date? When would you like to begin?"

"The sooner the better, so far as I am concerned. How would to-morrow do?"

"It would do perfectly for me. Then we will say to-morrow morning at nine. And as to you, Mrs. Schiller, if I should look in at your studio shortly after twelve, would that be convenient?"

"Quite," she replied. "I shall have just finished my morning's work. And now," she added, "as we have emptied the teapot, and I expect that you have some further arrangements to discuss, I had better make myself scarce."

She rose and, having shaken hands with the two visitors and announced that she would let herself out, bestowed a parting smile on Mr. Vanderpuye and bustled away.

The sound of the closing outer door brought the conversation back to the portrait and the "further arrangements", but with the details of these we are not concerned. Finally it was decided that the portrait should be a three-quarter length presenting the subject in his barrister's wig and gown, standing with a brief in his hand as if addressing the court, and having settled this and the question of costs, the two visitors rose to depart.

"*Au revoir*, then," said Mr. Vanderpuye, "or, as the Hausa men say in my country, '*Sei Gobe*' – '*Until To-morrow*'. Nine o'clock sharp will see me on your doorstep."

"And twelve o'clock sharp on Mrs. Schiller's," added Tom, with a sly smile.

Mr. Vanderpuye smiled in return. Whether he also blushed there was no means of judging.

Chapter V
A Trivial Chapter,
But Not Irrelevant

The vague hopes which Tom Pedley had conceived that a friendship between his new patron and Lotta Schiller might relieve him to some extent of the lady's society were more than fulfilled, for very soon it began to appear that Mr. Vanderpuye was not merely to share the burden of that intimacy – he had in effect stepped into the reversion of Tom's status as Lotta's sole male friend. Not that Tom was totally discarded by her. She still made occasional appearances in the studio, but those appearances tended in a most singular manner to coincide with the presence there of Mr. Vanderpuye.

There was no mistaking the position, nor, indeed, was there any concealment of it. The impulsive and susceptible African gentleman made no secret of his admiration of the fair and sprightly Lotta, or of the fact that they spent a good deal of time together, while as to the lady herself, she was at no pains whatever to disguise the new relationship. Thus Tom, guided by the light of experience, watched with grim amusement the development of the familiar symptoms, noted that Mr. William Vanderpuye had been promoted to the style and title of "Billy" – with or without the customary enrichments – and that Mrs. Lotta Schiller had ceased to command a surname.

The portrait progressed steadily but, being a nearly complete life-size figure with some accessories, its execution involved a considerable number of sittings, though Tom often saved time by working at the accessories in the intervals, and as it grew towards completion its quality began to show itself. It was a tactful and sympathetic portrait. There was no flattery. The likeness was faithfully rendered, but it was an eminently becoming likeness, presenting the sitter at his best, and if there was any tendency to stress the more favourable points, that merely reflected Tom Pedley's ordinary attitude towards his fellow creatures.

From time to time Lotta dropped in at the studio (usually about twelve) to inspect and criticize, and Tom listened to her with delighted amusement. Gone was all the clap-trap about representationalism and imitative art. She was now the frank and honest Philistine. Unlike the art critics from whom she had borrowed her "highbrow" phrases, who dismiss the "mere resemblance" in a portrait as a negligible irrelevancy, she was out for the likeness and nothing but the likeness, and as it approached the final stage, even she was satisfied.

"Do you think it is like me, Lotta?" Vanderpuye asked anxiously as they stood before the canvas. "I hope it is, but it seems a little flattering."

"You are a silly, self-depreciating little ass, Billy," said she. (Billy stood a trifle over six feet in his stockings). "You don't realize what a good-looking fellow you are."

"Well, my dear," he rejoined, regarding her with a fond smile, "I am always willing to learn, especially from you."

"Then," said she, "you can take it from me that the handsome legal gentleman in the picture is a faithful representation of my friend Bill, and not flattered in the least. Isn't that so, Tom?"

"I think so," he replied. "I have painted him as I see him and as his friends see him, and I hope I have done him impartial justice."

Tom's view was confirmed by another of "Bill's" friends – to wit, Mr. Polton, who made occasional visits and followed the progress of the work with the deepest interest, a sort-of proprietary interest, in fact, for it transpired that it was at his instigation that the portrait had been commissioned when photographs had been tried and found wanting. The confirmation came on a certain occasion when the four interested parties were gathered around the portrait, now practically finished, to discuss its merits.

"The art of painting," Mr. Polton moralized, "seems to me almost like a supernatural power. Of course, I can do scale drawings to work from, but they are only diagrams. They don't look like the real objects, whereas with this picture, if I stand a little way off and look at it with one eye closed, I seem to be actually looking at Mr. Vanderpuye."

"Yes," Lotta agreed, "it is a perfect representation, almost as perfect as a photograph."

"I beg your pardon, ma'am," Polton objected, "but it is a good deal more perfect. You can't do this sort of thing by photography."

"Not the colour, of course, but I meant the representation of form."

"But, ma'am," Polton persisted, "there is something more than form in this portrait, something that photography can't do. I tried one or two photographs of Mr. Vanderpuye when I was teaching him the technique, but they were quite a failure. The form was perfectly correct and they would have been excellent for identification, but there was something lacking, and that something was what we might call the *personality*. But that is just what the portrait has got. It is Mr. Vanderpuye himself, whereas the photographs were mere representations of his *shape*."

Tom nodded approvingly. "Mr. Polton is right," said he. "Photography can give a perfect representation of an object, such as a statue or a building, which is always the same. But a living person changes from moment to moment. A photograph can only show the appearance at a given instant, but the portrait painter must disregard the accidents of the moment and seek out the essential and permanent character."

This seemed to be quite a new idea to Lotta, for she exclaimed, "Really! Now I never thought of that, and I am rather sorry, too, because I had meant to ask Mr. Polton to take a photograph of Bill just as he is posed for the painting. But if it would not be a true likeness, I shouldn't care to have it. Still, it's very disappointing."

"There's no need for you to be disappointed, ma'am," Polton interposed. "If Mr. Pedley would allow me to take a photograph of the painting, you would have a portrait with all the qualities of the original except the colour. It would be a true copy."

Lotta was delighted, and most profuse in her thanks. She even informed Mr. Polton, much to his surprise, that he was a duck.

"What size, ma'am," he asked when the permission had been obtained, "would you wish the photograph to be?"

"Oh, quite small," she replied, "so that I could have it mounted in a little case that I could carry about with me, or perhaps in a brooch or pendant that I could wear. Would that be possible, Mr. Polton?"

"Oh, certainly, ma'am but, if you will excuse my mentioning it, a brooch or a pendant would not be so very suitable for your purpose because, when you were wearing it, the portrait would be visible to everybody but yourself."

Lotta laughed. "Of course," said she. "How silly of me, and exhibiting the sacred portrait to strangers is just what I don't want to do. But what would you suggest?"

"I think," he replied, "that the old-fashioned locket would answer the purpose best."

"A locket," interposed Vanderpuye. "What is a locket? You will pardon me, but I am only a poor ignorant African."

"A locket, sir," Polton explained, "is a sort of pendant, usually of gold, forming a little flat case which opens by a hinge, and displays two little frames. Sometimes there used to be two portraits, one in each frame, but more commonly one frame contained a portrait and the other a lock of the – er – the selected person's hair, either plaited and made up into a tiny coil, or arranged in a flat spiral."

Vanderpuye chuckled gleefully. "I like the idea of the locket," said he, "but I am afraid you would get into difficulties with my hair."

461

"Not at all, sir," replied Polton. "Each of your hairs forms a natural spiral like a little watch-spring. That is one of the African racial characteristics. Shall I show you?"

He produced from his pocket a pair of watchmaker's tweezers and a pair of folding scissors and, having picked up a single hair from Vanderpuye's head, cut it off neatly, laid it on a white card, and passed it round for inspection.

"How perfectly lovely!" Lotta exclaimed. "It is, as you say, exactly like a tiny watch-spring. Yes, I will certainly have a locket."

"If you wished to extend the spiral," Polton suggested, "so as to fill the frame, it could easily be done by using two or three hairs."

"Oh, but that would spoil it," she protested, "and it is so beautiful. No, just one perfect little watch-spring in the middle of the space. Don't you agree with me, Bill?"

"Certainly, my dear," he replied with a broad smile, "especially as it would exhibit a racial characteristic. But how are we going to get the locket? Are they still to be obtained in the shops?"

"I expect they are. But I don't want a shop locket. It would be a soulless, machine-made thing, unworthy of my beloved Bill and his charming little watch-spring. What do you suggest, Mr. Polton? I suppose you couldn't make a locket for me, yourself?"

"So far as the mere construction is concerned, of course, I could make a locket. But I am not a goldsmith. The design would have to be made by an artist. If Mr. Pedley would make the design, I would carry it out for you with great pleasure."

"Oh, but how kind of you, Mr. Polton! You are really too sweet. I think I have already remarked that you are a duck."

"I think you have, ma'am," he replied with a somewhat wry crinkle, "and I beg to thank you for the – er – for the compliment."

"Not at all, Mr. Polton. And now, Tom, about this locket. Can you design it?"

"Yes," he replied. "I have done some designing for goldsmith's work and a simple locket would present no difficulty, especially as I should be collaborating with Mr. Polton. If you like, I will make one or two sketches for you to see, and we can then discuss the question of ornament."

"Yes, that would be very nice of you, Tom, and you must let me know what it will cost."

"That is not your concern, Lotta," said Vanderpuye. "It is to be a gift from me."

462

"How very noble of you, Bill. Of course that will make it much more precious, and I accept gratefully on one condition, which is that you have a locket, too, and that you let me give it to you."

"But men don't wear lockets, do they?" he asked.

"They used to," said Tom, "before the arrival of the wrist-watch. The locket was usually suspended from the watch-chain."

"Well," said Vanderpuye, "as you see, I carry a pocket watch on a chain, as a wrist-watch is not very suitable for the Tropics, so I am eligible for a locket, and I should very much like to have one with a portrait of Lotta and a lock of her beautiful golden hair. Would you two gentleman accept the commission?"

The two gentlemen agreed that they would, where upon Lotta objected, "But you have no business to offer the commission. That is my affair, seeing that the locket is to be a gift from me."

Vanderpuye smiled blandly. "The commission," said he, "was offered and accepted without prejudice as we say in the law. The other question is for separate consideration. Now we have to arrange details. The locket is to contain a portrait and a lock of golden hair. The hair presents no difficulty, as it is obviously available. But what about the portrait? Should we ask Mr. Polton to do us a little photograph?"

"No you don't," exclaimed Lotta, "and I am surprised at you, Bill, when you've just heard what these two experts said about portrait photographs. No, it shall be a real painted portrait. I will paint it myself, and then I shall ask dear Mr. Polton to make a little photograph of the painting, and I am sure he won't refuse."

"Certainly not, ma'am," said Polton. "It will give me great pleasure, and I think it a most excellent idea. It will be a memento in a double sense – a portrait of the giver and a specimen of her handiwork."

Vanderpuye, however, was less enthusiastic. (He had seen "the giver's handiwork" and Polton hadn't.) "Why not let me commission Mr. Pedley to paint a portrait?" he suggested.

"You'll do nothing of the kind!" she replied. "The locket is to be my gift and I want the portrait to be my very own work."

There was nothing more to be said. Vanderpuye looked a little glum, and Tom, too good-natured to be simply amused, was regretful. A vivid recollection of "The Madonna" suggested breakers ahead and a disappointment for Mr. Vanderpuye. But he made no comment. Perhaps the future might develop some way out of the dilemma.

A few days later at the last of the sittings, a few final touches were added, and the portrait being now entirely finished, Tom escorted the sitter to the frame maker's to advise him as to a suitable frame. When this business had been disposed of, Tom produced one or two sketches

463

which he had roughed out in the interval showing alternative designs for the two lockets. The one for the standing figure was a rather long ellipse, while the other, to hang on the watch-guard, was considerably smaller and circular in shape. Both forms were shown with alternative designs of decoration, in simple embossed metal, in coloured enamel, and with set stones.

"If you will be seeing Mrs. Schiller, you might show her the sketches," said Tom, "and talk them over with her, and if you both approve of the circular shape for the smaller one, you might remind her to design her portrait to fill the circular space so that the head is not too small."

"I shall be seeing her in about half-an-hour's time," said Vanderpuye. "We are lunching at a place which she has discovered in Soho, so we shall have an opportunity to discuss the designs. But I think we should both like take your advice on the matter."

"Yes," Tom agreed, "a little discussion and explanation might be useful, as the sketches are rather slight. Perhaps, when Mrs. Schiller has finished her portrait, we might all four meet at the studio and make the final arrangements."

"I will suggest that to her," said Vanderpuye, "and I will let you and Mr. Polton know when the portrait is ready. I wish," he added, confidentially, "that she had agreed to your painting it. Her style of work doesn't seem to me very suitable for a portrait but, of course, I am no judge. What do you think?"

Tom's opinions on the subject were perfectly definite, but his reply was discreetly evasive.

"I have never seen a portrait by her, so I can hardly judge, but we will hope for the best."

With this, by way of avoiding a dangerous topic, he shook Vanderpuye's hand cordially and the two men went their respective ways.

The meeting took place about a week later, the day and hour having been decided by Polton and, somewhat before the appointed time, that cunning artificer made his appearance and forthwith set to work. From one of his numerous and capacious pockets he produced a small folding camera which, when it was opened, was seen to be fitted with a level and a sighting frame.

"I haven't brought a stand," said he, "as I thought that an easel would be more convenient and more rigid. Can you lend me one?"

"Yes," replied Tom. "I have one unoccupied, a heavy one with a lifting screw, which will answer your purpose perfectly. It is as steady as a rock."

464

He drew it out from its corner and trundled it across to a place opposite the portrait, when Polton took charge of it, placing his camera on the tray and, with the aid of the sighting frame, adjusting the relative positions of the camera and the portrait until the latter exactly filled the space of the frame. Then he made the exposure, and was in the act of winding on the exposed film when the sound of the studio bell announced the arrival of the other two parties to the symposium. As they entered and Polton made his bow, it seemed to him that Vanderpuye's expression lacked its usual geniality, in fact, the African gentleman looked undeniably sulky. On the other hand, the fair and volatile Lotta was in the best of spirits, and apparently quite pleased with herself.

"Why," she exclaimed as she bounced into the studio, "here is my dear Mr. Polton, improving the shining hour like a pre-punctual duck and all ready to begin work." She shook his hand warmly and continued, "And what a darling little camera. But isn't it rather small for that big portrait?"

"It is going to be quite a small photograph, you will remember, ma'am, not more than an inch-and-a-half high."

"Yes, of course. How silly of me. Are you going to take the photograph now?"

"I have taken it already, ma'am, and I shall have great pleasure in taking your own when it is available."

"It is available now," said Lotta, opening her handbag and taking out an envelope about eight inches by six. "I made it quite a small painting as you see, but I dare say it will be big enough."

"The size is amply sufficient," Polton replied, "as it has to be reduced so much."

He took the envelope which she handed to him and, opening the flap, tenderly drew out a small mounted watercolour, which he regarded with a reverential smile. It emerged with the back uppermost but, as he quickly turned it over, the smile faded from his countenance and gave place to an expression of astonishment and dismay. For some moments he stood speechless and rigid, staring incredulously at the thing which he held in his hand. Then he cast a furtive glance at the artist and was reassured to find her watching him with a sly smile. Obviously it was a joke, he decided, but he was too discreet to say so. He would lie low and let the situation develop.

"Well, Mr. Polton," said Lotta, "how do you like it?"

"Since you ask me, ma'am," he replied with a cautious crinkle, "I really don't think you have done yourself justice.

"You wouldn't have me flatter myself, would you?" she demanded.

"Oh, no, ma'am," he replied. "But there was no need to. You had only to represent yourself exactly as you are to produce a very charming portrait."

Lotta laughed gaily. "Thank you, Mr. Polton, for a very neatly turned compliment."

"It's no compliment at all," Vanderpuye burst in. "Mr. Polton is perfectly right. What I wanted was a likeness, but this portrait isn't like you a bit. I should never have recognized it. What do you say, Mr. Pedley?" But Tom, who was looking at the portrait over Polton's shoulder, emulated the latter gentleman's caution.

"Of course," said he, "it is not a literal representation. But then it isn't meant to be."

"Exactly," Lotta agreed. "The mere physical resemblance is not what I was aiming at. This portrait is not a work of imitative art. It is a work of self-expression."

The argument between Lotta and Vanderpuye was pursued for some time with some heat, not to say bitterness. But it led nowhere. Lotta was immovable, and Vanderpuye had at length to retire defeated. Meanwhile Polton, having realized to his amazement that this preposterous thing had to be taken seriously, took it seriously and, without further comment, stuck it up on the easel beside the other portrait and gravely proceeded with the photograph. When he had finished and handed the portrait back to its creator, the sketches for the lockets were produced and discussed at some length, the conclusion reached being that both should be decorated with a simple design in *champlevé* enamel, and that the details should be left to the designer and the executant.

"And that appears to be all," said Lotta, bestowing the "self-portrait" in her handbag.

"Excepting the hair, ma'am," Polton reminded her. "If I may be permitted to take a sample for each locket, I shall be able to get on with the work without troubling you further."

From his inexhaustible pockets he brought forth a couple of seed envelopes, a pair of tweezers, and a pair of folding scissors, all of which he laid on the table. Then, beginning with Vanderpuye, he separated one of the little crisp curls and cut it off flush with the skin, putting it at once into one of the envelopes, on which, having sealed it, he wrote, "*W. Vanderpuye, Esq.*"

Lotta watched him with a smile and commended his caution.

"It would be a bit awkward if you had two unlabelled envelopes and didn't know which was which. Now, how much of mine do you want? Be thrifty, if you please. I can't have you leaving a bald patch."

466

"Certainly not, ma'am," Polton assured her. "A dozen hairs will be enough, and they will never be missed."

By way of confirmation, he counted them out one by one, and then, gathering up the little strand, cut it through close to the roots. Having twisted the strand into a loose yarn, he coiled it neatly and slipped it into the envelope, which he sealed and inscribed with the name of "*Mrs. Lotta Schiller*".

This brought the proceedings to an end and, when Polton had put the two precious envelopes into a stout leather wallet and stowed the latter in a capacious inner pocket, Lotta and Mr. Vanderpuye rose together to take their departure and, having shaken hands with Polton, went out escorted by their host.

When the latter returned to the studio, he discovered his collaborator seated opposite the clock, apparently regarding it with intense concentration. He looked round as Tom entered and, gazing at him with wrinkled brows, exclaimed solemnly, "This is a most extraordinary thing, sir."

"What is?" asked Tom, looking at the clock and not perceiving anything unusual about it.

"I am referring, sir, to this portrait of Mrs. Schiller's. I am utterly bewildered. At first, I took for granted that it was a joke."

"Vanderpuye didn't," Tom remarked with a grin.

"No, indeed. But do you understand it, sir? To me, it looked exactly like the sort of portraits that I used to draw when I was a boy of ten, and that other little boys used to draw. But I suppose I must have been mistaken. Was I, sir?"

"No," replied Tom. "You were perfectly right."

"But," Polton protested, "Mrs. Schiller is a professional artist, as I understand. Can she really paint or draw?"

"Since you ask me, Polton, I should say that she can't. She draws in that way because she can't draw in any other."

"But what an amazing thing, sir. If she can't draw or paint, how does she manage to practise as an artist?"

"I don't know," replied Tom, "that it's quite correct to describe her as practising as an artist. She has never sold any of her work and never exhibited any. By the term 'practising artist', one usually means an artist who gets a living by his work. Still, there are painters whose work is no better than hers who exhibit and even sell. You can see their stuff in the various freak exhibitions that appear from time to time in London. That is how Mrs. Schiller got her ideas. She went to one of these freak shows which was being boosted by the art journalists, and she thought that the stuff looked so easy to do that she decided to try whether she couldn't do

467

something like it. So she tried, and found that she could. Naturally. Anyone could – even a child, and some children can do a good deal better."

"But does anyone take these works seriously?"

"Seriously!" exclaimed Tom. "My dear Polton, you should read the art critics' notices of them and then see the mugs, who want to be thought 'highbrow', crowding into the galleries and staring, open-mouthed, at what they believe to be the last word in progressive art. But to do them justice, they don't often buy any of the stuff."

"And the painters, sir, who produce them? Are they impostors or only cranky?"

"It is difficult to say," replied Tom. "The early modernists were, I think, quite sincere cranks. Some of them were admittedly insane. But nowadays it is impossible to judge. For the mischief is, you see, Polton, that if once you accept incompetent, childish, barbaric productions as genuine works of art, you have thrown the door wide open to impostors."

"And what about Mrs. Schiller, sir?"

"Well, Polton, you have seen her. She certainly isn't mad, and she certainly can't paint, and my impression is that she knows it as well as you and I do. But what her motive may be for keeping up the pretence is known only to herself."

Polton pondered awhile on this answer. Then he raised another question.

"I am rather puzzled, sir, as to her relations with Mr. Vanderpuye. She is, I understand, a married woman, so those relations are not very proper in any case. But there seems to me something rather unreal about them. From their behavior, you would take these two persons for very devoted friends, if not actually lovers, and that, I feel sure, is genuinely the case with Mr. Vanderpuye. But I have my doubts about the lady, and if she is an impostor in one thing, she can be in another. But I am like you – I can't imagine a motive for imposture. Of course, Mr. Vanderpuye is a rich man, but I don't, somehow, suspect her of trying to get money out of him. And yet I can't think of any other motive. In fact, I can't make it out at all."

"Is there any need to make it out?" asked Tom. "It isn't our affair, you know."

"Excepting that Mr. Vanderpuye is my friend, and a very worthy, lovable gentleman. I shouldn't like him to get involved in any unpleasantness."

"Quite right, Polton," Tom agreed, "but I don't see what you can do beyond keeping your weather eyelid lifting, and that you seem to have been doing."

468

Which observation having closed the discussion, the two parties to it transferred their attention to the sketches and the consideration of the technical details connected with the goldsmith's art.

Chapter VI
The Forest of Essex

On a certain evening early in November, Tom Pedley, having put down his canvas-carrier to free one hand, inserted his latch-key, and pushed the gate open. Then, according to his invariable custom, he withdrew the key and pocketed it before entering, and as he did so, happening to glance up the street, he perceived Lotta Schiller and her friend Billy just turning the corner and approaching. He had not seen either of them for more than a fortnight – not, in fact, since the frame-maker had carted away the portrait and the two lockets had been delivered to their respective owners, so he thought it proper to pause at the open gate to exchange greetings, especially as they had already seen him and notified the fact.

"Where have you been all this time, Tom?" exclaimed Lotta as they met on the doorstep. "I haven't seen you for ages."

"Well, I haven't been in the same place all the time," Tom replied. "To-day I have been in Epping Forest. Doing a bit of landscape painting for a change after the portrait."

"Epping Forest," repeated Lotta. "How delightful. I've never been to Epping Forest. May we come in and have a look at what you've been painting?"

"Do, by all means," Tom replied heartily. "The picture isn't finished, but it will give you an idea of the place."

They entered together, and Tom, having unstrapped the carrier, placed the canvas on the easel at an angle to the great window.

"The light isn't very good," said he, "but you can see what the forest is like."

"Yes, indeed," she exclaimed enthusiastically, "and it is perfectly lovely. It looks like a real forest."

"It is a real forest," said Tom. "It is a surviving remnant of the primeval forest of Britain, and there is quite a lot of it, still."

"But how thrilling! A primeval forest! Have you ever seen a primeval forest, Bill?"

"Yes," said Vanderpuye. "I have seen the great forest that covers Ashanti, and it is something like this painting. The African forest trees are probably a good deal more lofty than these, but it is difficult to judge from a picture."

470

"It is almost impossible," said Tom, "without figures or animals to give a scale. I think of putting in one or two deer."

"But there aren't really any deer there, are there?" asked Lotta.

"Bless you, yes," he replied. "Deer, foxes, badgers, and all sorts of wild beasts. It is a genuine forest, not a mere park. And there are two ancient British camps. I pass one of them on the way to my pitch."

"It sounds like a most heavenly place!" said Lotta. "And to think that I have never seen it, though it is so near London. It would be delightful to spend a day there. Don't you think so, Bill?"

Bill agreed with enthusiasm, as he usually did to Lotta's suggestions.

"Then that is settled. We will have a day rambling and picnicking in the forest, and Tom shall show us the way. Oh, you needn't look like that. We shan't hang about and hinder you."

"I wasn't looking like that," Tom protested. "I shall be very pleased to show you the way there and start you on your ramble. My picture will be ready to go on with in three or four days, say next Thursday. How will that suit you?"

"It will suit me perfectly," she replied, and Bill having concurred, she added, "I suppose we shall have to take some food with us. How do you manage, Tom?"

"I take my lunch with me, but you needn't. There is an excellent inn near High Beach called the King's Oak, where you can get refreshment for man and beast."

"I don't quite like that expression," said Lotta, "as only one of us is a man. But never mind. Now let us settle our arrangements. I think we had better meet and start from here, as I am here already and Bill isn't a Londoner. Give us a time, and then we will go and leave you in peace."

Tom suggested nine o'clock on Thursday morning and, this having been agreed to, his visitors departed, whereupon, having cleaned his palette and washed his brushes and himself, he proceeded to lay the table – including in its furnishings Polton's incomparable tankard – opened the haybox, and settled himself with deep satisfaction to the disposal of his evening meal.

Punctually, on Thursday morning, the two ramblers made their appearance at the rendezvous, and a few minutes later the party set forth for Fenchurch Street, Vanderpuye carrying the strapped stool and easel. An empty first-class compartment being easily obtainable at this time in the day, they took possession of one and, having deposited Tom's impedimenta on the hat rack, lit pipes and cigarettes, and prepared to enjoy the journey. And a very pleasant journey it was (excepting the stop at Stratford, when mephitic fumes from some chemical works poured into the compartment and caused them hastily to pull up the window-glasses). Lotta was in buoyant spirits and rattled away gaily between the puffs of her cigarette, while the two men smoked their pipes and allowed themselves to be entertained.

"For a painter, Tom," she remarked, as the train drew out of Woodford Station, "I consider you extraordinarily unobservant. You actually haven't noticed my beautiful new locket."

As a matter of fact he had, and thought it slightly unsuitable to the occasion.

"You are quite wrong, Lotta," said he. "My eyes have been glued to it ever since we started, and I have been thinking what a remarkable genius the fellow must have been who designed it."

"Now listen to that, Bill," said she, selecting a fresh cigarette from her case. "Isn't he a conceited fellow? Brazenly fishing for a compliment, and he won't get one."

"I knew that," retorted Tom, "so I supplied the compliment myself. But it really does look rather fine, thanks to the brilliant way in which Polton carried it out."

Lotta laughed scornfully. "Now he's pretending to be modest. But it's no use, Tom. We know you. Still, I agree that the little man did his part beautifully, and I am grateful to both of you, to say nothing of the generous giver."

Here she bestowed an affectionate smile on the gratified Vanderpuye, who smiled in return as a man can afford to smile who has such a magnificent set of teeth. There followed a brief interlude in Lotta's babblings while she lit and smoked the fresh cigarette. A few minutes later the train slowed down, and Tom, reaching down his property from the rack and slipping the strap of the satchel over his shoulder, announced, "This is our station," and prepared to open the door.

As the train came to rest, Vanderpuye once more relieved Tom of the folded easel and the three emerged on to the platform. Passing out of the station, they walked up the rather dull village street until they came to a large pond on the border of the forest. Here Tom turned off into a path which skirted the pond and presently entered a broad green ride. A short distance along this he entered a narrow green ride that led off to the left up a gentle incline and then down across the end of a little valley, the marshy bottom of which was covered with beds of rushes.

"This hollow," Tom announced, "is called Debden Slade. May as well remember the name in case you have to ask the way. This path – what they call in the forest a green ride – leads, as you see, up the hill

472

and directly to the corner of the ancient British fortification, called Loughton Camp, and passes round two sides of it."

"But you are going to show us the way to it," Lotta stipulated.

"Yes, I am coming with you as far as the camp and, when you have seen it, I will set you on your road before we separate."

"I suppose," said Vanderpuye, "you know your way about the forest quite well?"

"Yes," Tom replied. "I have done a lot of sketching and painting here in the last few years. It is quite easy to find your way about the forest after a little experience, but at first I always used to bring a large-scale map and a compass. This is the camp that we are approaching, the south side. We shall pass round it to the north-west side, and there our roads diverge."

"But I don't see any camp," said Lotta, looking vaguely into the dense wood which seemed to close the green path that they had been ascending. "I can only see a high bank covered with a mass of funny little trees that look as if they wanted their hair cut."

"It isn't very distinct," Tom admitted, "except on the map. But you must bear in mind that it was built two- or three-thousand years ago or more, and that it has probably not been occupied since the Roman invasion. In all those centuries, the forest has grown over it and more or less covered it up. But you can make it out quite well if you climb up the bank through the trees and let yourself down into the enclosure. Then you can see that there is a roughly four-sided space enclosed by high earth walls or ramparts. But as it is all covered by a dense mass of those small trees, you can only see it a bit at a time."

"But why are the trees so small?" Lotta asked. "There doesn't seem to be a single full-grown tree among them, though, from what you say, they have had plenty of time to grow."

"They are not young trees," said Tom. "They are old dwarfs. The people of this manor used to have lopping rights. Consequently all the trees, as they grew up, were pollarded and, every year the new branches that sprouted from the crown were lopped off for firewood, with the result that the trees are gnarled and stunted. They are rather uncanny in appearance, but not very beautiful."

"No," agreed Lotta, "uncanny is the word. They look like little witches with their hair standing on end. But the whole place is rather weird and solemn, especially when one thinks of the dead and gone Britons and the centuries that the camp has been lying desolate and forgotten. Those holes in the bank, I suppose, have been made by animals of some kind."

473

"Yes. The small holes are usually rabbit burrows, the larger ones are fox earths."

As they had been talking they had walked slowly along the green path in the deep shade cast by the pollard beeches that crowded the high bank of the old rampart. Presently they turned the corner of the camp and passed along the north-western side, until they reached a more open space where the green ride grew broader and turned sharply to the left while a narrower path led on straight ahead. At the point where the two paths separated Tom halted and held out his hand for the easel which Vanderpuye was still carrying.

"This is where we part company," said he. "My way is by the little green path to Great Monk Wood, about three-quarters-of-a-mile farther on. Yours is by the green ride along the crest of the hill, a pleasant walk with a delightful view all the way."

"Yes," said Lotta, looking across the open forest that stretched away from the foot of the hill, "it is a lovely view, and it seems a relief to be out in the open, away from that gloomy old camp and those unearthly, weird little trees. And yet, somehow, I find a curious fascination in that ancient fortress. I should like to get inside the walls and see what a British camp was really like. Wouldn't you like to explore it, Bill?"

The amiable and accommodating Bill expressed the strongest desire to explore the camp and the profoundest interest in the Ancient Britons and their works.

"Well," said Tom, "you can't explore it to-day, because you would want a map and a compass and you ought to have a copy of the plan that was made when the Essex Field Club surveyed the camp. I have one filed away somewhere, so if you propose to make a serious exploration, I can lend it to you with a map of the forest and a compass. But now you had better stroll across to High Beach and learn to find your way about."

"Yes," agreed Vanderpuye, "that will be best, especially as we have brought no refreshment, and you say that there is an inn at High Beach where we can get some lunch. But we shall want you to direct us."

"It is perfectly plain sailing," replied Tom. "You see that clump of elms in the distance?"

"I see a clump of trees, and I take your word for it that they are elms."

"Well, they are at High Beach, so if you keep your eye on them you can't go wrong. You have to follow this green ride along, the crest of the hill. About half-a-mile from here you will cross the Epping Road and half-a-mile farther on you will come to a green ride at right angles to this. Turn to the left and go along it and you will come to the King's Oak inn, where you can stoke up if you want to. High Beach is only a few minutes' walk from the pub along the same ride. So now you know all about it."

He put the easel and canvas-carrier down on the turf and shook hands with the two ramblers, wishing them *adieu* and a pleasant journey. Lotta smiled slyly as she shook his hand and remarked to her companion, "That means that he has had enough of our society, so we had better make ourselves scarce. Come along, Bill."

The pair turned away to start on their walk, but Tom did not immediately resume his journey. His hands being free, he took the opportunity to fill his pipe in a leisurely fashion. But when it was full and ready for lighting, he still stood at the parting of the ways, following with a meditative eye the progress of the two adventurers as they stepped out briskly along the broad green ride. Once more Polton's question recurred to him: What were the relations of these two persons? They had the manner of an engaged couple which they certainly were not, but were they lovers or only friends? In his own case, Lotta's behaviour – apart from the verbal endearments – had been scrupulously correct. True, he had given her no opening for anything different, but still the fact remained that she had never made the slightest approach. Were her relations with Vanderpuye of the same platonic order? It seemed doubtful, for the conditions were not the same. Vanderpuye was no unwilling partner to this intimacy. From the first he had been Lotta's ardent admirer, but from admiration to passion is but a short step, and passion, in his case and hers, could but lead straight to disaster.

Thus Tom cogitated as he stood looking at the two receding figures. Many a time in the months that followed did that scene recur to him, the long, straight, grassy ride with the figures of the man and woman stepping forward gaily and now growing small in the distance. And still his eyes followed them with an interest which he could not explain, until they reached a point where the ride described a curve, and here Lotta, glancing back and seeing him still standing there, waved her hand to him, and Vanderpuye executed a flourish with his hat. Tom returned their farewell greeting, and a few moments later they entered the curve and vanished behind the roadside bushes, where upon he lit his pipe, picked up his fardels, and set forth along the little green path for his pitch in Great Monk Wood.

He had told himself, and Polton, that the nature of Lotta's relations with her African friend was no affair of his. And it was not. Nevertheless, as he strode along the narrow track through the silent and lonely forest, the question still occupied his thoughts, especially the question as to what was to be the end of it, for neither of the pair – and certainly not for Lotta – had he any strong personal regard, but he was a kindly man and it irked him to think of these two, heading, as he feared, for trouble. Particularly was he concerned for Vanderpuye, who, as an African, probably passionate and impulsive, and inexperienced in European ways, was the more likely to get himself into difficulties and to bear the brunt of any unpleasant consequences. For he was a barrister with a position to maintain and a future to consider. It would be a grievous thing if he should be involved in a scandal at the very start of his career.

At this point in his reflections he arrived at the forest opening which was the subject of his painting. He laid down his burdens, took off his satchel and, having identified the holes in the ground made at his last sitting by the feet of his stool and easel, unpacked the latter and set them up in the old position. Then he fixed up the canvas, set his palette, made a careful and critical survey of his subject and compared it with the half-finished painting, and straightway Lotta Schiller and her African friend faded from his thoughts and left him to the untroubled consideration of his work.

It was a lovely day despite the lateness of the month, and a beautiful scene. The noble beeches still bore many of their leaves, though these had now exchanged the tender green of summer for the gorgeous tints – all too fleeting – that marked the waning year. For four delightful hours Tom worked industriously, painting at the top of his form and enjoying every moment. Not a human creature came near him in all that time, though he received occasional visits from the non-human people of the forest, as the landscape painter commonly does. An inquisitive squirrel played peep-bo with him round a tree and then came down and danced around him within a few feet of the easel. A pair of friendly blackbirds pursued their business close by, and once or twice a couple of the dark-coated forest deer stole across the opening, apparently oblivious of his presence.

At the end of the second hour he took what workmen call a "beaver", a modest meal of bread and cheese (whereby the squirrel benefited to the extent of some morsels of bread and a piece of cheese rind), with a draught of beer from a large flask. Then once more he took up his palette and brushes and worked away steadily until the changing light told him that it was time to go, when he packed up tidily, lit his pipe, picked up his kit, and started back by the way he had come. At the junction of the two paths he paused to look along the green ride, though the afternoon was still young and his friends would hardly be returning so early. Nevertheless, as he took his way round the camp and back past the pond, he kept a half-unconscious look-out for them, and even at the

476

station as he paced the platform they were still in his mind until the train came in and bore him away alone.

During the next few days his thoughts turned occasionally to his two friends, with vague speculations as to how they had fared in the forest. He had rather expected a visit from Lotta and, on the strength of that speculation, had looked out the map, the compass, and the plan of the camp to hand to her when she should call. But to his surprise – almost to his disappointment – she made no appearance and, eventually he decided that she had given up the project of exploring the camp and, having put the things back in their usual receptacles, he dismissed the matter from his mind.

Yet, as the days passed without the expected visit or even the customary chance meetings in the street, her complete disappearance from his orbit impressed him as a little odd. He was even faintly displeased, a state of mind which he, himself, recognized as rather strange and perverse. For it was only a few weeks ago, when he had been the unwilling *cher ami*, that his chief desire in life had been to be rid of her, whereas now, though he felt no great concern, still he would have been quite pleased to find her on his doorstep. Once he had even contemplated calling to make inquiries, but discretion prevailed. He had no desire to revive that troublesome intimacy.

It is probable that, if nothing further had happened, the passing of Lotta out of his life would have been accepted and presently ceased to be noticed. But a new circumstance tended to revive his curiosity. Returning one day by way of Cumberland Market, and thus passing her house, he noticed that her brass plate was not in its usual place. It was not a fixed plate permanently secured to the wall, but was held in place by removable fastenings, and it had been Lotta's custom to take it down in the evening and replace it in the morning. Thus, when he noticed its absence, he assumed that she had merely forgotten to fix it up and thought no more about it. But, happening on the following day to glance at her door and again noting the absence of the plate, he gave the matter more attention, with the result that, after several daily observations, he decided that the plate had disappeared for good. Then, again, he had thought of calling, but now he was restrained by a fresh consideration. Possibilities which he had dimly envisaged might have become realized, and if so, it were well for him not to meddle in Lotta's affairs. On the other hand, he was now definitely anxious and a little disturbed, particularly on Vanderpuye's account, and it seemed to him that a few discreet inquiries through a third party might elicit the facts without committing him in any way.

Now the obvious third party was Mr. Polton. He was in touch with Vanderpuye and was certainly keeping an eye on the course of events. But the question was, how to get at Mr. Polton. Tom had never ventured to call on him, as he resided on the premises of his employer, Dr. Thorndyke, and an uninvited visit would have seemed somewhat of an intrusion. Of course, he could have written to Mr. Polton, but that would have involved a direct inquiry, which he wished to avoid. His idea was that if he could contrive a meeting with his ingenious friend, the required information could be made to transpire naturally in a judiciously managed conversation, without his asking any questions at all.

The problem was, therefore, to find a pretext for a visit to Polton, a convincing pretext which would account for his having called rather than written. To the solution of this problem Tom addressed himself and, being an eminently straightforward man, little addicted to pretexts of any kind, he had to give it a disproportionate amount of attention. And then the problem solved itself. Happening to pull out a drawer in which he kept miscellaneous oddments, he discovered in it the pedometer which he had been accustomed to carry on his expeditions in search of landscape subjects. For years it had served him well, but latterly it had become erratic in its action and so unreliable that he had ceased to carry it. So he had put it aside, intending some time to take Mr. Polton's opinion on it. But out of sight had been out of mind and the matter had been forgotten. Now, however, it gave him not a mere pretext but a reasonable occasion for the visit.

Accordingly he dispatched a short note to Polton, announcing his intention to call and, if an interview should not be convenient, to leave the pedometer for a diagnostic inspection, to which Polton replied by return with a cordial invitation and the necessary directions to his domain in the premises.

Chapter VII
Of a Pedometer
and a Tragedy

At four o'clock precisely, on a bright December afternoon, Tom Pedley arrived at the entry of Number 5A King's Bench Walk, having made his way thither very pleasantly through the old-world courts of the Temple.

For a few moments he paused to examine with an artist's appreciation the fine red brick portico (commonly attributed to Wren). Then he entered and, following Polton's directions, ascended the stairs to the landing of the "*Second Pair*". As he reached it a door opened, and his host came out to meet him.

"This is very pleasant, sir," said Polton, shaking hands warmly. "I don't often have a visitor, being a solitary worker like yourself, so your visit will be quite a little treat for me. Will you come into the laboratory? We are going to have tea in my room upstairs, but I am boiling the kettle here to avoid smoking it on the fire."

As they entered the large room Tom glanced about him curiously, noting that some of the appointments, such as a joiner's bench, a lathe, and a large copying camera, hardly accorded with his conception of a laboratory, and that a handsome copper kettle, mounted on a tripod over a Bunsen burner and a fine old silver teapot seemed to have strayed in from elsewhere.

"Perhaps, sir," suggested Polton, "we might have a look at the pedometer while the kettle is getting up steam."

Tom fished the instrument out of his pocket and handed it to him, whereupon, having opened the glass back, he stuck a watchmaker's eyeglass in his eye and examined the visible part of the mechanism.

"There doesn't seem to be much amiss with it," he reported, dancing the instrument up and down to test the lever. "Just a matter of wear. The little spring click has worn short and tends to slip over the teeth of the ratchet wheel. That is a fatal defect, but it's easily mended, and I may find some other faults when I come to take it down, as we say in the trade – that is, take it to pieces. At any rate it will be none the worse for a clean-up and a touch of fresh oil."

"I am afraid I am giving you a lot more trouble than I expected," said Tom.

Polton looked up at him with his queer, crinkly smile.

"Trouble, sir!" he exclaimed. "It is no trouble. It isn't even work. It will give me several hours' pleasant entertainment, and I am much obliged to you for bringing me the instrument."

In confirmation, he produced from one of his innumerable pockets a small portable screwdriver and seemed about to attack the pedometer forthwith, when the kettle intervened by blowing out a jet of steam, whereupon he replaced the cap of the screwdriver, returned it to his pocket, and proceeded methodically to make the tea.

As he led the way upstairs, carrying the teapot while his guest followed with the kettle, Tom remarked on the comeliness of the latter.

"Yes, sir," replied Polton, "it's a fine old kettle. They don't make them like that nowadays. I found it in a marine store in Portugal Street. Came from some old lawyer's chambers in Lincoln's Inn, I expect, and very shabby and battered it was, but I put a bit of work into it and made it as good as new. You see, sir, I rather take after you. I like the common things that I use and live with to be good and pleasant to look at."

His statement was borne out by the aspect of the spacious room on the "Third Pair" which they now entered, where a tea-table, flanked by two easy chairs, stood before the fire. Tom, having deposited the kettle on a trivet, out of reach of the smoke or flame, sat down in the chair allocated to him and surveyed the prospect, while Polton did the honours of the tea-table, noting the well-filled book-shelves, the one or two pictures on the walls (including his sketch for *The Eavesdropper*, simply but tastefully framed) and a four-fold screen which he suspected of concealing a bed. It was all simple and plain, but the room and everything that was in it appealed quietly to Tom's rather fastidious taste, even to the quaint old cottage clock that hung on the wall and hardly disturbed the silence by its homely tick.

"This is my private domain, sir," said Polton, "but I don't spend much time in it. The laboratory is really my home. I am an inveterate mechanic, always happiest at my bench. That pedometer of yours is quite a windfall for me. May I ask how long you have had it?"

"I should say about a dozen years," replied Tom.

"And do you find it fairly accurate? The experts on surveying dismiss the pedometer as a mere useless toy. What is your experience of it?"

"It is accurate enough for my purpose," Tom replied. "I'm not a surveyor. I don't deal in inches, but I find that it agrees pretty closely with maps and milestones, and that is enough for me."

"The reason that I asked is that I had thought of getting one for Mr. Vanderpuye to take back with him. There won't be many milestones in his country."

"Is Mr. Vanderpuye going back to Africa soon?" Tom asked with suddenly awakened interest.

"Not very soon," replied Polton, "because he has joined the Bar Mess at the Central Criminal Court and is attending the court regularly – that is, he has been since Mrs. Schiller went away."

"Oh, she has gone away, has she?" asked Tom, considerably startled.

"Yes, sir, and I hope she will stop away, for before she went, he used to neglect his work terribly. I am very much relieved that she has gone."

"Do you know whether she has gone for good?"

"I am afraid not, sir. Of course, I couldn't ask any questions, but I gathered from Mr. Vanderpuye that she had gone to stay with some friends at Birmingham. How long she will be away I have no idea, and I don't believe he has."

"I suppose you don't know whether he corresponds with her?"

"I don't actually know, sir, but I think not. My impression is that he doesn't even know her address. Queer, isn't it? But then she's a queer woman. With all her flighty ways, she is uncommonly good at keeping her own counsel."

This last observation rather impressed Tom, for now, reflecting on it, he suddenly realized how very little he knew about this strange woman. However, she was not his concern now that his anxieties on Vanderpuye's account had been dispelled and, as he had obtained the information that he had come to seek, he began to consider whether it was not time for him to go. Polton had duties of some kind, and a prolonged visit might be inconvenient. But when he made tentative signs of departure, his host protested, "You are not going on my account, sir, I hope, because the Doctor is dining out to-night and I've got the evening to myself. Besides, now that he has given me an understudy to carry on in my absence, I am much freer than I used to be. Of course, I mustn't detain you if you can't spare the time, but – "

In effect, Tom was very glad to stay, and said so and, accordingly, having filled his pipe (at Polton's invitation), settled down to spend a very pleasant and interesting evening. For his host, although "an inveterate mechanic," possessed a wealth of information on all sorts of curious and unexpected subjects, and when they had examined the remarkable technical library, the pictures on the wall, and the picturesque old clock (Polton's chiefest treasure, a relic of the home of his childhood, which had come to him on the demise of a certain Aunt Judy), they subsided into their respective chairs to gossip discursively on the various subjects in which they had a common interest, with a general leaning towards "antiques".

"To return to your pedometer, sir," said Polton, when Tom finally rose to depart, "I shall look it over in my spare time, but it won't take long. When it is done I will bring it round to your studio, if you will tell me when I shall find you at home."

"It's very good of you, Polton, but I think you had better settle the time. I can always stay in if I want to."

"Then, sir, I would suggest next Thursday, about three o'clock if that will suit you."

"It will suit me perfectly," said Tom, taking up his hat and stick and, having thus made the assignation, he shook hands with his host who, nevertheless, escorted him as far as the laboratory floor where they parted, Tom to make his way homeward and Polton, probably, to launch the attack on the pedometer.

During the next few days Tom gave only an occasional passing thought to Lotta. He was completely reassured. There had been no elopement or scandal of any kind, and that was all that mattered to him. As to the woman herself, he could only echo Polton's wish that she might stay away as long as possible, and if she should never come back, her absence would create a void not entirely unacceptable. In fact, he began to hope that she had passed out of his life – that he had, at last, really finished with her, and from vaguely hoping came gradually to believe that it might be so.

The disillusionment was sudden and violent. It synchronized with the arrival on the appointed day of his pedometer-bearing friend. At three o'clock to the minute on Thursday afternoon the studio bell rang, and Tom, hurrying out at the summons, found Mr. Polton on the wide doorstep. But he was not alone. Sharing the doorstep with him was an anxious-looking woman whom he recognized as his next-door neighbour, Mrs. Mitchens, who was also Lotta's landlady. He had been on bowing terms with her for some years but had never spoken to her, except to wish her good morning, and he now wondered what her business with him might be. But he was soon enlightened, for almost as he appeared at the door she asked in an agitated tone, "Could I have a few words with you, Mr. Pedley?" (On which Polton tried to efface himself and prepared to slink in by the half-open door.) "It's about Mrs. Schiller, sir."

As she spoke the name Polton halted suddenly, and tried to look as if he were not listening.

482

"I have come to you, Mr. Pedley," Mrs. Mitchens continued, "because you were a friend of hers and I thought you might know what has become of her. I haven't seen or heard of her for quite a long time."

"Oh, that's all right, Mrs. Mitchens," Tom answered cheerfully. "She has just gone away to stay with some friends at Birmingham."

But Mrs. Mitchens did not look satisfied. "It's very strange," she objected. "She never said anything to me about going away, and the rent hasn't been paid, though she was always so punctual. You are sure she has gone to Birmingham?"

Tom reflected for a moment and then, turning to Polton, asked, "What do you say? Are we sure?"

"Well, sir," was the reply. "I wouldn't put it as high as that. I was told by Mr. Vanderpuye that Mrs. Schiller had told him that she was going to stay with friends at Birmingham. That is all. We don't actually know whether she has or has not gone."

"Then," said Mrs. Mitchens, "I am afraid she has not gone."

"Why do you say that?" Tom asked.

Mrs. Mitchens appeared to be in difficulties. "I hardly know how to express it," she replied, "but there's something wrong in her rooms. My husband and I have both noticed it, and it seems to be getting worse."

"I don't quite understand," said Tom. "What is getting worse?"

"It is difficult to explain," she replied, "but if you will be so good as to step into the hall, you will understand what I mean."

Tom showed no eagerness to accept this invitation, but Polton, now all agog, requested the lady to lead the way and followed her with a purposeful air while Tom brought up the rear, and watched her gloomily as she inserted her latch-key.

But Mrs. Mitchens was right. No sooner had they entered the hall and shut the outer door than they both understood perfectly what she had meant. But the realization affected them differently. Tom shrank back with an expression of horrified disgust towards the outer door, whereas Polton, having sampled the air by a little diagnostic sniff, took the definite initiative.

"I presume, madam," said he, "that this door is locked?"

"Yes," she replied. "Locked from the inside."

"Well," said Polton, "that room ought to be entered, at once."

"That is what my husband said, and he tried it with one of our keys, but unfortunately the key is in the lock, and he didn't like to break the door open."

"No," Polton agreed, "it is better to use a key if possible. May I ask whether the lock has been used much?"

483

"Yes," she replied, "constantly. Mrs. Schiller always locked the door at night and whenever she went out."

"Ha," said he, "then it should turn pretty easily. It is sometimes possible," he continued reflectively, with his hand in an inner pocket, "to persuade a key round from the outside if it isn't too stiff. Now, I wonder if I happen to have anything in my pocket that would answer the purpose."

Apparently he had, for as he stooped to peer into the keyhole, his hand came out of the pocket holding an object that looked somewhat like a rather unusual pocket corkscrew fitted with some stout angular wire levers. One of these he inserted into the keyhole and pried about the interior of the lock while Mrs. Mitchens gazed expectantly at his hand, which concealed both the keyhole and the instrument.

"Yes," said he, "the 'thing'." And as he spoke, the lock clicked, the instrument was withdrawn (disappearing instantly into the pocket whence it had come), and Polton turned the handle and tried the door, shutting it again immediately.

"It isn't bolted, you see, madam," said he, stepping back to make way for her.

She showed a natural reluctance to enter that mysterious and ominous room, but after a few moments' hesitation she grasped the knob, turned it softly, opened the door and stepped in. But even as she entered she uttered a low scream and stood stock still with the doorknob in her hand, staring before her with an expression of horror.

"Oh, the poor thing!" she exclaimed. "She has made away with herself. Do, please, come in and look at her."

On this, Polton entered the room followed by Tom, and for a while both stood by the door gazing at the tragic figure sitting limply with dropped head in a little elbow chair that had been drawn up to the table. The right arm hung straight down while the left lay on the table and, close to the discoloured hand was an empty tumbler and, a few inches away, a small glass water jug and a little bottle containing white tablets.

"Poor creature!" moaned Mrs. Mitchens. "I wonder why she did it, so bright and cheerful as she always seemed. And how dreadful she looks, poor dear. I should never have recognized her."

Polton, meanwhile, had cast a keen glance round the room, and now, stepping forward, leaned over the table to scrutinize the tumbler and the bottle of tablets.

"What is in that bottle?" Tom asked.

"Cyanide of potassium," was the reply.

"That is a strong poison, isn't it?"

484

"A most deadly poison," Polton replied, "and extremely rapid in its action – quite easy to obtain, too, as you see from the label on this bottle – '*Photographic Tablets*'. Easy to get and hard to trace."

"The tracing of them won't be of much importance in this case," remarked Tom, "as she poisoned herself. The question is: Why on earth did she do it?"

From the poison Polton turned his attention to the corpse and, as he stood gazing at the dead woman, an expression of surprise and perplexity stole over his face. At this moment a beam of pale autumn sunlight shone in through the window, lighting up the fair hair to the brightness of burnished gold. This appearance seemed further to surprise Polton for, with a distinctly startled expression, he stepped close to the corpse and, delicately picking up a small tress of the golden hair, held it close to his face, and scrutinized it intently. Then as if still unsatisfied, he gently raised the bowed head and looked long and intently into the poor bloated, discoloured face. Tom and the landlady both watched him in astonishment, and the former demanded, "What is it, Polton?"

Polton, still holding the head erect, replied impressively, "This woman, sir, is not Mrs. Schiller."

"Not Mrs. Schiller!" the landlady echoed. "But she must be. Who else could she be, locked in here in Mrs. Schiller's room?"

"This is certainly not Mrs. Schiller," Polton persisted. "I ask you, sir, to come and see for yourself. You knew her better than I did. You will see that the hair is the wrong colour and the features are different."

"I noticed the hair when the sun shone on it," said Tom, "and it struck me as being somehow changed. But as to the features, I should say that they are quite unrecognizable."

"Not at all, sir," replied Polton. "The skin is bloated, but there is the nose. That is unchanged, and so, more or less, is the chin. And there are the ears, they are hardly affected at all. You had better come and have a look at her as the identification is most important."

Thus urged, Tom plucked up courage to make a close inspection, and as Polton held the head up, he examined first the profile and then the ears. A very brief scrutiny satisfied him, for, as he backed away from the corpse, he announced, "Yes, Polton, you are right. This is not Lotta Schiller. The nose and chin look the wrong shape, but the ears are quite conclusive. They are of an entirely different type from Lotta's, and differently set on the head."

"You really think, sir," said the landlady, "that this poor creature is not Mrs. Schiller?"

"I feel no doubt whatever," he replied, "and very much relieved I am that she is not."

485

"So am I, for that matter," said Mrs. Mitchens. "But how on earth does she come to be here? Locked herself in, too. It's an absolute mystery."

"It certainly is," Tom agreed. "But it isn't our mystery. It will be for the police to solve it."

"That is true, sir," said Polton, "though perhaps it may be more of our mystery than you think. But, of course, the police will have to be informed at once, and it will be for them to find out who this poor woman is, and how she came to be here. But there is one question that I should like to settle now, that is whether she took the poison herself, or whether it was given to her by someone else."

"But," Tom objected, "the police will deal with that question. It isn't our affair."

"It is not, sir," Polton admitted. "But I should like to know, just for my own satisfaction. Do you happen to have a piece of fairly stiff smooth paper about you?"

With a rather puzzled air Tom brought out of his pocket the artist's notebook that he always carried.

"Will that do?" he asked. "If it will, you can tear a leaf out, but don't take one with a drawing on it."

"I won't tear the leaf out," said Polton. "It will be handier in the book, and I shan't want to keep it."

He took the little canvas-bound volume and, watched curiously by Tom and the landlady, went over to a small writing-table on which lay, beside the blotter, a rubber stamp and an inking-pad.

Taking up the latter, he carried it across to the table at which the dead woman was sitting, when he once more examined the tumbler as well as he could without touching it.

"The finger marks," he observed, "look like those of a left hand, and as the left hand is near the tumbler we will try that first."

Very gently, to avoid disturbing the body, he raised the hand and, grasping the thumb, pressed it on the inking-pad. Then, laying down the pad and taking up the book, he brought the inked thumb over a blank page, pressed it down lightly and withdrew it. In the same way he took an impression of each of the four fingers, the group of prints being arranged in a line in their correct order and, as soon as he had finished, he carefully wiped the traces of ink from the fingertips with his handkerchief. Softly laying down the hand, he placed the open book by the side of the tumbler and carefully compared the prints on each.

"Well," said Tom, "what do you make of it?"

"The prints on the tumbler are her finger-prints all right," replied Polton. "Would you like to see them?"

Tom's principal desire now was to escape from the charnel-house atmosphere of this room but, as Polton evidently wished him to see the prints, he went over to the table.

"My prints are very poor, smeary impressions," said Polton, "but you can see the patterns quite well. Look at the thumb-print with that spiral whorl on it, and compare it with the one on the tumbler. You can see plainly that it is the same pattern."

"Yes," Tom agreed, "I can make that out quite clearly, but the patterns of the fingers don't seem so distinctive."

"No," Polton admitted, "they are rather indistinct for some reason, especially in the middle of each print. But still, if you compare them with the tumbler, you can see that the patterns are the same."

"I'll take your word for it," said Tom, "as you know more about it than I do. And after all, it isn't our affair whether she took the poison herself or not. Of course, the police will settle that question, and if you take my advice, you will say nothing about these finger-prints. The authorities don't much like outside interference."

"I think Mr. Pedley is right," said Mrs. Mitchens. "We don't want to appear officious or meddlesome, and we certainly don't want to offend the police."

"No, ma'am," Polton agreed, "we do not. It will be much better to keep our own counsel – which, in fact, is what I had intended to suggest. I made the trial just to satisfy my curiosity as to whether it was a case of suicide or murder."

"Well," said Tom, edging towards the door, "now we know, and the next question is, who is to inform the police?"

As he raised the question he looked significantly at Mrs. Mitchens, who replied gloomily, as they retired to the hall, "I suppose, as I am the householder and Mrs. Schiller's landlady, I had better go. But I can't tell them much, and I expect they will want to question you about Mrs. Schiller."

"I expect they will," said Tom, "but, meanwhile, I think you are the proper person to give the information."

With this view Polton agreed emphatically and, by way of closing the discussion, softly drew the key out of the lock, closed the door and, having locked it, withdrew the key and handed it to the landlady. Then he and Tom, after a few words of condolence with Mrs. Mitchens, took their leave and made their way to the studio.

"Pah!" exclaimed Tom, taking several deep breaths as they emerged into the open air. "What a horrible affair! But I suppose you are used to this sort of thing."

"To some extent, sir," replied Polton. "I have learned from The Doctor not to allow my attention to be distracted by mere physical unpleasantness. But what a mysterious affair this is. I can make nothing of it. Here is a woman, apparently a stranger, locked in Mrs. Schiller's room with Mrs. Schiller's key. All sorts of questions arise. Who is she? How did she get that key? Why did she come to that place to commit suicide – if she really did commit suicide? And where is Mrs. Schiller? The police will want to find answers to those questions, and some of them will take a good deal of answering, I fancy."

"Yes," Tom agreed gloomily, "and they'll look to us to find some of the answers. It is going to be an infernal nuisance."

When they had washed – which Tom did with exhaustive thoroughness – in a big bowl in the studio sink, they resumed the discussion while they laid the table for tea and boiled the kettle. But nothing came of it beyond bringing to light, the curious difference in their points of view. To Tom, the tragedy was repulsively horrible, and his connection with it profoundly distasteful. Interest in it or curiosity he had none.

Polton, on the other hand, so far from being shocked or disgusted, seemed to savour the details with a sort of ghoulish relish and fairly to revel in the mystery and obscurity of the case, so much so that Tom's repeated efforts to divert the conversation into more agreeable channels failed utterly and, for the first time in his experience, he was almost relieved when the time came for Polton to return to his duties.

"Well, sir," the departing guest remarked as he wriggled into his overcoat, "this has been an eventful afternoon. I have enjoyed it immensely." Here he paused suddenly in his wrigglings, gazing at Tom in ludicrous consternation. "God bless me, sir," he exclaimed, "I had nearly forgotten the pedometer. I have cleaned it up and put it in going order, and I have fitted a new regulator with a micrometer screw and attached a watch-key to turn it with. You will see at once how it works, but I have written down a few directions."

He produced the instrument, wrapped in tissue paper, and laid it with the little document on the table. Then, deprecating Tom's grateful acknowledgments, he shook hands and bustled away, en route for The Temple.

Chapter VIII
Revelations

When Polton's departure had left him to the peaceful enjoyment of his own society, Tom Pedley tried to dismiss from his mind the gruesome experience of the afternoon and settle down to his ordinary occupations. But try as he would to forget it, that dreadful figure, seated at the table, intruded constantly into his thoughts and refused to be dislodged, and when, later in the evening, the studio bell announced a visitor, he resigned himself to the inevitable, and went out to the gate, where, as he had expected, he found a police officer waiting on the threshold.

"You'll guess what I have come about, sir," the latter said, genially, as Tom conducted him to the studio, "just to make a few preliminary inquiries. I am the coroner's officer and it is my job to find out what evidence is available for the inquest."

"Well, Sergeant," said Tom, "I will give you all the help I can, though I am afraid it will be mighty little. However, if you will take a seat and tell me what you want to know, I'll do my best. Perhaps a glass of beer might be helpful."

The sergeant agreed that it might, and when he had been settled in an easy chair by the fire with a jug of beer and a couple of glasses on a small table by his side, and had – by invitation – filled and lighted his pipe, the inquisition began.

But we know what Tom's information amounted to. Of the material facts of the case he knew nothing. The dead woman was a stranger to him, and even Lotta Schiller was little more. Indeed, as he strove vainly to answer the sergeant's questions, he was surprised to find how completely ignorant he was of her antecedents, her position in the world, her friends and relations – of everything, in fact, concerning her except the little that he had gathered from direct observation.

"Seems rather a mysterious sort of lady," the sergeant remarked as Tom refilled his glass. "Pretty discreet, too, not given to babbling. Is there anybody that knows more about her than you do?"

Tom suggested Mr. Vanderpuye, but as the latter's address was unknown to him, he referred the sergeant to Mr. Polton.

"That's the gentleman who unlocked the door from the outside," commented the sergeant. "Handy gentleman he must be. Yes, I'd like to have a word with him, if you would tell me where to find him."

"He is a laboratory assistant to Dr. Thorndyke of 5A King's Bench Walk, and he lives on the premises."

At the mention of "The Doctor's" name, the sergeant pricked up his ears.

"Oh, that's who he is," said he. "Would be a handy gentleman, naturally. I'll just pop along and see what he can tell me. Do you think it is too late to call on him to-night?"

Bearing in mind Polton's intense interest in the case, Tom thought that it was not, whereupon the sergeant, having finished his beer and reloaded his pipe, prepared to depart.

"We shall want his evidence," said he as he moved towards the door, "to prove that the door was really locked from the inside, and as to yourself, sir, although you don't seem to have much to tell, I expect you'll get a summons. Something new might arise which you could throw light on. However, the inquest won't be opened for some days, as time has to be allowed for the analysis after the *post mortem*."

Events justified the sergeant's forecast. In due course the summons was served and, at the appointed place and time, Tom presented himself to give evidence if called upon. He arrived a little before time and thereby secured a reasonably comfortable Windsor armchair, in which he sat at his ease and observed the arrival of the other witnesses, among whom were Mrs. Mitchens, his friend Dr. Oldfield, Polton, and Vanderpuye – who arrived together – and last, no less a person than his old acquaintance, Detective-inspector Blandy.

"Hallo, Pedley," said the doctor, taking the adjoining chair. "Sorry to see you mixed up in a disreputable affair like this. Extraordinary business, though, isn't it? Ha, here comes the coroner and the jury. They've been to view the body, I suppose, and look as if they hadn't enjoyed it. Well, how are you? I haven't seen anything of you for quite a long time – not since you took up with that painted Judy that I have seen you gadding about with."

Tom reddened slightly. He had, in fact, rather neglected his friends since Lotta had taken possession of him. However, there was no opportunity to rebut the accusation, for the coroner, having taken his seat and glanced round at the witnesses and the reporters, proceeded to open the inquiry with a brief address. It was a very brief address, no more than a simple statement that "We are here to inquire into the circumstances in which a woman, whose name appears to be Emma Robey, met with her death. I need not," he continued, "go into any particulars, as these will transpire in the depositions of the witnesses, and by way of introducing you to the circumstances I will begin by taking the evidence of Sergeant Porter."

490

On hearing his name mentioned, Tom's new acquaintance took up his position at the table and stood at attention while he disposed of the preliminaries with professional swiftness and precision and waited for the next question.

"I think, Sergeant," said the coroner, "that you had better just tell us what you know about this affair," whereupon the officer proceeded, with the manner of one reading from a document, to recite the facts.

"On Thursday, the 30th of December, 1930, at 3:46 p.m., Mrs. Julia Mitchens came to the police station and reported that she had found in a room in her house the dead body of a woman who was a stranger to her, and who had apparently committed suicide by taking poison. She stated that the room had been let to, and was ordinarily occupied by, a Mrs. Schiller, but that the said tenant had been absent from her rooms for some time and that her present whereabouts was unknown. In answer to certain questions from me, she gave the following further particulars – " Here the sergeant gave a more detailed account of the events, including the unlocking of the door by Mr. Polton, " – with some kind of instrument – " which we need not report since they are already known to the reader.

On receiving these particulars, he had accompanied Mrs. Mitchens to her house and had been admitted by her to the room, where he found the corpse and the other objects as she had described them. Having given a vivid and exact description of the room, the seated corpse, the tumbler, and the poison bottle, he continued.

"As the circumstances were very remarkable, I decided to make no detailed examination without further instructions and, accordingly I came away, having locked the door and taken possession of the key, and returned to the station, where I made my report to the Superintendent. When he had heard it, he decided that it would be advisable to inform the authorities at headquarters of the facts so far known and directed me to telephone to the Criminal Investigation Department at Scotland Yard, which I did, and was informed in reply that an officer was being dispatched immediately. I also telephoned to the Divisional Surgeon, acquainting him with the facts and asking him to attend as soon as possible.

"In about twenty minutes, Inspector Blandy of the C.I.D. arrived by car and, almost at the same moment, the Divisional Surgeon, Dr. Oldfield. Acting on instructions, I conducted them to the house, Number Thirty-nine Jacob Street, and admitted them to the room. When the doctor had made his examination he went away, but I stayed for about ten minutes to assist the inspector with his examination. Then I handed him the key and came away, leaving him to continue his investigations."

At this point the sergeant made a definite pause, looking inquiringly at the coroner, who said, in answer to the implied question, "Yes, Sergeant and, as Inspector Blandy is here to give evidence, I don't think we need trouble you for any further particulars, unless the jury wish to ask any questions."

The jury did not, and accordingly, when the depositions had been read and signed, the sergeant retired to his place behind the coroner, and the name of the next witness, Dr. Oldfield, was called.

The doctor, like the sergeant, made short work of the preliminaries and, having been accommodated with a chair and started by the coroner, reeled off his evidence with similar ease and precision. But we need not report it verbatim. The general description of the corpse and its surroundings merely repeated that of the previous witness, but from this the doctor continued.

"I examined the body carefully as I found it, especially in relation to its position in the chair. It seemed very insecurely balanced. In fact, it appeared to be supported almost entirely by the arm which was extended on the table. When I lifted this clear and let it hang down, the body slipped forward in the chair and would have slid to the floor if I had not propped it up."

"You seem to attach some significance to this condition," said the coroner. "What did it suggest to you?"

"I think it is a fact worth noting," the doctor replied cautiously, "but I would rather not go beyond that, except to say that it seemed somewhat against the probabilities. I should have expected that at the moment of death, when all the muscles suddenly relaxed, the body would have slipped forward out of the chair."

The coroner pondered this careful answer for a few moments, and then asked, "Could you judge how long the deceased had been dead?"

"Only approximately. I would say about three weeks."

"Did you discover anything further?"

"Not on this occasion, but I examined the body very thoroughly at the mortuary and drew up a detailed description, mainly for use by the police. Do you wish me to give those details?"

"It is not actually necessary," the coroner replied, "but perhaps it would be as well to put the description on record in the depositions. Yes, let us have the full details."

The witness accordingly proceeded: "The body was that of a woman of about thirty, apparently married, as she was wearing a wedding ring, but there were no indications of her having borne a child. Her height was five-feet-six-and-a-quarter inches, weight one hundred and twenty-four pounds – eight-stone-twelve. Figure spare – in fact, definitely thin.

492

Complexion fair, hair flaxen or golden. Its length suggested that it had been bobbed some time ago, now a little below the shoulders. Eyes apparently grey, but it was impossible to judge the exact tint owing to the condition of the body. For the same reason, the features were a little obscure but it could be seen that the nose was rather small, of the concave type, with a slight prominence on the bridge. The mouth medium-sized and apparently well shaped. The ears were more distinctive and less changed. They were slightly outstanding, thin in all parts with hardly any lobule, and set obliquely on the head. The line of the jaw was also markedly slanting, and the chin was pointed and slightly receding.

"As to the identity of the deceased, I was present when the clothing was removed from the body and I examined each garment. Two of them were marked in ink with the initials '*ER*.', one was marked in ink '*E. Robey*', and a small fancy handkerchief in the skirt pocket bore the name 'Emma' embroidered in white silk. That completes the description of the deceased."

"Yes," said the coroner, "and a very full and clear description it is. There ought not to be any difficulty in getting the body identified. And now we come to the question of the cause of death. Were you able to ascertain that?"

"Yes. The cause of death was poisoning by potassium cyanide. The dose taken was very large, fully sixty grains, and death probably occurred almost instantaneously, or, at most, within a minute or two."

"Is potassium cyanide a very powerful poison?"

"Yes, very. It contains prussic acid in a concentrated form and acts in the same way and with the same violence and rapidity."

"What is the lethal dose?"

"It is usually given as less than five grains, probably as little as two-and-a-half grains but, as in the case of most poisons, the effects vary in different individuals. But a dose of sixty grains is enormous."

"Did you make the analysis yourself?"

"Yes, in conjunction with Professor Woodfield. When I made the *post mortem*, I removed the organs and took them in sealed and marked receptacles to the laboratory of St. Margaret's Hospital, where the professor and I made the analysis together."

"The poison was derived, I suppose, from the tablets of which we have heard?"

"So one would have assumed, and analysis proved that the tablets were really composed of potassium cyanide. But when we came to make the examination, a very curious fact transpired. The quantity of the poison taken was at least sixty grains, the tablets were shown by the label

493

on the bottle to contain five grains each, and we verified this by analysis. The quantity taken was therefore equal to twelve tablets. But there were not twelve tablets missing from the bottle. The label showed that the bottle, when full, had contained fifty tablets of five grains each, so that if twelve had been consumed, there should have remained thirty-eight. But there were forty-three, or five more than there should have been."

"That doesn't seem to me very conclusive," the coroner objected. "There might have been some error in filling the bottle. Don't you think so?"

"No, sir," Oldfield replied firmly. "We excluded that possibility. I purchased two fresh bottles from the makers, and the professor and I each counted the tablets. There were exactly fifty in each bottle, and the important fact is that each bottle was quite full. Neither would hold another tablet. Then we tried the bottle that was found on the deceased's table, and the result was the same, it would hold fifty tablets and not one more. A single extra tablet prevented the complete insertion of the cork."

The coroner appeared deeply impressed. "It is a most extraordinary thing," said he, "but there seems to be no doubt of the facts. Can you suggest any explanation?"

"The only explanation that occurs to me is that the poison taken was not derived from the tablets at all. Part of it certainly was not, and if a part came from another source it is most probable that the whole of it did. The facts suggest to me that a solution of the cyanide was prepared in advance, and that it was this solution which was swallowed by the deceased. But that is only my opinion."

"Exactly. But if your view is correct, why were the tablets there?"

"That," Oldfield replied, "is not strictly a medical question."

"No," the coroner agreed with a smile, "but we needn't be too pedantic. You have considered the question, I think, and we should like to hear your conclusion."

"Then I may say that the tablets appeared to me to have been put there designedly to support the idea of suicide."

The coroner apparently considered this a rather lame conclusion, for he did not pursue the subject, but returned to the analysis.

"Did your chemical examination bring out anything more?"

"Yes, another very significant fact. At my suggestion, Professor Woodfield tested the material for morphine, and I assisted him. The result was that we discovered undoubted traces of the drug, though the condition of the body did not admit of anything like a reliable estimate of quantity. But morphine was certainly there, and in an appreciable amount, as was proved by our getting a positive reaction. A very small quantity would not have been discoverable at all."

494

"Can you give us any idea as to the amount that had been taken?"

"We agreed that our results suggested a full – but not very large – dose. Not more than a third-of-a-grain, or at the outside, half-a-grain."

"But isn't half-a-grain rather a large dose?"

"It is a very large dose if given hypodermically, but not so excessive if swallowed. Still, one doesn't usually give more than a quarter-of-a-grain."

"You said just now that the morphine test was made at your suggestion. What made you suspect the presence of morphine?"

"It was hardly a suspicion. The possibility occurred to me, and it seemed worthwhile to test it."

"But what suggested the possibility?"

"The idea arose from a consideration of the extraordinary circumstances of this case. Taken at their face value, the appearances point definitely to suicide. But yet it is impossible to rule out the alternative of homicide by the forcible administration of poison. It is very difficult, however, to compel a person to swallow even a liquid against his will, and the attempt would involve considerable violence, which would leave its marks on the body. But if the victim could be given a full dose of morphine beforehand, he would become so lethargic and passive that the poison could be administered quite easily.

"In this case, I searched carefully for bruises or other signs of violence but I found none, which seemed to exclude the suggestion of homicide, but only on the condition that no narcotic had been taken. It was then that I decided to test for the most likely and most suitable narcotic – morphine."

"And having found it, what do you infer? You seem to imply that its presence suggests homicidal poisoning."

"I would not put it as high as that, but if there should be other evidence creating a presumption of homicide, the presence of the morphine would be strong corroboration."

This completed the doctor's evidence and, when the depositions had been read and signed, he was informed that he was free to go about his business. He elected, however, to return to his seat to hear the rest of the evidence, and to jot down a few notes.

"I think," said the coroner, "that if we take the inspector's evidence next, we shall have all the known facts of the case and can fill in details later from the evidence of the other witnesses."

Accordingly, Inspector Blandy, having, at the coroner's invitation, taken possession of the vacated chair, bestowed a benevolent smile on the jury and ran off the preliminaries with the air of one pronouncing a benediction. Then, in reply to the opening question, he introduced his

495

evidence by a general statement which, in effect, repeated those of the preceding witnesses. Having described the room, the corpse, the table, and the various objects on it, he continued.

"When the doctor had finished his examination, I proceeded with my own, beginning with the tumbler and the water jug. On these were a number of finger-prints, mostly very distinct, and apparently, all made by the same hands. Those on the water jug were from a right hand and those on the tumbler were from the left. I took the finger-prints of the deceased on small cards and compared them with those on the tumbler and the water jug, and I can say, positively, that they were the same. All the prints on the jug and the tumbler were certainly those of the deceased's fingers, and there were no others."

"Would you regard that as conclusive evidence that the deceased took the poison herself?"

"No, certainly not. Anyone having control of the dead body could easily have taken the finger-prints of the deceased on the jug and the glass. The evidential value of the finger-prints is dependent on the other evidence."

"You have heard that the deceased was locked in the room and that the key was on the inside."

"Yes," the inspector agreed, beaming benignly on the coroner, "but I have also heard that the door was unlocked from the outside by Mr. Polton, and he could as easily have locked it from the outside, leaving the key inside. In fact, the thing is frequently done by criminals, especially by hotel thieves, who have a special instrument made for the purpose, somewhat like a dentist's root-forceps. With this they can grasp the key from the outside, unlock the door, commit their robbery and, when the go away, relock the door from outside, leaving the key inside."

"Have you any reason to believe that the door of the deceased's room was locked from the outside in this way?"

"Not with the instrument that I have mentioned. That instrument, having roughened jaws, usually leaves little scratches on the key. I examined the key for scratches, but there were none. Nevertheless, I believe that the door was locked from the outside and that a very simple improvised apparatus was used. Perhaps I had better explain the method before giving the reasons for my belief. The procedure – which is well known to the police – is this: The key is placed in the lock so that a quarter-turn will be enough to shoot the bolt, then a small rod such as a thick match, a skewer, or a lead pencil, is passed through the bow, or handle, of the key and a loop at the end of a length of string is hitched on to the rod. The string has to be kept fairly tight to prevent the loop from falling off. The operator now goes out, closing the door after him, keeping the tightened string in the space between the edge of the door and the jamb, and well above the level of the key, then he gives a steady pull at the string with the result that the leverage of the little rod turns the key and shoots the bolt of the lock. When the key has made a quarter-turn and locked the door, the loop slips off the rod, the string is pulled out through the crack of the door, and the little rod either drops on the floor or is flicked out of the key and falls some distance away."

The coroner looked a little dubious. "It sounds very ingenious," said he, "but rather risky for a person who has just committed a murder. Suppose the plan should fail."

"But it couldn't fail, sir," the inspector replied. "If it did not work the first time, all he would have to do would be to open the door and try again. Perhaps a demonstration will make it clear."

He opened the attaché case that he had brought with him and took out a flat slab of wood to which a lock had been attached and a through keyhole made. Inserting a key, he produced a thick match and a length of string with a loop at the end. Passing the match through the bow of the key, he held it there while he slipped the loop over it and drew the string fairly taut.

"Now," said he, "observe what happens. The key is towards you and I am on the outside of the door."

He held the slab firmly on the table, brought the tightened string round to the back, and gave a steady pull. Instantly, the key was seen to turn, the bolt shot out, the loop slipped off the match, and the latter, flicked out of the key, flew along the table.

The effect of the experiment was unmistakable. The jurymen smiled and nodded, and even the coroner admitted his conviction.

"And now, sir," said the inspector, picking up the match and viewing it through a lens, "I will ask you to examine this match. Near the middle you will see a little indented curved line on one side and, on the opposite side, about half-an-inch nearer the head, a smaller, less distinct mark. Then, at the other end of the match, where the loop of the string caught it, you will see four little dents, one at each corner, and if you place the match in the key, as it was when I pulled the string, you will see that the two dents on the side correspond exactly with the sharp edges of the key-bow."

He illustrated the method and then passed the match together with his magnifying glass to the coroner, who examined it with intense interest and then passed it to the jury.

"Well, Inspector," said the coroner when the match had gone the round, "you have given us a most conclusive demonstration, and I am

497

sure that we are all convinced of the practicability of the method. The next question is, Have you any evidence that it was actually used?"

The inspector's answer was to open once more his attaché case and take from it a corked glass tube containing a single large match, the end of which bore a spot of red sealing-wax. Then from his pocket he produced a key and, taking the match from its tube, laid it and the key on the table before the coroner.

"This match," said he, "which I have marked with sealing-wax to prevent mistakes, is, as you see, a large-size Bryant and May. I found it on the floor of the room (which I will call 'the deceased's room') under a small cabinet, two-feet-three-inches from the door. This is the key with which that door was locked. On the match are six indentations exactly like those on the other match, which you have. The two side indentations correspond exactly with the sharp edges of the key-bow. I have no doubt that this match was used to lock that door, and I am confirmed in this by having found on the arris, or sharp corner of the edge of the door, an indented mark at exactly the spot where the string would have passed round, as proved by actual trial. I can't produce the door, but I have here a heel-ball rubbing which shows the mark distinctly."

He handed the sheet of paper to the coroner, who, having examined the rubbing, and passed it to the foreman of the jury, turned once more to the witness.

"You have given us, Inspector, a very complete and convincing demonstration, and there now arises from it another question. This key which you have shown us apparently belongs to the door of the room in which the body of the deceased was found. But whose property is it? The presumption is that it belongs to the tenant of the room, Mrs. Schiller. But is it actually her key, or only one similar to hers? Can you tell us that?"

"Only by hearsay. I am informed by Mrs. Mitchens that this key is the actual key that she gave to Mrs. Schiller. She can identify it by a mark that was made on it. As she is one of the witnesses, she can give you the particulars first-hand, but I think there is no doubt that this is Mrs. Schiller's own key."

"Then the next question is: Where is Mrs. Schiller?"

The inspector smiled a pensive smile. "I wish," he replied, "that I could answer that question. Ever since the discovery, we have been trying to get into touch with her, but we cannot learn anything as to her whereabouts. She is said to be in Birmingham, but that is a rather vague address even if it is correct. We have advertised in the papers, asking her to communicate with us, but there has been no reply."

"In effect, then, she has disappeared?"

"That is what it seems to amount to. At any rate she is missing."

"The importance of the matter is," said the coroner, "that if this is her key, there must have been some kind of contact between her and the deceased."

"Precisely, sir," Blandy agreed. "That is why we are so anxious to get into touch with her."

This was the inspector's final contribution and, when he had signed the depositions and retired to his seat, the name of Julia Mitchens was called, and that lady proceeded to give her evidence, which was largely negative. She had never seen or heard of a person named Emma Robey. Of her tenant, Mrs. Schiller, she knew practically nothing. The lady had engaged the ground-floor rooms, furnished, but had added some furniture. No references were given but the rent was paid – in cash – monthly, in advance. She had said that she needed no attendance but wanted to be left alone to do her work, which was that of an artist. Witness seldom saw her excepting when she paid the rent. She was pleasant in manner but not intimate. She had a separate electric bell with a small brass name-plate under it, and a removable brass plate on the wall, which she took down every evening. She had her own latch-key and keys of the bedroom and the sitting room. The bedroom door was kept locked, and she always locked the sitting room door when she went out.

The witness never saw any visitors except Mr. Pedley and a black gentleman, and them very rarely. Had known Mr. Pedley by sight for some years. Does not know whether Mrs. Schiller ever stayed away from home. Had noticed the absence of the plate from the wall for about three weeks and, later, had become aware of an unpleasant odour in the hall.

"To come back to the subject of the keys," said the coroner. "A key was found in the lock of the sitting room door. If Inspector Blandy will lend us that key for a moment, can you tell us for certain whether it is the one that you gave to Mrs. Schiller?"

"I am sure I can, sir," was the reply.

Here the inspector produced the key and, having taken the precaution to tie a small piece of string round the bow, passed it to the coroner who handed it to the witness.

"Yes, sir," said Mrs. Mitchens after a single glance at it, "this is Mrs. Schiller's own key."

"You speak quite confidently," said the coroner. "How are you able to distinguish this key from all other keys?"

"It is this way, sir," she replied. "When Mrs. Schiller engaged the rooms there was a big old-fashioned lock on the sitting room door with a large clumsy key. Mrs. Schiller found this very inconvenient, so I got the locksmith to fix a more modern lock with a smaller key. He supplied two keys with the lock and I decided to keep one in reserve in case the other should be lost, but I thought it better to mark the two keys to prevent mistakes, so my husband filed a nick on the handle of the one that Mrs. Schiller was to have, and two nicks on the other to show that it was the duplicate. This key has one nick, so it must be Mrs. Schiller's, and here is the duplicate with the two nicks on it."

As she spoke, she took a key from her handbag and laid it, with the other, on the table.

The coroner took up the two keys and having rapidly compared their bows, passed them to the jury, from whom they presently found their way back to their respective owners.

"This evidence," said the coroner, "is very important and perfectly conclusive. We now know for certain that the key which was found in the door was Mrs. Schiller's own key. How it came there, Mrs. Schiller alone can explain. I suppose," he added, turning to the witness. "You cannot give us any hint as to where she may possibly be?"

"No, indeed, sir," was the reply. "I had no idea that she had gone away, and when I first noticed the – er – *unpleasantness*, I thought she was lying dead in her room."

"By the way, you had the duplicate key. Why did you not try to enter that room?"

"We did try, sir, but the other key was in the lock."

"Yes, of course. Well, Mrs. Mitchens, you have given us some very important evidence, and now, if nothing else occurs to you I think we need not detain you any longer."

The next witness was Tom Pedley. But Tom knew nothing about anything, and said so. To his relief no questions were asked about Lotta's artistic abilities, and the only contribution that he made was a brief history of his acquaintance with Lotta, a very definite statement of his relations with her, and a rather sketchy description of the expedition to Epping Forest, that being the last occasion on which he had seen her. He was followed by Nathaniel Polton, who testified that the door was undoubtedly locked when he tried it and, from the smoothness with which the key turned, he inferred that the lock had been kept oiled. He had had no difficulty in unlocking it with a simple bent wire appliance (which he had unfortunately forgotten to bring with him) and could with equal ease have re locked it. He knew nothing of Mrs. Schiller, who was virtually a stranger to him.

The evidence of the last two witnesses had been "harkened to" by the jury with somewhat languid interest, but when the name of the next witness was called and the rather commanding figure of Mr. William

Vanderpuye arose, attention was visibly sharpened. Realizing this, the new witness, striking in appearance and faultlessly "turned out", seemed, naturally, a little self-conscious as he walked across to the table but, having been sworn, he stated his personal particulars – as a barrister of the Inner Temple – confidently enough and thereafter gave his evidence clearly and with perfect dignity and composure.

Of the tragedy, itself, he knew nothing, and had heard of it first from the coroner's officer. He had never seen or heard of a person named Emma Robey, and the circumstances connected with her death were entirely unknown to him. This closed the first part of his examination and the rest of his evidence was concerned exclusively with Lotta Schiller. Having described the opening of his acquaintance with her in Tom Pedley's studio, he answered the coroner's questions frankly and fully though he volunteered nothing.

"Did you see much of Mrs. Schiller?" the coroner asked.

"Yes, for a time I used to see her almost daily, and we often spent whole days together."

"And how did you spend your time on these occasions?"

"Principally in seeing the sights of the town: Theatres, concerts, cinemas, museums, and picture galleries. We took our meals at restaurants."

"Did you usually meet by appointment?"

"No, I nearly always called for her at her rooms, and saw her home at night."

"When you saw her home, did you go into the house?"

"No, never. I just saw her to her door. When I called for her, I used sometimes to go in for a few minutes, but never at night."

"I am going to ask you a question which you are not bound to answer if you have any reasons for objecting. It is this: What were your exact relations with Mrs. Schiller? Were you just friends, or were you on affectionate terms, or were you, in effect, lovers? Remember, I am not pressing you for an answer."

"There is nothing that I need conceal," Vanderpuye replied calmly. "We were rather more than ordinary friends. I may say that our relations were affectionate, at least on my side, I can't answer for her, though she seemed rather devoted to me. But we certainly were not lovers."

"You were not, for instance, on kissing terms?"

"No, I never kissed her. She made it quite clear that kissing was not permissible."

"Reference has been made to certain lockets that were exchanged. You would not regard them as love-tokens?"

"No. They were made at her suggestion to serve as souvenirs when I should have gone back to Africa."

"When did you last see Mrs. Schiller?"

"On the eighteenth of November, the day of our trip to Epping Forest which Mr. Pedley has spoken of."

"Would you give us some particulars of what happened after you parted from Mr. Pedley?"

"We walked across to High Beach, as he had directed us, and had lunch at the King's Oak. Then we went for a ramble in the forest and soon lost our way. After wandering about for a long time, we met a forester who directed us to Loughton and, with some difficulty, as it was then getting dark, we found our way there and eventually caught a train to London. I saw her home and said good-night to her on her doorstep at about half-past-nine. It was in the train that she first told me that she was going to stay with some friends at Birmingham."

"Did she give you her address there?"

"No. She said that it would be best that no letters should pass between us, and that she might be visiting friends elsewhere, but she promised to let me know when she would be returning, though she did not know when that might be. Since then I have neither seen her nor heard from her."

This was the substance of Vanderpuye's evidence and, after one or two further questions, which elicited nothing new, the coroner glanced through his notes.

"I think the witness has told us all that he knows about this strange affair and, unless the members of the jury wish to put any questions, we need not detain him any longer."

He glanced inquiringly at the jurors and, as no one made any sign, the depositions were read, the signature added, and the coroner, having thanked the witness for the frank and helpful way in which he had given his evidence, released him, whereupon he retired to his chair beside Mr. Polton.

The next witness – who proved also to be the last – was a small elderly woman of somewhat foxy aspect who advanced to the table with a complacent smirk and gave her evidence readily and with obvious enjoyment. Her name was Jane Bigham, address 98 Jacob Street, no occupation except that she supplemented the small income left to her by her late husband by knitting socks and other articles for sale. She usually sat at the window, partly for the sake of the light, but principally because, being an expert knitter who had no need to keep her eyes on her work, she could entertain herself by observing what was going on in the street. She knew all her neighbours by sight and a good deal about their habits and doings, and as her house was exactly opposite that of Mrs. Mitchens, she had often seen Mrs. Schiller. She remembered that lady moving in with her little bits of furniture about six months ago, and the brass plate being fixed up. ("Which I went across the very same day to read the name on it.")

"You seem to have taken an interest in Mrs. Schiller," the coroner remarked with a smile.

"I did sir. I wondered what a woman like her was doing in our quiet street with her paint and her powder and her high-heeled shoes. In fact, I suspected that she was no better than she ought to be."

"Very few of us are, Mrs. Bigham," said the coroner, "but it is not a crime to wear high-heeled shoes or to paint and powder. Most women do nowadays."

"So they do, sir, the more shame to them. At any rate, within a week of her coming, I saw her go to Mr. Pedley's door and ring the bell, and when he opened the door, I could see that he didn't know her, and looked as if he didn't want to. But she went in and stayed half-an-hour. After that she often used to go there, and once or twice Mr. Pedley went to her rooms about tea-time, and sometimes they used to come home together as if they'd met somewhere.

"Then, a month or two later, a black gentleman appeared on the scene – the one that has just given evidence, Mr. Vanderboy. At first he used to go to Mr. Pedley's, and she seemed to know that he was there for she would slip round and ring the bell and then she and Mr. Vanderboy would come out together. Then he took to calling for her and they would go off together and not come back until night – sometimes quite late."

Here an intelligent juryman protested that, "We had all this before," and the coroner agreed that, "We had better get on. Will you kindly tell us," he continued, "when you last saw Mrs. Schiller."

The witness directed a baleful glance at the juryman and replied after a resentful sniff, "About three weeks ago, it would be. I saw her come home with Mr. Vanderboy about half-past-nine at night and, by the look of her, I reckoned she's had a drop too much."

"What made you think that?" the coroner demanded.

"Well, sir, she looked a bit unsteady on her legs, and she held on to his arm, which was not her 'abit. And then when they came to the door, it was him that put in the latch-key and opened it and helped her in."

"Did he go into the house?"

"Yes, and he stayed there about an hour-and-a-half, for I saw him come out at a few minutes past eleven. I just chanced to go to the window at that time – " (The coroner smiled grimly at the coincidence.) " – and there he was coming out carrying a bag – or a small suitcase it might have been – which he hadn't got when he went in, and mighty careful he was not to make a noise, for, instead of slamming the door, he put in the latch-key and closed the door without a sound. Which was curious, for it seemed as if he had a latch-key of his own."

"Did you ever see Mr. Vanderpuye go into the house on any other occasion?"

"Well, I can't say that I ever did. But if he had a latch-key – "

Here the intelligent juryman interrupted with the question. "Can the witness swear, sir, that the man she saw was Mr. Vanderpuye?"

"What do you say, Mrs. Bigham?" the coroner asked. "Are you perfectly certain that the man was Mr. Vanderpuye?"

"Well, sir, he certainly looked like him. Besides, who else could he have been?"

"The question is, did you clearly and definitely recognize him as Mr. Vanderpuye?"

"Why, as to clearly and definitely recognizing a person across the street on a dark December night, and no streetlamp near, it's hardly possible. Of course, I couldn't see the colour of his features, but he looked to me like Mr. Vanderboy. Besides, who else could he – ?"

"Never mind who he might be. Can you swear that he was Mr. Vanderpuye and not some other man – Mr. Pedley, for instance?"

"Lord! I never thought of that. Perhaps you're right, sir, being next door, too. But no, it couldn't have been, because I saw him walk away towards Hampstead Road."

"I was not suggesting that the man was Mr. Pedley. I was merely giving an instance. The fact is that you did not actually recognize him at all. You assumed that he was Mr. Vanderpuye. Is that not so?"

The witness reluctantly admitted that it was, and the coroner then proceeded to the identification of the woman with a similar result. There had been no actual recognition. The witness had taken it for granted that she was Mrs. Schiller because "she certainly looked like her, and then who else could she be?" *etcetera*.

By this time the coroner and the jury had had enough of Mrs. Bigham, who was, accordingly, dethroned and sent back regretfully to her chair. Then Mrs. Mitchens and Vanderpuye were recalled and briefly re-examined, but neither could throw any light on the incident. Mrs. Mitchens and her husband were early birds and usually retired to their bedroom in the second-floor back at ten o'clock, and Vanderpuye repeated his statement that he had never entered the house at night. This completed the evidence and the coroner proceeded at once to his brief but lucid summing up.

"I need not, members of the jury," he began, "weary you with a recapitulation of the evidence which you have listened to so attentively, but merely suggest to you the conclusions which seem to emerge from it. Our function is to ascertain when, where, and how the deceased, a woman of whom we know nothing but that her name was Emma Robey, came by her death. The place we know was 39 Jacob Street, the exact date is less certain, but the death occurred about three weeks before the discovery of the body on the thirtieth of December – that is, approximately on the ninth of December. The cause of death was a very large dose of potassium cyanide either taken by the deceased herself, or given to her by some other person. If she took the poison, herself, she may have done so inadvertently, or with the deliberate intention of taking her own life. If it was given to her by some other person, that person is guilty of wilful murder.

"There are thus three possibilities: Accident, suicide, and murder. Accident we may dismiss, since there is no evidence suggesting it, and we are left with the alternatives of suicide and murder. Now what evidence is there to support the theory of suicide? There are two facts which, taken together, seem at the first glance to point conclusively to self-destruction. First, the finger-marks on the tumbler and water jug were undoubtedly those of the deceased's own fingers. Secondly, the deceased was found alone in a locked room with the key on the inside of the door. These two facts, as I have said, seem to furnish convincing evidence of suicide. Nevertheless, it is worth noting that an experienced police surgeon and an experienced detective-inspector both appear to have suspected from the first and in spite of that evidence that this was a case, not of suicide but of murder, and when they came to give evidence, they gave substantial reasons for their suspicions. Let us consider first the evidence of Inspector Blandy. From him we learn that the evidence of the finger-prints is practically worthless since they could easily have been made by a murderer from the victim's fingers after death.

"Then we come to the locked door. Now, the fact that Mr. Polton unlocked that door from the outside and could as easily have locked it destroys at once the conclusive significance of that item of evidence. It proves that it was possible for the door to have been locked from the outside. But the inspector's evidence goes further. It goes to prove that the door was, in fact, locked from the outside. I need not remind you of his convincing demonstration, but I must impress on you the enormous evidential value of the match which he found. That match bore marks that exactly fitted the bow of that particular key, and also the clear impression of a loop of string. It was found close to the door in the position in which one would have expected to find it if it had been used in the way which he described and demonstrated, and the door itself bore a mark of the exact kind and in the exact place in which it would have been made by a taut string used in that way On the supposition that the door had been locked from the outside, with a match and string, all those appearances are perfectly consistent and understandable. On any other supposition they are completely incomprehensible. I submit that there is no escape from the evidence of that match. We are compelled to believe that the door was locked from the outside and therefore that it could not have been locked by the deceased.

"The doctor's evidence concerning the morphia – or morphine, as it is now usually called – which he found in the body, and the significance which he attached to it, was very striking, but it became much more so when we had heard the evidence of Mrs. Bigham. We may disregard her identification of the two persons whom she saw as a mere guess, and probably wrong at that. But what her evidence did prove was that on a certain dark night about three weeks before the discovery of the body (which had been dead about three weeks), a man and a woman entered that house by means of a latch-key.

"Now, who were these two persons? Let us first consider the woman. Mrs. Bigham assumed that she was Mrs. Schiller, from which we may infer that she either was Mrs. Schiller or a woman who might have been mistaken for her. But the deceased was actually mistaken for Mrs. Schiller by Mrs. Mitchens and Mr. Pedley, both of whom knew the latter well. It is thus possible that the woman seen by Mrs. Bigham was Emma Robey, and it is here that the doctor's evidence is so important. The woman looked to Mrs. Bigham as if she were the worse for drink, and the medical witness swore that the deceased had taken a considerable dose of morphia. But a person under the influence of morphia might easily be mistaken for one under the influence of alcohol. So that the evidence establishes a rather strong probability that the woman Mrs. Bigham saw was actually the deceased.

"Now let us consider the man. Of his personal appearance we can say no more than that Mrs. Bigham took him to be Mr. Vanderpuye and that there was probably some general resemblance as to age and figure. That, however, is a mere surmise. But there are three facts which seem to be profoundly significant. This man opened the door with a latch-key, but as he might have received it from the woman, that circumstance has no great importance. The three strikingly significant facts that I allude to are: First, that he still had the key in his possession when he came out, second, that he took extraordinary precautions against noise by easing the door to with the key, and third, that when he came out he was carrying a bag or suitcase which he was not carrying when he went in.

506

"What was he doing with that latch-key, which was certainly not his, whomever he was? The strong suggestion is that he had kept it for the express purpose of shutting the door silently. But why that strange, stealthy exit? Why was he so anxious that his departure should not be known to the inmates of the house? Finally, whose bag was it that he was carrying, and what was in it? When we ask ourselves those questions, remembering that this man had been in the house, apparently alone with the woman, for an hour-and-a-half, the answer seems to be that his behaviour is singularly suggestive of that of one escaping from the scene of a crime and taking with him certain incriminating objects connected with it. That, I say, is the suggestion. It is nothing more, taken alone. But taken together with the evidence of the doctor and the inspector, it is, perhaps, more than suggestion. That is for you to judge. When you consider your verdict, you will have to decide between two alternatives: Did the deceased meet her death by her own act or by the act of another? Did she commit suicide or was she murdered? That is the issue, and I leave you to consider it."

The silence that settled down on the court as the coroner concluded his address was of short duration, so short as to suggest that the jury had already made up their minds, for within a couple of minutes the foreman announced that they had agreed on their verdict.

"We find," said he, in answer to the coroner's question, "that the deceased died from the effects of poison, administered to her by some person unknown."

"Yes," said the coroner, "that is a verdict of wilful murder. I shall enter it as such, and I may say that I am in full agreement with you."

This brought the proceedings to an end. The witnesses, spectators, and reporters rose and began to file out of the court. Dr. Oldfield bustled out to his waiting car with the inspector, and Tom Pedley, Polton, and Vanderpuye went off together en route for the studio.

507

Chapter IX
Where is Lotta?

The inquest and the events which had preceded it had broken in on the quiet current of Tom Pedley's life ,leaving him somewhat unsettled, and as the day following the inquiry found him disinclined for regular work, he devoted it to a survey of his stock of materials and the drawing up in his notebook of a list of deficiencies. The process disclosed the fact that the book which he was using was nearly full and that he had no other to replace it. Now, Tom's notebooks were no mere ready-made productions which could be bought when required. They had been designed by him, with careful thought as to suitability of size, shape, thickness, and binding, and were specially made for him of a selected paper which was good for pen or pencil, or, at a pinch, a wash of colour, by the artists' colourman in the Hampstead Road. He usually ordered a dozen at a time, and each one, as it became used up, was provided with a date label on the back and was stowed away on a shelf with its predecessors to form part of an ever-growing series.

It was an admirable plan, for not only did the series furnish a store of material for reference but, since Tom invariably dated his sketches no matter how slight, and even the written notes, the collection served as a fairly complete diary and a record of his doings and his whereabouts on a given date. Accordingly, having added to his list a dozen of the indispensable notebooks, he set forth at once for the establishment of the provider.

As he turned the corner of Jacob Street into the Hampstead Road, he perceived, a short distance ahead, his old acquaintance Inspector Blandy in earnest conversation with Mrs. Bigham, and as he had no desire for a meeting with either the inspector or Mrs. Bigham (whom he privately regarded as an inveterate "Nosy Parker"), he mended his pace and assumed an air of intense preoccupation. But it was of no use. Both saw him at the same moment, and the inspector, hastily detaching himself from the lady, advanced to meet him, holding out his hand and beaming with benevolence.

"This is a stroke of good fortune for me," he exclaimed, pressing Tom's hand affectionately, "I have been wanting to have a word with you and now here you are."

Tom agreed, cautiously, that there he was and waited for developments.

"The matter is this," the inspector explained, "We have been trying to get into touch with Mrs. Schiller, but we haven't succeeded. Either she hasn't seen our advertisements or she is keeping out of the way and, as she won't, or at least, doesn't, come forward, we must take more active measures. To do that, we must have a full and exact description of her, and the question has arisen, how are we to get it? Now, as soon as that question arose, my thoughts naturally turned to you. Mr. Pedley, I said, with his remarkable powers of observation and his wonderful visual memory, will be able to give us a description that will be as good as, or even better than, a photograph."

"Is Mrs. Schiller under suspicion?" Tom asked, warily.

"Suspicion!" the inspector repeated in a shocked tone. "Certainly not. Why should she be? But she could give us invaluable information respecting that key, for instance, and perhaps about Mrs. Robey and those other unknown persons. I trust you won't refuse us your help. It is to her interest as well as being a matter of public policy that this mystery should be cleared up."

"I shouldn't be prepared to give a description offhand," said Tom.

"Of course you wouldn't," Blandy agreed. "The visual memory must have time to operate – but not too much time, as the matter is urgent. I suggest that you think it over and jot down a few notes."

"And post them to you," Tom suggested, hopefully, but the inspector amended, "Hand them to me, personally. You see, they might need some explanation and amplification. Would it be possible for me to call for them at your studio this evening?"

Deciding that it would be best to get the business over at once, Tom assented and, when the hour of 7:30 had been agreed on, he shook the inspector's hand and left him to rejoin Mrs. Bigham (who had been lurking observantly in the offing) while he hurried away to the shop of the artists' colourman.

Having transacted his business there, he came away and, turning northward, started on a brisk walk through the quiet squares to consider the situation. The whole affair was extremely distasteful to him. He had no love for Lotta Schiller, but she had been in a sense his friend, and his natural loyalty revolted against the idea of his aiding the police in their pursuit of her, for that was what it amounted to, in spite of Blandy's indignant protest. Obviously, she was under suspicion, but to what extent and how justly Tom did not like to ask himself. However, he had no choice. A crime had been committed, and it was his duty as a good citizen to give what help he could to the police in their investigation of it, and having reached this conclusion, he turned his face homeward to give effect to it.

Once embarked on the description, he carried it out with his customary thoroughness. On one of the few remaining pages of his notebook, he jotted down his recollections of Lotta, point by point, referring back to the memory sketches that he had made of her for details of the profile, and trying to visualize her as completely as was possible. The result rather surprised him, for though he had seen her often enough and observed her with a certain disapproving interest, he had not expected that his memory would have yielded a description so vivid and so full of detail.

When he had completed his notes, he took a sheet of paper and wrote out a fair copy, thereby making the production of the notebook unnecessary, and he had but just finished this when, punctually to the minute, the studio bell rang, whereupon he pocketed the notebook and went out to admit the inspector.

"This is extraordinarily kind of you, Mr. Pedley," said Blandy as he entered and smiled a general benediction on the premises, "to let me take up your valuable time in this way. But I mustn't take up too much of it. Are these the notes?"

He picked up the copy which Tom had placed on the table and, laying down a portfolio that he had brought (which Tom instantly recognized as Lotta's) glanced rapidly through the notes, while Tom speculated anxiously on the significance of the portfolio.

"Astonishing!" Blandy exclaimed as he finished the preliminary reading. "One might have thought that you had the lady before you as you wrote. What a wonderful thing is the artist's visual memory. You seem to have observed and remembered everything, even to the difference between the two ears. By the way, what exactly does a Darwinian tubercle look like? Perhaps a slight sketch on the back of this paper – "

Tom took the copy from him and, turning it over made a rapid but careful pencil sketch of a right ear, showing the feature in question.

"Oh, thank you," said Blandy, taking the paper from him. "I see. This little projection on the edge is the tubercle. But tell me, does this drawing represent that particular ear in other respects?"

"It does as nearly as I can remember."

"That is good enough for me. And now with regard to the hair, I am not quite clear about that. You say, '*Hair unusual in colour, between light brown and flaxen, but of a peculiar texture which makes the colour seem variable.*' Could you amplify that description?"

"Well," said Tom, "I am not very clear about it myself, as I have never seen any other hair quite like it. I might compare it to shot silk. You know what that looks like – changes in colour when you move it

510

about and let the light fall on it differently. Green, it may be, in one position, and violet in another. Of course, Mrs. Schiller's hair doesn't change to that extent, but it does seem to change – quite golden in one light and almost brown in another."

"You don't think it may have been dyed or faked in some way?"

"That is possible. Light hair dyed black sometimes looks red or purple when the light shines through it, but I never got the impression that her hair was dyed. However, I expect you know more about faked hair than I do."

The inspector admitted that it might be so and, having entered the "amplification" on the back of the sheet, put one or two questions concerning the other items of the description. When these had been disposed of, he carefully put away the document and, after a few moments' reflection, asked, "By the way, Mr. Pedley, when did you last see Mrs. Schiller?"

"On the day of the Epping Forest jaunt, I parted from her and Vanderpuye close by the Ancient British camp, they taking the green ride towards High Beach and I going on to Great Monk Wood. We said 'Good-bye' at the corner, and I never saw her again."

"Rather odd, that. Don't you think so?"

"I did at the time, but then I didn't know she was going away. In fact, I expected that she would look me up within a day or two, and I even got out a map of the forest and a large-scale plan of the British camp to show or lend her."

"Why did you do that?" asked Blandy.

"I thought she intended to make another visit there. She seemed greatly interested in the camp, and she proposed to Vanderpuye that they should come another day and explore it and, as he agreed, I took it as a settled thing."

"You don't happen to know whether they did make another visit there?"

"They couldn't have done, as Vanderpuye never saw her again after that night. You heard him say so at the inquest. But what I can't understand is why she made the proposal when she had already decided to go to Birmingham."

"Yes," the inspector agreed, thoughtfully, "it does seem a bit inconsistent. I wonder – "

But what he wondered never transpired, as he left the sentence unfinished and Tom did not pursue the subject. A brief silence followed. Then the inspector said, taking up the portfolio, "I am going still further to trespass on your forbearance. Would you be so very kind as to look at these paintings of Mrs. Schiller's and give me your opinion of them?"

511

"I am not a critic, you know, Inspector," Tom protested. "My job is to paint pictures, not to judge other people's work."

"I know," said Blandy, "and I understand your delicacy. But the point is this: Is Mrs. Schiller an artist at all or is she an impostor? Now, look at that." He drew forth the painting of *Adam and Eve* and laid it on the table. "It looks to me like a child's drawing, and not a clever child at that."

Tom had to admit that it did. "But," he added, "there is a new fashion in art which accepts childish drawing as the real thing. I don't understand it, but the highbrow journalists do. Why not get an opinion from an art critic?"

Blandy shook his head. "That is no use to me, Mr. Pedley. I don't want to hear a man expound theories or spin phrases. I am out for facts. Now you are a genuine artist. I can see that for myself. You know what a competent artist is like, and I ask you to tell me, in confidence, whether Mrs. Schiller is a *bona fide* artist or only an impostor. Remember, I am a police officer seeking information, and I think you ought to be frank with me."

"Well, Inspector," said Tom, "if it will help you, I will tell you what I know, but I don't want to offer mere opinions. I know that Mrs. Schiller can't draw and can't paint, and that she seems to have no natural aptitude for painting. Whether she is or is not an impostor, I can't tell you. If she honestly believes that she is an artist, she is suffering from a delusion. If she knows that she is not an artist, but pretends that she is, she is an impostor. That is all I can say."

"It's enough for me," said Blandy. "I can answer the other question for myself. And now I will just pop round and put this portfolio back where I found it, and I can't thank you enough, Mr. Pedley, for the generous way in which you have placed at my disposal your vast stores of knowledge and experience and your really astonishing powers of memory."

With this final flourish, he shook Tom's hand affectionately and allowed himself to be escorted to the gate.

Having launched his visitor into the street, Tom returned to the studio breathing more freely and hoping that he had now heard the last of the unpleasant affair in which he had become involved. And, in the days that followed, that hope seemed to be justified. Gradually he drifted back into his ordinary ways of life, now working in the studio at a new subject picture and now going forth in overcoat and warm gloves to make a rapid winter sketch in some accessible country district. An occasional glance at a newspaper told him that the mysterious Emma Robey was still unidentified and that the search for the equally mysterious Mrs. Schiller

512

had yielded no results. But beyond a faint curiosity as to what part Lotta had played in the crime and a hope that she was not in for serious trouble, he was not much interested. His principal desire was to be left alone to get on with his painting.

About three weeks later he made a fresh contact with the case, but it was such a slight one that, at the moment, it caused him no concern. It is true that when, in answer to the summons of the bell, he went out to the gate and found Inspector Blandy on the threshold, he was slightly disturbed until that officer announced his harmless mission.

"I am ashamed, Mr. Pedley, to come pestering you in this way, but I won't detain you a minute. You were so kind as to mention, when I last called on you, that you had put out a plan of the British camp at Loughton to show or lend to Mrs. Schiller. Now I have come to ask if you would be so very good as to let me see that plan."

"But, of course, Inspector," Tom replied, ushering him into the studio. "Do you want to look at it here, or would you like to take it away with you to study at your leisure?"

"That is a most generous suggestion, sir," said Blandy (who had obviously come to borrow the plan). "I didn't dare to make it myself, but if you would be so extremely kind – "

"Not at all," Tom replied, opening a cupboard and running his eye along the shelves. "Ah, here we are. It's really a pamphlet, you see, with a folded plan bound up with the text, so you've got all the information together. I hope you will find it useful, and you needn't be in any hurry about returning it."

He handed the little volume to the inspector, who, having glanced at it, slipped it into his pocket and then tactfully retired, discharging volleys of thanks on the way to the gate. When he had gone, Tom returned to the studio and prepared to resume his work but, for once, his curiosity was definitely aroused. It had really been a rather odd transaction. For what purpose could the inspector require the plan? And why had he suddenly developed this curious "interest" in the British camp? These questions Tom continued to revolve in his mind at intervals for the rest of the evening, but answer there was none. He could make nothing of it, and at last put it away with the reflection that he could only wait and see what came of it.

He had not long to wait. On the following morning when he went forth to do his modest shopping, he was confronted with a staring poster outside the newsagent's announcing in enormous type: "*Jacob Street Murder: Dramatic Development*", and straightway went in and bought a paper. A single glance at the scare headlines on the front page enlightened him sufficiently as to the purpose of the inspector's visit and he folded up the paper and pocketed it for more leisurely perusal when he had finished his shopping.

At length, having completed his round, he re-entered the studio, deposited his parcels on the table, drew out the paper, and subsiding into the easy-chair, read through the account in all its detail. Omitting the typographical flourishes, it ran as follows:

*Yesterday morning a forester, making his round through that part of Epping Forest which constitutes Loughton Manor, made a startling discovery. Following the green path that skirts the ancient British earthworks known as Loughton Camp, he noticed among the roots of the trees halfway up the bank, and nearly hidden by the fallen leaves, a lady's handbag. Climbing up the bank and brushing aside the leaves, he picked it up and, having noted the initials, "L. S." on the outside, opened it to see if it bore any clue to the identity of the owner. Inside it he found, among other things, a leather card case containing a number of visiting cards, and on drawing one out he read on it, "*Mrs. L. Schiller, 39 Jacob Street, Hampstead Road, London*".*

Recognizing the name from the Press notices that he had read, he immediately realized the importance of the discovery and proceeded without delay to Loughton Police Station, where he delivered the bag to the officer in charge and described exactly the place where he had found it. A preliminary inspection showed that the bag contained, in addition to the visiting cards, two objects of considerable interest. One was a small blue handkerchief bearing the name, "Lotta", embroidered in blue silk, in one corner, and closely resembling the handkerchief found on the person of the murdered woman, Emma Robey. The other was a leather key-pouch with a separate swivel for each key. There were six swivels but only four keys, and it could be seen, by the distinct impressions on the leather, that the two missing keys were, respectively, a latch-key and the key of a room door or the door of a large cupboard. Having made his inspection, the superintendent reported by telephone to headquarters at Scotland Yard, and meanwhile dispatched a detective officer to accompany the forester to the place where the bag was found, to mark the spot and to keep it under observation until he was relieved.

514

In reply to the telephone message, the superintendent was informed that a C.I.D. officer was being sent down to conduct inquiries, and about an hour later a police car arrived bearing Detective-Inspector Blandy and Sergeant Hill, both of the C.I.D. These two officers, having seen and taken possession of the bag, were conducted to the spot where the local detective was waiting and, with his assistance and that of the forester, they made a systematic search of the immediate locality. As nothing further came to light there, they climbed the bank and descended into the area of the camp, where they separated and carried out a methodical search of the ground, which was covered by a dense growth of pollard hornbeams and a thick mantle of dead leaves.

For some time the search was without result, but at length it was rewarded by a new and most significant discovery. Tucked away in a hollow between the roots of a small hornbeam, the sergeant espied a gold locket, whereupon he signalled to the inspector and meanwhile made a distinguishing mark on the tree. Examination of the locket showed it to be a handsome and valuable trinket, richly ornamented with enamel and bearing the engraved initials, "L. S.", and when it was opened, one side was seen to be occupied by a portrait of a black gentleman in a wig and gown while the other held what at first looked like the hair-spring of a watch but was in fact a single coiled hair of the African type, presumably from the head of the legal gentleman.

The rest of the search yielded no further discoveries, but these two relics of the missing woman furnish abundant material for speculation, for instance –

Here the writer illustrated the point by various speculative suggestions, which we need not quote, and to which Tom paid little attention as they contained nothing that he did not know. But as he reflected on the facts disclosed, certain uncomfortable questions presented themselves and demanded answers.

What had really happened to Lotta? Had she been lured to that solitary place and made away with? That was the plain suggestion, and it seemed to be the one adopted by the police, judging by the inspector's sudden interest in the plan – after the finding of the locket – which hinted at a further and more thorough exploration. But what could she have been doing in the forest? When and why had she gone there? Who was her companion, and what was the connection between the new tragedy and the murder of Emma Robey? That there was some connection seemed to be proved by the vanished keys and the curious resemblance of the two handkerchiefs, and this latter seemed to hint at some complicity on Lotta's part.

But it was all very obscure and confusing. Tom could make nothing of it and finally decided to wait for further developments, and meanwhile to avoid as far as was possible letting his thoughts dwell on it – which was a decision more easily formed than carried out, for though he had never had any great liking for Lotta, it troubled him deeply to think that any mischance might have befallen her and still more to suspect her of a guilty connection with a most atrocious crime.

Chapter X
The Camp Revisited

Once again, Tom Pedley stood at the parting of the ways outside the ancient British camp looking thought fully along the broad green ride that leads towards High Beach. Under the grey winter sky the scene lacked the beauty and gaiety that had charmed him when he had last looked on it, with the late autumn sunshine lighting up the gorgeous raiment of the beech-trees and sprinkling the bushes with gold and the turf with emerald, yet the picture came back to him, not for the first time, with singular vividness, the two figures stepping out gaily and babbling cheerfully as they went, dwindling to the eye with every pace, and at last, halting at the curve to make their farewells. Little had he thought as he returned Lotta's greeting that he was looking his last on her, that the wave of her hand was a final farewell and that as she turned and disappeared round the bend, she had passed out of his ken forever.

His presence in the forest was not entirely voluntary. He had not wanted to come. But his friend, Polton, had entreated him so earnestly to seize this opportunity (which he, the said Polton, had secured), that Tom had not the heart to disappoint him. So here he was, taking as little advantage of the opportunity as he could decently manage with due regard to his friend's feelings.

The occasion was the complete and final exploration of the ten or twelve acres of land enclosed by the ramparts, with the object of clearing up the mystery of Lotta Schiller's disappearance. The *prima facie* appearances strongly suggested that she had been murdered, and if she had, the overwhelming probability was that her body had been concealed in this enclosed space. Hence, the police, feeling that all doubts on the subject should be set at rest as soon as possible, had decided that the suspected area must be examined with such conclusive thoroughness as to settle the question finally.

But there was a difficulty. Since the camp was scheduled as an ancient monument, promiscuous digging was inadmissible. That difficulty, however, was easily disposed of. To an expert eye, any disturbance of the surface, no matter how artfully disguised, is instantly discernible, and there is no lack of expert eyes in the Criminal Investigation Department. Eventually it was arranged that the Office of Works should send a representative and that the C.I.D. officers, under Inspector Blandy, should be assisted by certain competent volunteers from the Essex Field Club, and by Mr. Elmhurst, the eminent Kentish archaeologist, whose great experience in the excavation of ancient sites had commended him both to the police and the Office of Works. Thus was ensured a most complete exploration of the precincts with security against possible damage to the camp from an antiquarian point of view.

Now, it happened that Mr. Polton got wind of the proposed investigation and was forthwith all agog to be present, for that cunning artificer had followed with eager, almost ghoulish, interest every phase of the crime whose discovery he had witnessed. And now the final act of the tragedy was about to be played with the possible exhumation of a corpse as its climax. It was too much for him. By hook or by crook he must manage to secure a front seat. And he did. By an artful and persuasive offer to his old acquaintance, Inspector Blandy, of assistance in the matter of photography and plaster moulding, he succeeded in extracting an invitation from that suave and polite officer. But more than this, representing to the inspector the invaluable service that Tom Pedley might render in identifying objects or remains (and really convincing him this time), he got the invitation extended, much more to his own satisfaction than to Tom's. So here they were with the assembled explorers, Polton following every movement with devouring interest while Tom browsed about in the neighbourhood of the camp and made occasional visits of inspection.

The examination was conducted with professional thoroughness. The precincts being marked out into sections by pencil lines on the plan, each section was pegged out on the ground and dealt with exhaustively before passing on to the next. No labourers were employed, the whole procedure being carried out by the skilled explorers, who tenderly removed the thick mantle of dead leaves, almost leaf by leaf, to ensure that the actual surface should be exposed quite undisturbed. And it was well that they did, for the very first section uncovered showed the traces, faint but quite recognizable, of two pairs of feet, those of a man and a woman.

"They are not very good prints," said Blandy when Polton offered to take casts and a photograph. "Made through the leaves, apparently. We'll cover them up for the present and see if anything better turns up."

Accordingly an empty sack was laid, carefully, on the footprints and the examination proceeded. The next section showed more prints, but these also were rather shallow and blurred, suggesting some thickness of dead leaves between the feet and the earth, and so it went on for two more sections, each showing faint impressions of the two pairs of feet, and all of them displaying the prints of those feet in parallel pairs, implying that the two persons were walking side by side.

518

At this point the inspector, who had been anxiously poring over the plan, called out to Sergeant Hill, "Aren't we getting near the tree that we marked, Sergeant? I put a pencilled cross on the plan, but that was only guesswork, away from the place."

"I think you are right, sir," the sergeant replied, "it was somewhere about here. I'll just go on ahead and see if I can find it."

He walked forward, treading delicately on the russet carpet of leaves and peering among the weird-looking dwarf beeches and hornbeams that jostled one another in the precincts, like a crowd of fantastic hamadryads, and spread out their contorted roots over the surface. Then he disappeared into the miniature forest, and for a time, soft rustlings from the coppice announced his unseen activities. Suddenly, a louder sound, as of a falling body, with expletory accompaniments, was borne to the inspector's ears, and a few moments later the sergeant reappeared with a slightly uneven gait.

"Tripped over one of those damned roots," he explained, stooping to rub his right foot, "but I found the tree, sir, and laid my handkerchief at the foot of the trunk so that we can't possibly miss it."

Meanwhile the explorers went on steadily with their work and, having at length uncovered the surface of the whole section and minutely examined every square inch of it, proceeded to peg out the next under the direction of Mr. Elmhurst, who wielded a surveyor's tape and entered the particulars on his copy of the plan. In the course of his measurements he encountered the marked tree, which was contained in the new section and which, having been exactly located by means of the land-tape, acquired "a local habitation and a name" on the plan.

"Now," said the sergeant, "we ought to see what that locket meant. Something must have happened, and it must have happened just about here, and I think it would be as well to lay down some sacks for the workers to stand on."

This suggestion was adopted and, when the sacks had been spread on the ground, the whole company of explorers concentrated on this region, clearing a broad track towards the tree and scrutinizing each handful of leaves as it was removed. The ground thus uncovered still bore the imprints, faint and blurred, of the two pairs of feet, which continued evenly side by side until they had been traced to a point within a few yards of the tree. Then there was a sudden change in two respects. No longer dim and faint, the footprints were now clear, sharp, and deeply impressed in the moist, clayey soil, and in place of the orderly, parallel lines, there appeared a confused welter of footprints pointing in all directions and overlapping and partially obliterating one another over a considerable area. From this a line of prints led in the direction of the

519

tree, but although both pairs of feet could be distinguished, they were no longer side by side. Both led straight ahead and both had conspicuously deep toe-marks, but whereas the woman's footprints were in some places trodden into, those of the man were all whole and undisturbed.

"Seem to tell their story pretty plainly, don't they?" said the sergeant, viewing the whole group critically from his sack, and addressing Mr. Elmhurst.

"So it appears to me," the latter replied. "My reading of them is that the couple walked together to this place, side by side, and apparently quite amicably. Then the man made a sudden attack and there was a struggle which ended in the woman escaping and running off, pursued by the man."

"That's about what it amounts to," the sergeant agreed, "and now the question is, what was the next act? For the Lord's sake be careful in uncovering the rest of the tracks."

But the caution was unnecessary, for all the explorers were now on the tiptoe of expectation, and the position of the tracks being known, they were able to work from the sides and avoid the risk of treading on the prints.

"It is a bit of luck for us, sir," the sergeant remarked to Blandy, "that the prints that matter most should happen to be the clearest. The ground here must have been uncovered at the time, and the leaves blown over it afterwards. I only hope the rest of the tracks will be as distinct.".

"It's of no great importance," the inspector replied. "We know they were here, and we know who one of them was. The real question is: What has become of the woman?"

A couple of minutes later, that question seemed on the way to being answered for, opposite the marked tree and extending several yards beyond it, was an area of heavily trampled ground on which the impressions of the two pairs of feet were so intermingled and confused that hardly a complete footprint was distinguishable. And the sergeant's hopes were realized. The imprints had evidently been made on bare ground and the few that were whole were deep and remarkably distinct.

"Well, sir," said the sergeant, "there seems to have been a pretty considerable dust-up. He didn't have it all his own way. I wonder how – "

He did not finish the sentence, for the inspector was not listening. His sharp eye had apparently noticed something ahead, for after one long and intent look accompanied by the inevitable smile, he advanced over the uncleared leaves with a sack in either hand to a spot beyond the tree where the clearance was still in progress. Here he laid down one sack, and standing on it, stooped low and pored over the ground at his feet.

520

After a full minute's scrutiny, he stood up and looked significantly at the sergeant, who had followed him.

"Yes, sir," said the sergeant, "I see what you mean. This is where it ended. There's a clean-cut groove made by her heel as she slipped, and there are two marks that show, plainly, the heel ends of her shoes. She must have been lying down on her back to make those marks. And I seem to make out an impression of the body."

"'Seem'," the inspector repeated impatiently. "It's as plain as a pikestaff. She came down on that group of footprints and flattened some of them out. You can see where her shoulders came, and beyond them a faint mark where the head would have been, and right underneath us is a slight flattening of the footprints where the hips would have rested. It is not very clear, but it is just in the right place."

He drew a spring tape from his pocket and, stooping down, measured the distance from the two heel impressions to the middle of the ill-defined flattening.

"Yes," he reported with his thumb on the tape. "Thirty-three inches, and her height was about five-feet-seven. And now the question is: What happened next? She couldn't have got up without making some very characteristic foot-marks, and there aren't any. But there are one or two very distinct prints of the man's feet, and they seem to be on top of the others. Let us see where they go to."

He picked up his sacks and, followed by the sergeant, moved forward over the heaped-up leaves by the side of the uncovered track, following eagerly with his eyes the footprints that the clearance had disclosed, until he reached the place where the work of clearing was still going on.

"Only a single line of footprints, you see," he remarked. "Not a sign of the woman, though. If she had come this way, her heels at least would have shown plainly. What do you think of these prints? Do they strike you as specially deep?"

"I was just wondering," the sergeant replied. "They ought to be if he was carrying a woman who might have been nearly as heavy as himself. But it's rather hard to judge."

"It is," Blandy agreed, "and when you have judged, it's only an opinion. What we want is an actual measurement. I wonder if Mr. Polton has brought his plaster outfit."

"If he hasn't, we have," said the sergeant, who slightly resented the presence of the unofficial interloper, "and we are quite competent to do the job."

"Of course we are," said Blandy, tactfully using the first person, "but Polton isn't only competent, he is a first-class expert. We must see if he has brought his kit."

There was no difficulty in finding out, for Polton, thrilled by the discovery of the "signs of a struggle" had been unobtrusively following the inspector with a gloating eye fixed on the tell-tale markings. When the inspector broached the subject to him, his eyes glistened.

"Yes, sir," he replied eagerly. "I've got a good supply of the best sculptor's plaster and enough water to start with. As you want the moulds for measurement, it will be necessary to include the surface of the ground immediately surrounding the footprint."

"Exactly," replied Blandy. "That's the idea. Give us an edge that can be measured."

"And as to a control, sir? When I have made a mould of one of these prints, would you like me to do one of those where the two parties were walking together?"

"Certainly, if you will be so good. We must have the means of comparison to ascertain whether these prints are deeper than the others."

With these instructions, Polton hastened away to the entrance to the camp, where he had deposited his kit, and returned carrying a heavy suitcase and a three-pint can of water. The inspector selected a sample footprint, Mr. Elmhurst marked its position on his copy of the chart, with a distinguishing letter, and Polton opened his case and fell to work. Meanwhile, the explorers, still following the tracks, had uncovered another fifty yards, along which the solitary walker could be traced, now with difficulty where he had apparently tramped over the thick coating of leaves, now quite easily where he had trodden on the bare earth. But for the moment the inspector let them work unheeded while he and the sergeant and Mr. Elmhurst stood by and watched Polton's rapid and skilful manipulation of the plaster.

"Don't you usually spray some varnish into the footprint before pouring the plaster?" the inspector asked.

"Not in clay, sir," Polton replied. "Clay – moist clay like this – takes the plaster quite kindly and gives a beautifully sharp mould. Besides, sir, there are the measurements. They will be very delicate, and even a thin film of varnish might affect them.

"Very true, Mr. Polton," Blandy agreed. "We must be correct to a hair's breadth."

Accordingly the moulder proceeded with his task and, having poured the plaster and put in the iron wire reinforcements, was watching the surface as it solidified when one of the explorers approached hurriedly, holding some object daintily between his finger and thumb.

522

"We found this, Inspector, among the leaves just at the foot of the bank," he announced as he delivered the object – a painted wooden button – to Blandy. "I thought I had better bring it along at once."

"You are extremely kind," said Blandy, taking the button from him and regarding it with mild interest. "Then you have actually reached the bank?"

"Yes, and there are footmarks on it – rather indistinct but quite unmistakable – and there is a broken branch which seems to have given way when the man caught hold of it climbing up the slope."

"And the footmarks? Any trace of the woman?"

"No, unless that button belonged to her, which seems rather probable."

"It does," said Blandy, "but probability isn't much good." He looked at the button reflectively and then held it out towards Polton, who took it from him and, having examined it minutely, handed it back.

"I can't identify it, sir," he announced regretfully, "but then I shouldn't be likely to, having seen so little of the lady. But Mr. Pedley might. He used to see her pretty often – and there he is, coming up the track at this very moment."

As Tom approached rather wearily along the uncleared border of the track, the inspector hailed him and held out the button, whereupon Tom quickened his pace.

"This button has just been picked up, Mr. Pedley," said Blandy. "Can you tell us anything about it?"

Tom took it from him, and after one brief glance, replied, "Yes. It is a button from Mrs. Schiller's jacket."

"You speak quite positively," said Blandy. "Do you mean that she had buttons of this kind on her jacket, or that you can definitely identify this button? To me, it looks like an ordinary trade button such as you can see at Woolworth's."

"That is what it was, originally," replied Tom. "Just a plain wooden button covered with a pink cellulose glaze. But she had a fancy for decorating the set with a painted design, and she consulted me about the method of doing it. I recommended her to use ordinary oil paint varnished with copal, and when she had painted them, as she hadn't any copal varnish, she brought them to me and I put a coat of varnish over them. This is certainly one of those buttons. I recognized it at a glance by the material, the technique, and the design, which I think represents some sort of flower."

"Then," said Blandy, "you could swear, positively, in a court of law, that this button was actually on Mrs. Schiller's jacket?"

"Certainly I could," Tom replied. "I saw the buttons on the jacket – which, by the way, was a green jacket, and here is a thread of green silk still sticking in the eye of the button."

"Yes," said the inspector, verifying the fact as Tom returned the button. "Very complete, very conclusive. I wish some of the other evidence was as good."

He carefully wrapped the button in an envelope from his wallet and, having bestowed it in an inner pocket, turned to the volunteer who had brought it.

"I will come back with you and get you to show me exactly where you found this button. Have they completed the clearance of the bank?"

"No, Inspector. They had only begun, but we could see the footmarks on the slope as the leaves hadn't settled there very thickly."

"Then perhaps there may be something more to see by this time," said Blandy, and with that he started off along the edge of the track, accompanied by his informant and followed by the sergeant and Mr. Elmhurst, but not by Polton, who dared not leave his half-made mould.

When the party arrived at the bank, the inspector's hopeful surmise was justified. The footmarks on the steep slope, indistinctive as they were, told their story plainly enough. The unknown man had climbed the bank more than once, apparently helping himself by the lower branches of a pollard beech, one of which had broken under his weight. In one place, an elongated mark showed where he had slipped, and in another, deep heel-marks furnished evidence that he had descended the bank into the camp at least once.

"Looks as if he had gone to the top of the bank to see if all was clear on the other side," the sergeant remarked, "and then come back to fetch something, and we can guess what that something was."

"There is no need to guess," said Blandy. "Look at this."

Standing on the swept-up leaves at the side, he pointed to two small and faint impressions on the cleared ground, each of which was accompanied by a little sharp-edged dent.

"You're right, sir," agreed the sergeant, craning forward eagerly. "Those are the prints of the back parts of a pair of feet, and those little sharp-edged marks show that they were a woman's feet. No man's heel would make a mark like that."

At this moment Polton came bustling up with his suitcase and water can. Setting the former down on the leaves, he opened it and took out a bundle of lint, from which he extracted the newly made mould, and offered it for inspection.

The sergeant looked at it and chuckled. "It's quite uncanny," said he, "looks just like the sole of a white shoe, and for purposes of comparison it is as good as the shoe itself. How would it be, sir, for Mr. Polton to make a plaster mould of these two impressions?"

"Just what I was thinking, sergeant. What do you say, Mr. Polton? Have you got a fair supply of plaster?"

"I've got enough for three or four more moulds if I'm careful," Polton replied, "and these little shallow impressions wouldn't take much. I should have plenty for those other prints that have to be done."

"Thank you," said Blandy. "It's rather important, as the moulds will probably show the forms of the heels more clearly."

Accordingly, Polton set to work at once while the inspector resumed his examination of the bank, climbing to the top and scrutinizing the ground narrowly. Here he found obscure traces of something having been dragged across the top and, what was more significant, a tiny thread of green silk caught on the ragged end of a broken twig. This he put in the envelope with the button and wrote on the outside a short descriptive note. Then he descended the outer slope of the bank and anxiously surveyed the ground at its base. But here the appearances were unpromising in the extreme, for he was now on the green ride, the ancient and well-trodden turf of which yielded no impressions whatever, as he ascertained by walking a few paces and noting the total absence of any resulting footprints.

"Well," he said gloomily to Mr. Elmhurst, who, with the sergeant, had followed him down, "this looks like the end of the trail. Can you see which way he went?"

Elmhurst shook his head. "Nothing lighter than a horse would leave visible traces on this turf. We shall have to try to pick up the tracks farther afield, if he really carried the body out of the camp. It isn't certain that he did. We haven't finished clearing the surface yet, and until the whole of the camp has been examined we can't be sure that the body is not concealed in it, after all."

But the inspector was not comforted by this faint encouragement.

"No," he admitted, "but we've followed the tracks to the top of the bank and it's pretty clear that he came out that way. Still, you are quite right. We mustn't leave any possibility untested."

The pursuit was accordingly suspended for the moment. Elmhurst went back to the explorers and resumed the systematic examination of the camp, Polton, having finished the small moulds (which showed clearly the backs of a woman's high-heeled shoes) returned along the tracks and made a "control" mould of the man's footprints, where he was walking with his companion, one of the woman's at the same place, and one of the two feet of the prostrate figure near the tree, and in all these cases he photographed the impressions before making the moulds.

All this, with necessary adjournments for refreshment, took time, and the daylight was already failing when Mr. Elmhurst sought out the inspector to make his report.

"Well, Inspector," said he, "she isn't here. Every inch of the camp has been examined, and there is no trace whatever of any disturbance of the surface. Of course, this elaborate procedure was hardly necessary, but it is all to the good. It settles the question beyond any possible doubt."

"It does," Blandy agreed gloomily. "But it is a disappointing result."

"I am afraid it is," Elmhurst admitted. "Still, it is conclusive, and it doesn't close the inquiry. If she isn't here, she must be somewhere else and," he added encouragingly, "you've got all the rest of the forest, with the ponds and lakes, as a possibility."

Blandy smiled, less benevolently than usual. "The idea of a man," said he, "strolling about the forest, even at night, carrying the body of a good-sized woman, doesn't appeal to me. However, I suppose we shall have to consider the possibility."

Thus, unsatisfactorily, ended the exploration which had seemed in the morning so promising. It was not the end of the search. On succeeding days, the police, aided by the foresters and local members of the field club, roamed through glades and thickets, now carpeted with fallen leaves, seeking in vain some trace of the missing woman. The ponds at the Cuckoo Pits and various other sheets of water were dragged, the margins of streams searched for footprints, but nothing came of it. When all was done, and the search was at last abandoned, Inspector Blandy's verdict was justified. The marks on the summit of the rampart were "the end of the trail". There Lotta Schiller, dead or alive, had vanished, whither or in what state no man could tell. She had gone, taking with her the secret (if it had been known to her) of the mysterious death of Emma Robey and of the name of her murderer.

Doubtless the police kept her in mind and continued their inquiries, but if so, no faintest whisper of any discovery ever transpired. To Mr. Polton, with his dossier of newspaper cuttings now tidily put away its appropriate shelf, the failure was a deep disappointment which he hoped was not final. To Tom Pedley, it was something of a relief, and as the weeks passed into months and the months into years, the memory of those tragic incidents faded by degrees until it was almost too dim to be painful.

Part II – The Unknown Factor
Narrated by Christopher Jervis, M.D.

Chapter XI
Mr. Penfield Opens the Ball

The mountain that was in labour and brought forth a mouse is familiar to us all, but none of us, I suspect, and certainly not I, have ever heard of a mouse that was in labour and brought forth a mountain. Yet, since we are dealing with impossibilities, the one metaphor seems as good as the other. But I shall not argue the question. The second metaphor occurs to me only as illustrating the truth that trivial actions of unimportant persons may generate disproportionately momentous results, a proposition that is obvious enough to be grasped without any metaphor at all. And as to its application to the strange and tragic story that I have to tell, perhaps I had better leave that to develop in due course, merely remarking that the name of the super-prolific mouse was Nathaniel Polton, and that he happened to be our laboratory assistant and Dr. Thorndyke's devoted henchman.

Our direct contact with the case occurred quite casually. The occasion was a visit of our old friend, Mr. Joseph Penfield, of George Yard, Lombard Street, to our chambers at 5A King's Bench Walk. Ostensibly, it was a professional consultation, but conducted with Thorndyke's habitual informality – an informality which at once scandalized and delighted our legal friends.

At the moment, Mr. Penfield was seated cosily in an easy-chair drawn up before the fire, with his toes on the kerb and his silver snuff-box and a glass of sherry on a small table by his side.

"Well," he said, "that seems to dispose of all my difficulties. Now I know all about it, or think I do, thanks to your learned and lucid exposition. I suppose that a solicitor of nearly forty years standing and experience ought not to have required it, but somehow, when I come here to discuss points of law with you, I feel like a mere schoolboy."

"It is a very misleading feeling," said Thorndyke. "The fact is that you usually consult us on problems that are outside your own special province and inside ours. On questions of property law or conveyancing you could probably make us feel like schoolboys, whereas on subjects such as survivorship or presumption of death, in which medical or scientific knowledge is helpful, the advantage is with us."

"That is true," Mr. Penfield agreed, with more emphasis than the rather obvious explanation seemed to merit. "Very true."

He paused with a reflective air, looking steadily at the fire. Then, having refreshed himself with a delicate pinch of snuff and an infinitesimal sip of sherry, he continued. "I am glad you mentioned the subject of presumption of death, because it happens to be one in which I am somewhat interested at the moment."

"Are you proposing to make an application?" Thorndyke asked.

"No," replied Penfield. "On the contrary, I am considering the expediency of contesting one. I have not quite made up my mind but, as I am executor and trustee for the person whose death it is sought to presume, the onus seems to rest on me to contest the application. My duty is obviously to consider the interests of my client and, since the presumption of death is not the same thing as the fact of death, there is always the possibility that the person who is presumed dead may be in fact alive. It would be exceedingly unpleasant if, when death had been presumed and the estate distributed, the client should turn up alive and demand an account of my stewardship. I should feel very unhappy if I had acquiesced passively in the application."

"I suppose," Thorndyke suggested, "there are substantial grounds for believing the person to be dead?"

"There must be. The case for the application is that there is good reason to believe that the person was murdered and, though there is no direct evidence of the murder and the body was never found, the person has never been seen or heard of since the date of the presumed crime. As that date is so recent – only about two years ago – a substantial body of circumstantial evidence must be available to render the application possible. But I have not gone into that question."

"And as to the collateral circumstances – I suppose you know all about them?"

"Indeed I don't, and I am not much interested in them, since they can hardly be material to the issue. The question is whether this woman is or is not presumably dead. That is all that the court has to decide, and that is all that interests me."

"So," I remarked, "your client is, or was, a woman."

"Yes, a Mrs. Schiller."

"Not Lotta Schiller!" I exclaimed.

"Ah. Then you know the name, and perhaps some of the circumstances?"

"We do, indeed. Polton was acquainted with the lady, and he took an almost morbid interest in the circumstances of her disappearance. He has collected every scrap of information bearing on it and he was actually present at the search for the body, making moulds and photographs of the footprints. He probably has the photographs still."

"Ha!" said Mr. Penfield. "Very interesting, though a footprint seems rather to connote a living person. However, what you tell me puts an end to my hesitation, I shall contest the application if I can secure your support. What do you say?"

"I say, yes, certainly," replied Thorndyke. "The case is entirely within our province."

"It is more than that. You not only have the general knowledge and experience, but you have the particular knowledge of the facts of this case, which should be invaluable in cross-examination. And then," he added with his queer wry smile, "you have the further attraction to me that you are able to prepare your own brief."

"Let us rather say, part of it," said Thorndyke. "We must depend on you for the general facts of the case. There is the motive, for instance. Why does someone want to presume this woman's death? Who are the parties? Is the husband one of them?"

"He is not. No doubt he would be interested to know whether he is a husband or a widower, but he is not interested in the legal sense. He has nothing to gain, and he is not a party to the application. The motive is a sum of about twenty-thousand pounds, and the applicant is the sole beneficiary under Mrs. Schiller's will, who stands to gain that sum of money if the application succeeds. These facts do not seem very relevant to the issue, which is simply whether the woman is alive or dead, but I agree that you will want a general outline of the case. Perhaps a brief sketch of the history of my relations with Mrs. Schiller might do for a start. The details could be filled in later."

Thorndyke having agreed to this suggestion, Mr. Penfield took a pinch of snuff and began his narration.

"About five years ago – I can't give you exact dates or figures as I am speaking from memory – but a little over five years ago, Mrs. Schiller came to my office to ask me to draw up her will and to take custody of it and of certain monies in her possession. She was a stranger to me, but she brought a letter of introduction from one of my clients – now the deceased – and I agreed to undertake the business, though I was not very favourably impressed by the lady herself – a flashy, golden-haired baggage, painted like a clown and powdered like a miller, and very free and easy in her manners. However, it was a small affair and perfectly simple, a matter of about three-hundred pounds, left by the will to one sole beneficiary, so I drafted a short will in her presence, read it over to her and, at her request, appointed myself sole executor. Having made an appointment for the following morning, I got the will engrossed and made the necessary arrangements with the bank.

"When she arrived on the following morning, bringing with her the money in notes, some further arrangements had to be made. As she was in the habit of moving about a good deal and had no permanent address, she wished me to act as her man of business and manage her financial affairs, such as they were. I need not go into details. The arrangement constituted me her agent with power to receive and pay monies on her account, and when the will and the other document had been signed and witnessed in my office, the transaction was complete. She left my office immediately and I never saw her again or received any communication from her."

"She left you her address, I suppose?" said Thorndyke.

"Yes. She was then living in lodgings at a place called Linton Green – Corby Street, I think, was the exact address – and I remember that the landlady's name was Wharton. But that is of no consequence, as she had left those lodgings when I made my inquiries and the landlady did not know where she had gone. She had promised to keep me informed of her whereabouts when she changed her address, but she never did, which, for a time, was no concern of mine, as I had no occasion to communicate with her.

"But then there came a new development. A certain rather wealthy man – a Mr. Charles Montagu – died. (I regret to say that he, also, was murdered. It is a distinctly unsavoury case altogether.) Well, this man had bequeathed to a certain Miss Dalton a sum of about twenty-thousand pounds. There was some delay in regard to the probate of his will owing to the fact that some large payments – over a thousand pounds – had been made in cash and not accounted for in the books. Another unsavoury detail, for there could hardly be a doubt that those payments represented blackmail, especially as the man was murdered. However, the will was eventually proved, but the probate was barely completed when Miss Dalton died.

"It then appeared that she had made a will leaving the bulk of her property to Mrs. Schiller, who, as the residuary legatee, became entitled, also, to the twenty-thousand pounds. But now there was a fresh difficulty. Not only were the whereabouts of Mrs. Schiller unknown, but it was not certain that she was alive, or even that she had been alive at the time of Miss Dalton's death. On this question I could, of course, give no information. I tried to get into touch with her through the usual channels but had no success, and so this matter remained in abeyance for a time.

"Then the position was clarified in a very startling manner. There was yet another murder – (I must really apologize for these sordid details!) – and it appeared that Mrs. Schiller was under some suspicion of being at least an accessory. That, however, does not concern us. The material fact is that she was proved to be alive and, consequently, the bequest took effect, and I duly notified the claim on her behalf, disregarding the criminal details. But the astonishing thing that now transpired was that she had been living all this time at a place called Jacob Street within a short bus ride of my office.

"But the uncertainty which had just been cleared up was almost immediately succeeded by another, which is the one that concerns us. First, Mrs. Schiller disappeared. Then traces of her were discovered which led the police to believe that she had been murdered. But no body was found and no actual proof of death was obtained. On the other hand, the woman has never been seen or heard of since the disappearance. It appears that the police have made all possible inquiries, but have not been able to discover any traces of her. Their attitude, I understand, is entirely noncommittal, she may be dead or she may be alive, but there is no positive evidence either way.

"So that is the position, and our function – or perhaps I should say *yours* – will be to examine the known facts and assess the probabilities. If there are clearly good grounds for presuming death, it might not be worthwhile to do more than watch the case in my absent client's interest. We shall be better able to judge when we know exactly what facts the applicant relies on."

"Then," said Thorndyke, "I take it that you have not yet received copies of the affidavits?"

"No. I have had no formal notice of motion, only an informal, and quite friendly, notice of the proposed application. And, for my part, I am not going to be unnecessarily contentious. I don't particularly care whether the woman is alive or dead. I am only doing what I conceive to be my duty to an absent client, and I shall certainly not oppose the application if, when you have examined the facts, you think it ought to succeed. As soon as I receive the copies of the affidavits, I will let you have them, and you can then advise me as to our further proceedings."

This concluded the business and, shortly afterwards, Mr. Penfield rose and, having pocketed his snuff-box and waved away the proffered decanter, shook our hands and departed.

"Quite a promising case," I remarked when he had gone, "though Penfield does not seem enthusiastic. But he never is if there is any criminal element. It will be interesting to see what sort of case the applicant's lawyers have made out."

"I expect," said Thorndyke, "that they will take the same line as Penfield has taken."

"Yes," I agreed, "and, after all, it seems a perfectly logical view, though I suspect that you won't concur. But really all that the court has to decide is whether the probability that the woman is dead is so great as to justify the presumption that she is dead. The various collateral circumstances do seem, as Penfield maintains, to be irrelevant."

"The question is," Thorndyke replied, "what is meant by 'collateral circumstances'? Penfield is assuming that facts and circumstances which appear to have no bearing on the main issue are irrelevant and may be disregarded. But until those facts are examined, it is impossible to say whether they are or are not relevant. It is a capital mistake to classify facts in advance as relevant and irrelevant, and to limit consideration of them to those which appear relevant."

"Still," I persisted, "there are the plain physical facts, and if they are such as to establish an overwhelming probability that the woman was murdered, the various other facts, such as her personal character and way of life, for instance, do really seem to have no bearing. The simple issue is whether she is dead or alive. If she is dead, that issue is settled. How she came to die or what were the factors that brought about her death are interesting questions, but not material to the issue. However, the known facts may not be conclusive enough to justify a decision. We shall be better able to judge when we have seen the affidavits."

"I don't expect that they will tell us anything new," said Thorndyke. "We have heard the whole story of the search from Polton and Elmhurst, and we read the account of what happened at the time. We probably know all the facts on which the applicant will rely, judging from what Penfield said."

"You may, but my recollection of them is rather dim. I am afraid I did not quite share Polton's enthusiasm. After all, it was no special concern of ours."

"Then," said Thorndyke, "let me refresh your memory. Put in a nutshell, the case amounts to this: A woman was murdered in Lotta Schiller's rooms at Thirty-nine Jacob Street. The person who committed the murder let himself in with Lotta Schiller's keys."

"Or perhaps with some similar, or skeleton keys," I suggested.

"No. One key was found in the lock and conclusively identified as Lotta's own key. At the time of the discovery of the murder, Lotta had already disappeared and could not be found or heard of by the police. Some time later – I have forgotten the dates – her handbag was found on the bank enclosing the British Camp in Epping Forest. It contained a key-pouch from which two keys were missing, one being the latch-key and the other the key of the room in which the murder seemed to have taken place. Inside the camp the police found a locket belonging to Lotta – incidentally, made by Polton – and containing a portrait of our friend, Vanderpuye."

"Yes, I remember that. Poor Vanderpuye! He will wish he had gone back to Africa when he hears that the scandal is going to be revived."

"Probably," Thorndyke agreed, "though his evidence will refer only to the date on which he last saw Lotta. But to continue: As the finding of these things indicated the probability that the woman had been murdered and her body disposed of in the neighbourhood, the police arranged an exhaustive search of the camp for further traces of her, dead or alive. The result of that search was the discovery of a series of footprints, apparently of a man and a woman, which proceeded side by side to a point near the place where the locket was found. Here the ground was trampled in a way that suggested a struggle, and there was a rather obscure impression of a woman's body lying in a supine position. From this point the footprints continued, but they were those of the man only. There were no further footprints of the woman, and it is suggested that the impressions of the man's feet were somewhat deeper than they had been before.

"The single track of footprints crossed the camp to the north-west side until they reached the enclosing bank, and here some further discoveries were made. It was seen that the man had climbed up the bank twice – the first time apparently to reconnoitre. Near the foot of the bank was another, very obscure, impression of a woman's body lying on the ground. Near it a button was picked up. It was a very distinctive button, painted by hand, and was conclusively identified by a Mr. Pedley as a button from Lotta's jacket. On a broken twig, halfway up the bank, a wisp of a green material was clinging, and this shred Mr. Pedley identified as exactly similar to the material of her jacket and dress. Finally, at the top of the bank, the earth showed marks as if some heavy object had been dragged across the summit.

"That, as Inspector Blandy put it at the time, was 'the end of the trail'. On the outer side of the bank was the turf of the green ride, which would not have shown impressions in any case, but the fact is that no tracks or traces of any kind were found outside the camp, while inside the enclosure, there was no sign anywhere of the ground having been disturbed. It can be taken as certain that the body – if there was a body – was not buried in the camp, and no traces of either the man or the woman could be discovered anywhere else.

"Those are the facts that I think we shall find embodied in the affidavits, together with evidence that the woman has not been seen or heard of since her visit to the forest with Vanderpuye. On them will be based the application for the court's permission to presume that Lotta Schiller is dead, and I ask you, Jervis, as an experienced medico-legal practitioner, whether you still think that collateral facts, such as the woman's personal character and way of life, are not material to the issue."

"I still don't see that they are," said I, "though, as you apparently do, I suppose I am wrong. But it seems to me that the facts that you have stated point very strongly to the conclusion that the woman was murdered and her body concealed somewhere in the forest. There appears to have been an adequate motive for the murder. To get possession of the keys and to eliminate a person who might have been dangerous, for it is practically certain that Lotta Schiller would either have known or guessed who committed the murder in her rooms.

"The prima facie evidence that she was murdered seems to me extremely strong, and when we add to it the fact that she has never since been seen or heard of, the probability becomes overwhelming, and certainly enough, in my opinion, to warrant the presumption that she is dead."

"*Q.E.D.*," Thorndyke commented with an appreciative chuckle. "You have put the case for the applicant with admirable lucidity. Unfortunately, it is that case that we have to demolish if we can do so by fair means and consistently with what we believe to be the truth. Wherefore I now call upon my learned friend to bring his mighty intellect to bear on the opposite proposition. Come, now, Jervis, here is an opportunity to exercise your wits and utilize your experience. You have just given a masterly exposition of the reasons for presuming that Lotta Schiller is dead. Now cross over to the other side and see what reasons you can find for presuming that she is alive."

With a strong and growing suspicion that I had, as usual, overlooked some material fact, I promised to reconsider the case and, as a first indispensable step, to refresh my memory as to the whole set of circumstances, to which end I repaired to Polton's lair and, having conveyed to him the tidings of the proposed application, had no difficulty in obtaining the loan of his voluminous collection of newspaper cuttings, which I bore off to study at my leisure.

Chapter XII
Tom Pedley Receives Visitors

The question with which Thorndyke had closed his narration had rather taken me aback, but what had really surprised me was his clear and complete recollection of the case in all its details. Yet it ought not to have surprised me, for the thing had often happened before, but I always failed to allow for a fundamental difference between us: Thorndyke was a genuine criminologist and I was not. By me, the report of a criminal case was read with mild interest, and then, if it did not concern us, was straightway dismissed and forgotten.

Not so Thorndyke. To him, every case was a problem, and if there was any element of mystery or obscurity, he would study it, evolve one or more possible solutions, and retain the case in his memory until it was cleared up – if ever it was – and the actual solution was disclosed. It was a useful habit, for, apart from the mental exercise amounting in effect to experience, there was the practical advantage that if an obscure case was ultimately referred to us – as often happened – it found Thorndyke fully informed as to the facts and perhaps with a solution already arrived at.

This, I suspected, was the present position. Reading attentively through Polton's collection of reports, I realized that the whole case, including the murder of Emma Robey, was profoundly mysterious. But I also realized the significance of Thorndyke's question: Lotta Schiller was definitely implicated in the murder.

This, Penfield would have said, was not material to the question whether she was dead or alive. But it *was* material. The disappearance of a person who is under suspicion in regard to a murder calls for a much more critical consideration than that of a person who has no known motive for disappearing.

In due course the notice of motion was served on Mr. Penfield, and copies of the affidavits were sent on to us, and as I read them through, I saw that Thorndyke had been right. The facts sworn to were concerned exclusively with evidence of Lotta Schiller's death. The murder of Emma Robey was referred to only incidentally (in an affidavit by a Mrs. Bigham) in connection with the man who, accompanied by a woman, had let himself into the premises of 39 Jacob Street with a latch-key. Evidently, the inference advanced by the applicant would be that this man had already murdered Lotta Schiller and possessed himself of her keys.

Thus the case for the application was fairly clear. We could see what "the other side" proposed to prove and, taking the facts at their face value, it was a reasonably good case. But the next question was: What did Thorndyke propose to prove, and what was he going to do about it? Assuming – as I did – that he had already considered the case and probably arrived at some provisional conclusions, my expectation was that he would follow his usual practice and begin by seeking to enlarge his knowledge, by searching for some new facts to supplement those already known, and mighty curious I was as to what line his investigations would take, and not a little surprised when his intentions were disclosed.

"So," he remarked on the following day, "my learned friend has studied the affidavits and the Poltonian Dossier and now knows all the available facts? Probably he has found them a little sketchy?"

"On the contrary," I replied, "I thought that we had a pretty full account of the case. What more do you want to know?"

"I want to know all that I can learn. For instance, there is Lotta Schiller, the central figure in the case. What do we know about her? She is little more than a name, a sort of algebraical symbol. I want to turn her into a real person – to know what she was like, physically, mentally, and morally."

I was about to object that such knowledge was not likely to help us much in opposing the application, but fortunately I saw the red light in time.

"And how do you propose to get that knowledge?" I asked

"The most likely source is Mr. Thomas Pedley. He, apparently, knew her quite intimately, and should be able to tell us quite a lot about her. So I wrote to him a day or two ago, and he has kindly given me an appointment for to-morrow afternoon. May I take it that I shall have your support at the interview?"

As it happened, fortunately, that I had the afternoon free, I accepted gladly – indeed, I may say eagerly. For my curiosity about this visit was intense. That its object was simply to get a description of Lotta Schiller's appearance and personality seemed incredible, and I hoped that by listening attentively to Thorndyke's questions I might get some inkling of what was really in his mind.

Jacob Street we found to be a shabby, old-fashioned street turning out of the Hampstead Road, in which Mr. Thomas Pedley's studio was distinguishable by a green-painted wooden gate bearing the number *38A* in well-polished brass characters, and by a small brass plate at the side inscribed "*T. Pedley*" surmounted by a shining brass bell-knob. A tug at this resulted in the distant jangling of a large bell, followed by the opening of the gate and the appearance thereat of a big, hearty, pleasant-faced man who surveyed us for a moment with a friendly blue eye and then, apparently recognizing us or taking our identities for granted, bade us "come along in", whereupon we followed him along a stone passage and across a small yard to the studio, the size of which, and especially of the great north window, I found quite impressive.

"It is very good of you, Mr. Pedley," said Thorndyke, "to let us come here occupying your time with matters in which I don't suppose you are much interested."

"Oh, I am interested enough," replied Pedley, "but I am afraid you will find me rather disappointing, for I really know nothing about Lotta Schiller or her affairs."

"Well," Thorndyke rejoined with a smile, "that is a fact, to begin with, and not entirely without significance. But at any rate, you know more about her than I do, so I stand to learn something."

"I am afraid it will be mighty little," said Pedley. "But perhaps a cup of tea may brighten my wits. Yours probably don't need any brightening."

He led us across to the tea-table which had been placed, with three armchairs, in front of the fire and, having installed us, proceeded to make the tea at a gas-ring by the large sink, and while he was thus occupied I cast inquisitive glances around, and was not a little impressed by the fine china and elegant table appointments and the various signs of a refined and fastidious taste in the furnishing of the place, which contrasted rather oddly with the sink, the cooking stove, and the working appliances.

"I think," said Pedley when he had poured out the tea and taken his seat, "that, as you know what information you want and I don't, you had better treat me as a witness. You ask your questions, and I will answer as well as I can."

"Very well," said Thorndyke, producing a notebook and opening it. "Then, as I have never seen Mrs. Schiller and have no idea what she was like, we will begin with her personal appearance. Can you give me a description of her?"

Pedley was obviously astonished – as well he might have been – but he replied readily enough. "Yes, I can do that all right, for it happens that Inspector Blandy made the same request, and I drafted out an exhaustive description and gave him a copy. I can show you the original draft."

He went to a shelf on which was a long row of linen-bound books, each having on its back a paper label bearing a date.

"Let me see," said he, running his eye along the row, "it would be about 1930. Yes, here we are."

He picked out the little volume and brought it to the table, explaining, as he turned over the leaves. "This is the notebook that I was using at the time. It contains all sorts of notes, sketches, drawings, and written memoranda and, as I date every entry, it serves well enough as a diary. This is the draft that I made for Blandy."

He handed the open book to Thorndyke, who glanced through it rapidly though with close attention and, I thought, some signs of surprise.

"But, Mr. Pedley," he exclaimed, "this is an extraordinarily complete description. You seem to have observed everything and forgotten nothing."

"Well, you see," Pedley replied, "that is an artist's job, to look at things attentively and remember what he has seen. But I am glad you approve. Blandy was quite pleased, though he wanted one or two points elucidated."

"For instance?"

"Well, there were the ears. He asked me if I could draw them from memory, which, of course, I could and did."

"He was quite right," said Thorndyke. "A drawing is better than the best verbal description. I wonder if you would kindly do the same for me?"

Though still looking a little puzzled, Pedley complied readily. On a small cartridge paper block he drew, very deliberately and yet quickly, a pair of ears, facing each other.

"There," he said, taking off the sheet and handing it to Thorndyke, "you see they are just normal, well-shaped ears with a small Darwinian tubercle on the right one. I have marked in the line of the jaw to show how they were set."

Thorndyke thanked him for the drawing and, having examined it, put it away carefully in his wallet. Then, glancing once more at the description, he said, "There is one point here that seems to require some amplification. You say that the hair had some peculiarity of texture that made it seem variable in colour. I don't quite understand that."

Pedley grinned. "Blandy again," said he. "He didn't understand it and neither do I. So I couldn't tell him anything beyond the bare fact that it certainly did seem to change colour in different lights. The change was very slight and I don't suppose the majority of people would have noticed it at all. But there it was, and I've never seen any other hair like it before or since."

"Do you think," I suggested, "that it might have been dyed or faked in some way? Women do all sorts of queer things to their hair in these days."

538

"I thought of that," replied Pedley, "but there was one circumstance that seemed to exclude it. Dyed or faked hair, as you know, won't bear close inspection, especially at the roots. But Mrs. Schiller had no objection at all to a close inspection. When Polton wanted a sample of her hair, she made no difficulty but let him cut it off himself. He separated out a little tress and cut it off close to the roots, exposing the skin of the scalp and, apparently, he noticed nothing unusual there."

"Did you ever mention the peculiarity to her?" asked Thorndyke.

"No, and I don't think she was aware of it herself."

"By the way," said I, "what did Polton want a lock of her hair for?"

"He was making a locket for Mr. Vanderpuye, and it was arranged that there should be a specimen of her hair set in one side to face the portrait in the other."

"Oh, yes, I remember the locket – the two lockets, in fact – but they were empty when I saw them. I never heard what was to be put in them."

"As to the portrait in Vanderpuye's locket," said Thorndyke, "was it a miniature or a photograph?"

"It was a photograph, but not from life. She painted a self-portrait in watercolour and Polton did a reduced photograph of it."

"Was it a fairly good likeness?"

Pedley grinned. "It wasn't a likeness at all. There was no resemblance whatever to Lotta, and hardly any to a human being."

"But I wonder Vanderpuye didn't object," said I, "seeing that a likeness was what he wanted."

"He did – in fact, he was really angry. He wanted me to paint or draw a portrait of Lotta of which Polton could make a reduced photograph to fit the locket. But she would not have it, nor would she allow Polton to do a photograph of her. She insisted that the portrait should be her own work, and from that she wouldn't budge. So poor Vanderpuye had to accept her drawing, but I shall never forget Polton's face when he first set eyes on it. He thought that it was a practical joke, but he realized his mistake in time."

"But what was it like?" I asked, a little bewildered by his account of the incident.

"It was a drawing of a woman's head such as might be done by a child of nine or ten – not a clever child, mind you, but just an ordinary child with no natural aptitude for drawing."

"But," I exclaimed, "I don't understand this. Wasn't she a professional artist?"

"She claimed to be one but, of course, anyone can call himself an artist. The fact is that she couldn't draw and she couldn't paint."

"Do you mean that she drew badly," Thorndyke asked, "or that she, literally, couldn't draw at all?"

"Her drawing," replied Pedley, "was like that of an ordinary child, and I am quite sure that she couldn't do anything different."

"This is rather remarkable," said Thorndyke, "and it suggests one or two questions. The first is as to her state of mind. Was she cranky enough to believe that she really could paint?"

Pedley chuckled. "Blandy again," said he. "That is what he wanted to know and I rather dodged his questions. But I won't hedge with you because I have thought the matter over since, and I have come to the conclusion that she was a rank impostor. There was nothing cranky about her. She was a pretty shrewd, level-headed young woman, and I am sure that she had no delusions about her painting. It was a deliberate fraud. What her object was in posing as an artist, I have no idea, but what I am quite clear about is that she just took advantage of the present fashion for freak pictures and started producing freaks. Anybody can do it. All you have to do is to paint something quite unlike a normal picture and leave it to the highbrows to explain it to the multitude. But she knew all about it, and she had got all the highbrow jargon at her finger-ends."

"That," said Thorndyke, "partly disposes of the next question, which is how she maintained the pose. Did she ever offer her work for sale?"

"No. She spoke of an intention to send some of her stuff to an exhibition, but she never did send any."

"I suppose she signed her pictures with her own name?"

"She didn't sign them at all, properly speaking. She used a cipher – a sort of conventionalized flower with a little circle on each side of the stalk."

"It all sounds rather tortuous and secretive," I remarked.

"Yes," Pedley agreed, "but she was secretive in everything. Polton first drew my attention to her capacity for keeping her own counsel. But the secrecy about her paintings I don't understand. It looks rather as if the artist pose was a temporary stunt which she meant to drop when it had served her purpose, whatever that may have been."

"It does," said Thorndyke, "and yet the brass plate by her door seems to exclude the idea of secrecy. It was a public announcement."

"It wasn't very public," replied Pedley. "It was only a small plate, about six-inches-by-four, with just the bare name in small copper-plate script. It wasn't very easy to read from the pavement even when it was new and, by the time she had kept it polished for a few weeks and rubbed most of the black out of the engraving, it was nearly illegible. No passing stranger could have read it."

"That seems to answer my objection," said Thorndyke. "And now, to come back to the description. I suppose you don't possess a photograph of her?"

"No," replied Pedley, "and I never saw one."

"Did you ever draw a portrait of her?"

"Not from life. I had thought of suggesting that I should paint her portrait and then I decided that I had better not. But I made one or two trial sketches from memory to see how a profile portrait would look. They are in that notebook that you have. Would you like to see them?"

"I should, very much," replied Thorndyke, handing him the book and watching him, expectantly, as he turned over the leaves.

"This is the best one," said Pedley, passing the book back, "and as the others were preliminary trials, we can disregard them."

Thorndyke examined the drawing with deep interest, as also did I, though what chiefly interested me was the liveliness of the representation and its finished character. It might have been a careful drawing done direct from the model.

"This is rather more than a sketch, Mr. Pedley," said Thorndyke. "It gives the impression of an actual portrait but, of course, I can't judge as to the likeness. What do you say about it? Is it really like her?"

"Yes," replied Pedley. "I should say it is quite a good likeness."

"Do you think it would be recognized by anyone who had known her?"

"Oh, certainly. Looking at it now, after all this time, it recalls her to me perfectly. You see, in drawing from memory one instinctively chooses the most characteristic and easily remembered aspect."

"Yes, I see that," said Thorndyke. "But you seem to have a rather remarkable memory."

"Not remarkable," replied Pedley. "I have a good memory, and I have made a point of training it. But, in effect, all drawing is memory drawing. You can't look at the model and draw at the same time. You have, first, to look at the model with concentrated attention and try to memorize the part you are working on. Then, as a separate act, you draw it, and then you compare what you have drawn with the actual facts and correct your drawing if necessary. Memory drawing is only the same thing with a longer interval between seeing and drawing."

Thorndyke pondered this with his eyes fixed on the portrait. At length he said, "If this is a perfectly recognizable likeness of Lotta Schiller, it may be of some importance as the only existing record of her personal appearance. I wonder if you would allow Polton to bring a camera here and take a photograph of it."

541

"Of course I would, with the greatest pleasure. But why take all that trouble? Better just slip the book in your pocket and let me have it back when you have done with it."

"That is very gracious of you, Mr. Pedley," said Thorndyke, "and it will certainly be much more convenient. I didn't like to ask you for the loan, as I understood that the book contained some private memoranda."

"You needn't have been so punctilious," Pedley replied with a smile. "I have no secrets and, if I had, I shouldn't write them in my notebook. No, Doctor, I give you the free run of the book if the sketches and notes are of any interest to you. Perhaps you might like to see the finger-prints that Polton took from that poor murdered woman. They are in the book somewhere. Shall I see if I can find them?"

"I don't know that they are of much interest now," said Thorndyke, handing him the book nevertheless, "excepting as to Polton's improvised method of taking them."

"And his motive for doing it," I added. "It wasn't a very correct proceeding, and I never understood why he wanted to meddle."

"I think that is pretty clear," said Pedley. "He wanted to know, then and there, whether it was a case of suicide or murder. Ah, here are the prints."

He returned the book to Thorndyke, who, notwithstanding what he had said, looked at the rather feeble impressions with some interest, which seemed to deepen as he looked, for, presently he produced his lens from his pocket and made a closer examination, finishing up by viewing the prints with the book held at arm's length.

"Quite a creditable performance," he remarked, "considering the very inadequate means. What do you think of them, Jervis?"

He handed me the book with his lens, and I examined the prints with some curiosity.

"Yes," I agreed, "they are not bad, rather weak and faint, but you can make out the pattern quite clearly, even in the last three fingers, where the impression seems to have partly failed. I shall make a note of the method for use in a similar emergency. And, by the way, the method is not new to us. The original *Thumbograph* was provided with an inking-pad."

I returned the book to him and, when he had closed it and slipped it into his pocket, I waited expectantly for the next question. But there was none. Apparently the "examination in chief" was finished.

I say "apparently", for with Thorndyke you never knew when the examination had really ended. He had a way of directing a conversation without appearing to and thus allowing the information that he was seeking to transpire, as it seemed, spontaneously, and I had a faint

542

suspicion that, on the present occasion, Pedley was being gently guided along the paths of reminiscence in the desired direction.

And yet it seemed incredible, for though Pedley's account of his relations with Lotta Schiller was amusing enough, described in his quaintly humorous way, it was utterly trivial and seemed to have no bearing whatever on our problem. The way in which she had opened the acquaintance by a transparent pretext and thereafter adopted him as her dearest friend, in spite of his struggles to escape, was rather funny, but relevant to nothing that concerned us. At least, so I judged, though even then my judgment was confounded by Thorndyke's concentrated attention to these trifling reminiscences and by the little aids to amplification that he applied.

"It is a quaint picture," he remarked with an appreciative chuckle. "The masterful lady and the lover *malgré lui.*"

"Not lover," protested Pedley. "There was not even a pretence of that."

"But you seem to have been on quite affectionate terms," Thorndyke maintained.

"On her side only," said Pedley, "and that was all bunkum. It was just a pose, like her painting. But it was very queer. I never understood what her game was. She called me 'Tom' from the very beginning, and soon it came to Tom, dear, or darling or duck. But it was all verbal, there was no demonstration of affection. Anyone listening in an adjoining room might have taken us for an engaged couple, but our actual behaviour was perfectly matter-of-fact."

"Do you mean that there were no physical endearments? Did she, for instance, never kiss you?"

"Lord, no! I shouldn't have let her. But she never made any approach to that sort of thing. As I say, it was purely verbal. I took it to be just a silly habit of speech, especially as she used the same terms to others. Why, she even called Polton a duck, and as to poor Vanderpuye – but his case was different. He took the endearments quite seriously. Still, even he was not on kissing terms. He swore, at the inquest, that he had never kissed her, and I suspected that he had made an attempt and not brought it off."

"Very odd," Thorndyke commented, "particularly as the modern woman seems to be so far from squeamish in such matters. Did the verbal endearments extend to written communications? How did she address you in writing?"

"She never did, and I am glad she didn't, for if her handwriting was at all like her drawing, it would have taken some deciphering. But she never wrote to me, and I gather that she never wrote to Vanderpuye. It almost looks as if she avoided putting any of her nonsense down in black and white, though there was nothing very incriminating in it."

"Not incriminating," said Thorndyke, "but, after all, she was a married woman, and compromising letters are apt to be dangerous things if there happens to be an unfriendly husband in the background."

"I don't think her husband was unfriendly. The position seemed to be that they had separated by mutual agreement and gone their respective ways, simply ignoring the marriage. On the few occasions when she referred to him, she did so without the slightest trace of animosity."

"Apparently she was not very communicative about him."

"No, he was rather a shadowy figure. All I learned from her was that his name was Carl, that by profession he was a sort of travelling wine merchant, that he was, in a sense, domiciled somewhere in Germany, but spent most of his time rambling about the Continent with occasional visits to this country and the United States. That is all that she let drop. Of course, I never asked any questions."

This apparently exhausted Pedley's store of reminiscences, for the conversation now drifted in the direction of his work and mode of life, and when he had shown us some of his paintings and taken us on a personally conducted tour of his premises, including the very pleasant little cubicle bedroom that he had built in a corner of the studio, we felt that we had stayed long enough.

"It is most kind of you, Mr. Pedley," said Thorndyke, "to have let us take up so much of your time and to give us so much help in our inquiry."

"I am glad to hear that I have been helpful," replied Pedley, as he escorted us along the paved passage. "It seemed to me that I was ladling out some rather small beer. But I enjoyed doing it. To a solitary man, a real good chin-wag comes as a refreshing novelty."

With this exchange of courtesies and a hearty handshake we took our departure and, crossing the Hampstead Road, set a course for the Temple by way of the less-frequented back streets. For some time we walked on in silence, but presently, according to custom, I ventured to put out a cautious feeler.

"Pedley's estimate of the conversation was rather like my own, and we are probably both wrong but, apart from the description and the portrait (the value of which is not obvious to me), I don't see that we have learned anything very significant."

"That," replied Thorndyke, "must be because you have not got the issues in this case clear in your mind."

"But I think I have. The simple issue is whether or not Lotta Schiller is presumably dead."

544

"Yes, but put it another way. Either the woman is dead and her body concealed in some unknown place, or she is alive and keeping out of sight. The issue is between the alternatives of a concealed dead body or a concealed living person."

"She would be mightily well concealed to keep out of sight for two years with the police on the look-out for her all the time. I should have thought it practically impossible, considering all the modern means and facilities at their disposal."

"Still," said he, "the possibility of her being alive is the one that concerns us, and the value of the information that we have got from Pedley is in its bearing on that question. What I recommend you to do is this: When you get home, while the matter is fresh in your memory, take a sheet of paper and write down a full report of our conversation with Pedley. Then read it over and extract from it any facts, explicitly stated or implied, without regard to their significance, and write them down on another sheet. Finally, consider those facts, separately and together, in relation to the two alternatives that I mentioned. I think you will find Mister Pedley's small beer more nourishing than it appeared at the time."

Chapter XIII
Thorndyke Becomes Secretive

Thorndyke's suggested procedure for extracting the nourishment from Mr. Pedley's "small beer" – which I duly put into practice – proved highly effective. But yet it was not effective enough, for while it brought into view several facts which might be important in certain circumstances, it threw no light on their application to our present problem, wherefore, and because the reader, quicker in the uptake than I, has no doubt already noted them, I shall make no further reference to them. But if not very enlightening, my study had the effect of stimulating my curiosity as to what was in Thorndyke's mind. That he had a definite theory concerning Lotta Schiller's disappearance, and that his theory was strictly relevant to the main problem I had no doubt, and since I could make no guess as to the nature of that theory, I could only seek enlightenment by observing his proceedings and trying to deduce their object. This, however, turned out a complete failure, for the more I saw of his methods, the more bewildered I became, and the less able to connect them in any way with Mr. Penfield's case. I shall therefore put my observations briefly and baldly on record without unnecessary comments.

A few days after our visit to Pedley, Thorndyke, when he came into lunch, took from an inner pocket a couple of documents and deposited them in the cabinet in which such things were usually kept, and I noticed that they went into the drawer which contained Mr. Penfield's papers.

"You have been to Somerset House," said I, having recognized the official copies.

"Yes," he replied. "An unnecessary visit, perhaps, but one never knows what unexpected questions may arise during the hearing, so I have provided myself with certified copies of two of the wills concerned in Penfield's case. We have a copy of the third, Lotta Schiller's."

"Whose are the other two?" I asked.

"One is that of Barbara Dalton who left the twenty-thousand pounds to Lotta. The other is that of a Mr. Charles Montagu, which contains, among many other legacies, the bequest of twenty-thousand pounds to Barbara. Would you like to look over them?"

"No, thanks," I replied. "They don't interest me, unless they contain something unexpected or curious. Do they?"

"No, they are quite simple and straightforward and, of course, they are not disputed."

"Then I think we can leave them to Penfield, if they come into the case at all."

Thus the matter was dismissed, leaving me with a faint feeling of surprise that even Thorndyke should have concerned himself with such remote antecedents. But apparently it was only another instance of his almost fanatical insistence on knowing all the facts.

The next proceeding of his that attracted my attention had, at least, some connection with Penfield's case, though I failed utterly to discover any relevancy. It took the form of an exhaustive interrogation of Vanderpuye, of whom we now saw a good deal as the Long Vacation had brought him back from his travels on the Southeastern Circuit. It was not, of course, a formal interrogation, which would have been quite alien to Thorndyke's usual methods. But Vanderpuye was perfectly willing to talk about his liaison with Lotta Schiller – it had been the great adventure of his life – and a little skilful guidance of the conversation brought out all the details. But of these conversations, which seemed to elicit nothing that was new even to me, I shall record only one, and that one chiefly because it led to further activities on Thorndyke's part. We had been discussing Pedley's portrait of Vanderpuye and the incidents connected with the painting of it, when my colleague led off in a new direction with the remark, "It was a very successful portrait, a faithful likeness and an extremely becoming one, too. I am rather surprised that you did not get Pedley to paint one of Lotta. I should have thought that you would have liked to have a portrait of her."

"I should," Vanderpuye replied emphatically, "and I begged her to let him paint one of her, but she refused flatly. It was at the time when the lockets were being made, and I wanted him to paint her portrait so that I could have the original to hang beside my own and a little photograph of it to carry about with me in my locket. But she was most obstinate and perverse. She insisted on painting the portrait herself, and she wouldn't even agree to letting Polton take a photograph of her for the locket. It was really very awkward. I had seen her work and I knew that she couldn't paint a portrait, but she stuck to her decision, and I had to accept her self-portrait. But I was very annoyed."

"Then I infer that it was not a very good likeness?" Thorndyke suggested.

"Bah!" exclaimed Vanderpuye. "It was not a likeness at all. But you can see for yourself." And, as he spoke, he unshackled the locket from his watch-guard and handed it to Thorndyke, who carefully prised it open and looked curiously at the little portrait.

"I was going to remark," said he, "that as I have never seen the lady, I could hardly judge the likeness. But I see that I was wrong. This drawing only faintly resembles a human being and certainly could not be a recognizable likeness of any particular person. By the way, did she give you the original drawing?"

"No, she never offered it to me, and I should not have accepted it if she had."

"I ask," said Thorndyke, "because her work as an artist may have some bearing on the case that is pending, and I should have liked to produce a specimen. But this is rather small, particularly if the judge's eyesight should happen to be at all defective. What do you think, Jervis?"

I took the locket from him and gazed in astonishment at the incredibly crude and childish drawing – though Pedley's description had prepared me for something abnormal – which, small as it was (about the size of a shilling) offered evidence enough of the artist's incompetence. But I couldn't understand Thorndyke's difficulty, and said so.

"I don't see that the size matters. It would be quite simple to make an enlarged photograph – that is, if Vanderpuye would give his permission."

"But of course," protested Vanderpuye. "I should be delighted to help in any way. By all means take the locket and let me have it back when you have done with it."

Thereupon, having thanked the owner warmly, Thorndyke slipped the little bauble into an envelope and folded it up securely, but I noticed that instead of locking it up in the cabinet according to his usual custom, he stowed it carefully in an inner pocket. It was a small matter but it attracted my attention, and when, on reflection, I realized how adroitly Thorndyke had managed to obtain possession of the trinket without asking for the loan, I began to suspect that there was more in the transaction than met the eye. Accordingly, I followed the fortunes of the locket closely to see whether any ulterior purpose should come into view. But apparently there was none. On the following day Thorndyke handed the locket to Polton, who gazed at it fondly and then returned it.

"I don't want the locket, sir," said he. "You are forgetting that I did the miniature. I have the original negative that I made from the drawing, which will be much better for doing the enlargement as it is a good size already."

"Of course," said Thorndyke. "My wits must have been woolgathering. Why didn't you remind me, Jervis?"

I replied that my wits were probably on the same quest, as I had suggested the borrowing of the locket, but protested that no harm had been done.

548

"No," he agreed, turning the locket over in his hand, "and I am glad to have seen the little bauble again. It is a charming specimen of goldsmith's work and it does Mr. Pedley and his executant very great credit. How on earth did you manage, Polton, to work the hair into that beautifully regular spiral? Hair isn't a very kindly material, is it?"

"It's all right, sir, if you know how to manage it. I just soaked two of the hairs from the little tress that I had cut off and wound each of them tightly on a thin steel spindle. Then I carefully heated the spindle and, when it was cool, the hair slipped off in a little close cylinder like a cylindrical spring. After that, it was quite easy to work it into a flat spiral on the card."

"So you used only two of the hairs. What did you do with the remainder of the tress? Did you throw it away?"

Polton crinkled slyly. "No, sir," said he, "I've got the regular craftsman's vice. I never throw anything away. You see, even a hair comes in handy, if it's long enough, to string a small bow for use on the turns. Would you like to see what's left of it?"

Without waiting for an answer he went to one of his innumerable cabinets and, from a labelled drawer produced a seed envelope inscribed in pencil "*Mrs. Schiller's Hair*", which he handed to Thorndyke, who drew out of it a little tress of pale brown or dull flaxen hair neatly tied up with bands of thread.

"I don't see anything unusual in it," said I, as Thorndyke held it at arm's length in the light of the window.

"No," he agreed, "but we haven't Pedley's trained colour sense, and probably the peculiarity that he described would be noticeable only in large masses. But it couldn't have been very conspicuous even then, as nobody else seems to have observed it."

He pulled the tress out taut and, having measured it against a two-foot rule on the bench, wrote the length ("*Nine-and-a-half inches*") on the envelope. Then he re-coiled the tress and slipped it back into its receptacle.

"I am going to rob you, Polton," said he. "This specimen had better go with the rest of the possible exhibits, and on the remote chance of its having to be produced in court, you may as well sign your name on the envelope under the description."

This ceremony was duly performed and, when Thorndyke had declined my derisive offer to witness the signature, he put the envelope in his wallet and we then reverted to the enlargement of the portrait.

I make no comment on these proceedings, having already said that I found myself utterly unable to connect any of them with Mr. Penfield's problem. Nor shall I, for obvious reasons, say anything about certain other activities which Thorndyke carried on in his private laboratory with the door locked, which from experience I judged to be experiments connected with his inferences from the facts known to me. No doubt they would have been highly revealing if I had known what they were but, in accordance with the queer convention that existed between us, by which Thorndyke gave me every opportunity to observe the facts but refused to disclose his inferences or hypotheses until the case was concluded, I was left in the dark, and even Polton, bursting with curiosity, could only gaze wistfully at the locked door.

Of what went on, then, in the private laboratory, I had no knowledge at all, but in two other instances I was permitted, so to speak, to inspect the backs of the cards. Thus, on a certain day, returning at lunch time, I perceived my colleague pacing up and down the lower end of King's Bench Walk in earnest conversation with one Mr. Snuper. Now, Mr. Snuper was a very remarkable man. Originally a private inquiry agent, he had been employed by Thorndyke on one or two occasions to collect information or to keep certain persons under observation, but he had proved so ingenious, resourceful, and dependable, that Thorndyke had engaged him permanently, and a very valuable member of our staff he had proved in making inquiries and observations where it was undesirable for us to appear.

But what could this meeting portend? Usually, Mr. Snuper's appearance foreshadowed some more or less sensational developments. But at present the Schiller case was the only one that we had on hand in which sensational developments were possible, but of that case we seemed to be in possession of all the relevant facts. Our problem was concerned with the application of those facts and seemed to offer no opening for Mr. Snuper's activities.

But my bewilderment reached a climax that very evening when, entering our sitting room, I found Polton placing an easy-chair before the fireplace and setting beside it a little table on which were a whisky decanter and a box of cigars. I watched him with growing suspicion, and when he added an awl, borrowed from the workshop, suspicion grew into certainty.

"Expecting the superintendent?" I asked.

"Yes, sir," he replied. "Mr. Miller is coming by appointment at half-past-eight."

"You don't know what about, I suppose?"

"No, sir, I do not. I suspect it is that Schiller case, but that is only a guess, and I don't mind telling you, sir, that I am fairly eaten up with curiosity. I can see that there is something in the wind, and that somebody is going to get a surprise."

"What makes you say that?"

"Oh, I know the symptoms of old, sir. The Doctor is in one of his exasperating moods, as secret as an oyster and as busy as a bee. He has been locked in his laboratory doing all sorts of things that are really my job – developing photographs, mounting specimens for the microscope, making micro-photographs, and the Lord knows what else. I know that much, because I've done the clearing up after him."

I laughed at his undisguised inquisitiveness, but not without sympathy.

"It seems to me," I remarked, "that you have been doing Snuper's job, keeping what the plain-clothes men call 'obbo' on the Doctor."

"Well, sir, there's no harm in keeping him under observation when his actions seem to invite it, and I believe he likes to be watched. It's part of the game. Why, only this morning I saw him colloguing with Mr. Snuper on the Walk. He knew I could see him from the window. And now there's Mr. Miller coming, and he isn't giving much away. And what do you make of that?"

He produced from his pocket a little slip of mahogany about four-inches-by-two, in which was a shallow, elongated cavity about two-and-a-half inches by one, with straight sides and rounded ends, and a little round hole about a sixteenth-of-an-inch wide, just outside the middle of the cavity.

"I made it from the Doctor's own full-scale drawing," Polton continued, "and, as he said nothing about its purpose, I suspect it is part of the surprise packet."

"It looks rather like some sort of a microscope slide," I suggested, but at this moment, as a quick footstep became audible ascending the stair, Polton picked up the slide and returned it to his pocket, smiling guiltily as the door opened and Thorndyke entered.

"I see we are to have the pleasure of a visit from Miller," I remarked.

He glanced at the little table and then asked with a smile, "Is that information received or observation and inference?"

"Both," I replied, "but the inference first. It was the awl that clinched the diagnosis."

"Yes," Thorndyke chuckled. "It is wonderful how Polton remembers all the likes and dislikes of our visitors. He would have made a perfect innkeeper. How do you do it, Polton?"

"Well, sir," he replied with a gratified crinkle, "the proper study of mankind is man, and that includes Mr. Miller – and by the same token, here he is."

551

The crescendo of approaching footsteps culminated in the characteristic knock and, as Polton threw the door open, the superintendent entered and saluted us with a comprehensive smile, which took in the three easy-chairs and the small table.

"It's nice to see you all again," said he, when the preliminary greetings and hand-shakings – which included Polton – had been disposed of. "Quite a long time since I was here. Don't get many excuses to come now that I am kept bottled up in the office."

We chatted inconsequently for a minute or two and then adjourned to the chairs, when Thorndyke and I lit our pipes while Miller carefully selected a cigar and Polton poured out the whisky.

"Well, Doctor," said the superintendent, thoughtfully operating with the awl on the proximal end of the cigar, "I've managed your little business. Rare job it was, too. Had to get the Assistant Commissioner's permission, of course, and he wasn't at all ready to give it, but I showed him your letter and coaxed him a bit and at last he gave way. But he wouldn't have done it for anyone else, and no more would I for that matter, and he stipulated that the information was to be considered strictly confidential and personal to you."

"You know that you can depend on my discretion, Miller. But supposing it were required to be used in evidence? May I take it that he would consent?"

"That you would have to settle with him. You weren't proposing to challenge the conviction, I suppose?"

"No. The conviction, whether good or bad, is no affair of mine."

"I wonder what is your affair – and so did the A.C., especially what you wanted the finger-prints for. However, I suppose we shall know in due course, as you seem to hint that you may need our collaboration later. At any rate," he concluded, producing a bulky, sealed envelope from his pocket, "here is the dossier of the worthy Louisa Saunders, if that was her name – apparently it was, as it agreed with the initials on her clothing – all complete: Personal particulars, finger-prints, prison portraits, summary of the police-court proceedings, everything that you asked for, and you notice that the envelope is sealed with wax and marked 'Secret Documents'."

He delivered the package to Thorndyke, with a malicious leer in my direction and, when my colleague had thanked him very warmly for his friendly offices, the transaction was concluded and the conversation drifted into other channels, mostly connected with the work of the Criminal Investigation Department. But though the superintendent's "shop" talk was highly interesting to listen to, it does not belong to this history. Nor was I very attentive to it, for my mind was occupied with the questions, Who the deuce was Louisa Saunders, what concern was she of ours, and what could Thorndyke possibly want with her finger-prints?

These questions, and the mystery surrounding the dossier, gave me abundant material for thought during the next few days, as, apparently, in a different way, they did to Thorndyke. For once more, to Polton's exasperation, he locked himself in his laboratory and resumed his mysterious doings, and as these appeared, from Polton's reports, to be mainly of a photographic nature, I surmised that he was making reproductions of the *"Secret Documents"*, but for what purpose I could not even guess.

Thus the time ran on, the Long Vacation ran out, and the day fixed for the hearing drew nearer. Once or twice we had communications from Mr. Penfield, chiefly relating to Thorndyke's request that certain witnesses should be summoned to appear in court for cross-examination on their affidavits, and once I observed among the letters delivered by the first post a large, well-filled envelope addressed to Thorndyke which looked to me like a report from Mr. Snuper. But that was only a guess, though Snuper's handwriting was a good deal more distinctive than his person.

Otherwise Thorndyke's preparations seemed to be complete, so far as I could judge with no knowledge whatever as to their nature, and I looked forward eagerly to the approaching date of the hearing, when, as I hoped, the obscurities in which I groped vainly should be made clear.

Chapter XIV
The Probate Court

The morning of the day appointed for the hearing found us with all preparations completed and – speaking for myself and Polton – all agog for the opening of the play. As the Law Courts were close at hand, Thorndyke and I put on our wigs and gowns before starting and, thus figged out and accompanied by Polton carrying a small suitcase, we set forth betimes, crossing the Temple by way of Crown Office Row and Fountain Court and finally emerging from Devereux Court into the Strand opposite to the main entrance of the Royal Courts of Justice and, crossing the road, entered those august premises and made our way to the court in which the hearing was to take place.

With the exception of the usher and Mr. Turner, Penfield's managing clerk, we were the first arrivals, but shortly after us came Mr. Longford, the applicant's solicitor, escorting his client, Miss Dalton, and a gentleman whom I correctly diagnosed as Mr. Carl Schiller. As we knew Mr. Longford slightly, we exchanged a few words of greeting, and he then introduced us to his two companions, and as we were making polite, but not too topical, conversation, we accompanied it by a mutual inspection.

Miss Dalton, "The Applicant", was a decidedly good looking woman of about thirty-five, but I was not much interested in her, my attention being more attracted by Mr. Schiller, whom I took the opportunity to examine as closely as good manners permitted. Not that he was a particularly striking personality, but he was (or had been) the husband of the mysterious Lotta, and he had the added interest of being present to learn whether he was a presumptive widower or only a mere husband. So I looked him over as we talked (as also, I noticed, did Thorndyke) and listened critically to his speech, in which I detected a faint German accent which seemed to agree with his rather Teutonic appearance. He was a smallish man, about five feet seven, spare and slight in figure, long-necked and bottle-shouldered, blond in complexion, with a rather scanty moustache and beard of a delicate ginger tint and eyes of a peculiar greenish-hazel. His eyebrows were considerably darker than his beard, rather broad, and set in an almost straight horizontal line. As to his hair, it was probably of a similar colour to his beard or perhaps lighter, but as he had greased it with grease in order to comb it smoothly back over the crown of his head, I was unable to judge. On the whole, I considered him a fairly good-looking man, and our brief contact left me with a rather favourable impression.

During our short talk there had been other arrivals. Mr. Lorimer, the applicant's counsel, had entered in wig and gown and was now in close conference with Mr. Longford at the solicitor's table. Mr. Pedley had slipped in and quietly seated himself on a back bench where, presently, he was joined by Inspector Blandy and by two middle-aged women who arrived together and who, having espied Pedley, at once seated themselves beside him. But the most interesting arrival to me was a rustic-looking gentleman who drifted in by the swing door and, having gazed about him vaguely, wandered slowly up the court towards the solicitor's table, for in him, with my usual start of surprise, I suddenly recognized the inscrutable Mr. Snuper.

He certainly enacted the part of a country cousin to a finish. The mixture of curiosity and boredom with which he stared about him was absolutely convincing, and the dropsical watch which he drew from his pocket and solemnly compared with the clock might have been an heirloom from some ancestral yeoman. But what was he doing here, masquerading under our very noses? Unable to imagine what his function could possibly be, I determined to keep an eye on him and try to solve this mystery for myself. But now the clock on the gallery announced the near approach to the hour and bade us take our seats, which we accordingly did. Miss Dalton was given a chair at the solicitor's table, Mr. Schiller selected a front bench with a restfully high back, Snuper shuffled into a seat behind him, and Mr. Lorimer joined us at the counsels' bench, and hardly had we taken our places when the usher threw open the door beside the bench and the judge bustled in and took his seat.

I looked at him with a good deal of interest since, as there was no jury, the decision of the case lay with him. But apart from this, I was attracted and interested by his personality, which was in several respects of an unusual type. He had none of that monumental repose that one associates with the occupants of the judicial bench. In fact, he was the liveliest judge that I have ever met. He bobbed up and down in his chair, he turned to confront each speaker whether witness or counsel, and leaned out sideways to address them with a curiously friendly and confidential air in keeping with his general conduct of the proceedings, which was that of carrying on a sort of family consultation.

Nor was his vivacity only bodily. He was very much alive mentally and seemed to follow every stage of the proceedings with intense, almost eager interest, watching the speaker and dropping in occasional comments in a quick emphatic manner entirely free from judicial

555

solemnity. But he was an excellent judge, attentive, helpful and friendly, and as informal as was permissible in the circumstances.

When his Lordship had settled himself in his chair and had taken a rapid survey of the court, he turned expectantly towards Mr. Lorimer, the applicant's counsel, who thereupon rose to open his case.

"Is the application opposed?" the judge asked, when Mr. Lorimer had set forth the nature of the case.

"I am not quite clear, my Lord, as to the extent of the opposition. No affidavits have been filed in answer, and there have been no pleadings."

The judge glanced inquiringly at Thorndyke, who thereupon rose to explain. "The position, my Lord, is this: The executor of Lotta Schiller's will is also her solicitor and man of affairs and, as the legal presumption at present is that she is alive, he has thought it necessary to safeguard her interests by ensuring that all facts adverse to the presumption of death are brought to the notice of the court."

"But you have filed no affidavits?"

"No, my Lord but, if, in the course of the hearing, it should seem to be necessary, I shall ask for an adjournment to enable me to file affidavits in answer or to call witnesses."

The judge smiled pleasantly. "I see. The good old principle of not leaping before you come to the stile. Very well."

He nodded to Mr. Lorimer, who continued, "As this is an application to presume death, the facts in issue are those relating to the probability of death, but it seems to me desirable that I should, very briefly, explain the circumstances which have made this application necessary.

"About five years ago – on the 16th August, 1928, to be exact – Lotta Schiller executed a will leaving the whole of her very small property, about £300 in all, to her friend, Barbara Dalton, or, if Barbara should die before her, to Barbara's younger sister Linda. At about the same time, Barbara made a will in similar terms with the difference that she gave her chattels, excepting her violin, to Linda. The violin, with the residue of her estate, about £250, was left to Lotta. Thus, at the time, these two wills were quite unimportant. But on the 28th of May, 1930, a certain Mr. Charles Montagu died, and it then appeared that by his will a sum of £20,000 was left to Barbara Dalton and a similar sum to Linda. These bequests seem to have been quite unexpected by the beneficiaries, and it may have been that Barbara might have made some modification of her will if there had been time. But there was not. For some reason, a considerable delay occurred in the probate of Mr. Montagu's will, and in the meantime Barbara died. Then, since Lotta Schiller was the residuary legatee under Barbara's will, the further sum of £20,000 accrued to her.

556

"But now a new difficulty arose. When it came to distributing Mr. Montagu's estate, the whereabouts of Lotta could not be discovered. The usual advertisements were issued but there was no response. So for a time, the matter remained in abeyance. It was not certain that she was alive, and there was the added difficulty that, not only could the money not be paid to her, but no evidence existed that she was entitled to it, since it could not even be proved that she had been alive at the time of Barbara's death.

"Then came an announcement in the papers of Lotta's sensational disappearance and the suspicion that she had been murdered, and the astonishing fact transpired that, all this time, she had been living in lodgings at 39 Jacob Street, Hampstead Road. Either she had never seen the advertisements or – which seems incredible – had ignored them. But, however that may have been, as soon as Barbara's executor became aware that Lotta either was, or had recently been, alive, he endeavoured to get into touch with her, but without success. Nor have his efforts, repeated from time to time, had any better results, and now, after the lapse of two years, since it appears nearly certain that Lotta Schiller is dead, Miss Linda Dalton, the surviving beneficiary under Lotta's will, acting on the advice of her solicitor, is applying to the court for permission to presume the death of the testatrix in order that the will may be proved. As the facts on which we rely in support of the application are principally those connected with the disappearance of the testatrix, I shall now proceed to a more detailed account of that incident.

"On the 16th of July, 1930, Lotta Schiller engaged furnished rooms at 39 Jacob Street, Hampstead Road. She gave no references but paid a month's rent in advance, and that payment and all subsequent payments were made in cash, although she had a banking account, which suggests that, for some reason unknown to us, she did not wish to disclose her whereabouts to any of her friends. This suggestion is supported by the fact that during the whole of her residence in Jacob Street, she made no local acquaintances excepting Mr. Pedley, an artist who lived next door, and Mr. Polton and Mr. Vanderpuye, both of whom were introduced to her by Mr. Pedley.

"During this time she seems to have made a pretence of practising as an artist, but this must have been a mere pose, as we have evidence that her work was quite incompetent, which is not surprising, seeing that she had never previously been known to paint or even to draw. However, it enabled her to strike up an acquaintanceship with Mr. Pedley which soon grew into definite friendship, and thereafter she used frequently to visit his studio. In this way she presently made the acquaintance of Mr. William Vanderpuye, a barrister of the Inner Temple, who came to the studio to have his portrait painted by Mr. Pedley. This new acquaintance soon ripened into a quite intimate friendship, accompanied on her side by unabashed flirtation and on his, perhaps, by real affection."

I need not report the rest of Mr. Lorimer's opening, since it dealt with matters with which we are familiar and which have already been recorded. In close and conscientious detail he described all the circumstances connected with Lotta Schiller's disappearance, including the murder of the ill-fated Emma Robey and the search by the police for Lotta, the discovery of the relics and, finally and at considerable length, the exploration of the ancient British camp and the various efforts which had been made during the last two years to get into communication with Lotta.

Meanwhile, since I was not much concerned with the speech, I entertained myself by observing what was going on in the court – watching the judge, who was listening with an air of intense concentration to the counsel's recital, the one or two strangers who drifted in by the swing door and soon drifted out again, and especially Mr. Snuper. Not that he offered much entertainment. At first he had seated himself directly behind Mr. Schiller, but had gradually worked his way along the bench, apparently to get nearer to the speaker, and there he sat listening open-mouthed, seeming to be as much engrossed with Lorimer's recital as the judge himself. As to Mr. Schiller, after the opening statement, he appeared to take little interest in the proceedings, having, no doubt, heard it all before. Most of the time he sat with his eyes closed, his head reposing restfully against the high back of the seat as if he were asleep, though, from time to time, he opened his eyes and even raised his head to look about him, but subsided almost immediately into his former semi-somnolent state.

It was during one of these temporary awakenings that a very odd thing happened. Mr. Lorimer had come to the end of his narrative and was just beginning his argument, when Mr. Schiller opened his eyes and looked drowsily at the counsel. Then, suddenly, his eyes opened wide and a most strange expression of dismay appeared on his face. I looked at him in astonishment. He seemed to be making an effort to move, but his head remained fixed as if it were attached to the back of the seat. Almost immediately his predicament was observed by Mr. Snuper, who hastily slid along the seat towards him, at the same time fumbling in his pocket. I heard him murmur, "Don't move, sir," and some other words which I could not make out and, as he spoke, I saw him quickly open a pair of folding pocket scissors. Then, with these in his hand, he leaned over the back of the seat, and the next moment the prisoner was free, smiling a little wrily, tenderly feeling the back of his head, and looking round curiously at the spot on the bench-back which Snuper was now carefully scraping with a pocketknife.

What he was scraping I could not see, but there must have been some foreign matter on the bench-back, for I saw him hold up the knife for Mr. Schiller's inspection and then wipe it on an envelope which he produced from his pocket and returned there after having folded it. But even then he was not satisfied, for he continued his scraping, wiping the knife on another piece of paper, and finally, having felt the surface with his hand, gave it a vigorous rub with his handkerchief. Meanwhile, Mr. Schiller, having acknowledged Snuper's services with a smile, moved along the bench and, taking the precaution to examine the surface by sweeping his hand over it, leaned back and once more closed his eyes.

It was a queer episode, trivial enough to a casual observer and over in less than a minute – apparently unobserved, too, excepting that the judge cast one quick, inquisitive glance during the scraping operation. But its triviality was not quite convincing to me, and I continued to keep an eye on Mr. Snuper, notwithstanding that he was now once more the open-mouthed listener, and I noticed that he seemed to be imperceptibly creeping along the bench towards its farther end. He had just reached his goal when Mr. Lorimer's speech came to an end and, as the counsel sat down and preparations were being made for the reading of the affidavits, I saw him rise and, having anxiously consulted the ancestral turnip, steal away quietly towards the swing door and vanish without a sound. So whatever his purpose might have been in attending at the hearing, it had apparently been achieved.

The first of the affidavits to be read was that of Thomas Pedley and, as it set forth all the material facts, I did not quite see why Thorndyke had asked for his attendance for cross-examination. Nor did my colleague elicit any new facts of importance. His purpose was evidently to stress the significance of those facts that had been stated, and this he did most effectually.

"You have said, Mr. Pedley," he began, "that you were somewhat intimately acquainted with Mrs. Schiller for about five months. During that time, did you learn much about her as to her past history, her former places of abode, her friends and her relatives?"

"No," replied Pedley. "She never referred to her past at all, and she never mentioned any friends or relatives except her husband, and she only referred to him on one or two occasions, and then very slightly."

"Would you be able to recognize her handwriting?"

"No. I have never seen any writing of hers."

"But the signature on her pictures?"

"She did not sign her pictures. She used a conventional mark somewhat like a flower."

"Did you ever see a portrait of her husband or of herself?"

"I never saw a portrait of her husband, and the only portrait of herself that I ever saw was one that she drew for reduction to put into a locket that she was to give to Mr. Vanderpuye."

"Was Mr. Vanderpuye satisfied with her portrait?"

"No. He begged her either to let me paint her portrait or to ask Mr. Polton to take her photograph. But she refused absolutely. She insisted on painting the portrait herself, and did so."

"Was her portrait a good likeness?"

"It was not a likeness at all. It bore no resemblance to her."

"Do you recognize this?" Thorndyke asked, handing a mounted photograph to the usher, who passed it to the witness.

"Yes," Pedley replied with a faint grin. "It is a photograph of Mrs. Schiller's portrait of herself."

"And do you recognize this locket?"

As he spoke, Thorndyke produced from the suitcase Polton's mysterious wooden slide, on which Vanderpuye's locket had been fixed by a clip, opened to show the miniature and the hair, and provided with a pair of lenses, one over the portrait and the other (a coddington) over the hair.

"Yes," replied Pedley as the usher handed it to him, "it is Mr. Vanderpuye's locket, and it contains Mrs. Schiller's portrait of herself and a specimen of her hair."

Here the locket and the photograph were passed up to the judge, who looked first at the photograph and smiled broadly and then peered through the lens at the miniature and compared it with the photograph.

"Yes," he remarked, "one can readily believe that this is not a good likeness, unless the testatrix was a very unusual-looking woman." Before returning the "exhibit", he applied his eye to the other lens and examined the hair. Then he turned sharply towards Pedley and asked, "Was there anything at all peculiar about Mrs. Schiller's hair?"

"Yes, my Lord," was the reply, "but I can't say exactly what it was. There seemed to be something unusual in its texture."

"Ha," said the judge, "so it appeared to me. However – "

Here he handed the locket to the usher and, as the latter conveyed it to Mr. Lorimer, he seemed to reflect on the circumstance as if it had suggested some idea to him. Lorimer, on the other hand, was not interested at all, bestowing only an impatient glance at the two exhibits and pushing them along the desk to Thorndyke, who passed them on to me. Naturally, remembering Pedley's description of Lotta's hair, I

560

examined it with keen interest, but the light was not good enough, and the magnification not sufficient to show much detail. All that I could make out was a faintly speckled appearance quite unlike that of normal human hair. Reluctantly I returned the exhibits to Thorndyke, who, when he had put them back into the suitcase, resumed his cross-examination.

"Apart from this drawing of Mrs. Schiller's, have you ever seen any portrait of her?"

"No portrait drawn from life. I once drew a portrait of her from memory."

"Is this the portrait that you drew?" asked Thorndyke, handing to the usher Pedley's own notebook, fixed open with a rubber band, and a photograph.

Pedley looked at them with a shy grin and replied, "Yes. The original drawing is in the book, and this is a photograph of it."

"Is the portrait a good likeness?"

"I should say that it is a fairly good likeness. I think it would be recognizable by anyone who knew her."

The book and the photograph were passed up to the judge, who inspected them with apparent interest, and from him they were conveyed to Lorimer, who glanced at them almost contemptuously and pushed them along to Thorndyke. Evidently the learned counsel regarded my colleague's proceedings as a regrettable waste of time, and he made no secret of his relief when Thorndyke sat down, indicating that his cross-examination was finished.

As Lorimer made no sign of re-examining the witness, and it was now within a few minutes of the luncheon hour, the judge announced the adjournment, where upon we all stood up, his Lordship whisked out by the private door, Polton hurried forward to seize the suitcase, and the occupants of the court trooped out by the swing door. We followed almost immediately and, issuing into the Strand, set a course for our chambers by way of Devereux Court.

Chapter XV
Mr. Lorimer Objects

As we approached the end of Crown Office Row I observed with interest, but no surprise, a rustic-looking person who appeared to be making a leisurely survey of the old houses in King's Bench Walk. Needless to say it was Mr. Snuper, apparently unconscious of our existence until Thorndyke, with the nearest approach to eagerness of which he was capable, accosted him. Then he turned with a start of surprise, and he and my colleague drifted down the Walk together, apparently in earnest conversation. I slowed down my own progress to keep an eye on them, for I was devoured by curiosity as to Snuper's proceedings in court, but there was little to see and less to hear, for neither of them was addicted to shouting, and they were near the garden end of the Walk before any visible action took place. Then I thought I saw Snuper hand something to Thorndyke, but I could not see what it was and, as it disappeared instantly into my friend's pocket, I judged that it was lost to me – at least for the time being – whereupon I abandoned my spying and hurried indoors in quest of lunch.

As the table had been laid by Polton's deputy, who was in the act of bringing in the food, I sat down to wait for Thorndyke's arrival, but when he looked in a few minutes later, it was only to beg me to proceed with the meal in his absence.

"I have a little job to do in the laboratory," he explained. "It will only take me a minute or two, but there is no need for you to wait."

Accordingly, as we had to be back in court punctually, I lifted the cover and fell to, but in less than five minutes Thorndyke joined me and, looking at him critically, I seemed to detect, under his habitual impassiveness, an expression of satisfaction and even of elation, suggesting that the "little job" had turned out a success. Which led to speculations on my part as to the nature of that little job, and in particular, whether it had any connection with Mr. Snuper's activities. But, of course, I asked no questions and, equally of course, Thorndyke volunteered no information.

When the hearing was resumed after lunch, Mr. Lorimer rose to request that Miss Linda Dalton's evidence might be taken next, to enable her to catch a train and, as the judge raised no objection, she took her place in the witness-box and her affidavit was read. Most of it was concerned with her claim under the will, but it finished up with the statement that she had last seen Lotta Schiller early in June 1930, and that since then she had received no communication from her nor had any knowledge of her until she heard of the disappearance.

When the reading was finished, Thorndyke rose to cross-examine.

"Do you happen to remember what kind of dress the testatrix was wearing when you last saw her?"

Miss Dalton smiled. "I do, indeed," she replied. "It was a very ugly dress and I thought it rather eccentric. The bodice and skirt were a sort of dull violet, and there was a broad turn-down collar of a deep orange and sleeves of the same colour. It was a dress that one could not forget."

"Did the testatrix play any musical instrument?"

"Yes. She played the violin."

"Did she spend much time practising?"

"Latterly, she did. My sister Barbara used to make a little income by playing in a small orchestra – at a cinema, I think – and she got Lotta an engagement at the same place, and they used to practise together and, of course, she was playing for some hours every day in the orchestra."

"You will, of course, remember her appearance quite well. Will you look at this portrait and tell me whether you consider it a good likeness?" As he spoke he handed to the usher a photograph which I saw was the reproduction of Pedley's drawing.

Miss Dalton looked at it rather blankly.

"Is this supposed to be a portrait of Lotta?" she asked, "because I don't think it can be. I can't discover the faintest resemblance to her."

Glancing at Lorimer, I thought I detected a faint smile on his face. The judge, on the other hand, looked surprised and keenly interested and, when the photograph was passed up to him, he examined it closely, turned it over to examine the back, on which a number had been pencilled, and made a note.

Meanwhile, Thorndyke had produced a small portfolio which was handed to the witness.

"In that portfolio," said Thorndyke, "are half-a-dozen photographs. Will you look through them and see whether any of them resemble Lotta Schiller?"

Miss Dalton glanced quickly at the first two which came to hand but at the third she paused. Then she took it out and said, "This is a portrait of Lotta Schiller, a very odd one, but an excellent likeness. And so is this other one," she added, taking it out and holding it up.

"You feel no doubt that those two photographs are portraits of Lotta Schiller?"

"None whatever. They are both unmistakable."

The two portraits were now passed up to the judge, who examined them with intense interest and compared them minutely with Pedley's drawing. When he had looked at the backs and made his notes, he passed them down, but still seemed to reflect with a rather puzzled air, and when they reached me I could understand his surprise, for the discrepancy between the drawing and the photograph seemed incredible in the case of a competent artist like Pedley. However, there was no time to consider the point, for Thorndyke had finished his cross-examination and, a minute later Miss Dalton left the box and, with a wave of the hand to Mr. Schiller, tripped out of the court.

The next witness was Mrs. Mitchens, whose affidavit set forth concisely the facts known to her relating to the case from the 16th of July, 1930, when Lotta engaged the rooms, to the time of her disappearance, including the finding of Emma Robey's body. When the reading was finished, Thorndyke rose and led off with the question, "Would you recognize Mrs. Schiller's handwriting if you saw it?"

"No," was the reply. "I have never seen her handwriting, she had no occasion to write to me – at least she never did write and, as she always paid her rent in cash, there were no cheques."

"Did she ever play any musical instrument?"

"No, never, but she had a violin. I didn't know it until after she had left, but then, as I was going through her things to store them, I found it under the bed."

"When you were going through her things, did you come across a dress with a violet bodice and skirt and orange-coloured sleeves and a broad collar of the same colour?"

"No indeed, sir, and I don't think Mrs. Schiller would have worn such a dress. Her costumes were usually rather quiet and tasteful. But I only found one or two dresses, and I am sure there was nothing of that kind among them."

"When Mrs. Schiller engaged your rooms, did she give you any references?"

"No. She paid a month's rent in advance – in cash."

Here Thorndyke again produced the portfolio and, when it had been handed to the witness, said, "I want you to look through those portraits and see if you can find any that you think is like Mrs. Schiller."

Mrs. Mitchens turned over the first two portraits and then, as she came to the third, she picked it out and, holding it up triumphantly, announced, "That is Mrs. Schiller."

The judge, who had been watching eagerly, now held out his hand for the identified portrait, and when it was passed up to him, he looked at it with intense interest and, leaning out towards the witness, said, "Now,

Mrs. Mitchens, are you perfectly sure that this portrait is really like Mrs. Schiller?"

"I am perfectly sure, my Lord," she replied. "It's a speaking likeness."

On this his Lordship scribbled a note and then asked to have the portfolio handed up to him. When this had been done, he picked out two photographs and passed them down to the witness.

"Did you look at these two portraits?" he asked.

"Yes, my Lord," she replied, "but they are not Mrs. Schiller. They are not the least bit like her."

The judge noted down the answer and then, having passed the portfolio back, nodded to Thorndyke, who now put his final question.

"Did Mrs. Schiller ever receive visitors?"

"Only Mr. Pedley and Mr. Vanderpuye. I never saw anybody else."

On this, Thorndyke sat down, and when Mrs. Mitchens had been released from the box, the name of the next witness – Mrs. Bigham – was called, and a very unprepossessing woman advanced with something of a swagger. The evidence contained in her affidavit was of some importance in regard to the disappearance, but when it came to cross-examination, Thorndyke confined himself to the question of identification. Producing the inevitable portfolio, and passing it to her, he asked, "You say that you knew Mrs. Schiller well by sight. Do you think you would be able to recognize a portrait of her?"

"I am quite sure I should. I've got a rare memory for faces."

"Then will you look at the portraits in that portfolio and tell me whether any of them appears to be a portrait of Mrs. Schiller?"

Mrs. Bigham opened the portfolio with a judicial air and, pursing up her lips, glared critically at the top photograph and thrust it over with the remark, "That ain't her," and passed on to the next, which she dealt with in the same fashion, and so on with the others until she came to the fifth, at which she gazed intently for an instant and then, picking it out and holding it aloft with the face towards us, exclaimed, "That's her."

I recognized it as the reproduction of Pedley's drawing, and so did the judge, who listened with rapt attention for the next question.

"You are quite sure that that portrait is really like Mrs. Schiller?"

"Lord, yes," was the reply. "It's her spit image. I reckernized it at the first glance."

"There are two others that I want you to look at very carefully. They are numbered three and four."

The witness turned over the photographs and selecting two, held them up for our and the judge's inspection. They were the portraits that had been identified by Miss Dalton.

"If you mean them," said Mrs. Bigham, "I can tell you that they ain't Mrs. Schiller. Nothink like her."

"You are quite sure of that?"

"Positive. They ain't no more like her than what I am." With this answer Thorndyke appeared to be satisfied, for he asked no further questions and, when he had sat down and Mrs. Bigham had – somewhat reluctantly, I thought – vacated the box, I waited with some interest for the next item, and when it came, it was not altogether unexpected. For some time past, I had noticed signs of restiveness on the part of the learned counsel for the applicant, and I was not surprised, for I had an uneasy feeling that Thorndyke had been taking some slight liberties with the legal proprieties. That was evidently Mr. Lorimer's view, and he now gave expression to it.

"I am unwilling, my Lord," he began, "to occasion delay in the hearing, but there seems to have been a departure from customary procedure on the part of the opposition to which I feel bound to object. My learned friend appears to be raising an entirely new issue, of which we have had no notice, and supporting it by the production of documents – to wit, photographs – the existence of which has not been disclosed to us."

"Yes," the judge agreed with a smile, "the learned counsel does certainly seem to have sprung a little surprise on us."

Here he cast a somewhat quizzical glance at Thorndyke, who thereupon rose to reply.

"I shall not deny, my Lord, that some apology seems to be due to my learned friend, but I would submit that the raising of a new issue is only apparent. There are really two issues in this case: One is whether the person known as Lotta Schiller, who disappeared in Epping Forest is, or is not, presumably dead, the other is whether that person was the testatrix. We have all assumed that Lotta Schiller of Jacob Street and Lotta Schiller, the testatrix, were one and the same person. There seemed to be no reason to question the identity. Nevertheless, I considered it desirable, *ex abundantia cautelae*, to test the correctness of our assumption, with the surprising result that there now seems to be some doubt whether we are not dealing with two different persons."

Lorimer and the judge both smiled appreciatively at Thorndyke's ingenious evasion, and his Lordship replied, "That is quite true, though it does not answer the learned counsel's objection. But the question of identity has been raised, and it has evidently got to be settled before the other issue can be considered. So the problem now is, what is to be done about it? You mentioned at the opening that you might ask for an adjournment to enable you to file affidavits in answer or to call witnesses. Are you going to apply for an adjournment now?"

"I think, my Lord," replied Thorndyke, "that, in view of the conflict of testimony, some new evidence is required, and I should wish to call witnesses but, as those witnesses would have to attend for cross-examination, there seems to be no object in filing affidavits, and time would be saved by not doing so. We are now at the week-end, and I submit that if your Lordship would consent and my learned friend would agree, he and I might confer in the interval and thereby avoid the necessity for an adjournment."

The judge looked a little dubious at this suggestion but, as Lorimer signified his agreement and was evidently anxious to get on with the case, his Lordship consented to the arrangement and adjourned the hearing for the week-end.

As the court rose, Lorimer turned to Thorndyke and spoke to him in a low tone. Then they walked together to the solicitors' table and apparently held a short discussion with Turner and Longford, at the end of which they came back and we set forth in company towards the Temple.

"We have arranged about the conference," said Thorndyke. "The solicitors prefer to leave the matter for counsel to settle, so Lorimer and I are going to dine together and then adjourn to his chambers for the pow-wow. That will leave us a free week-end."

Accordingly, when he had shed his wig and gown, he went off with his learned opponent and I saw him no more until about eleven o'clock, when he turned up at our chambers in obviously good spirits.

"Well," I asked, "how did you get on with Lorimer?"

"Admirably," he replied. "He is quite a reasonable fellow and I had no difficulty in getting him to see my point of view. I had to tell him more than I wanted to, but as we were alone it didn't matter."

"And what did you arrive at?"

"We agreed to treat the question of identity as a separate issue to be settled definitely before going on to the main issue. I made him understand that whichever way it went the result would not affect his case."

"The devil you did!" I exclaimed. "I should like you to make me understand that. It seems to me that if you make out your contention of two different persons, his case collapses at once."

He regarded me with an exasperating smile. "That, you know, Jervis, is because you have not been following the evidence in this case, or have not reflected sufficiently on its significance. Turn it over in your mind between this and next Monday and see if you cannot anticipate the revelation that I hope to make at the next hearing."

With that tantalizing hint I had to be content. Of course, I did not trouble to "turn it over in my mind". I realized that Polton had been right as usual. Thorndyke's devilish machinations in his laboratory had been the prelude to "a little surprise for somebody", and I was going to be one of the surprised.

Chapter XVI
Superintendent Miller Intervenes

Of what took place during the week-end I am not very clear. On the Saturday Thorndyke was out and about most of the day making, as I assumed, his final arrangements, which assumption was confirmed by a late telephone message from Superintendent Miller asking me to "Let the Doctor know that Miss Rendell has been warned and will attend court on Monday." Who Miss Rendell might be I had no idea and I did not inquire. For the time being, my curiosity was in abeyance.

One small piece of enlightenment I did indeed acquire. Finding Polton at a loose end in the laboratory, I attacked him facetiously on the subject of Mr. Snuper's watch, which I suggested was a disgrace to an establishment that included on its staff a first-class artificer. "Really," I concluded, "I think you ought to provide him with something less prehistoric for the credit of the house. Just get him to show it to you."

Polton regarded me with a cunning and crinkly smile. "I've seen it, sir. In fact, I made it. But it isn't a watch, though it has hands that you can set to time for the sake of appearances. It is really a camera, but Mr. Snuper carries his watch in another compartment of the same pocket."

"A camera!" I exclaimed. "But it can only be a mere toy."

"Well," Polton admitted, "it isn't much of a camera, just a makeshift. But it answers Mr. Snuper's purpose, as you can use it anywhere without being noticed, and a poor photograph is, for him, better than no photograph. It is a record, you know, sir."

"And what sort of picture does it give?"

"Better than you would think, sir. The negative is half-an-inch-by-five-eighths, and it will bear enlarging up to four-inches-by-five. It has a beautiful little lens and the definition is perfect. Perhaps you would like to see it. I've got it in for recharging."

He produced the illusive turnip from a drawer and exhibited it with excusable pride, for it was a miracle of ingenuity, with its arrangement for changing the film, which also set the shutter, and that for setting the hands. But almost more surprising were the tiny negatives, microscopically sharp, which Polton also showed me, and the clear and admirable enlargements, which caused me to view the turnip and its creator with a new respect.

The following day Thorndyke spent mostly in his private laboratory, making, as I supposed, some final preparations for the resumed hearing.

But I had no idea what they might be, nor did I speculate on the subject. I had given the problem up, and reserved my curiosity for the promised revelation on the morrow.

Apparently I was not alone in this attitude, for, when we took our places in court on the Monday morning, I detected in Mr. Lorimer an air of lively expectancy, and the judge, as soon as he had nipped into his seat, glanced at the counsel for the applicant with evident curiosity, whereupon Lorimer rose to make his announcement.

"During the week-end, my Lord, I have conferred with my learned friend, and we have agreed, with your Lordship's consent, to treat the question of identity as a separate issue, to be disposed of before taking any further evidence on the main issue."

"That seems a reasonable proceeding," said the judge. "Evidently it would be futile to consider the presumption of death until we know whose death it is sought to presume. Are there any new witnesses?"

"Yes, my Lord. I am calling Mr. Carl Schiller, the testatrix's husband, whose affidavit has been filed. When he has given his evidence, as I have no other witnesses to identity, I have agreed that my learned friend should, with your Lordship's consent, produce his evidence forthwith."

The judge nodded, and thereupon Mr. Schiller stepped into the witness-box and stood there, listening attentively while his affidavit was read. It was quite short, setting forth merely that he had not seen or heard of, or from, his wife for more than three years, and that he had no knowledge whether she was alive or dead. When the reading was finished, Lorimer took the portfolio, which was handed to him by Thorndyke, and passed it across to the witness.

"There is some conflict of testimony, Mr. Schiller," said he, "as to which of the portraits in this portfolio is a true portrait of your wife. Will you kindly look through them and see whether you can settle the question for us?"

Mr. Schiller opened the portfolio and went systematically through the whole of its contents – some seven or eight photographs. Having looked at them all, he selected one and held it up for inspection, and I saw that it was Pedley's drawing, or rather the reproduction of it.

"This," said he, speaking with a perceptible German accent, "is the only one that seems to me to resemble my wife, and it is quite a fair likeness. The others I do not recognize at all."

I was a good deal surprised, and so, I think, was the judge, for Schiller's evidence directly contradicted that of Miss Dalton (who was not present on this occasion). However, there was nothing to be said as the witness had looked carefully through the whole set of photographs and, as neither the judge nor Thorndyke questioned the evidence, the witness was released and returned to his seat – or rather to a seat at the extreme end of the bench, and Thorndyke called his first witness, a Mrs. Matilda Wharton, whereupon a pleasant-looking elderly woman stepped into the box.

"What is your full address, Mrs. Wharton?" Thorndyke asked.

"I live at 16 Corby Street, which is a turning out of the Linton Green Road."

"Have you ever been acquainted with Mrs. Lotta Schiller?"

"Yes. She lodged with me for about three years."

"Did her husband live with her?"

"No. He travelled about a good deal, but when he was in London he used to call on her and they used to go out together. But he never lived in the house. I think he used to stay at hotels."

"On what kind of terms were they?"

"They seemed quite friendly though not affectionate, but shortly before she left there seemed to have been some sort of disagreement, for she became rather strange in her manner and appeared to avoid him."

"When, and in what circumstances, did she leave you?"

"She left me on the 13th of June, 1930. She went out one morning and never came back, but she sent me a telegram saying that she had gone away and would write. She never did write, but a couple of days later her husband came to the house and told me that she had been suddenly called abroad and that she would not be coming back for some months. He paid what was owing and took away her belongings, including her violin. I have never seen or heard of her since."

"Was there anything remarkable about the manner of her departure?"

"Well, it was rather strange. She said nothing about going away before she went out, and she had nothing with her but the things that she stood up in."

"During the time that she lodged with you, did she receive many visitors?"

"No. The two Miss Daltons used sometimes to call to see her or to take her out, and once or twice Mr. Montagu – the poor gentleman who was murdered – came to see her or to fetch her out."

Here Thorndyke gave me – and not me alone – the first of the surprises by producing from the suitcase a small oil painting, which I recognized as a sketch of Pedley's that I had seen hanging on the wall of Polton's private room.

"I want you, Mrs. Wharton," said he, passing it across to her, "to look at this painting and tell me whether the figures in it suggest any particular persons to you."

The witness examined the painting closely and then at arm's length.

"Of course," she said cautiously, "I can't recognize any of these people, but the woman looks to me very much like Mrs. Schiller."

"In what respect is she like Mrs. Schiller?"

"I think it is chiefly the dress. It's rather a peculiar dress, and Mrs. Schiller had one just like it. In fact, she was wearing that very dress on the morning that she went away. But the figure is like her, too, and the colour of her hair. Still, it is only a resemblance. I don't say it actually is her. You see, there are no features to recognize it by."

"And as to the other figures: Do they seem to suggest anybody that you have known?"

Mrs. Wharton again looked at the picture critically. At length she replied, in a rather doubtful tone, "It's only a mere guess, as they have their backs to us, but I think the taller of the two men rather reminds me of Mr. Montagu. I often used to see him in the street, and he was always dressed in this way, and he had a habit of gesticulating with his umbrella as he talked, as this man seems to be doing, and the umbrella in the picture seems to have an ivory handle as his hand. And he seems to be about the right height, comparing him with the other man. Still, I don't profess to be able to recognize him."

"Of course you can't," said Thorndyke, "but I must compliment you on your memory and powers of observation. And now I will try you with something that it is more possible to be certain about."

Here he produced the inevitable portfolio and passed it across to her. Meanwhile the picture was handed up to the judge, who looked at it curiously and returned it, and I noticed that Lorimer examined it with more than his usual faint interest in exhibits. But attention was now focused on Mrs. Wharton, who, at Thorndyke's request, was looking very carefully through the collection of portraits. When she had examined them all, she very deliberately selected two, which she held up with their faces towards us, and which I could see were the two that Miss Dalton had recognized.

"These," said she, "are portraits of Mrs. Schiller. They aren't very flattering, but they are quite good likenesses."

The judge inspected them with a surprised and rather puzzled expression and then glanced at Thorndyke, who, as he received the portfolio, took from it Pedley's drawing and passed it across to the witness.

572

"What do you say to this? It is supposed to be a portrait of Mrs. Schiller. Is it a good likeness?"

The witness looked at it with evident surprise. After a prolonged inspection she handed it back, shaking her head.

"I don't think it can have been meant for Mrs. Schiller," said she. "It doesn't seem to me to be like her at all. It looks like quite a different person."

This evidently completed his Lordship's perplexity, for he asked that the portfolio should be passed up to him and, when he had it, he laid the three portraits in a row on his desk and made a prolonged and careful comparison. But clearly he could make nothing of them, for he finally gathered them up and, glancing at Thorndyke with raised eyebrows, handed back the portfolio.

Among the new arrivals in court I had noticed a rather prim-looking lady dressed in a neat and becoming uniform which associated itself in my mind with the idea of "chokee" – formerly known familiarly as "the jug". And so it turned out to be, for, when Mrs. Wharton had vacated the box – there being no cross-examination – the lady in question took her place and, facing Thorndyke with professional composure, introduced herself as Miss Julia Rendell, a Female Officer at Holloway Prison. Thereupon, Thorndyke produced the everlasting portfolio, but he did not on this occasion pass it across to the witness. Instead, he opened it and, selecting from the collection the two photographs which Mrs. Wharton had identified, sent them across for the lady's inspection.

"Do you recognize those two photographs, Miss Rendell?" he asked.

"Yes," she replied promptly. "They are incomplete copies of two prison portraits of a prisoner named, or known as, Louisa Saunders."

"Do you recognize these two?" he asked, handing over two other photographs which he had just fished out of the suitcase.

"Yes. They are the original portraits, or facsimile copies of them."

"Are they good likenesses of Louisa Saunders?"

"Yes, quite good. I recognized them at once."

"When did you first see Louisa Saunders?"

"On the 13th of June, 1930 at the evening receptions. She had been arrested that morning and remanded in custody."

"Do you know any particulars of the charge on which she was arrested?"

"Yes. I accompanied her, with some other remands, to the police court and was present at the hearing. She was charged with having uttered a forged one-pound note and with having in her possession four other forged notes."

"Did she plead '*Guilty*' or '*Not Guilty*'?"

"'*Not Guilty*'. She said that the notes had been given to her in a bundle and that she had no suspicion of their being bad notes."

"Was any evidence given to show that she knew the notes to be bad notes?"

"No. The only evidence against her was that she had offered the bad note in payment for some goods that she had bought, and that she had the other notes in her possession. But, as she would not give any account of herself or say where she had obtained the notes or who had given them to her, she was convicted and sentenced to six months' imprisonment."

"Is that, in your experience, a usual sentence for this offence?"

"No. I should say that it was an unusually lenient one."

"Did the prisoner give any address?"

"No. She would give no account of herself whatever except her name."

"Was there any evidence that Louisa Saunders was her real name?"

"None beyond the fact that her clothing was marked with the initials '*L. S.*'"

"Was she a married woman or a spinster?"

"She refused any information about herself but, as she was wearing a wedding ring, we entered her as a married woman."

"While she was in prison, was her hair cut?"

"No. It was rather short when she came in and, as she was perfectly clean, there was no necessity."

"Do you remember how long it was when she was discharged?"

"So far as I remember, it was about down to her shoulders."

"On what date was she discharged?"

"On the 12th of December, 1930, at noon."

"I suppose you don't know whether anybody met her when she left the prison?"

"As a matter of fact, I do. I happened to be going out of the prison at the same time, and I saw a man who seemed to be waiting for her at the corner of Hilmarton Road. At any rate, she crossed the road and joined him."

"Do you remember what he was like?"

"Not very clearly. I did not notice him particularly and should not know him if I were to see him. All that I remember about him is that he seemed to be a fairly well-dressed man and rather short."

"You saw the prisoner, Saunders, at receptions on the day of her arrest, you accompanied her to the police court, and you saw her in the street when she left the prison. Do you remember how she was dressed on those occasions?"

574

"I remember that she was wearing a rather conspicuous dress with sleeves a different colour from the bodice and skirt."

Here Thorndyke produced Pedley's sketch and passed it across to the witness.

"I want you," said he, "to look carefully at that picture and tell me whether it recalls anything to your memory."

The witness looked at the painting attentively for a few moments, and then replied, "The woman in the picture reminds me strongly of Louisa Saunders. She is like her in figure and in the colour of her hair, and the dress is exactly like the one that Saunders was wearing when she came to the prison and when she left it. Of course, I can't identify her as Saunders because the face is not recognizable, but otherwise the resemblance seems to be complete."

This concluded the examination-in-chief and, as Thorndyke sat down, Lorimer rose to cross-examine.

"Is it not rather remarkable," he asked, "that you should have so clear a recollection of this prisoner after the lapse of so long a time?"

"I don't think so," she replied. "A prison officer is expected to be able to remember and recognize persons, and Saunders was a rather unusual prisoner. Most of the women who come in at receptions are of the lowest class, and then the dress that she was wearing was a distinctly striking one. And," the witness added with a deprecating smile, "a female prison officer, like any other woman, is apt to have a good memory for an unusual dress."

"This one," his Lordship remarked, "certainly seems to have made a deep impression on the ladies who had seen it, judging by the evidence, as they all remembered it clearly. But the photographs give a very misleading rendering of it, though one can see that the sleeves and collar are of a different colour from the bodice. The painter has still some advantage over the photographer."

"In the matter of colour, my Lord," said Lorimer. "Not in respect of personal identity. I do not admit that the figure in the painting has been identified."

"No, no, no!" exclaimed the judge. "I was referring only to the colour of the dress. No one has suggested that there has been actual identification of the person."

With this, Lorimer opened a new subject. "You have said that you were present at the police court proceedings. Was any evidence produced to show that the accused had any guilty knowledge of the character of the notes?"

"None except the fact that she had the notes in her possession and had passed one of them."

"Was there any evidence that her explanation of the way she came by those notes could not be true?"

"No. But the trouble was that she refused to say where she got the notes or who gave them to her."

On receiving this answer Lorimer discreetly closed his cross-examination, having apparently made his point, which seemed to be that the accused might quite possibly have been innocent, the conviction notwithstanding. Why he should stress this point I could not quite see, unless he was beginning to entertain the same suspicion as that which was creeping into my own mind.

I had listened to Miss Rendell's evidence with intense interest – indeed, I had been considerably startled, not only by the identification, but by the curious coincidence of dates. But my interest was feeble compared to his Lordship's. The new identification had evidently astonished him and, when the date of the prisoner's arrest was mentioned he hurriedly turned over his notes and made some comparisons, and when the photographs were handed up to him, he spread them out in a row and rapidly compared them. There was no need for a prolonged examination, as I realized when they reached me, for the two pairs appeared to be from the same negatives. The only difference was that the "originals" showed a black batten with the prisoner's name chalked on it fixed across the chair and occupying the foot of the portrait, whereas, in the "incomplete copies" the batten had been masked out.

But there were other interested listeners besides the judge and me. Mr. Schiller, although he still made a show of keeping his eyes closed, was evidently wide awake. Inspector Blandy followed the evidence with close attention, and Superintendent Miller, who had slipped quietly into the court some time previously with my friend, Dr. Oldfield, was listening and watching attentively, though he must have known all about Miss Rendell's evidence.

As the latter lady made her dignified exit from the box, the judge cast a quick, expectant glance at Thorndyke. Then the name of the next witness was called, and Dr. James Oldfield came forward and presented himself to be sworn and to give evidence.

In his case, as in that of the previous witness, the examination began with the passing across of the two "incomplete copies".

"Will you look at those two photographs, Dr. Oldfield," said Thorndyke, "and tell us whether they seem to be portraits of any person whom you have ever seen?"

Oldfield examined the photographs closely for nearly a minute, and as he looked at them, there stole gradually over his face an expression of surprised recognition. At length he replied cautiously, "These photographs appear to me to be portraits of Emma Robey, the woman who was murdered about two years ago at 39 Jacob Street, Hampstead Road."

"Can you say definitely that they are portraits of Emma Robey?"

"I don't like to swear positively, that they are. The woman had been dead about three weeks when I examined her body, and some changes had occurred. But I feel a strong conviction that these are portraits of her. Would it be permissible for me to refer to my notes?"

"When did you take the notes?" the judge asked.

"I made them in the mortuary in the presence of the body, and I compared and verified them, point by point, after I had written them."

"Then you may certainly refer to them," said the judge.

On this, Oldfield produced from his pocket a small book and, opening it at a marked place, made a systematic comparison of the notes and the photographs. When he had finished, he announced, "I have compared the description in the notes, detail by detail, with the photographs, and I find that they agree in every respect except one. That is that the hair in the photograph is considerably shorter than the hair of the corpse when I examined it."

"Did you note the exact length of the hair?"

"I did not measure it, but I noted it in the description as just down to the shoulders."

"With that exception, you find complete agreement between your description and the photographs?"

"Yes, the agreement is complete in every detail."

"And, apart from the written description, do you recognize the portraits as being like Emma Robey?"

"Yes. As soon as I saw the photographs I felt that they were portraits of somebody whom I had seen, and when I tried to recall who that somebody was, I suddenly realized that she was Emma Robey. I may say that I have now no doubt that these are really portraits of her."

At this point my attention was attracted by Mr. Schiller, who had suddenly awakened, and now, pulling out his watch and glancing at it with a startled air, stood up abruptly and, with a little bow to the judge, began to make his way slowly and silently towards the door. As he rose, so also did Inspector Blandy and Superintendent Miller, both of whom moved off unobtrusively in the same direction. I followed the three figures eagerly with my eyes as they converged on the exit, Schiller leading and slightly quickening his pace. One by one they passed out, and as the door swung to noisily, after the last of them, the judge (who had also been observing the exodus) took the photographs in his hand

and remarked, "This is a most extraordinary affair. These portraits have now been confidently identified as three different persons."

"My submission is, my Lord," said Thorndyke, "that those three are one and the same person."

"That would seem," the judge began, but at this moment a heavy thump on the swing door sent it flying inwards and, through the opening came a sound as of several persons scuffling, mingled with low but excited voices. Then, in the midst of the confused noises, a pistol shot rang out. And as the door swung to, the sounds became more muffled and distant. After a short interval, at a sign from the judge, the usher hurried towards the door and, having peered out cautiously, disappeared, and the door swung to after him. There was a brief silence during which we all waited expectantly. Then the usher reappeared, in company with Superintendent Miller, and announced, "This officer, my Lord, has a communication to make to your Lordship."

The judge made no comment but looked inquiringly at Miller, who stepped up to the bench and made his "communication".

"I have to inform your Lordship," said he, "that Mr. Carl Schiller has just been arrested on a charge of having murdered his wife."

"Is it permissible," asked the judge, who seemed more interested than surprised, "for you to give any particulars of the charge?"

"It is quite permissible, my Lord," replied Miller, "as the prisoner will be brought before a magistrate immediately. The arrest was made on an information sworn by Dr. Thorndyke, and the charge is that the accused did, on the 12th of December, 1930, at Number 39 Jacob Street, Hampstead Road, murder his wife, Lotta Schiller, by forcibly administering poison to her."

"Ah," said the judge, "Thirty-nine, Jacob Street. Then the Epping Forest tragedy, if there ever was one, is irrelevant to the case of this poor woman?"

"Quite irrelevant, my Lord," Miller agreed.

The judge reflected for a few moments, then, addressing the court – that is to say, the counsel and solicitors – he said, "You have heard this officer's remarkable announcement. Obviously this new information involves at least the suspension of these proceedings. If there is evidence that Lotta Schiller was murdered, there must be evidence that she is dead, and if her death can be proved, that proof excludes the idea of presuming it. The hearing will therefore be adjourned *sine die*."

On this, we all rose. The witnesses – there were no spectators – faded out of the court, and we were preparing to depart also. But the judge made no sign of retiring. Instead, he craned out of his seat towards Thorndyke and, in a low voice, suggested his desire for a little further enlightenment. Accordingly Thorndyke stepped over to the bench, and Lorimer and I had no false delicacy about following him.

"Well, Doctor," said the judge, "as you seem to have been making use of the Probate Court for your own purposes, I think that the least you can do is to satisfy our legitimate curiosity. Now, what I want to know is, what has happened to the woman who personated Lotta Schiller at 39 Jacob Street, and what part did she take in the crime?"

"There was no woman, my Lord," replied Thorndyke. "The person who was known at Jacob Street as Lotta Schiller was Carl Schiller, dressed and made up as a woman."

"God bless me!" exclaimed the judge. "It sounds incredible. I suppose you have clear evidence as to the identity?"

"Yes," Thorndyke replied. "The two persons are identical in their physical characteristics, in size, eye-colour, form of features, and in the exact shape of the ears."

"That won't carry you very far in support of a capital charge," the judge commented.

"No," Thorndyke agreed. "It would be of no use excepting for corroboration. But there is one piece of evidence that is quite conclusive. Providence has been kinder to us than to the criminal. It happens that Carl Schiller has a most unusual type of hair."

"Ha!" the judge exclaimed. "There is something queer about the hair, is there? I thought, when I looked at the locket, that it was odd-looking hair. Very unusual, is it?"

"It is more than that, my Lord. It presents one of the rarest of anomalies. This ringed hair, as it is called, each hair being marked by alternate light and dark bands, is of such extreme rarity that, in the whole of my professional experience, I have never before met with a case. Only a very few examples exist in museums."

"That is fairly impressive," said the judge. "But the specimen in the locket, which, I suppose, is what you rely on, appertains to the lady. Do you know as a fact that Carl Schiller has hair of this character?"

"I do," replied Thorndyke. "There, again, Providence has been kind to us. During the last hearing, a very curious accident happened in court. Mr. Schiller's head became in some way stuck to the back of the bench, and it was necessary for a person who was sitting in the bench behind him to cut the hair in order to liberate him. The piece of hair which was cut off came into my possession and, of course, as soon as it was examined with the microscope, the murder was, literally, out."

The judge's eyes twinkled. "Ha!" said he. "Now I wonder how that gentleman's head became stuck to the bench? Do you happen to know?"

"I don't actually know," Thorndyke replied, "but I have certain suspicions."

"So have I," said his Lordship.

Chapter XVII
Observations on the
Art of Disguise

It might perhaps be of interest, if space permitted, to describe in detail the trial of Carl Schiller for the murder of his wife, Lotta. But space does not permit, nor is there any need for such description, since all the facts brought forward in evidence against him are known to the reader of this narrative. It is, however, one thing to know the facts, but quite another to perceive their application or the inferences deducible from them. I had known all the facts that were known to Thorndyke, but it was not until I had heard him reconstruct the course of the investigation that I perceived their exact connections and understood how, by piecing them together, he had evolved his startling conclusion.

The trial had run its course to its inevitable end. The jury, without leaving the box, had brought in their verdict of "Guilty", the judge had pronounced sentence of death, and the prisoner had descended the stairs from the dock, vanishing for ever from the sight of men, and the spectators, having thus witnessed the fall of the curtain, rose and began to surge out through the open doors. I followed them as soon as I could and, presently, in the great hall, encountered Polton, Pedley, and Vanderpuye, whom I joined to wait for Thorndyke.

For my part, I had looked on at the unfolding of the drama, at the piling up of the deadly evidence, with no single twinge of pity or compunction, even when the judge had assumed the black cap and pronounced the final words of doom. But it was otherwise with our two friends. For them it had been impossible, as they looked on the white-faced brute in the dock, facing his accusers like a caged wild beast, to forget the ties of friendship and even of affection that had once bound them to him. Looking at their pale and troubled faces, I realized that it had been a painful ordeal which had left them shocked and saddened. So, too, Thorndyke, when he came out and joined us, was instantly aware of their distressed state of mind and, with his invariable sympathy and kindliness, sought for some means of distracting their thoughts from their late painful experience.

"I am wondering, Polton," said he, "whether the resources of 5A King's Bench Walk are equal to an impromptu dinner for five?"

"The resources of Number 5A, sir, are unlimited," was the confident reply, in a tone of persuasive eagerness.

"Then," said Thorndyke, "I am in a position to ask our two friends to give us the very great pleasure of their society this evening."

He glanced inquiringly at Pedley and Vanderpuye, both of whom accepted the invitation with almost pathetic promptitude, whereupon Polton excused himself and darted off like a lamplighter, while we, since it was still some time short of any reasonable dinner hour, meandered down the Old Bailey to Ludgate Hill in search of a much-needed cup of tea. When we had disposed of this, with as much lively conversation as Thorndyke and I could produce for the occasion, we set forth at a leisurely pace for the Temple by way of the Embankment.

Polton's estimate of the resources of 5A King's Bench Walk was justified by the result, though I suspected that the Rainbow or some other excellent Fleet Street tavern had been pressed into service. But however that may have been, the dinner to which we sat down in due course did credit to the establishment, handsomely supported as it was by the products of our own cellar, which Polton had raided to some purpose (though his own place at the table was marked ingloriously by a bottle of lemonade). The unobtrusive service was conducted by William, Polton's domestic understudy, aided by a mysterious stranger of waiter-like aspect, who lurked in the background performing curious feats of legerdemain with dishes and covers but never intruding into William's domain.

The opening stages of a good dinner "when beards wag all" are not adapted for sustained conversation. So, for a time, what talk there was concerned itself for the most part with cheerful trivialities. But at the back of all our minds was the drama which we had seen played out to its tragic end a few hours before, and inevitably it had to come to the surface sooner or later. But it was not until the manducatory pace had slowed down and the wine had circulated that the subject, hitherto taboo, was broached, and even then only indirectly.

"Before I forget," said Thorndyke, "let me make restitution." He produced from his pocket Pedley's notebook and Vanderpuye's locket and, pushing them across the table towards their respective owners, added, "There is no need for me to tell you how much I am indebted to you both for the loan and the use of these things. You have heard the evidence and you know what invaluable light they threw on the mystery."

Pedley took up the book and pocketed it without remark, but Vanderpuye hesitated, looking at the little bauble as it lay on the table with intense disfavour. Eventually, however, he picked it up and dropped it into his pocket with something of a gesture of disgust.

"Your property, Polton," said Thorndyke, "is, as you see, on the mantelpiece, and is now at your disposal, with many thanks for the loan."

"You were very welcome, sir," replied Polton, "but I think that the loan benefited me more than it did you. It has given the picture a new interest for me, whereas I don't see that you got much help from it except for the colour of the lady's dress."

"I think," said Thorndyke, "that when you hear the whole story, as you shall some day, you will find that the picture played a more important part in the investigation than you have realized."

"If it did," said I, "there is at least one point that I have missed, for I had the same idea as Polton – in fact, I rather wondered why you produced the picture in court at all."

"The principal object in producing it," he replied, "was to help the witnesses to remember the dress. The photographs gave no such help, but the dress was of vital importance in fixing the dates. A further purpose was to ascertain whether the figure of the woman was recognizably like Lotta Schiller."

"Yes, but you seem to hint at some other function that the picture served, and you hint at some future occasion when we shall hear the whole story of the investigation. But why a future occasion? We are all here, and I think we are all in the same condition as to our interest in the case. Speaking for myself, I am still mystified. I have heard all the evidence and found it perfectly conclusive, but what I cannot understand is how you came to build up the whole scheme of evidence out of nothing. Where did you get your start? What first put you on the track? It seemed to me that from the moment when Penfield proposed the case, you went straight ahead as if you had a considered theory already in your mind."

"But that, in effect," he replied, "was the actual position. When Penfield informed us of the impending application, he was not, so far as I was concerned, opening a new subject, but only introducing a new phase of a problem that I had already considered in some detail. But the story of the investigation is a rather long one and, if you all really want to hear it, you had better draw up your armchairs round the fire and prepare yourselves to listen in comfort."

There was no doubt about the desire to hear the story. Polton was "on broken bottles" of curiosity, and our two guests, each in his own way, were eager to learn how the tangled skein had been unravelled. Accordingly we drew the armchairs up to the fire and Polton placed conveniently by them the little tables with their decanters and cigar boxes, while William and the alien waiter – who now came out into the

583

open – swiftly cleared the table of its now irrelevant burden. Then, when the two operators had finally departed, Thorndyke began his story.

"The account of the actual investigation has a necessary prologue, necessary because it explains how suspicion first entered my mind in the absence of any positive suggestion from without. Jervis knows, because I have often told him, that in the early days when I had little or no practice, I used to occupy myself in the study of hypothetical cases. I would consider how a particular crime could be planned and executed with the greatest amount of security against detection and, when I had established the principles, I would apply them by working out in detail an imaginary crime. Then I would study this crime to discover its weak points and the signs by which it might be recognized in real life. The method was a really valuable one, for a hypothetical crime, systematically studied, yields practically as much experience as a real one.

"Now, the most important crime from a medico-legal point of view is the deliberately planned murder. Accordingly, I gave special attention to this type of crime and, after trying over a number of different methods, I decided that by far the most secure from the chance of detection was that of a fictitious person. It seemed to me that if this method were skilfully planned and efficiently carried out, it would be almost undetectable."

"I am not quite sure," said Vanderpuye, "that I understand what you mean by creating a 'fictitious person'."

"Well, let us take an imaginary case. We will suppose that a man whom we will call John Doe has some reason for wishing to eliminate a certain person. That person may be an unwanted wife. John Doe may wish to marry another woman, or he may be haunted by a blackmailer. The reason, whatever it may be, is a permanent one. The person whom he desires to eliminate is an abiding hindrance to happiness or a menace to his safety. Now, supposing him to adopt my method, let us follow his procedure.

"He begins by assuming a disguise which so far alters his appearance that he would not be easily recognized by anyone who knew him, and that gives him certain new and easily recognizable characteristics."

"That would not be particularly easy," I remarked.

"It would not," Thorndyke agreed, "but we will consider that question separately. Now we will assume that John Doe has so disguised himself and has taken a new name. Let us say, Richard Roe. Under that name he takes up his abode in a neighbourhood where he is not known and there assumes a character which will bring him into fairly close contact with a limited number of people. He may open a shop or an

584

office or practise some kind of avocation whereby he will become well known by the inhabitants of the neighbourhood and more intimately known by a few, and in that way he will carry on for some months – at least, until he has become a well-established character in the locality.

"Then he proceeds to commit his crime, at his own selected time and place. He is not hurried. He can make his arrangements at his leisure. He has no occasion to take any measures for concealment of the identity of the criminal. On the contrary, the more definitely the crime is connected with Richard Roe, the more perfect will be his security. All that is necessary is to avoid any actual witnesses of the crime or any need for him to escape quickly. Probably the most perfect method would be to lure the victim to his premises and, having committed the murder, to lock the corpse up in those premises and quietly take his departure.

"He is still, you see, not hurried or in any danger. He simply sheds his disguise and now has no connection with the murder. Some days, or perhaps weeks, will elapse before the body is discovered, in which time he can go abroad or to a distance, write to his friends describing his travels and, in due course, after a discreet interval, return to his usual places of resort and to the circle of his old acquaintances.

"Meanwhile the body has been discovered and the police are in full cry after the murderer, Richard Roe. They have an excellent detailed description of him, vouched for by a number of reliable witnesses who knew him quite intimately, and would certainly recognize him if he were produced. But he never is produced, for, in the moment when John Doe shed his disguise, Richard Roe ceased to exist. The police are, in fact, searching for a purely imaginary person."

"Yes," said I, "it certainly appears to be a very perfect scheme. But yet there seems to me to be one snag. The victim is in some way connected with John Doe, and it might be noticed that the murder is very opportune for him. For instance, the murdered person might be his unwanted wife, with whom he is known to have been on bad terms."

"I don't think that there is much in that," Thorndyke replied. "You see, the identity of the murderer is not in question. He is a known person – Richard Roe – and, consequently, no suspicion can possibly fall on any other person. Still, the matter is worth noticing. It would undoubtedly add to the murderer's safety if the corpse also could be disguised or rendered unrecognizable. We will bear that fact in mind. And now let us consider the question of disguise, remembering that a mere stage make-up would be useless – that it would have to be efficient out of doors in daylight and that it would have to be used constantly over a considerable period of time.

585

"To change a man's appearance so completely that his friends or acquaintances would not recognize him is not easy. But it can be done. There used to be a wig-maker in Russell Street, Covent Garden, who made a regular profession of the art of disguising, and who was able to produce the most surprising transformations. But his methods were rather elaborate, the results not at all comfortable to the subject and, in continuing cases, the clients had to attend daily to have the make-up renewed. This would hardly do for a long-term disguise, and certainly not for an intending murderer. He would have to do his own make-up, and it would require to be reasonably comfortable.

"However, we need not dwell on the difficulties of purely male disguise, for there is another kind that is comparatively easy and extremely convincing: Change of sex. When it is possible, it is completely effective, for a marked change of appearance can be produced with very little actual disguise. And the change of appearance becomes of less importance, since the change of sex creates a new personality. To his new acquaintances John Doe is a woman, and if any of them should subsequently meet him, a slight resemblance to that woman would pass unnoticed.

"Moreover, the present fashions are favourable to such personation. Women's hair is worn in all sorts of ways, from a close crop to a mop of fuzz, and it is not only waved or curled artificially, but is also dyed or bleached, quite openly and without exciting remark. Again, there is the extensive make-up, which is almost universal and is a recognized fashion: The painted lips, the tinted and powdered cheeks, the false eyelashes, and the pencilled eyebrows. All these materially alter the appearance, and by management could be made to alter it profoundly. A man, by simply dressing as a woman and adopting a feminine mode of wearing the hair, with some use of the lipstick and the eyebrow pencil, would at once be considerably disguised, probably enough to pass unrecognized by persons who knew him only slightly, and if he had previously worn a beard or moustache, his appearance would be totally changed. Even his friends would not recognize him.

"But it is a method that is subject to very severe limitations. To certain types of men it would be impracticable. For a tall man it would be very unsuitable. A six-foot woman would be rather remarkable, but conspicuousness is what a disguised man would need to avoid. Then a dark man would be almost impossible, for no amount of shaving would get rid of a dark beard, and no paint or powder would cover it up. A man with a bass voice would also be impossible. It is difficult to modify the voice appreciably, and anything like an assumed voice would attract

586

attention. Other peculiarities such as a very large nose or marked hairiness of the chest or limbs would create difficulties.

"And now let us see what would be a really suitable case, remembering that the object is to produce a woman of an ordinary type whose appearance would not attract notice. He would be the opposite of the types which we have excluded – that is to say, he would be a rather small, slight, blond man with somewhat small features, a light voice, and not too much hair on his chest or limbs. Such a man, if he shaved twice a day and used the make-up judiciously, might pass as a very ordinary-looking woman, provided that, before making his appearance in his new character, he let his hair grow long enough to allow of some kind of feminine mode. And, conversely, if one suspected a woman of being a man in disguise, one could postulate a man of this type as the one to be sought for, and such a suspicion might reasonably arise if a woman who had committed a crime disappeared immediately and permanently."

"I should have thought," said I, "that the voice would have created a difficulty."

"I think you exaggerate the difficulty," he replied. "There are voices which are unmistakably masculine or feminine, but there are a good many others – more, I think, than we realize – that are not at all distinctive. Between a deep female voice, especially if the lower register is habitually used, and a light male voice, there is very little difference. On hearing such a voice proceeding from another room, it is often difficult to say whether the speaker is a man or a woman. The fact is that our ideas are based on extreme or typical forms.

"And now to resume our argument. We have considered only physical disguise, change in appearance. But there is also what we may call psychological disguise, the adoption of feminine habits and modes of behaviour and the creation of circumstances suggesting a feminine personality. These would act by suggestion and leave observers with an unshakable conviction of the personator's sex, the more powerful because unconscious. But the most convincing of all would be a love affair with a man, preferably a somewhat scandalous one which would give rise to gossip. The suggestive effect of this would be intense. It would completely forestall any possible question as to the sex of the personator.

"Incidentally, we may note that the latter would be wise to associate with women as little as possible, for women, having an intimate knowledge of the ways of their own sex, might notice some discrepancy of habit or behaviour into which a man might be betrayed by the lack of such knowledge.

"And now, having considered the 'fictitious person' method in the abstract, we may proceed to observe its application in the case of '*R. v. Schiller*'."

He paused to pay certain little attentions to his guests. Then, when our glasses and pipes were recharged and Polton had refreshed himself with a pinch of snuff, he commenced his narration.

Chapter XVIII
The Investigation Reviewed

"It would be a paradox," Thorndyke began, "to say that the unravelment of the complex scheme for the murder of Lotta Schiller began before the murder was committed, but it is a fact that, as each of the later developments came into view, it found me with a body of considered data to apply to the solution of the problem presented. At first, this was not an investigation *ad hoc*. Until Penfield proposed his case to me, I was an outsider, watching with little more than academic interest the unfolding of a train of events in which I was not personally concerned. Hence, when the question of the Presumption of Death was raised, I had not to embark on an investigation *de novo*, but only to test and verify conclusions already formed.

"For me, the starting-point was the murder of Charles Montagu. The interest of that crime from a medico-legal point of view lay in the unusual method adopted by the murderer – the forcible administration of poison. But there were other elements of interest and, thanks to Polton's enthusiasm, we were kept fully supplied with the published records of the case. We had the lurid descriptions of the murder and of the mysterious artist on whom suspicion at first lighted, and a full report of the inquest, but above all, we had Pedley's remarkable little picture of Gravel-pit Wood.

"That picture made a deep impression on me. There it is on the mantelpiece and, if you will look at it attentively, I think you will understand its effect on me. There are three figures. One, the taller man, was recognized by Blandy as Charles Montagu, and there we see him going to his death. The shorter man must have been the murderer, and we can see him there, leading his victim to the appointed place. But to me, the most impressive figure was that of the woman. Who was she, and why was she there? Obviously she was spying on the two men, and apparently trying to hear what they were saying. The strong suggestion was that she was in some way related to one of them and, since she never came forward to give information, the natural inference was that she was related to, or connected with, the shorter man. For, if her relations had been with Montagu, she would surely have denounced the murderer.

"But, above all, what impressed me was the terrible position that this unfortunate woman had placed herself in, the dreadful peril in which she stood. For her life hung on a thread – the thread of her silence. If she

589

had not actually witnessed the murder, she certainly knew who the murderer was. A word from her could have sent him to the gallows, and she alone in all the world had that fatal knowledge. It was an awful position. The man had committed his crime and vanished without leaving a trace. He must have believed himself to be absolutely safe, and yet, in fact, his life was in this woman's hands. If ever an inkling of the truth should leak out, she was doomed. The ruthless ferocity of the crime made that practically certain.

"I must confess that the thought of the dangers that encompassed that unhappy woman caused me a good deal of discomfort, which was revived from time to time when I used to see the picture hanging in Polton's room, and I was haunted by an uneasy expectation that, sooner or later, I should hear of the murder of some woman which should justify my forebodings. But the months passed, and I began to hope that the woman had had the wisdom to keep her secret and that the danger had passed.

"Then, at last, came the murder of Emma Robey and, immediately, my suspicions were aroused. It was a bizarre, theatrical crime with many curious features, but the one that instantly attracted my attention was the method adopted by the murderer – the forcible administration of poison. Not only was it the same method as that employed in the murder of Montagu, but the poison used was the same poison.

"Now, when we consider the inveterate tendency of criminals to repeat their procedure, it is evident that this similarity of method suggested at least a possibility that the murderer of Emma Robey might be the same person as the murderer of Charles Montagu, and if that possibility were entertained, it carried with it the further possibility that poor Emma Robey might be the woman in the picture. There was, of course, no evidence that she was. All that could be said was that, in the only respect in which comparison was possible – the colour of the hair – they were so far alike that they might have been the same person. And at that I had to leave it for the time being. I waited hopefully for Emma Robey to be identified, assuming that, when she was, we should get into the world of realities. But she never was identified and, after a time I decided, as also, I think, did the police, that Emma Robey was a fictitious name and that the marking on the clothing was a plant, done deliberately to confuse the issues. But who she really was remained a mystery.

"And now we come to another remarkable feature of this strange crime. I mean the absence of any real attempt to conceal its authorship."

"You are not forgetting the locked door," I reminded him, "and the elaborate suggestion of suicide?"

"No," he replied, "but I don't regard that as a serious attempt. The police did not entertain the idea of suicide for a moment, and neither did I. The whole circumstances shouted 'murder'. Nor did the murderer seem to expect that the pretence would be accepted. Otherwise she would have made the discovery herself and called in the police. But she would not run this risk but took the more prudent course of absconding, and in doing so, frankly abandoned the pretence of suicide."

"But," I objected, "why the pretence at all?"

"It seems to me," he replied, "that there were two objects. First, it was a 'try-on', a gamble on the infinitesimal chance that the appearance of suicide might be accepted. What the criminal thought of that chance may be judged by the fact that she did not stay to see whether it came off. She preferred definitely to incriminate herself by flight. As to the other motive, we shall come to that presently.

"To return to the crime, I repeat that, disregarding the pretence of suicide, there was no attempt to conceal the identity of the murderer. There was the corpse in Lotta Schiller's room, locked in with Lotta Schiller's key, and Lotta, herself, nowhere to be found. When once it was decided that this was a case of murder, Lotta was the obvious presumptive murderer. She alone had access to the rooms and there was no one else on whom any sort of suspicion fell. All that remained for the police to do was to arrest her and bring her to trial.

"But Lotta had disappeared, and notwithstanding the most intense and energetic search, the police failed to discover the slightest trace of her. Now, as Jervis remarked recently, it is not very easy, in these days of telephones, wireless, and a very perfect police organization, for a known person to disappear without leaving a trace, especially a rather conspicuous person like Lotta Schiller. Yet no sign of her was discovered until the finding of the handbag in Epping Forest.

"I am inclined to regard the planting of those relics in the forest as a tactical mistake. It never deceived the police, though Blandy very wisely made a search so exhaustive as to settle the question for good. Of course, the absence of a body damned the scheme. If there had been a murder, there must have been a body in the camp, and there would not have been those admirably selected clues, and the appearances could have been so easily produced by one person with two pairs of shoes. The only effect on the police was to confirm their conviction of Lotta's guilt and to spur them on to further efforts to lay hands on her.

"But as you know, their efforts failed utterly, though the search never entirely ceased during the two years that followed, for Scotland Yard has a long memory and does not readily accept defeat.

591

Nevertheless, in all that long pursuit, not the faintest trace of Lotta Schiller ever came to light.

"So much for the crime itself. Now let us see how these developments appeared to an experienced and deeply interested onlooker. To me, the most striking fact was the one which I have just mentioned, the virtual acceptance by the criminal of the authorship of the crime. Apart from the perfunctory suicide tableau, which the murderer obviously did not rely on, there was not the slightest effort to dissociate Lotta Schiller from the murder. Indeed, it almost seemed as if the onus of the crime were being deliberately cast on her.

"This curiously defiant attitude interested me profoundly. What could it mean? This was no crime of impulse with an unpremeditated flight. It was a carefully prepared murder, the procedure of which had been arranged and considered in advance. The only explanation that suggested itself to me was that Lotta Schiller had never been in any danger at all – that before the crime was committed, a means of escape had been provided, so secure as to render any other precautions unnecessary. And here, I think, we have the principal motive for the suicide deception, to disguise the criminal's confidence in her immunity from the danger of discovery.

"But what could be the nature of this infallible means of escape? I could think of only one, and the facts fitted it so perfectly that I adopted it as a working hypothesis. I decided that here, for the first time in my experience, I had met with a criminal who had put in practice my method of the fictitious person – that Lotta Schiller was a disguised person with a fictitious personality who, having committed the murder, had simply dropped the disguise and forthwith had virtually ceased to exist.

"You will see how completely this hypothesis agreed with and accounted for all the circumstances. It was just a reproduction of the case of John Doe. Here, in the assumed character of Lotta Schiller, he lures his victim into his premises, in which everything has been prepared, commits his murder at his ease without danger of disturbance or interruption, removes all in criminating traces and, in this case, arranges the sham suicide tableau, goes away, removes his disguise, if he has not removed it already and, having now changed back into the personality of John Doe, watches unconcernedly the pursuit of the non-existent Lotta Schiller. If he had been perfectly wise, he would have left it at that, but he was not perfectly wise, and he elected to play the fool in Epping Forest and thereby offer to the police an unnecessary suggestion of deception.

"Having accepted this hypothesis, I asked myself the further question: Assuming Lotta Schiller to be a disguised person, who and

592

what was the real person, and what was the nature of the disguise? Was she really a woman, or was she a man disguised as a woman? I decided, for several reasons, that she was more probably a man. In the first place, as I explained just now, change of sex is, as a long-term disguise, much easier and far more effective than any other kind. Then the crime looked like a man's crime. Poisoning is characteristically the woman's method, but not forcible poisoning. That requires such an amount of strength as to make it certain that the crime can be carried out. Then there was a curious little point that cropped up in the evidence at the inquest and that seemed to me very revealing. In proof of the essentially proper character of his relations with Lotta, Vanderpuye swore that he had never kissed her, that she had absolutely forbidden any intimacies of that kind.

"Now, if we assumed that Lotta was a woman, this was rather extraordinary, considering that their relations were almost those of lovers. But if we assumed that Lotta was a man, the anomaly was quite easily explained. By careful shaving, a blond beard can be rendered quite invisible. But it cannot be rendered impalpable. By the sense of touch – especially the touch of the sensitive lips – the invisible stubble would be instantly detected. Hence, in such a case, physical endearments would have to be avoided most strictly.

"The position, then, at this stage, was that I believed the murderer of Emma Robey to be some unknown man at whose identity I could not even make a guess, for he had vanished without leaving a trace – or rather, I should say, leaving only deceptive traces in the form of a well-known but non-existent woman.

"But there remained the problem of Emma Robey herself. As the time ran on and the police failed to discover any missing woman of that name, it began to dawn on me that here, probably, was another fictitious person, that the marked underclothing had been a 'plant', and that there was no such person as Emma Robey. But if there was not, then who was the murdered woman? Again, it was impossible to make even a guess, though, at this time, when I used to look occasionally at the picture in Polton's room, I would ask myself whether it might not be that the two unknown figures in that picture were Emma Robey and her murderer.

"But this was mere speculation. It could not be tested or verified and it led nowhere. As the months slipped by and no new facts came to light, it began to look as if the Jacob Street murder would have to be added to the long list of unsolved mysteries. And so the matter rested for a couple of years. And then came Mr. Penfield, and with his arrival on the scene my role of the detached onlooker was exchanged for that of an authorized investigator.

"Now, before Penfield had spoken a dozen sentences, I saw that we were going to get some important new light on the problem, for we were now in a world of realities in which systematic inquiries were possible. But from Penfield himself, as he sketched out his case, I gathered several illuminating facts. Let us see what they were.

"First, we learned that Lotta Schiller was a real person. But Penfield's case dealt with two Lottas, one, the testatrix, who was certainly the real Lotta, and another, the lodger at 39 Jacob Street, who was assumed to be the same person.

"Then we learned that there was some sort of connection between Lotta and Charles Montagu. The nature of it was not clear, but there had certainly been a contact of some kind.

"We learned, further, that Montagu had apparently been blackmailed, and that the blackmail had been assumed to be connected with the murder.

"Then Penfield could give us the address where Lotta was lodging when she was last heard of, and we gathered the significant fact that those lodgings were near Gravel-pit Wood.

"Finally, Penfield gave us a description of Lotta. It was very sketchy but, such as it was, it seemed roughly to agree with what we knew of the appearance of Lotta the lodger (as we may for convenience call her, to distinguish her from the testatrix, whom we may call, simply, Lotta). But it agreed equally well with the woman in the picture and with Oldfield's description of Emma Robey.

"Here, then, was some valuable new material and, as soon as I had settled definitely with Penfield, I proceeded to sort out the facts and to seek to add to them. I began by inspecting Lotta's will at Somerset House and trying to memorize her signature and, as a matter of routine, I secured copies of the wills of Montagu and of Barbara Dalton. From the former of these I learned nothing fresh, and from Barbara's only one trivial and apparently insignificant fact, which was that she had bequeathed all her chattels to her sister Linda, with the exception of her violin, which she gave to Lotta, from which it was reasonable to infer that Lotta was able to play the violin. But that fact, though I noted it, seemed to have no possible bearing on our inquiry.

"And now I addressed myself to the really important question: Was the lodger at Jacob Street the same person as Lotta the testatrix? The most likely source of the relevant facts was Mr. Thomas Pedley, with whom I accordingly communicated without delay and, having received from him a most gracious invitation, I descended on him, supported by Jervis, at the appointed time.

"I must admit that, whatever my expectations may have been, the results of that interview were beyond my wildest hopes. Tom Pedley was a mine of information. He was a first-class observer, with an indelible memory and the valuable gift of imparting his knowledge by means of drawings. I need not go into details as most of them are known to you, but I will take the results in order.

"First, we learned that Lotta the lodger was a sham artist, an absolute sham, a complete impostor. Pedley assumed that she was posing deliberately for some reason unknown to him. This was an important fact, for, to this extent at least, she was masquerading in a false character.

"Next, we learned that, although Pedley had been on terms of fairly intimate friendship with her for many months, he knew absolutely nothing about her as to her past history or her friends or relations, excepting the rather shadowy husband. In respect of everything concerning herself, she was uncommunicative to the point of secretiveness.

"Then there were two very significant facts. One was that Tom had never seen her handwriting, and apparently no one else had, for she never wrote either to Tom or to Vanderpuye, and avoided the use of cheques by paying her rent in cash. She did not even sign her pictures. The other was her perverse refusal to have either a drawing or a photograph of her made for the locket, coupled with the fact that her own self-portrait bore no resemblance to her whatever. The great significance of these two facts was that, when the woman disappeared, all traces of her personality disappeared, too (as she believed). No portrait remained to be shown, studied, or compared with any known person, and no scrap of writing, or even the recollection of any, to be compared with letters or documents. The two facts, taken together, offered a distinct suggestion of preparation for a disappearance.

"The forced friendship with the remarkable manifestations of affection – entirely verbal and unaccompanied by any kisses or other physical endearments – was significant, especially as the woman seemed to have no other friends until Vanderpuye arrived and became the object of similar platonic affection. But I have already referred to the value of a flirtation as support for a 'change of sex' disguise.

"And now we come to the description and the incomparable notebook. That description was quite masterly, and to me an unexpected windfall. For, if I was right in my suspicion that Lotta the lodger was a man disguised as a woman, this description, with its wealth of exact detail, was substantially a description of the man himself. Thus, we learned that the woman's height was about five-feet-seven without her high heels, that she had ears of a certain distinctive shape (of which Tom gave us a drawing), and that her eyes were of a greenish-hazel. Now, these were characteristics that no disguise could appreciably alter. It followed, therefore, that the man, if he existed, must be about five-feet-seven inches in height, must have ears of that particular shape, and greenish-hazel eyes. But Tom was able to supplement this description by an excellent memory drawing, the existence of which had been unknown to Lotta.

"But the real windfall was the hair. As soon as I had heard Tom's description I realized that we had got a means of definite and certain identification, since Vanderpuye's locket contained an authentic specimen which could be examined. For the condition was obviously abnormal. I suspected it to be ringed hair, since there seemed to be no other possibility but, whatever it was, the microscope would make its nature clear. So we had got one totally unexpected item of evidence.

"It was, however, not the only one. Another point of unexpected importance emerged when Tom, in handing us his notebook, showed us the finger-prints of poor Emma Robey. They did not appear to be of any interest as the unfortunate woman was dead and buried, but I looked at them to see how Polton's improvised method had answered, and then I made a curious discovery. The finger-prints showed that Emma Robey had been a violin player."

"How did they show that?" Vanderpuye interrupted, eagerly.

"By the signs of pressure and friction on the fingertips," Thorndyke replied. "You must remember that finger-prints show other things besides the distinctive pattern – thickenings, for instance, of the epidermis due to particular ways of using the hands. Thus a professional violinist or a regular player develops thickenings of the skin – little corns, in fact – on the tips of the four fingers of the left hand which are used in stopping the strings. They do not appear on the fingers of merely occasional players, and so are indicative of the professional or serious player. The traces that they leave on the finger-prints are quite characteristic since they are raised above the general surface and, owing to their hardness, the pattern tends to be worn flat. These, by the way, were not at all well marked, just little areas of indistinctness in the centre of each print. Still, they were quite unmistakable, and they established beyond doubt that Emma Robey had been a regular violin player.

"The significance of the discovery remained to be proved. I had inferred that Lotta Schiller had been a violin player, but the inference might have been wrong. Meanwhile, the evidence, such as it was, supported the suggestion that Lotta Schiller and Emma Robey were one and the same person.

"These were the chief facts that we learned from Tom Pedley, and you will see that it was a rich haul, for these facts were the foundation of my case. When we came away from the studio I had the skeleton of the case sketched out pretty completely in my mind. Of course, that case was purely hypothetical, and it might be entirely fallacious. Its truth or its fallacy could be tested only by further investigation, and I applied myself forthwith to the task of verification.

"The first step was to examine the locket, which Vanderpuye very kindly placed at our disposal. I took it up to the laboratory at once and examined it under the microscope with a strong top light. A single glance showed that the hair was ringed hair, though, owing to its light colour, the rings were quite indiscernible to the naked eye or even through a weak lens. But with strong magnification it was perfectly clear, so we now had an infallible touchstone which could be applied confidently to any individual suspected of being Lotta the lodger.

"But we had to find that individual, and we had to seek further evidence as to whether Lotta the lodger was or was not a fictitious person. But this question was closely bound up with that of the identity of Emma Robey, for if Emma was, as I suspected, Lotta Schiller, then Lotta the lodger must be someone else. Accordingly I turned my attention to this question, and I began by ascertaining the latest date on which the real Lotta had been seen alive. Now, we knew from the affidavits that she had never been seen by any of her friends after she had left her lodgings at Linton Green. From that time she was never heard of by them until her reported disappearance in the Forest.

"The first thing, then, to be done was to find out the exact date on which Lotta disappeared from her lodgings, to which end I dispatched the invaluable Snuper to Linton Green to make inquiries of Mrs. Wharton, Lotta's landlady. He began by asking if she could give him Mrs. Schiller's present address, which, of course, she could not, but instead gave him those particulars which you have heard in evidence.

"This information did not appear to help us at all, for, as Lotta left her lodgings in the morning of the 13th of June, 1930 and the lodger did not appear in Jacob Street until about a month later, there was nothing to show that they might not be one and the same person. So I had to look for evidence elsewhere, and I did not quite see where I was to look for it. The position was very tantalizing. I had the finger-prints of Emma Robey and, if I could only have compared them with those of Lotta Schiller, the question would have been settled. But where was I to look for them? There is only one place in which the finger-prints of unknown persons may be found: Scotland Yard. But it seemed practically useless to look for the finger-prints of Emma Robey in that place, for whether she were or were not Lotta Schiller, she was presumably a respectable woman. Still, it was not absolutely impossible that they could be there and, since there was no alternative, and that I might feel that I had left no possibility untested, I made a good photograph of the finger-prints in the notebook and, armed with this, went to the Yard and sought out our old friend, Miller. He made no difficulty about taking me round to the Finger-print Department and presenting my photograph of the prints to the search officer. And then, behold the miracle! The finger-prints of Emma Robey were actually in the files and, of course, there were also the prison photographs and a summary of the particulars.

"At first it seemed as if the discovery did not help us much, for the name attached to the prison portraits was Louisa Saunders. We seemed merely to have got another unknown person. But the particulars were much more enlightening. It was noted that the prisoner's underclothing was marked with the initials L. S., which agreed with the name that she had given, Louisa Saunders, but it agreed equally well with the name of Lotta Schiller. The most striking fact, however, was that Louisa had been arrested in the afternoon of the 13th of June, 1930 – the very day on which Lotta had left her lodgings, and after her departure from them. The agreement was so complete as to be almost conclusive.

"But there was yet another agreement. From Mrs. Wharton, Snuper had learned that Lotta was practically a professional violinist. But the finger-prints of Louisa Saunders were obviously those of a regular violin player. The impressions of the corns were extremely well marked, and now I understood why they had been so ill-defined in Emma Robey's prints. During the imprisonment the corns had atrophied from disuse, and become worn down.

"The facts thus disclosed left no doubt in my mind that Louisa Saunders was really Lotta Schiller and, since Louisa was certainly Emma Robey, it followed that Emma Robey was Lotta Schiller. From this it followed that Lotta the lodger was some other person, and the question was, who could that person be? And now it was possible to suggest an answer to that question. The telegram that Mrs. Wharton had received had certainly not been sent by Lotta, for it would have disclosed her address, which she had refused to give to the police. But since Carl Schiller had called at the lodgings later to settle the rent and remove Lotta's possessions, it was evident that he knew where his wife was. Apparently, he had sent the telegram to prevent Mrs. Wharton from making inquiries about her missing lodger. Evidently, then, there were reasonable grounds for suspecting that Lotta the lodger was in fact Carl Schiller. But nothing more than suspicion. It had yet to be ascertained that his physical characteristics were such as to make the disguise possible, and this could not be decided until I had seen him or obtained a detailed description of him.

"At this point, it became necessary to take Miller into my confidence to some extent, as I needed his help for the next stage of the inquiry. He was perfectly willing, personally, to let me have copies of the prison portraits and the particulars, but he asked for a letter which he could show to the Assistant Commissioner, whose permission was necessary, and I accordingly sent him one, with the result that, as you remember, he called on me and brought the copies with him. Of these prison portraits I made copies with the name board masked out and put them, with a photograph of Pedley's portrait and a few dummy portraits, in a portfolio to be produced in court.

"And now I was ready for the opening of the case in the Probate Court, when I hoped to make the decisive move. But I was in a difficulty in regard to the procedure, for the correct course would have been for me to disclose the information that I possessed to Penfield, who would have passed it on to the other parties. But this was clearly impossible. Very unwillingly, I was compelled to adopt the quite irregular course of proceeding without the disclosure of material facts or discovery of documents, in the hope that I should be able to make my essential points before Lorimer objected.

"But I must admit that I was far from confident that morning when we set out for the Probate Court, for I had to settle certain questions, and to settle them quickly, and the opportunity might be lacking. And the results might not be those which I expected, in which case I should have to start the whole inquiry afresh. I have seldom been more anxious about a case than I was on that morning.

"The questions that I had to answer were: First, was Louisa Saunders actually Lotta Schiller? Second, did Carl Schiller's physical characteristics agree with Tom Pedley's description of Lotta the lodger? Third, had he ringed hair? The first question would probably be easy to dispose of, but the other two were subject to all sorts of contingencies. In the first place, Carl might not be there, although I suspected that he would, for his absence would be rather remarkable, considering his obvious interest in the case and the fact that his affidavit had to be read and that I had asked for his attendance. But even if he answered the description, there was the difficulty of obtaining a specimen of his hair. I had discussed this matter with Snuper and we had considered a number of plans but, in the end, I had to leave it to his ingenuity and readiness to take advantage of any opportunity that should present itself.

"You know what the upshot was. When Schiller was introduced to us, I saw at a glance that he agreed perfectly with the description. He was about five-feet-seven inches in height, he had greenish-hazel eyes, his ears exactly resembled Pedley's drawing, and the right one had a small Darwinian tubercle while the left had none. His profile, where it was not concealed by the beard, corresponded perfectly with Pedley's portrait and, as he was talking with Jervis, I noted that his smooth, high-pitched voice would have passed quite well as a woman's voice. The agreement was complete. There was not a single discrepancy and, for my part, I had no doubt that here was Lotta the lodger, the murderer of Lotta Schiller.

"But my belief was not to the point, nor did it amount to certainty. There remained the question of the ringed hair. That was the final test, and you will notice that it acted both ways. Lotta the lodger certainly had ringed hair. If this man had ringed hair, he was certainly the lodger. If he had not ringed hair, he was certainly not the lodger, no matter how complete was the agreement in all other respects. So that the identity of this man still remained to be proved, and I considered very anxiously whether it would be possible to get the sample of hair that was necessary for the proof or disproof. It looked an almost impossible task.

"I glanced towards Snuper, who had followed us into the court, and made the agreed signal to indicate his quarry, whereupon he got to work with his ridiculous little camera and managed to take two excellent profile portraits. Then he subsided into his seat and lay in wait for his victim, who presently seated himself close by, and then, as Lorimer made his opening speech, leaned his head against the back of the bench and closed his eyes.

"I watched Snuper anxiously and could see that he was keeping in close proximity to Schiller's head. But that was all that I could see, for Snuper has all the conjuror's skill in concealing his movements and diverting the attention of the onlookers. What he actually did was to wait until Schiller raised his head for a moment and, in that moment to deposit a thick smear of a quick-drying adhesive on the back of the bench just where the head had been resting. It was a most audacious proceeding but apparently no one noticed it – not even Schiller himself. And it was perfectly successful, as I realized in the sequel, for, the next time that Schiller tried to move his head, it was stuck fast to the back of the bench and had to be released by Snuper's scissors. Then I saw what had happened and was on tenterhooks while Snuper scraped away the adhesive – ostensibly to clean the back of the bench – for fear the judge should intervene and impound the scrapings for examination. However, all went well, and Snuper took an early opportunity to escape, and then I knew that the sample was safe, whatever it might turn out to be.

"You know, in effect, what the result was. When we arrived at the Temple in the lunch interval, I found Snuper waiting for me, modestly

600

triumphant at his success, and received from him his little camera and a folded envelope which enclosed some sticky material and a small tuft of hairs. I need not say that I lost no time in taking the latter up to the laboratory for examination. There I picked out a few hairs and, laying them on a slide with a drop of bergamot oil and a cover-glass and, placing the slide on the stage of the microscope, put my eye to the eye-piece.

"It was a dramatic moment, for the life of Carl Schiller hung on the answer to my question. And the answer was given at the first glance. The hairs were ringed hair, plain and unmistakable, and it was now certain that Lotta the lodger and Carl Schiller were one and the same person. But that person was the murderer of Emma Robey, and the final question that remained was whether Emma Robey was the same person as Lotta Schiller.

"I went back to the court, confident of being able to dispose of this question before the inevitable objection. And so it turned out. When Linda Dalton identified the prison portraits, my case was complete, for her identification was so confident and positive that it left no doubt in my mind, and I now knew that abundant confirmation could be obtained. Lorimer's objection came too late to hinder me, for I could, if I had chosen, have had Carl Schiller charged then and there."

"Why didn't you?" I asked. "Why did you go on with the case in the Probate Court?"

"The rest of my proceedings," he replied, "were for the benefit of the police. They would want to be able to make out a *prima facie* case before they committed themselves to an arrest and, in fact, I had promised Miller to provide him with enough evidence for the purpose. But it was as important to me as to him, for we had to make sure of a committal. It would have been a disaster if the case had failed in the magistrate's court. Besides, the latter proceedings were a sort of rehearsal, they enabled us to see exactly what evidence we could produce at the trial.

"Well, I have now retraced the course of the investigation and you can see how the mass of circumstantial evidence grew up as each successive fact came into view. There is no need to go into details of the preparation of the case, such as the composite photographs and the other exhibits which were produced in court, nor to speculate on those questions of which we shall never know the answers."

"That is all very well, sir," said Pedley, "for the learned lawyer and scientist, but simple folk like myself would like to have some sort of answers to those questions. For instance, I should very much like to know why the deuce Schiller elected to take up his abode next door to me and adopt me as his dearest friend. It could hardly have been a mere coincidence."

"No," Thorndyke agreed, "that seems incredible. But if it would comfort you to guess at his motives, I think you have something to go upon. He would have been looking about for a suitable neighbourhood where he was not known and for a likely stranger to adopt as a friend. He would have seen your name and address mentioned in the papers as that of the 'mysterious artist', and he might have noted that, as you never came forward to give information and appeared to have been unaware of the murder, you were certainly not a busy or inquisitive person. Your neighbourhood was perfectly suitable to him, and your profession ideal for the purpose of striking up an acquaintance, provided that he could pose as a fellow artist, and that the present fashion for childish and barbaric painting made quite possible, with a judicious use of the current jargon. I think he made a very good choice."

"I should have thought," Pedley objected, "that the fact of my having seen him in the wood that day would have put him off."

"But, my dear Pedley, he didn't know that you had seen him. You are forgetting: The police kept your information to themselves. It never appeared in the papers. And after all, though you had seen him, you never recognized him. No, my friend, I don't think that there is much mystery about his having selected you, but there are some other questions that are a good deal more difficult to answer."

"You mean," I suggested, "how it happened that Lotta allowed herself to be convicted of an offence that she had not committed – for I have assumed that Schiller planted those notes on her, deliberately, and that she knew it, though, of course, she couldn't guess at his object. But why didn't she say where she had got them?"

"Probably," Thorndyke replied, "she was so terrified of him, knowing him to be a murderer, that she did not dare to put the blame on him, and it is even possible that she accepted the prison willingly as a sanctuary from him. But we shall never know the actual facts, and it is not very profitable to speculate on them."

"You speak, Jervis," said Vanderpuye, "of his object in planting those notes on her. What was his object?"

"I take it," said I, "that his object was to get her safely out of the way while he was making his preparations to personate her, and be ready to make away with her when she came out, before she had time to get into touch with her friends, and I assume that he knew that she would rather go to prison under a fictitious name than make a scandal and exasperate him. What do you say, Thorndyke?"

"I think you are probably right," he replied, "but we don't know, and we never shall. Nor does it really concern us. We knew enough to defeat a really talented criminal, and that should satisfy us."

"Even though," I suggested, "it knocks the bottom out of the infallible scheme of Mr. John Doe?"

"But does it?" he retorted. "I think, Jervis, you are overlooking some very material facts. In the first place, Schiller did not carry out John Doe's programme completely, and it was his departure from it that was his undoing. John Doe, having committed his crime, simply shed his disguise and disappeared, leaving no trace and, thereafter, making no sign. If Schiller had done this, no question would ever have arisen. But he elected to stage the bogus murder in the Forest, and thereby left a loose end.

"Then you are overlooking the enormous effects of unforeseeable chance. The ringed hair was a chance in a million, and that of Polton's taking the dead woman's finger-prints and Pedley's preserving them was almost as great. Yet, if you subtract those two infinitely improbable circumstances, there is no case left. Schiller would have been perfectly safe, for I could never have got beyond the stage of suspicion.

"Further, you overlook the fact that, in spite of all these adverse effects of chance, Schiller's scheme did succeed. For two whole years he was at large and totally unsuspected. It is an actual fact that when Penfield came to me, not a single individual in the world, except myself, had any doubt that the person who disappeared in the Forest was really Lotta Schiller. Even the police, who rejected the bogus murder, did not question the identity."

"Still," I persisted, "the undeniable fact is that his scheme did fail, and that he is going to be hanged."

"Yes," Thorndyke admitted, "his scheme was defeated by the unforeseen and unforeseeable. His failure illustrates the truth of Herbert Spencer's dictum that social phenomena are too complex for prevision to be possible. But without prevision, no plan can be devised that will certainly produce the effects intended. That is where social reformers and all sorts of other planners fail. They take no account of the unknown factors. But it commonly happens that the unknown factors turn out to be the operative factors, as they did in the case of Carl Schiller."

"That is very true, sir," said Vanderpuye, "and the operative unknown factor in his case was the existence of a gentleman named John Thorndyke."

The End

About the Author

Richard Austin Freeman was born on April 11th, 1862 in the Soho district of London. He was the son of a skilled tailor and the youngest of five children. As he grew, it was expected that he would become a tailor as well, but instead he had an interest in natural history and medicine, and so he obtained employment in a pharmacist's shop. While there, he qualified as an apothecary and could have gone on to manage the shop, but instead he began to study medicine at Middlesex Hospital.

Austin Freeman qualified as a physician in 1887, and in that same year he married. Faced with the twin facts of his new marital responsibilities and his very limited resources as a young doctor, he made the unusual decision to join the Colonial Service, spending the next seven years in Africa as an Assistant Colonial Surgeon. This continued until the early 1890's, when he contracted Blackwater Fever, an illness that eventually forced him to leave the service and return permanently to England.

For several years, he served as a *locum tenens* for various physicians, a bleak time in his life as he moved from job to job, his income low, and his health never quite recovered. However, he supplemented his meager income and exercised his creativity during these years by beginning to write. His early publications included *Travels and Live in Ashanti and Jaman* (1898), recounting some of his African sojourns.

In 1900, Freeman obtained work as an assistant to Dr. John James Pitcairn (1860-1936) at Holloway Prison. Although he wasn't there for very long, the association between the two men was enough to turn Freeman's attention toward writing mysteries. Over the next few years, they co-wrote several under the pseudonym *Clifford Ashdown*, including *The Adventures of Romney Pringle* (1902), *The Further Adventures of Romney Pringle* (1903), *From a Surgeon's Diary* (1904-1905), and *The Queen's Treasure* (written around 1905-1906, and published posthumously in 1975.)

In approximately 1904, Freeman began developing a mystery novella based on a short job that he had held at the Western Ophthalmic Hospital. This effort, "31 New Inn", was published in 1905, and it is the true first Dr. Thorndyke story. In 1907, the first Thorndyke novel, *The Red Thumb Mark*, was published.

From Thorndyke's creation until 1914, Freeman wrote four novels and two volumes of short stories. Then, with the commencement of the

First World War, he entered military service. In February 1915, at the age of fifty-two, he joined the Royal Army Medical Corps. Due to his health, which had never entirely recovered from his time in Africa, he spent the duration of the war involved with various aspects of the ambulance corps, having been promoted very early to the rank of Captain. He wrote nothing about Thorndyke during this period, but he did publish one book concerning the adventures of a scoundrel, *The Exploits of Danby Croker* (1916).

Following the war, he resumed his previous life, writing approximately one Thorndyke novel per year, as well as three more volumes of Thorndyke short stories and a number of other unrelated items, until his death on September 28th, 1943 – likely related to Parkinson's Disease, which had plagued him in later years. He is buried in Gravesend.

If you enjoy Dr. Thorndyke, then you'll love
The MX Book of New Sherlock Holmes Stories
Edited by David Marcum
(MX Publishing, 2015-   )

"This is the finest volume of Sherlockian fiction I have ever read, and I have read, literally, thousands." – Philip K. Jones

"Beyond Impressive . . . This is a splendid venture for a great cause!
– Roger Johnson, Editor, *The Sherlock Holmes Journal,*
The Sherlock Holmes Society of London

Part I: 1881-1889
Part II: 1890-1895
Part III: 1896-1929
Part IV: 2016 Annual
Part V: Christmas Adventures
Part VI: 2017 Annual
Part VII: Eliminate the Impossible (1880-1891)
Part VIII – Eliminate the Impossible (1892-1905)
Part IX – 2018 Annual (1879-1895)
Part X – 2018 Annual (1896-1916)
Part XI – Some Untold Cases (1880-1891)
Part XII – Some Untold Cases (1894-1902)
Part XIII – 2019 Annual (1881-1890)
Part XIV – 2019 Annual (1891-1897)
Part XV – 2019 Annual (1898-1917)
Part XVI – Whatever Remains . . . Must be the Truth (1881-1890)
Part XVII – Whatever Remains . . . Must be the Truth (1891-1898)
Part XVIII – Whatever Remains . . . Must be the Truth (1898-1925)
Part XIX – 2020 Annual (1882-1890)
Part XX – 2020 Annual (1891-1897)
Part XXI – 2020 Annual (1898-1923)
Part XXII – Some More Untold Cases (1877-1887)
Part XXIII – Some More Untold Cases (1888-1894)
Part XXIV – Some More Untold Cases (1895-1903)

In Preparation
Part XXV – 2021 Annual

. . . and more to come!

The MX Book of New Sherlock Holmes Stories
Edited by David Marcum
(MX Publishing, 2015-   )

Part VI: *The traditional pastiche is alive and well . . . .*

Part VII: *Sherlockians eager for faithful-to-the-canon plots and characters will be delighted.*

Part VIII: *The imagination of the contributors in coming up with variations on the volume's theme is matched by their ingenious resolutions.*

Part IX: *The 18 stories . . . will satisfy fans of Conan Doyle's originals. Sherlockians will rejoice that more volumes are on the way.*

Part X: *. . . new Sherlock Holmes adventures of consistently high quality.*

Part XI: *. . . an essential volume for Sherlock Holmes fans.*

Part XII: *. . . continues to amaze with the number of high-quality pastiches . . .*

Part XIII: *. . . Amazingly, Marcum has found 22 superb pastiches . . . This is more catnip for fans of stories faithful to Conan Doyle's original*

Part XIV: *. . . this standout anthology of 21 short stories written in the spirit of Conan Doyle's originals.*

Part XV: *Stories pitting Sherlock Holmes against seemingly supernatural phenomena highlight Marcum's 15th anthology of superior short pastiches.*

Part XVI: *Marcum has once again done fans of Conan Doyle's originals a service.*

Part XVII: *This is yet another impressive array of new but traditional Holmes stories.*

Part XVIII: *Sherlockians will again be grateful to Marcum and MX for high-quality new Holmes tales.*

Part XIX: *Inventive plots and intriguing explorations of aspects of Dr. Watson's life and beliefs lift the 24 pastiches in Marcum's impressive 19th Sherlock Holmes anthology*

Part XX: *Marcum's reserve of high-quality new Holmes exploits seems endless.*

Part XXI: *This is another must-have for Sherlockians.*

The MX Book of New Sherlock Holmes Stories

Edited by David Marcum

(MX Publishing, 2015-   )

Also From MX Publishing

Traditional Canonical Sherlock Holmes Adventures by
David Marcum
Creator and editor of
The MX Book of New Sherlock Holmes Stories

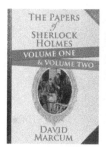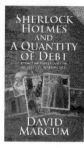

The Papers of Sherlock Holmes
"The Papers of Sherlock Holmes *by David Marcum contains nine intriguing mysteries . . . very much in the classic tradition . . . He writes well, too.*"
– Roger Johnson, Editor, *The Sherlock Holmes Journal,*
The Sherlock Holmes Society of London

"*Marcum offers nine clever pastiches.*"
– Steven Rothman, Editor, *The Baker Street Journal*

Sherlock Holmes and A Quantity of Debt
"*This is a welcome addendum to Sherlock lore that respectfully fleshes out Doyle's legendary crime-solving couple in the context of new escapades . . . .*"
– Peter Roche, Examiner.com

"*David Marcum is known to Sherlockians as the author of two short story collections . . . In* Sherlock Holmes and A Quantity of Debt, *he demonstrates mastery of the longer form as well.*"
– Dan Andriacco, Author

Sherlock Holmes – Tangled Skeins
(Included in Randall Stock's, 2015 Top Five Sherlock Holmes Books – Fiction)
"*Marcum's collection will appeal to those who like the traditional elements of the Holmes tales*"
– Randall Stock, BSI

"*There are good pastiche writers, there are great ones, and then there is David Marcum who ranks among the very best . . . I cannot recommend this book enough.*"
– Derrick Belanger, Author and Publisher of Belanger Books

Sherlock Holmes in Montague Street
by Arthur Morrison
Edited, Holmes-ed, and with Original Material
by David Marcum

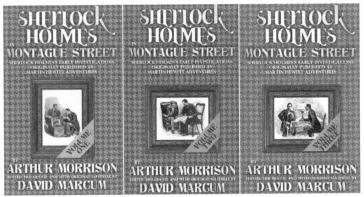

Separate Paperback Editions

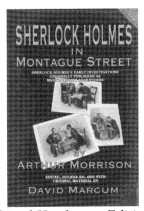

Combined Hardcover Edition

*"It's been suggested that Hewitt was the young Mycroft Holmes,
but David Marcum has a more plausible and attractive theory
– that he was Sherlock, early in his career as an investigator
. . . these are remarkably convincing in their new guise."*
– Roger Johnson, Editor, *The Sherlock Holmes Journal*,
The Sherlock Holmes Society of London

MX Publishing

MX Publishing is the world's largest specialist Sherlock Holmes publisher, with several hundred titles and over a hundred authors creating the latest in Sherlock Holmes fiction and non-fiction.

From traditional short stories and novels to travel guides and quiz books, MX Publishing caters to all Holmes fans.

The collection includes leading titles such as *Benedict Cumberbatch In Transition* and *The Norwood Author*, which won the 2011 *Tony Howlett Award* (Sherlock Holmes Book of the Year).

MX Publishing also has one of the largest communities of Holmes fans on *Facebook*, with regular contributions from dozens of authors.

www.mxpublishing.co.uk (UK) and *www.mxpublishing.com* (USA)

Lightning Source UK Ltd.
Milton Keynes UK
UKHW040722010421
381362UK00001B/2